'If any ambitious TV producers are looking for a multi-part fan-

'In just a few years Robert V.S. Redick has developed into one of
the most exciting voices in fantasy'   *Fantasy Book Critic*

'Redick pulls off epic fantasy with a great deal of style, giving his
readers everything they want along with a big bag of surprises'
                                                                          Starburst

'Robert Redick is an extraordinary talent'
                        New York Times bestselling author Karen Miller

'The adventure is nonstop, the characters powerfully endearing,
and the world-building meticulous'   Paul Di Filippo

Also by Robert V.S. Redick from Gollancz:

ROBERT V.S.REDICK

THE NIGHT OF THE SWARM

Copyright © Robert V.S. Redick 2012

All rights reserved

The right of Robert V.S. Redick to be identified as the author
of this work has been asserted by him in accordance with the
Copyright, Designs and Patents Act 1988.

First published in Great Britain in 2012 by
Gollancz
An imprint of the Orion Publishing Group
Orion House, 5 Upper St Martin's Lane,
London WC2H 9EA
An Hachette UK Company

This edition published in Great Britain in 2013
by Gollancz

1 3 5 7 9 10 8 6 4 2

A CIP catalogue record for this book
is available from the British Library

ISBN 978 0 575 09779 7

Typeset by Input Data Services Ltd, Bridgwater, Somerset

Printed and bound by CPI Group (UK) Ltd, Croydon, CR0 4YY

The Orion Publishing Group's policy is to use papers
that are natural, renewable and recyclable products and
made from wood grown in sustainable forests. The logging
and manufacturing processes are expected to conform to
the environmental regulations of the country of origin.

www.redwolfconspiracy.com
www.orionbooks.co.uk
www.gollancz.co.uk

To those who still read with wonder

There cannot be, confusion of our sound forgot,
A single soul that lacks a sweet crystalline cry.

W.B. Yeats, 'Paudeen'

And they're only going to change this place
By killing everybody in the human race.

The Police, 'Invisible Sun'

Prologue

A battle is ending in the heart of a black wood. From the surrounding treetops it is all oddly peaceful: the late moonlight, the
curve of the river, the grassy clearing on its banks, the ruined tower
like a broken bottleneck thrust against the sky. No shouts from
the combatants, no clashing of steel. One can even hear the crows
across the water, rejoicing in the almost-dawn.

But distance deceives. A little closer, and we find the grass is
scorched, the river furious, the stairs of the ruined tower slick with
blood. And at the foot of the stairs a dozen figures crouch: all
wounded, all contemplating death; in a minute's time they will be
slain by sorcery. They bend low, squeeze tightly together. They are
surrounded by a ring-shaped pit, and the inner edge of the pit is
crumbling toward their feet.

Above their heads shimmers a dull halo, resembling a mist or
cloud of insects. It is neither; it is the whirling of enchanted blades.
They have cut someone already; a fine haze of blood thickens the
air. The blades, as may be expected, are descending. The ring-
shaped pit bristles with spikes.

Crude horrors, these; but so is the confluence of powers that
has willed them into being. High on the tower wall stands a mage:
skeletal, staring, hideous at a glance. He is gripping the hair of
another, a ragged beast of a man, and gesturing at the unfortunates
below. The ragged man is drooling, his gaze empty of all comprehension. Tight to his chest he holds a little sphere of darkness, so
black it devours the moonlight, so black it troubles the eye.

Movement, suddenly: a third figure has crawled up from

behind. A youth, dripping wet, bleeding, his look of fury rivaling the mage's own. Unseen, he staggers closer, holding what can only be a blackjack. With a spasm of regret he strikes down the ragged man. There is a crack of breaking bone.

The whirling blades vanish, and the pit. The ragged man falls dead, and the sphere slips from his grasp. Among the crouching figures, a young woman closes her hand upon a sword hilt. Above, the sphere of darkness is rolling towards the wall's sheer edge. The mage lunges, catches the sphere at the last instant, and with it clutched in both hands, he falls. Before he is halfway to the ground, the future of Alifros takes shape.

The touch of the sphere is death, even to one as powerful as this. Death consumes him, hands to wrists to elbows. Thirty feet from the ground his arms are dead. And yet he smiles. He is speaking an incantation. Beside the tower, the surface of the river convulses, and something thin and dark leaps out of it, skyward. The mage tries for a glimpse, but at that instant the young woman strikes with rare perfection. Her blade sings. The body lands headless on the earth.

The dark splinter, however, continues its ascent, like a fish that leaps and forgets to fall. Up through mist and cloud it stabs, above the paths of hawks and falcons, above the spirit highways of the murths, until at last it touches the shores of that greater ocean, the void from whence we came. But no further: it has work to do in Alifros, tireless work.

Northwards it passes, turning and tumbling like a shard of glass, over the mountains, the dew-damp woods, the lowlands where villagers are waking, muttering, hitching oxen to the plough. By the time it reaches the ocean it has doubled in size.

I

The Victors

11 Modobrin 941
240th day from Etherhorde

No sunrise in his life – and he has watched hundreds, being a tarboy – has ever made him sentimental, but now the tears flow fast and silent. He is standing in the river with the water to his knees. Voices from the clearing warn him not to take another step, and he knows the danger better than they. Still he cannot believe that anything will harm him now. The sun on his brown, bruised face declares him a survivor, one of the lucky ones, in fact so lucky it staggers the mind.

He can hear someone singing, haunted words about remembered mornings, fallen friends. He lifts a hand as though to touch the sun. Tears of gratitude, these. By rights they should be dead, all of them. Drowned in darkness, smothering darkness, the darkness of a tomb.

Footsteps in the shallows, then a hand touches his elbow. 'That's far enough, mate,' says a beloved voice.

Pazel Pathkendle gives a silent nod.

'Come on, will you? Ramachni has something to tell us. I don't think it can wait.'

Pazel bends and splashes water on his face. Better not to show these tears. He is not ashamed; he could not care less about shame or valour or looking brave for Neeps Undrabust, as good a friend as he could ever hope for. But tears would make Neeps want to help, and Pazel the survivor is learning not to ask for help. Friends have

3

just so much to give; when that is gone there's no hand on your elbow, no one left to pull you ashore.

He turned to Neeps and forced a smile. 'You're a mess.'

'Go to the Pits,' said the smaller tarboy. 'You didn't come through this any better. You look like a drowned raccoon.'

'Wish I felt that good.'

Neeps glanced down at Pazel's leg. '*Credek*, it's worse than ever, isn't it?'

'The cold water helps,' said Pazel. But in fact his leg felt terrible. It wasn't the burn; that pain he could tolerate, or at least understand. But the incisions from the flame troll's fangs had begun to throb, and itch, and the skin around them was an unhealthy green.

'Listen, mate, the fighting's over,' said Neeps. 'You show that leg to Ramachni. Not in an hour or two. Now.'

'Who's that singing? Bolutu?'

Neeps sniffed; Pazel's dodge had not escaped him. 'Bolutu and Lunja both,' he said. 'A praise song to the daylight, they told us. I think the dlömu are all sun worshippers, deep down.'

'I'm joining them,' said Pazel, his smile now sincere.

'Rin's truth!' said Neeps. 'But right now I just wish I could thank the builders of the tower, whoever they were.'

Pazel looked again at the massive ruin, and struggled as before to picture it intact. He could not do it; what he imagined was just too big. The absurdly gradual curve of the wall, the fitted stones large as carriages, the seven-hundred-foot fragment jutting into the sky: the tower would have dwarfed the greatest palaces of Arqual in the Northern world, along with everything he had yet seen in the South. And Neeps was right: it was the tower, as much as Ramachni's magic or Thasha's brilliance with a sword, that had saved their lives.

For they were still within the tomb – a living tomb, a tomb made of trees. Days ago, hunting the sorcerer Arunis, they had found themselves standing above it: a crater so vast it would have taken them days to walk around, if they had not known that Arunis waited somewhere in its depths. A crater which they at first mistook for an enormous, weed-covered lake. But it was no lake. What they had at first taken for the scummed-over surface was in fact a lid of leaves: the huge, flat, rubbery leaves of the Infernal Forest. Pazel had been reminded of lily pads blanketing a mill pond, but these pads were fused, branch to branch, tree to tree, all the way to the crater's edge.

The entire forest lay sealed beneath this skin. Beneath four such skins, as they had found on descending: for there were older leaf-layers beneath the topmost, all supported by the straight, stony pillars of the trees. Like the decks of a ship, each layer was darker than that above. Below the fourth level their descent had continued for several hundred feet, until at last they reached the forest floor.

Not a drop of rain or beam of sunlight could ever touch that floor. It was a hell of darkness they had wandered into. Seven of their party had fallen in that hot, dripping maze, where giant fungi exhaled mind-attacking spores, and bats smothered torches, and the trees themselves lowered tendrils, stealthy as pythons, strong enough to tear a man limb from limb.

The Infernal Forest. Did any place in Alifros better deserve its name?

But here in the forest's very heart was a refuge, an oasis of light. The ruins held the trees at bay, and the standing wall cut through the leaf-layers to open sky. Moonlight had been dazzling enough after so much blindness. The sun was pure, exquisite joy.

'Of course, there's plenty of thanks to go around,' said Neeps. 'Old Fiffengurt, to start with, for giving you the blackjack. And Hercól for the fighting lessons.'

'You fought like a tiger, mate,' said Pazel.

'Rubbish, I didn't. I meant the lessons he gave Thasha, all those years. Did you see her, Pazel? The *timing* of it? The way she pivoted under Arunis, the way she swung?'

'I didn't see her kill him.'

'It was beautiful,' said Neeps. 'That's an ugly thing to say, maybe. But Pitfire! It was like she was born for that moment.'

'She wasn't, though, was she?'

Neeps shot him a dark look. 'That's enough about *that*, for Rin's sake.'

They walked in silence to the foot of the broken stairs where the others were clustered, listening to the dlömu sing. Thasha, who had made love to him for the first time just days ago – a lifetime ago – stood before him in rags. Her skin a portrait of all they'd passed through. Bites and gashes from the summoned creatures they'd fought here at the tower's foot. Scars where she'd torn off leeches as big around as his arm. Blisters from the touch of flame-trolls. And blood (dry, half-dry, oozing, rust-red, black) mixed with every foul substance imaginable, smeared and splattered from her feet to her golden hair. She caught his eye. She was smiling, happy. You're beautiful, he thought, feeling a fool.

This was love, all right: wondrous, intoxicating. And at the same time harrowing, a torment more severe than any wound. For Pazel knew that Thasha, in a sense quite different from the others, should no longer be standing before him.

Fourteen left alive: just half of those who had set out from the city of Masalym and stormed into the heart of this deadly peninsula in a single furious week. Pazel looked at them, the victors, the sorcerer-slayers. It would have been hard to imagine a more crushed and beaten company. Split lips, bloodshot eyes. Ferocious grins bordering on the deranged. Most had lost their weapons; some had lost their shoes. Yet the victory was real; the great enemy lay dead. And given what the fight had taken from them, it was a wonder that madness only flickered in their smiles.

Hercól Stanapeth had almost *literally* been crushed, beneath an enormous stone hurled by Arunis. He was on his feet, though: crouching over a pile of tinder, whirling a stick in an effort to start a fire. Pazel's sister Neda was helping, scraping bark and twigs together with her bloodied hands. Beside them, the two black-skinned, silver-eyed dlömu were bringing their song to an end.

6

Another hour, another day, let our unworthy kind
Feel Thy returning light and say that yet within the mind
We guard the long-remembered joys, too sudden then for song
The fire of youth that time destroys: in Thee it blazes on.

'Well sung indeed,' said Ramachni. 'And fitting words for a day of healing.'

'Is it to be such a day?' asked Bolutu.

'That is more than I can promise,' said Ramachni, 'but not more than I hope for.'

Ramachni was a mink. Slender, coal black, with very white fangs, and eyes that seemed to grow when they fixed on you. Like all of them he carried fresh wounds. A red welt crossed his chest like a sash, where the fur had been singed away.

It was a borrowed body: Ramachni was in fact a great mage from another world altogether, a world he declined to name. Arunis had been his mortal enemy, and yet it was Arunis who had clumsily opened the door between worlds that let Ramachni return, just hours ago, at the moment of their greatest need. He had taken bear-form during the fight, and matched Arunis spell for spell. But Arunis' power, though crude, was also infinite, for he had had the Nilstone to draw upon. In the end Ramachni had been reduced to shielding them from the other's attacks, and the shield had nearly broken. What was left of his strength? He had told them he would return more powerful than ever before, and so he clearly had. But he had not come to do battle with the Nilstone. Had this battle drained him, like the fight on the deck of the *Chathrand*? Would he have to leave them again?

'There,' said Hercól, as a wisp of smoke rose from the grass.

'What good is a fire,' said Lunja, the dlömic soldier, her face still turned to the sun, 'unless we have something to cook on it?'

'Don't even *mention* food,' said Neeps. 'I'm so hungry I'm starting to fancy those mushrooms.'

'We must eat nothing spawned in that forest,' said the other dlömu, Mr Bolutu, 'yet I do need flame, Lunja, to sterilise our knives.' He looked pointedly at Pazel's leg. Bolutu was a veterinarian: the only sort of doctor they had.

'We will have something to cook,' said Hercól. 'Cayer Vispek will see to that.'

The *sfvantskor* warrior-priest smiled. Neda, his disciple *sfvantskor*, did the same. 'We eating goose,' she said.

'There you go again,' said the old Turach marine. He frowned at Neda, his wide mouth indignant. 'You call that Arquali? "We eating", indeed. How do you expect us to understand you?'

'Enough, Corporal Mandric,' said Bolutu. But the Turach paid no attention.

'Listen, girl: We *will* eat, someday. We *ate*, long ago. We *would* eat, *if* we had a blary morsel. Which one do you mean? In a civilised language you've got to specify.'

'Yes,' said Neda, 'we eating goose.'

She pointed at the river. On the far side, eight or ten plump grey birds were drifting in the shallows. Cayer Vispek's eyes narrowed, studying them. Neda glanced at Pazel. Switching to Mzithrini, she said, 'Cayer Vispek can hit anything with a stone. I have seen him kill birds on the wing.'

In the same tongue, Pazel said, 'You saw him almost kill *me* with a stone, remember?'

She looked at him as only a sister could. 'No,' she said, 'I'd forgotten all about it.'

Neda spoke with bitter sarcasm. Years ago their mother had changed them both with a great, flawed spell: the only one she had ever cast, to Pazel's knowledge at least. It had nearly killed them, and had plagued them with side effects that persisted to this day. But it had also made Pazel a language savant, and given Neda a memory that appeared to have no bounds.

Pazel doubted that Neda could control her Gift any better than he could his own. But he was certain she recalled that night when they were at last reunited, and the violence that had erupted minutes later.

'Did you expect my master to kill you?' she asked suddenly.

'I don't know,' said Pazel. 'Yes, I suppose.'

'Because we're monsters?'

'Oh, Neda—'

'Heartless creatures with their barbaric language, barbaric ways. Your Arquali friends will tell you all about it.'

'Next you'll be calling *me* Arquali again,' said Pazel.

To his surprise, Neda did not rise to the bait. She looked furtively at Thasha, as though ashamed of herself. 'I have said too much already,' she said. 'We of the Faith do not speak against our betters, and this morning I swore kinship with her.'

'That doesn't make Thasha your better, does it?'

His question only made things worse. Neda flushed crimson. 'I could not have struck that blow,' she said.

Pazel's anger vanished; he found himself wishing he could take her hand. They had left home barely six years ago, but at times it felt like sixty. Neda had gone to the Mzithrin Empire and become a warrior-priest: she was Neda Pathkendle no longer; they called her Neda Ygraël, Neda Phoenix-Flame. But Pazel had been captured by men of Arqual, the *other* great empire of the North, and the Mzithrin's enemy. It was Arqual that had invaded their home country, broken up what remained of their family. Arqual that had made him a tarboy, the lowest kind of shipboard servant. Arqual that had sent the soldiers who dragged Neda, screaming, into a barn.

Becoming a tarboy had been merely the best of the awful choices before him. It was not clear whether Neda understood that choice, or could forgive it. But something had changed in the last few days. Her glances, even the sharpest ones, had a little less of the *sfvantskor* in them, and a little more the elder sister.

'When do we march, Hercól?' asked Neeps abruptly. 'Tell me it won't be sooner than tomorrow.'

'*When's* just one of the questions,' added Big Skip Sunderling, the blacksmith's mate from the *Chathrand*. 'I'm more worried about *how*. Some of us ain't fit to march.'

'We will do as Ramachni commands,' said Hercól. 'You have

followed me thus far, but make no mistake: he is our leader now.'

'I would be a poor leader if I drove you on without rest,' said Ramachni. 'We need food as well, and Bolutu and I must do what we can for the wounded. And for all of us there remains one grim task before we depart.'

'Do not speak of it just yet, pray,' said a high, clear voice.

It was Ensyl, with Myett close behind her, scrambling down the broken staircase. At eight inches, neither ixchel woman stood as tall as a single step, but they descended with catlike grace, copper skin bright in the sun, eyes of the same colour gleaming like coals. Each carried a bulging sack, fashioned from bits of cloth, over her shoulder.

'We have ventured high up the wall in search of breakfast,' said Ensyl, lowering her burden with care. 'The wind is ferocious above, though you cannot feel it here. But it was worth the struggle: these dainties, at least, did not come from the forest.'

The humans sighed: within the sacks lay twenty or thirty eggs. They were of several sizes and colours; the most striking were perfectly round and gleamed like polished turquoise.

'There are strange birds aloft,' said Myett. 'Some have claws halfway down their wings, and hang by these from the rock face. Others are so small that at first we took them for insects. Atop the spire there are nests the size of lifeboats, made of moss and branches. We did not see the birds that built them.'

She looked sourly at the faces above her. 'You giants won't be happy until you boil these eggs into hard rubber, of course—'

Big Skip seized an egg. Tilting his head backwards, he cracked the shell against his lower teeth, emptied yolk and white into his mouth, and savoured both in silence a moment. Then he swallowed. A shiver passed through his big frame.

'Tree of Heaven, that's good,' he said.

The remaining humans dived on the eggs. Pazel gulped his down in one swallow; Thasha licked the inside of her shell like a cat cleaning a dish. Ensyl grinned; Myett pressed her lips tightly shut.

Bolutu did not partake, however. Lunja took an egg and held it up before her eyes, as though considering. 'No more,' she said at last, returning it. 'We have swallowed enough little suns, who served in the armies of the *Platazcra.*'

'Little suns?' said Pazel.

'For our people,' said Bolutu, 'to eat an egg is an act of great pride – unhealthy pride, my father used to tell me.'*

'In Bali Adro today, only soldiers and royals may eat eggs,' said Lunja. 'We turn it into another bit of flattery for the Empire. *"The sun itself we shall devour, in time."* If I were still in Masalym, I should have to eat this egg, and say those fatuous words, or be accused of disloyalty.'

'That's a blary shame,' said Mandric, licking his fingers.

Ramachni neither ate nor spoke. His watchfulness soon gave the others to realise that the 'grim task' would not long be put off. They finished quickly, leaving a few eggs for later, and turned their attention to the mage.

'Hercól,' he said, 'is the Nilstone safe?'

In answer the swordsman pointed gravely at a small mound of rocks, carefully arranged beside the tower wall. Through the spaces between the rocks Pazel could see the Nilstone's inverse glow, its blacker-than-all-blackness, and felt a touch of that deep, flesh-chilling aversion the relic always produced in him.

'We have one sturdy sack in which to bear it,' said Hercól, 'but I will wrap the Stone first in whatever spare cloth we can find. No one will die of an accidental touch.'

Ramachni nodded. 'We will not leave this place before tomorrow,' he said, 'and I will confess to you that I am not sure how the deed is to be done. Walking would be terribly dangerous: there are few ways out of the crater at all, and most of the openings that do exist are traps, designed to lure prey down to the forest floor and

---

*The notion is of ancient standing. In the oldest dlömic tales, the figure doomed to some pride-provoked catastrophe frequently begins his errors with a meal of eggs. - EDITOR

keep them there. I had hoped that the river could carry us to freedom, for it does flow out of the forest at some point. But the river has dangers of its own, and it winds like a snake – and besides, we have no raft. The wood of the great trees is so dense that it sinks like stone.'

'There are young pines by the forest's edge,' said Cayer Vispek, gesturing, 'but they are few and small.'

'We have a final problem, alas,' said Ramachni. 'The fireflies cannot go with us.'

Cries of dismay. 'You can't mean it!' said Big Skip. 'Go blind again into that mucking forest?'

'I did not say *blind*,' said Ramachni, 'only without the fireflies. They are fragile creatures, and I can ask little more of them.'

'Ramachni,' said Bolutu, 'can you induce the *nuhzat*?'

Lunja shot him an appalled glance. Pazel too was startled: the *nuhzat* was the ecstatic dream-state of the dlömic people, and when it struck they exhibited all sorts of odd behaviours and abilities. But it had become extremely rare – so rare indeed that most dlömu were afraid of it.

'I have done so,' said Ramachni, 'in the distant past.'

'Madness,' said Lunja.

'Or salvation,' said Bolutu. 'Sergeant Lunja, we were both in *nuhzat* in the Infernal Forest. I heard your singing, and I saw your eyes: black as midnight they were. When the torch went out, I found that the *nuhzat* had given me a kind of inverse sight. It was frightful and bewildering, but I could make out the shapes of trees, mushrooms, people. As a last resort we might link the party together with rope, and you and I could lead them.'

'Only if the *nuhzat* gave you that exact gift again,' said Ramachni, 'and that no one can guarantee. There is a reason your dream-state was never harnessed as a tool of warriors or athletes, Bolutu. It is by nature a wild condition, a wayward grace. It liberates, but it does not willingly serve.' He turned to Ensyl and Myett. 'I wish we had spoken before you climbed the ruins. A bit higher, and you might have described the land downriver for us.'

'We will climb again,' said Ensyl.

Myett shot her a hard look: *Speak for yourself.*

'A noble offer,' said Ramachni, 'but let us stop thinking of our escape for a while. The time has come: we must burn the sorcerer.'

He nodded at a giant cube of rock some twenty yards away: one of the structural stones of the broken tower. In the grass about it Pazel could see one withered arm, sticking out from behind the stone. The fingers were desiccated, curling like strips of parchment. The hand seemed almost to beckon him.

'Arunis is slain,' said Ramachni, 'but his death opens the way to dangers that were absent before. To begin with, I expect he was using his arts to hide from Macadra.'

'Macadra!' cried Lunja. 'The Emperor's mage? What has *she* to do with Arunis?'

'She may pose as a servant of your Emperor,' said Ramachni, 'but that sorceress has long since become the keeper, rather than the kept. In any case, Macadra Hyndrascorm covets the Nilstone as much as Arunis ever did, and will be seeking it with all her powers. Worse still, Macadra can draw upon the might of a whole empire in her hunt. Indeed she *is* the Empire of Bali Adro, at least for purposes of violence and intrigue. We are fortunate to be so far from any town or garrison. But this wilderness cannot protect us for long.'

'That's how it is, eh?' said Mandric. 'We were hunters, and now we're prey?'

'Let us hope it will not come to that, Corporal,' said Ramachni. 'I do not think that the Nilstone itself calls out to any mage; otherwise Arunis would have plucked it from the seabed off the Haunted Coast with far greater ease. But the corpse of a mage is very different. Magic leaks from it as well as blood, and by that magic it shines like a beacon-fire on a hilltop. We must snuff that beacon quickly, or she will know it for Arunis. It may already be too late.'

'Why burn him?' asked Dastu, the young Arquali spy. 'Why not toss him into the river and be done?'

Pazel looked at Dastu with a calm, cold hate. Like Neeps and Thasha, he had once considered the older youth a friend – before he had revealed himself as a protégé of Sandor Ott, the Imperial spymaster. Before his betrayal had exposed their resistance to Ott's plans, and seen them all sentenced to death as mutineers. Captain Rose had suspended that sentence, but he had not pardoned them – and Pazel doubted any of them could pardon Dastu, either.

'You know we can't just toss the body in,' said Thasha. 'That's no normal river. It's a path between worlds.'

Dastu shrugged. 'If you're telling the truth—'

'If?' said Pazel. 'Damn it all, Ibjen was right next to me. I saw him – taken. Like a leaf in a hurricane, carried off Rin-knows-where.'

'That's the idea, Pathkendle,' said Dastu. 'Arunis will just disappear.' Then he jumped, as though struck by a sudden thought. 'Gods of death, have we all gone simple? The Nilstone! We can throw the Nilstone into the River of Shadows as well! Right here, this very morning. No one will ever see it again.'

Utter silence. Dastu looked from face to face. 'What's the matter now?' he demanded. 'Isn't this what you lot have been seeking? A way to toss the Nilstone out of Alifros?'

'Yes,' said Hercól, 'but not this way.'

'He has a point, though,' said Mandric. 'You've always said it can't be destroyed.'

'Nor can it,' said Ramachni, 'and indeed the Nilstone *must* be hurled into the River of Shadows – but where it exits this world, not here where it enters.'

'Is that so crucial?' asked Lunja doubtfully.

'Utterly,' said the little mage. 'The stone belongs in the world of the dead. My mistress Erithusmé tried with all her might and wisdom to send it back there. She failed – but she had a glimpse of how it might be done, in the last days before Arunis drove her into hiding.'

Pazel glanced at Thasha, but her eyes were far away.

'We know the task before us. The River flows into death's

kingdom at the point where it leaves Alifros, and nowhere else. That is where we must take the Stone.'

'And that place is the island of Gurishal,' said Dastu. 'But Ramachni, it can't be done! Gurishal is on the western edge of the Mzithrin Empire. We're standing by a river in a wasteland on the far side of the Ruling Sea, hurt and hungry and lost.'

'While the hag who controls *this* whole blary Empire is out hunting for the Stone,' put in Mandric, with a bitter laugh. 'Us, take the Nilstone to Gurishal! It's worse than ludicrous. It's a deathsmoker's dream.'

'The cause is not hopeless yet,' said Ramachni, 'and whatever the odds, we must try.'

'We've heard that one before, haven't we?' said Dastu. 'Just before you led us into battle, and Arunis nearly skinned us alive. Only now the odds are even worse. There's no ship waiting for us at the coast, Ramachni. Only enemies, with Plazic blades that make them itch for murder, and sea-weapons like nothing the North has ever dreamed of. And there's *still* worse, by the Blessed Tree. Didn't you say that the River of Shadows almost always flows deep underground?'

'In this world, yes,' said Ramachni.

'Then what if that's the case on Gurishal? Master Ott has studied the island for forty years. Alyash *lived* there. Neither of them ever spoke of any strange river, any doorway to a land of death. What if it's buried, eh? What if we do get there – miracle of miracles – and find that the River's under a mile of stone?'

'Then we dig,' said Ramachni, 'but we will not cast either the Stone or the sorcerer's corpse into the River here.' The mage spoke quietly, but there was cold steel in his voice. 'Would you throw poison into a stream, Dastu? That is a crime, even if it be a stream you yourself will never drink from. That, in fact, is how the Nilstone came to enter Alifros to begin with – a selfish and a careless act, by one who wished only to be rid of it quickly. That is how its long history of ruin here began. Impossible, you think our goal? Do not believe it. This night past we killed Arunis, and ended his thirty

15

centuries of power and scheming. Today we work. Tomorrow we will do the impossible again.'

But even today's task promised to be hard. The trees shed few branches, and the mushrooms, though plentiful, were too wet for burning. Hercól forbade anyone to venture into the forest beyond the nearest trees, and for once not even the *sfvantskors* were inclined to argue.

Still, the banks of the river yielded logs and sticks, and with persistence they achieved a respectable bonfire. Hercól and Cayer Vispek lifted the headless corpse and tossed it heavily atop the blaze.

'Stand away!' said Ramachni. 'Do not breathe the smoke. Curses may linger anywhere about the corpse.'

The fire quavered; the flames licking the body turned a strange, dark red. Pazel worried for a moment that they had not gathered enough fuel for the task, but it was soon clear that no such danger existed. The flames grew tall and voracious, gobbling the corpse. Pazel glanced at Ramachni and saw that he was very still, facing the fire with his cut eyes tightly closed.

You're helping, aren't you? Then you're not entirely drained.

Thasha came up next to Pazel and leaned gently against his side. 'Burn,' she whispered, eyes locked on the corpse.

He understood how she felt. Arunis had started everything. All the scheming and most of the deaths traced back to him. Arunis had made the puppets dance, even those who never guessed they were puppets, even those with puppets of their own. Pazel knew that he hated Arunis, but right now he felt nothing but an over-powering desire to see the process through. *Let the body become ash, the ash blow away, the world start to heal and forget this monster ...*

A look of peace crept over the watching faces. If evil could die, perhaps good might grow. And now a great mage was leading them, not attacking. Why shouldn't they prevail? For the first time in many days Pazel let himself think of his mother and father, the old life, the far side of the world. It no longer seemed quite so absurd to hope that one day, somewhere, they might all be—

'The head,' said Ramachni suddenly, opening his eyes. 'What has become of the sorcerer's head?'

'I was about to fetch it,' said Cayer Vispek. 'It lies there behind the stone.'

'Do so quickly,' said Ramachni, 'while the flame is at its height.'

'I will go, Master,' said Neda.

She ran behind the great carved stone. When she returned a moment later, Pazel knew that the horror was starting again.

The thing in Neda's hands was not the mage's head. It was a large yellow mushroom, one of the few that sprouted in the clearing. Neda held it at arm's length, her lips curled in wary disgust. Already she was preparing to throw it in the fire.

Cayer Vispek snatched at her arm. 'Are you mad, girl?' He knocked the mushroom from her hands. Neda cried out, reaching for it, and Vispek slapped her across the face. 'You're charmed, you're magicked!' he shouted, and dashed behind the stone himself.

'Have a care, Vispek, the same may befall you!' cried Hercól, racing after him.

'Rin's eyes, it's right there on the ground!' cried Ensyl. She was pointing at the Turach's helmet.

'Be still, I have it!' shouted Vispek, returning. In his hand was a fistful of grass.

Something close to panic seized the company. The world was off-balance; the fire was suddenly dying, and a noise like laughter echoed through the ruins. Pazel whirled, and saw the gory head a stone's throw away. He rushed towards it, calling desperately to the others: but no, it was further off, almost under the trees. Neeps and Mandric were making for different parts of the forest, pointing and shouting; others were racing back to the burning corpse. Stones, mushrooms, clods of earth, weeds, eggs, boots, were hurled into the fire.

'Hold!'

Ramachni's voice cut through the mayhem like a scythe. The distant laughter ceased; the world rebalanced itself. The mage, looking very small, stood beside the mushroom Neda had brought in the first place.

The party reassembled. Ramachni's white teeth flashed. 'Come here, young *sfvantskor,* and finish your work. But this time, speak your prayer as if you mean it.'

Neda hesitated, one hand touching the cheek her master had slapped. 'The prayer?' she said.

'Child,' said Ramachni, 'that hand is too close to your mouth.'

Neda's hand fell like a stone. Thoroughly unsettled now, she knelt before Ramachni. She put out a hand towards the mushroom, made a fist, and shouted several words in Mzithrini, the language of her faith.

And suddenly they all saw it: the gaunt, cruel, mud-caked, gore-splattered head. The eyes were closed and the mouth hung wide. Below the chin, Thasha's cut was remarkably neat.

'Old Faith prayers are rich in antidemonic patterns,' said Ramachni, 'and the oldest and most uncorrupted of them, the songs of Tzi-Haruk and Lisériden, were taken from the guardian-spells laid down in the Dawn War. They have almost gone cold, those ancient spells. But a few embers remain alight.'

'Our prayers are not hexes, wizard,' said Cayer Vispek sternly.

'Nor is a bucket a well,' said Ramachni, 'although it serves to lift well-water.'

There came a sharp rasp of steel on steel. Hercól had drawn Ildraquin, his black and ancient sword. With great care he drove the tip of the blade into the severed neck, and lifted the head from the ground.

'Antidemonics?' he said. 'Do you mean to say that Arunis counted *demons* among his servants?'

'Perhaps,' said Ramachni, 'but Arunis never dedicated himself to the summoning arts: in that discipline Macadra was ever his superior. I think it more likely that he has coaxed a lesser fiend or two into serving him, in exchange for future rewards. Arunis, after all, sought nothing less than godhood, and in his fevered investigations of the several worlds, he found at last a kind of schooling that promised just that. He set out to end life on Alifros for one reason only: because that was the task *assigned* him, in his third millennium of studies. Those studies he had all but finished. The freeing of the Swarm of Night, and through it the destruction of the world, together comprised his last, horrid test.'

'His exams,' said Pazel. 'Fulbreech called them his exams. It seemed too horrible to be true.'

'Yet it is,' said Ramachni. 'Greysan Fulbreech could never have imagined such a depravity, any more than he could have imagined what would come of pledging himself to Arunis. What he witnessed in the depths of the Forest was too much for his weak soul. I think he saw the faces of that deathless circle Arunis hoped to join. The hand that killed Fulbreech was a merciful one.'

Ibjen's hand, Pazel thought. The dlömic boy had sworn an oath before his mother: never to fight or even bear a weapon. Fear had not been enough to make him break that oath; but mercy had, in the end. Pazel glanced at the dark river. Was the boy still alive? Had he been swept already into some strange, forbidding world?

'There should be a scarf,' said Thasha suddenly. When the others looked at her, she said, 'You can't have forgotten. His white scarf. He was *never* without it on the *Chathrand*.'

Pazel remembered: that ratty, worn-out cloth. 'Thasha's right; he never took the blary thing off. But I don't remember seeing it here. Does anyone?'

The others shook their heads. Pazel and Thasha looked at each other uneasily.

'Hercól,' said Ramachni, 'take the head to the fire. We have laboured long for this day.'

'Your labour is not done.'

Everyone cried out: it was the head itself which had spoken, in a voice like moaning wind. The dead eyes snapped open; the dead lips curled in a sneer. Hercól placed both hands on Ildraquin. At the sword's tip, the knob of flesh and bone was moving, twisting, staring with hatred at them all.

'Arunis!' cried Ramachni. 'We have sent you from this world!

Death's kingdom is your dwelling now. Go quietly; you know the agonies reserved for those who will not.'

'Death's kingdom cannot hold me,' said Arunis. 'Do you hear, rat-mage? We of the High Circle are death's masters, not its slaves. We brew death in our stomachs. We spit death where we will. Your own deaths I will prolong beyond the compass of your shabby minds, and every instant will be a symphony of pain.'

'You have no other window on Alifros,' said Ramachni. 'Your body is burned already; this last foul tool will follow. Spit, viper! Spit your curses among the damned, for they are the kin you have chosen.'

The head's pale eyes swivelled. 'Has your mage called this victory?' it asked the others. 'He lies, then. For Erithusmé is dying, dying in the body of that wanton girl.' The eyes flicked in Thasha's direction. 'You have failed. She will never return. And I have done all that was asked of me. I have brought the Swarm of Night into Alifros, and it will sterilise this world, as a doctor does his hands before a surgery. Nothing will be left that walks or breathes or grows beneath the sun. Wait and see if I lie, maggots. You will not be waiting long.'

'It is true that we are done with waiting,' said Hercól, advancing to the fire. The head writhed and roared. Hercól drew Ildraquin back for the fling – and reeled, almost dropping his sword.

Where the head had dangled a moment before, the tiny body of an ixchel woman hung impaled. A beautiful woman, writhing in agony. Pazel could not help himself: he cried aloud, and so did several others. The woman was Diadrelu – Dri – Hercól's lover and their cherished friend. She had perished months ago. They had given her body to the sea.

A tortured moan escaped Hercól's chest. Ramachni was on his shoulder in an instant, whispering. Ensyl too raced up Hercól's side, and out along the arm that held Ildraquin. 'Put her down, put her down!' she shouted through her tears.

'*Stop!*'

It was Dri's voice. She could see them. Desperately she waved

for Ensyl to be still. Then her eyes moved back to Hercól. 'Arunis
... being helped ... the demon-mage ... Sathek.'

'Sathek!' cried Neda and Cayer Vispek.

Dri's face was almost mad with pain. She looked again at Ensyl
and switched tongues, falling into the speech of ixchel, beyond the
range of human ears. Ensyl nodded, weeping uncontrollably. Then
Diadrelu placed a hand flat on either side of Ildraquin and swept
them all with her eyes.

'No quitting,' she said, and pushed herself free.

The tiny body fell to earth. Hercól lunged, but Ramachni was
faster. Pouncing on Diadrelu, he sank his fangs into her side, and
with a sharp twist of his body, flung her into the fire. Hercól did
not make a sound, but he shuddered, as from a death blow. Yet
even as Diadrelu struck the flames, she vanished. In her place the
sorcerer's head reappeared, mouthing a last, voiceless curse.

Hercól walked out among the reeds by the river's edge, with Ensyl
on his shoulder. They sat there, half-hidden, and their sounds of
grief floated softly over the clearing. Thasha pulled Pazel and
Neeps into her arms and wept. The tarboys stood numb, holding
her between them. Pazel could not say exactly where his own tears
had gone. He only knew, as he had that morning in the river, that
he couldn't afford them. *Your labour's not done.* Manifestly mucking
true. Friends had died, he was still standing. Bring on the next
thing, the next kick in the gut.

'It was her,' Thasha kept repeating. 'It was really her.'

'Yes,' said Ramachni. 'Arunis was using her, of course. But being
fearless, she sought to turn his torture to our advantage. Even in
death she has not given up the fight.'

Neda and Cayer Vispek stood gaping. Corporal Mandric shook
his head in disbelief. Humans no more cried for ixchel than a dog
did for its fleas.

As for Myett, she raced away from them all up the broken
stairs. Eyes dry, thoughts black. She could not bear to think of
them looking at her. With compassion, maybe, with forgiveness.

She had watched Hercól broken once already, at the moment of Diadrelu's death – her real death on the *Chathrand*, which Myett had helped bring about. She had taunted him, called him goat, satyr, sexual freak. All for Taliktrum. All to justify the extremes he was going to, the messianic make-believe, the killing of his rivals, the killing of his aunt.

Didn't you know? The question chased her, nipped her heels. Didn't you know it was false, the way Taliktrum excused his own brutality (I am your deliverer, the one to whom vision is given; I am my own reason why)? Couldn't you see it in his violence, his fear? After each encounter with Diadrelu he would rage at Myett, or strip and straddle her like a rapist, or worst of all sit quivering alone. *Didn't you know it was a lie?* Of course, of course. But she had managed not to know. She kept the knowledge hidden, a black stone in her stomach, until the day that Taliktrum himself could bear the lie no more.

She understood at last why he had cast her off. Taliktrum had shed family blood. And every glimpse of Myett had reminded him of the deed. It could never be otherwise. Even if he lived, and she found him, somewhere in this vast, vicious world – even then, it would lie between them. She climbed on, heedless of the growing wind, the slickness of the weathered stones.

Pazel sat staring into the fire. He could smell Arunis burning. It sickened him, and yet he craved the smell. There could never be enough proof that the mage was gone. Hercól and Ensyl were still crouched by the river. Neeps was walking up and down with Thasha, who was too distraught to hold still. Dastu sat a few yards from Pazel, likewise studying the fire.

'Muketch,' he said, 'I've been meaning to thank you.'

Pazel turned to him, benumbed. 'To thank me?'

'For what you did on the tower. You saved us, every bit as much as Thasha did.'

Pazel swallowed. 'I killed a man in the process.'

Dastu shook his head. 'Not a man.'

Pazel sighed and nodded. True enough: the *tol-chenni* had never had a human mind. It had been born with animal intelligence, and its parents had been the same. But its grandparents, or great-grandparents: who had they been? Shopkeepers in Masalym? Teachers, maybe? Newlyweds, with dreams for their children?

Some questions (many questions) were better left unasked.

'You've learned some fighting skills,' said Dastu.

Pazel shook his head. 'Only a little, from Thasha and Hercól. I'll never be really good.'

Pazel recalled a time when the compliment would have felt like a gift. He had once thought of Dastu as his best friend among the tarboys, after Neeps. He had delighted, secretly, in the fact that Dastu was pure Arquali, and yet free of the contempt for conquered races that infected so many. He'd adored the older boy. Everyone had: even those who never looked at Pazel or Neeps without a sneer.

Then Dastu had turned them in for mutiny.

Of course they *were* mutineers, Pazel and his friends. They'd met in a lightless room in the bowels of the *Chathrand*, to plan their takeover. Their true enemy was Arunis, but there had been no way to fight him without defying Captain Rose.

Pazel looked pointedly at Dastu. 'You still think we should be hanged?' he asked.

Dastu looked away. 'I'm loyal to Arqual. I swore an oath to my Emperor, and to the Service.'

'That's a yes, is it?'

The older youth shrugged. 'Doesn't matter what I think. Not to anyone. Pitfire, it hardly matters to *me*. Listen, Muketch: we have to toss the Nilstone in the river. Not on Gurishal. Right here. I know what Ramachni says about poisoning a well. But we have no choice, no other chance. And think of it this way.'

He scooped up two handfuls of dirt. 'Suppose we set off for Gurishal – somehow.' He let one handful sift through his fingers. 'The Stone remains in Alifros. The Swarm grows, the world is destroyed. That *will* happen. We'll struggle on awhile, then we'll fail, and everything will go to pieces. Look around and tell me I'm wrong. Look at us, Muketch; look at your leg. Think of where we are.'

'Denial is death,' murmured Pazel.

The other boy looked up sharply. 'Rin's truth, that is.' He opened his other hand, gazed at the sandy earth. 'But in another world, who can say? Maybe they're stronger, maybe they have great lords or wizards who'll know what to do with the Nilstone. All we know is what happens if it stays here.'

'That's all we know,' Pazel agreed.

Encouraged, Dastu leaned closer, lowering his voice. 'Bolutu's dead set against it, just like the mage. But there's one good thing about being here, in this Godsforsaken wilderness. You know what I mean. We outnumber them. We humans outnumber the dlömu, and if we know what's good for us we'll stick together. Do you understand me, Muketch?'

Pazel looked at him a moment. 'Yes, I think I do. And just now I was thinking of what you said that day, when I asked why you'd betrayed us. You told me to save my breath. That nothing I could say would make a difference to you, because you had your loyalties straight. Well, so do I, and they begin with Ramachni. Without him Arunis would have beaten us a long time ago.'

'Arunis nearly killed us last night. Because of Ramachni.'

Pazel shook his head. 'In *spite* of him. I won't help you, Dastu. And you're not getting near that mucking Stone by yourself. We'll carry it to Gurishal, somehow. And you know what else? You're here for a reason. Doesn't Ott always boast about leaving nothing to chance? He sent you along to help us on this mission, not to hinder us. Are you going to obey him or not?'

Dastu let the second handful of earth dribble to the ground. When his hand was empty he looked up at Pazel. His eyes were bright and accusing.

'You still don't see it, do you? We're trapped here. We're going to die in this place. We nearly killed ourselves getting here and now we are mucking *buried alive*.'

Hercól and Ensyl came back to the group around the fire. 'My mistress has not finished the dark journey,' said Ensyl.

'Not finished?' said Big Skip. 'What do you mean, by the Blessed Tree? Is she dead or not?'

'Her body died,' said Hercól, 'but her spirit has yet to pass into death's kingdom. She is holding herself back in order to help us. All this time she has lingered in some strange place between the lands of light and darkness.'

'In Agaroth,' said Ramachni. 'The Border-Kingdom. I have walked those dark hills myself, long ago in my youth. Many linger in Agaroth, hoping to finish some deed in this world, or because they fear the next.'

'Ensyl,' said Thasha, 'did Dri say anything more, in your tongue?'

'Yes,' said Ensyl. 'She said he was furious that he'd been tricked by Erithusmé.' She glanced at Pazel. 'You heard as well, didn't you?'

Pazel nodded. 'She said that Arunis had done everything he could to bring the Stone to Gurishal – until he learned that we could get rid of it there – and that now he'll do everything he can to *stop* us from taking it to that island.' Pazel looked at Ramachni, shaken. 'He learned the truth here in the forest, didn't he? Maybe with the Nilstone's aid. And Fulbreech overheard. But what if he hadn't? What if he'd died before we found him? We'd still have no idea where to take the Nilstone. *Credek*, we'd have no chance at all.'

'What if Fulbreech lied?' asked Lunja.

'Excellent question!' said Mandric. 'That boy was more crooked than a back alley in Ulsprit. What if he decided to stick it to us one last time?'

'I don't think he lied about Gurishal,' said Neeps.

The others looked at him. 'Oh yes,' said Dastu, 'your famous *hunches*. Your nose for lies.'

Neeps glared at Dastu. 'It's not a blary hunch,' he said. 'Think it through. If you *can't* reach the world of the dead from Gurishal, then what did Dri mean about Arunis being tricked?'

'If, if, if!' said Dastu. '*If* that was really your crawly friend who spoke to us. *If* she has any idea what Arunis is really up to. *If* the sorcerer didn't tell Fulbreech exactly what to say when we found him.'

'Mage,' said Cayer Vispek, turning to Ramachni, 'now that the sorcerer's body is burned, how much power remains to him?'

'In this world?' said Ramachni. 'Not much, I hope. But I am troubled by that missing scarf; we must search the ruins again before we leave.'

'There's one more thing,' said Ensyl. 'Dri said that Arunis spoke the truth about the Swarm.'

Ramachni's eyes darkened. 'This much is true: that the Swarm is drawn to death, and grows stronger when deaths are numerous. It belongs in the Border-Kingdom, patrolling that great and final Wall, beyond which stretches the land of the dead. Where the Wall crumbles, the Swarm holds back the dead, lest they flood into living lands and despoil them. That is its purpose: a vital purpose indeed. But it was *never* meant to be in the living world, or to encounter living beings, and here its work can only bring disaster. It will fall upon death, immobilizing the souls of the fallen. But when it falls upon the living, they too shall die – and feed the Swarm. The cycle can only accelerate, you see: with each death, the Swarm will grow stronger. Unless we rid the world of the Nilstone, the Swarm will come to blanket earth and sky, and smother every living thing beneath its pall.'

'But Ramachni, this makes no sense!' said Bolutu. 'Why should the Swarm have such power here? I have read many treatises on magic, including your own. The Swarm should be weak here in Alifros, if its power comes from elsewhere.'

'Not while the Nilstone remains in this world,' said the mage. 'You see a dark sphere, Belesar, but the Stone is also a puncture wound, and it is through that wound that the Swarm's power floods into our own.'

'Where has the Swarm gone, Ramachni?' asked Hercól.

'Away in search of death,' said the mage. 'Like water flowing downhill, it will go where death is strongest – to some unhappy corner of Alifros beset by plague or famine – or war.'

26

'War,' said Thasha. 'It all fits, doesn't it? Arunis did everything he could to start a war between Arqual and the Mzithrin. And we made it easy for him, both sides did, with all our greed and hate and holy nonsense.'

She looked pointedly at the *sfvantskors*. Silence fell. The North, the humans' battered homeland, was briefly, painfully present.

'I think war is getting now,' said Neda.

'There you go again,' said the marine.

Pazel lay on his stomach on a wide, flat stone, and Ramachni jumped up beside him and licked his ankle. A cool painlessness flowed from the mage's touch into his wounded leg; soon the whole limb felt heavy and remote. Then Bolutu came towards him with a knife, and they made him look away. Pazel could not feel the touch of the blade, but he heard a faint slicing sound as Bolutu cut out the dying flesh. Afraid he might be sick, he forced his thoughts elsewhere.

'Where is Myett?'

Bolutu frowned and glanced upwards. 'She has scaled the tower anew. Ensyl plans to go looking for her. Be still now, let me work.'

He bandaged Pazel's leg with scraps of cloth washed clean in the river, and Ramachni set a paw on the wound and spoke a few soft words. The delightful coolness grew stronger, but Ramachni warned him that the pain would return. 'I would fear for your leg if it did not,' added Bolutu.

'The bite will heal,' said Ramachni, 'but the damage may be of more than one kind. The jaws of the flame-trolls are ghastly pits, and just what foulness lurked in the one that gnawed you I cannot tell. Of course you were not the only one bitten – Mandric and Lunja both need tending – but the fang that pierced your leg went especially deep. You must keep your eye on that leg for years.'

'If I live to have such problems I'll be glad,' said Pazel.

But his words touched a deeper fear, resting like a stone in the pit of his stomach. 'Ramachni,' he said, very low, 'Neeps is the one I'm worried about.'

'He fears for his Marila, and their child,' said Bolutu.

'It's not just that, Bolutu,' said Pazel, glancing nervously at the rest of the party. 'It's the mind-plague.'

Bolutu started. '*Jathod*, I smelled it! The sharp smell of his sweat, like lemon peel. I had forgotten what it was like.'

'For Rin's sake, don't tell anyone,' said Pazel. 'Thasha knows, but no one else does. Not even Neeps has guessed.'

'I know of his condition,' said Ramachni. 'We can discuss it further after you sleep.'

'Can you cure him?'

Ramachni sighed. 'Pazel, your friend is succumbing to one of the most powerful spells ever cast in Alifros. It has already destroyed the minds of every human south of the Ruling Sea. The spell's caster herself proved powerless to stop it. Before I try to do what my mistress could not, I must have help. You know where I hope to find that help, I think.'

Pazel glanced at Thasha. He took a deep breath. 'I know,' he said, 'but you've made a mistake. There isn't going to be any help from Erithusmé.'

'We shall see,' said Ramachni gently.

'I don't think you understand,' said Pazel. 'It didn't work, she hasn't come back. Thasha is still just Thasha.'

'She was never *just* Thasha, my lad,' said Ramachni. 'And now I must insist that you *sleep*.'

The last word was like a finger snuffing a flame. Pazel barely had time to lay his head on the stone before sleep engulfed him, blissful and profound. In the stillness of the clearing he dreamed of a typhoon, and the *Chathrand* running north again, racing on madcap winds, chasing or giving chase. The whole crew was reunited, the dead and the living alike, and Captain Rose was on his quarterdeck, raging and gesturing, shouting orders, cursing ghosts. Pazel stood in the lashing rain, and Thasha was near him, her eyes bright as sparks, her pale skin luminous, as on the night when they had made love beneath the cedar. And somewhere in the darkness of the ship Pazel could feel the Nilstone, throbbing, pumping death through the ship and the storm and the world like a malignant spirit, like a great black heart.

Myett had climbed three hundred feet before she realised that she did not wish to die.

She knew the difference between flirting with death and hungering for it, wanting it with her soul. She had known the latter condition, and once, very nearly, succumbed. This was different. The impulse to destroy herself weakened with every yard she ascended.

She'd been in earnest that other time, however. Sealed in the *Chathrand*'s flooding hold, blind drunk, heartbroken. It was luck that had saved her: luck and the Masalym shipwrights. If the draining of the ship had been delayed another quarter-hour, they'd have found her body clogging the pumps.

Three hundred feet brought her to the level of the bottom-most leaf-layer, where the wind began. She held tight, feeling the still-pleasant burning in her muscles, the strength in arms, fingers, ankles no giant could ever attain. She was wedged in a crack that ran like inverse lightning up the tower wall. The strange birds wheeled around her, crying. Afraid she'd come for what was left of their brood.

The alternative to death had been this expedition, this crossing of battle-lines. She had spent most of the voyage fighting Ensyl and Diadrelu and their giant friends. Myett had been as committed as any ixchel to the hatred of human beings, and heaven knew there was reason for it. But loyalty to her lover had been the bedrock of that hate. She had cleaved to Taliktrum, Diadrelu's nephew, before and after his rise to power. After he became a visionary, Myett had argued with the doubters, rabidly insistent that he was all that he claimed. Too funny. All along the debate had been with herself.

She could not pinpoint when the change had come. After the flame-trolls, surely, and before the catastrophe in the forest. Was it the night she dreamed her grandfather's death, and woke sobbing, bewildered, unable to recall for nearly half a minute that she'd left him safe and sound on the *Chathrand*? Was it when the giants wept for their dead, and she had nowhere to be but right there beside them, witnessing grief that looked and sounded for all the world like ixchel grief? Or the night she saw Thasha and Pazel Pathkendle slip away to make love, and followed them, unseen of course, and vaguely disappointed to learn that this, too, was not a thing her people did better than giants.

Four hundred feet, and the rim of the crater was in sight. A tearing wind broke around her, trying her grip. The crack had narrowed, too: Myett found fewer places to wedge her body, rest her weight. She could see the large, shaggy nests atop the pinnacle, now, and one grey wing, spread wide to bask in the sun.

Whenever it had happened, the change was real. She stood with Ensyl, now – and heaven help her, the giants. The humans. She would have to remember to hate them, secretly, remind herself of what they were. Or else become one. That was Diadrelu's choice, and Ensyl's. Myett would never go that far, never risk becoming a mascot. But the quest was hers now, and she would give more than they did, more than they ever could. It had become a cause to live for, rather than a slower, grander way to die.

She stopped. Her muscles twitching, her fingers raw. She was a hundred feet above the highest leaf-layer, seeing the wider world for the first time in days. She knew that the descent would take all her strength, if indeed she had not gone too far already. The wind tore at her, but she would not retreat without the view she'd come for. Aching, she leaned out from the wall.

The ruins stood almost exactly at the Forest's centre. To the south, dark hills pressed close to the crater's rim. A shimmer of reflected sunlight marked the place where the mighty Angungra cut through the crater wall and swept away, into a deepening gorge. A mist hung over that gorge, and beyond it there were mountains, lower than the cold peaks they had passed through, but tight and forbidding all the same. And endless, too: if they somehow escaped this Forest they would have little choice but to brave those mountains – with no guide who had ever set foot there, no notion of what lay beyond.

Or almost none.

There is hope downriver, between the mountains and the sea. The strange message from Vasparhaven, the Spider Temple, came back to her with sudden irony. Hope. Maybe it was out there, somewhere, hidden in this great arbitrary maze of a world. But what of it? The notion seemed cruel, like showing a coin to a beggar, then tossing it away into a field.

Carefully, she turned to face the north. The snow-capped range through which they had come loomed dark and massive. Astonishing to think that a footpath snaked through those peaks, and down again, to the city where they'd left their ship, their one real hope of any life save the life of castaways. To say nothing of kinfolk, clan brothers and sisters, her grandfather ... and Taliktrum.

He was back there in Masalym. The only ixchel in that vast city of dlömu. Her lover, exiled by his own choosing. And by the impossible, the suffocating neediness of their clan.

I should be with you. I should have sought you out.

Nonsense, of course. Taliktrum had spurned her, called her *an entertainment.* If Myett had abandoned both the ship and this expedition, if she somehow found him in that huge dark hive of a city, Taliktrum would only have called her a fool. And been right in doing so. Myett was done with foolishness: she too had made decisions, chosen sides. It was a strange fate, to be fighting alongside giants, sworn enemies, for an abstraction called the world. But Myett knew what she and Ensyl could give them, how ixchel skills might help them all survive, and that certainty of being needed was what one felt in a clan.

It was not passion, not 'starlight in the blood' as the poets had it, not the bliss she had felt when Taliktrum was at his best, when he managed to be loving and kind. But it was good, they were good; even Hercól had forgiven and embraced her. She looked down, mapping out her descent.

Then her brow furrowed. What was blocking the sun?

Instinct came too late. Myett's hand flew to her knife, but the hawk was already on her, grey wings filling her vision, shrill cry rending the air. Talons longer than her arm bit into her flesh.

She was crushed, barely able to breathe. But as the hawk wheeled away from the tower she managed to pass the knife from her half-pinned arm to her teeth. Her thoughts exploding. She would fall. She would die. She would work the arm free, stab the bird, master it, make it land. No quitting. No quitting. The talons moved. Her arm slid free.

At once she buried the knife in the bird's leg. Its reaction was swift and violent, a sharp jerking stall, and Myett was thrown, whirling, falling, falling to her death. The sun whirled, the earth flashed in circles around her, the tower wall surged by faster and faster, she was dead, she was surely dead, a life of lust and bitterness and rage—

The hawk snatched her from the air. Myett felt its black beak tighten as it pulled out of the fall, straining, the tug of the earth so strong she thought her ears must be bleeding. Then they rose above the top leaf-layer and shot away to the south, and the hawk passed her back into his claw, slick now with the blood she had drawn. One eye, coral-red and brilliant, fixed upon her.

'If you fight me,' said the hawk distinctly, 'I will pinch that arm until it dies.'

2

Flesh, Stone and Spirit

11 Modobrin 941
240th day from Etherhorde

The mighty are beggars, child. They rattle silver cups by the roadside, pleading for love.

Dlömic folk song

Sandor Ott paced the cabin in a circle. His movements as always were fluid, measured, utterly precise. He spoke no offhand words, made no careless sounds, revealed nothing but what he chose to in the cast of his old, scarred face. His hands hung loose; his knife was visible but sheathed. As he walked, his eyes remained fixed on the circle's centre: the spot where Captain Nilus Rotheby Rose sat scowling, fidgeting, in a chair barely large enough to accommodate his bulk.

The captain's eyes were bloodshot; his red beard was a fright. It was his own day cabin he sat in, under the assassin's gaze. The chair was the one he usually gave to the least favoured guest at his dinner table.

Rose crossed his burly arms. Sandor Ott continued circling. For some reason he had also brought his longbow – huge, stained, savage – and propped it near the stern galleries, along with several arrows. Target practice? Shooting gulls from the window? Rose scratched the back of his neck, trying to keep the old killer in sight.

Maybe he would never speak. It was even possible that his

thoughts were not with the captain at all, no matter how much he drilled with his eyes. Some people whittled sticks when they were concentrating. Sandor Ott tormented people, stripped their certainties away, needled them with doubts.

There was a small table within the captain's reach, and a flagon of wine atop it. Rose snatched it up and pulled the stopper. His grip was weaker than a year ago: he had lost two fingers in a fight with Arunis. Rose had trod on one of them, heard the knuckle crack beneath his boot. Horrible the things that came back to him, the sensations one was powerless to forget.

He raised the flagon, then paused and removed a small object from his mouth. It was a glass eyeball, beautifully rendered. Yellow and black, orpiment and ebony, arrow-slit iris of a jungle cat. A leopard, to be precise: the symbol of Bali Adro, this Empire twice the size of Ott's beloved Arqual, if the dlömic freaks told the truth. They'd handed Rose the taxidermed animal (sunbleached, moth-gnawed, deeply symbolic in some way he cared nothing about) just hours before the ship's departure from Masalym. A gesture of goodwill to let a human captain hold the carcass, during those last hours in port. No matter the captain's own concerns. No matter that he loathed all things feline, beginning with that vile Sniraga, purring even now beneath his bed.

He drank; Ott circled. In Rose's closet, Joss Odarth was snickering about modern naval uniforms.[*]

Monster. Fool. You have blinded the Leopard of Masalym. So the freaks had shouted, and of course it was true. The first eye had come loose when he'd handled the carcass a bit too roughly, clubbed the topdeck with it in fact; the second he'd pried out with a spoon. Thinking all the while of the Tournament Grounds, where his crew had been imprisoned, and from whence twenty-three men had escaped one panicky night into that great warren of a city, and never returned.

---

[*]Jossolan 'Snake Eyes' Odarth, Captain of the I.M.S. *Chathrand*, W.S. Years 593-624. Killed in a brawl on 2 Modobri 627. - EDITOR

Damn your soul for all eternity, Ott! Whatever you mean to do, get on with it!

Rose squeezed the eye in his sweaty fist. He had tossed the leopard ashore when the mooring-lines were freed, just as tradition demanded. And they'd caught it, those dlömic mariners. They'd even cheered a little: the tail had not brushed the ground, and that meant splendid luck. Then they'd noticed the missing eyes and stared in horror at the departing ship. Rose had grinned and popped the eye into his mouth. He had traditions of his own.

He would keep it; there was power in a little theft. One day it would gather dust on his mantel, declaring with its stillness that this *was* a mantel, in a house without ladderways or a brine reek from the basement, a house that never rolled or pitched or pinwheeled; Gods, how he hated the sea.

Nonsense, nonsense. A frog could not hate the mud that made him; a bird could not hate the medium of the air. He was fatigued; he needed protein; where in the Nine Pits was Teggatz with his tea? He put the eye back in his mouth. Better to keep it there, clicking against his molars, studying his tongue, watching his words before they left his—

'Riding pants!' said Sandor Ott.

Rose inhaled the eye. His face purpled, his vision dimmed. The old killer sighed and bent him double; then came a stunning blow between his shoulders. The eye shot from his mouth, and the hated cat, Sniraga, chased and batted it across the floor.

'Now sit up.'

Rose did not sit up. He was thinking of the augrongs, Refeg and Rer. It was just possible that he could oblige the huge anchor-lifters to kill Sandor Ott, battering through a wall of Turachs, lifting the spymaster, breaking him over a scaly knee. But what if the Turachs killed the augrongs instead?

'Kindly look at me when I am talking,' said Ott. The captain stared hard at the floor. Vital to resist, vital to deny: if he caved in on small matters, the larger would follow.

'Boots,' Ott snarled. 'Buckskin gloves. A spare belt buckle, a fifth of rum. Powdered sulphur in your socks. A little whetstone for your axe. But the pants, Captain: they tell the whole tale. They'd been altered that same afternoon: bits of leather trim were still in Oggosk's sewing basket. The hag stitched them especially for you, with thick pads in the seat, lest that treacherous arse develop saddle sores. You truly meant to go through with it. To abandon your vessel, your crew. To run off with Hercól and Pathkendle and Thasha Isiq.'

'Only to the city gate,' said Rose. 'Only until I was sure we'd seen the last of them.'

'And for this you kept the witch up all night sewing pants?'

Rose sat up heavily. 'They're not idiots,' he said. 'They had to believe I meant to join their daft crusade.'

Sandor Ott stopped pacing directly in front of Rose. He put his hand in his pocket and withdrew a small lead pillbox. He held it close to the captain's face.

'These?'

'Sulphites,' said the captain, 'for my gout.'

Ott extracted a pill, crunched it in his mouth. He turned and spat on the polished floor.

'Waspwort,' he said, 'for altitude sickness.' The spymaster's gaze was very cold. 'You were going with them over the mountains. It was no bluff at all.'

Rose dropped his eyes. 'It was no bluff,' he said.

'I am empowered by His Supremacy to punish you with death,' said Ott. 'You were given command of the most crucial mission in the history of Arqual, and you tried to shrug it off and flee. That is criminal dereliction of duty. Your life is justly forfeit.'

'We both know you're lying,' said Rose. 'Emperor Magad gave *you* into *my* service, not the other way around.'

'Have you believed that all along?'

The captain's face darkened. 'I am the Final Offshore Authority,' he said.

'Treason nullifies such authority,' said Ott. 'You would do better to concentrate on providing reasons I should *want* to keep you

36

alive. For at the moment, Captain, I have not a one.'

His hand shot out, seized the captain's own. Then he pointed to a short scar, healed but plainly visible. 'How did you get this?' he said.

'From that miserable Sniraga,' said Rose, flicking his eyes towards the cat.

'Stop lying to me, bastard. That's the mark of a blade tip. A sword, I think. Who the devil lunged at you with a sword?'

'It was the cat, I say. Have a look at her claws.'

Ott shook his head in disappointment. He turned and walked to the gallery windows, swept the curtains aside. Grey daylight flooded the chamber, refracted through a haze of cloud. It was midmorning but the sun could have been anywhere – high or low, east or west. They were in the shallows of the Ruling Sea, two days out from Masalym, running west along the endless length of the Sandwall. Running for their lives.

'Our relationship,' said Ott, 'must proceed henceforth on a new footing, or death alone can be the result. And speaking of death, three mutineers remain at liberty among the crew. It would be better if you dispensed with them, rather than I.'

'That matter is decided for now,' said Rose. 'I have suspended their punishment. There were mitigating factors.'

Ott shook his head. 'For certain crimes there is no atonement. You will hang them.'

Rose erupted to his feet. 'What are you proposing? To hang a pregnant girl from the crosstrees? To hang the quartermaster who saw us across the Nelluroq alive?'

'You condemned them yourself,' said Ott. 'And haven't I heard you tell your officers that they must never issue a command they're not willing to enforce? What is the difficulty? The girl Marila is nothing: a stowaway who fell in with Pathkendle's gang, and spread her legs for one of them. Fiffengurt's skills are redundant, as long as you're alive. And Mr Druffle is a tippling buffoon.'

'He claims he was too drunk to know that he'd been brought to a gathering of mutineers,' said Rose.

'Is that one of your mitigating factors? Go ahead, extend that reasoning to the entire crew. Amnesty for drunkards. Pickle yourself before you challenge my command.'

Rose's mouth twisted. The spymaster looked caught between amusement and outrage. 'You can't have gone soft?' he demanded. 'You, Nilus Rose? The man I watched strangling Pazel Pathkendle in the liquor vault? You, who sent a boatload of men ashore to pick apples, then sailed away and abandoned them at the approach of a hostile ship?'

'My hand was forced. As you would know if you had not been imprisoned.'

'But I *was* imprisoned, Rose – and once freed, I dealt with those who had imprisoned me, and rid the ship of them.'

'That remains to be seen.'

'You're splitting hairs, now,' said Ott. 'Some of the crawlies fled into Masalym. Others we killed. They are gone, neutralised. That is how one deals with enemies, unless one prefers to be dealt with.'

He looked out through the curtains again. 'I remember when you tossed a man from this window,' he said. 'Mr Aken, the honest company man, the quiet one. You could hear the wheels turning in his mind, you said, and for all I know you spoke the truth. But listen once and for ever, Captain: the wheels in *your* head are loud as grinding stones. You will not deceive me. When you feign madness, I know it. Just as I do when true madness directs your steps. Your plan to abandon ship was not one of the latter cases. You were deliberate. You had better tell me why.'

'Go rot in the Pits.'

Not a flicker of response passed over Ott's face. He waited, looking out over the sea.

'You can't sail this vessel,' said Rose. 'Elkstem can choose a heading, and Fiffengurt trim the sails, but neither can manage eight hundred men. Who's going to keep them working as a team, as a family? Haddismal, at spear point? Uskins, who nearly put the ship at the bottom of the sea? You?'

'What is the danger you haven't spoken of, Captain?'

'You know the danger,' said Rose. 'There's a she-devil of a sorceress bearing down on Masalym, in a vessel packed with dlömic warriors. Macadra, she's called. Arunis' rival, the one who stayed behind when he crossed the Ruling Sea and set about teaching us to destroy each other. With your expert help, of course.'

'Stick to the point,' said Ott.

'The point, bastard, is that she wants the mucking Nilstone, and we can't assume she'll believe it when they tell her Arunis took it away over the mountains. And even if she does believe, she may still want this ship. Pitfire, she may want *us*: human beings, to torture or take apart. Or breed. We were their slaves, once, and could be again.'

'What is the danger, Rose?'

'Gods below, man! Isn't that enough?'

'We stand a fine chance of evading pursuit,' said Ott. 'Something else weighs against our chances. Something so terrible you'd rather abandon this *family*, and run away in shame.'

Rose lowered his chin, glowering. His mouth was tightly closed.

'You are asking yourself what kind of force I mean to apply,' said Sandor Ott. 'It does not involve pain – unless things go very wrong, that is. It will be worse than pain. But you should know that I never discuss my techniques. Some things are better demonstrated than described.'

'The trouble,' said Rose, 'is that you won't believe me.'

'That is not your concern. Speak the truth. What were you running from?'

Rose looked the assassin in the eye. 'Not running *from*,' he said. 'I was running *to*. The worst danger's not the one that's chasing us. Stanapeth and the tarboys and Thasha Gods-damned Isiq: they're in the right. You don't like it; nor do I. But it happens to be true. We're going to be slow-roasted, all of us, the whole Rinforsaken world, if Arunis finds a way to use the Stone in battle.'

As Rose was speaking, Ott had once more grown still. Now he walked to the cabin door and opened it an inch. A Turach was stationed there, barring entry. Ott gestured, and the Turach passed him a pair of objects. A small glass pitcher and a shallow bowl.

Ott closed the door and returned, and Rose saw that the pitcher held a few ounces of milk. Ott knelt beside the captain's desk, not far from where Sniraga crouched, tail twitching, watchful. He poured the milk into the bowl and set the bowl on the floor. Then he stood and walked to the gallery window. He picked up the bow and notched the arrow to the string.

'You hate this animal,' he said.

Sniraga raised her head, considering the proffered milk. Rose's eyes widened. 'Lower that bow, Spymaster,' he said.

'In killing her I'll be doing you a favour, no doubt. You've thought of doing this so many times, but something has always stopped you from acting on the impulse.'

'Nothing will stop me from avenging myself on you, if you harm the creature.'

For the first time, Ott smiled. 'Halfwit. If only I could let you try.'

Sniraga nosed forward. It had been many weeks since she had tasted milk.

'Speak the truth, Rose. Otherwise you may consider this a fore-taste of something much slower and crueller I'll be doing to your beloved witch. Is she your aunt or your mother, incidentally? Or are you still unsure?'

'I can state my motives,' said Rose, 'but I can't make you hear. Put the bow down. That's an order.'

'You are right in one respect,' Ott continued. 'I won't be killing you. Not until the mission is completed, and Arqual's victory achieved.'

'That day will never come!' Rose exploded from his chair, prompting Ott to bend the bow. 'Damn you to the blackest hole! *Forget the mission!* It's a fever dream. A lie you hawked to that deathsmoke-addled Emperor of yours.'

'I will not tolerate slander of Magad the Fifth,' said Ott, taking aim.

Rose was bellowing. 'Greater Arqual, the defeat of the Mzithrin

– rubbish and rot. One of these sorcerers is going to clap hands on the Stone and make sausage out of us. Out of your precious Emperor, out of Arqual and the Sizzies and the whole Rinforsaken North. Blind fool! You're a soldier in an ant war, and the mucking anteater's coming down the trail.'

'Rose,' said Ott, 'do you recall that you'd become a disgrace? Removed from command by the Chathrand Trading Family, wanted in twenty ports, living off the last spongings from your creditors? Do you know what a boon of trust His Supremacy gave you, when he restored you to the captaincy of the *Chathrand*, and gave you nominal command of this mission you advise me to forget?'

'We will see how nominal it is when the waves hit eighty feet,' shouted Rose. 'As for that *boon*: rubbish again. Put the bow down, Ott. The game was never winnable, but without me you couldn't even play. You didn't dare attempt the Ruling Sea – put the bow down, I say – without Nilus Rose at the helm. I alone know the soul of this vessel. I alone have the sanction of the ghosts.'

'You alone *see* them.'

Rose's body was rigid. 'I am the captain of this ship. You are an adjunct, a supernumerary. If you challenge me openly you will bring anarchy down upon us all. That's as clear today as it was when your mucking Emperor—'

Ott's bow sang. There was a caterwaul (horrid, held) and Sniraga became a red tornado of fur and fangs and blood. The arrow had pinned her tail to the floor.

Rose leaped on the hysterical creature. He was bloodied instantly from hands to shoulders, but he wrenched the arrow free. Sniraga flew from beneath him, crashing against furniture, painting the room with the red brush of her tail. Ott leaned on his bow and laughed.

Then the wailing changed. Rose turned, bewildered; Ott snuffed his laughter. A second cry, a human cry, was drowning out Sniraga. It rose through the floorboards, a voice they had not heard in months. The only voice as deep as the captain's, or as cruel as Ott's.

'WHERE IS IT? WHO TOOK IT? FAITHLESS VERMIN, PARASITES, OFFAL WORMS! UNCHAIN ME! BRING IT BACK TO ME NOW!'

Alongside the screamer, other voices began to rise, shouting in fear and wonder. Then commotion at the door. Ott dashed to it, flung it wide. A gnarled stick poked him in the chest, and Lady Oggosk, tiny and raging, hobbled into the room.

'He's dead, Nilus, get up! He's dead, he's dead, he's alive!'

'Duchess—'began Rose.

'Is she mad, Rose?' Ott demanded. 'Who is dead? Who is shouting below?'

'Nilus, your arms are soaked in blood!' shrieked the witch. 'Get yourselves together, you pair of fools. The sorcerer's been killed, and Pathkendle's charm is broken. The spell-keeper was *Arunis*, all along. Do you understand now, Sandor Ott?'

A wild gleam lit the spymaster's eye. He flew from the cabin, shouting at the Turachs to clear a path. Rose looked at Oggosk, but there was no hope under Heaven's Tree of explaining, so before she noticed Sniraga he charged after Ott. He had a presentiment of disaster. It grew with each roar from below.

Sailors thronged the topdeck; some of them already knew. The captain waved them off, needing to see it before he heard them speak, needing to mark the disaster with his eyes. Down the broad ladderway called the Silver Stair he plunged, bashing aside Teggatz and his tea service, bellowing at dolts who froze at the sight of him, walking right over a topman who had fallen flat in his haste to get out of the way. Everyone below was shouting. He could hear the panic in their throats. He plunged out onto the orlop deck, raced through the fire-scarred compartments, and stepped at last into the manger.

Great devils, there he was.

A huge, hideous man, seventy if he was a day, raged into the centre of the chamber, his bare feet stamping in an effluvium of grime, straw and fresh blood. In his eyes was more mad viciousness than Rose had glimpsed in any living soul. The Shaggat Ness, the lunatic king, the most hated man in Mzithrini history. He was tangled in chains looped around an indestructible wooden stanchion. But the chains had been placed to secure a statue, a lifeless thing of stone, for that is what the man had been for five months.

No longer. The mink-mage had told Arunis he could only reverse the spell when someone aboard the *Chathrand* died. If Lady Oggosk was correct, that someone was Arunis himself. *What happened? Did he die trying to master the Stone? Could that gang of children and mutineers possibly have killed him?*

No time to wonder. The Shaggat was gesturing, flailing with both hands: the unharmed right, and the dead, scarecrow-stick left, the hand that had seized the Nilstone. His jaws were wide, his screams insufferable, a bomb that kept going off, *Where is it, who stole it, bring it to me, you lice.*

His eyes found Rose. He lunged, and the stanchion shook.

Sandor Ott rubbed his chin. He stood with Sergeant Haddismal and several other Turachs, conferring quickly, eyeing the Shaggat like a rabid dog. Ignus Chadfallow, the Imperial Surgeon, was in the room as well, bending down to talk to old, befuddled Dr Rain, whose gape of horror made him look like an eel. The captain stepped towards them – then leaped sideways with a curse. The Shaggat had lunged at him again.

'BRING ME THE NILSTONE! BRING IT! BRING IT!'

'Monster—' said Sandor Ott.

'I WILL PACK YOUR MOUTH WITH SCORPIONS AND GLASS!'

'Listen—'

'I WILL TEAR OFF YOUR MANHOOD AND THROW IT TO MY HOUNDS!'

'Your toe.'

'BRING ME THE – WHAT?'

'Your toe.'

The Shaggat looked down. And dropped in his chains, howling, seizing his foot with his one living hand. The foot was gushing blood: where the big toe should have been was an open wound.

Undrabust!

It came back to Rose in a flash: how Neeps Undrabust had pulverised the Shaggat-statue's toe with a lump of iron. Arunis had managed to heal the other damage, the long cracks in the Shaggat's stone arm: wounds that would have killed a living man. But he had forgotten the toe.

A sailor appeared in the doorway, clutching Dr Chadfallow's medical bag. The surgeon and Sandor Ott rushed to the man. Chadfallow seized the bag and withdrew a folded cloth and small blue bottle. He glanced dubiously at the Shaggat.

'This will suffice, but how exactly—'

Ott snatched both items, uncorked the bottle and sniffed. He coughed, then doused the rag with the contents of the bottle. The doctor retreated as a cloying smell of spirits filled the room. The Shaggat raised his head too late. Ott threw himself on the huge man, and caught his chin in the crook of an elbow. The mad king erupted, clawing at him, crushing him against the stanchion, rolling atop him on the bloody floor. The Turachs surged forward, weapons drawn.

'Hold!'

Ott's voice, loud in the sudden silence. The Shaggat's bellowing had ceased. His arms went limp, and he toppled over in his chains.

Sandor Ott hurled the rag away. 'Stop the bleeding, fools!' he said. Then he too collapsed. During the struggle his face had been only inches from the rag.

A cold claw touched Rose's elbow. Lady Oggosk was there, suddenly, her shawl splashed with blood and fur, staring up at him with her milk-blue eyes. 'They will press you harder than ever, now that he's returned,' she said. 'Do not yield to them, Nilus. You know what must be done.'

Rose studied the two men at his feet. He felt a bottomless disgust. The mastermind of Arqual and his tool. *Better for everyone if they had strangled each other, if that sleep were the sleep of death.*

But what of Nilus Rose? He had sworn to his father that he would bend these creatures to his will. But that was only hubris – the kind of talk his father wanted to hear, demanded to hear. Over and over, decade after decade. The long, daft proof of their power. The family epic. Rose had never stopped writing it, even though a fool could tell you that the premise was absurd.

'He was unhinged before, or partly so. Now I fear his derangement is complete.'

Dr Chadfallow lowered himself stiffly into a chair, scanning the other faces around the table. The wardroom was cool, bathed in grey-blue light from the glass planks in the ceiling. Old Dr Rain took the chair to his right, glancing at Chadfallow with a mixture of jealousy and gratitude; it was only through Chadfallow's courtesy that he'd been included at all.

Fiffengurt, the quartermaster, sat down as well, glancing at the other faces as though tensed for a fight. *That one will take it badly*, thought Rose, studying him.

Fiffengurt was almost old. He had white whiskers and a rogue eye that spun randomly in its socket. He looked anxious, and more than a little guilty. Chadfallow, Rose saw now, was much the same. *Allies of Pathkendle and company – even the doctor has at last chosen sides. I must expect the worst from both of them.*

No one looked healthy, in point of fact. No one but the ghosts. Three had slithered into the chamber when the door was ajar. Captain Kurlstaff was among them, his pink blouse faded, his painted lips the colour of a man's intestines, his battleaxe huge and unwieldy in the crowded room. He watched the living with interest. He was the only one of the *Chathrand*'s former commanders with whom Rose deigned, at times, to consult, although today the old pervert merely stood and stared.

At least Kurlstaff had the decency not to sabotage the meeting. Captain Spengler was rummaging in the chart locker behind Rose's head. And Maulle, the pig, had actually taken a chair, in which he slouched and squirmed and bit his fingernails. The man had the worst facial tic Rose had ever seen; when it happened his face compressed like a sponge, and a puff of chalk powder lifted from his ancient wig.

'Sir?' said Chadfallow.

Rose pivoted away from the ghosts. 'So the Shaggat is mad,' he said. 'Is that news, Doctor? Have you nothing else to report?'

Chadfallow took a careful breath. 'The Shaggat is seventy-four years old. And he has just suffered traumas that would strain the faculties of any man. The touch of the Nilstone. The killing fire that ran up his arm. The transmutation into a dead statue, through Pazel's Master-Word, and this morning's reversal. But above all, he is disturbed by the loss of the Stone. To gain it was his life-long obsession. He thinks the Gods themselves chose him to wield it, along with that lesser artefact, Sathek's Sceptre. And because he cannot have had any sense of time's passage while enchanted, he must perceive that the Stone has just been taken from him.' Chadfallow shook his head. 'His mind is warped beyond all healing, now. What you saw is likely all that remains.'

Old Dr Rain cleared his throat. 'He exhibits a certain *unease*, Captain Rose. That is to say, he is uneasy.'

Rose turned him a choleric stare. The old medic looked quickly at Chadfallow.

'I cut off the dead hand,' said Chadfallow. 'He felt nothing. Below the wrist the limb was dry and brittle. It's a wonder it did not break during that wrestling match.'

'It did not break, because I did not break it,' said Ott. 'What else?'

Chadfallow shrugged. 'His body is otherwise sound. The man is a war elephant. You've heard the legend about the arrow that broke off in his chest, the head of which was never extracted? I saw the scar, I felt the hard nub with my fingers. The wound was two inches above his heart. There are flecks of iron embedded in his left eyeball, too, and signs that his feet were blistered by walking through fire, or over coals. He is indestructible, in a word. Only his mind has failed, and that utterly.'

Rain cleared his throat again. 'In professional terms – that is, in proper language, medical language—'

'Stop your fidgeting, dog!' snapped Rose. He was addressing Captain Maulle, but Rain flinched as if struck.

Haddismal was scowling. 'The Shaggat's mad, but he ain't an animal. The good doctor exaggerates.'

'Agreed,' said Ott. 'You're distorting your own diagnosis, Chadfallow, because you wish our cause to fail. In violation of your medical oath, to say nothing of your oath to His Supremacy.'

Chadfallow bristled. 'You saw it yourselves,' he said. 'That man raged for six minutes without a glance at his own maimed foot. He might have bled to death without noticing the wound.'

'And blary good riddance,' said Mr Fiffengurt, the quartermaster, unable to contain himself.

Sandor Ott turned his gaze on Fiffengurt. 'Another proud son of Arqual,' he said. 'What has happened to all your friends, traitor?'

Fiffengurt's bad eye drifted. But the other was clear and sharp, and he trained it now on Sandor Ott.

'My friends are right here,' he said, thumping a fist to his chest. 'Where are yours, exactly?'

A frigid silence followed. Then Ott said, 'Captain Rose may have his reasons for delaying your execution—'

'He does,' said Rose. 'The word is seamanship, and it cannot be wasted.'

Fiffengurt did not smile – Rose would get no smile out of him, not in this lifetime – but a certain grim pride showed in his face.

'Seamanship,' said Ott, 'just so. Yet this voyage will end one day, Mr Fiffengurt. And when you step ashore, so shall I.' He turned back to the others around the table. 'As for the Shaggat: hysteria is rarely permanent. Through all the years of his ascendancy he was prone to fits. They form part of the legend of his greatness.'

'They can't have been like *this*,' ventured Elkstem, the sailmaster. 'He'd never have been able to lead no rebellion. He was screaming like a stuck pig.'

'I doubt we shall ever see another display like this morning's,' said Ott. 'And if we do – well, Doctor, I did not add you to this mission because I loved your company. You earned great fame with diseases, but your talents go further, don't they? Before the miracle with the Talking Fever, you had another specialty. A rather lucrative one, at that.'

Chadfallow started. 'You're mistaken,' he said.

Ott raised an eyebrow, smiling.

Dr Rain snapped his fingers. '"*Ignus Chadfallow, Sedatives and Stimulants,*"' he said. 'Remember, Ignus? You gave me your card at the Medical Academy dinner, in the spring. I have it right here ....'

The old man fumbled in the pockets of his threadbare coat, at last producing what looked like a mouse's nest. Tearing open the fluffy wad, he extracted a crushed and soiled square of parchment. He held it up, beaming. Chadfallow stared in disbelief.

'That card is twenty-six years old,' he said.

Ott leaned over and snatched the card from Rain. He squinted. '"*Compounds to Induce Tranquillity and Peace of Mind.*" Capital, Doctor; the Shaggat Ness is in good hands. Besides, we do not require the murdering genius of his youth. All he needs is that apocalyptic impulse, and enough coherence to put his fanatics once more on the path of war.'

'And the Nilstone?' asked Rose.

Ott shook his head. 'The Nilstone is behind us. And despite the Shaggat's obsession, the cursed thing was never part of our plan. It nearly killed him, after all. Let it remain here in the South. If it has truly caused the death of Arunis, so much the better. Our concern is to finish the task His Supremacy placed before us, with all dignity and speed.'

'Dignity,' said Chadfallow.

He spoke the word softly, but it still conveyed the bitterness of a lifetime. Captain Kurlstaff, breaking his silence, said, 'I like this doctor, Rose. But the spymaster wants him dead.'

'Hold your peace, Ott,' said Rose. 'I have not brought you here to bicker like tarboys.' He turned to Fiffengurt, and barked suddenly:

48

'Where in the Black Pits is the first mate? Did I summon my deck officers or not?'

'I conveyed your order to Stukey myself, Captain,' said Fiffengurt. 'He only grunted at me through his door.'

'Uskins missed his noon log entry as well, sir,' put in Mr Fegin, who had recently been promoted to the rank of bosun. 'Perhaps he's ill?'

Rose looked at the doctors, who shrugged. 'He's not been to sickbay,' said Chadfallow.

The captain's fury was a live coal in his chest. 'Find the duty clerk, Mr Fegin,' he said, very low. 'Tell him to inform Mr Uskins that if he is not here within three minutes he will be tied to the mizzenmast with a vat of excrement from the chicken coops, and not released until he drinks it.' He paused, then shouted: 'Go!'

Fegin was off like a greyhound. The captain spread his hands flat on the table, glaring at the faces around him. 'Why do ships sink?' he asked them. 'Imprecision, that is why. Laxity and sloth, and men who look the other way. That will never be while I command this ship.'

He took care not to glance at Sandor Ott. But a part of him knew that his words were for the spy, a reminder of what Rose alone could deliver.

'We are being hunted, gentlemen,' he said. 'In all likelihood that sorceress has reached Masalym by now, and learned that we have fled. Whether or not she realises that we don't have the Nilstone, she'll want to take us – and she has the right ship for the job. The *Kirisang*, also known as the *Death's Head*. The vessel's every bit as large as the *Chathrand*, and a warship through and through. Or so Prince Olik claimed. Of course I do not trust him, or any other dlömu. But we have seen Bali Adro firepower for ourselves.'

He gave them a moment to remember it: the horrific armada that had passed so near them, great squalid ships held together by spellcraft, bristling with terrible arms.

'Now take heart, for Arunis *is* dead. Lady Oggosk sensed it, and the Shaggat's return to life is the proof. He is gone, and the

Nilstone is gone, and the ship is both provisioned and repaired. You may have heard that there was a hairline crack in the keel—'

They had *not* heard: Fiffengurt and Elkstem gaped, struggling to contain themselves.

'—but I assure you that rumour is false: no ship of mine will ever touch the Nelluroq with a damaged keel. No, the *Chathrand* will not disappoint us. The sorcerer is gone, and if any crawlies remain, we shall deal with them as with any vermin.

'In short, gentlemen, we are done with the South. The last stage of this mission lies before us. We must find our way to Gurishal. The Shaggat must go to his tribe, to wreak havoc in the heartland of the Mzithrin. Only then will we be suffered to return to Arqual, and our families.'

Ott and Haddismal looked deeply content. The others showed varying degrees of confusion. 'But sir,' said Fiffengurt, 'ain't it nearly time to land our men on the Sandwall? We talked about it just yesterday. Men with mirrors, to relay the all-clear signal from Masalym, when it comes.'

'We will be landing no one on the Sandwall,' said Rose.

'How, then,' said Chadfallow, 'are we to know when Macadra has left the city, and what course she is on?'

'I say again, no need.'

'But I don't understand, Captain,' said Fiffengurt. 'How will we know when it's safe to return for Pazel and Thasha and the others? Can Lady Oggosk tell you that as well?'

'Oggosk has nothing to tell me in this regard,' said Rose, 'because we are not going back.'

The explosion was just as he had foreseen. Chadfallow and Fiffengurt rose, shouting in rage. 'You wouldn't dare, Captain!' thundered the quartermaster. 'Leave them behind? How can you even jest about such a thing?'

'I make no jests,' said Rose.

'You will *not* do it!' shouted Chadfallow. 'What's more, you dare not. The Nilstone—'

'—is in Hercól's hands,' said Ott, 'or perhaps those of the

Masalym Guard who rode with him. In either case we can do nothing about it. Believe me, I hate to leave a thing of such power unclaimed. It would be a great joy to present it to our Emperor.'

Chadfallow was gaping. Fiffengurt was nearly out of his head. He stepped towards Rose, hands in fists. Sergeant Haddismal, grinning, merely seized his arm. Ott was watching Chadfallow with lively curiosity. Neither the spy nor the Turach bothered to stand up.

'This is unthinkable,' said Chadfallow, shaking with rage. 'Even for you, Rose. We gave you our trust.'

'Oh, Doctor, you're priceless,' laughed Sandor Ott. 'You gave nothing of the kind. Tell the truth, old man: you never expected to see them again. You knew they were choosing exile among the fish-eyes for the rest of their days – indeed, that that was the best possible outcome for the ardent fools, and far from the most likely. I'm not calling you a coward, sir. You might even have joined them, if I'd allowed it, for you're quite fond of your family of criminals. But of course I could not allow it. We have over seven hundred men left to care for, and no doctor but you, save that, that—'

He gestured vaguely at Rain, whose eyes tracked his moving hand, befuddled. Ott and Haddismal roared with laughter.

'Prince Olik's brief rule in Masalym will already have ended,' said Rose, speaking over them. 'Macadra will likely kill the man, if she can do so quietly enough. In any case, she will replace him with one of her servants. Ott is correct, Doctor: you knew from the start that we would not return. So did your friends who went ashore, in their hearts.'

'You yourself planned to go with them,' said Chadfallow, staring rigidly at Rose. 'What if Ott had allowed you to join the expedition? Do you think for one instant that if Mr Fiffengurt had taken command, he would have abandoned you?'

'Ott did not prevent me going ashore,' said Rose.

At that Spengler paused in his rummaging, and spat. 'You're a liar, Rose. He hog-tied you. You should boot that spy's arse right over the rail.'

'Pointless speculation,' said Ott. 'I would have compelled Fiffengurt to sail on, whatever his preference might have been. No, our dalliance with traitors has run its course. If there was any justification for their presence aboard, it lay in their efforts to thwart Arunis and drive him from the ship. That work is done, but His Supremacy's great task is not.'

Fiffengurt's face had turned so scarlet that Rose half expected to see blood filling the whites of his eyes. Chadfallow was restraining him by force. The doctor's jaw was clenched, as if words he dared not utter were caught between his teeth. He drew a deep, shaky breath. 'Sandor Ott,' he said, 'you're a man of immense talents, immense energies and strength.'

Smiling broadly, as though preparing for a grand entertainment, Ott leaned back in his chair and placed his hands behind his head.

'You are the personification of commitment,' the doctor continued. 'That I would never deny, although I differ with your choice of loyalties. You might have grown very rich, without ever leaving Etherhorde; you might have settled for exploiting your office. You did not. You chose one task and pursued it selflessly, and with skills like no other man alive. I say all this because I wish you to know that I am not blinded by the animosity between us.'

Haddismal appeared to be preparing some caustic remark, but Ott wagged a finger at him for silence.

'Now all I ask,' said Chadfallow, 'is that you try to see beyond that hatred yourself. The emperor you serve has long counted me among his irreplaceable servants. In his name, let me ask ... a favour of you. Let the men be landed on the Sandwall, and await the signal from Masalym. Let us wait for them here, as we discussed. Only for a fortnight – your plans for the Shaggat will not be harmed by such a small delay. Let us see if Macadra departs, and whether Pazel and the others return. They need not trouble you, now that Arunis is gone. They can be kept in the brig – all of them, all the way to Gurishal and beyond. But do not leave them here, to grow old and die among the dlömu, never seeing human faces again.'

Ott's smile had faded into something more thoughtful. Haddismal too had shed his look of mirth.

'Rose, you must put a stop to this,' said Kurlstaff. 'You're the blary captain, not the spy. He should be seeking that boon from *you*.'

Rose looked the ghost in the face but said not a word.

'I am begging you, Mr Ott,' said Chadfallow. 'But more importantly, I am appealing to the idealist in you – the loyal soldier. Your dedication to Magad the Fifth is a passion in your heart, like all human loyalties. Pazel, Thasha, Hercól Stanapeth – their passions are no different. Consider them misguided, consider them mad if you must. But see what you share with them – it is conviction, sir, a willingness to risk one's very life for what one holds most dear.'

Ott was frowning now. His eyebrows knitted, and the scars about his eyes were lost for a moment among the wrinkles.

'Not just their lives,' said the doctor softly, 'but their souls. They are in the land of the mind-plague. They may all become animals, brainless *tol-chenni*, if we abandon them. Mr Ott, do you imagine that they would take such a terrible risk if they did not believe it was essential? Is that not what *you* believe of Arqual's conquest of the Mzithrin? Disagree with them all you like – but do not condemn them in this way. To do so is to condemn yourself.'

The room was silent. Even Spengler had turned away from the cabinets to gaze at the Imperial Surgeon. Ott himself was looking down at the table. He blinked, a quizzical light in his eyes.

'A good speech, Doctor,' he said. 'It's plain to see why His Supremacy needed your diplomatic skills. But you've left out a key detail, I think.' He raised his eyes. 'You're his father, aren't you? Pathkendle's father. You cuckolded Captain Gregory while he was away at sea.'

Silence. The living and the dead were still. Then Chadfallow, never shifting his gaze from Sandor Ott, said, 'Yes, I did. And Pazel is my son, that's true.'

'Are you the girl's father as well? Did you sire a future *sfvantskor* on that woman?'

'Neda is Gregory's daughter,' said Chadfallow stiffly. 'She was born before I ever knew him, or Suthinia Pathkendle.'

'You were wise not to lie,' said Ott. 'That would have ended the discussion. But one thing still perplexes me, Doctor. Why lie to the boy? He asked if he was your son just before leaving the *Chathrand*, I believe. And you denied it to his face.'

Chadfallow looked shocked. Though why should he be, thought Rose, to learn that the spymaster continued to spy?

'You let him depart thinking himself the son of that traitorous freebooter, that nobody,' said Sandor Ott. 'Why?'

The doctor's hands were trembling slightly. 'I made a rash promise,' he said at last. 'To his mother, the night she told me that the child was mine. She was afraid of losing her son, as she was already losing Captain Gregory. She feared that Pazel would choose me over her one day, if he ever learned the truth. And so I swore I would never tell.'

'It has cost you a great deal to keep that promise, I think,' said Ott quietly.

Chadfallow nodded. 'Yes, it has,' he said.

'Hmm, so,' muttered Ott. 'You wish us to give them a fortnight. To catch up and rejoin us.'

'Nothing more,' said Chadfallow. 'A fighting chance, sir. In Magad's name.'

Ott looked sidelong at Haddismal. Then he rose to his feet and started for the door. He waved his hands as though relinquishing the matter. 'This means the world to you, apparently,' he said.

'Do you mean—'

'You served Arqual truly, once,' said Ott. 'I haven't forgotten.'

Chadfallow closed his eyes, his shoulders bowed with relief. Mr Fiffengurt put a shaky hand on his arm.

Then Rose glanced up to see that Ott was ushering Turachs into his cabin. Haddismal barked a code word, gesturing at the doctor and Fiffengurt, and before either man had time to react they were seized, and the door slammed anew. Ott struck Fiffengurt in the stomach, lightning-fast, dispassionate. The quartermaster doubled over, labouring to breathe.

The soldiers threw the struggling doctor to the floor and stretched him out, a man on each thrashing limb. They beat him, slapped him so hard that the outlines of their fingers appeared like strips of white paint on his cheeks. Sandor Ott let himself into Rose's sleeping cabin, and returned with a pillow, fluffing it in his hands.

'*Credek*, he's in for it now,' said Captain Maulle.

Ott tossed the pillow to Haddismal, then knelt and tore open Chadfallow's jacket, sending buttons flying. He drew his long white knife, slipped it under the doctor's shirt, and cut the fabric from collar to waist. He did the same with each leg of the doctor's trousers. The doctor's skin was very pale. His limbs were muscular but the joints looked stiff and swollen.

'Be gentle with his hands, we need them,' said Ott to the marines. Then he nodded to Haddismal, who lumbered forward and knelt by the doctor's head. Using both hands, the sergeant held the pillow down over Chadfallow's face, leaning into it with the whole of his bulk. The doctor kicked and thrashed, but the Turachs held him firmly. A muffled howl escaped the pillow, but it did not carry far.

Fiffengurt tried to lunge and was brought down with a second blow. The ghosts were backing away. Death, for some reason, could always be counted on to unnerve them.

Ott pinched the doctor's skin appraisingly, as a tailor might a jacket he was preparing to trim. Then his knife-hand moved in a blur, and an arc of scarlet appeared on the doctor's breast. Chadfallow's writhing did not change: he was suffocating; the pain of the cut passed unnoticed.

Ott studied the wound a moment. His hand flicked again. The second cut, three inches lower, was exactly the same shape and length as the first. Rose found himself admiring the man's concentration. Two more strokes followed, curling this time, bisecting the lines in a graceful pattern.

Captain Kurlstaff moved away from his ghostly companions.

He flowed through the crowd, through the table, and solidified again by Rose's chair. 'You whore's bastard! Make him stop! You're the captain of this ship!' Rose sat as if turned to stone.

The doctor's movements grew erratic. Ott picked up speed, moving from chest to stomach to legs, violating the doctor's body with the precise but impulsive movements of a painter surrendering to inspiration. Blood ran in stripes over Chadfallow's limbs, trickling into the remains of his clothes.

At last Ott gestured to Haddismal, and the sergeant removed the pillow. Dr Chadfallow was barely conscious. Blood foamed about his lips. He had bitten his tongue.

'In Magad's name,' said Sandor Ott.

Thumping footsteps outside the cabin. Mr Uskins, the disgraced first mate, pushed open the door. He was terribly dishevelled, his hair untrimmed and greasy, his uniform lumpy and stained. He gaped at the scene before him, then broke into a smile of glee.

'Look at the Imperial Surgeon! How the mighty are fallen, eh, Captain Rose? How the highborn are brought to heel!'

Fiffengurt was sobbing. Chadfallow moved feebly, leaving smears of blood. Captain Kurlstaff stared at Uskins with vague apprehension. There was a white scarf knotted at his neck.

Ott cleaned his knife in Chadfallow's hair, then stood and stretched his back, wincing with pleasure. 'Spread him out,' he said.

The Turachs pulled at Chadfallow's wrists and ankles until the doctor lay spreadeagled on his back. Unbuttoning his fly, Ott began to urinate on the man, methodically, face to feet and back again.

'The trust we put in you,' he said, 'makes your defection all the more base. It is not only treasonous but hurtful to His Supremacy. It is a crime against – what did you call it, Doctor? – the soul.'

The room grew rank. Chadfallow groaned and spat but could not move. Ott paused, chose a new position, began again, soaking the doctor's wounds and shreds of clothing. When he finished, he went to the table and gathered the linen napkins and tossed them at the doctor. 'Clean yourself,' he said. 'Rose, I am sorry this occurred in your cabin. Tell the steward to clean it with vinegar and lye. I believe this concludes our business, gentlemen. Let us hope for favourable winds, and a swift departure for the North.'

3

A Leopard Hunt

He heard the dogs behind him at midday, while he rested near the mountain's peak. He had the telescope out and trained on the inlet. When the baying started he swung the instrument back down the mountain in the direction of the city, and swore.

'Are they hers, Prince?' asked the ixchel man on his shoulder.

'Oh yes, they're Macadra's.'

That ancient sound, the war-bay, the summons to their masters: here is the blood you want. He could see five dogs on the mountain, huge and lean and red. They were racing up the dry ridge like furies, cutting the switchbacks, tearing through brush. Their deep chests heaved like bellows. Their wide paws gripped and pulled. *Athymar* eight-fangs, bred for murder, the dogs that bit and never let go.

'They have our scent,' said the ixchel.

'My scent, Lord Taliktrum,' said the prince. 'I doubt they would know what to make of your own.'

Prince Olik Bali Adro, rebel and fugitive and distant cousin to the Emperor, allowed himself a last glance at Masalym below the mountain: her layer-cake loveliness, her waterfalls, the River Maî winding through her like a sapphire braid. City of marvels, and of fear, with its wealthy households squeezed together like a rosebud at the apex, and the poor adrift in the crumbling labyrinth below. He had ruled Masalym for something less than a week. This morning, he had barely escaped it with his life.

Five dogs, five *athymars*. He did not want to fight them. He did not, in truth, want them to exist. Dogs had a beauty and a purity no dlömu ever matched. They would work or fight as their keepers required, go through battle and flames and savage landscapes that bloodied their paws. They would serve until their bodies broke, or their hearts. And they would kill him regardless of Imperial law.

'She has branded them on their hindquarters,' he said. 'That seems a senseless act. Who would be fool enough to try to steal those monsters, I ask you?'

'Prince?' said Taliktrum.

'Hmm, yes?'

'Put that scope away and run.'

The prince lowered the telescope, considered the dogs without it, the distance they had travelled in the last few minutes alone. 'Quite right,' he said, and let the instrument fall from his hands.

He ran west along the summit trail, through the hyssop and giant rosettes. No cover, nothing to climb. He saw his own dogs loping parallel to him, dispersed as he'd ordered them to be. The nearest were keeping him in sight; those further out watched their companions. All nine could be called in with a gesture to help him fight. But his dogs were smaller creatures, a mixed pack of hunters and scouts. They could fight, certainly: they had been trained by the Masalym Watch. But the slaughter, the maimed animals – no, this was not the place to make a stand. What he needed now was distance from Masalym, and the servants of Macadra Hyndrascorm that streamed from it in all directions.

Prince Olik had already killed once that morning. Barely an hour up the Rim Trail, with the huge cliffs called the Jaws of Masalym open beneath him and the thunder of the great falls reverberating in his bones, a pair of riders had suddenly rounded a bend and spotted him, and the one in the lead had charged. The prince could not help but feel a moment's fright. He had lived so long in safety, protected by his face and name: a face it was every citizen's duty to know; a name that meant death to anyone who touched him. When he fled beyond the Empire they had made him a target, but here, all his life, they had accustomed him to invulnerability. Each time he met a citizen who feared Macadra more than the ancient law, it was as if a crack had opened in the bedrock of the earth.

Still, the prince had not hesitated. He had killed them, those men who had been his subjects only the day before: the first as he tried to run Olik down with his spear, the second as he raised a bugle that would have sealed his fate. Lucky kills, both of them. Yet he had no luck with the horses, which bolted riderless back down the ridge.

Two hours later the sun was fully risen, and the prince stood atop the headland, wild rosemary about him and Taliktrum on a stone nearby, looking down at the *Kirisang*, the *Death's Head*, Macadra's hideous ship. 'Why, it's almost a twin of the *Chathrand!*' the ixchel had exclaimed. And of course that was true: though much older and heaped with strange Plazic weaponry, the *Kirisang* was a *Segral*-class ship like the one the humans had arrived in. Olik turned away from the sight: he knew that Macadra herself was on that ship, unless she had gone ashore to look for him. The sorceress had not stirred from Bali Adro City in thirty years, but lust for the Nilstone had drawn her out.

Then the prince had raised his eyes and looked north, through the gap in the Sandwall where the *Chathrand* had sailed five days before. 'I wonder if they are truly out there, waiting for an all-clear signal, so that they might return and collect their missing crew. Rose's eyes were shifty when he promised to do so. And that bloodthirsty Mr Ott never left him alone. "Stath Bálfyr, Captain; our goal is Stath Bálfyr." He was in a fever to reach that isle.'

'He should not have been,' Taliktrum had replied. 'If they ever do reach Stath Bálfyr, it will be the end of the voyage for them all.'

'You sound quite sure of that.'

'I am,' said Taliktrum, 'but ask me no more about it, Sire. There are some oaths even an exile must keep.'

He was a cipher, this tiny lord who'd saved his life. The prince knew almost nothing about ixchel. They had suffered under the Platazcra, but their own habits of secrecy disguised the extent of their persecution. They were found occasionally aboard boats plying the Island Wilderness, and were said to be tolerated by the people of Nemmoc and other lands west of Bali Adro. Yet Taliktrum had given him the impression that the Northern ixchel who had come with the *Chathrand* were of a very different sort: rigidly communal, even indivisible in their clan structure and ethos of 'us' before 'me'. Which made Taliktrum's own defection rather startling. On the headland, with as much delicacy as he could muster, Olik had asked Taliktrum if he regretted leaving his people behind. Taliktrum had stared hard at the sea.

'I left myself no choice,' he said. 'I am like the hunter who falls into his own snare. I could blame my father, of course: he persuaded us all to go hunting to begin with. But I took up the horn and blew until my face was red. And when my father became frail I named myself not just the master of the hunt, but its guardian spirit, a visionary, a prophet.'

'You do not strike me as so proud.'

Taliktrum laughed. 'I might have before,' he said, 'but even that would have been an illusion. Pride did not lead me on, though at the time even I thought it had. No, I named myself a prophet as an act of rebellion. I lacked the courage to turn from my father's path, so I tried to escape another way: by going too far. Unfortunately, my own people called my bluff.'

'By believing in you?'

Taliktrum had nodded. 'And trapping me, thereby. I could not deliver what I promised them, and so I fled. And when I had been gone a little while, free from their needy eyes, my mind cleared and I saw my own need at last. But before I could return and claim her, I saw her vanish into this wilderness, joining you giants in the hunt for the Nilstone, abandoning the comfort of the clan. She was the one of vision. I was the blind fool who never saw her until she was gone.'

They raced on up the slope. The prince was vaguely disgusted with himself: a mere five hours and he was winded, and the path had not been that steep. He should have started earlier; he should have spent the night on this mountain.

'The hounds are closing already,' said Taliktrum. 'Mother Sky, but they're fast.'

'Wait until they reach level ground,' said Olik.

'I'd rather we didn't, Sire.'

If he had started at dusk yesterday he would have reached the Sarimayat River by now, and could have sent the dogs safely home. Now look at him: desperate, pretending to a calm he didn't feel, hoping for a miracle, or the kind of strength he'd not felt in a decade.

Your strength, for example, he thought, glancing at Taliktrum out of the corner of his eye. If an ixchel stood six feet tall, and his strength were raised proportionally, well, the prince wasn't quite sure what that would mean, but something astonishing. Taliktrum stood eight inches tall and could leap forty from a standstill.

There were rocks by the sea cliff, however. Tall rocks, and many. On an impulse, the prince dived from the trail and ran among them. He had rope. Perhaps there was a way down the cliff where they could not follow, or even a path along the shore.

Or no path. They are almost upon you. Best be ready for an ocean swim.

But a swim to where? Last night in Masalym he had studied maps, traced his possible avenues of escape. He'd known Macadra was coming, bearing down on the city in the *Death's Head*, knew she thought the Nilstone might still be there and would commit any atrocity to obtain it. The Stone was not there, of course – but was Arunis? Olik had sworn not to abandon the city until he could swear to its citizens that the sorcerer had fled. At last Hercól Stanapeth's fire-signal from the mountains let him do so. But by then Macadra's ship was already in the harbour, and Olik had barely managed to slip away.

The river, he thought. *The Sarimayat. You can lose them there, hide your scent, crawl out after sunset on the nether shore. Gain that river and you live.*

'Prince, you must abandon these rocks,' said Taliktrum. 'They can trap you here. This was a mistake.'

The ixchel was right again: he should have crossed the summit at a dead run and simply hurled himself down the western slope. Or called his pack in to fight at his side. The prince had no illusions about his talents. He was a passable swordsman, nothing more than that. His strength was archery, but he had no bow. What he did have were nine *kryshoks*: steel disc-blades, each the width of his palm, and bulging slightly at the centre with the weight of lead. They were less accurate than arrows, but no less deadly when they found their mark.

'A vantage,' he said to Taliktrum. 'Find me a vantage point, an outlying rock. Some of them will follow their noses in here. I want to be waiting where they emerge.'

Taliktrum nodded, seeing the plan. He crouched tight as the prince grabbed him bodily. Olik threw him high, like a ball, and at the zenith of his ascent Taliktrum spread his arms, thrust deep into the gauntlets of the swallow-feather suit, and soared west over the rocks.

Behind him, the *athymars* suddenly bayed: a deeply chilling sound. They were on the summit. Olik dashed, slipping and squeezing through tight places in the rocks. *Macadra would not use* athymars *if she meant to take me alive. They will devour me, probably, devour the evidence. And she will still have them slaughtered and cremated, lest their stomachs be opened by the Platazcra Inspectorate, looking for fragments of a missing prince.*

Taliktrum returned, alighted on his shoulder. 'That way, run,' he gasped. 'It is far, but no other place will serve.'

The prince ran where he was told. The dogs' howls echoed among the rocks. If they caught him here, with no throwing-room, no room even to swing a sword ....

Grey fur: the prince wheeled, groping for his dagger. But it was only Nyrex, his pack leader, a great rockhound with the tented ears of a fox. Her mouth was foamy with exhaustion and her tongue lolled like a skinned eel, but her eyes still begged for orders.

'Out of these boulders, out! Scatter!' Olik flung his arm, and the dog sprang away like a hare. Then the prince emerged from the rocks, and Taliktrum pointed to the one that stood apart. Flat-crested: fine luck. He raced the sixty feet and vaulted onto the stone. Eight feet: tall enough. But the rear of the boulder had a shelf halfway up its side. Bad luck. He lay flat at the centre of the stone.

'Circle me at dog-height,' he told Taliktrum. 'Can you see me? Quickly, pray!'

Taliktrum flew low about the stone, arms working furiously. He landed, rolling, by the prince's arm. 'You're hidden from view,' he said. 'But Prince, their noses—'

'Yes,' Olik whispered. 'I'm counting on it. When I toss you again, Lord Taliktrum, you must fly off shouting – and not return until the killing's done.'

'I've fought dogs before, Olik.'

'No you haven't. Not like these.'

He slid his hand into the leather pouch that held the *kryshoks*, dealt out four upon the stone, as though preparing for a round of cards.

Taliktrum shook his head, frowning. 'If they wait at a distance, for the rest of the pack—'

'Silence,' said the prince, 'they are here.'

He caught the sound of their panting, the low *huff*s they directed at one another. Olik tried not to breathe. Four *kryshoks* beside him; one in each hand, three left in the pouch.

Wait.

A sharp yip: that was Nyrex. The brave creature was still on the mountaintop, somewhere, trying to draw them off. The *athymars* growled at her, but they were not really tempted. Sweat was running into Olik's eyes. The panting drew nearer. It was on both sides of his rock.

Wait.

Three were here for certain, probably four. They were trotting in small circles now, orbiting him, the scent always returning them to this spot. He drew a finger along the knife-edge of the *kryshok*. Sniff, step, pant, sniff again. He could feel the pulse of his own blood. Then, all in the same moment, the pack grew still as stone.

Olik hurled Taliktrum skyward. The ixchel man shot away like a living, screaming arrow. The dogs' heads turned – and Olik rose and struck.

A *kryshok* could pierce welded plate, cut through chain mail like straw. Olik flung his arms out, snapped his wrists, making himself want to kill them. One. Two. The third so near it sprayed his legs with blood. The fourth was airborne before he could draw another *kryshok*, but only its forelegs reached the rock, and he sent it tumbling with a kick. He whirled, drawing his sword, and plunged it into the chest of the fifth dog in mid-spring. It knocked him flat; it had found the ledge and used it. Even as it died the creature bit him, and he screamed with pain. Four fangs locked on his arm. Never mind, where was the other? Where was the dog he'd kicked?

Then he knew. He rolled over, in agony, and lifted the eighty-pound corpse. Its eyes still on him, he smashed forward, and caught the last dog as it leaped. But it was wiser now. It snarled and clawed and soon Olik was retreating, still parrying with the dead dog's body, still trying to free his sword.

The dog came on, a burning fuse. There was no more room to retreat. Then suddenly the *athymar* whirled in place and there were two dogs, fighting, falling, dropping from the stone. It was Nyrex, fearless Nyrex, a dog he had purchased barely a week ago, a dog about to give her life. They rolled, cyclonic, a single entity at war with itself.

He couldn't wait. Nyrex would be shredded; the *athymar* could not possibly lose. He drew a *kryshok* and hurled it blind into the tangle of limbs with all his might.

A death-howl soared above the bedlam for an instant. Then silence. Olik found that his eyes were pinched shut. He forced them open: Nyrex stood over the *athymar*, dripping blood. The *kryshok* had severed the spine of the larger dog.

The prince slid down the back of the rock, dragging the corpse of the dog whose jaws had locked. He inspected Nyrex: she had scratches and a torn ear. 'A torn ear!' he shouted aloud. 'Finest beast, that's a mark of honour! But you're a disobedient bitch – I told you to stay clear of this fight.'

'Just as well she had other ideas,' said Taliktrum, landing on the rock once more.

Prying open the jaws of the dead *athymar* was a foul business. When at last the prince succeeded, he groped for his tiny medical kit and washed out the four fang wounds with spirits of copperwood, then bound his arm with gauze. He called Nyrex and began to clean her ear. She whined and turned her head sharply.

'Those were fine kills,' said Taliktrum gruffly.

'They should never have happened,' said Olik. 'I should have seen to my own horse yesterday, not obliged a servant to do it for me. You can't blame the man for disappearing with his steeds. Law or no law, Macadra's wrath could fall on anyone who aids me.'

'You are most forgiving of betrayal,' said Taliktrum.

'I prefer to see myself as pleasantly surprised by loyalty,' said Olik. 'My mistake was betting my life on it.' He glanced up at the ixchel. 'At the river I will disperse the pack entirely, except for Nyrex here. She will bear you until we take to land again. Hold still, girl! I'm almost done.'

The dog was squirming, pulling away from him. She had grown abruptly tense, gazing back the way they had come. Olik stilled his hand. He rose, and motioned Taliktrum to be silent.

There it was. More baying. More *athymars*. A dozen more, at least.

Olik dug the *kryshoks* from the corpses, wiped them hastily on their fur. He tore his shirt, gave the pieces to his own dogs, sent out in a fan shape across the mountain. Then he ran as he had not run in ages. His jacket chafed, but Taliktrum needed something to grip. Olik was light-headed from the loss of blood. The ruse with his shirt-scraps might buy him a few minutes. And it might buy him none at all.

The trail returned to the cliffside. They had descended from the summit, but not very far; there were miles of high country yet. And the sea? It boiled and foamed below them – so *very* far below. If it came to that he would dive; Taliktrum could fly to some crevasse in the cliffs and hide until the *athymars* withdrew. Every healthy dlömu was a diver; and every Bali Adro prince leaped from the Hyrod Cliffs before his thirteenth year. But this jump would be from twice that height or more, threading a needle between rocks, and the wind gusts could toss him anywhere, or turn him sidelong at impact, which would be death. It was a leap Imperial champions would shy from. A very last resort.

He counted his blessings. Good shoes, good footing. Enemies who announced that they were coming to kill you while still far away. Taliktrum, this gruff comrade-in-arms. And the dogs, with their flawless loyalty, of the kind that worked so much evil between men.

A mile swept by. From a hilltop, well inland, two shepherds gazed at him in wonder, surrounded by their milling flock. Then came a stone wall. Then a meadow, and a patch of wild sage.

'Smell that!' said Taliktrum. 'You should stop and roll!' But the prince shook his head.

'Not strong enough to hide my scent. Worse, it would give them two scents to follow, once they guessed what I'd done.'

Another ridge, another breathless climb. At the top he surprised a hermit poking a fire by the trailside. The man fled with a squeal, leaving behind his water jug. Olik drank deeply from it, then tossed the jug over the cliff. Better that way. The dogs might harm the old man if anything he owned smelled of the prince.

'*Héridom*, I could have used a sip myself,' said Taliktrum. 'Never mind, keep moving; you're too visible here, and – *skies of fire, Olik, what is* that?'

Something whirled overhead, dark and viciously fast. Olik turned, chasing it with his eyes as he groped for his sword. But what he saw was so appalling that for a moment he could only stare.

It was a smoke cloud, or a swarm of insects, or a nightmare fusion of both. It was miles above them, probably, and fast as a shooting star. Jet black, opaque, and yet *writhing* as it flew like a nest of maggots. To his horror the thing slowed momentarily, as if pulled in two directions at once. Then it resumed its westward course, and soon dwindled to a speck.

'Blood of devils,' said the prince. 'Did you see it? Do you know what that was?'

The dogs were whimpering. The prince himself felt ill. 'I don't know,' cried Taliktrum, shaken. 'How could I know? Tell me!'

'That was the Swarm of Night. That was the doom foreseen by the spider-tellers, the doom that travelled with your ship.'

'There was no such monstrosity aboard the *Chathrand*!'

'No, but there was the Nilstone, and a sorcerer itching to use it. Well, he has used it, my lord. He has brought the Swarm back to Alifros, to kill and to feed.'

A sudden howl. Olik started. Four or five miles back along the trail, upon a knob he'd crossed thirty minutes ago, stood an *athymar*. It was looking straight at him – but its eyes were not the equal of its nostrils, and Olik reflected that there was some chance at least that it did not yet know what it saw. He might be just another shepherd, another hermit.

Even as the prince watched, more dogs came up behind the first. Some of them lay down upon the hilltop.

'They must be winded,' said Taliktrum. 'They started out in the wrong direction, after all, and had to double back when the first ones caught your scent. They may have run twice as far as those you killed.'

'They are not tired enough,' said the prince. '*Jathod*, look at them all.'

The dogs kept coming: ten, now fifteen. 'Very well,' said Olik, 'we are going to start off walking. No, better yet – hobbling. Old. I think I can imitate a bent old hermit. And then, if they let me hobble around that curve in the trail there, we shall fly. Watch them, Taliktrum, and tell me if they start to move.'

He bent his knees, and his back. The performance was harder than he'd imagined. For the first time since his departure from Masalym, the prince felt afraid. It was this slowness, this charade. It made him aware of the trembling of his skin.

Halfway to the curve. The dogs remained still. 'I count nineteen,' said Taliktrum.

'My lord,' said the prince, 'do you know what the *nuhzat* is?'

'I heard you speak of it, that night on the derelict boat.'

The night Taliktrum had saved him, striking down his assassins with a poisoned blade. 'The last man to fall,' said Olik, 'the one Sandor Ott kicked to death. He was in *nuhzat*. That is why he began to fight so well.'

'What of it, Prince?'

'I will be in *nuhzat* soon; I can feel its onset already.'

'Ah!' said Taliktrum. 'Is that good luck or bad?'

Before Olik could answer the pack behind them erupted in howls. 'They're coming, they're coming like fiends!' cried Taliktrum. Olik burst into a run, his dogs flowing beside him, and this was it, no more resting, no more tricks. Only speed. He swept around the bend, clawing at the rocks for purchase, gravel scraping under his heels. The path was narrow; there were sheer falls on his right. He flew headlong, screaming at his dogs to keep their distance: one stumble and the *athymars* would have them.

His throat was raw. This was a long descent – but was it *the* descent, the start of the river valley? No, damn it all, there was a plateau before him yet. And structures. Many structures. Could he possibly be approaching a town?

The ridge grew steeper. The earth sheared off in patches beneath his feet. It was like skiing at one of the Emperor's mountain retreats, that freefall sensation, one's balance miraculously restored again and again. He thought of his mother. *You'll know a world beyond me, Olik, a world I'll never see. If there be peace in your lifetime perhaps you'll be an artist, and paint the glories of this kingdom – I mean the beauty of it, not the deeds. If there be war, you'll fight.*

'There are riders with them!' cried Taliktrum. 'Seven riders!

Olik, you must go faster! On that plateau they'll run you down!'

I'm not one for fighting, Mother; I've told you I can't stand the blood.

'Prince Olik!' Taliktrum was shouting in his ear.

I know that about you, darling. That's why you'll matter, when the world looks back. Others will be bloody-minded; you'll fight to bring us to our senses.

If he had wings sewn to his arms he would spread them now, and lift like a falcon from this wounded earth. But instead there came a quietness, and a change in the light. The *nuhzat* had begun.

Thank you, Mother. Thank you for easing this pain.

For his raw throat, the burning in his chest, the ache of his bitten arm: gone. Nothing hurt any more, and yet his senses were rarefied and keen. And he was running faster, much faster. Already the buildings were flying by.

'That's it! Don't stop!'

They were ruins. Not ancient, merely old. He was sprinting down the centre of a wide, dead street, his own dogs barely matching his pace. Then he remembered: *Ved Oomin. Human Settlement.* The words in pale red ink upon his map. This was a township, wiped out in the mind-plague and never settled again.

Sudden snarling behind him. He could not look back; he was a running spirit, an idea of speed. Taliktrum shouted that the first *athymars* were catching up with his pack. Olik clenched his teeth and ran faster. The village was ending. A ruined wall crossed his path. Olik cleared it in one bound.

Steel horseshoes on cobblestones. The riders were behind him. 'They have bows,' said Taliktrum. 'Never mind, they're not using them; it's still the dogs you've got to outrun.'

Tombstones. Human graves lost in brambles and weeds. Names melting with the years, souls fallen like raindrops in this silent land.

Another wall, another leap. And now he was in forest, wet and tangled. He slashed through vines and cabbage palm and tall soaked ferns. Bad luck. The forest would slow him more than the dogs.

Then the ground began to drop, steeply. At last, he thought, the descent.

'There's the blessed river!' cried Taliktrum, 'but Prince, they're too close! You must push one more time, a little faster, do you hear? Olik, *you will not make it at this speed.*'

Half a mile, less. Then came an explosion of canine fury. On his right, two dogs were rolling, a coil of fur, claws, teeth. Olik shouted to the rest of his pack: *Go free, disband, leave the fight and turn home.* But there was Nyrex, keeping pace with him, disobedient again. She caught his eye. So much trust in that creature, so much unwarranted faith.

Taliktrum was screaming: 'Faster, faster! *Hérid aj,* man, you're almost there!'

A quarter mile. The final stretch looked terribly steep. An arrow flew past him, wildly off the mark. His pursuers were desperate; they could see the river too.

A last scramble before him. Maybe a leap from the high green banks. 'Pitfire, you're doing it!' cried Taliktrum, almost laughing in his amazement. 'You're losing them, man, you're the royal leopard incarnate!'

Of course he was; he was Bali Adro. There was no stopping his family. Given time they would conquer the sun.

Then an *athymar* caught his heel.

It was a nip, not a bone-crushing bite, and yet it was enough to send him sprawling. Any semblance of control was gone; the world spun madly. But the *athymar* had fallen, too. Nyrex had pounced on it, and the three of them and half a ton of loose jungle soil were rushing for the river; it was a landslide with heads and limbs, his boots fending off the *athymar*, its four fangs seeking him, Nyrex tearing at the larger dog's hindquarters and—

Freefall.

The banks were high, all right. They plummeted in their squall of mud and debris, revolving helplessly, and then they struck and it was done.

Olik was in the water, and Nyrex surfaced beside him, paddling.

The *athymar*, not five feet to his left, had struck a fallen tree projecting out into the river. Dead already, it hung before them, impaled on a jagged branch.

Arrows fell. On the banks fifty feet above them, the other *athymars* were massed and baying. They pulled away from the shore into the swifter current, the rushing chariot that would bear them away. A mad river, a beautiful thing, burrowing deep into the Peninsula and the wild lands that remained.

But before they gave themselves to the current, Olik made for a rock, and Nyrex came up beside him, and they waited there, struggling to be still. Olik watched the shore, murmuring the hope-chant that for the dlömu takes the place of prayer. But no winged shape flew to him out of the jungle, only arrows and sounds of rage. The *athymars* jostled along the banks, now and then looking back over their shoulders.

Olik knew that the riders would soon brave that last slope, and spy him, and that once they did they would never turn back. He made a small sound of grief. If there was a lonelier soul than Lord Taliktrum's, he could not have said whose it might be.

The prince and his one companion swam away.

4

Fires in the Dark

12 Modobrin 941
241st day from Etherhorde

The raft did not inspire confidence. The party stood around it, staring; none of them could quite believe what they had built. 'It looks like a pig's stomach tied to a loom,' said Neeps.

'Your imagination does you credit,' said Bolutu.

'It is sturdy enough,' said Hercól, 'but I dare say it will be like no float any of us has ever taken.'

'I don't like it,' said Dastu, probing the raft with his foot.

'What would you like?' Pazel asked him. 'In case you haven't noticed, we don't have a highway to follow.'

'Or wings to fly,' said Ensyl, gazing upwards.

Thasha felt a stab of grief. It was about this time yesterday that Myett had been taken. Pazel had slept through the tragedy, but Thasha had seen Ensyl leap up as though stabbed, hearing what they could not: a fellow ixchel's cry. Looking skyward, they had all seen the bird of prey, fighting in midair with something gripped in its talons, before beating a swift path to the south. They had raced up the stairs, crying Myett's name. Ensyl had continued far up the ruined wall, her shouts and wails so eerily silent to human ears. She had come back stone-faced. 'We are thirteen now,' she'd said.

Of course Dastu had a point about the raft. It was a freakish thing. Its body was a huge bladder-mushroom, a tendril-fringed bag some fifteen feet in diameter. Half the party had ventured into the forest in search of such a fungus, Ramachni lighting the way, one last time, with fireflies. Thasha had joined the search: loath as she was to set foot in that hot, dripping hell, the thought of waiting for others to return from it was worse.

And light made all the difference. Beneath the bright canopy of insects the forest had mostly shrunk from them, closed its petals and pores. The flesh-eating trees withdrew their tentacles; the lamprey-mouthed fungi turned away. What could replace the fireflies, once the journey resumed?

It had taken hours to locate a bladder of the right size, and immense care to drain it from a single incision and cut it free of the ground. Even emptied, the thing was heavy, like a great rubbery hide. They slogged back to the clearing with it draped on their shoulders. When they arrived it was well past sundown. A fire burned in the clearing, with two geese roasting on spits, and when she tasted the sizzling meat Thasha groaned with pleasure.

'I am telling you, no?' said Neda, catching Thasha's eye. 'My master is best to kill with a stone. He is hitting anything, whatever you want.'

There were a handful of young pines in the clearing; those who had remained behind had felled and stripped them already. When dawn came, they had notched the soft wood with swords, tied them into a square frame with the vines that boiled at the forest's edge, and woven a net of these same vines on which to rest the giant bladder. Then everyone had helped to stuff the bladder like a cushion, with anything that would float: dry grass, hollow reeds, a spongy moss that grew on the ruin's north face. At last, using Ensyl's sword like a sewing needle, they had stitched the incision shut as best they could.

'It should carry us as far as the forest's edge,' said Hercól, 'provided we keep that hole above the water line.'

The sun was by now almost straight overhead. They ate a hurried meal of cold goose. Then Ensyl brought something from among the stones, and Thasha felt the ache again, worse than before. It was a rough pine carving of a woman, standing straight, arms raised high like a child who expects to be lifted in its mother's arms.

'Farewell, sister, honour-keeper, brave daughter of the clan,' she said, bending her voice so the others could hear her. Then, methodically, she broke the statue into twenty-seven pieces, and wrapped each one in a bit of cloth. Everyone but Dastu had contributed a scrap or two from their clothing. Ensyl gave the parcels to the stream one by one, and Thasha blinked back tears. If Myett had died among them, it would have been parts of her body in those little shrouds. Thasha had witnessed it before, this grisly rite, an assurance that no trace of the dead could ever be found by humans, and thus endanger the clan. Even funerals were part of the ixchels' struggle to survive.

The ceremony over, Hercól brought out the sack containing the Nilstone (another sort of death-parcel), and tied it firmly near the centre of the raft. Ramachni circled it once, his black fur raised. Then he turned and looked at the others.

'The sorcerer's reek is still about the Nilstone,' he said. 'Stay as far from the sack as you can. If anyone should reach for it, we must assume his mind is under siege, and stop him by force.'

'To do so would be simple mercy,' said Hercól. 'Four men on the *Chathrand* touched the Stone, and four men's bodies withered like leaves in a fire. Come, it is time we left this place.'

Together they dragged the raft into the shallows. Hercól and Vispek held the frame as the others scrambled aboard. The raft heaved and shifted, but it bore their weight. They spun away from the clearing, pushing off with long poles, and Thasha felt the current gather them into its arms.

Big Skip laughed aloud. 'We're ridin' a blary jellyfish,' he said. 'By the Tree, I hope I live just to hear what people say when we tell 'em.'

'They'll say we are liars,' said Bolutu.

'Be still, now,' said Ramachni. 'We are above the very spot where the River of Shadows roars up most powerfully into the Ansyndra. The blend of shadow and water is very thin here. If we do not sink in these first minutes we may have hope for the rest of the journey.'

They brushed the side of the tower where it jutted out into the stream. 'We *are* sinking!' cried Ensyl. And it was true that the raft was suddenly very low, ripples and wavelets lapping over the frame.

'Spread out! Lie flat!' Ramachni hissed, and they hurried to obey. The raft was teetering, one side and then another vanishing beneath the surface. Thasha lay on her stomach, half submerged, watching the river slosh around the crude surgical scar in the middle of the raft. She prayed, a reflex. The water black and chilling. They knocked along the tower wall, spinning like a leaf, then gyred out into the swifter current.

No one was laughing now. Thasha was dizzy and cold. She sensed a frightful nothingness below her, as though an endless black cavern waited for her there, lightless and roaring with wind; and this river surface, delicate as a soap bubble, was all that held them above its maw.

They sank lower still, clinging to the frame and to one another. The craft was all but submerged; the hole was like a pair of sealed lips just inches above the water. Helpless, Thasha watched the first surge of water pass over it. There were oaths. A second surge followed. Air bubbled around the wound.

And then, by the Blessed Tree, it stopped. The raft held steady, and – was she imagining it? – even began to rise. Thasha glanced at Ramachni, wondering if he had cast a spell after all. They rose higher, and picked up speed. 'We're out of it, aren't we?' said Pazel.

'The worst of it, yes,' said Ramachni. 'Almost pure shadow lay beneath us for a moment. It was there that the Swarm of Night burst forth into Alifros, when our enemy called it yesterday. The further we drift from that spot, the thinner the darkness beneath us – but do not be deceived. The Ansyndra will go on mixing with the River of Shadows for hundreds of miles. We must try to avoid swimming – and never, ever dive.'

They were far from shore, now. Thasha looked back but could not see the campsite, the place where they had bled and triumphed, where she had killed a mage but failed to become one herself, where Ramachni had at last been free to tell her the truth of her birth. A strange truth, an awful truth. She had thought herself the child of

Erithusmé; now she knew that she *was* the great mage, one soul shared between them: Erithusmé's soul. The wizardess had sparked life in the sterile womb of Thasha's mother, but not as an act of kindness. She had needed a hiding place, as her enemies closed in. She had bricked up her memories and magic behind a wall in the back of the unborn child's mind. Out of everyone's reach, even the girl herself. For seventeen years Thasha had lived in ignorance of that wall and the force behind it.

And now she had to let it out. Ramachni had told Pazel that they could not win otherwise. In fact Ramachni had believed that his mistress had *already* returned, after Thasha beheaded Arunis. But it was Thasha who had done that killing, not Erithusmé. Arunis' head had told the truth: Erithusmé could not return. The wizardess might have dismantled her own wall, but the young girl had built another. No one knew how or why, least of all Thasha herself. She only knew that it had to be broken.

'The current is swift,' said Hercól. 'Very soon we must face the darkness again.'

Thasha gazed ahead, where the vast trees arched out over the river, their thick leaves fusing together, shutting out all light. She felt Pazel's hand on her own and gripped it fiercely, caught his eye and saw the love there, and marvelled. How he steadied her. The things he did without speaking a word.

'Listen, now, for I have a solution of sorts,' said Ramachni. 'There is a light peculiar to this forest, produced by the plants and mushrooms themselves. Your eyes cannot perceive it, but mine can. I can share my vision – but with no more than two of you at a time. We must defend the raft, three at a time. Come here, Thasha and Neeps; you shall be the first.'

'Why the boy?' said Cayer Vispek. 'He is brave-hearted, but new to the warrior's arts.'

'Trust his choices, Cayer,' said Hercól.

Thasha and Neeps crept close to Ramachni. 'Shut your eyes, and cover them as well,' he said.

Thasha obeyed. A moment later Neeps gave a yelp of pain. 'Keep your hands in place, Neeparvasi Undrabust!' snapped Ramachni. 'Do not move until I speak!'

Thasha was shocked; Ramachni had never snapped at anyone before. His paw touched her chin, lingered there a moment, withdrew. Thasha waited. 'I don't feel a thing,' she said at last.

'That is because you listen to your betters,' said Ramachni. 'Lunja, come closer. If this knave has not seared his eyes with daylight, you must lend him your sword.'

They were back in the forest: Thasha could feel its hot, moist breath on her skin. The noise of the river grew, as though it were echoing in a cave. 'Keep your eyes covered,' said Ramachni, 'until we round the first bend, and the clearing is gone from sight. Not long now—'

Such heat! Already Thasha longed to splash water on her face. But when at last the mage told them to uncover their eyes she forgot everything but the message of her eyes.

A purple radiance, a kaleidoscope of melting images and hues, flooded her vision. She stretched out her arms and could not see them. She blinked, and the radiance moved. Slowly the kaleidoscope began to settle, the colours to sharpen and divide. There were her hands, two flickering lights. Here was the raft, a spinning pool of jade, and her friends like burning spirits upon it. And the forest, *Aya Rin!* Endless, vast pillars of tree trunks, supporting the distant roof of joined leaves, in which veins burned like hot wires, and eye-stabbing colours flashed like wormy lightning and were gone.

Along the banks, the riot of mushrooms overwhelmed her: they bled colour and form in such profusion that she simply had to look away. The river itself had become a thing of glass, revealing a second forest of water-weed and knobby coral-like growths beneath their feet. Some reached to within a few yards of the surface; in other places the lights flickered from startling depths. There were fish like tiny particles of fire, fish as large as sharks with glowing gills, fish that resembled arrows, hatchet-heads, stingrays, moths. And under everything ran veins of darkness, pulsing, impenetrable, but thinning like ink as they rose. Thasha shuddered: *those* were the depths she had sensed at the beginning, when they had almost sunk. Veins of shadow from the River of Shadows. The blood of another universe, leaking into their own.

'Well, I'm not blind,' said Neeps, 'but Rin's gizzard, Ramachni: wouldn't it have been easier to light some magic lamp, if you can't bring back the fireflies?'

'Savant!' said Ramachni. 'Thank heaven we brought you along.' Then, more gently, he added, 'I considered it, lad. And of course I could produce such light at need. But a mage-lamp bright enough to pierce this River's depths would make us visible for miles about. It would also take more from me than sharing my vision. I prefer to do as much as possible with as little as possible, for now.'

Thasha felt a nervous tightening of her limbs. *He's been drained. He gave all his strength fighting Arunis, keeping us alive.*

But Ramachni, as if reading her thoughts, added, 'My powers are far from spent – but we are far from our goal as well. And no rest in this world will allow me further magic than what I harbour within me now. Do you remember when I spoke of carrying water across the desert, Neeparvasi?' He sighed. 'There is a final desert before us. My powers must see us across it, to the place where our work is done at last.'

'And then you'll return to your own world, and recover,' said Pazel. 'Won't you?'

The little mage did not answer. Thasha's fear redoubled. *He came back through this River, but he can't go home without my clock. He's trapped here, unless we somehow make it back to the ship.*

Then she recalled the first time she had seen Ramachni drained of magic, in Simja, after their first great fight with Arunis. He had warned them that he had no choice but to leave. *If I do not go while I have the strength to walk away, I shall still depart, by burning out like a candle.*

He wasn't risking exile by standing with them now. He was risking death.

The three of them took up positions at the edges of the raft. The others, perfectly blind, kept low and still. The hardest job was keeping the raft off the coral-like growths and fallen tree limbs. They loomed up suddenly, and Thasha and Neeps had to scramble to pole the raft left or right. 'Faster!' Ramachni chided them. 'One scratch from below and our proud ship could sink! Above all, do not lose your balance! We have no means of stopping for you – or of knowing what lurks in these waters. Thasha – on your right!'

Over and over they lunged with the poles. The light was deceptive: what they took for coral proved a surface mirage; what looked like soft weeds would resolve into a branch. There were also dangers from above: vines that stuck to them like taffy, or burned at the touch – and the groping white tentacles of the trees themselves. Neeps and Thasha hacked at them, and lengths of the tentacles fell upon the raft, still writhing, among their blind companions.

The struggle went on and on. Thasha's head hurt and her eyes were throbbing. Tentacles snatched at them; a spiny fish leaped onto the raft and flopped about like a living pincushion; a storm of bats swept around them in a cloud. The river curved and twisted and appeared to have no end.

When Hercól and Bolutu relieved them at last, Thasha dropped beside Pazel and pulled him close. He fumbled for her, bathed her face with a river-wet rag. She put her lips to his, forced his mouth open, kissed him in hunger and exhaustion. Before the kiss was over Ramachni's magic left her and she was blind.

She lost track of the hours. Hercól and Bolutu's shift ended; Pazel and Cayer Vispek took their places. Thasha found being blind and motionless every bit as awful as manning the poles. Every sound became a danger. Every tilt or shudder in the raft meant they were sinking at last. But somehow the vessel bore them on, mile after lightless mile.

There were spells of calm, in the deep centre of the river where no snags threatened them, no tentacles groped. During her second shift Thasha was paired with Pazel. She watched Ramachni's mage-sight come over him: a gasp, disorientation, finally a grin as his eyes met hers. They shared a strange privacy for a time. Thasha waited until the mage looked elsewhere, then leaned close to Pazel and mouthed *I want you,* and laughed when he nearly dropped the pole. After their shift Pazel sat beside her, kissed her, slipped a hand beneath her ragged shirt. Thasha laughed again and pushed his hand away. Pitfire, he'd thought she was serious.

Later she must have dozed. A hand touched her again, but it was not Pazel. It was Big Skip, shaking her by the shoulder and whispering: 'Lady Thasha, wake up. Something's amiss.'

She bolted upright. The raft was not moving. 'What happened? Did we wreck?'

'Softly!' came Hercól's voice. 'We are not wrecked but beached in the shallows, and we are all of us blind. Ramachni has cancelled the seeing-spell. There was a strange sound from behind us. Like thunder, or a monstrous drum.'

'Where has Ramachni gone?'

'Up a tree, with Ensyl,' said Bolutu. 'We couldn't talk him out of it – or very well prevent his going. Hark!'

This time she heard it: a deep rumbling, far off but furious. An eruption, or the peal of some war drum of the Gods. The sound rolled past them like a storm front. When it ended the silence was profound.

'Closer, this time,' whispered Bolutu.

'What he is wanting in the tree?' hissed Neda. 'I think to climb is not sensitive.'

'Sensible, lass,' corrected Mandric.

'The sound came from outside the forest,' said Pazel. His voice was oddly strained. Thasha reached for him, wishing she could see his face. 'Pazel?' she said.

His arm trembled beneath her fingers. 'My mind-fit's coming,' he said. 'Soon, I think. And it's going to be a bad one.'

Dastu muttered a curse. 'Brilliant timing, *Muketch,*' he added.

'Your hearing is sharpened, then?' asked Cayer Vispek.

'Yes, it is,' said Pazel. After a moment, he added, 'Ramachni's singing to himself, up in the tree. I think he's weaving a spell. And that wasn't thunder, Hercól. It was a voice.'

'A voice,' said Dastu, scornful. 'You're mad as a mudskipper, Pathkendle. What sort of voice?'

Pazel was silent for a very long time. Then he said, 'A demon's?'

Even as he spoke, light appeared: a stabbing red light that made them all recoil. Wincing, Thasha forced herself to look: the glow came from about a quarter-mile away, at the height of the forest roof. Already it was growing, spreading. 'Tree of Heaven, that's fire!' said Mandric. 'The mucking forest is on fire!'

'Do not move!' said Ramachni suddenly. Thasha heard the mage and Ensyl scrambling aboard, felt Ramachni's sleek shoulder brush her arm. 'Be silent, now,' he said, 'and whatever happens, do not leave the raft. We are in unspeakable danger.'

The light became a sharp red ring: the leaf-layer, burning outward from a central point, like dry grass around a bonfire. The fire's glow danced on the river beneath it, and soon the red-rimmed hole was as wide as the river itself. But there it stopped. The blinding light faded, leaving only a fringe of crackling fire, and another light replaced it: pale blue and gentle. It was the Polar Candle, the little Southern moon. The fire had burned through all four leaf-layers and opened a window on a clear night sky.

Oh Gods, it's true.

In the fiery gap a monstrous head had appeared. A hideous sight: part human, part snake, larger than the head of an elephant. Fire dripped from its jaws, dark runes were etched upon its forehead, and its eyes were two great yellow lamps. A long neck followed, snaking in through the burning hole. The lamp-eyes swung back and forth, casting the trees in a sickly radiance. When they passed over her, Thasha felt a prickling in her mind. She shuddered. Now it was Pazel's turn to reach for her, pull her close. The lamp-eyes returned. When they touched the raft again they grew still.

Deep within Thasha's mind, another being sensed those eyes, and reached out for them as if to feel their heat. Another being, who did not fear them as Thasha did.

No girl, not another. Your maker, your soul-sharer. The part of you that's lost.

Beside her, Ramachni tensed, bearing his tiny teeth, flexing his claws one by one. Then the creature roared: a deafening, complex blast of noise that shook them to their bones. Beside her, Pazel's face showed a horror unlike that of the others, and suddenly she knew that he was understanding. His Gift had given him this creature's language; there was meaning in that awful sound.

Ramachni turned suddenly to look upstream. To Thasha's amazement the creature did the same, breaking off its roar and turning its fell eyes away from them. It looked very much as if both mage and monster were straining to catch some far-off sound. Thasha listened but heard nothing at all.

The creature faced them once more, and spat a meteoric glob of liquid fire, which hurtled towards them with a whistling noise, tore through the low vines at the river's edge, and exploded in the shallows thirty feet from the raft. Over the wall of steam Thasha saw the snaky neck retract upwards. She caught a glimpse of ragged wings, spreading, filling, and then the beast was gone.

Ramachni was the first to move, stretching out catlike on the raft. 'Well,' he said, as fire fell sizzling around them, 'now we have faced a *maukslar* out of Neparv Nédal. I am afraid we must get used to such things.'

'What – what—' The old Turach found no other words.

'A *maukslar*. A demon.' Pazel's voice was hollow. Dastu stared at him, aghast.

'The beast was a scout from Macadra,' said Ramachni. 'I did not know she had grown strong enough to pluck servants from the City of the Damned. She must have wagered her very life on obtaining the Nilstone. I wonder how much she knows of us, and our friends on the ship.'

'Why did the thing not attack?' demanded Hercól.

'It was never certain we were here,' said Ramachni. 'Some hours ago it reached the clearing, and pawed the ground where we burned the sorcerer's remains. I sensed it then, and shrouded us in a mist, and the demon turned away. But as you see, I should have done more. When it came racing back, I threw the mightiest hiding-charm I could fashion over us all. It was not quite enough, alas. The creature smelled something. It would have rushed straight at us, probably, if not for that … flash.'

'Flash?' said Pazel.

'Of spellcraft,' said the mage. 'Somewhere miles to the east, another power showed itself – for the blink of an eye. That blink saved us. The *maukslar* has flown off to investigate. And we must go too, before it decides to come back.'

'Those marks upon its forehead,' said Pazel. 'I couldn't read them all, but one of them said *Slave*. In the creature's own language.'

Neeps turned to him, startled. 'Your Gift just—?'

'Yes.' Pazel stared at his friend in some consternation, as if the idea was still sinking in. 'Pitfire, mate,' he whispered, 'I – I – *Thaaurolllllllgafnar, madocrón,* Oh *credek*, get it out of me, Ramachni, pull it out, pull it out—'

More ghastly, barrel-deep sounds escaped his chest. Terrified, he stuffed a hand into his mouth. His jaw went on working, biting down; his lips struggled to form words. 'Neda!' shouted Ramachni. 'Come and help your brother!'

'How help?' she cried, rushing forward.

'Not with your babyish Arquali, lass! Speak Ormali with him. Tell him anything, nursery rhymes if you like – only fill his ears, and do not stop speaking until he does. Pazel will master the demon-tongue, but first he must subdue it, or it will drive him mad.'

'I am six years not speaking Ormali!' said Neda, looking side-long at her master. 'Is heretic's tongue!'

Pazel sank to his knees, gabbling and moaning. 'It is your birth-tongue, girl!' said Cayer Vispek. 'And you are *sfvantskor,* foe of devils! Obey him!'

Neda bent and took her brother in her arms. '*Kuthyn, kuthyn, Pazeli,*' she said. Pazel fought her, but Neda's arms were those of a warrior-priest. He took his hand from his mouth and spat the ugliest sounds Thasha had ever heard. Neda gripped him tighter, pressed her cheek against his own, her lips against his ear as she spoke. They fell; she rolled him onto his back. They looked like lovers, coming together after bitterness or pain.

But already Pazel was quieter. His eyes streamed with tears. Thasha reached out for him, but Hercól gently caught her hand.

'You are not the one to help him, this time,' he said.

'His mind-fit—'

'Has not yet begun,' said Ramachni. 'This is different: a human mind forced to reckon with the language of the Pits. And lest we all face a reckoning with that beast, we must go.'

He gave the mage-sight to Dastu and Lunja, and they poled the raft away from the shore. The journey resumed; the forest once more went on the attack. The hot air pressed down on them like a blanket soaked in bathwater.

Blind again, Thasha listened to Pazel's moans, Neda's soft chatter in a tongue she didn't understand. She was jealous of Neda, and tried to be amused by the fact. She could hear what her father would say: *You're a fool beyond all redemption, Thasha Isiq*. With a smile to make it clear that he thought nothing of the kind.

Her father. By now the admiral would have heard that she was alive, for all the good it would do him. Once again she thought of the odds of ever returning to the North, seeing him again, kissing his bright bald forehead. What was he doing now? Pazel's mother had said only that he lived, in her single dream-visit with her son. Was he still in Simja, playing the part of Arqual's ambassador to that island nation? Or was he back in Etherhorde, under the thumb of Emperor Magad, and Sandor Ott's network of spies?

She dipped a hand in the river, splashed tepid water on her face. No use dwelling on the bad possibilities. Then Neeps groped towards her and took her hand. He was trembling. Thasha found his cheek and kissed it, tasting lemon sweat, and steeled herself not to cry. No use, no use. She wished for somebody to fight. He embraced her, clumsily. 'Don't worry,' he whispered, 'I know what's going to happen to me.'

Neeps stayed close to her after that. She sensed the fear in him and tried not to return it. 'Nothing's going to happen,' she told him, much later. 'You're tired, and you're a fool. Stop thinking that way.' When her next shift came she stole glances at him: awake, alert, casting his blind eyes about as if searching for something. Each time she spoke, Neeps lifted his head in her direction.

The hours passed, her shift ended; she was exhausted and filthy and bruised. She wanted to go to Pazel and hold him, but he was still sleeping peacefully, and Neeps looked cornered, lost. As the seeing-charm faded and the darkness flooded back, she went to him and knelt.

'You need a shave,' she said, as brightly as she could manage. 'Marila wouldn't know her husband.'

Neeps smiled, touching his woolly chin. Then he raised his hand to his temples and the smile disappeared. 'I can feel it already,' he said. 'Like an empty spot inside me, a place I can't go any more.'

'Just go to sleep, you donkey. When was the last time you slept?'

This time he didn't smile. Thasha took his hand. As her blindness gathered she watched his face disappear.

She slept, Neeps' arm over her shoulder and the world's horrors forgotten, and the woman that was part of her and yet a stranger walked the catacombs of her mind, seeking egress, seeking light. She would fail of course. Thasha's mind was a salt cavern beneath a desert, no mouth, no tunnel to the surface, no way in or out. The woman knew this better than Thasha herself; she knew every inch of the place, could have drawn it from memory, walked it in the dark. She had lived there seventeen years.

'Light! Light!'

Was she dreaming? Was that Ensyl, tugging at a lock of her hair? Someone whistled, bodies were stirring on the raft. Neeps just groaned and pulled her closer.

Ensyl tugged at her again. 'Wake up! Look around you!'

Thasha raised her head, wincing. There was light, natural light, gleaming along one side of the trees ahead.

'It stings at first, doesn't it?' said Lunja.

'I don't care if it stings for a week,' answered the Turach.

The river had narrowed; the raft was tumbling around a curve. All at once something dazzling spun into view. After a few painful blinks, Thasha realised she was looking up at high cliff walls, glowing in the midday sun.

Neeps twitched, and Thasha looked at him again. He was awake, still holding her. Their faces were inches apart.

Then Pazel said, 'We did it.'

He extended a hand to each of them. If he was disturbed to find them nesting like two spoons, his face showed no sign. They rose awkwardly, and Pazel threw his arms over their shoulders. They had reached the forest's edge. Before them, the Ansyndra flowed out through a great crack in the crater and into a canyon of grey-blue stone.

'Chins up, you dolts, we're alive,' said Pazel. Thasha gripped him tightly, felt Hercól's hand squeeze her shoulder, and brushed it with her cheek. Gratitude was all she felt, so fierce and pure that it was almost pain.

'Rin's eyes, I never thought we'd make it,' said Big Skip.

'Some of us did not,' said Hercól.

Thasha squeezed her eyes shut. The image of Greysan Fulbreech, paralysed and mad, had suddenly risen before them. The Simjan youth had betrayed them, but he had betrayed himself long before. She had tried to fall in love with Fulbreech: had hoped, maybe, that his charm and handsome body would save her from the frightening, foolish immensity of what she felt for Pazel. Then, at Hercól's insistence, she had used him: played the infatuated young woman, dazzled by his attentions, hungry for his touch. All with the aim of ferreting his master, Arunis, from his hiding place on the *Chathrand*. It had worked; they had found the sorcerer, kept him from killing anyone else on the ship.

But in the end they could do nothing for Fulbreech.

They were small matters, of course: his death, the soldiers' deaths, the death of Ott's agent Mr Alyash. The death of Jalantri, the young *sfvantskor* who had fallen in love with Pazel's sister. The disappearance of Ibjen, the dlömic boy, into the River of Shadows. The deaths of the hunting dogs who had followed them under the trees.

Small change, trivial losses, compared with the gigantic horror they were trying to prevent. Thasha knew this, and knew also that she would never believe it in her heart.

When she opened her eyes the raft had cleared the forest's shadow, and they were free.

'Can you guess how I got *this* one, Thasha?' asked Neeps.

'No,' Thasha mumbled. She did not particularly want to learn, either, or to see another of his scars. Both he and Pazel looked barbaric in the sun. Thasha glanced at their ten-day beards and thought of pig bristles, and wondered that she'd managed to kiss Pazel without scratching herself raw. No denying how strong they'd become, though. The tarboys matched her in muscle, now, and that was shocking. If she wrestled either of them she'd have to rely on skill alone.

They had floated for several hours through the silent canyon, the sun playing hide-and-seek in a white fog that was gathering near the clifftops. The walls of the canyon were sheer to about a hundred feet, then broke into forbidding crags and boulders. The company squirmed and shifted. Holding still on the jittery raft was becoming a kind of torment.

'My little sister bit me, that's how,' said Neeps.

'You must have deserved it.'

Neeps laughed aloud, as though she had said something very clever. Thasha smiled to hide her unease. Since that unexpected embrace in the forest Neeps had not left her side. Thasha had never seen him like this: so soft-spoken, so confiding. He talked of his brother Raffa's treachery, those two pounds of Sollochi pearls chosen instead of Neeps' life – and how his desire to kill Raffa had turned slowly into a desire to convince him, 'intellectually, like', that he had chosen wrong. He talked of his grandmother's battles with crocodiles, the whistle his grandfather invented that could call catfish, the girl at the docks in Etherhorde who'd fancied him, and her gangster uncles who had made sure that they never exchanged more than burning looks. Neeps did not speak once of Marila.

Now the canyon's heights were lost in the mist. 'We're still trapped,' said Corporal Mandric, staring up into the haze. 'Mind you, I'm glad to be out of that mucking forest. But sooner or later we've got to find a way to scramble out of here.'

'And what then?' said Big Skip. 'Getting out of the Forest alive was all I could think about, but there are hard choices waiting for us now. The road back to Masalym will be a dark one.'

'Only if you take it,' said Ramachni.

'*If?*' said Cayer Vispek. 'Great mage, how could we do otherwise? We have no notion of what lies ahead. We know nothing of this peninsula except that it is vast and desolate, and that the sea lies much further to the west than we have travelled thus far. We must go back.'

'There's the small matter of the flame-trolls to consider,' said Corporal Mandric.

'Not to mention that iron ladder that came loose from the cliffs under Ilvaspar,' said Pazel, 'and that cliff was much higher than these. Without that ladder there's no way up.'

'A *sfvantskor* takes such hurdles as gifts from the Unseen.'

'Gods of death, he's serious,' said the Turach, amiably enough.

'It is true that we know little of the trail ahead,' said Ramachni, 'but we know a great deal about what awaits us back in Masalym.'

'Our ship is there, maybe?' said Neda.

Ramachni sighed. 'Hercól, it is time you settled that particular question.'

'Agreed,' said the swordsman. While the others looked on, uncomprehending, he moved carefully to the raft's edge, as far from the Nilstone as possible. There he knelt and lay Ildraquin across his knees.

'What is this?' said Vispek. 'More enchantment in the sword?'

'The same, Cayer,' said Hercól. 'You know that Ildraquin can guide its wielder to any soul whose blood it has drawn.'

'You proved as much with Fulbreech,' said Lunja. 'What of it?'

'The morning we left the *Chathrand*, I drew the blood of Captain Rose.'

'Pitfire, now you tell us!' cried Thasha. 'Why were you keeping *that* a secret?'

'You're talking about that scratch on his wrist, aren't you?' said Neeps.

'Of course,' said Hercól, 'and I assure you it was done with his co-operation. As for my silence, the fact is that I hardly dared to think of Rose myself. The sword can follow but one blood-trail at a time, and if ever you turn aside, the trail goes cold, and cannot be found again. I dared not take that risk with Fulbreech: he was our only link to the Stone. But now—'

He slid the blade a few inches free of the scabbard, and sat with his hand upon the pommel, closing his eyes. The party fell silent, watching, and Thasha saw the frown begin at the corner of his eyes. Then he opened them and looked gravely at Ramachni.

'They are gone,' he said. 'Far from Masalym, and sailing further by the day. Since yesterday they have sailed northwards almost two hundred miles.'

'Damn the lying dogs!' exploded Mandric. 'They promised to return for us! All that about laying low in them islands outside the whatsit, the Northern Sandwall, sending lamp signals, waiting for that hag Macadra to clear out!'

'Perhaps she is in Masalym yet, or her ministers,' said Ramachni. 'Either way, Prince Olik will have been deposed. Do you see how foolish we would be to return, Cayer Vispek? Only death awaits us there.'

'Northwards,' said Dastu, clearly shaken. 'So they mean to cross the Nelluroq, and abandon us for good. We'll never see home again.'

Hercól looked at Dastu with compassion. 'When did you last see home, lad? When you walked the streets of Etherhorde as a spy? When you sat at your mother's table, concealing the fact that her son was learning to slit throats, hide bodies, brew tasteless poisons? Even if you do return to Etherhorde, you will remain a creature of the shadows, pretending to a life more than living it, unless you break with Sandor Ott. Your home was lost the day you joined the Secret Fist.'

'Go drown yourself,' snapped Dastu, 'although drowning's a lot kinder than what's in store for the rest of us. We're going to live and die in this Rinforsaken country, surrounded by their sort—' he waved at Bolutu and Lunja '—and treated like animals, like apes. That is, if we don't *become* apes, the way your tarboy pet—'

Thasha's fist closed; she saw herself breaking Dastu's teeth, saw the same rage in Pazel's eyes. But before she could move, something whirled at the youth. Ensyl had leaped with that matchless ixchel speed onto Dastu's shoulder. One hand gripped his ragged shirt. The other held her sword against the soft flesh beneath his eye.

'If you *dare* say another word—'

Dastu held his breath, motionless but for his darting eyes.

'Ensyl,' said Ramachni, 'come away from the youth.'

Silence. The raft bobbed and spun. Then, quick as a grasshopper, Ensyl sprang away from Dastu and landed by Hercól's foot. She kept her eyes fixed on Dastu as she sheathed her blade.

'This is a new life, with new requirements,' said Ramachni, 'and first among them is that we stand together. Let the old hates languish: you will find they vanish like dreams, if you permit them to.'

'Don't imagine that I mock your past allegiances,' said Hercól, 'for were they not mine as well? We need your skills, Dastu of Etherhorde. Stand with us, I say.'

Dark emotions played over the youth's face. He touched his cheek near the eye. 'Those crawlies nearly sank our ship,' he said. 'I don't know why you brought a pair of them along. But one's dead. Get rid of the other, and then talk about standing as a team.'

'Some are more wedded to hate than others, Ramachni,' said Ensyl.

'My mother's table,' sneered Dastu. 'Maybe that's how it was for you, Stanapeth, with your farms and manor houses. But as for me, I *found* my home when I joined Master Ott. The first in my mucking life. I'm not about to toss it off and go seeking another, though that's clearly the fashion in this company.'

The fog lowered. The canyon walls faded in and out of sight. It was disconcerting, but safer, Thasha knew: if the *maukslar* returned they would be hidden almost as well as before. The river ran swift, and looking down into its depths Thasha still imagined she could see veins of darkness, and feel the vertigo of endless space.

At some point in the afternoon, Lunja suddenly called for silence. A faint, deep noise was echoing down the canyon.

'Hrathmog drums,' said Lunja. 'The creatures send messages in this way. I have heard them often on the road to Vasparhaven.'

Thasha tensed. She had seen a single hrathmog, dead in the jaws of one of the great catlike steeds called *sicuñas*. Even dead it had been menacing, an axe-wielding, fur-covered humanoid with enormous arms and a mouthful of knifelike teeth. 'Do you think they've spotted us, Lunja?' she asked.

Lunja shook her head. 'When hrathmogs spot an enemy their drums fall silent, unless they fear a rout. The silence itself alerts other bands of the creatures. We guardians of Masalym have learned this through many ambushes, many deaths.'

The drums sounded again, even more faintly – but this time the echo came from downriver.

'They're just saying hello, I shouldn't wonder,' said Big Skip. 'Eight bells, and howdy-do-sir.'

'Well,' said Hercól, 'better to learn of them while they are still at a distance.' He squinted at the canyon walls, and Thasha could almost hear his thoughts: *Hard climbing. For some of us, impossible.*

They floated on, and heard no more of the drums. Soon Neeps was beside her again, uncomfortably close. Thasha tried to draw Pazel into their chatter, but he was keeping far from them both, which maddened her. She was terrified for Neeps. He was Pazel's best friend; this behaviour had to be a side-effect of the plague. He reached for her hand, and she let him hold it. She couldn't bear the thought of hurting him, in what might be his last days of human life.

Sometimes he grew flushed with excitement. 'I didn't expect this,' he said. 'What I'm feeling. It's so good.' Thasha turned away, wiped her eyes. Would they have to tie him like an animal? Would he have lucid moments, aware of what he'd become?

Late afternoon, a sandy beach loomed out of the fog: it was an island, crowned with oaks and cedars, splitting the river in two.

'Left or right?' asked Bolutu.

'Neither,' said Hercól. 'Twenty minutes ashore, to wash and stretch our limbs.'

They beached the raft. Neeps bounded up and helped Thasha to her feet. She saw Pazel glance in their direction and turn quickly away.

'Some of the vines have broken,' said Hercól. 'Come here, Neda, and help me lift the frame. You too, Undrabust.'

Thasha felt like running. She marched up the foggy beach and stepped into the trees. After a dozen yards she stepped behind an oak, then leaned out to look back at the shore. The others had stayed close to the raft. Pazel bent and tried to help with the repairs, but Hercól waved him firmly away – in her direction, as if by chance. She could have hugged him. Nothing escaped her mentor.

When Pazel drew near, she whistled softly, then beckoned him near and hid again. Eventually she heard his footsteps approaching. When she could stand it no longer she stepped out and dragged him behind the tree.

'You blary *imbecile*,' she said. 'Why didn't you help me with him?'

Pazel made no reply. He shrugged off her hand and walked deeper into the mist-shrouded trees. Furious, she plunged after him. The land rose, and they scrambled up the brief incline. When the ground levelled off the mist was brighter, and a pale green moss covered the feet of the oaks.

Thasha cornered him against a fallen tree. 'I could kill you,' she said. 'You just mucking *stood* there! Couldn't you see how bad he was getting?'

Pazel nodded.

'Look at me, you sorry—'

He kissed her, gently at first, then with abandon, his hands under her clothes, his hips pressing hard against her. Thasha gasped; her arms went around him, and for a moment she did not know if she was struggling or urging him on, helping him free of his trousers, giving in to his need and her own. His eyes were half-shut, he was devouring her with kisses, how could she stop him, how could she keep these boys from pain?

'Thasha—'

'Stop talking. Stop talking.'

He had a hand between her legs; she had her shirt up so that her breasts could touch his skin. This was the end, they were ruined. She was going to scream.

He was still. She hadn't screamed but her mind had gone elsewhere. Those were only his fingers, his fingers; she had lost all restraint but he hadn't, thank Rin. Her mind was racing, bliss and sadness and memories and mad notions of her destiny, all bent by the prism of his touch. *That wanton girl*, Arunis had cackled. Not everything he'd said was a lie.

Warm rain on her shoulder: Pazel was crying. 'Neeps wanted this,' he said.

'Maybe. Yes.'

'I was trying not to hate him. I was so angry I could barely breathe. I couldn't look at the two of you.'

'It's not his fault,' she said.

'I know, I know. And it doesn't matter, either. If it helps him somehow I don't care what you do.'

They still had not moved. 'It wouldn't help him,' she said. 'Making love doesn't protect you from the mind-plague.'

'Maybe it does, though. Maybe he senses something. Like animals do when they're sick.'

'No,' she said. 'If this were enough, humans would still be here, wouldn't they? Besides, he and Marila did it eight times—'

'*Eight?*'

'That's what she told me.' Thasha kissed his cheeks, his eyelids. 'Pazel ... you were in *nuhzat*, just now.'

'What?'

Appalled, he tried to break away, but Thasha held him tight. 'Hush, hush. It was over in seconds. But I saw your eyes change, turn solid black like Ramachni's. It was beautiful, you were beautiful. That's when ... I stopped thinking.'

He was barely listening. 'It's the second time it's happened to me,' he whispered.

Thasha knew that only dlömu could experience the *nuhzat*, that waking trance with its visions and powers, its fear. Dlömu, and in the rarest of cases, humans who had been raised by them. Or loved them. She knew also that Pazel had slipped into *nuhzat* in the temple at Vasparhaven. He had told her that much. But he had told Neeps more – and Neeps, in his disordered state, had babbled some of it to Thasha.

'You were with a dlömic woman,' she said, hoping she didn't sound accusatory.

'No!' said Pazel. 'I mean, yes. But not *with* her, not like this. I can't explain.'

She did not like the change in his voice, or the way his eyes stared past her as he spoke. 'Anyway,' he added, 'I'm not sure she was a dlömu.'

'What else could she have been?'

Pazel hesitated. 'A spider,' he said at last.

'You're insane,' said Thasha. 'Or I am. Oh *credek*. Pazel, listen: we can't do this any more. Not until we're safe somewhere. You know that, don't you?'

His answer was a kiss. She returned it, not caring if the kiss meant yes or no, for the blackness was flickering in his brown eyes again, and her youth was her own and not Erithusmé's, that was as certain as his beauty, his urgency, the rising of the sun.

She turned from him again.

'It's too dangerous,' she said. 'This time I wouldn't have stopped.'

'I *didn't* stop,' he said. 'I just – it was just—'

'Oh, Pitfire.' Thasha stepped back, lowering her shirt. 'That's it. I can't end up like Marila. You have to promise me you'll stay away.'

He laughed, reached to touch her again. Glaring, she caught his hands.

'Night Gods, Thasha,' he said. 'A few minutes ago you wanted to kill me because I *was* keeping away. Listen, stop worrying—'

'Oh, why should I worry? *You* listen, you blary ass. This time we got lucky. The first time I kept my head. No more.'

He was fumbling with his trousers, which were literally held up with string. Loving him desperately, she gripped his chin and raised it.

'Promise.'

She was quite certain about what she was doing. Pazel, however, managed to surprise her again: he turned and rushed down the hill in the direction of the raft. Suddenly she realised that he was limping. *You idiot!* she thought. *Why did you let him climb the hill?*

She closed her eyes. His stubbornness had left her shaking with rage. When she looked again Pazel had vanished in the fog.

Once more she bolted after him. She had no clear idea of what would happen when she caught up – tears, apologies, violence? *Aya Rin, don't let him fall on that leg.*

She reached level ground. The fog was now so thick that she could see just a few trees ahead of her, and only realised she was nearing the shore when the earth grew sandy among their roots. Where had he gone? She drew a breath to shout, but some instinct for caution made her hesitate. She rushed forward to the river's edge. There was no one in sight. Had they descended the wrong side of the island? Of course not, there was the raft, and—

Pitfire!

Thasha drew her knife, whirled into a defensive stance. The raft was destroyed. The vines cut, the bladder-mushroom slashed – and the Nilstone gone. The ropes that had secured its sacking trailed in the water. Footprints surrounded the raft, a confusion of footprints, radiating in all directions from the shore. She could see no other sign of the party.

As ever in a crisis, she thought of Hercól, his wisdom and severity. Her mind became clear. She bent low beside the nearest footprints. River water was trickling into the heels, softening them even as she watched. *The prints were only seconds old.*

She turned at bay. Now she heard it: a wide, dispersed sound, as of many persons or creatures moving in near-silence. The heart of the sound was at too great a distance to be coming from the island itself. *The shore, then. Or other boats.* Whatever it was, the party was no longer alone.

Thasha stepped carefully away from the raft, then turned and darted along the shore, putting distance between herself and that unseen host. She had taken no more than ten steps when Pazel materialised out of the fog.

'Don't move, Thasha,' he hissed.

Pazel was stock-still. And the next instant she saw why. A hrathmog stood facing him, gripping a huge, double-bladed axe. Water dripped from its black fur; long white fangs showed in its mouth. The shoulders beneath the crude leather jerkin were enormous.

The creature's eyes were fixed on her, now. It stood head and shoulders taller than either of them. She held her breath, muscles twitching with apprehension. The hrathmog fingered its axe.

Then Pazel spoke: a single word in a hard, guttural tongue such as Thasha had never heard. The creature gave an uncertain reply, its voice like the growl of a bear.

'It's afraid of us – afraid of humans,' Pazel murmured in Arquali. 'It said it didn't know this island belonged to the Lost People. That it was ordered here by its chief on the far shore. That it's sorry for disturbing our rest.'

'It thinks … we're dead?'

Pazel nodded, then spoke again in the hrathmog's tongue. The creature shuffled back a step. 'Where are the others?' Thasha whispered.

Pazel shook his head: no idea. The hrathmog lowered its axe. Thasha imagined it was breathing easier. She was not.

'The raft's destroyed,' she said.

Pazel shot her a look of dismay. Then his eyes snapped back to the creature. 'Right,' he said, 'we're ghosts, see? And we're just … going to … back away.'

They began a slow retreat, foot by careful foot. 'Into the river,' he said, 'just until we're out of sight. Then we'll swim.'

'Not too deep, though,' she said. 'Ramachni warned us—'

'I know.'

They backed offshore until the water reached their knees. The hrathmog watched, unmoving. Already its form was dimming in the fog. Pazel murmured a last word to the creature, and Thasha silently exhaled. His Gift had just saved them again.

Then her legs collided with something in the water. She whirled. A second hrathmog was floating beside her, face up. An arrow protruded from its throat. Although quite dead, the creature still gripped the arrow shaft with one hand.

Whose arrow? Their party had no bows.

Suddenly the hrathmog on the island rushed forward, narrowing its eyes. When it saw the body it threw back its head and gave a monstrous howl. From the far shore, dozens of voices rose in answer. But the hrathmog did not wait for its comrades. The two hairless creatures were not ghosts but tricksters, murderers. It raised its axe and charged.

Thasha grabbed Pazel by the shirt and flung him behind her. They stumbled backwards, flailing for deeper water, but then the hrathmog raised the great axe over its head, preparing to hurl it, and Thasha saw her death. The water had slowed her. She was offering the blade her chest.

The beast hurled the axe. But as it stepped into the throw, a second arrow pierced its calf. The hrathmog stumbled, the blow struck the water a foot from her chest. As the creature charged, Thasha groped for the weapon, pulled it from the river bottom, and swung.

How weak, how feeble, but somehow she'd cut the creature's hand. She kicked backwards, swimming now, screaming at Pazel to *Go go go!* The hrathmog snatched at the weapon; Thasha flung it away. *Chase it, chase it please!* The hrathmog lunged and caught her by the leg.

Thasha's knife flashed: now both its hands were bloody. Then those maimed hands caught her by the throat.

It tried to close, to bite. She forced an arm under its chin. They fell back into deeper water, the current whirling them downstream. Her knife was gone; Pazel groped for her and was gone; hairy thumbs dug into her windpipe. She twisted, clawed at its eyes. She was failing, the thing was killing her, it was just too strong.

All at once a spasm shook the creature. Pazel was on its back, his head over its shoulder. The creature screamed; its hands released Thasha and seized Pazel and hurled him away, and in the half-light she saw that Pazel had most of its ear in his teeth.

In a killing frenzy the hrathmog dived after Pazel. She clung to it, knowing it would tear her lover to pieces. The creature dragged her on, heedless – and then, suddenly, it was dead. Other beings surrounded them. Knives flashed. Dark blood billowed from the hrathmog's neck.

She was choking: she must finally have gasped. Her vision dimmed and a roaring filled her ears. Her last sensation was of the veins of darkness in the river's depths, coiling about her ankles, pulling her down.

5

———❦———

Monday, 21 Modobrin 941. A dlömic woman spat a seed into the waves today & made me cry. She never saw me watching her. First her lips worked round & round, then her face lifted & she made kissing-lips & when the seed flew her eyes tracked it like a gunner his cannonball. At first I couldn't account for my tears; then I knew I was seeing my Annabel on a picnic, with a sweet green mush-melon, spitting seeds in Lake Larré, the juice runnin' down her lovely chin.

Nine days since the Shaggat's waking, the torture of Chadfallow, the proof that Rose has ceded his captaincy in all but name to Sandor Ott. We are blazing west by northwest under topgallants & triple-jibs, over waves like rounded hills, putting mile after mile between us & our abandoned shipmates. *Coward, traitor, fair-weather friend*: at night the accusations churn my stomach, though no one makes them but me.

A queer dark spot in the sky this morning. It moved closer & we saw it was a solid mass, very low in the sky. We beat to quarters, ran out our guns. The object bobbed & turned. It seemed adrift in the air, & with indescribable horror we saw that it was the bow of

---

*The quartermaster's first journal was stolen and partly destroyed by Mr Uskins. The second was locked in the secret wall cabinet in Thasha Isiq's cabin in the stateroom of the *Chathrand*. These journals filled two of the opulent blank books left on board by Admiral Isiq. The third and final journal, however, was written in a slender notebook that Fiffengurt kept in his breast pocket. He claimed that it was a gift from Prince Olik before the ship departed the city of Masalym. - EDITOR

a sailing ship, fifty feet of hull & deck & shattered framewood, the stump of a foremast, the whole bowsprit thrusting upwards like a narwhal's tusk. Rin as my witness, the thing looked *torn*, like a heel of bread from a loaf. Two cables reached skyward from the anchor ports, a quarter-mile maybe, & at the end of 'em we could now see one of those weird sky-sails used by the dlömic armada: half kite, half balloon, kept aloft by some power none of us could explain. The wreck blew right over us, some hundred feet above our forecastle. There were flames inside her, & dlömu, living dlömu, holding fast to the rigging & rails. They looked down at us & I expected to hear calls for help, but they were silent. Maybe they thought us phantoms, heralds of doom, as their cousins did that first night in the port in Masalym.

No one spoke, no one could. One of those poor devils jumped for our rigging but of course at that speed it just tore through his hands like razors & then his foot grazed something & he turned & reached the deck headfirst & Heaven's Tree, how I wish I'd shut my eyes.

If only someone up there had thought to drop a rope. We might have reeled them down with the capstan, spread combat netting between the yards. They could have jumped & lived. As it was the wreck drifted northwards, gaining height. For hours we watched it dwindle against the sky.

I am done with journal-keeping. Let oblivion take these memories. Anni will have had the child by now; Rin knows how she'll care for the little thing, or who she'll turn to for comfort. Goodbye to you, journal. You're a womanish weakness I've indulged & that is the true reason I kept you a secret. No more entries, no more pain. Goodbye I say. The end. Let me be an animal that labours for his food bag, a dumb brute who does as he's told.

Wednesday, 23 Modobrin 941. But what I'm told – the miracle that Rose would have me work – is to keep their spirits up. 'Make them hope a little longer, Quartermaster,' he says. 'You're honest, & you're an ally of Pathkendle & Company. It falls to you.'

Make them hope. I close the door to his cabin, walk ten paces. Before me is a man I recruited off the streets of Etherhorde, a pious youth as I recall. He's in a deathsmoke trance. I remember what I said to him, in that tavern doorway on a cool summer's eve: 'Finest run you'll ever make, & the easiest. Due west to Simja, feasting & carousing at a festival that'll be the envy of your grand-kids, the pomp & splendour when we give away the Treaty Bride. Then due east to Etherhorde again, and ninety cockles in your purse by midwinter.' I believed all that myself – wanted to believe it, needed to. My own pay for that easy run would have let me clear Anni's parents' debts, with maybe a bit left for a humble wedding.

Now here the fellow stands, reeking, mouth agape, so fogged he doesn't know me, or his peril should he draw the captain's eye. He is a Plapp, & when I alert his brother gangsters they whisk him down to the hold to sleep it off – or to look for his stash, or both.

That was midday. At three bells there's a tarboy before me, hor-rified, whispering that a group of thugs is working the berth deck, snatching boys from their hammocks at night, clapping hands over their mouths & bungin' 'em in the lockers until they bleed. At five bells another deathsmoker appears in the galley, in worse shape than the first. He's a Plapp as well, but this time the Burnscove Boys get to him first, & turn him in. I suppose his execution will follow.

Someone is knocking at my door: more bad news, or else Uskins, drooling & vague, with a word from the captain. I should have married her in secret. I should have told her old dad to get stuffed.

Thursday, 23 Modobrin 941. There is heat in Rose's innards yet. I went straight to him with the tarboys' problem, having some inkling that the crime would touch a nerve. That it did: hardly had I spoken when he exploded out of his stuporous slouch & thundered to the cabin door, bellowing for the nearest lieutenant. A moment later he was back, questioning me furiously about the incident. He was taking it very hard by the look on his face, & then he shook my hand. I did not dream that: Captain Nilus Rotheby

Rose shook my hand, & did not bite it either. A knock at the door. He scowled & shoved me, but I didn't mind. The boys would be safe. As I left I saw who was waiting to enter: Sergeant Haddismal & the Bloody Son.*

Later there are distant explosions in the south, & flashes like bubbles of fire – rising, bursting, gone. The War Furnaces, whisper the dlömu. Fed not with coal but lead and diamonds, and above all eguar bones. Machines so huge & hot the discharge can be seen these hundreds of miles. The lads just stand & stare, as if the Nine Pits were gaping open there on the horizon, as perhaps they are.

'Do they threaten us, away out here?' I ask the dlömic commander, a thick-chested fellow whose long, fleshy earlobes make me think of soup spoons.

He shrugs. 'When I saw the armada pass by Masalym, I thought, "They've emptied all the shipyards of Orbilesc & Bali Adro City; there mustn't be a boat left to watch over the heartland." I was wrong. Those sorts of flares, you see them only when a warship launches. Part of the fleet is still here. We'll be in danger if they spot us.'

'We're flying the Bali Adro flag. Won't that help?'

Only to a point, he says. When they run out of enemies, they fire on one another, ram one another, close & grapple & kill. The eguar gave them indescribable power, but it also made them frenzied & fearful, almost rabid. 'And a rabid dog must bite *something*, after all.'

He is a good fellow, Spoon-Ears, but he never cheers me up.

So we run & run, with many a backwards glance. Lady Oggosk crouches topside day after day, like a gargoyle, staring in the direction of the Sandwall, which most days one needs a telescope to see.

---

*A Turach, one of the original Etherhorde hundred. The marine earned his nickname at the age of twelve, when he killed his father with a maul after learning that the man had raped his younger brother. Fiffengurt's intervention probably led to the surprise Turach patrols of the berth deck that began at this time, as well as the threats posted in the ladderways, promising castration on the blacksmith's anvil. – EDITOR

Felthrup, of all Rin's creatures, has taken to chatting with her, & even sits in the old crone's lap. The vicious Sniraga, who used to kill rats by the score for food & pleasure, wails & flicks her ruined tail but will not touch him. When the hag wants Felthrup's company she sends Sniraga to howl outside the stateroom, & the cat leads Felthrup to her door like a bodyguard. Mr Teggatz watched them walk by & cracked his knuckles & burbled cryptically:

'Cat takes rat, bah ha! Quite enough, quite enough. Cat takes *orders* from rat? Topsy-turvy. It's the end of the world.'

Monday, 28 Modobrin 941. If Teggatz is right about the approach of doomsday we could well be the last to know it. There is no one & nothing out here. We could be launched already into the heart of the Ruling Sea, save for those brief glimpses of the Sandwall, & the meekness of the waves, which have not topped fifty feet. Some land mass ahead must be taming them, unless the lions of the deep have all turned lambs.

Rose navigates by Ott's ancient map & a fine dlömic chart provided by Prince Olik, but the former is a faded scrap & the latter only depicts the margins of the Island Wilderness. Our immediate goal: Stath Bálfyr, that last bit of Southern land, from which place Ott's sniffing about in books & archives back home produced detailed course headings for our run across the Ruling Sea. We stand a fair chance of locating the island, too: Prince Olik ventured there in his youth & has pencilled in his best guess at its location.

And what a great black joke if we succeed.

For we've kept the secret so far – 'we' being just myself & Marila & Felthrup, now the others have departed. Alone on the *Chathrand* we know that those course headings are a perfect crock. They don't point to Gurishal, that blighted kingdom of the Shaggat Ness. I doubt they point to any safe, sound path across the Nelluroq at all. Ott's chart is a forgery, but this time he was not the forger. The ixchel have used us, used us like the great oafs we are, used this ship to ferry them back to Stath Bálfyr, their homeland, from whence we stole them centuries ago. Now all the little people have gone, vanished into thin air.

That is nonsense, of course: they are flesh & blood, not pixies. They are also a brave & decent people, no more vicious or deluded than we ourselves, & more committed to one another by far. Probably they slipped ashore in Masalym, to try their luck on some less lethal ship. Rin save us, if men will rape tarboys half their size, what will they not have done to tiny ixchel, in the silence of attics, laboratories, holds?

But now that the ixchel are gone, should I tell? Should I try to persuade Ott that his whole mad circumnavigation of Alifros is based on a lie? Soon enough I'll have no choice, for he means to start our northward run the minute Stath Bálfyr gives us our bearings. For the moment I see nothing to be gained by speaking up: Ott would insist on attempting the crossing anyway, & sooner, probably. Stath Bálfyr will not help us get home, but so long as we are searching for it we are at least on the same side of the world as our friends.

Tuesday, 28 Modobrin 941. Felthrup is sleepwalking. This is preferable, he declares, to not sleeping at all, by which malady he nearly perished on the Ruling Sea. Yet any sleep disorder in the rat should set alarm bells ringing throughout the *Chathrand.* His insomnia proved to be his way of fighting Arunis, who was attacking the minds of who-knows-how-many crewmembers as he tried to master the Nilstone.

He has come a long way as a dreamer, Felthrup declares. Time was that Arunis had infiltrated his dreams, & placed a lock on them, so that he could torture & interrogate the rat all night, & be certain Felthrup would be none the wiser by day. Now that lock is broken (another result of the sorcerer's death, maybe?) & Ratty can remember his dreams like anyone else: imperfectly, that is, & through the veil that falls with the opening of the eyes. I ask what he thinks he's searching for, when he roams the passageways, or bumps along the edges of the stateroom chambers in his sleep. 'The doors of a club,' he tells me cryptically. 'I have a friend there who might help us, if I can only find him.'

Marila has a little bulge at her beltline already, as though her stomach aspires to catch up with those round cheeks of hers. Felthrup tells me that she is 'miserable, weak, sickly, ill-humoured, dolorous', but he is distressed whenever one of us suffers a hangnail. What is certain is that Mrs Undrabust has no patience with the indignities of her condition. She storms about looking for work & grows irritated when the women steerage passengers – old spinsters to the last, since the desertions in Masalym* – coo & cluck at her & tell her she should be abed. Mr Teggatz lives in fear of her: she is usually famished but gags on his offerings. The tarboys are sniggering over a rumour that she begged the cook for a salted pig's ear, claiming it was for Thasha's dogs, & then was seen gnawing it herself on the No. 3 ladderway.

Dr Chadfallow, for his part, is healing – Ott knows just how far to torture a man – but he is broken in spirit, & does not hide the fact. 'I have chosen all the wrong paths in life,' he said this evening, as Marila & I changed his bandages. 'I should never have set foot in the Keep of Five Domes. I grew to like it there, among the jewels & courtesans. I thought I could stand beside Magad & nudge his Empire towards the good. I thought reason would prevail. Self-delusion, nothing more. The Emperor gelded me the day he called me to court.'

At that Felthrup began to leap up & down. 'The villain! The wretch! Was the operation terribly painful?'

'Hush, Ratty, it was a figure of speech,' I said. And to Chadfallow: 'All you could do was try, man. Nobody steers a ship but the captain.'

The doctor was having none of that. 'When a captain will not turn you must place another boat across his way. I should have fought Magad sooner, while there was still time.'

'You'd have made a lousy rebel,' put in Marila, who has a knack

---

* Fiffengurt refers to the escape of twenty-six crew and passengers into the streets of Masalym. These men and women could not be found before the *Chathrand*'s desperate flight. - EDITOR

for getting to the heart of things. 'You'd have just been hanged or stabbed or something. And then you'd never have invented your parasite pills, & I'd have died when I was eight.'

Chadfallow snorted, then winced with pain, but for a moment I saw pleasure in his eyes.

He is not alone in his melancholy, of course. Rose is still hermited in his cabin; Uskins still shuffles about like the walking dead. The men are grim, the tarboys witless with fear, the dlömu simply astonished. They hang together, these dlömu. Rin knows they must need the comfort of familiar faces, when all they see are pale humans, ghost faces to them, their country's exterminated slaves come back to life. They sleep on the boards, play a game with dice & chalk lines, exercise at dawn. Teggatz says they don't eat much – not more than half what a human eats – but after labour how they will gobble *mül*. I've watched 'em knead those sticky globs like bread dough, then chew & chew 'til a peaceful look steals over them, & they sleep. I've eaten the stuff myself (bland & vaguely foul it is) but still haven't a clue what's in it.

As I say, they're close. Still the ganglords smell fresh blood & are trying their luck at recruiting. This evening I heard Kruno Burnscove make a pitch to three of the youngest dlömu. Protection, he kept saying. 'At the darkest hour, you'll need more than forty brothers & sisters, won't ye now? Human beings are wicked, you have no muckin' idea. If we get lost out there, & the food gets low? You think them Plapps will settle for that dlömic putty you live on? Why, they'll kill you & cut out your fat & boil it up into a stew. They've done it on other ships, lads. There's witnesses aboard.'

He noticed me listening, then, but only smiled. What was I going to do about it?

'All lies,' I told the dlömu. 'Pay no attention, lads. There's strychnine on certain tongues.'

'He *would* say that,' Burnscove countered, pointing at me with a blackened nail. 'Let me tell you about the neighbourhood this one comes from—'

We bickered, but I could tell who had their ears. So could Kruno

Burnscove, whose twinkle kept on brightening. Rose still needs the gangs; their hatred of each other protects him from any serious threat of mutiny. Otherwise he'd long ago have cut the heads off those twin snakes.

Thursday, 31 Modobrin 941. A ghastly night. Marila came weeping to my door. Sharp pains in her gut, & vomiting too: the poor girl was a sight. I put her in my bunk & ran to Chadfallow, hating to think of him rising & tearing all his stitches. But Felthrup was there ahead of me (he is Marila's constant guardian in the stateroom), nipping at his ankles, chiding him to be careful.

'Dysentery, if she's lucky,' said Chadfallow. 'Nothing to do with the pregnancy – but I've seen it end a few. We must be ready for that.' He sent me dashing off to Teggatz with a fistful of herbs to brew into tea. By the time I got back to my cabin he & Ratty were there, & Marila was moaning. She threw up the first cup; the second gave her the runs. A crowd gathered in the passage, hushed & fearful. Of all forms of good luck that sailors believe in, a babe in a lawful, wedded womb is the most potent. Not the cruellest bastard aboard wanted her to lose the child.

Marila sipped that brew for hours, Teggatz rushing back & forth from the galley with fresh kettles, Chadfallow taking her temperature, sniffing her sweat, making her blow up little balloons & Rin knows what else besides, & Ratty flying about my little cabin like blary ball lightning, insisting that everything be 'perfect, please everyone, not good enough, passable, tolerable, tarboyish, rodent-grade – *perfect!*' & Marila herself moaning & squatting mortified on chamber pots behind a blanket. No blood, she'd say, & we'd all sigh & swear.

Very late, the symptoms broke. Marila lay still, breathing easier, & the crowd drifted away, smiling like children. In time she persuaded Chadfallow to go to his rest, & I sent Felthrup along behind to see that he did so. Marila fell asleep gripping my sleeve. I lowered myself to the floor & closed my eyes. If anyone can bring us hope it will be young Mrs Undrabust.

I dreamed of the other youths. Pathkendle toppling from a bridge. Undrabust knuckle-walking like an ape. Thasha trapped in stone like a fly in amber. I had the power to save them from those calamities, to pull them together in my arms, & wonder of wonders, when I did so we had all become the same age, each of us in our bursting prime, unbent & exuberant & delivered from fear. They're my kin, I thought, & why did it take so long to see it? For the journey was ended; someone was calling me away. And I only knew the place they had in my heart because I was leaving, because we'd never live beneath the same roof again. I woke stricken, on the point of blubbering tears.

Then my eyes snapped open. An ixchel was crouched on my foot locker, gazing at me. I started to rise, & knocked over the little stand with the tea kettle, waking Marila with a gasp.

The ixchel was gone. Surely I'd had a dream within a dream? 'What is it, what's happened?' cried Marila. Nothing, dear, nothing. Old men will have nightmares, they talk to themselves, you should never spend the night in their company.

But the vision troubled me throughout the day. For it was not just any ixchel* I'd dreamed about. It was Talag, their lord & elder, the embodiment of the clan. A genius & a fanatic, & a man who'd not be pried away from his people by any power on earth.

Friday, 1 Halar 942. By our shipboard reckoning it is New Year's Day. And thus the first day of spring in the North – though here the dlömu say that autumn has begun. And why should I expect anything comforting & familiar? Everything is backwards here. There are mould spores on the biscuits of a colour I've never seen in my life. There's a second moon in the sky. Creatures with the skin of black eels & spun-silver hair rule an empire, & humans – what are they? Formerly slaves; today nothing at all, a bad memory, a handful of mindless scavengers dying of hunger in the wild. Rin's

---

* Here Fiffengurt has rubbed out the word 'crawly' in favour of 'ixchel'. The racial slur never appears in his journals again. – EDITOR

mercy, what will happen to those we left behind?

The new year. Start of the twenty-ninth in the reign of that crooked man I shall never again call His Supremacy. I once adored him, our Magad of Arqual. I knew he'd had a hand in driving Empress Maisa from the throne, but the fact never troubled me. She was corrupt & twisted, she had to be – my schoolteachers had told us so. Never mind that the Abbot's Prayer we said every morning had included a plea to Rin for her safekeeping. One morning she was our Empress; the next her portrait came down, & we were told that she was a villainess, & had been 'mercifully' allowed to flee into exile. They spoke of her with shame, that day. The following morning no one spoke of her at all. The last time I pronounced her name it was to my brother Gellin, & he hushed me angrily. 'Don't you *ever* pay attention, Graff? We're not to mention that whore. She's a stain on Arqual & best forgot.'

I didn't argue. He was right; I was certain of it. Our generation had rather too many certainties.

Thirty years would pass before I heard another tale of Maisa's overthrow. Hercól Stanapeth's was a darker tale, but I didn't have to be terrified or bullied into believing it. And we live (don't we now?) in the hope that it may yet end well.

Whatever the future holds, this new year is starting off as dismal as the inside of a shark. The men's feet drag, their eyes wear foggy veils of despair. They're haunted by this day, of what it could be for them, what it *has* been. The work furloughs, the gifts of candy, the kids screaming & hugging your knees. The games & laughter. The wine gulped, the girls kissed, the marriages consummated or destroyed. So precious, even the bad memories, here on an alien sea.

Then at midday Rose proves once more his gift for shocking us (the man's mind is a jungle; at any moment a bright bird may issue from it, or a gruesome snake). We're assembled on deck, even the late watch rousted & dragged into daylight, & there from the quarterdeck he bids us believe in the future: 'As I told you once before, lads, the future we can fight for, not be given.' He doesn't elaborate, mercifully enough: we are none of us open to pretty speeches any more. But he does bring forth the apple-cheeked Altymiran woman who helps out Teggatz in the galley. She's well liked, & has regained a bit of her plumpness on the rations provided by Prince Olik. She also turns out to have the lungs of a choir mistress, & she sings us a naïve little melody about the lambing-time in Arqual, & blast me if she doesn't turn us all to lambs for ninety seconds or so.

Next comes his real trick: the old fox suddenly produces *thirty bottles* of aged juniper *idzu*, secured in his cabin since Etherhorde, he says – but in what rat-proof, wave-proof miracle of packing I should like very much to know. The men don't care to ask: tarboys have brought our tin cups from the galley & are passing them quickly. Rose breaks the sealing wax & pours a thimbleful. Before a silent ship, he drinks, swallows, considers. Then he nods & looks at us.

'No better *idzu* could I obtain in the capital,' he said softly, 'and I would have you know two things. First, neither I nor anyone aboard has partaken of this store, until this moment. Second, that I am a fair judge of liquor—' there are chuckles at the understatement '—& this drink is fine. Truth be told, it surpasses the drink they plied me with in the Keep of Five Domes, when I dined with the Emperor's sons. If it were possible, I should declare it fit for you – fit for the most capable & dauntless men ever born beneath the arc of heaven, born to make mockery of hardship, born to crack an old, bedevilled skipper's heart with pride. I should like to declare it that good – but nothing is that good. It is all I have to give you this New Year's Day. A drink, & my promise to fight for our lives, hard as it may be to find the path to their salvation. Drink now to its finding, men of the *Chathrand*. That is all.'

The crew roared. Staggered, I looked out over that throng of wretches. Plapps & Burnscovers, sailors & Turachs, even some of the folk we'd blary kidnapped on Simja: all cheering. They hadn't even tasted the drink, but what did it matter? The Red Beast had praised them to heaven, & they loved him, suddenly. The drink went round, it was ambrosial & strong as the devil's mead. 'He's not just our captain, he's our father!' shouted a young midshipman, & seconds later I heard a song we used to sing in Temple School, on the lips of hundreds of overgrown boys:

> *Father dauntless, we're your lads, through cold and darkness wending.*
> *Climb we will that blasted hill,*
> *Lonely, sad but marching still*
> *Father fearless, lead us on, the night is surely ending.*

They pressed close to him. Rose never did smile: that would have diluted the effect. He only nodded, urging them to drink, & the *idzu* was gone before anyone could get too afflicted. They went singing to their stations, those wretches. I turned & slipped through a crowd of bewildered dlömu, making faces at the strange stuff in their cups & stranger joy in the humans around them, & then I saw Sandor Ott at the No. 4 hatch, looking over the scene with a certain abhorrence. I could have laughed. *This is why you need him, killer. This is why you don't dare make a final enemy of the man.*

Saturday, 2 Halar 942. The second day of any year is a disappointment. This one was marked by weird & hideous events. The predawn watch came off their shift wild-eyed & swearing: one of them had heard music in the darkness, flutes, but no players could they find, aloft or below. Already the talk is of ghosts. Did you see ghosts, I enquire? Well no, Mr F, not as such. But who made that music, eh? A fevered imagination, that's who, I told 'em, but I wasn't getting through. Ghosts, they insisted. Of course Rose's endless mutterings on the subject have made it hard for even the natural sceptics among them to hold steady.

At two bells, the expected cry finally comes: land ahead, a mist-fuzzed shadow, & another spotted minutes later, further west. They are the Sparrows, the dlömu aboard tell us: little no-count islands, but for any ship with business in the Island Wilderness the sight of them marks the moment for turning away from the continent once & for all. With double hands on the braces we're soon tacking northwards. I look back & cannot see the Sandwall. But when I close my eyes I see their faces, plain as my hand: Thasha & Pathkendle, Undrabust & Hercól. I don't believe in prayer, & yet I pray.

Five bells. I'm on the berth deck (routine inspection, no whimpering tarboys any more) when from the orlop below comes a howl such as man gives only when running for his life. I'm down the ladderway in seconds, with Teggatz & the tarboy Jervik Lank on my heels & Mr Bindhammer racing ahead. Rin save us, who do we see but the purser, Old Gangrüne, running like a lad of twenty, & just behind him a mountain of red muscle & white tusks & slobber. It's the Red River hog — the same mucking animal that disappeared in the rat war — fat & huge & furious, & before we can do more than gawk they're both around the bend in the corridor.

Alas for Gangrüne it was a dead-end passage. We charged in, screaming, but the beast was already goring the man, waving him about on its tusks like a dishrag. We attacked & a horrid melee it was. No boar in Alifros compares to a Red River either in size or sheer mean mordaciousness. Bindhammer was trampled. Jervik stabbed the beast in the jaw but his little knife broke off at the hilt. Teggatz had brought a meat cleaver & lopped a slab of pork from one fatty shoulder. The hog turned screaming & caught his arm near the elbow, & you could see his arm would not long inconvenience those boltcutter jaws, so I drove my knife into the neck of the beast, once, twice, thrice, & the third time it screamed again & backed off Teggatz & smashed me up against the wall. I lost my knife. I locked my hands on those tusks but they were slippery with blood & then it chomped me, Gods of Death, it's a wonder this left hand ain't in its belly right now.

I have Jervik to thank for that. He picked up the cleaver & proceeded to carve his way into the hog's right buttock, deranged & deadly he looked, & the hog whirled & trampled him worse than Bindhammer, & Pitfire if all four of us weren't down, bleeding, beaten flat & the hog not remotely tired of thrashing us, & a few men I'd like to vivisect just gazing meekly around the corner, & then a huge shadow & a roar & Refeg the augrong lifted the beast off Jervik, smashed it left & right, shattering the walls, & then his brother Rer caught up from behind & bit down on one huge kicking hog-leg. A crack, a squeal. The thing kept fighting. They had to tear it apart.

Tonight we are all still alive, though Bindhammer's lung is collapsed & he fights for breath, & Jervik is so bruised & battered he can scarcely move. But the hog! I know its history: that fool Latzlo meant to sell it to the highest bidder, for the feasts after Thasha's wedding. He'd fattened it out of his own purse, all the way to Simjalla City. Of course neither he nor his prize pig ever made it ashore.

Where can the beast have hidden, all this time? The answer is nowhere. We run a tight ship; nothing half its size could be overlooked for long. I think back to the ixchels' accusations, when they were still in charge: that we were hiding cattle & goats somewhere aboard. They claimed they'd heard the creatures, a moo-moo here, a bleat-bleat there, & we just laughed in their faces. No one is laughing any more.

Jervik lies in sickbay. I brought him a new knife: a fine blade with a walrus-ivory handle & a locking hinge. It had belonged to Swellows, the first bosun on this voyage, but in this case I didn't mind raiding the locker of a dead man. Swellows had bragged about winning it in a tavern by cheating at spenk, & had made other, fouler remarks about how it was just the tool for a necklace-fancier.* Jervik was pleased & didn't ask where the knife had come from. What he did ask, to my surprise, was when we'd be turning back for Pazel & Co.

I stumbled a bit. 'That … ain't quite clear.'

---

*A collector of ixchel skulls, which some men wore about their necks in the odd belief that it would improve their virility, especially if the wearer himself had beheaded the corpses. – Editor

He lifted his black & blue face from the pillow. 'Wha?'

'The captain ... hasn't made me privy to the plan.'

Jervik squinted at me. 'Yer leaving 'em behind, ain't ye?'

I expected a grin. If he'd given one I think I might have snatched that knife back from him & stabbed him in the ribs. Instead I saw the same distress in his face that I was feeling myself. I was floored. I bent down in the chair & fiddled with my shoe.

'Lank,' I whispered, 'what am I missing, here? Did you all become friends before they left?'

He scowled. 'I ain't good enough to be their friend. Not after wha I done. But I'm on your side, all right. Them others, Rose, Ott, they can all bite my—'

'Hush! They'll kill you.' I ran a hand through my hair. 'You can't shoot your mouth off about this, d'ye hear? But you're perfectly right: Ott means to sail north & abandon them all. I don't think the captain wants to, although with Rose it's blary hard to tell. But Ott has the Turachs behind him, so what he wants, he gets.'

'I'll cut him open. And Rose too.'

I looked at him. 'That was my promise to Lady Thasha. That I'd stab Rose dead if he tried to sail away & leave them here. But who would it help, lad? Are we going to seize the *Chathrand* & sail it back to Masalym? And what if they're not waiting for us in Masalym? What if they're making for some other port?'

'Then it's hopeless. Bastards, whoresons—'

'It's not hopeless. You know what they're made of, Pathkendle & Thasha & Hercól. And there's Turachs with 'em too, & eight dlömic soldiers. But if we're going to see 'em again, I think they will have to come to *us*.'

'Come to us! On what boat, Mr Fiffengurt? And how would they know where to look?'

I toyed with mentioning Stath Bálfyr, & the master plot of the ixchel. I considered trusting him with the knowledge of Hercól's sword. What could be gained by either confidence, however, save further danger for us all? 'They'll know,' was all I managed to say.

He nodded, & I left him to his rest. A new ally, in the person of Jervik Lank. There's no end to wonders under Heaven's Tree.

Teggatz reassembled the hog (Refeg & Rer did not eat it; they live on a diet of fish meal & grains) & roasted it in the galley stove, with cooking sherry & dlömic onions & snakeberries & yams. Everyone aboard got a bite of that beast, & it was sumptuous beyond all telling. I was wrong: Latzlo is no fool. For such a splendid pig the royals on Simja would have showered him with gold. I took him a plate. He nibbled with tears in his eyes.

As for the officers, we ate in the wardroom. Uskins joined us for the first time in days, looking like something a dog had tired of chewing, as Sergeant Haddismal informed him to general delight. Rose & Ott were elsewhere, which made for looser tongues, & I dare say the rich food made us wild. Fegin told us about one such hog that got loose in a slaughterhouse in Ballytween & killed every man in the place, & seven delivery boys one after another, & the foreman who came to see why the packing was so slow.

'And they all *knew* about the hog. It didn't just appear like a fairy.'

'This weren't no mucking fairy,' said Haddismal.

Mr Thyne speculated that the hog might have gotten into a dark corner of the hold & gone to sleep – hibernated, in a word. The notion brought jeers. 'Listen to the company man! Telling *us* about pigs!'

'The Red River is on Kushal,' I explained. Seeing his blank look, I added: 'Where it's warm all the time. No need to hibernate if you're a tropical pig.'

'Latzlo hid the creature,' said Haddismal, matter-of-fact, 'and I hope Rose hangs him from the yards by his thumbs. No worse money-grubber alive than that man. You heard him in the passageway: "My property, my investment." Gangrüne & Bindhammer lying at his feet, half killed, & he's got eyes only for this.' He waved at the platter of bones. 'He's the guilty party, no doubt about it. Still thought he could sell it, I shouldn't wonder.'

'Sell it to whom?' asked Mr Elkstem.

'To us, of course. Later on, when the fresh food ran out, & we got hungry again.'

'Brainless twit,' said Uskins, through a mouthful.

Haddismal looked at him with contempt. 'That depends on who he's compared with,' he said, & chuckled at his own jest.

'I wasn't speaking of Latzlo,' said Uskins.

Our busy jaws stopped dead. Haddismal stared in amazement. Uskins normally flinched at the very sight of the marine, who smacked him about with some regularity. But now he just went on eating.

'I didn't quite catch that remark,' said Haddismal, low & deadly.

Uskins shrugged, chewed faster. Haddismal kept drilling him with those eyes, then slowly shook his head, as if he'd decided Uskins wasn't quite worth interrupting his dinner for. The rest of us exchanged glances, started breathing again. Thyne hiccupped. Haddismal took another rib from the platter.

'This hog was smarter than you on a good day,' said Uskins.

The Turach exploded from his chair. Thyne & Elkstem dived out of his path as he rounded the table.

'Because nobody *kept* it, you see,' said Uskins, the only one of us still seated. 'It was woken, intelligent, & we're eating it anyway, how d'ye like that, Sergeant, hmm? The Sizzies always did call us cannibals.'

The Turach was reaching for Uskins' collar, but he froze there, agog. Now we were all shouting at the first mate, in rage & disgust. *Woken?* What in the brimstone Pits did he mean?

Uskins swallowed a large gristly bite. 'Of course woken,' he said. 'How do you think it got away from the rats? Day after day in that wooden crate. Thinking, knowing its circumstances. Knowing it was travelling to its death. What did piggy do? It watched & waited. And when the rats came it kicked that crate to pieces & fled into a vanishing compartment. Just like mages have done for hundreds of years. Just as Miss Thasha used to do, in olden times, when the ship was hers. The cows & goats went too, but they were just lucky.'

He pushed more flesh into his mouth. 'Uskins,' I said, 'the hog never talked.'

'Neither do I, most days,' he said. 'Why talk when nobody listens? You're a bilge-brain, too.' He gave me a meaty grin. 'What would it say? "Hello, Mr Latzlo! It's your thousand-pound piggy, let me out & I'll play nice with you, I'll fetch your slippers, I'll never bite off your head."'

'Raving lunatic,' said Haddismal.

Uskins lurched forward & dragged the whole platter to himself, knocking his plate to the floor. He began to eat with both hands, chin low, making slobbery sounds like a dog. Yet somehow he managed to keep talking.

'Vanishing compartment. Vanishing compartment. The same trick the crawlies pulled to escape us – they never went ashore, they'll be back to fight us yet – the same trick that let Arunis hide so long in the—'

Smack. His face went right into the pile of meat, as though shoved by an unseen hand. He began to squeal & writhe, in terrible fear, & it took all of us to restrain him, & hours for him to wear himself out. He is in his cabin now, strapped to his bed lest he hurt himself. A few of us are taking turns watching over him; I am writing this by his bedside in fact. I've tried to talk with him, to tell him that whatever's happening is not his fault. When I raise the candle he stares at me with the blank eyes of an ape.

6

School Mates

14 Modobrin 941
243rd day from Etherhorde

'Barley and rye,' shouted Captain Gregory Pathkendle, stretching his arms up the halyard.

'And a fair lady's thigh.'

The five men hauled as one. They shouted the refrain philosophically, without a hint of arousal or mirth. Admiral Eberzam Isiq hauled too, sandwiched between the bald man with hoop earrings and the white-haired giant. For Isiq the work was agony: needles of pain danced from his heels to his spotted, shaking hands. And yet he hauled, and knew he bore a share (a paltry, old-man's share) of the weight. The yard rose. The sail billowed out. Forty years, forty years since he'd worked a boat that eight men could handle alone.

'Brandy and tea.'

'And a fair lady's knee.'

They hauled a third time, and a fourth. The topman kept the sail knife-edged to the wind. Spray doused the men on the line (cold spray; it was late winter in the Northern world) and the tarboy tossed wood shavings under their feet for traction. Isiq smiled, his mind as clear as his body was tortured. Nothing had changed, everything had changed. One day you're that tarboy, insolent and quick. The next you turn around and you're old.

'Honey and bread.'

'And a fair lady's bed.'

'*To us all, brave boys, they will come to us all,*' sang Gregory, and made fast the halyard to the cleat. The men dropped the slack end; Isiq groaned and staggered away.

Before he had gone three paces Captain Gregory was on him, seizing the admiral's hands and turning them palms-upward for inspection. The hands were rooster-red, the blisters already forming. Captain Gregory shot him an angry look.

'Pace yourself,' he said. 'Torn hands don't earn their keep.'

'Oppo, sir,' said Isiq, with just a hint of irony.

Captain Gregory didn't smile. His finger jabbed Isiq smartly in the chest. 'Get fresh with *me*, you old walrus-gut, and you'll—'

Cannon-fire. Both men snapped to attention, twin hounds on a scent. By old habit Isiq found himself counting: sixty, eighty explosions, double broadsides, two ships lacerating each other at close range, and chaser fire on the margins. Gregory ran forward, shouting for his telescope, though it was a bit too soon to see the fighting.

They were near the mouth of the harbour, Simjalla City dwindling behind them, the western headland rising fast on the port bow. The little two-master creaked and wallowed. *Dancer*: her name seemed almost cruel. A light clipper, she might have had some simple beauty in her prime. Today she looked one storm away from the salvage yard. Her deck was bowed. Her mainsail had a stitched-up tear as long as Isiq's leg.

A blur of wings: the little red tailor bird was circling him, panic-stricken. 'Is it war, Isiq, are we going to war?'

He held up his hand, and the woken bird touched down for an instant, its wings still churning the air. 'Not on this vessel,' said Isiq. '*Through* it, perhaps, but that is for the captain to decide. All the same, you should stay below.'

'But the sounds—'

'Are nothing, as yet. Say that to yourself, each time the guns go off: it is nothing, it is nothing, it is still nothing. Let that be your task: to say it until it feels true. You must master that racing heart, Tinder, if you're to help in days ahead.'

The bird quieted a little. He was proud to be needed. Proud also of the name Isiq had given him: Tinder, fire-starter, the one whose patient friendship had fanned the dark stove of Isiq's memories back into a blaze.

'The dog is more frightened than I,' said Tinder.

'Have him do the same,' said Isiq. 'Go on; I'll visit you presently.'

Tinder flew below, and Isiq looked back over the stern, one final time, at the city of Simjalla. A laugh escaped him: a laugh of pain and amazement. The *Dancer* stood almost exactly where the *Chathrand* had, six months ago, when Isiq first looked on that lovely city, her white sea wall and hilltop groves, her modest spires and the lush green mountains behind. Isiq had looked out from his stateroom window, then. He had arrived as Ambassador of Arqual, ended the next day as a prisoner of Arqual's spy service. He had lain for nearly two months in a dungeon forgotten by the citizens above, in unspeakable darkness, worshipping a glow between the locked door and the door frame, a light so faint he could barely see it with his eye pressed to the crack. And the rats: he had beaten those bastards, a swarm of gigantic, thinking rats that had boiled out of that dungeon and nearly destroyed the city from within. He had fought them with his hands, his feet, his wounded mind; and he had lived because he had to. Because there were bigger rats to kill.

Of course he had also lived because the King of Simja, Oshiram II, had not wished him to die. He had misjudged Oshiram: he knew that now. At their first encounter he had thought the young king a dandy, a spoiled child of the forty years' peace Arquali soldiers had purchased with their blood. But a dandy would never have taken on the Secret Fist. A dandy would have shunted him into an asylum to die a quiet death. Or packed him onto the first boat out of Simja, heading anywhere. Good luck Ambassador, don't write, don't remember us if you please. A dandy would not have obliged his own doctor to treat such a hazardous patient, nor given him a fat purse of gold, nor smuggled him out through the spy-infested streets to the cottage where Captain Gregory waited to receive him, along with his radiant ex-wife, Suthinia.

Rin keep you, Oshiram of Simja.

That had been over a week ago. Gregory had planned to sail the very morning after Isiq appeared at his doorstep, and had raced off in the night to make arrangements. Isiq had stayed up talking to Suthinia, whom the dog and the bird knew simply as "the witch", and everything he learned about her was fascinating. She was indeed a mage, though not a mighty one. She had given Pazel his Language-Gift, and the terrible fits that came with it. And she had come over the Ruling Sea to fight Arunis, with a great company that had been almost entirely slaughtered.

Isiq had gone to sleep at last upon a quilt on her floor. Less than an hour later Gregory shook him roughly awake. There was no sign of Suthinia.

'What is it? What is it?'

'The mucking Secret Fist,' said Gregory, shoving Isiq's boots onto his feet. 'They're raiding the house across the street. Get up, move, or we'll be dead in seconds.'

They fled by the back door, careening like a pair of clumsy thieves. Flames danced in an upper window across the avenue. Down a short alley they dashed, then turned and ran flat out for several long city blocks, the dog racing ahead to check the corners. At last Gregory let them pause for breath in a doorway.

'Why were they across the street?' Isiq demanded, gasping.

'Because it's my house,' said Gregory. 'That hovel we put you in was Suthee's.'

They're still apart, then. Isiq despised himself a little for the elation he felt.

'And also,' added Gregory, 'because someone's ratted on me, told the Fist that I had human cargo to move. I help the odd debtor escape from Simja, before your good king's bailiff can lock him up.'

'Why does the Secret Fist care about debt-dodgers?'

'They care about me,' said Gregory. 'Just a little, fortunately. But a little attention from those bastards—'

'I know.'

Gregory winced. 'Yes indeed, your pardon. *Credek*, this used to be so easy! I tell you, since Treaty Day my job's been nothing but a headache.'

'Why is that?'

The smuggler glanced at him over his shoulder. 'Because a long time ago I gave my name to one Pazel Pathkendle – my name and precious little else. And rumour has it that on Treaty Day Pazel did a splendid job of pissing off the Imperial Spymaster.'

So did I, thought the admiral.

As if divining his thought, Gregory added, 'They weren't looking for you, Isiq. If they knew you were alive I couldn't do a thing for you. No one could, not even the king.'

'All the same, I am sorry about your house.'

Gregory shook his head. 'Suthee told me the place had too many windows. I do hate it when she's right.'

They moved on, turning at the next corner, creeping in the shadow of a high brick wall. Another turn, and they were in a narrow lot, stepping through trash and reeking puddles, until at last they reached a padlocked gate. Cursing, Gregory rattled it, again and again, looking back fearfully the way they'd come. Then soft footsteps, young feminine fingers on the iron bars, and a woman's elfin face smiling through them, warily.

'Rajul!' said Gregory. 'We're not here for you – for any of you. This is the man I spoke of, the one you're to ask no questions about. Give me that key, girl. He will pay you more than handsomely.'

They had stowed Isiq in a dovecot on the brothel roof. Utterly safe, perfectly wretched. The cooing of the birds indistinguishable from the moans of clients in the chambers below. Eight frigid, lice-bitten days, and he didn't mind any of it. He had a pact of sorts with the Gods of Death: those cruel, unfashionable Gods, the ones the monks called 'hermits in the hills'. They would let him live each day so that he might amuse them with greater folly the next. If they had let him perish in Queen Mirkitj's dungeon, they'd never have seen him fight the rats. And if he died here of some dove-shit disease – oh, the sport they'd be missing, the spectacle!

The women brought him food and water and bad wine, and left with his gold. Isiq dared not sit near the window, but he could lie on his stomach and raise himself on his elbows, peeping down at the port district, and a stretch of land beyond the city wall. He saw the little Simjan fighting fleet – aging, third-rate frigates of forty or sixty guns, some of them built in Arqual itself – gamely holding the mouth of the bay. He saw the little charity ships built by the Templar monks, rushing to the docks with wounded civilians. He saw the wrecking crew at work on the Mzithrini shrine.

King Oshiram had told him about the shrine. The Babqri Father had been killed there, just after Treaty Day, and to the Mzithrini way of thinking such an illustrious death made the place unclean, from the first drop of blood until the end of time. The Mzithrini delegation had abandoned Simja. Now, months later, they were paying Simjan labourers to tear the once-holy shrine apart, and to cast the stones into the sea.

They had still been at it, that chiselling, hammering mob, when Gregory and two of his officers had come for Isiq, declaring it time to make a run for the *Dancer*. Gregory had thanked the presiding madam with a shameless kiss. Once aboard the vessel, Suthinia had glared at Gregory, and even more so at Isiq, who had brought peril on them all.

Now, as the little two-master picked up speed, Isiq looked across the water at the low hill where the shrine had stood. The work was finished, the shrine was gone; even the jade dome with its silver inscriptions had been given to the waves. *Once defiled, for ever unclean ... can we ever hope to understand the Western mind? And without understanding, is there any hope of sharing Alifros in peace?*

More cannon-fire, distant but steady. Isiq sat down against the wall of the quarterdeck, watching the young men scramble. No work for him now, except to stay out of their way. He stretched out his legs, rubbed the knee he'd wrenched during his escape from Simjalla Palace. The witch had touched him there, and the pain had lessened instantly, but now—

'Legs in!' barked Gregory, storming by. 'Damned if the old man's not a menace!'

Isiq folded his legs. *Pazel's father is a right bastard offshore. And just as well, just as well.* Isiq would stand for any badgering, so long as men did their job. It was sloth and lies and clumsiness that could doom them, and those he would never tolerate in anyone again.

Of course he had no authority on this smuggler's boat. But he had power. He looked at his feeble, mutinous hands. How fast it had come back: the power, the certainty of strength. The knowledge that he had one fight left in him, and that its outcome would determine the worth of his whole life.

All thanks to the witch and her astonishing news. *Thasha is alive.* On the far side of the Ruling Sea, and in danger – but alive, and trying to return. Pazel still with her, and Neeps Undrabust, and thank the good Lord Rin, Hercól. If anyone could protect her it was Hercól. And yet the witch appeared to believe that Thasha herself would decide the battle ahead, and who was Isiq to say that she was wrong? *Thasha feigned death on Treaty Day. She fooled the sorcerer, fooled Sandor Ott. My blessed, brilliant girl.*

But – a mage? A spell-weaver like Suthinia? The witch herself had said no, not like her. 'Thasha's power is unfathomable. Think of me as a little trembling flame, your daughter as a wildfire roaring on a hill. If only she has unlocked that power. If only she's found the key.'

Slam, slam. Heavy guns, close action. Isiq heaved to his feet and gazed north, wishing his eyes could pierce the headland. On the other side of it men were dying, their bodies scorched or shattered. Isiq felt cold in his heart. The Third Sea War. Men were already calling it that. After soldiering away his life he'd turned to diplomacy, to peacemaking, his goal to prevent the 'Third Sea War' from ever becoming an entry in the history books to come. And here it was, breaking out around him.

No matter. It would not be like the other two. There would be no illusions, no despised Sizzy horde, no blameless Arqualis, no songs about the Blessed and the Damned. If he had his way, there would only be accounts of its brevity: the war that endured just a month, just that last sad week of winter – and many longer chapters on the peace that followed, Alifros renewed and hopeful, a spring rebirth.

For the witch had told him of a second miracle: the miracle of Maisa, Empress Maisa, rightful ruler of Arqual, the one to whom he'd sworn his oath. The one whose own nephew, the usurper Magad V, had vilified her and driven her into exile. An old woman the world had left for dead.

He had thought her dead too, and told them so. Gregory had laughed and pulled at his pipe. 'You come with us, Isiq. You'll see how dead she is.'

The witch had turned her eyes on him fiercely. 'It was convenient, wasn't it? To assume she'd died. Better to justify serving her pig nephew all these years.'

'Things were never so simple,' he'd objected. 'Arqual needed a monarch; we had nearly lost the war. And we were told horrid things about Maisa. That she'd looted the treasury, corrupted children, taken flikkermen to bed. I was just a captain, then. It was decades before I caught a whiff of the truth.'

The witch had glowered at him. 'Explain it to your Empress,' she'd said.

The giant lumbered up to Isiq and held out a hand. Despite his pale hair he was not more than thirty, and probably younger. 'We're coming into the Straits of Simja,' he said. 'You'll want to see, won't you, *Vurum*?'

Isiq grasped the hand, and the giant raised him effortlessly. *Vurum*, Grandfather: the huge fellow had taken a liking to him.

The explosions quickened further. Isiq heard the giant muttering beneath his breath: 'Fear rots the soul and gives nothing, but wisdom can save me from all harm. Fear rots the soul and gives nothing, but wisdom ....'

The Seventh Rule of the Rinfaith. The man was trembling. Isiq reached up and seized his elbow.

'Tell me the rest of the Rule.'

The giant stammered. 'I shall ... I shall cast off the first for the second, and guard the sanctity of the mind.'

Isiq nodded. 'Keep a clear head, and listen to your captain. When the time comes you'll do him proud.'

'Oppo, *Vurum*.' The giant managed a shaky grin.

'Where's your sword, lad?'

'Belowdecks, like everyone else's. The captain doesn't want us armed yet. We're not supposed to look dangerous.'

'In that case you'd better go about on your knees.'

This time the grin was wider.

At the bows Gregory stood beside the witch – shoulder to shoulder, husband and wife. Both swore it was over, a marriage doomed from the start and ended wisely, decisively, when Gregory ran off into the shadow-world of the freebooters, the smugglers of the Crownless Lands.

Pazel's mother. And the love of Ignus Chadfallow's life. Isiq had seen her that first night, outside her little house in Simjalla, but this was his first glimpse of her by daylight. She was tall and slender. Despite the chill her sea-cloak was thrown open, and her long black hair blew free in the wind. Isiq found himself longing to seize handfuls of that hair, to run his dry fingers through it, to hold it against his face. She was still lovely, and must have been heart-troubling in her youth. *You're an imbecile, Gregory.* Whatever riches the man had earned, whatever freedom, whatever wild couplings with pirate girls or harlots on Fuln – he had walked away from *that*.

She turned and caught him staring. 'M'lady,' he said awkwardly, with a slight bow.

'Murderer,' replied Suthinia Pathkendle.

'She's startin' to like you, Isiq,' muttered Gregory, his telescope raised. 'That's more or less how she used to greet me, when I came home from abroad.'

'*When* you came home,' said Suthinia.

'Every night or two I say a little prayer for Neda,' Gregory continued. 'The fates got it backwards with that girl – gave her my looks and Suthinia's lovely disposition.'

'And Pazel?' asked Isiq. 'Do you say no prayers for your son?'

Gregory and Suthinia both visibly stiffened. 'Pazel's never forgotten,' said the captain, as Suthinia gazed hard at the sea.

Isiq too averted his eyes. *It's true then. Pazel is Chadfallow's boy, not Gregory's at all.* The doctor had been in love with Suthinia Pathkendle all the years Isiq had known him. And he had been stationed in Ormael in the twenties, hadn't he? Just when the witch must have conceived. Isiq stole another glance at the two of them. *Watch your mouth, old fool.*

'She spies on their dreams, you know,' said Gregory, earning a look of rage from his wife.

'I did not know,' said Isiq.

'Oh yes,' said the captain. 'She has two vials of dream-essence, whatever that is, and when she warms them against the side of her face she can tell what they're dreaming. She even *entered* one of Pazel's dreams, and talked to him at some length. But it made his fits worse, and she had to promise not to do it any more.'

'It's none of his business, Gregory!' hissed Suthinia.

'She might still be able to speak with Neda – but then Neda's gone and become a crazy priestess, and it mustn't look good for a crazy priestess to have a witch for a mum. But Suthee looks and listens all the same. Because who knows? Maybe their dreams can give us some idea of where they've all washed up, and what they're facing. Last night, for instance, she saw them floating down a river on a giant cow's stomach – inflated, you understand – and doing battle with a – Pitfire!'

They had just cleared the headland, and there beyond it was war. Enormous, horrific. A great line of Arquali warships began a mile or two from beyond Simja's rocky terminus and ran away northwards, bow to stern, bow to stern. And west of them, in a curving, swift-running line: the white ships of the Mzithrin. Both sides belching fire, selectively where the lines diverged, frantically where they neared. At the closest point the battle was an orgy of blackness and flame, the ships' masts rising out of the gushing, enveloping smoke. The tarboy brought a second telescope: Isiq reached for it automatically, but Suthinia turned and snatched it; the scope was for her, of course.

Isiq squinted, shading his eyes. Plenty of death to go around. Ships on both sides maimed and burning, some limping out of formation, others helpless and adrift. A Mzithrini Blodmel was canted over on her beam-ends: fouled on a reef, most likely. Nearer at hand, an Arquali vessel was sinking fast, the decks awash, the men streaming out of her in crowded lifeboats.

Gregory pointed at the doomed ship. 'That's the *Vengeance*, I believe. One Captain Kesper. You know him, Isiq?'

'I know him. And the *Vengeance* as well. I trained on that ship, by damn.'

'Hmph!' said Gregory. 'Now Arqual will be wanting a *Vengeance II*. Maybe they can give it to Kesper's son.'

Kesper, dying before his eyes! Isiq squinted at the line, wondering which of the young men he'd commanded were out there, dying in a battle that should never have begun.

'Humourless old dog, Kesper,' said Gregory. 'Lend Isiq your scope, won't you, Suthee, there's a good girl.'

Suthinia gave her ex-husband a withering glance. The man liked to bait her; who wouldn't? Nonetheless she slapped the telescope into Isiq's waiting palm.

The carnage was worse than he'd thought. The Mzithrini were outnumbered but they had the wind, and their ships were smaller and faster. Where the Black Rags' line bent closest to the Arqualis they were emptying their guns, one after another, then heeling about and running west. They were giving better than they got, and it was all the Arquali cruisers could do to hold the line.

Isiq felt his chest constricting. Just as well he'd bucked up the giant lad when he did. He was not sure he'd be able to manage it now.

'Who is winning?' asked Suthinia.

The captain and the admiral glanced at each other. 'No one, I think, m'lady,' said Isiq. 'This battle is immense, to be sure, but it is just one battle, and little tactical change will come of it. The Mzithrinis cannot push east through the Straits, not with the heavy cannon on Cape Córistel, and the Third Fleet massed and waiting in the Nelu Peren. Nor can Arqual extend its reach far to the west. There is no base to hold, no part of the Mzithrin lands we can reasonably contest.'

Suthinia gaped at the carnage. 'Do you mean to say the Arqualis will withdraw?'

'Both sides, most likely,' said Gregory, 'after dark.'

'Then why are they fighting?' cried Suthinia. 'Why did the Arqualis leave the Straits to begin with? What in the Nine Pits is this *for*?'

Huge and sudden flames from one of the Mzithrini ships: her powder room had exploded. A quarter of her portside hull simply flew out in burning fragments, a whirlwind of fire that raced horizontally over the water and across the deck of the Arquali warship that had bombarded her. The rigging of the Arquali ship bloomed bright orange; tiny figures leaped burning into the sea.

Gregory looked at Suthinia and shrugged. 'Practice?' he said.

Eberzam Isiq lowered the telescope. His hands were shaking. 'You mean to run *that* gauntlet?'

Now Gregory was amused. 'Not to your taste, old man?'

'Tell me your mucking intentions, or send me below if I'm no use.'

'My mucking intentions are to leave these poor sods behind by nightfall, to stay out of the crossfire *and* the lee shore *and* that blary boat-gobbler of a reef, to lighten your purse by three-quarters, to get close to the Arquali flagship – and incidentally you'd better find me that flagship – and finally, to be sure none of your ex-protégés see your face. So yes, I will be stashing you below, and not very comfortably, I'm afraid. Enjoy your liberty while you can.'

'You *are* a pig, sometimes, Gregory,' said Suthinia. 'Enjoy *that*? Do you enjoy it when your mates in the Fens get slaughtered?'

'It's a pleasant morning all the same. Look at them clouds, Suthee. That one looks like a sheepdog.'

'Go rot in the Pits. They're his countrymen. You didn't even ask if Kesper was his friend.'

'Didn't need to ask,' said Gregory.

Isiq cleared his throat. 'Your heart is kind, Lady Suthinia—'

'Put your eye to that blary scope!' she said. 'Tell Gregory what we're looking at. You're the war-maker, and that's your fleet.'

'Alas for Arqual, that is merely a squadron.'

Suthinia's eyes danced with fire. 'You spent your life among those people. You must know something about them – something beyond how to make them tear defenceless cities apart.'

Isiq raised the telescope. *Rin's heart, that's much woman.* A few hours in her presence and he'd stopped craving deathsmoke. And who knew? A few days, if they lived that long, and the witch might cure him of missing Syrarys as well. Just as well that she despised him and all he stood for. There was no room for love in his plans.

So: northwards. Three impossibilities to choose from. You could tack west for hours, in plain sight, and hope the Mzithrinis give you the freedom of the waters they held. You could run between the opposing forces and be pulverised. Or you try to slip east of the action, between the Arquali line and Cape Córistel. And that option was at least as mad as the others. Yes, there was a fair mile between the battle-line and the sawtooth rocks of the Cape. But the wind was onshore, and would contend with the *Dancer* league by league, trying to drive her onto those rocks. Such a wind called for prodigious leeway: a good skipper would sail another eight or ten miles west, before starting his northward tack. Of course that wasn't going to happen today: that whole Arquali squadron would have been better off eight miles west. The Black Rags were not letting it happen.

Gregory had them on a beam reach, sailing right into the slaughter. It was tactical, of course: you needn't chase a boat that was coming straight for you. But soon enough he'd have to show his hand. They had to round Cape Córistel: Isiq knew no more than that. What cove or uncharted island or waiting boat they were making for neither Gregory nor Suthinia would reveal. Beyond the Cape lay the Chereste Sands, a long flat dunescape separating the Gulf of Thól from the vast, steaming Crab Fens. Isiq had guessed at first that they would make a landing there and trudge into the interior – but King Oshiram had heard that Arqualis were holding the Cape, with great guns hauled from Ormael, ready to blast any Mzithrinis who broke through the line. They would not put ashore on the Chereste Sands.

Could they be bound for Tholjassa? Maisa had indeed fled to that mountainous land, decades ago, with her two young sons. Naval gossip had confirmed it, along with the fact that Sandor Ott had pursued them, assassinated the children, brought them back to Etherhorde on slabs of ice as warnings to any future foes, royal or otherwise, of His Supremacy Magad V. Isiq had always assumed Ott had killed the mother as well. Halfway measures were not to his liking.

The cannon roared. They crept nearer the mayhem. Before them a Mzithrini ship dragged herself to shelter behind the line, trailing rigging, her foremast in pieces on the deck. Then Isiq saw what he'd been looking for. Behind the Arquali warships, lighter auxiliary craft were running the line, bringing fresh powder and replacements for fallen men. One of these, a sizeable brig, was trimming her sails afresh. Isiq pointed to her with the telescope.

'Breakaway, Captain. They've been ordered to pay us a visit, sure as Rin made rain.'

'We'll be ready.'

'Is that certain?' asked Isiq. 'You've never dealt with the navy until you've seen them on a war footing.'

'What will they do to us?' asked Suthinia.

Isiq looked at her. 'Anything remotely useful in a fight they'll appropriate,' he said, 'water and provisions included. Then they'll turn us back to Simjalla, and they won't listen to a word we have to say.'

The brig heeled round, and her sails began to fill. 'They're on intercept, true enough,' said Gregory. 'Right, old man, we'll have to make them listen, won't we?'

Isiq made no reply. It was of course quite possible that they were going nowhere, that Maisa was long dead, that Gregory and his wife were lunatics. More likely they were just fools, used to trickery and luck, and the successes available to the bold in a place as chaotic as the Crownless Lands. Gregory was known as a dogged fighter and a slippery eel. But his fame had been earned in peacetime, and this was war again, Gods forgive us, Imperial war.

She might also be alive, but senile and hopeless. That would be a joke to Ott's liking, to kill her sons before they could grow up and menace him, and leave the broken mother to rave and wither and divert the energies of those who might oppose the usurper – to concentrate them behind a single, hopeless symbol of what they had lost.

Of course the woman they were rushing to meet might simply be an impostor. None of these people had seen Maisa before her fall, and the Empress had suffered few to paint her portrait: 'That nonsense can wait,' she'd said in Isiq's hearing, 'until we finish this war.' The admiral smiled. An impostor, wasn't that likely? Some card sharp of an actress, washed up, nothing left to lose. What better role to play than that of long-lost Maisa, the answer to the dreams of desperate men?

The brig fired a warning shot. 'They outgun you, Captain,' said Isiq.

'As we have no guns, that's sure to be true.'

Isiq shook his head. Luck was like deathsmoke: start relying on it, and your soul gets lazy, until you can't recall how you ever did without it. Then one day it's snatched from you. Prayer stops working; the Gods tire of your flattery. The scales tilt; you slide into the abyss.

But not today, Gregory Pathkendle. Madman or gambler, you'll not lead us to our deaths. His eyes slid surreptitiously about the deck. It was true; the men had all stowed their arms elsewhere. But he, Isiq, still had the dagger from King Oshiram, and the stiletto he'd killed a man with the week before. *I don't wish to, Gregory. I like you and your people. But I'll do it, by all the Gods. I'll put my hand on the scales.*

'Have you seen Tholjassa in winter?' asked Gregory suddenly. 'Horrific place. The sea fog blows in and freezes, inches thick. You take a chisel to your doors to get them open. I saw a monk pull the bell for morning service and his blary hand froze to the chain, Rin blast me if I lie.'

'Of course it's a lie,' said Suthinia. 'You're never up in time for morning temple.'

'Just for that I might really take you there, Suthee. How about it, Isiq?'

The admiral just shook his head. Gregory was bluffing: the *Dancer* would never reach Tholjassa, not with the light provisions they had aboard. Nor had Gregory made any hint that such a three-week voyage lay before them. Where in Alifros were they going, then? Some river north of Córistel, winding back into the Fens? Some island cave? Or could Gregory possibly mean to sail further along the shore?

Isiq started at the thought. *Further along* meant the Haunted Coast, a three hundred-mile nautical graveyard, the place ships went to die. No law held sway there, and no naval commander would dare take his boats among those shifting sandbars, those rip currents and sudden, enveloping fogs. Smugglers braved its waters, and pirates certainly, but the Haunted Coast harvested its share of those maniacs as well. Treasure seekers simply never left alive.

With one infamous exception, that is. Arunis had pulled the Nilstone from those waters, and escaped with his life.

And the sad truth was that the tarboys had helped him – unwillingly of course. Pazel and Neeps Undrabust had been Arunis' captives, and the mage had dropped them into those waters to seek the Stone or drown in the attempt. Pazel, amazingly, had succeeded. Isiq had questioned the tarboys about the affair, but found them both (and his daughter, for that matter) strangely averse to talking of that particular day. 'Pazel had help,' Thasha had told him when pressed, and Isiq knew somehow that she was not referring to the other divers, or the mage.

The Haunted Coast. It made a horrid kind of sense. Isiq knew for a fact that Gregory sailed there: it was the only place on the mainland still open to freebooters, the only place not yet beneath the heel of Arqual or the Mzithrin. Hardly surprising, that: it was the devil's own shoreline. Like many naval commanders, Isiq had seen it from a respectful distance. He never wished to see it again.

'New colours on the Arquali ship, Captain,' shouted the bald man with the hoop earrings, snapping. 'Three diamonds – and a red stripe below, by the Tree!'

Three diamonds: *Strike sail and hold position*. One red stripe: *Obey or expect to be fired on*. He glanced at the bald man. What had he expected in the middle of a firefight? *Sail on, and Rin speed your journey?*

Captain Gregory was laughing. 'Take in one reef, boys; let's not make it too easy for them. Now tell me, Admiral: where's the man in charge of this fleet?'

'Squadron, sir. And I'd imagine he's in the vanguard, third or fourth position. If I had to guess, I'd try for that great bear of a cruiser with the gilded stern.'

'The *Nighthawk*,' said Gregory. 'Fine and dandy! That's our new heading, bosun. Now get below with you, Isiq. Tull here will tell you what's what.'

He gestured at the bald sailor with the earrings. The man stepped forward, sour-faced, and subjected Isiq to an insolent examination. 'Can he keep his mouth shut, Captain?' he demanded.

'I can if I'm given a reason,' said Isiq.

The man's eyes pouted. He turned and led Isiq down the ladder-way, past the galley and the lightless berths. The door at the end of the passage was narrow as a cupboard. When Tull opened it a rank smell leaped out at them.

'Terrible,' he said. 'There's flies, too. Step in there and give me your pants.'

'My ... ?'

'You heard me, strip 'em off. And be quick, old man, I'm not here to make merry.'

He tugged irritably at Isiq's arm. Isiq whirled, slammed him hard against the wall, set his his elbow to the grubby neck.

'Explain yourself,' he said.

Tull was suddenly meek. 'It was the skipper's idea. He says you're to play a wounded man, a goner. I'm to strap the blubber on your leg is all. And to bandage your head and neck. And you're not to talk, nor sit up, nor do nothing but point at your throat and gurgle.'

Isiq hesitated. He was a guest on Gregory's ship, and the instinct to respect another captain's authority ran deep. But he had come to doubt his instincts, the 'standards of the Service', his lifelong crutch.

There was no help for it, though. He was in these smugglers' hands. He released Tull and unbuckled his belt.

The 'blubber' was a hideous masterpiece: a thick, stinking sleeve of boar flesh, rotting in places, bloody everywhere, and clearly the source of the stench that filled the *Dancer*'s tiny sickbay. When Tull slid it over his naked leg, Isiq feared he might vomit. The thing mimicked the swelling of a diseased limb. Mid-thigh it bore a ragged wound, clotted with dry black blood. Tull provided him with a coat as well – filthy, partly burned – then helped him to lie back on the boat's one sickbed. He dressed the false leg in soiled bandages, then moved on to Isiq's head and neck. When he was finished only the admiral's mouth and left eye remained uncovered.

'Your captain's a whorespawn,' said Isiq. 'Why didn't he tell me this was the plan?'

No comment from Tull; but when Isiq had lain still awhile, Gregory himself ducked into sickbay and made a brief inspection.

'Perfect! You stink like a butcher's privy.'

'You rotter.'

'Suthinia made a joke, can you believe it? "He shouldn't gripe; when they snuck him out of the King's residence he played a corpse in a coffin. He's moving up in the world." Not bad, eh? Here's a bloody rag for you.'

'How thoughtful.'

'Cough into it when they ask you to speak. But perhaps they'll only ask you to nod and the like. Remember, you're one Lieutenant Vancz of the I.M.S. *Rajna*, sunk three days ago by the Mzithrinis.'

Isiq started. 'There was such an attack. Oshiram spoke of the *Rajna*; he said her sinking was the talk of the island.'

'And well beyond. The real Vancz died, but they're not to know that.'

'Who was he?'

'No one important. That's the beauty of it, you see?'

A great volley of explosions shook the *Dancer*. This time Isiq heard the distant screams that followed. 'I do *not* see, Pathkendle. How will all these shenanigans get you past the fighting?'

'No time to go into it. Just lie still and keep quiet, and remember that you're supposed to be at death's door. This will all be over soon.'

He turned on his heel to go, then looked back sharply at Isiq. 'And show Tull a little courtesy, won't you? He's good at what he does.'

The door closed. Isiq lay still, feeling his age, listening to Gregory bellow: *Strike the mains, all hands assemble, no arms on your person if you please.* Flies buzzed his ears. Suthinia opened the door and looked at him, amused. Then the smell of the place hit her; she gagged and fled. Isiq's face burned. He felt as though she'd caught him at something naughty.

Not long thereafter Tull rushed in with a handbag, wearing some sort of gown, and proceeded to sit beside the bed with his eyes closed.

'What in the nine putrid Pits—'

'Hush,' said Tull, swaying slightly.

'Is that blary perfume?'

'Burn ointment. For your leg, old fool. Now don't distract me – I'm in character, like. Also, they're here.'

It wasn't a gown; it was a surgical bib, and the bag was a doctor's.

The man had removed his earrings, too. *I'm out of my depth*, thought Isiq.

His countrymen were abusive when they drew alongside the *Dancer*. They howled at Gregory: did he know how mucking fortunate he was they hadn't blown his hull out from under him?

'When Arqual tells you to strike sail, you *strike* it, dog! What were you blary thinking?'

Isiq did not catch Gregory's answer, but the Arquali reaction was plain.

'The commodore? You lying, pig-faced, dung-eating smuggler! Take this boat, Sergeant! You curs get down on your knees. *Now*, damn you, or we'll shorten your legs with our broadswords.'

A great thumping and swearing followed. Men were leaping aboard the *Dancer*, the ladderways thundered with boots. The door flew open, and an armoured Turach stood there, dagger drawn. He screamed at Tull to get above with the other sailors.

'My patient's dying,' said Tull.

Holding his breath, the marine plunged into the sickbay and dragged Tull out by the collar. 'Lie still, Vancz!' Tull cried as he went.

The next time the door opened it was Gregory and the Arquali captain himself: as young as he'd sounded, and as fierce. 'Gods of death, is that man even *breathing*?'

'Not for long,' said Gregory. 'I told you there was no time to waste. Darabik will skin us both if—'

Despite himself, Isiq twitched. *Darabik? Purston Darabik?* He started to rise, then checked himself and fell back.

'There, you see?' cried Gregory, making the best of Isiq's blunder.

'I see a half-corpse who knows the commodore's name,' said the Arquali. 'We'll need more proof than that, dog. Get me the letter you spoke of.'

Mr Tull wormed back into the chamber. He reached into Isiq's bloody coat and removed an envelope. He held it up before the others. 'Sir, he's very poorly, very weak. I've done what I can, but that leg—'

Heavy fire, and a cry from the Arquali vessel. The captain snatched the envelope and tore it open. He glanced from the letter to Isiq and back again. Then he stormed out, with Gregory on his heels. Tull leaned close to Isiq's ear and whispered, 'You scared me silly. I thought you were going to get up and dance.'

He might have, too. Purston Darabik. Purcy! Was *he* commanding the squadron? They were old mates, same year at the Academy; Isiq had even courted one of his sisters before Clorisuela entered his life. So had half the navy, went the joke. Darabik was one of nine children; the other eight were girls.

There was a great deal more shouting, over the endless bombardment. The Arquali captain returned and asked if the patient could be moved. 'Are ye trying to be funny?' said Tull. 'The man is gangrenous. He nearly bled to death on the *Rajna*, he's burned, his spleens are granulated; he's half delirious with pain. Move him! You might as well just stick him a few times and be done with it, you nasty—'

The commander slammed the door. Tull and Isiq sat rigid, listening. But they did not have to wait long for the orders to start to fly: *Get up! Get this garbage scow underway! And stay in our lee, good and close, or we'll put more holes in you than a blary bassoon – if the Mzithrinis don't do it for us.*

Isiq turned his bandaged head. 'Spleens?'

'Everyone's a critic,' muttered Tull.

They were underway again. The blasting of the cannon grew almost intolerably loud, and now the screech of flying ordnance reached their ears as well. He could smell the powder-smoke. From the topdeck, Suthinia cried out at something she saw. Vividly he imagined his arms about her, protective; then the image changed to her clawing at his eyes. To fall for a witch: Rin forbid. She might end up like Lady Oggosk, a mad crone in bad lipstick and jewels.

The flies lifted with each explosion. Tull mumbled about his 'life as an actor'. Isiq reflected that it might do them no good whatsoever to find Darabik. His old mate was an Imperial officer at war.

He, Isiq, was simply a mutineer, an enemy of Magad V, the man on the Ametrine Throne.

Eventually he realised that the battle noise had peaked and begun to fade. He waited; other Arqualis were hailing the brig, scandalised and doubtful: 'You have the commodore's *what?*'

At last the *Dancer* slowed, and a great shadow darkened the skylight. Isiq heard the groan of huge timbers, the voices of sailors two hundred feet overhead. They were alongside one of the warships, perhaps the *Nighthawk* itself. He heard the faint rattle of davit chains as a small craft was set afloat.

'Concentrate,' whispered Tull.

A new set of Turachs stormed through the *Dancer*. Gregory was questioned, insulted, abused; Tull was frisked, even Isiq was briefly inspected. 'You're Vancz?' He answered with a croak. A soldier began to pluck at his bandages, and Tull flew into a convincing rage. Then a voice Isiq knew well – velvety, but somehow no less dangerous for that – spoke a single word, and the Turachs straightened and marched out. They thumped their spears in the passage, a formal salute. The door opened, and Purston Darabik stepped into the room.

Isiq did not breathe. The commodore was his own age exactly, but look at him: old, severe, impossibly eminent and grey. He flicked a hand at Tull. Wordlessly, the smuggler fled the room, and Darabik closed the door behind him. His turquoise eyes drilled into Isiq, and there was no doubt whatsoever. He was not deceived by Gregory's flimflam, nor the false leg, nor the room's withering stench. He knew who lay before him. His hand rested on his sword.

They had not always been friends. As boys in Etherhorde they had built rival forts in Gallows Park, and the raids with slingshots and clods of mud had been fierce, until they'd united against a larger gang from Hurlix Street. At the Academy, when Darabik learned that Isiq was courting his sister, he'd taken his prospective brother-in-law out for a brandy. 'Take your time with the decision,' he'd said, 'but if you wound her honour I'll knock your teeth out the back of your skull.'

Darabik crossed and uncrossed his arms. His eyes grew thoughtful; he rubbed his face. 'Oh,' he said, rather loudly. 'Oh, Vancz, dear fellow. So be it, if that is truly what you want.'

Then, as Isiq lay dumbfounded, the commodore knelt beside the bed. His face had changed; a new light gleamed in the bright blue eyes. Leaning very close to Isiq's ear, he whispered, 'Admiral Isiq. You're a blary magician. You're alive.'

'Purcy.'

'Don't move, sir. Don't speak above a whisper. I dare not reveal your presence, not even to my closest aides. The Turachs would kill us in a heartbeat. I don't know who'll stand with us, yet. Not many. Not enough.'

'What do you mean, stand with us?'

'Admiral—'

'Call me Eberzam, for Rin's sake.'

Darabik nodded slowly. Eminence notwithstanding, he was nervous in the extreme.

'I saw her, Eberzam. With my own eyes. Gregory's her transport, and her go-between. I gather he has been for a decade.'

Isiq felt a tingling in his limbs. 'Maisa,' he said. 'But Purcy, where is she, and what does she hope for? Has she an army, has she ships?'

'Of course not! She's in deep hiding, with her loyalists. And they are not many. Magad's forces could snuff her like a match. The fact is, this is suicide. That she's survived all these years is a blary miracle, but it can't go further. We're simply too few.'

Isiq studied him. Then he raised himself to one elbow, pulled the bandages away from his face, staring hard into the commodore's eyes.

'It will go further,' he said. 'You and I will see to that, when Her Majesty calls us to the task. It will go as far as Etherhorde, and the Chamber of Ametrine, and that chair that belongs to our Empress alone.'

Darabik met his gaze. A fierce delight shone in them suddenly. 'You're a mad bastard, Eberzam.'

'You have no idea.'

Darabik glanced quickly at the skylight. 'I can't stay; it looks odd enough that I came at all.' He looked down sharply at Isiq. 'You've lost three fine women, Eberzam. I'm very sorry.'

Isiq shook his head. 'Just one, just my dear wife. Thasha lives, Purcy. And Syrarys was a traitor. It was Sandor Ott who sent her to my household. She was poisoning me for years.' Isiq hesitated. 'With deathsmoke.'

'Lord Rin above!'

'I have beaten the drug.' Isiq saw doubt in the commodore's face, and added quickly, 'How did Gregory convince your men to let me through? Who did he claim I was?'

Darabik's mouth twisted slightly. 'Who you should have been, Isiq. My brother-in-law. Only the way Gregory's playing it, you're mortally wounded, and desperate to get home to Tholjassa to see my sister one last time.'

'Which of them went to Tholjassa, by damn?'

'No one did. But I stopped telling the men about my sisters years ago. They only mixed the stories up.'

It was a grim effort at levity. Isiq smiled anyway, wondering why Darabik had never made admiral. The man had iron strength; his men both feared and loved him, and that was the navy ideal. He'd won more fights than the Lord Admiral, almost as many as Isiq himself.

'Purcy, you're losing ships out there. What's the reason for this engagement?'

'The reason?' Darabik's voice was suddenly bitter. 'Does there have to be one, Eberzam? Officially, the Emperor and the Lord Admiral decided they had to know how serious the Black Rags were about holding the Gulf of Thól. Well, here's a shocker: they're mucking serious indeed. They'll throw *blodmels* into the effort, they'll launch waves of ships from the Jomm. You don't have to be an old relic like me to guess that. You don't need to have been in the last war personally. You could talk to old boys in Etherhorde; there are plenty of us around. I suppose you could even cross the street from the club to the naval library and read a Gods-damned mucking book. The Admiralty Review of the last war, for instance. Or the one before that. Of course there's another way, Isiq – much grander, much more exciting. You can throw your advance squadron at the enemy like a fistful of dirt.'

'Now *you* had better lower your voice.'

Embarrassed, Darabik collected himself. 'I'm presuming a lot, aren't I? Literacy in Naval Command. A disinclination to get your boys carved up. Arqual standing for more than bloody-mindedness and greed.'

This is why he's still a commodore, thought Isiq.

'You'll be reprimanded if word gets back to Etherhorde. Letting a freebooter past your line of control. Even a well-known neutral, like Gregory Pathkendle.'

'I'll give it some thought,' said Darabik, 'after I save as much of my squadron as I can.' He grew still a moment, looking hard at the admiral.

'We wiped our plates with 'em, didn't we?'

'Who?'

'That gang from Hurlix Street.'

Isiq nodded. 'That we did, Commodore. It was a strong alliance we made.'

Darabik pressed his forehead hard against Isiq's. 'Gods above, let you be all that you appear. Let Maisa be strong and healthy; let others rally to her side. Because we can't stay long in the shadows; sooner or later they'll find us out. We've gone too far already, Isiq. You know that, don't you?'

'Oh yes,' said Isiq, 'we've declared war on the Secret Fist.'

The commodore declared them non-combatants, bound for Tholjassa on a mercy mission, and the reconnaissance brig escorted them along the rest of the line. For ten miles they sailed untroubled, but at the northern edge of the engagement the Mzithrinis opened up with long-range fire. The brig shielded them, and lost a mast for her troubles. She slowed, and before Gregory could reduce speed to match her a lucky 32-pound ball skipped over the waves and split the *Dancer*'s port rail and crushed her only tarboy dead against the mainmast. Isiq had just shed his disguise, and climbed to the topdeck to find Gregory on his knees, head bowed, the youth's bloody corpse in his arms.

By sunset the captain was telling jokes again, but his voice and face had changed. The whole crew felt it, and they sailed into darkness without banter or songs. At dinner Isiq sat alone with his bowl of rice and cod, until Suthinia appeared and sat across from him, stone-faced, with a bowl of her own.

'That tarboy could not make conversation to save his life,' she said, chewing. 'But he was Gregory's favourite all the same.'

'In this little crew, you mean?'

Suthinia shook her head. 'At sea Gregory has no favourites; he's marvellous that way. The boy was his favourite child. Of some twelve or more. This one's mother is with Maisa; she'll be waiting for us when we arrive.'

7

On Sirafstöran Torr

14 Modobrin 941
243rd day from Etherhorde

When he woke, Pazel could hear only ringing, as though a bell that never faded had been struck inside his head. He could feel the water sloshing in his ears, and imagined what Ignus Chadfallow would say. *Three near-drownings in a single week. You'll be lucky if your hearing ever returns.*

It was dusk. Pazel was being carried up a steep hillside; the surrounding pines were low and dense, and the sharp smell of resin filled the air. He was clinging to the back of a slender being with olive-green skin and black feathers for eyebrows. *A selk.* Pazel had met one only the week before, in the temple of Vasparhaven, the first and only such encounter in his life.

The selk who carried him was a woman. She was strangely beautiful, though it was a severe kind of beauty, and quite unlike that of any human or dlömu. The other two were men. All three wore plain grey tunics. No shoes, no helms or armour. But on their belts they wore swords, long straight blades that glistened red in the dying sunlight, as though made not of steel but coloured glass.

'Thasha—'

The selk woman looked back over her shoulder. 'The golden-haired one is alive and well, friend human,' she said. 'Your other friends escaped as well. Be still now; it is not much further.'

The mist had disappeared. Pazel saw they had carried him right out of the canyon, up some narrow crevasse. He was stiff and cold, but immensely relieved. Everyone had survived, and who had come to their aid but the selk. The selk! Pazel had reason to think that they were both wise and good: certainly Kirishgán, the selk friend he had made in Vasparhaven, had treated him with kindness. Theirs was an ancient people, Kirishgán had claimed: nomads, wanderers, philosophers of a sort. And they had suffered terribly in Bali Adro, whose maddened warlords had blamed them for the decay of their enchanted Plazic weaponry, and tried to exterminate the race. They had come harrowingly close to success.

Where had these selk come from? Were they the 'hope' of which Kirishgán had written, in his cryptic message? He had been strangely elusive on certain questions, saying that there were subjects he was forbidden to discuss. Still, Pazel found it hard to imagine that Kirishgán's people could mean them anything but good.

Pazel's head began to clear. He remembered selk hands raising him from the river's depths. He'd seen Thasha vanishing below, lost his head, tried to shout, and nearly swallowed the hrathmog's bloody ear.

He touched his jaw, found it tender and swollen. *I tore off its ear with my teeth. Like an animal.* And he wondered if the scent of lemons was in his sweat.

What had happened next was a blur in his memory, though he recalled a fist thumping his back, and crawling from the river onto a warm, flat rock – and Ensyl appearing from somewhere, pulling his eyelid open with her hands, sighing with relief when he managed to focus.

There came a sudden *pop*, and his hearing returned. He swallowed: his ears hurt, but the ringing noise was gone. And at the same moment Pazel's Gift surged to life. The selk were conversing quietly, and their tongue had a soft, swift music like rain on leaves. *Sabdel,* he thought. *Their native tongue.* Pazel had never heard the language before, but his Gift pounced, and in a heartbeat it was his.

'They really are human beings,' said the one who carried him.

'Surely that proves they came out of the River? What else could they be but castaways?'

'With two dlömu for travelling companions?' said the other. 'And an ixchel woman, and a mink?'

'All very strange,' agreed the selk bearing Pazel. 'Their wounds are recent, also, and not the work of hrathmogs. And this boy has a spell under his tongue.'

'The girl has another sort of wound, Nólcindar. Could you feel it? A fracture, a broken soul.'

'I did not touch her,' said the first selk. 'But the smallest – he is far along with the mind-plague. Poor boy! I wonder if he knows.'

'*I* wonder if the others have it. And what about that bundle, that the tall one feared so much to lose? No, they are not simple castaways. Something about them troubles me.'

Pazel coughed. The selk looked back over her shoulder. Switching to Imperial Common, she said, 'How is it with you, friend human?'

'I'm just fine,' said Pazel. 'I can walk.'

The selk lowered him gently to his feet. 'Walk this last stretch, then,' she said, 'but tell my brothers and sisters how Nólcindar carried you, or they will think me lazy.'

She sounded youthful, but Pazel knew better than to trust impressions. Kirishgán had sounded youthful too – even when remembering a time before the founding of Bali Adro itself. Pazel looked up and down the trail. 'Thasha – the girl, did you see what happened to the girl?'

'The golden-haired one is alive and well,' said the selk who had carried him. 'And far more precious to you than gold, to judge by how often you have called her name.'

'And the others?'

'They await you. Come, we are almost there.'

As soon as he began to climb, Pazel felt the weakness in his leg. The pain that Ramachni's spell had eased was returning, creeping outward from the wound. It had not been wise to blunder about on that foggy island, either. But soon the slope grew gentler, the trees taller and further apart. Voices reached him: the voices of his friends. Pazel almost broke into a run. There sat all his party, save Thasha and Ramachni, along with many selk. They were drinking from small silver cups, among the ruins of some ancient structure, now overgrown with trees. Big Skip saw Pazel first: 'There he is, the boy who wouldn't sink!'

They all greeted him warmly – even Dastu gave him an uncertain smile. But Neeps stared anxiously down the trail. 'Where is she, mate?' he said. 'How could you leave her behind?'

Before Pazel could answer, a selk called out from deeper among the trees. 'Patience, Mr Undrabust,' he said. 'She will be here, as I promised. She has only made a kind of … detour.'

The selk who had spoken came nearer. He was not the tallest of the group, but there was a firmness to his voice and a fluid ease to his movements that made one think of great strength. He looked at Pazel for a moment in silence, but with a lively warmth.

'You are a fighter to be reckoned with,' he said, 'even weaponless and drowning. I have seen nine thousand years of bloodshed, alas. But never have I seen a human bite the ear from a hrathmog.'

The others turned to stare at him. 'You did … *what?*' said Neeps.

Pazel nodded, feeling his jaw.

'He has been cruelly tested,' said Hercól. 'All of us have been, on this journey.'

'Few come this way of whom that could not be said,' replied the selk. 'But where has your weasel gone? Did it run away?'

'It is a mink,' said Hercól.

Pazel looked at him, baffled. *It?* Then Cayer Vispek, standing near him, gave his arm a surreptitious squeeze. All at once he understood: Ramachni had not announced himself. He was pretending to be a mascot, a normal animal tagging along in their wake. Pazel was abruptly on his guard. Did the selk threaten them after all?

'The creature is not quite tame,' said Bolutu, 'but it will not stray far from us.'

The selk leader smiled. 'Well,' he said, 'here is a companion of yours who did stray, though I doubt that will happen again.'

He clapped his hands, and a dog raced out from among the selk. The travellers shouted with astonished joy: it was the same white hunting-hound that had journeyed with them from Masalym, one of three that had followed them into the Infernal Forest. Lunja fell on her knees and embraced the animal: Pazel had never seen the stoic warrior closer to tears. *Bali Adrons and their dogs*, he thought, but there was a lump in his own throat as well. He bent, and the dog licked his hand. The animal had followed him and Thasha to the riverside where they had first made love.

'He swam out of the Forest, close to death,' said the selk. 'Tooth-fishes were gnawing at a wound in his side. But he is a sturdy animal with a great will to live.'

'He was Commander Vadu's favourite,' said Lunja. 'I never learned his name, but from now on I will call him *Shilu*, Survivor.'

Bolutu turned and bowed deeply to the selk leader. 'We are in your debt, *alpurbehn*,' he said.

Once more Pazel's Gift went to work: *alpurbehn* was *elder brother* in Nemmocian, another graceful Southern tongue. Bolutu had used the word as an honorific, a formal endearment.

The gesture was not lost on the selk. Their leader nodded cordially to Bolutu. 'I am Thaulinin, of the line of Tul,' he said. 'I have led these walkers since the fall of the Mountain Kings. However cruel your trials, they have not robbed you of courtesy – nor of all good luck. We were making to ford the Ansyndra not far from the island where we found you. If we had chosen any other crossing we would never have seen you at all. We knew there were hrathmogs afoot, but we sought no fight with them.'

'I still don't understand how you rescued me,' said Pazel.

'We are strong swimmers,' said Thaulinin, 'almost the equal of dlömu, in fact. You were choking; we drew the water from your chest and pulled you to safety. Your companions we helped away before the hrathmogs sent their scouts to the island. And we destroyed your raft, fascinating vessel though it was. You could have ridden it no further in any case: the hrathmogs have a camp on the riverbanks, two miles downstream. Come and rest now,

Pazel Pathkendle. Our wine is somewhat fairer than river water, as you will learn.'

Something in the selk's account of their rescue struck Pazel as incomplete. He could not quite put his finger on it: the dense fog, the extraordinary coincidence of their discovery … Thaulinin, meanwhile, was leading them deeper into the glade. Pazel saw that the fallen stones marked the outline of a small keep or fortress. Most of the walls had toppled to knee-height, and moss grew over them. But soon they reached a spot where the hillside opened in an arch of fine workmanship, bricks of red stones alternating with others cut from the blue-grey rock of the canyon walls, and the keystone was engraved with the figure of a running fox. At the threshold a fire danced within a ring of stones, and two selk were roasting a hare upon a spit. Torches shown deeper within the ruin.

'Where have you brought us, elder?' asked Lunja.

'These are the remains of Sirafstöran Torr, where once stood a palace belonging to Valridith, a dlömic monarch, whose lands were easternmost of the Mountain Kingdoms of Efaroc. The outer walls enclosed the whole of the glade, but the keep was entered here, through the side of the hill. For most of his life Valridith governed this land with kindness, and wisdom enough. But in his last years he grew suspicious, obsessed with the power of neighbouring kingdoms, indignant at the smallest complaints brought by his people. "These are the hairline cracks in my kingdom," he used to say, "and through them I feel a wind blowing, the cold wind of the grave." His only comforts were his son and daughter, who were both fair and gentle. The young prince he sent west to Bali Adro, with orders to seek a marriage – any marriage – within the Imperial family. The lad never returned from the capital, and what happened there is a mystery to this day.

'Whatever the truth, Valridith was heartbroken, and swore on the charnel-stone of his family that he would protect his daughter better, and choose a husband for her himself. It was a rash oath. For years he kept it merely by forbidding her to travel beyond his inner kingdom. Mitraya was her name, and she was full of love for her father, and all the people of the Torr. The joy of his autumn years, she was – until the day he promised her to a petty tyrant, whose aggressions he hoped to placate. But Mitraya would not oblige him, for she loved another. The king had never been crossed by one of his own, and he imprisoned her in this fortress, swearing he would not release her until she consented to the match. She took her own life, after four years of captivity.'

'I recall her face in the window there,' said another selk, gesturing at a heap of crumbled stone. 'We would bring her wild grapes in autumn. She could smell them when the breeze was right.'

'After she died, her father went mad with remorse,' said Thaulinin. 'He threw his crown into the Ansyndra, and ordered this palace destroyed. When the work was done he paid the labourers handsomely and cut his own throat.'

Dastu shrugged. 'Old tales,' he murmured.

But Thaulinin heard him, and shook his head. 'Not very old. This spring it will be three hundred years. I came here the morning after; the king's blood still stained the earth. About where you are standing, in fact.'

A slight commotion made Pazel turn. Thasha, escorted by two selk, was marching towards them, shivering. He ran to her; she threw her arms around his neck. She was soaked with river water, cold as a fish.

From the corner of his eye, Pazel saw Neeps, standing near them, his arms half-raised. He had been on the point of embracing her himself. Their eyes met; Neeps reddened suddenly and turned away.

Thaulinin called for a blanket. Neeps, his face still averted, spoke in anguish: 'Where *were* you?'

Thasha winced. Letting go of Pazel, she went to Neeps and pulled him close, and whispered something consoling in his ear. Pazel felt his heart beating wildly. *She's doing the right thing. She's making him feel better. Don't be jealous, you fool.*

The blanket came, and Neeps spread it over her shoulders. 'I sank,' said Thasha, 'through the river, and down to … the other river.'

'Yes,' said Thaulinin. 'You fell into the undercurrent of Shadow – faster than your friend here, much faster. As if the River were calling you. But Nólcindar dived in after, and brought you back when the current ebbed. She is best of all of us at Shadow-swimming.'

'I was falling,' said Thasha. 'The water beneath me disappeared. There was nothing I could catch hold of – just wind and darkness – and some vines, I think.'

'She behaved strangely there, Thaulinin,' said the woman, Nólcindar. 'We took shelter in a moth-cave, out of the wind, while I waited for her strength to return. She recovered more quickly than I expected – indeed she jumped to her feet, and it was all I could do to prevent her leaping into the shaft. She was not afraid in the least. She looked at me and said, "Unhand me. I must visit the Orfuin Club."'

Thaulinin glanced sternly at Hercól. 'And yet you tell us you did not come here from the River of Shadows.'

'I spoke the truth,' said Hercól.

'Nine humans, in a land where humans are extinct. An ixchel woman, thousands of miles from the nearest clan. And a package that reeks of sorcery. You do not wish to name this thing, but you tell us that if we so much as cut away the cloth, we may die. That Macadra craves it and will try to steal it. And that you carried it to Bali Adro in an ancient ship, over the Nelluroq, only to lose it to a thief in the city of Masalym. A thief who brought it here.

'All this in good faith I have tried to believe. But many are they who come ashore in Alifros from the River of Shadows – some by accident, others by dark design. If you are strangers to the River, how is it that this girl longs to visit the Orfuin Club, that most celebrated tavern in its depths? Think well before you answer! I have patience with many things, but lies are not among them.'

'Nor have we misled you, though we have not told all,' said Hercól.

'The evil thing you carry – *that* came out of the River, did it not?' demanded Thaulinin.

No one answered him. For a moment there was no sound but that of the crackling fire.

'Perhaps I will not return it, until you choose to speak.'

The faces of the selk, which had been so friendly, were now quite cold. Some rose slowly to their feet. Still more had gathered, from within the keep and without.

'I think it will be best for all of us if you disarm,' said Thaulinin.

Indignant cries. Pazel's company drew closer together. 'We are most of us disarmed already,' said Hercól, 'but by misfortune, not threat. Before we surrender the few blades we still possess, I would ask for your word: to restore to us that which we carried, and let us go unhindered.'

'I will make no promise before I see this thing,' said the selk leader. 'Why do you not tell us your mission plainly? That is a small courtesy to offer those who have just saved your lives.'

'And if we cannot?' asked Hercól.

'Then I cannot return your parcel,' said the other.

Very slowly, Hercól reached back over his shoulder and drew Ildraquin from its sheath. 'You have lived a long time,' he said, 'and seen much that is in Alifros, but you will have met with few swords like this one, and no swordsman like the one before you. I would shed no blood today. But some of us are oath-bound to a certain task, and we are very far from its completion. We can afford no further errors, *alpurbehn* – including errors of trust.'

'We would make the same mistake,' said Nólcindar, 'if we let you take this thing and go your way. Perhaps you will use it to attack us from behind.'

'Do we strike you as so depraved?' asked Ensyl.

'I do not think so,' said Thaulinin, 'but you are creatures of the moment; your whole lives are as a single week in the life of a selk. You did not live through the Lost Age, or the Worldstorm. You do not recall the War of Fire and Spells, when tools of great evil were scattered over Alifros, and scarred its very bones. I do not know what is in your package, but a force bleeds from it that burns my hands, and I have seen what such power can do.'

'You must know also that such tools are beyond the use of simple beings like ourselves,' said Bolutu.

'Always before that was so,' said Thaulinin, 'but then you dlömu robbed the graves of the eguar, and fashioned blades from their bones. Into the hands of generals and warlords and petty royalty they went. Look now at the bonfire that was Bali Adro! The waste, the martial lunacy, the slaughter of peoples near and far.'

Of selk, Pazel recalled with a shudder. *Rin's eyes, what are we doing? They could kill us here and now.*

'You make your case poorly,' said Nólcindar. 'If you are truly the simple folk you claim, then perhaps you cannot do great harm with this thing – but you are not the ones to guard it, either. Where you set it down, a stand of trees may die, a field wither, a trickle of rain become an acid that scars the land.'

'Is that any of your concern?' said Dastu. 'I thought you were wanderers, just passing through.'

The selk looked at Dastu in silence. A few wore expressions of sorrow; many more of rage. Thaulinin's eyes held both.

'Our people do not think in this way,' he said. 'We have no permanent home, it is true. But that is only because everywhere is home. When the Platazcra burned the forests of Ibon, we mourned those trees. When madmen poisoned Lake Elsmoc, we wept. Harm elsewhere is harm to us, a despoiling of our home. There are in truth no countries. There is only Alifros: one land, one ocean, drowned in a common sea we call the air. You may say we *pass through* a place, but we never truly leave it. Nor do you, though a part of you ceases to believe in what you cannot touch. An endearing quality, perhaps – but only in the very young.'

'*We are all young beneath the watchful stars,*' said Pazel.

Every selk head turned. Pazel was almost as startled as they: he had spoken without a moment's forethought.

'Where did you hear those words, human?' asked Thaulinin.

'From one of your people, in Vasparhaven. He said the stars would wait out our errors, and perhaps even forgive them. Those were his last words to me. But he gave us a written message, also:

he told us there was hope downriver, between the mountains and the sea. I think he wanted us to find you, Thaulinin. His name was Kirishgán.'

'Kirishgán!' This time surprise contended with a joy the selk could not disguise. Kirishgán was in Vasparhaven Temple? Why, how, when had Pazel seen him? To the latter question Pazel replied that it had been little over a week.

'He expected to leave the temple the day after my visit. He'd been there for nearly three years. He said he'd learned Spider-Telling. But I know he was eager to return to the outer world.'

'A world that has missed his wisdom,' said Thaulinin. 'This is a heart's prayer answered. Forty full moons have come and gone since our brother departed. We feared the worst. He has been marked for death by the Platazcra.'

Then his face turned stern once more. 'I do not doubt that Kirishgán hoped we would meet – but not, I think, for the reasons you imagined. We will feed you, treat your wounds, even guide you from this wilderness. But we will not return your death-bundle. And you will not take it by force.'

At that Cayer Vispek drew his sword as well – and instantly, twenty selk blades whistled from their sheaths. Thasha, wet and shaken as she was, groped for Arunis' knife but found it gone.

'We may surprise you,' said Hercól, 'though Death alone will smile on what we do here today.'

'Death and the *maukslar* searching these hills,' said a voice from above.

It was Ramachni, curled on a high pine branch, ten feet over-head. 'Never fear,' he added quickly, 'the demon is still far from us. I have been keeping watch by the clifftops; I caught his reek upon the breeze.'

Thaulinin glanced sharply at his people. 'Eyes forward! Do not let the creature distract you from the fight!'

'Ramachni, what are you *doing*?' cried Thasha. 'How long have you been watching us?'

'Long enough for both sides to show their firmness, as I hoped they would,' said the mage. 'Be at peace, one and all: you may trust each other now.'

'I tire of these pleas for trust,' said Nólcindar. 'Keep to your tree, little mink, and spare us your fibs and fantasies.'

Ramachni rose to his feet. His black eyes bore down on them, and no one below dared look elsewhere.

'You have all shown your readiness to die for Alifros,' he said, 'but to serve it you must live. Away with your weapons! If you shed blood here there will be no one left to remember, no songs about the second tragedy of the Torr. There will be only darkness, the last pall of death drawn over this world. You know of what I speak, Thaulinin Tul Ambrimar. Shall I give it a name?'

The selk leader waved urgently. 'Not here!' he said. 'But I think I can name *you*, now, trickster. You have taken a body unknown to me, but your voice is another matter. It is little changed since the Battle of Luhmor, my lord Arpathwin.'

Ramachni's ears twitched. 'Arpathwin,' he said, '"Still Flame". So your people cheered me that morning, over the howling of the Demon Prince we had subdued. No, my voice has not changed, but how your world has, in twelve swift centuries. *Arpathwin*. I am glad to hear it on a selk tongue once again.'

He descended the tree, and when Thasha bent down he sprang to her shoulder, where he curled like a living scarf about her neck. 'But why did you not speak at once?' said Thaulinin. 'You have walked with us in the Sabbanath Fields, brought us hope in the Twelve Years Winter, built the trap with your great mistress that holds the arch-demon even today. Can you be in doubt of your welcome here?'

'Had I spoken sooner,' said Ramachni, 'you would not have learned that my friends are equally deserving, and equally without fear. But I might pose the same question to you, master selk. For you have shadowed us, I think, since before we left the confines of the Forest.'

Thaulinin was startled; but he nodded briskly. 'You were not difficult to follow, being blind within the wood. Yes, we watched you from afar.'

'And from afar you raised the commotion that made the *maukslar* turn away?'

After a brief hesitation, the selk said, 'That was not our doing.'

He made a small gesture of his hand, and his warriors stood down, sheathing their swords. 'But Arpathwin: must we hide? Is the demon approaching?'

'No, it has flown east,' said Ramachni. 'to scour the Ghelvi Marshes. Return it may, but now that I have its scent I may hope to give us fair warning. Nor will the hrathmogs find you on these heights, as I expect you know already.'

'Then draw near, friends – and no more questions until you are warm and well fed.'

The selk pressed the newcomers close about the fire. They gave them the entire hare, along with handfuls of nuts they had roasted on the coals, and small, delicious fruits one could eat whole, and more bread and wine. Pazel was amazed at how quickly their friendliness returned. They smiled, took delight in watching the humans eat, rushed for new provisions as they thought of them. How was it possible that just minutes ago they had come so close to killing one another?

While they ate the selk brought instruments from within the keep – curious fiddles, wooden pipes, a small silver harp – and played softly, while those at the edges of the fire matched their voices to the music, very low. Pazel strained to catch the words, and was amazed that he could not: the language refused to be named, to be captured by his Gift. For a moment he panicked: when his Gift stopped catching languages it meant his terrible fits were about to descend, maiming him with noise. He went rigid, fighting the urge to leap up and run from the circle. Music was torture at such times.

But the attack did not come. And as he calmed himself, Pazel realised that the music was of a beauty such as he had never heard in life or dream: swift, gentle and elusive, the song of a child that runs alone through a wood at sunrise. But no, he thought, that's not right, it's more the music of the very old, in their last or next-to-last summer of life, but so adept at memory that they could still hear and see all that such mornings had revealed to the children they had been, so many centuries ago. And yet he still had it wrong, for something in the music told Pazel that the selk knew neither childhood nor age as humans did. They knew loss, however: every quiet phrase evoked the memory of something fine that had perished or departed, moments of bliss that shattered as soon as they were felt, loving glances that pricked the heart like a needle and were gone.

The food was soon exhausted, but their cups were refilled, and the musicians played on without a moment's pause, as though the song they were immersed in had no true beginning or end. The stars appeared among the trees. By their faces Pazel knew that the others were caught up in deep and private emotions, but whether of sadness or joy he could not tell.

The music ended the only way it could: suddenly, in the middle of a phrase. In the abrupt silence, Thaulinin said, 'Your death-parcel lies within the mountain. I will have it brought out to you now.'

'Let it stay there,' said Ramachni. 'When I show it to you in the morning, you may wonder that we did not beg you to keep it.'

'I start to wonder that already,' said Thaulinin. 'Whatever help I can offer shall be yours. If you wish to resume your journey on the morrow, I will send guides with you, that you may find the safest paths. But I warn you that the way is long. The selk run quickly over field and marsh and mountain, but even for us it is twenty days to the sea.'

'Twenty!' said Corporal Mandric. 'By your leave, Mr Ramachni, we're in no shape for a forced march.' He gestured at Lunja. 'Otter here shed her boots in the Forest; she has thorns in her pretty webbed feet. So does Brother Bolutu. As for Pathkendle, he'll drop before you can say field amputation. That mucking troll nearly chewed him like chicken bone.'

'There is no other way,' said Thaulinin. 'I have told you already that hrathmogs hold the river. In earlier times I might have bargained with them to let you pass, but not today. They have learned the value of handing goods or captives to the Ravens, and Macadra pays particularly well for any curiosities fished out of the River of Shadows.

'Even afoot, the way is perilous. All the ports and coastal townships from Masalym to Orbilesc are under strict Bali Adro control. Some are being torn apart by infighting, as the madness of the Plazic blade turns general upon general, prince against prince.'

'Not here in the interior, then?' asked Ensyl.

'Not yet,' said the selk. 'These wildlands are still considered too troublesome to conquer – but that does not mean that they are safe. Far from it! Macadra is very powerful, but to summon a *maukslar* she must have given the blood of her own withered veins. If she lusts so deeply for your death-parcel, she will not stop there. Her agents will be groping inward from the coast, and they may take many forms. Plazic squadrons, mercenaries, hrathmog collaborators, murths: she has employed all of these in the past. The selk are adept at eluding such tentacles – and even hacking them off when they grope too far. But the sea belongs to Bali Adro. If with great care and fortune you should reach the coast, what then?'

'We have a ship of our own,' said Neeps.

'Had, you mean,' said Dastu. 'They've abandoned us. Hercól proved that with his sword-trick, remember?'

'I proved only that they are making for the Island Wilderness – currently,' said Hercól. 'But come, tonight is spent. Let us cast about no more for answers. By daylight we may find our path clearer than we think.'

No words could have been more welcome. Still Pazel felt that Hercól was merely putting the best face he could on terrible circumstances. The selk were kind to offer help, but for all their age and wisdom they were just twenty nomads, living by what they carried on their backs. *And what about Neeps?* If the selk could do nothing for him, Pazel would beg Ramachni to try deeper magic. He could not just watch and wait.

The selk led them into the ancient fort. The dim lamplight flickered over pale marble columns, and alcoves and doorways intricately carved with figures of men and beasts. The chambers were many and mostly dark, and Pazel thought an air of sadness hung about them. But the eyes of the selk gleamed in the lamplight, and their voices were bright and clear.

The ruin clearly served as a way station, not a permanent home. Still their hosts had made it clean and comfortable; in the room where the company was to sleep, deer skins had been spread over beds of pine needles. 'Rest well, and fear nothing,' said Thaulinin. 'Tonight at least you will be as safe as ever you were aboard your ship.'

'That is less comforting than you intend,' said Hercól with a smile, 'but we thank you all the same.'

'I would speak with you a while longer, Thaulinin,' said Ramachni.

'Then go elsewhere, Rin love you,' Big Skip implored. 'Mages and selk may be able to do without sleep, but I'm staved through, and my hold's filling fast.'

The selk leader laughed. 'Come, wizard. You have many years to account for.'

He took a lamp from one of his men and led Ramachni from the chamber. The other selk departed, and the company settled down on the deerskins. Most slept like the dead, but Pazel tossed and turned, helplessly awake. Like feral cats, the dark possibilities of what lay ahead prowled through his mind, scratching, spitting, clawing him further from sleep.

The whole coast in the hands of the Ravens. No way out, tentacles closing in. And the Swarm of Night growing larger, like a tumour, like a shroud. Better to have stayed on the Chathrand. *Better a hrathmog spear through the gut.*

Someone in the room was whispering, praying; or had he dreamed that, just moments ago?

Arunis reached back into this world to frighten us, to try to break our nerve: You killed me but you didn't; Thasha cut off my head but she

*failed. Erithusmé is dying, dying inside her. And without Erithusmé
you have no hope.*

Lies, hatred. Poison spewed from a dead man's lips.

*Try this one, then: Arunis would have died weeks ago on the
Chathrand, if you hadn't interfered. All your fault: his escape, this exile,
the deaths in the Forest, the loosing of the Swarm.*

This is what it felt like to go crazy, to be whittled down to madness by your guilt.

Pazel tried to turn his thoughts in a sunnier direction. Thasha.
He could still feel her touch. It did not long cheer him to think
of her, though. She'd wanted him to promise to keep his distance.
Would she ever understand that he had refused out of fear for her?
That it was their lovemaking, more than anything else he'd found,
that drove the haunted look from her eyes?

Pazel rubbed his face in the darkness. He was haunted too, in
an entirely different way. When Thasha kissed him, undressed
him, nothing else mattered under Heaven's Tree. But afterwards …
afterwards, he thought of Klyst, the murth-girl. Which was weird
in the extreme.

Murths were a kind of half-spirit, as best Pazel could understand. Klyst, a sea-murth, had appeared to him twice in the flesh,
and vanished both times with the suddenness of a candle flame.
Since the crossing of the Ruling Sea he never saw her at all.
But now and then he could feel her longing for him rise out of
nowhere. It was an accident, that longing: her people used infatu-
ation-charms to lure humans to their deaths, and killing Pazel was
all she'd had in mind at first. But Pazel's Gift had made her spell
backfire. She thought she loved him. She tried to persuade him to
abandon everything, humanity included, and live with her beneath
the sea. And she had placed a tiny shell beneath the skin of his
collarbone and called it her heart. He could feel the shell with his
fingers, that unmistakable bulge. It was sleeping; Klyst could not
find him at this distance, apparently. But why was it so hard not to
think of her? Was it guilt, that she should be suffering for his sake?
Was it fear for her and her people, if they should fail in their quest?

A shroud, a pall, a black smoke filling room after room ....

No good; he was more exhausted than when he first closed his eyes. He sat up and quietly pulled on his boots. He was longing for fresh air.

The passage outside the chamber was deserted and still. He moved left, feeling his way along the passage. Somewhere ahead there was a glimmer of light. As he walked it brightened, until at last the passage opened on a broad stone patio, built against the back of the hill. It overlooked a long valley, awash in the light of both moons, and rimmed on the far side by the jagged mountains he had glimpsed a week ago, before their descent into the Forest. He was high enough to see them again, and marvelled at their sheer number, and how their white peaks gleamed like mother-of-pearl.

Just beyond the patio, a narrow track wound down the side of the hill. And there with a start Pazel saw a lone figure, walking swiftly away. He was tall and moved with grace, despite a certain urgency to his step, and on his belt hung a long straight sword: one of the weapons of the selk.

Even as Pazel reached the balustrade, the figure slowed, as though sensing someone behind him. Without stopping he glanced over his shoulder.

'Kirishgán!'

Pazel did not shout, but he called out loud enough for the other to hear. It was unmistakably Kirishgán, his friend from Vasparhaven, the only selk he had ever seen before that day. As he looked up at Pazel, Kirishgán did stop – but only for a moment, as though ceasing to move required some great effort on his part. Then he turned and hurried on, down into the shadow of the hill.

Pazel called out a second time. The selk was gone, but he had looked at Pazel, recognised him. Was he dreaming? No, impossible: he was perfectly wide awake. Then he turned and looked again at the rocky hill above the patio. Thaulinin's troop was sleeping there, under the open sky, curled like deer in the high brittle grass. Some few slept together, limbs entwined, but whether for love or simple warmth he could not guess. As Pazel watched, a blue selk eye opened here and there – single eyes, not pairs – and glowed briefly, firefly-bright, before drifting shut again.

Keeping watch in their sleep.

Then more than ever, Pazel understood that they were among beings unlike themselves, far stranger than dlömu or flikkermen, or any other race he had encountered.

Dawn brought driving rain. The selk were awake and afoot, and they fed the company and brought them cups of steaming tea – and yet something in their eyes had changed. The hostility had not returned, but in its place had come caution and amazement, and perhaps a hint of fear. Pazel was unsettled. Had they unwrapped the Nilstone? Had one of them, Rin forbid, been so mad as to touch it? Or was his glimpse of Kirishgán somehow known to them, and for some reason forbidden?

Ramachni and Thaulinin arrived just after breakfast, and the mage looked pleased, but Thaulinin's face was drawn like that of all his people. 'We have ranged the hills all night, Arpathwin and I,' he said, 'and we have travelled even further in our speech, and into darker realms. I know the task you are about, and repeat my offer of help.'

'And *I* repeat: we ain't fit to march,' said Mandric. 'Twenty days! I'd give us two, before someone goes lame outright – provided you let us rob you of all the food in your larder, Mr Thaulinin.'

'I can see your wounds for myself,' said Thaulinin, 'and they are not to the flesh alone. No, you cannot march to the sea – not yet. And you cannot wait here for the hrathmogs or the Ravens to find you. But there is a third choice, if you will take it.'

'What choice is that?' asked Thasha.

'Shelter and healing, until you are fit for travel, and your scent goes cold,' said Thaulinin. 'More than that I cannot say. But I think you will be satisfied, if you place yourselves entirely in my hands.'

The party stirred uneasily. 'What would you require of us?' asked Hercól.

'Sleep,' said Thaulinin. 'A profound sleep, aided by a plant I have gathered this evening with Ramachni. It will not harm you, but it will allow us to do a thing we may not do in the waking presence of any non-selk, ever, by an oath as old as these very hills.'

Now there were open grumbles. 'Last night you drew swords against us,' said Cayer Vispek. 'Now you ask for blind trust.'

'I do not ask for it,' said Thaulinin. 'I merely name it as a condition of my greater help.'

'And you should agree,' said Ramachni, 'for I guess already what it is that our host offers but cannot name, and it is a distinction offered to few in the history of this world. And what Thaulinin has not mentioned is the grave risk that *he* would take on our behalf. By helping us he will face the judgement of his own people, and should they find him in the wrong he will be imprisoned to the end of his days. For a selk, such punishment is worse than death. Indeed many take their own lives rather than be kept from walking freely over Alifros.'

Pazel looked sharply at the crowd of selk. That was it; that was the reason for those chilly, fearful eyes. *It's not just Thaulinin. All of them will be held responsible, all of them will be judged.*

Thaulinin looked down at Ensyl. 'The plant does not work on the little folk,' he said. 'You will not sleep, but must be kept from seeing us, and confined.'

'Caged?' Ensyl bristled, backing towards the wall. 'For an ixchel that is a vile proposal. Few of us who enter cages have ever left alive.'

'Didn't stop you from caging *us*,' growled Mandric.

Dastu crossed his arms. 'I say, no thanks. I say we'll take our chances on the trail.'

'Then you getting die,' said Neda, 'like stupid Alyash, like so much crew on *Chathrand* ship.'

'Don't lecture me, girl,' snapped Dastu. 'How many Black Rags *getting die* when Rose blew your fancy ship out of the water?'

'Peace, Dastu!' said Hercól, stepping between them. 'Thaulinin, we must speak apart before we answer you. Be patient with us, pray.'

'Go and speak, then,' said Thaulinin, 'but it is your fate that begs a swift decision, not the selk.'

The party withdrew to their sleeping-chamber to debate, and soon their voices rose in argument. Dastu did not wish to have anything more to do with the selk, and Mandric and Lunja rejected the leap of faith Thaulinin demanded. Big Skip and Ensyl seemed torn. The shouts grew heated. Only Ramachni stood silent. Pazel looked at him in frustration. *Why doesn't he say anything?*

'I do not like blind choices either,' said Hercól, 'but we will not heal our wounds on a death march, nor fill our stomachs crouching here underground.' He looked at Mandric and Lunja. 'You are both soldiers, trained to trust in weapons more than words. So are Neda and Cayer Vispek. But self-reliance is not always the wisest path. When they surrendered to us – to their arch-enemies – it was an act of courage.'

'It was the only choice, save starvation and exile,' said Vispek.

'And that is exactly where we stand today,' said Bolutu.

'Nonsense!' said Mandric. 'You might as well say that them two were fools to surrender – they've ended up starved and exiled anyway, and in a worse fix than if they'd stayed on the Sandwall.'

'Worse?' said Vispek. 'You did not see the shipwreck near our camp, full of dlömu with their throats slit, and the word *Platazcra* scrawled in blood across the deck.'

'And you're exaggerating anyway, Corporal Mandric,' said Thasha. 'The selk have already fed us, and given us shelter.'

'And played pretty music,' scoffed Dastu.

Lunja glanced at him curiously. 'We have a saying in Bali Adro: *The singer is more truthful than the talker, and the harp more truthful still.*'

'Very nice,' said Mandric, 'but I still don't fancy getting poisoned.'

'I'm with you there,' said Big Skip. 'We'd wake up *confused*, he says? Pitfire, we went through that with the mushroom-spores in the Forest! It was blary unnatural.'

'These creatures aren't natural either,' said Dastu, 'and they're shifty as midges, by damn. Anyone who trusts them is a blary fool.'

'I'll trust them,' said Neeps.

Everyone stopped talking and looked at him. 'They know a lot,' he said. 'Maybe they can help me. And maybe some of you have the mind-plague too, and don't know it yet. I doubt they have a cure, or they'd have used it before the humans died out. All the same, I'll stay with them. I'm no use to anyone if I turn into an animal, and—' he looked at Pazel and Thasha, blinking '—it's getting harder to think.'

His friends rushed to embrace him. Pazel had to turn his face away, lest Neeps see his tears. Hercól said, 'Trust is dangerous, but less dangerous than acting in fear. Come, we must decide. Will you not take the hand extended?'

'No!' said Dastu. 'Have you all gone soft? They want the Nilstone! Last night they were on the verge of gutting us over it, like so many fish. They found out we had a mage and decided the fighting-odds weren't as good as they'd figured. Now they're counting on desperation to make us walk into their trap.'

'Did you hear nothing in the music?' asked Ramachni.

Dastu turned to him, startled. 'You too? What's so special about that blary music?'

'Almost everything,' said the mage. 'It was a part of the *Cando Teahtenca*, the Creation-Song of the Auru, First People of Alifros. It was the Auru who built the tower where we fought Arunis, to guard the River and issue warnings; the Auru whose final charge in the Dawn War drove the Gorgonoths back into the Pits; the Auru whose spell of beauty still rings in certain hearts, like the note of an enchanted bell struck ages ago. They have all gone from the world, but it is said that among the most ancient selk there are a few who walked with them in their twilight, and heard their songs entire. Perhaps Thaulinin erred with us in the matter of the Nilstone. But the selk apologise with gifts, not words, and that rare music was a gift given to few.'

Another silence fell. Then Lunja said, 'I will trust them. To do otherwise is folly.'

Mandric looked at her, wrathful. 'You're right, Otter, damn your sweet eyes.'

Dastu laughed scornfully, but he knew he stood alone. 'We'll regret this,' he said. 'If we're lucky enough to do any regretting, that is. If those monsters let us wake up.'

His eyes, or the black humour in his voice, reminded Pazel powerfully of something, but he could not say what. They filed back to the entrance hall, and found Thaulinin's people ready. One selk approached each traveller, holding a piece of something fleshy and brown. 'We must watch you swallow,' said Thaulinin. 'Fear not; we will catch you if you fall.'

Pazel's heart was racing. The selk who had carried him up the hill stepped forward with a peculiar smile, and immediately pressed the fleshy thing between his lips. It was tart and slimy. The selk looked at him, waiting. Pazel chewed.

The rain froze motionless in the sky.

'Swallow,' said the selk. But his voice was odd, and Pazel saw with a jolt that his upper and lower teeth were fused together, and stretching like toffee with the movement of his jaw.

'Ramach— Ramachni,' Pazel sputtered, fearing suddenly for his own teeth.

'Mushrooms!' howled Big Skip. 'Rin's eyes, these are straight from the Infernal Forest, ain't they?'

The air was gelatinous. The selk's smile was a blur. Pazel dropped to his knees. Beside him, Dastu was laughing again, loud and bitter, and suddenly Pazel knew what he was reminded of. Dastu had never sounded so much like his master, Sandor Ott.

8

The Hidden and the Dead

A man cannot hide from the truth, outlaw the truth, spit in the face of truth, and then in good conscience punish those whom he discovers have given up trying to tell him the truth. Such behaviour is indefensible in a king. He would do better to probe the reasons for their secrecy, which are most often grounded in despair at his rule. The wise king will reward these truth-tellers, as he would the doctor who arrests his blindness before it is complete.

– Preface to the *Life of Valridith* by Thaulinin Tul Ambrimar

4 Halar 942
263rd day from Etherhorde

'What happens if they separate?'

Felthrup glanced up from the *Merchant's Polylex*. Marila's voice was trembling, although her face, as usual, remained impassive. She had paused with a Masalym fig halfway to her mouth.

'Separate, my dear?'

They were both on Thasha's bed, Marila with her feet up, shoulders propped against the wall. Amber evening light fell on her round face and dark, salt-brittle hair. She bit down on the fruit and it ruptured with a squeak.

'They're all right together,' she said as she chewed. 'Pazel has his fits, but the others protect him until they're over. Thasha goes blank, like she's sleepwalking, or very far away – but Pazel and

Neeps coax her out of it. Neeps—' she drew a sharp breath '—
is a fool, of course, but the others can keep him from exploding.
Sometimes. What if they get separated, though? Who will look
after them?'

Felthrup could smell the fear on her skin. Humans could not
detect that smell, did not know they produced it; but rats knew.
Many a colony owed its life to that particular scent. Humans had
warning bells, drums, criers who ran through the streets. Rats had
their noses. When enough humans began to exude the smell of
fear, rats ceased their scavenging and dashed for the warren, and
did not move until it faded.

Marila shook her head. 'Forget it,' she said. 'I just can't seem to
quit imagining things. Blary waste of time.'

This is how she asks for comfort, he thought.

'It was a great company that set out from Masalym,' he said.
'Humans, dlömu, ixchel, horses, dogs. We must have faith in them,
as they did in one another.'

Marila turned her gaze to the window. They had left the
Sparrows Islands behind and were skirting the edge of a bigger
land mass called *Vilgur* or *Vulgir* – 'Peaceful' was the translation
the dlömu had offered, and that was accurate enough. A broken
black mound rising whale-like from the glaucous sea. Cubes and
polygons, wave-tortured, algae-crowned. Yes, it was peaceful in its
lifelessness.

'I don't want to visit Oggosk,' said Marila.

'The duchess is peculiar,' said Felthrup, 'and I will never trust
her fully – certainly to the ixchel she is a merciless foe. But she is
equally a foe of Arunis – or was, if he is truly dead. And she has
taken a strong interest in Thasha from the start.'

'A nasty interest. She threatened to punish Pazel terribly if he
didn't stop loving Thasha. She might as well have ordered him to
stop eating, breathing. Having a heart.'

'That is why we must go and see her,' said Felthrup. He tapped
the *Polylex*. 'She wishes to consult this book. She wishes for it with
unspeakable intensity, though she tries to hide the fact. We are in

a position to name our price, my dear Marila. And we may begin by demanding that she tell us everything she knows about Lady Thasha.'

'Mr Fiffengurt dreamed he saw Lord Talag.'

'How you *do* jump from thought to thought,' said Felthrup admiringly. 'Some of us only creep, meandering, myopic, dragging our bellies in the dust. You leap with the freedom of a gazelle.'

She gave him an odd look. 'My belly will be dragging soon enough.'

Should he laugh, should he sympathise? What if the child had the father's temper, the mother's gift for stuffing feelings in a closet, leaning hard against the door?

'Listen to what I've found in the *Polylex*,' he said, playing it safe. He cocked an eye at the tiny print. '"*Within the cave all was ice-sheathed, and the corpses were as figures under glass. But when she reached the chamber where Droth's Eye had fallen it was warm as a summer's eve, and a light that was not her torchlight shone about her, pale and deathly.*"'

'You've found it!' said Marila. 'Erithusmé's story! So that old Mother Prohibitor told the truth, it *is* written down! But we've searched and searched, Felthrup. Where was it hidden?'

'Under *Raptors*.'

'Raptors?'

'Birds of prey, my dear. The great hunters of the air. Eagles, falcons, hawks, marapets, osprey, kunalars, the rare nocturnal—'

'All right!' said Marila. 'Raptors, naturally. It makes no sense at all.'

'On the contrary, it makes perfect sense, if your goal is to conceal forbidden histories in wild thickets of words.'

'I suppose *Droth's Eye* is the Nilstone,' said Marila, 'since that's what she's supposed to have found in the ice cave. Go on, read me the rest.'

Felthrup found his place and continued:

All about her lay death's monuments, testimony to the killing power of the Orb. Yet Erithusmé did not fear, and that was ever her salvation. She went straight to the Eye and clasped it in her hand, and felt only a little prick, as of a dull needle scraping. The Eye was far too heavy for its size, and the girl thought at first that she would never lift it. At last, with both hands, she raised it to her chest, and thereupon her very desire to bear its weight did change her, strengthening her body, and that was the first deed of magic the great wizardess ever performed. And the second was to shape the ice into stairs and level passages for her return to the surface. Little control did she have of this sudden power: the ice melted and soaked her, and the stairs were cracked, and once the very mountain shook, and rocks fell crashing about her. She never quailed, however, and came at last into the daylight again.

There in the plain below waited the King of Nohirin in his pavilion, surrounded by the eight hundred soldiers who dared not enter where the young girl had gone alone. When Erithusmé descended, the king praised her, then roughly demanded the Orb, saying, 'This tool would never profit a peasant's daughter. Give it to me! It belongs in royal hands.' But the girl drew back, and reminded him of his promise. 'One falcon of my choice from your covey did you swear to give me, O King,' she said. 'And my choice is there on your huntsman's arm.'

The king was angry, for she had chosen his favourite. 'I will send a suitable bird to your father's homestead,' he told her. 'Now give me Droth's Eye.'

Still Erithusmé did not yield. The king shouted to his guard, and they moved to seize her. And not knowing what she did. Erithusmé raised the Orb before her with a cry, and the king and his eight hundred were swept away in a whirlwind of terrible force, and found later throughout the countryside, crushed against cliffs, impaled on trees and steeples. But the bird flew to her arm and became her companion, and journeyed with her far over Alifros aboard her ship.

When fresh carrion is plentiful the raptor may not bother to

171

*hunt, though it will rarely pass up the incautious mouse or field
rat—*

'Oh, I say.' Felthrup shook himself, and looked up from the *Polylex*.
'It's all birds from that point on,' he said. 'Nothing more about
Erithusmé, under *Raptors* at least. Not so useful, was it? We knew
the outline of the story already.'

Marila gazed down at the book. 'It does tell us one thing.
Erithusmé could use the Nilstone from the moment she touched
it. And not just for simple tricks. If the book's telling the truth, she
had huge powers from the start. And all because she lacked fear.
That's strange too. What sort of person lacks fear *entirely*?'

'But she did not,' said Felthrup. 'That at least is how Thasha
heard the story from the Mother Prohibitor. That little nee-
dle-prick became a slight burning, then a stronger pain, and each
year she kept the stone it grew worse. And when Erithusmé con-
sulted the High Priestess on Rapopalni, she was told no mortal
being can ever be wholly emptied of fear – and that consequently
the stone *would* kill her in time. And Thasha believed the same
would happen to her, only faster.'

'*Much* faster,' said Marila, nodding. 'We talked about the
Nilstone, once. During that week when the boys weren't speaking
to us. She thought it would take the stone about three minutes to
kill her, if she was rested and could put up a good fight.'

'Three minutes!' said Felthrup. 'Then I hope she never touches
it at all.'

'But even three minutes makes her – different,' said Marila.
'Everyone else who touches that blary thing dies before they can
scream.'

'Unless they've drunk of the wine of Agaroth,' said Felthrup.
Marila looked at him blankly. 'Ah, but you weren't there, were
you? It was in the Straits of Simja, just after the Shaggat Ness was
turned to stone. Ramachni spoke of an enchanted wine from the
twilight kingdom, used by the Fell Princes when the Stone was
in their possession, long eons ago. The wine made them fearless

enough to survive the touch of the Stone. Though I doubt it helped their judgement when they used it.'

'What happened to that wine?'

Felthrup's nose twitched. 'What do you think, my dear? They drank it up. You can find it in the *Polylex* under the heading *Incontinence, Sins of.*'

Marila laid a hand on the delicate paper of the book. 'We know Erithusmé and Thasha are connected. Thasha knows that herself. When we were locked up in the Conservatory, there was even talk that Erithusmé could be her mother. Thasha went sort of crazy once, and began talking in someone else's voice. Maybe that voice was Erithusmé's. Neeps thought so.'

Marila fell abruptly silent. Then she rose to her feet, startling rat and dogs alike.

'I don't know what we think we're accomplishing. What does all this matter, if we never see them again? No, that's not what I'm trying to say. It matters, *they* matter. But we don't.'

She touched her belly, unconsciously. The rat wished for human arms, for limbs that could embrace and protect. Fear was so easy to smell, so terribly difficult to lessen.

I must return to the River of Shadows, he thought. *I must find Orfuin and beg for aid. Somehow we must reach them, if they yet live. Or free ourselves from hope if they do not.*

'I can't stand thinking of him,' Marila whispered, as if ashamed of the admission.

'You must,' said Felthrup. 'Not thinking of him is a human sort of trick, and not a very clever one, my dear. Some pain it is folly to avoid. Think of him, ache for him. Let that longing bring you the strength to do what he would wish you to do.'

Marila blinked at him. 'How did you learn to think that way?'

Felthrup tilted his head as though to say he had no idea. He could not bring himself to admit that he was quoting from a volume of melodramas Admiral Isiq had left in his cabin, under the pillow.

Marila closed the *Polylex* and stepped to the wall. Running her fingers along the rough planks, she found the spot she wanted and pushed. There was a click, and Felthrup saw the outline of the hidden cabinet where they stored the irreplaceable book. Marila clawed it open and slipped the *Polylex* inside.

'Come on,' she said. 'Let's see if we can get something out of the witch.'

They left the stateroom, Thasha's mastiffs leading the way. In truth, Felthrup had his doubts about their errand as well. Lady Oggosk (with that certainty of obedience she always displayed) had simply ordered him to produce the *Polylex*. 'I'm not Arunis, I won't steal it from you,' she had declared. But she had turned from him as she spoke the words, as though afraid of what her face might reveal. Inwardly, Felthrup had panicked, matched her evasion with one of his own. He would have to speak to Marila, he'd said, for he could hardly fulfil her wishes alone. Priceless and forbidden books were not to be dragged about in sackcloth, were they?

Convince her! Lady Oggosk had replied, adding that the very survival of the *Chathrand* was at stake. After that she'd shut her mouth, waiting for him to go. It was not for rats to question the Duchess of Tiroshi.

He did not like to cross the witch, despite her curious transformation into his protector and confidant (if such a word could ever apply to one so crafty and calculating). And yet the book was in his trust, his and Marila's. And so he had questioned further.

'Forgive me, lady, but you had best make a stronger argument. Recall if you will that the Mother Prohibitor herself told Thasha to share the book with no one.'

Lady Oggosk had thrown a hairbrush at him. 'The Mother Prohibitor!' she shrieked. 'Is she aboard? Did she ever do anything for Thasha Isiq, save imprison her, and teach her how to snare a man with hips and eyelashes? Did she ever raise a finger against the sorcerer, or the excesses of the Secret Fist? I am the one who sacrificed! That woman stayed in Etherhorde to raise catfish.'

Felthrup shuddered. He knew his favour with the witch could vanish as quickly at it had appeared. He had no idea why she considered him important. Before Masalym she had hardly spared him a glance. Now for some reason she had let it be known that he was under her wing – that the man who laid a finger on the *Chathrand*'s sole surviving rat* would answer to her. In her cabin she regaled him with stories of her first excursions with Captain Rose, her low opinions of certain crewmembers (most crewmembers), her hatred of Mzithrinis, her delight in the harm done to them by the Shaggat cult.

Most disturbing were her hints about the Swarm of Night, which she said was growing like an invisible tumour. 'It is here, in Alifros,' she would tell him. 'Some monster has brought it back – Arunis, possibly, before he fell. I can feel it, the way Rose feels the distribution of cargo in the hold. I can feel the Swarm unbalancing the world.'

They passed through the invisible wall. 'Not that way,' said Marila, as Felthrup started up the Silver Stair. 'I don't want the whole ship to see us heading for her door. Let's cross the lower gun deck. Nothing much happening there.'

They descended, and set out across the deck. Light poured in through the glass planks in the ceiling, making the floorboards gleam. Beside the open gunports, black cannon waited, like coffins at the doors of some vast crematorium. It was very quiet: Felthrup could hear the island's shore birds, smell the flat nickel-smell of the rocks. The few sailors at work here tried, as always, not to stare. 'Evening, Mrs Undrabust,' some murmured, while others considered them coldly. Felthrup was grateful for Jorl and Suzyt. Opinions about the four youths (Marila stood for all of them, now) ran from wary affection to hatred. Some blamed them for all the

---

*Felthrup clearly thought himself alone, but the forensic record leaves no doubt that he was mistaken. A few rats almost certainly boarded the *Chathrand* while she stood in the Masalym drydock. Their skulls reveal a fourth molar in the upper jaw, a telltale difference from their Northern cousins.- EDITOR

disasters of the voyage; others said that they were the only reason the ship was still afloat.

The dogs' mouths watered when they passed the galley. Felthrup knew the cause, for he could smell it too, however faintly: the Red River hog. Mr Fiffengurt had promised to save an ounce of its fat for each mastiff, but the gift had never come. When Felthrup had mentioned it, the quartermaster had looked rather ill and changed the subject.

Suddenly the noses of both animals dropped to the floorboards, as though pulled by strings. Felthrup and Marila stared. The dogs' great bodies quivered. 'They've picked up a scent,' said Marila, 'but it's nothing in the galley, is it? Look, they're following it away.'

The dogs padded forward, entranced. Felthrup rushed after them, trying to rid his nostrils of their sweat and breath and dander. He sniffed, sneezed, sniffed again. Then he looked up at Marila, amazed.

'Ixchel,' he said.

Marila's eyes went wide. 'Two of them, probably,' said Felthrup, 'and not more than an hour ago.'

'Ixchel!' said Marila. 'But they haven't been seen in weeks! Are you sure?'

'I spent a month sniffing them out when I first boarded the *Chathrand*, my dear. I hunted for them ceaselessly; I thought we might be friends. You know what became of that endeavour. Still I could no more mistake the smell of ixchel than I could the shape of my paw.'

The dogs had turned the corner at the cross-passage. When Felthrup and Marila caught up they found the animals whining and scratching at a rather decrepit length of floorboard. They were not unheard of, these points of decay. In Masalym the crew had been absorbed with major repairs; only now could they be spared for such smaller jobs, and Mr Fiffengurt's checklist was immense. The plank before them had a two-inch gap at one corroded corner: more than enough room for an ixchel to pass through.

Felthrup tasted the air above the gap. 'They passed through

here, between the floorboards and the ceiling of the orlop deck, and then to portside.' He looked up at the girl again, suddenly excited. 'And I must follow! Quickly, while no one's about! Raise that plank a little! Help me squeeze through!'

'Squeeze through? Are you joking?' said Marila.

'Decidedly not! This is great good fortune! It could be weeks, months before we catch their scent again. Even now it is fading. I might have missed it without the aid of the dogs.'

'You can't just go down that hole.'

'My dear, you know nothing of the art of the squirm! There have been studies, we rats can pass through any hole wider than our heads, as measured at the lower mandible—'

'Felthrup—'

'That is all one need verify, the mandibular axis, the yaw of the jaw—'

Felthrup jumped. Marila had just stamped her foot down over the gap.

'Take a look at your foot, you silly ass.'

Felthrup swallowed. Marila had a point: his left forepaw had never recovered from his first encounter with the ixchel. Lord Talag and his men had sealed him in a bilge pipe. Only at the last second, by jamming his paw between the pipe and its lid, had he escaped suffocation.

'Yes, yes, I fell into their trap,' he admitted, 'but Marila, you did not know the *Chathrand* in those days. Everything was different. We had not met Diadrelu, or heard of Arunis or the Nilstone, or guessed that we would all be fighting together to survive. When Lord Talag caught me he did not even believe I was a woken rat. But in time he came to respect me – even thanked me for my courage, and offered me the services of his cook. They have no reason to hate me now.'

'Talag didn't have a reason to *start* with.'

'But he knows me; they all do. Diadrelu called me her beloved friend.'

'They killed her too.'

Swift and certain logic. But Felthrup was not about to be turned. 'Remove your foot!' he hissed. 'Someone is coming! Sweet friend, we must know how many ixchel are left alive, and reason with them, before they try something atrocious at Stath Bálfyr.'

'Something atrocious – you see? Not everything has changed.'

A man *was* coming; he could feel the thump of footfalls in the boards. 'Oh dearest girl! Fond, caring, maternal Marila—'

'Don't call me *that*.'

No reaching her, no use! Felthrup spun in a circle. He could taste it, the burn of breaking faith, the horrid knowledge that even with loved ones, speech could be impotent, language something less than grace. 'Why are you crying?' said Marila, and then Felthrup bit her through the boot.

She screamed and danced away. The dogs howled. Mr Coote appeared at the corner, shouting, 'What's wrong, Miss Marila? The little baby? Is it time?'

'No! Pitfire!' She pointed, but it was too late already. Tufts of black fur edged the gap in the planks. Felthrup had done it; he was gone.

He was in darkness now, in the six-inch crawlspace between the floor of the lower gun deck and the ceiling of the orlop. The scent led straight to portside. He struggled to crawl in perfect silence, unscrambling the message from his nostrils, alert to the least movement of the air.

He ploughed forward through the velvety dust. When the scent trail reached the inner hull it veered right. Another scurry, his mind awash with thoughts of how to greet them, what he should say. Talag had ideas of honour: strange ideas, but no less powerful for their strangeness. The key was to access those ideas. *We are comrades in arms, Lord Talag, never mind the arm you mangled, why kill me before we chat a little, why kill me period, spear in haste regret at leisure, my enemy's enemy is my friend, and by obverse induction my friendly enemy is a, is—*

He stopped, nostrils flaring. They had stood here, the ixchel, not thirty minutes before. And then they had disappeared.

Rin's eyes, not again.

Felthrup circled, listening, feeling, tasting the air. The scent was gone; it led to this spot and vanished without a trace. When it came to hiding, rats were experts, but the ixchel were master magicians. He rolled over, pressed an ear to the boards. Nothing but men's distant footfalls, and the slosh of the sea. He hissed: 'Come out! It's only Felthrup! I'm a friend, today and evermore!' No sound, not even an echo.

'Don't do this! Suspicious ninnies! I won't betray your hiding place!'

The silence mocked him. They could be somewhere close at hand, smiling. Even fondling their spear-tips, circling, tightening the noose.

He blew one nostril and then another, inhaled deeply, struggling for even the most distant ghost of a scent. Nothing. He pressed his mangled paw against the boards, drew the tender flesh back and forth. What was he thinking? That he would find a hinge, a hair-line crack, the outline of an ixchel door? But such doors were never found. What a dreamer he was. Rose had torn the ship apart and found nothing. The ixchel would be seen again when they wished to be, and not before.

'We're stronger together,' he told the darkness. 'We have to stand together, with the humans as well, mind you. Or we're doomed.'

Felthrup put his head down on his paws. He was lying to himself. He didn't fear the ixchel closing in silently to spear him. No, what he dreaded was their absence, their refusal of his peace overtures, their continued loathing for the giants and anyone tainted by their favour. He was not much thinking about where that loathing could lead. He was only feeling the waste: the colossal, shameful waste. *You were right, Marila. You can love language and its promise of a straight sunny boulevard, a common currency of the heart. But that's your faith only, and it moves not mountains. They're not listening, those mountains. They're happy where they stand.*

He blinked.

Something had happened. A finger of cold had touched his stubby tail. He turned about, feeling: there was a large droplet on the plank. He touched his tongue to the water. It was salty – and what was far stranger, *clean*. This was no seepage, no condensation. This was a splash of fresh seawater, fallen from above, and yet somehow deep in the bowels of the *Chathrand*.

He turned away, crawled a few feet, stopped to think again. He touched the board six inches overhead. Then he turned and nosed his way back to where the trail disappeared. The wet spot was still there. He reached up again. This time his paw met with nothing.

Felthrup stared upwards. There was clearly another hole, larger than the one he'd squeezed through. By why was there no light from the gun deck, with all those open ports? Nervously, he rose on his haunches. There! He felt the edge of the opening, ran his paws about its perimeter. It was about ten inches square.

He rose higher – and light stabbed his eyes. By sheer instinct he ducked down again, and the light turned once more to blackness. Felthrup was shaken. It had been no lamp, but sunlight: the bright, cold glow of the sun through mist. And what else? The wind: he'd heard a moaning wind, and something that sounded very much like surf.

He stood mystified. Then, with a gasp, he saw the whole thing, what had become of the ixchel, why Rose had never found a trace.

'Felthrup?'

Marila's voice, faint and distant. She was still waiting for him. But no, he couldn't go back to her, now. He stood on his hind legs again, and the sunlight poured over him, and the wind and surf resumed. He pulled himself through the gap, onto chilly boards. He looked around. He was right where he expected to be, upon the lower gun deck, some fifty yards from where he'd left Marila. And at the same time he was somewhere utterly alien. Somewhere he had never hoped to see.

The deck was severely tilted, as if the ship stood almost on her beam-ends. And it was still, perfectly still; and not a soul was to be seen. The cold sunlight flooded in through the gunports, and further off, the tonnage shaft, which was cluttered with hanging debris. Felthrup climbed for the gunports, shining above him like skylights. Afraid that his body would betray him, that he might panic and run, dive for the square hole behind him. And even more afraid that if he did so, he would find that the hole had disappeared.

This is not a dream. Not a night journey from which I will wake safe and sound in my hatbox. So why does it draw me like a dream?

As he neared the gunports the surf grew louder. The cannon and their carriages were gone – no, there they lay below him, in a heap against the starboard hull. Some of the gunport doors lay with them; others dangled from their hinges, rusted and cracked. And there was another sound, a low, violent booming, reverberating in the planks beneath his feet.

He felt a cold sea-spray. He was almost blinded by the sun. *Not a dream*, he thought again, and crawled out through the port.

The wind swallowed his cry of horror. This was the *Chathrand*, all right – but only her carcass, beached and broken, utterly destroyed. She lay half-embedded in sand, and waves the height of houses were thrashing against her. Below, her keel was split, her frame-timbers shattered. A good third of her hull was simply lost, devoured by the sea.

Felthrup turned in place. Her mainmast still stood, absurdly proud, jabbing at the scudding clouds. The other masts were gone. Likewise the bowsprit, the forecastle house, and every trace of rigging save a few blackened strands still knotted to the rusted cleats. Her bell was gone; her paint was gone. The deck cannon were filled with twigs and seaweed. Bird nests. This *Chathrand* had been here for decades.

But where was *here*? An island. A low and empty place, not more than a mile long, and tortured by those thundering rollers. Beach grasses, terns and plovers, white bleached shells. No trees, unless those growths at the island's centre were stunted trees. And no other land, anywhere. The *Chathrand* had died quite alone.

A feeling like intoxication boiled up in the rat. He knew the legends about magical doorways on the Great Ship, and the 'vanishing compartments' they led to. Marila and Thasha had stumbled through one such door themselves, and ended up on a *Chathrand* from long ago, crewed by barbarous men. But he, Felthrup – he was seeing the future, obviously. Decades or centuries from now, this would be the Great Ship's end: beached and ruined on this nothing of an island, lost in the Ruling Sea. The ixchel had hidden not in space, but in time.

Then Felthrup saw the burial yard.

It stood above the beach, where the grasses were thick and the land looked almost stable, almost safe from being washed away in a storm. Rock cairns, the marooned sailors' grave markers, surrounded by the rotted posts of what had once been a fence, a wall against the wind and sand.

Felthrup thought his heart would burst. At least some of the crew of this other *Chathrand* had made it ashore, and lived here for a time, and perished. Who were they? In his own time the Great Ship was six hundred years old, and had changed hands, owners, nations, countless times. How many more had she known, before this lonely end?

'You can still read the inscriptions,' said a voice above him.

He jumped – and nearly became the next one to die. The hull was wet and slick with algae. He tore at it, digging in with his claws, jabbing with his incisors, and just managed to regain his balance. Above him, on the broken topdeck rail, crouched an ixchel he had never seen before. He had a broad face and small bright eyes, a black sash around his upper arm, a spear crossed over his knees. The man was smiling, but Felthrup did not much like the smile.

'Three inscriptions, anyway, etched in stone. The others are gone, or unreadable. Come up now, rat.'

'Cousin!' cried Felthrup. 'I must assure you that I am not here to spy out your secrets.'

'You've done that already.'

'My purpose is to give knowledge, not extract it.'

'Climb. You're not safe where you are.'

At that moment half a dozen ixchel appeared on either side of the man with the sash. They were armed and muscular, with shaved heads, and they looked down at Felthrup with the hungry eyes of hawks. Felthrup recognised their faces, but he did not know their names. He doubted that they were concerned for his safety.

'I know what you mean to do,' he shrilled. 'You would wait for us to reach your homeland, and then swarm back through that hole and attack.'

'Roast me, lads, he's seen right through us,' said the man, as those around him laughed. 'We give up a good home in Etherhorde. Fight giants and rats, storms and starvation, lose a fifth of our clan. And then, just as we near Stath Bálfyr, we *attack*. Sinking the ship, maybe, in typical crawly fashion. Or whispering a bad heading into Rose's ear. So that we can all drown together within sight of dear old Sanctuary-Beyond-the-Sea.'

He made an impatient gesture. 'I won't waste a weapon on you, beastie. If you will not climb, we will throw refuse down until we knock you into the waves.'

Felthrup turned to leap back through the gunport – but of course, they had closed in behind him, five more shaven-headed spearmen. They did not want him returning just yet.

You dug this burrow, Felthrup. Stop squirming and dig your way out.

He climbed. It was not as slippery as he feared: the curve of the hull worked in his favour. He reached the rail, and the ixchel roughly pulled him up. Oh, the wasteland of the topdeck! Holes, cracks, chasms. Splinters, rotting spars, rusted chains. Felthrup struggled to contain his tears.

'Well,' said their leader, 'we're not dead yet. Now you know.'

'You won't believe me, sirs, but I am glad of it – overjoyed.'

'You're damned right I don't. I am Saturyk, His Lordship's chief counsel.'

A twitch passed over Felthrup, one he hoped the man could not read. *Saturyk.* He'd heard the name many times; Ensyl had called him 'the one whose hands go everywhere'. After the ixchels' seizure of the *Chathrand* most of the little people had come out into the open, some gloating, some quiet and thoughtful. Not Saturyk: he had remained in the shadows, rarely seen, never lured into conversation. Felthrup studied the man, and felt himself studied in return, with cold exactitude. *I know who you are,* he told the man silently. *You're their Sandor Ott.*

'I wish to speak to Lord Talag,' he said.

'No doubt,' said Saturyk, 'but your wishes hold no currency with His Lordship. You've shown us who your friends are. One of them likes to dine on our brethren.'

'You mean Sniraga? I am no friend of that cat! She is merely the familiar of Lady Oggosk.'

'Aye,' said Saturyk, 'and you're another. For your sake, I hope she doesn't try to use you against us. We keep a fine edge on our spears.'

Felthrup was confused, frightened, exasperated with himself and them. 'We are wasting time,' he said.

'There's a bit of truth at last. You came to talk, you claim? Talk, then, we're listening. For the moment.'

'Talag and I are better acquainted.'

Once again Saturyk's mouth formed that unpleasant smile. 'Only because you're not giving me a chance,' he said.

'Master Saturyk,' said Felthrup, 'I would kindly ask you not to favour me with a display of wit, or irony, or your rudimentary teeth. You have no order to kill me, or you should have done so already. You are presumably required to defer to your commander in anything so unlikely as a visit from the other ship. I will speak to Talag, none other. And put away your pricking tools. Only a fool points out that spears are sharp.'

He was shaking as he spoke, but he forced himself to look Saturyk in the face. The guards were enraged. 'He mocks you,' hissed one, passing his spear to another and drawing a knife. 'Give the word, and I will take another inch off his tail.'

Saturyk gazed at Felthrup, expressionless, his eyes like two copper nail-heads in the sun. 'Put the knife away,' he told his man at last. Then he turned and started across the topdeck, one hand beckoning Felthrup to follow.

They walked a practised path through the jagged timbers, the drifted sand. Felthrup's gaze slid down into the chasm of the tonnage shaft. There was light in the ship's depths: sidelong light from the hull breach; and the waves moved through her, pulsing, as through the chambers of a heart.

At the starboard rail, a thin rope had been fastened to a cleat. It ran inland, taut above the surf, to a point some thirty yards up the beach. 'Can you walk a rope, Mr Stargraven?' asked Saturyk.

'Hmph,' said Felthrup. He had been walking ropes since he was weaned. Indeed he was swifter than the ixchel, as they made their way ashore. Sometimes it was good to be a belly-dragger.

But the blowing sand became a torment as they descended, and by the time they reached the ground it was almost intolerable. Saturyk urged him quickly forward, and Felthrup saw that they were making for a narrow tunnel. Soon they were all inside: a buried length of bilge-pipe, leading uphill towards the vegetation at the island's centre.

'You placed this here?' said Felthrup, amazed. 'Such industry! How long have your people been passing through that door?'

No one answered. They crawled, single file. When the pipe ended they dashed again through the blowing sand and dived into another. This one was longer, narrower. At length it brought them to the very edge of the brush. There were trees, after all: tortured and shrunken, but still a bulwark against the howling wind.

They were marching on a footpath, now. Looking left and right, Felthrup saw other ixchel moving with them, half-hidden, gliding through the patchwork of light and shadow. He knew many by sight, a few by name. He thought of the three hours' peace in Masalym, when the dlömu had lavished food on them all. *How different it could have been. And perhaps it can be yet. Watch your words, my dear Felthrup, watch your manners.*

They had not walked five minutes when the brush opened into a clearing, framed by half a dozen crumbling, human-sized buildings. As Felthrup watched, the clan came out into the open, soundlessly. And it was the full clan: still hundreds strong. Never before had he seen ixchel children, wide-eyed, thoughtful; or the greatly aged, skinny and round-shouldered, but never bent like human elders.

How careworn they all were! It shocked Felthrup profoundly, this defeated look: they might have been castaways themselves. And they were angry, too: furiously angry. They stared at him as though unable to quite believe that he had come here, and Felthrup turned in a circle, meeting their eyes. No, they were not all furious. Some looked at him with fear, or simple bewilderment, and a very few with hope.

The buildings were mere shacks. They listed, nearly ready to topple. Every one of them built, of course, with salvage from the *Chathrand*. Here was a bench from the officer's mess. Here a wheelblock mounted on a post: one end of a laundry line, perhaps. And Rin's eyes! There was the ship's bell, set upon a great flat stone like a monument in a village square.

But this had never been a village. Only three of the buildings looked as if they had ever been suitable for living in. Another might have served as a barn, the last a storehouse. There was a well, a rusty anvil, the ghost of a fence. 'They brought a great deal ashore,' said Saturyk. 'At low tide the *Chathrand* is fully beached, and you can simply walk aboard.'

Felthrup could not find his voice. He knew these things. He knew the people who had touched them. Or at least their doubles, their shadow-selves.

They must have dreamed of rescue. Even here they did not give up. He looked at the bell: it would have taken eight men to carry it inland. *Even here they fought for dignity.*

Saturyk led him to the least dilapidated of the houses. The human door was shut fast, but at its foot the ixchel had carved one of their own. Saturyk gestured to one of his men, who opened the door and slipped inside.

'How long?' Felthrup asked.

'Since the wreck, you mean?' said Saturyk. 'Thirty-four years, if you trust the giants' memory.'

'You found written records?'

'Among other things.'

They waited. It was almost warm, here at midday and out of the wind. Almost. Felthrup tried to keep himself from imagining the island in a typhoon.

A sudden noise came from the woods, or beyond them perhaps. Felthrup turned in amazement. It was the lowing of a cow.

Saturyk gestured, and a number of the ixchel darted off in the direction of the noise. 'There are not many,' he told Felthrup. 'They must have been brought ashore and released.'

'And bred?' said Felthrup. 'Or is that the voice of a thirty-four-year-old cow?'

Saturyk looked at him with vague hostility. *Neither,* thought Felthrup. *That is one of the beasts that disappeared on the Nelluroq. They came here, those cows and goats and other creatures. There's another doorway on the ship!*

The man returned from within the shack and whispered in his leader's ear. Saturyk, clearly surprised, looked at Felthrup in annoyance. 'You're to be admitted,' he said. 'Follow me, and ask no questions.'

Inside it was dim rather than dark, for there were windows. The shack's single room was clean and ixchel-orderly: tiny crates lined up along one wall, dried foodstuffs hanging in garlands over-head. Along the opposite wall stood racks of weapons. Most of the chamber, however, resembled a military drill yard. There were lines chalked on the floor, and tightropes, net ladders, high jumps, a cat-shaped archery dummy bristling with arrows.

They never rest, thought Felthrup.

'Stop gaping,' growled Saturyk. Then he lowered his voice and added, 'His Lordship has a long list of worries, see? A great deal on his mind. So none of your chatter when you're in his presence. That's a *friendly* suggestion, believe it or not.'

'I shall be on my best behaviour,' said Felthrup.

Saturyk frowned; he was not reassured. Then he raised his eyes. Above them was a storage loft, its interior concealed by a tattered curtain. There was no ladder, but the ixchel had made a kind of staircase from a taut rope with many knots. Up they went, leaping and scrabbling. When they stood at last on the edge of the loft, Saturyk told him once more to wait. He slipped inside, and Felthrup stood staring at the ancient curtain. It had once been blue. And hand embroidered: leaf designs of some sort. And from the hem dangled a few limp threads, the remains of some decorative tassel.

Felthrup's nose twitched. Something was very wrong. He squirmed away from the curtain. Turned his back to it. Turned to face it again. 'No,' he said aloud, shaking his head human-fashion. He put out his paw and touched the material, drew it up against his cheek.

It was Thasha's blanket.

He squealed, horrified, and ran blind along the edge of the loft. It was hers, unquestionably: the very blanket he and Marila had been sitting on not two hours before. The wreck was not some alien *Chathrand* from hundreds of years ago, manned by long-forgotten strangers. It was his ship, his people. *They* were the ones who had been marooned here, who had lived out their lives on this fingernail of sand.

'*Aya Rin!* There are no Gods! Only cruelty and agony, endless suffering for all people, a mass of pointless woe!'

The curtain flew back, and Felthrup squealed again. Diadrelu's brother, Lord Talag, stood before him, a hand on the pommel of his sword.

He looked as strong and fit as Felthrup remembered him at their first encounter; he had recovered entirely from his imprisonment by the rats. Yet he was changed, and not for the better. There was a raggedness about his hair and clothing. Deep lines creased his face, and his eyes were spectral. Felthrup had the impression that Talag was both studying him closely and somehow not seeing him at all.

'Come here,' he murmured.

Talag turned his back and walked away. The loft was nearly

empty. There was a single chair, ixchel-sized, beneath the unglazed window; and a shape wrapped in oilskins about the size of a human's toolbox against one wall, and nothing more. Talag went to the chair and looked at it in silence. His back was to Felthrup; his hands were in fists.

'Do you know,' he said, 'that blasted magic wall is still intact? The whole ship is falling to pieces, washing out into the Nelluroq, and yet we still cannot enter the stateroom. My sister knew a way in, but I have not been able to find it. There could be bodies in that chamber for all we know.'

'My lord—'

'You are not vile, Master Felthrup. I know this. But you have come here for naught, and to your own misfortune.'

'I have come with a warning,' said Felthrup.

'How benevolent of you,' said Talag.

'You may jest, my lord,' continued Felthrup, 'but I fear my warning is dire.'

'Do you imagine we have abandoned all vigilance? We fled the *Chathrand* to avoid extermination, but some of us are always aboard. We know how she fares. How her crew's hopes are drying to dust. We know too that she is hunted, and that if it comes to open battle, she will lose. I went aloft when the armada passed in the gulf. I saw the devil-ships of Bali Adro. If you think to inform me that our lives are yet in Rose's bloodstained hands, do not bother. I know it all too well.'

'Your people see what is before their eyes, Lord Talag,' said Felthrup. 'But the greatest peril is not aboard the *Chathrand* at all. Nor has it been, since Arunis took the Nilstone ashore.'

'Your witch would have us believe that Arunis is dead.'

'Dead he may be, yet the Nilstone remains. And you who had a hand in its finding: you too must bear a part of the burden, and help to cast the Stone out of Alifros.'

'I played no part whatsoever in the finding of the Stone.'

Felthrup took a deep breath. He had forgotten how Talag lied.

'You passed Ott forgeries that made this whole journey seem

possible. Dri told us, my lord. Those chart headings, from Stath Bálfyr to Gurishal: you invented them. Without you Ott might still be conspiring in Castle Maag, and the Stone might yet be hidden in that iron wolf at the bottom of the sea. And if the Stone is now taken by Macadra then we shall never get it back, for she will enfortress herself in the heart of Bali Adro as she works to unlock its maleficent—'

'Felthrup, be still,' said Talag, startling the rat with the plainness of his speech. 'You will not persuade me, you know. We should never have paid attention to the squabbling of giants, their wars and sorceries and deceits. We use them, manipulate them. We are artists in that way. But we do not take sides in their intrigues. The ixchel know better, as a race, and have known for centuries. You should let me recount some of our legends, one day. They are nobler than anything you will find in giants' books. And they warn us, rat: never collaborate, never lower your guard. If you do so, the giants will step on you. Every time.'

'This is a new day, my lord. Ancient tales cannot show us the way forward. We must seek it ourselves.'

'You want me to intervene, do you not? To force the ship about, oblige Rose to sail back and look for your allies on the Bali Adro mainland?'

Lord Rin above! thought Felthrup. *Is he saying that he could?*

Talag raised his eyes to the window. 'I do not hate your Pazel Pathkendle, your Thasha Isiq,' he said. 'They saved twenty of my people from their own, on the day of slaughter in Masalym. But we are nearing Stath Bálfyr at long last. I will not sacrifice the dream of our clan for their sake – even if there were hope of finding them alive. My sister became a partisan in their factional wars, and the results were catastrophic.'

Felthrup squirmed. Impatience was making him short of breath. 'The catastrophe was brewing already,' he said. 'The choices of your noble sister prevented it from becoming absolute.'

'My escape from captivity prevented that.'

Lies, always lies. And worst of all, lies told to persuade no one but the man himself. *Turn and look at me!* he felt like screaming. *Stop talking to yourself!* But all he managed to say was, 'The Nilstone, the Nilstone is the danger.'

'We are not a superstitious lot,' said Talag, as if Felthrup had not spoken. 'We do not worship idols, or gather in temples to praise beings none can see. And yet we are a people of faith. It is our faith that has kept us alive.'

'Faith?' cried the rat. 'Gracious lord, what could possibly be more dangerous than faith? Did you not see enough of *faith* when you were held by Master Mugstur? Faith is for his kind, for the Shaggats and Sandor Otts of this world. Faith will kill you, if you let it.'

'The word means something else to us.'

'No, it does not,' said Felthrup. 'It means turning from what is plain to see. It means preferring stories to evidence – and this voyage has spread a banquet of evidence before you. I did not come to beg your aid for my friends' sake, Talag! I came because we must help their cause or be killed. The Nilstone—'

'Do not speak to me of the Nilstone!' roared Talag, spinning on his heel. 'I know its history as well as you! Giants use it to kill giants! And they will go on doing so, with or without it, as they have done through all the carrion-heap of their history! But there is a place in Alifros where they do not rule, and have not despoiled, and I am sworn to take my people there!'

'Then proceed!' squeaked Felthrup, hopping in place. 'Carry on, advance! Be firm and exalted!'

'Quit my presence, filth.'

'But Stath Bálfyr will be no refuge! There is no lasting refuge, here or anywhere. And we *are* filth, all of us, even you. You're living filth!'

'Saturyk!'

'That is how they think of us – the powers who set Arunis and Macadra to work on this world! Can't you see *anything*? Alifros is to be scrubbed! Sterilised like a ward before surgery! *Aya!*'

He leaped, and something whizzed past his head. Saturyk had

flown through the curtain, wielding a heavy chain. Felthrup began to run, hysterical, and the ixchel man sprinted behind him. They made a wide circle around the room. Talag stood impassive by his chair.

'Great Talag!' shrilled Felthrup. 'Such a wise, brave lordship! The true leader of his clan!'

More ixchel surged into the loft, shouting in their sibilant tongue. Felthrup leaped over one spearpoint and sprinted past another – why didn't they just skewer him, a voice inside him wondered – and then the chair itself attacked him, or seemed to. He flipped over it, striking his head on the floor. He came to rest with his bad leg under him, agonisingly twisted.

Talag himself had thrown the chair. His foot was on Felthrup's neck, and the tip of his sword was pricking the tender flesh of the rat's inner ear. He leaned low, elbow bent for a downward thrust.

'I choose to yield,' said Felthrup.

'Choose!' said Saturyk. 'You mad little squealer! You've got no more choice than a fly on a frog's tongue!'

'Silence!' cried Talag. He bent his head close to Felthrup, nearly whispering. 'A leader, you call me? Witless animal. Look where I have led them. To ruin, to exile on this sand hill, or a hopeless return to a ship full of murderers. I pushed my son until he snapped and took on the role of a messiah. A role in which he killed my sister, and came close to killing everyone aboard, and fled at last into a living death himself. I drove him to those acts of despair, and then condemned him for his choices. A leader! You are preaching to a dead man, Master Felthrup. But this dead man will kill you all the same.'

Saturyk and the others closed in, swords and spears lowered in a deadly ring. Felthrup squeezed his eyes shut. How had he failed to understand? Talag was the one in despair. The man was too wise to deny the truth for ever; now it had caught up to him with crushing weight. But in one thing at least, Talag was still gravely mistaken.

'Your son has not given up the struggle,' Felthrup said. 'Nor did he go ashore in Masalym to die.'

A new fury contorted Talag's features. 'You know something of Taliktrum? Tell me. But breathe a false word and I will puncture your skull.'

'Will you let me return to the *Chathrand*?'

'No bargaining. Speak.'

'I do not bargain, I was merely curious,' said Felthrup. 'And anxious, I might add, in the spirit of full confession. Anxious that you not puncture my skull, Lord Talag, nor indeed my eardrum, which is more imminent, … but never mind, I digress. The fact is that your son *has* taken sides, Lord. Indeed he saved the life of Prince Olik in the Masalym shipyard, and that act has made all the difference. For it was Olik who then took the throne of Masalym, however briefly, and dispatched the expedition to slay Arunis and recover the Stone.'

'You know it was Taliktrum?'

'Unless there was another ixchel with a swallow-suit on the Masalym docks. Hercól was there; he witnessed it. Taliktrum swept down and slew the assassins before they could slit the prince's throat.'

Talag's eyes filled with wonder. 'My son. He saved the Bali Adro prince?'

'Far more than that. He stopped Arunis that night; he stopped the triumph of the death-force Arunis serves. Not for the sake of humans or dlömu or even ixchel. He did it for Alifros, my lord.'

Felthrup did not add that Sandor Ott had been present as well, nor that Taliktrum had vanished before the fight was through. *Let him think the best of his son. For all I know it might even be true.*

'Your noble sister,' he said carefully, 'used to speak of *idrolos*, the courage to see. That is what will keep your people alive. Nothing else will do, I think.'

Talag did not move for several seconds. Then he straightened, withdrawing the sword from Felthrup's ear, the foot from his neck. Felthrup rolled onto his feet, still encircled by weaponry. Talag gestured to Saturyk.

'Assist me.'

Together the two men walked to the square shape against the far wall, and tugged the oilskin aside. Beneath it were two stacks of human-sized books. All were battered, and most had water-damage. With great care Talag and Saturyk removed one from the stack and carried it nearer the window. It was a thin, attractive leather volume. Talag opened it and began turning pages almost the length of his body. Finding the desired page at last, he stepped up gingerly onto the book, knelt, and read aloud:

'It is just as well Ratty left us, after tasting the blood of the keel. He did not want to, of course. We had to convince him he was doing it for us – that he might find a way to send a ship here, a rescue party. But he was doing it for us, anyway, by all the Gods. Someone has to remember all this. Someone has to heal. And why should it not be Felthrup, who loves reading more than any human I have ever known?'

He looked across the room at Felthrup. 'You can guess who wrote those words, can you not?'

Felthrup nodded, weeping inside. Only one person had ever called him Ratty, and that was Fiffengurt. The quartermaster himself had written these lines. In the future.

No, he thought furiously, *in one future. Someone else's. This end is not inevitable. It cannot be.*

'He was still alive when we first passed through the doorway and found the wreck,' said Talag, 'but he did not live long. He had been alone for three years already. The others had perished one by one.'

'But what is he talking about?' Felthrup whispered. 'How, how did I leave? And the blood of the keel?'

Talag shrugged. 'A mystery, that. Where the wreck's keel is split you can see the heartwood, and it is indeed a rich, dark red – but we have not ventured to taste it. But as for how you left, that is easy. You used the clock, of course. You crawled through it to safety in another world.'

'It is here? Thasha's magic clock is here?'

Talag nodded. 'And today it is but an ordinary clock. We forced opened the hinged face, and saw only gears. Your escape seems to have exhausted its power at last.' Talag closed the book. 'You may earn the right to read any of these, Felthrup, with time and good behaviour.'

'My lord, I do not know when I shall have such a luxury.'

Saturyk smiled, but hid it quickly when his leader frowned. Talag glanced at Felthrup again.

'You tried to warn us of the Shaggat, and later of the sorcerer. I doubted you then, but time has shown which of us was in the right.'

Felthrup bowed his head.

'All the same, you have tried to keep faith with too many. You have tried to pick and choose, allying yourself with these giants and not others; these ixchel rather than those. Such efforts were doomed from the start. You have ended up on no one's side.'

'No one's mindlessly, Lord Talag. Of that fault I am happy to be accused.'

'I cannot permit you to return to the *Chathrand*,' said Talag. 'You are incautious by nature, and might well reveal our secret doorway to the giants. If they should ever find it we will be trapped here, marooned. I'm afraid you must be our guest until the end.'

Felthrup had foreseen this, and had readied half a dozen arguments. But the resolve in Talag's voice made him suddenly quail. He was about to gush nonsense. He bit his own foot, holding it in. *Babble not! Babble won't do, darling Felthrup. You must reach him some other way.*

Talag, no doubt shocked by Felthrup's silence, came forward and placed his hand on the rat's bowed forehead. '"*Unhappy the man must ever be who confuseth love and loyalty,*"' he said, clearly reciting from memory. 'That is from one of our greatest poems.'

'In whose translation?'

'Mine,' said Talag. 'Come, rat; I have a last thing to show you.'

Ordering his guards to follow, he led Felthrup down from the loft and out of the building. There he paused and spoke to the clan in the ixchel tongue. The crowd began to disperse, studying

Felthrup as they went. Talag marched through them, leading Felthrup back among the trees.

They started off in the direction of the wreck, but at a certain point Talag left the trail and began to climb a steep ridge. Felthrup climbed easily enough, but the ixchel struggled, for there was as much loose sand as soil underfoot, and the wind grew stronger at each step.

As they neared the crest of the ridge, Talag glanced back over his shoulder. 'The expedition was never heard from again,' he said. 'On that point Fiffengurt's journals are quite clear. Pathkendle, Thasha Isiq and the others never rejoined the crew, and thus were saved the horror of the wreck.'

'Why do you tell me this?' asked Felthrup.

Talag was silent. But a moment later Felthrup saw the beginnings of an answer. They had reached the edge of the trees, and before them lay the burial yard.

It had been laid out so neatly: thirty or forty graves marked with little rock cairns, each with a square ballast brick at its foot. And there were not one but two walls against the wind: the failed wooden fence and a lower rock wall, still standing but half-buried in sand. The graves too were vanishing: some of the cairns barely poked above the drifts.

With his heart in his mouth, Felthrup crept into the yard. He did not want to be here. These deaths were not his shipmates'. This Alifros was not his own. When he departed it would close behind him like an evil eye, and he would not remember it – not think of it – not let it live in memory.

'That's old Druffle, straight ahead,' said Saturyk.

DOLLYWILLIAMS DRUFFLE. Felthrup could just read the letters carved in the soft stone of the ballast brick. Felthrup made the sign of the Tree, then shuffled quickly away. The ixchel, he saw, had not entered the burial yard: Talag was directing them to take up position around the perimeter. Death rites mattered enormously to the ixchel. Talag must have assumed that Felthrup would wish to pay his respects without delay. It was an honour, he supposed, that Talag had brought him here in person.

At long last he treats me as a woken soul.

Felthrup moved among the cairns. He could read few of the inscriptions: three decades of exposure to the elements had blurred most of the letters beyond recognition. But some were clear enough. Swift Dale, a tarboy – and yes, that was his brother Saroo's grave beside him. Banar Leef, the main-top man. Jervik Lank, the tarboy who had bullied Pazel cruelly, but in the end proved brave enough to change. Felthrup was not surprised by the words that ran beneath Jervik's name: A Man to Trust.

Then Saturyk caught his eye and beckoned. He was standing upon the stone wall, along the side of the yard facing the sea. Nervously, Felthrup leaped up upon the wall himself and began to approach. The ruined *Chathrand* sprawled below them, the single rope still stretched taut between the beach and the topdeck rail. But Saturyk was pointing to the grave at his feet.

'I've swept it clean for you,' he shouted over the wind.

The cairn was tucked right into the corner of the yard. The brick was disappearing under sand again already: Saturyk's efforts were being undone. Felthrup bent low and read:

Pazel Undrabust

He looked at Saturyk, then back at the marker. The name was clearly carved. 'What – who?' he shouted, frightened and confused.

'Marila's child,' said Saturyk. 'Born at sea, died on this sand heap. It's all in that journal, how she and Neeps chose names together, on their wedding night. Pazel, for a boy, and if it had been a girl—'

'Don't tell, don't tell me please! No more!' Felthrup cast himself down, giving way to his misery. *Her child!*

Saturyk stood awkwardly above him. 'Oh, buck up, now,' he said. 'That's no way to honour the fallen – see here, I didn't mean—'

From across the burial yard, Talag shouted what could only have been a reprimand. Saturyk protested loudly, pointing at the grave, making sweeping motions with his hands. Felthrup could almost feel the little body, so close to him, floating face up beneath him in the sand. Pazel Undrabust. A miracle, snuffed out.

Then Felthrup gasped. He was hearing it, small and imperious: the voice of the dead. *Run*, was all the child told him. And Felthrup obeyed.

He was twenty feet down the dune-face before he heard Saturyk's cry of rage. Then a hiss: the blurred shape of a spear bit the sand beside his paw. He ran as he had not done since the maiming of his paw, rolling when he fell, leaping when he recovered. Speed was everything, speed his one chance. He was faster than the little people on sand, on rope. But not on the deck, not ever. And two of the guards carried bows.

The wind brought snatches of their cries. He did not look back. Another spear flew past him, so close he had to swerve around it when it struck. Then he reached the broken anchor and began to scramble up the rope.

The first gust of wind nearly threw him down. He flailed with claws and teeth, and just managed to scramble back atop the twisted cord. The ixchel were close behind him, the archers taking aim. Felthrup scrambled up the rope in a frenzy.

A hand closed on his hind leg. Saturyk had leaped, six times his own height or more. Felthrup was pulled upside down. He whirled and bit, tasting ixchel blood, and Saturyk fell cursing to the sand.

He climbed faster. Beneath him, sand gave way to breakers, seething around the Great Ship. A fall now would be lethal. But the wind that had nearly killed him was now saving his life: the archers' shots were hopelessly astray.

He was falling! They had cut the rope from below! Screaming, Felthrup plummeted towards the sea. For an instant he seemed to be racing above the surf, like a skimmer about to catch a fish. Then the black shape of the hull blocked out the sky. He struck: red agony. The waves boiled over him, and he cried out defiance of death.

When the wave-surge passed he was against the hull, still gripping the rope, still in command of his limbs. He climbed. Nothing was broken, and even the pain was a distant thing. New shouts from ixchel: they had thought him dead for certain. Arrows fell around him, none too close.

Saturyk was screaming at his archers, abusing them. Felthrup was forty feet above the water, then sixty, then over the rail.

He looked back. The ixchel were milling at the surf's edge, racing back when the foam advanced, trying for impossible shots. Only Talag remained on the hilltop, motionless on the rock wall, watching.

'You see, Mr Saturyk, there are always choices,' shouted Felthrup.

'*Palluskudge*! Bastard!' Saturyk howled. 'You're mucking dead!'

'Not in this world,' Felthrup shouted back. Then he turned and ran for home.

9

The Editor Confronts Death

I had better let the cat out of the bag and confess that I do not love everyone equally. On certain figures in this narrative it is difficult to lavish warmth. Say what you like about their upbringing, their acquaintance with hunger, the bad company they kept in formative years: they are bad, they are hideous; and the sooner I can wash my hands of them, the better.

This morning a young man tried to kill me. He was a rude fellow and I did not treat him gently; but I did not kill him, either, and have worried since that this was a mistake. He may avoid me, forget me even; or he may return with others who know how the job is done.

It was early, the garden shadows still deep and promising, the flycatchers lancing above the roofs. Students in the Academy trudged by at the street corner, barely awake. I was feeling vigorous, if a little guilty. I had chosen to set my book aside and go walking, with a little hound for company and my ancient cane to lean on. There was a time when I made such choices easily, thoughtlessly. One plucks the last roses of the season with more attention than the first.

My would-be killer stepped out of a bush – fell out of it, really – and swept the dust and leaves from his jacket. He was well fed and short and perhaps a little cross-eyed. Chewed fingernails. Beginner's beard. The dog wagged its foolish tail.

'Professor!' cried the man, as though delighted by a chance encounter. He smiled a covert little smile to which I naturally took offence.

'The dog bites,' I said.

'Such a *distinct* pleasure!' he declared, ignoring my warning. His smile implied that we already shared a secret. He might even have groped for my hand, but one was in my pocket, the other fingering the cane with what I hoped was obvious intent.

I am very old and my face is disfigured. I draw stares but scarcely mind them. Either a person knows me, in which case he is humble and discreet; or he has never heard of me, in which case he is frightened and discreet. There are no catcalls or screaming children – yet. When I begin to move about on all fours it may be another matter.

This man was determined to show no disgust. He had a way of both looking and not looking at me. I gazed past him down the alley.

'My name is—' he began. And then, as if a more dramatic possibility had just occurred to him: 'My name is unimportant.'

'Quite so,' I agreed, and hobbled on.

I am occasionally sociable (hail falls occasionally in summer) but my time is too dear to squander on cheap theatrics. Today I had to write a difficult letter to my patrons about the state of *The Chathrand Voyage*. The bedclothes needed laundering, too, and my skin was itchy, aflame. My bones ached as they do all the time; walking soothes this misery, and others.

The man chuckled, but the sound died when he saw how swiftly I was leaving him behind. I may rely on the cane but I am a champion hobbler.

'Professor, wait!' He caught up to me and blocked my path. 'You haven't seen what I brought you.'

With a sly grin he drew some pages from his vest pocket and waved them at me, like a treat for which I could reasonably be expected to beg. Angry now, I sidled past him again, and he pouted.

'Can't you spare me a moment, sir? I waited hours in that hedge.'

'Hedge!'

I stopped short. Then I bit my tongue and looked at him, smouldering. He had tricked me into granting him my full attention.

Such a low tactic. To refer to a single, fruit-bearing, once-potted, certainly solitary plant as a *hedge*: intolerable, intolerable.

'If this is about demonology class, you've waited in vain. Professor Holub has taken over my teaching chair. Holub, with the dimples. The one the girls follow about.'

'I don't want demonology, Professor. I know exactly who you are, and—' his voice dropped to reverential tones '—who you *were*. In the Old World. In the beginning.'

Then I knew. He was one of the crazies, the fanatics who had decided (out of boredom, out of hope?) that *The Chathrand Voyage* was a sort of key to Creation, a guide to the universe and all it contained. One of my 'assistants' (a famished schemer with garlic breath) had planted the idea among the younger students, and like a virile weed it had proven impossible to kill.

'Listen,' I said, 'the *Voyage* is just a history. Old, long-winded, violent and obscure. There are others. The library is stuffed with them.'

'They told me you were modest,' he said. 'How could you be otherwise, when you knew *them*? The Heroes. In the flesh.'

'You refer to my shipmates?'

He nodded, awestruck.

'Dead,' I told him. 'All dead, every last one of them. Dead for centuries.'

'Not all,' he said, gazing on me as one might a relic in a tomb. Suddenly I was afraid he wanted to touch me, and backed away a step.

'I'll join them soon enough,' I said. 'Anyway, why can't you take a history for what it is, instead of whipping it up like a blary custard—'

'A whatty custard?'

'—into a religion, a myth? You lot amaze me. These were real people; they lived and breathed. They're not symbols, not lessons for your moral improvement. You make me wonder if the chancellor isn't right to want the whole manuscript tossed on the fire.'

'Of course he's not right!' cried the young man, trembling. 'So it's true, then, you're fighting with the chancellor? Has he really tried to censor parts of the *Voyage*? Why, why would he do such a thing?'

To the first question I replied that the chancellor and I never fought. To the second: yes, he tried. To the third: because he is a spineless man who does not wish this hallowed school to be engulfed in scandal, or even controversy. A coward, that is. A glad-hander, with everything to lose but self-respect, which was lost beyond retrieval before he ascended to his current post.

'And now, good day.' I moved to tip my hat, then recalled that I had left it behind, since the changing shape of my skull had made it uncomfortable. I walked on, but the young man pranced beside me, brandishing those grubby sheets.

'You must protect it from him,' he said. 'No other tale contains such wisdom, such *meaning*, such burning truths about the world gone by. Professor, admit it, won't you? My friends and I have guessed the truth anyway. You're telling the lost history of our race. The Heroes, they're our ancestors, the ones who founded our nation and our people, the blessed seed from which we sprang!'

I shook my head, but he ignored me, rhapsodising. 'Let it all be told! Let the world drink of their wisdom – drink deep, and feel the menace of the Swarm, the black fire of the eguar, the thousand beauties of Uláramyth! The tale must be published in all its glory! It must see the light of day!'

'If it's as dear to you as all that,' I said, 'why are you robbing me? The Uláramyth chapter isn't even finished yet. You've seen a stolen copy, you atrocious little grub.'

His mouth opened wide. My accusation had caught him off guard.

'I am not a grub,' he said, 'and if you'll permit me, it is only thanks to a so-called *stolen copy* – and what is stealing, Professor, really? – that I am here today. I've brought you a warning. You've made a terrible mistake.'

'Mistake?' I said. 'How could you possibly know if I made a mistake? Who the devil are you?'

'I speak,' he said, placing a hand on his chest, 'on behalf of the Greysan Fulbreech Self-Improvement Society.'

I blinked at him. 'A student club? A joke fraternity of some sort?'

'I am the Society's president.'

'You're a cuckoo bird.'

'We are the Sons of Fulbreech,' he said. 'He is the true and rightful Hero, and we knew it from the start. Of all your shipmates, only Fulbreech never slumbered, never waited for things to happen to *him*. He *made* history. He took matters in his own hands. When Thasha warmed to him and discarded Passive Pathkendle, we cheered. We knew that she and Fulbreech were destined to be father and mother to us all.'

I pushed by him, wincing as our shoulders bumped. There was no hope whatsoever in words.

He kept pace with me easily. 'Have you read the epic called *The Choices of Yung Fulbrych?*'

Idiotic question. My first published manuscript was, and remains, the definitive refutation of the *Choices*. 'That thing,' I hissed, walking faster, 'was written two centuries ago, to flatter a despot. Fulbreech died *two thousand* years ago. The author had no notion of what that boy's life and death amounted to – nor much curiosity, either. It is no record of our time on the *Chathrand*. It is a heap of bad verse, penned in the service of bigoted power and bamboozeldry, not revelation or learning.'

He was visibly mortified. I clicked my tongue. 'You object – to what? The notion that I was a witness, that I've been displaced in time?'

'Oh, no.'

'That your hero died? Pitfire, man, what do you think Fulbreech was? A visiting demigod? The angel of Rin?'

The lunatic shook his head. 'It is all right that you kill him, in your tale. We know he was mortal, though his aura, his essence – never mind, sir, that can wait. But the death you paint in Book Three! Unworthy, sir, unworthy. Greysan Fulbreech could not meet such an end. Have you never once reconsidered?'

'Reconsidered? I can't even *follow* you. That statement makes no sense.'

'Or perhaps,' said the man with a sudden twinkle, 'you're planning to bring him back? Perhaps his death was an illusion?'

I was starting to feel like a drowning man.

'So you stole a copy of the fourth volume,' I said slowly, assembling the pieces, 'hoping to read that Fulbreech had … come back?'

'Or never died, never died! The Infernal Forest was a place of illusions, wasn't it? Say it, Professor! You can trust me; I won't breathe a word.'

'Arunis broke his back, and left him in a tank of fungal acid. Then a dlömic boy drove Hercól's sword straight through his gut. He died.'

The man wilted where he stood. He stared unfocused at my chest. Almost inaudibly, he murmured, 'Those last words you say he spoke. They're false too, of course. They make him sound weak and mean and frightened.'

He shook himself, then barked at me: 'A villain, that's what you've turned him into. And that is a lie! Passive Pathkendle – what is he? A lucky fool, a sap. Fulbreech is Will Incarnate. Redeem him, reward him!' He waved the paper in my face. 'Professor, we of the Society have written four possible endings to *The Chathrand Voyage*. We ranked them for your convenience, but any one of them would be acceptable, provided – *Ouch!*'

My cane was stout ironwood, and I had brought it down hard on his toe. He hopped around me, squeezing his foot. My anger was only stoked by the ridiculous sight.

'I do not *invent*, sir. I was given access, nothing more. Access to the past, my own past, the one I shared with them. I write it, sort it, add the odd footnote when I must. I am not some wretched novelist, rubbing my hands together, spewing diversions for a penny a page! Believe what you like, worship whom you like. Just leave me in peace. My days are numbered, my hands are changing shape; my incisors bleed on the pillow at night.' I snatched his pages, shredded them, tossed the bits over my shoulder. 'Let me finish the story. After that you can do as you please. Forward, Jorl.'

I hobbled on. The man stood rooted to the spot. I turned the corner into the boulevard, saw the first bustle of students on the lawn – saw Holub himself, in his mob of nubile demonologists. I closed my eyes. Of all the weird marvels of this body, lust was the most pointless and intractable. I wondered if it would be the last to go.

Then Jorl snarled. I twisted, and the knife in the hand of the president of the Greysan Fulbreech Self-Improvement Society missed my cheek by a hair.

My nascent transformation has certain benefits, among them dexterity and strength. My leap amazed him, and hurt me terribly, but I landed squarely and had at him with the cane. He crumpled, all but falling into the dog's mouth, and for a few priceless seconds little Jorl could have been a mastiff like his namesake. The fool dropped the knife. His head was unprotected; I could have cracked it like an egg. Instead I hauled him up and shook him.

'Listen, fool. I write the truth as I knew it. Not what you prefer in your fever-dreams, nor the chancellor in his cowardice, nor the Young Scholars in their fashionable savagery, nor I in my pain. Fulbreech was a poisonous toad. You'll sanctify him over my dead body. Get hence.'

I shoved him away. The man fled, stumbling and bleeding, and Jorl chased him all the way across the lawn.

Historians battle for the future, not the past. Our tales of who we were shape what we believe we can become. When I began to write, the story of the *Chathrand* was a collection of fragments and folk-tellings, yarns shared at bedtime or beer-time, or Rin spare us, to prove some moral point. It was a myth; and now as copies circulate it may become scripture, for a benighted few. The chancellor would gild it, peddle it with nine parts sugar to one part truth. Or else burn it and bury me. I must work faster, before I cease to have hands, before he calls a doctor or a dogcatcher and has me led away. I must finish the tale, lest they finish it for me. And that would be horrific, a mashed-together monster, a lord or lady with the head of a beast.

10

Sanctuary

15 Modobrin 941
244th day from Etherhorde

When they realised that the selk had fed them mushrooms, Lunja and the Turach began to fight. The selk were ready, however: blindingly fast, they pounced on the two soldiers, seized their limbs, heads, jaws. Neither managed to spit the fungus out.

Ensyl watched, appalled. Bolutu succumbed first: eyes wide, he raised both hands as though trying to pluck fruit from a tree; then his knees gave way and he toppled gracefully into the arms of a selk. Pazel followed, then Thasha and Big Skip. Dastu laughed viciously before he dropped.

The others had time to sit down. Before his eyes closed, Hercól turned to Ensyl and reached out suddenly, his face full of longing. Ensyl drew a sharp breath. She had rarely been so unsettled by a look.

It was done; only she and Ramachni were awake. Thaulinin looked at the mink. 'I will not waste words on you, Arpathwin. You will sleep when you wish to, and not before.' He turned to where Ensyl stood backed against the wall. 'But for you it is time, lady.'

He beckoned, and a selk came forward holding a strange object. It was about the size of whisky jug, but made of hide stretched over a round wooden frame. At one end the leather thongs had yet to be tightened, leaving an opening like the mouth of a cave.

'A palanquin?' asked Ensyl dubiously.

'But without windows, alas,' said the selk. 'We lined it with the fur of last night's hare. You will find a water flask within, and food as well.'

'How long will I be held?'

'Not long,' said Thaulinin, 'and you will be most comfortable.'

Ensyl shook her head. *You're wrong there, giant.* It was quite true what she had said about her people and cages. Yet she had argued for this choice, and would not be the only one of the party to back down. Taking a deep breath, she bent to squeeze through the opening.

'I must ask for your sword,' said Thaulinin.

His request was reasonable: Ensyl could gouge a spyhole with a single thrust. All the same it was hard, unbuckling the tattered baldric, repaired so many times since Etherhorde. She felt naked as she laid the sword on Thaulinin's palm.

'I think I will travel with you, Ensyl,' said Ramachni.

'There is no need, Arpathwin,' said Thaulinin. 'You are no stranger here.'

'And yet I hardly resemble the Arpathwin of long ago,' said Ramachni. 'Nor do all your people know me, in any form. Besides, I also wish to be carried like a lump.'

Ensyl was delighted, even though the fit was rather tight when they had both crawled inside. Thaulinin bent to look through the opening.

'Two warnings, then,' he said. 'You must use no magic of any kind until we release you. And do not call to us, unless one of you should be dying. That is vital. You would place yourselves and all your friends in danger if you forced us to release you early.'

He closed the aperture, and Ensyl felt him tie the leather thongs. Then they were lifted and placed inside a sack of some kind. All was dark and close. Their little fur-lined room swayed, and by its motion Ensyl sensed that they were now dangling from a sling. Ramachni chuckled in the darkness. 'We shall make this journey like a pair of royals,' he said.

Or a pair of grouse, Ensyl thought. Aloud, she said, 'I am glad of your company.'

'I hope you are still glad when my fleas discover you,' said the mage.

They were already moving. Ensyl thought they must surely be descending the hill, but the selk carried them so smoothly that it was hard to be sure. The palanquin did not swing wildly about, or even tilt a great deal. She *was* comfortable, in fact.

'I could almost sleep,' she said aloud.

'You must certainly sleep,' said Ramachni. 'After all, we shall be in here for days.'

'Days!'

'When Thaulinin said, "Not long," he was speaking as a selk. Never mind; I shall do my best to entertain you. And don't bother to bend your voice, by the way: these ears of mine can catch your ixchel-speech perfectly well.'

She could hear the muffled sound of selk voices, and even more faintly, their feet. They were running through that hardscrabble landscape – running with a burden of eleven humans and dlömu, presumably – and yet she felt as though the palanquin were drifting on an untroubled stream. Ensyl had no sense at all of how far they had gone, and in the changeless dark she soon lost track of time as well. There were very few clues: a laugh, a soft command, the noise of a waterfall, a whiff of cool spray penetrating the sack.

'Ramachni,' she asked, 'have you been there before? The place they're taking us?'

'I cannot answer you,' he said. 'Indeed, you had better ask me nothing about our destination, for what binds the selk tongue binds mine also. But perhaps we should speak of other matters, while we may.'

'If you mean to ask me where my clan-brethren on the *Chathrand* disappeared to—'

'Dear me, lass! Nothing could have been further from my mind. No, I had quite another concern. I am thinking of your mistress, Diadrelu.'

Ensyl froze. 'What about her?' she managed to ask.

'She is in Agaroth, the halfway-land, the Border-Kingdom

through which the dead must journey, before they gain their final rest. Nearly all pass through it in a heartbeat or two – like birds, or shadows of birds, they flit over its twilight hills, and are gone. Your mistress descended, seized a branch, stilled the natural flight of her soul. To do this requires magnificent strength, which Diadrelu Tammariken had in abundance.'

'Yes.'

'And it requires something further, Ensyl. I think you know what I shall say. It requires love.'

Ensyl hugged herself in the darkness. She hoped Ramachni could not see the way he had in the Infernal Forest. She hoped he was as blind as she was herself.

'My mistress loved well,' she said. 'Hercól was a strange choice, a choice that would have brought her suffering, even in peacetime, if she had lived. But you know how it happens.'

'Do I?'

'There's a song,' said Ensyl, and recited:

> *One path through endless pathways, one string unwound from birth,*
> *Through the mountains or the marshlands, over blest or barren earth,*
> *One lover from the multitude, one seedling on the plain,*
> *It is the heart that chooses for us, and who may ask it to explain?*

'That is a human song. My mother heard me sing it once, and slapped me. But it made no difference; I sang it to myself all the more. And that's the point, you see. The heart goes its own way. You can reason with it a little. Not very much.'

'That is true of human beings generally,' said the mage.

Ensyl laughed aloud. 'We ixchel are exactly the same. My mistress used to call me headstrong, but who in Alifros was more headstrong than she? No one could turn her from a task. She would drive herself past all exhaustion, past the time when even the strongest of the young folk had gone to their rest, and then look at me suddenly and say, "Very well, I have dawdled long enough; it is time to start working." Do you know, I had to stand with my back to the door to make her eat? At day's end, when she bathed, I'd hide her trousers, offer her nightclothes only, or she would go out for a third or fourth patrol. Limits were for other people, not for Dri. I begged her to stay clear of Taliktrum, I warned her that he would strike—'

Ensyl broke off, or rather her voice quit of its own accord. There was a wall inside her, solid bricks in the back of her mind.

'Diadrelu loved you like a daughter, Ensyl,' said Ramachni.

'That's not what I wanted,' Ensyl heard herself say. 'I had a mother, she was a wine drunkard; she left us to join another clan when I was ten. I didn't need more mothering, Ramachni. I wanted Dri to love me as a mate.'

Ramachni lay still. *No tears, no tears*, thought Ensyl wildly. But how had he done it? How had he pulled those words out of her – those thoughts, forbidden and precious, the ones she never allowed out of her own stifling little cave? How had he made her know?

'Of all … curious things to tell a mage,' said Ramachni at last.

'You broke his rule,' said Ensyl. 'No magic, Thaulinin told you. But you did some anyway. You breathed a spell onto me.'

'You're wrong there, lass. I only listened. There is a greater magic at work here than my own, and that too we may call by the name of love. But why this shame? Does your kind condemn this kind of longing?'

'Yes. Oh, they'd not admit it – that would make us no better than most giants, and worse than some. For every human short-coming you'll find an ixchel ready to swear that we have no such problem. But in this case no one would breathe a word about it.'

'I have heard it said that ixchel do not speak of love.'

'Rarely the feeling,' said Ensyl, 'and never the act. *Some things aren't for telling* – that is all an ixchel will tell you. And I'm no different. I don't want to speak of what happens in the dark. Yes, I am ashamed. There is an order to our lives that the giants cannot comprehend; there are bonds between us that cannot be broken or changed. Dri took me as a student. I wanted more. That is greed, and unforgivable. Because we *are* different from humans in one way. The heart chooses, yes – but our heart is shared.'

'The clan above the self, is it?'

'Always.'

Ramachni sighed. Ensyl waited for him to say more, to reveal why he had felt it necessary to torture her thus with thoughts of Diadrelu. But the silence held, and the pain lay heavy on her, and fleeing it she tumbled into sleep.

How long that sleep lasted she did not know. Dreams assaulted her in fragments, waking moments came and went. She felt like a smooth stone rolled along a riverbed by a stream without end, without pity, over the rounded, polished details of her life. The palanquin swayed, the selk laughed faintly; the warm fur became Dri's hair as she scrubbed it, in the little herring-tin bathing tub on the *Chathrand*. Her mistress reached up and grasped her hand, soap-slippery fingers interlaced, she could have died of bliss in that moment. The palanquin shifted. Diadrelu was gone.

'A shared heart,' said Ramachni, as if no time had passed at all. 'That is a lovely idea, whether fact or communal fancy. But now I must tell you what I fear is occurring. Dri has stopped in Agaroth of her own free will. And Arunis is there with her, and they are fighting.'

'Fighting over what?'

'Over the fate of Alifros, and the outcome of our struggle. It is an unequal fight, of course. A mage has certain powers even in death. But take heart, for in Agaroth they are closer to equals than they ever were in life. And Diadrelu arrived long before Arunis, and has had time to prepare.'

'Prepare for what?'

'I do not know, Ensyl. I have journeyed through many worlds, but none so strange as the Border-Kingdom. Time and thought are different there. One comes to know things suddenly, and to find things merely by thinking of them, and yet losing and for-getting come just as quickly. And always one senses the nearness of that terrible wall at the edge of the kingdom, the seething wall, beyond which is death.

'As for Diadrelu, she is no slave to the sorcerer, though clearly it was through his power that she appeared beside our bonfire in the clearing. He offered her that chance, meaning to appal and sicken us with her agony – and in that he succeeded, of course. But he never counted on her strength. Even impaled, Dri spoke to us, warned us that Arunis is once more being aided by Sathek the Vile. Well, Arunis will not make that mistake again. Dri, however, will keep on trying to help us, to reach out to us. I do not know if she will find another means – but if she does, it will be through those she loved the best. So I must ask you, as I have asked Hercól, to be watchful. Look for her, listen for her. She might come at any time.'

'Or—'

'Never. That is possible too.'

Ensyl lay down on the pelt, curling on her side like an infant. Which was worse: to see her mistress as before, knowing she was dead and suffering or never to see her again? Ensyl felt a sudden, gut-twisting desire for the Nilstone: to touch it, to be obliterated, reduced to an absence, a negative, something that could not feel or think. *Look for her, listen for her.* The mage's request merely changed her curse into an obligation. She was already haunted by Dri; now she had to welcome that haunting, pry the wound open whenever it started to heal.

'I regret the pain I have caused you,' said Ramachni.

'You did not cause it,' said Ensyl. 'It was there already. Don't you understand that much? Ramachni, do mages take no partners, ever?'

'We do not, unless we cease to be mages.'

'And before? Were you never in love?'

When Ramachni answered her his voice was oddly hesitant. 'I will tell you this much. The life I lived before is gone, irretrievably gone. It is like the memory of a story – or a sailor's journal, perhaps. It resides whole and complete in my memory, but behind a wall of crystal through which no heat or sound may pass.'

'I'm sorry.'

'Yes, but I am not. My road has led far from that quiet beginning. I am myself. The life before was another's.'

He said no more, and Ensyl closed her eyes. Mercifully, oblivion found her again. This time it was far deeper and longer. She had many dreams, many half-wakings, and behind them all was a strange feeling of forgiveness, of sympathy for the folly of her kinfolk, even deluded Lord Taliktrum, whom Myett had loved with as much ferocity as she, Ensyl, had loved Taliktrum's aunt. Foolish Myett. But in the end, less foolish than Ensyl herself. She had at least confessed her love; Ensyl had hidden, smothered, her own. What if Ramachni was right to doubt the ixchel way? What if the one unforgivable thing was not her love for Dri, but her silence?

I will become a mage. I will transcend this life, set it in crystal, place it on a high shelf where it need never be touched.

Stillness. Ensyl rubbed her eyes. The selk were talking; the palanquin was resting on the ground. A moment later the thongs were loosed and sunlight poured through the opening. 'Come out, travellers,' said Thaulinin. 'You have missed all the rain.'

Out they climbed, stiff and dazzled. They were in a stone tunnel, low and round and stretching away in two directions as far as Ensyl could see. The tunnel was unlit, but its roof was pierced at regular intervals by smooth holes, and it was through these that the sunlight poured. About half the selk from Thaulinin's band were here. So was their party, though they yawned, and looked unsteady on their feet.

'Have we … arrived?' asked Pazel.

'Almost,' said Thaulinin, 'and that is good, for you were starting to toss and turn inside the slings by which we carried you. Can you manage these last three miles?'

The travellers assured him that they could, although Ensyl had her doubts. Thaulinin gestured to Nólcindar, who held up a bundle of green cloth, tied firmly with a rope. 'That is your special burden,' said Thaulinin. 'It is surprisingly heavy, for such a small thing. Who will carry it?'

The travellers looked at each other uneasily. The question had yet to arise. 'Be so good as to bear it these last miles,' said Hercól finally. 'We are … not quite ourselves. I for one am dizzy, and have the feeling that I have forgotten something, or several things perhaps. You drugged us, did you not?'

'With your consent,' said Nólcindar, 'though you were reluctant, truth be told.'

The hunting dog leaned wearily against Lunja's calf. 'You even drugged poor Shilu,' said Lunja, bending to caress the animal.

'And carried him,' said Thaulinin. 'He is not woken, but any animal can become so. And those who do retain their earlier memories, animal though they are. We can take no chances, in this troubled age.'

'I feel like I've slept for weeks,' said Thasha. 'How long was the journey, really?'

'Not weeks,' said Thaulinin, and his tone made it plain that he would say no more.

'But Thaulinin, where is Dastu?' asked Ramachni suddenly. 'I hope you did not forget him back at Sirafstöran Torr?'

A dark murmur passed among the selk. 'Do not jest,' said Thaulinin. 'The youth deceived us. He only feigned swallowing the mushroom, and the sleep it should have brought. When darkness fell on the first day of our journey, we rested atop a deep defile, and laid you all down in rows. He must have been watching through slitted eyes. As we lay there we heard the *maukslar* bellowing, far behind us on the Torr. We all turned, fearing the demon might come hurtling out of the peaks, despite the care we took to hide our trail. And it was while we were thus distracted that your companion rose and slipped away. We gave chase, but the defile branched into many chasms, and the bottom-lands were wooded and black. All the same I marvel that he escaped us. He must have run almost as fast and silently as one of my people.'

'What will you do?' asked Big Skip. 'Let him run?'

'By no means!' said Thaulinin. 'He can only work mischief, if he manages to stay alive. We will seek him high and low. This is my failure, and his capture will be my charge.'

'You may hunt long for him,' said Hercól. 'Dastu has great talents as a spy.'

'But no talent for trust,' said Nólcindar. 'He would have found only healing and friendship among us. I wonder where his suspicious nature will lead him. To our enemies? Can he have more faith in their mercy than our own?'

'The Secret Fist does not teach mercy,' said Hercól. 'Only power, and sometimes power means striking a bargain. Dastu has just one thing to bargain with: his knowledge of our mission. If he chooses to betray us to our enemies, he can.'

'There will be no *choosing*, if the *Duirmaulc*-Dweller* seizes him in its claws,' said Nólcindar. 'His mind will be shorn open, and his knowledge taken as a bear takes honey from the comb.'

'I think I want to go back to sleep,' muttered Pazel.

Thaulinin looked at him. 'Take heart,' he said. 'Twice before in my life I have seen Alifros brought to the edge of ruin, and twice before we clawed away from the precipice. And no matter what is to come, there remain the stars.'

'I just can't work out how that's supposed to be comforting,' said Pazel. 'The stars business, I mean.'

Thaulinin smiled. 'Perhaps one day you will. But whatever the future brings, you will be safe for a time in Uláramyth.'

Uláramyth! The word struck Ensyl like a thunderclap. She had heard it before, hadn't she? Where, when? She could not place it at all, and yet it felt intensely familiar, suddenly, like the name of some home or haven visited as a child, a place where she had been happy; a place lost early in life and never glimpsed again. The name had stirred a response in the others as well, she saw: there was a sudden radiance about them. She might almost have called it hunger.

---

*Here Nólcindar uses the correct term *Duirmaulc* (Auru, 'place of last curses') to refer to the bottom-most pit of the infernal Nine. Students of demonology, take note: Holub's *Dermac* is a vulgar corruption.

'Uláramyth,' said Ramachni. 'You have freed my tongue to speak the name. And to think I feared never to see it again.'

'You've been there?' said Corporal Mandric, shaking his head. 'Any place you *haven't* been?'

'I have been there, also,' said Thasha.

The others looked at her, startled, and Ramachni's dark eyes gleamed. 'Not you, Thasha,' he said.

A look of distance and distraction had come over Thasha. Pazel and Neeps drew close to her: they were all too familiar with that look. Thasha did not even glance at them. 'I've been there,' she insisted. 'With you, Ramachni; don't you recall?'

The mage said nothing. Doubt flickered suddenly in Thasha's eyes. 'No,' she said, 'I'm just confused. Forgive me.'

'Some know the place with their hearts, before their feet ever touch its blessed soil,' said Thaulinin. 'But come and see for yourselves.'

Hercól knelt, offering his shoulder, and Ensyl bounded onto it, steadying herself as always with a fistful of his hair. The tunnel rose gradually, winding like a snake. They moved from one pool of sunlight to the next. She saw that each roof-hole was in truth a shaft leading upwards some ten or twenty feet, and ending in a riot of greenery: ferns, flowers, trailing vines.

'I know what this tunnel is,' said Bolutu. 'It is a lava tube. Is that not so?'

'Well guessed!' said Thaulinin. 'Yes, the blood-fire of the mountain formed this entrance-road, and others. We have been walking it in darkness for some hours already, carrying you. The shafts illuminate only the last few miles, where the jungle above is guarded. Soon we will pass under the mountain, and be in darkness again.'

'Is the jungle guarded by the selk?' asked Ensyl, peering up through a shaft.

'Not here,' said Thaulinin. He stopped and smiled. 'Climb up, if you will, and look around. But on your life, do not go beyond the shaft!'

Ensyl glanced at Hercól. 'I ... will look, if you'll indulge me,' she said.

The leap into the shaft was easy, as was catching hold of the lowest vines. Up she went, hand over foot. The sun warmed her, and a wet, fetid jungle smell filled her nostrils. When she finally raised her head above the shaft, she thought she had never seen such a lovely forest. By the height of the sun Ensyl knew it was midday, but the fierce beams slipped through only here and there, and cool shadows abounded. Every shade of green was here in abundance, caught in a thousand forms of leaf and shoot and stem and creeper. Bright droplets sparkled on leaf-tips, and gleamed in spiderwebs flung like a ship's rigging from tree to tree. Birdsong fell in great melodious threads; bees flowed like minnows through a sunbeam, and on an outflung limb dangled an orchid in brilliant, blood-red flower.

Then Ensyl's breath caught in her throat. Beyond the orchid hung row upon row of white, ropy vines, straight as piano wire, and as taut. She knew those vines, and the trees they were part of. She looked around, wildly: there! Huge grey trunks, towering over the lesser trees. Far above, those trunks would open in slitted mouths. And those vines, so innocent and still – they could tear a man apart.

She descended in a flash. Back on Hercól's shoulder, she gasped, 'The trees, those hideous trees from the Infernal Forest. They're here.'

'They are not hideous to the selk,' said Thaulinin. 'We have taught them manners, and a wider diet than flesh. For sixteen centuries they have secured this eastern approach to Uláramyth. They would not harm you if we stood at your side.'

They walked on, still climbing. The light shafts ended; one of the selk lit a lamp. Then came a great iron portcullis, barring their way. On the wall beside it was mounted an iron wheel, larger than the wheel of the *Chathrand*. Thaulinin took a key from about his neck and slipped it into a hole at the wheel's centre. He turned the key clockwise, then gripped the wheel and spun it in the opposite direction. After a moment it began to turn on its own. Gears clattered, counterweights rumbled in the walls. The wheel spun faster. The great gate began to lift.

When everyone had passed within, Thaulinin removed his key, and ducked inside as the gate slowly descended. On they marched, faster now. A few of the selk asked Thaulinin's leave to run ahead, which he granted.

They're as eager as children, Ensyl thought.

A light wind began to blow in the tunnel – and with it came a song. Ensyl felt her heart lift suddenly. The music was high and mirthful, quite unlike the Creation-Song the selk had played for them in the ruins, and yet for all its joy, there was a strangeness to the song that unsettled even as it gladdened her. She could not tell if it was being sung or played on some strange wind instruments, nor even *where* it came from: ahead of them, or behind, or both?

'I think the music is in the wind itself,' she whispered to Hercól.

'And the stone,' he replied, gesturing. Now Ensyl saw that there were many small holes in the tunnel surface, scattered at random, and perhaps the music did come from them, indeed. She saw Thasha, her face still strange and radiant, put her ear to the wall.

'I remember,' she said. 'The singing mountain. Just the same as before.'

The selk bearing the lamp glanced at her and smiled. 'This tunnel we call *Ingva,* the Flute. It always plays to welcome the return of old friends.'

He blew out the lamp. In the deep darkness, the selk took up the song, full-throated and glad. A hand touched Hercól's shoulder, guiding him. They walked on, and now the tune became both march and madrigal, a walking-chant and a song of praise.

At last a new light gleamed before them. The tunnel was ending. There was a carved chamber ahead, and stairs climbing up into daylight. Figures appeared, and raised their arms in welcome, but no one called out; no one interrupted the song. They reached the chamber; Ensyl shaded her eyes. They reached the sun-drenched stair, they climbed, she saw it: *Mother Sky,* she thought, *there is goodness in the world after all.*

It was what her heart felt, senseless though it might be. She clung to Hercól with both hands. Uláramyth was a great, green bowl, a hollow mountain, roofless and miles wide. *A fire-mountain, a volcano*: but the fire was long extinguished, and the crater teemed with life. They had passed through the wall of the mountain and stood halfway up the inner rim. Sweeping down and away from them was a lush land of jungle, streams, ponds, rice paddies, water wheels, citrus groves, white boulders, stone houses of fluid line and growing roofs, black horses, painted horses, flocks of restless birds, domes, towers, moss-green ruins, thickets of willow and bamboo. Parts of the crater wall sloped naturally; others were carved into great terraces, sweeping about the valley in concentric rings. Ensyl's eyes devoured it all, spread there below her like a table buckling under the weight of treasure. So much was starkly visible, and yet there were hiding places everywhere: dense woods, dark tunnel-mouths, fog on a distant lake.

The staircase had brought them out onto a marble landing surrounded by willow trees. Ensyl raised her eyes: the upper rim of the crater was a circle of barren, toothlike stones, the highest of them sparkling with ice. There were no gaps, no fissures: Uláramyth was completely enclosed.

From the landing where they stood, many footpaths and staircases led away – up and down, and horizontally along the terraces – and by all of these routes selk were approaching. They sang as they converged on the newcomers. Some, with faces aglow, clasped the arms of Thaulinin and his party. If any were shocked to find living humans in their midst, they gave no sign.

The song ended, and in the silence Nólcindar came forward and placed the Nilstone at Hercól's feet, making a deep *thump* like a cannonball dropped on the marble. For a moment everyone was still. Then another selk woman came forward with a water jug. She held it out to Lunja, who was nearest her.

'Peace and the stars attend you, citizen,' she said.

'Joy to your home and hearth-kin,' replied Lunja, startled. 'Yet I fear you are mistaken. I have never been here before.'

'You are citizens nonetheless,' said Thaulinin. 'All who pass the threshold of Uláramyth are granted citizenship, and none may deny them the same. But as for me, Tisani, you had best send for shackles, and conduct me to the Armoured Chamber. I will stand bond alone, if the Five allow it. The choice to bring these travellers here was mine.'

'You must certainly go,' said the woman sadly, 'and perhaps the others may remain at liberty for now. Yet all who walked with you must be judged alike.'

'What, straight to jail, for bringing us here?' said Neeps.

'It seems an unmerciful law, to punish such an act of charity,' said Hercól.

'These are unmerciful times,' said Thaulinin, 'but I would have you know that I do this gladly, and fear no injustice at the hands of my people.'

'Nor will your people fail you, Ambrimar's child,' said a voice from below the terrace.

All the selk turned, and made a curious gesture: head slightly bowed, hands raised and open, as though to offer them in service. A figure was climbing the staircase with slow dignity. He wore a dark green robe, and a chain of thick silver rings about his neck, and on his head was a circlet of woven vines. He was the first selk Ensyl had yet seen who looked truly old – not just ancient, as they all did, but weathered, worn smooth, his flesh like driftwood on a beach. Ensyl found herself awed: how many years did a selk have to live before they took such a toll?

'You shall not wear irons,' he said, 'and if I am heeded at the council, your stay in the Armoured Chamber will be brief.' His old eyes passed over the newcomers. 'Two dlömu, one ixchel – and eight human beings, wondrous to our sight. It is almost exactly as we were told.'

'Told?' said Pazel. 'Told by whom, sir, if you please?'

The elder turned back to the staircase, gesturing. Shilu growled.

A huge, snow-white animal padded up the stairs. It was a wolf, and when it stopped beside the selk its shoulder was level with his waist. The creature's jaws lolled open, showing white teeth. Unblinking green eyes studied the newcomers.

'By me, Pazel, if you must know.'

That voice! The wolf turned slightly – and Ensyl cried out, and flung herself from Hercól's shoulder, not caring how hard she landed. And Myett, from her perch on the wolf's back, did the same, and they met and embraced at the centre of the landing, overcome as ixchel rarely let themselves be. Myett was safe, whole, healed, and Ensyl kissed her hands and her forehead, asking no questions, needing no answers. *Uláramyth, Uláramyth, for this I love you already.*

For Pazel too, the sight of Myett was overwhelming. He rushed to greet her, along with Thasha, Neeps and Bolutu. He had never quite trusted Myett: she had played a part in Diadrelu's betrayal, after all. But she was one of them. She had tried to make amends by joining this expedition. And after so much death, she had returned to them alive.

Over their joyous shouts Myett was saying that she had been seized by a woken hawk, and had been here for two days already. Like the selk themselves, the hawk had been terribly suspicious, and had left her with a pair of selk who happened to be circling east around the Infernal Forest, while it flew on ahead to share her story with Thaulinin.

'The two he left me with got a shock when the bird came back and said Thaulinin had found you, and decided to bring you here, and that I should be carried on ahead. But they obeyed, and tied me up in black cloth like a bundle of sticks. It's a wonder they didn't smother me.'

Her habit of gripe had not changed, Pazel saw. And yet it had, for though the words were the same ones the old Myett might have spoken, there was no rancour in her voice, this time. 'Even when I arrived, the selk had their doubts,' she added. 'They thought I was one of Macadra's spies.'

'And we feared the same of your companions,' said Nólcindar.

'It was not an unreasonable fear,' said Thaulinin. 'Macadra has heard of Uláramyth, and hates it, for she knows that the power here is not her kind – not the power of fear and threat, but of healing and nurture. She knows too that those who fight for the Vale do so freely, and with full hearts, while her armies serve with broken hearts, in terror and derangement, and longing for the Empire that was. She dreams that one day the bloodied flag of Bali Adro will fly over Uláramyth.'

'While we live it never shall,' said the wolf. Pazel jumped, and looked again at those green eyes. *Woken* eyes: once you saw it, the intelligence, you wondered how you could have ever failed to.

'That is certain, Valgrif,' said the old selk, 'but who knows how long we shall live? For the fight is coming; the mountains are encircled. Since you left us the noose has tightened, Thaulinin, and every day new servants march eastwards from the river's mouth. Yet I am sorry, Myett of Ixphir House, that we have been forced to take such precautions.'

'No ixchel could ever condemn you for them,' said Myett. Turning to her fellow travellers, she said, 'This is Arim, second eldest of the Lords of Uláramyth. Lord Arim, these people are my … clan.'

Pazel looked at her, startled. Myett had struggled with the word, and he knew the weight of her choice. To an ixchel, 'family' would have meant far less.

Lord Arim gazed at them piercingly. His gaunt face and fine eyelash plumes made him look like an old bird of prey. 'You are people of the *Chathrand*,' he said, 'and that alone would mark you as heralds of great change. The *Chathrand*, Erithusmé's Great Ship. When last I saw her, the wizardess stood upon the forecastle, holding the chains of the demon Avarice. "I will take this one across the sea to a place of punishment, Lord Arim, and return before two summers pass, and dwell with you awhile in the Vale." So she declared, on that storm-swept morning. But neither she nor the *Chathrand* ever returned across the Ruling Sea. Until today.

'Your sister Myett has told us many things,' the old selk went on, 'but she too has her secrets. She would not name the burden you carry. I will not name it either, although I could. It is the darkest thing to enter here in many centuries.'

Thaulinin, chastened, bowed his head. 'We must speak of it soon, my lord,' he said.

'Yes,' said Arim, 'we must. For the present, take it to the home we have prepared for you, and keep it there, guarded and unseen. Do not unwrap it, or carry it about, unless an elder be with you. Now then, wizard.' He looked at Ramachni. 'Why do you not speak? For I think you are an old friend returned.'

'I am that,' said Ramachni, 'and your eyes are as keen as ever, Arim, to spy me out in this disguise. You may call me by the name you chose yourself, on the bloodied sands of Luhmor.'

Cries of joy and wonder rose from many of the selk. 'Arpathwin! Arpathwin has returned!' But there were cautious looks too, as though darker memories had been stirred by the name.

The white wolf padded nearer to the travellers, lowering his head and sniffing. 'Lord Arim, they are gravely hurt,' he said. 'The flame-trolls have burned them, and the poisons of the Infernal Forest are in their wounds.'

The old selk walked forward until he stood among them, and turned from one traveller to the next, and his eyes were grave. He looked a long time at Pazel, and even longer at Thasha. But when he came to Neeps a flicker of pain crossed his face.

'The youths are burning, wizard,' he said.

'But with different fevers,' said Ramachni. 'We have great need of your physicians, my lord.'

'Go down into the city,' said Lord Arim. 'What can be done shall be done.' He turned once more to Pazel. 'But you we shall carry, child of the North, for your wound makes walking a misery, I think.'

Again, Pazel shook his head. 'You're very kind, Lord Arim, but I can manage.'

The others tried to persuade him, but Pazel was steadfast. It was true that his leg hurt terribly, and the descent looked very steep. And yet he wanted desperately to walk. He put an arm over Neeps' shoulder. 'Just help me, once more,' he said.

'Go then, citizens,' said Lord Arim. 'Valgrif will escort you, and keep me informed of your progress. Thaulinin, you may walk with them until your paths diverge.'

The wolf looked at the ixchel. 'You may ride together, if you like,' he said.

With Myett and Ensyl clinging to his back, the wolf led them downhill, by stairs and sloping paths. The way was narrow at first, and they walked single file, passing over bridges, along raised boardwalks through the rice paddies, beside small streams that trickled down from the heights. At times Valgrif led them through tunnels, where Pazel saw stairs and corridors leading deeper into the earth. Most of the time, however, they walked in bright sunlight. The paths grew wider, the descent less steep. They marched for half a mile through a stand of ancient oaks, where fat acorns snapped underfoot, and unseen creatures scurried in the brush.

Pazel's leg now ached unremittingly, and yet he found he could bear it more easily than he had feared. And at every turn he was struck by the beauty of Uláramyth, the moist health of its woods and meadows, the sheer variety of its forms of life. Water tanks teemed with fish; an ivy-shrouded doorway let into a hidden smithy; a troop of monkeys raced like agile spiders through the treetops, beehives hummed in a glade. There were few sounds of industry, and none of machines. They did meet with other selk, and occasionally passed groups of houses or workshops cleverly fitted into the landscape. But when he looked out across the sweep of Uláramyth, what he saw was less a city than a garden.

'I can't understand,' he said at last. 'How can all this *be* here, lost in the wilderness?'

Ramachni glanced up at him. 'After what you've seen of Alifros, lad? How could it be anywhere else?'

Pazel found no answer. Like Hercól, he had felt upon waking from the drug that his memory was impaired, along with his sense of time. The feeling was mostly gone, but he still wondered if he might be forgetting something.

They stepped through a gate in a hedge. Beyond it the trail forked, and Thaulinin took his leave of the party. The travellers showered him with thanks, but he waved them off, smiling. 'Rest and heal, and do not forget the world outside. That will be thanks enough.'

He turned and walked briskly away. Far down the trail ahead of him, Pazel saw a small house carved into a hillside. It had a door of iron, and its windows were barred.

The path was level, now; they had reached the crater's floor. Here the houses grew more numerous, and there were squares and meeting-places between them, and some larger buildings with great porches and balconies draped in flowers. They passed along the streets, under the eyes of the silent, olive-skinned people, until Valgrif stopped at last before a door in a stone wall. He barked once, sharply, and the door flew open.

A trio of selk came out into the street. They were doctors, they said, and bustled around the newcomers to prove it, studying them, touching their wrists and shoulders. They were quiet and serious. Pazel had the feeling that they were paying more attention to what they sensed with their fingertips than what they saw. The effect was unsettling.

'You've, er, never treated our kind, naturally,' grumbled Corporal Mandric.

The selk paused in their work, looking at him.

'Turachs, you mean?'

'Humans, human beings.'

'But of course we have,' said the doctor. 'All our lives – except for the last hundred years. Come in, strip off those rags.'

Inside, they found a series of airy rooms, furnished with beds, wardrobes, dressing tables, shelves of books. Other selk were at work here, and from a back room came the sound of water gushing into a basin, and a puff of steam.

'Your home, citizens, for as long as you stay with us,' said Valgrif.

'You can dine here, or in the great hall, or anywhere else you like. Of course you have the freedom of Uláramyth.'

Pazel stood in the centre of the large common room. His leg was throbbing so badly that he had broken out into a sweat, but the glad, dreamlike feeling was stronger than ever. He was thinking of Ormael. And as he glanced around he suddenly knew why. The chambers were uncannily like the house of his birth: the same simplicity, the same brightness and warmth. He turned to his sister, and she nodded, speechless. The dining table was the size of their old dining table, and pushed close to the window, just as their mother had liked. There was even a courtyard at the back with a small, spreading tree.

'It's not an orange tree,' said Neda.

In Ormael the soldiers had mutilated her tree, broken its limbs, hurled oranges through the windows of the house. Before they moved on to Neda. Pazel took her hand, expecting her to snatch it away. But she didn't. She even squeezed his hand in reply. Then Cayer Vispek said, 'Why should it be an orange tree, *sfvantskor*?' and Neda dropped Pazel's hand as though it burned.

Hercól set the Nilstone down beside Ramachni. He unstrapped Ildraquin, bent and tore off his ruined boots. Then he slid down against the wall. He sighed – and Pazel thought he had never heard a sound remotely like it from the warrior. *Rin's eyes, he's let his guard down.* For the first time since they'd met on the far side of Alifros, Hercól was not protecting anyone. His eyes closed, gentle and serene. He was off-duty. It made him look like another man.

The women moved to the back chambers to undress. One of the doctors was cutting away the left leg of Pazel's trousers. He stood thinking of Dastu in the mountains, where the hrathmogs hunted and the *maukslar* raged. *Do not forget the world outside.*

II

—◆◆◆—

Monday, 11 Halar 942. The great and deadly Empire of Bali Adro – where has it gone? To this day we have seen no ships but that flying fragment, no forts or garrisons on the islands but a few burned & abandoned. We expected to be fighting our way into the Island Wilderness; instead we are gliding through it without so much as a sighting of Imperial forces. Only far to the south & west, on the edge of the horizon, do we still see those flashes, and later hear a great slow *boom* like a rolling wave. Sometimes too there is an eerie shimmer that makes the dlömu point & whisper among themselves. I tell Spoon-Ears that his men are sounding more frightened than my own. He agrees. 'Their fear has a face,' he says. 'A woman's face, staring out at them from a white hood.' I know who he means, but can she be the force behind those great discharges? Is she mightier than Arunis ever was?

While I have him, I pop another question that's been haunting me, but this one I can only whisper: 'You worked on the *Chathrand*'s repairs, when she was in drydock?'

'I was present,' he says with a nod.

'Then tell me: is our keel cracked, by damn? Are we sailing with a broken spine?'

He shakes his head, & I breathe a great sigh of relief. 'But it *was* cracked, to be sure,' he adds. 'I saw the damage myself. Amidships, it was, close to her lowest draft.'

'You *patched* a mucking keel?'

His eyes glance left and right. 'Not at all,' he murmurs finally. 'That is what is so strange. The crack closed of its own accord.

When we came back it was gone – totally self-sealed, as if the wood were living flesh – but better even than flesh, for it healed with no scar. Not even the master shipwrights could find the spot again. But do you know what else is strange? That crack … *bled*.'

'Bled?'

'For the short time it was open, yes. Like young sapwood. I saw it myself: a thin, red-gold nectar. There were still drops of it about the keel when the crack disappeared.'

Nectar from six-hundred-year wood. Cracks that heal themselves. If I needed more convincing that the Grey Lady was like no ship afloat, I have it now.

The Island Wilderness is vast & varied, like a big plate dropped on stone & shattered into thousands of pieces. Those pieces lie flung over a greater expanse of sea than all the waters claimed by Arqual, where many a doughty sailor has passed his whole career. Only the southern third of the Wilderness is charted, & we are nearing the end of that region. Afterwards we will depend on what Prince Olik sketched back in Masalym, & the remarks he made to our sailmaster.

All this effort to find Stath Bálfyr, from which island we have course headings leading precisely nowhere: course headings fabricated years ago by one Lord Talag, for no other reason than to lure us there. And now Ratty's learned that Talag & his clan are still aboard, still waiting for us to reach their homeland, waiting for their moment to strike again. How will they do it? What will they try? Ratty thinks there is good in Talag yet, & that our best hope is to appeal to it. For myself I'm not interested in the mix of good or bad in the fellow. But I know this: a man who could shape his entire life around such a deranged & brilliant scheme as Talag's is capable of anything, mass murder included. If it is part of that scheme to poison us all on landing, he will do it.

Simply to wait for that moment would be lunacy. We must warn Rose, somehow, & hope he is calm enough to believe us – and then sane enough to turn back. That this would require defiance of Sandor Ott is a given, & not on Rose's part alone. Haddismal will be forced to choose between them, & heretofore whenever a choice has arisen he has stood with Ott.

Yet we must turn back. Without knowledge of the currents, we might wander in the Nelluroq until we die of thirst. And even if we managed to cross in safety, where would we emerge? We have no knowledge of our position relative to the Northern lands. We could arrive in the heart of the Mzithrin, & be sunk by the White Fleet. Or in Arquali territory, where our own dear Emperor has promised to kill us & our families should we return without completing the mission. We might get lucky & scuttle into some port in the Crownless Lands. But even if they granted us sanctuary, the news of the *Chathrand*'s resurrection would soon escape, & both would descend on our poor hosts in fury.

No, we must return to Bali Adro sooner or later, & seek better information from some quarter. So why haven't I told Rose yet, before we ran northwards for weeks? Do I fear that he too will take Ott's side? Am I that much a coward, after seeing what the spymaster did to Chadfallow?

Each day we creep nearer. The whole crew is yearning for Stath Bálfyr; you can hear it in their voices, see it in their darting eyes. They are dreaming of home, & in their morally weakened state they forget, for moments, all the heartless immensities of Alifros that lie between.

I am not immune from temptation. Our bow points north; my heart pulls north like a lodestone, & pays no heed to reason. Some nights I think of Anni & me together, keeping house, raising our little one, making sweet love. That is when I feel most evil: when I catch myself imagining such an end, without regard for the ones we're leaving behind.

Against such gloom Felthrup is my strange defender. He cannot say why, but he believes our friends will catch us yet. 'There is Ildraquin and its compass-needle power,' he reminds me, 'and more to the point, there is wisdom and fearlessness in that company.' But is there a blary boat, and could it ever catch up with the

Chathrand? A pity that there's no Ildraquin at our disposal. We speak of them like guests who are fully expected, just running a little late, when in truth we do not even know if they are alive.

I do not ply him with these doubts. What if his hope is but a shield against smothering despair? Ratty feels things so acutely; in many ways he too is like a child. But his understanding of things runs deeper than any child's – deeper than his few years of woken life can easily account for. 'My only gift is dreaming,' he told us recently, but that is a splendid gift in dark times. And it was his dreaming, they say, that saved us once before.

In another dream, however, he saw the face of Macadra, & that face is much on his mind. 'She too is searching for us,' he told me yesterday. 'She does not know if the Nilstone left Masalym by land or sea, & so she scours both. We have a head start, but she has engines of madness to propel her. We will not be alone out here much longer.'

And still there's nothing. Weird evening glimmers, a lost pelican, a peal of thunder on a day without clouds. I would almost prefer a sail on the horizon. Better to spot the wolves at a distance than to worry each day that they're padding behind you, sniffing out your trail.

Tuesday, 12 Halar 942. There are odd fish, & there is Uskins. Since this voyage began, our first mate has been a dandy, a despot, a pretender to noble blood, a torment to me personally, a whipping boy for Captain Rose & most recently a madman who gobbles pork. Now, apparently, he is a soul reborn. To the whole crew's amazement he has recovered his wits & his self-control. There can be no question of him returning to his duties (indeed he has had no duties pertaining to the ship's functions since the day he tried to plunge her to the bottom of the Nelluroq Vortex) but there is talk of him returning to his cabin, any day. For now he may be glimpsed walking the deck with Dr Chadfallow, looking saner (and better groomed) than he has since Etherhorde.

This very afternoon he came to me quietly, the doctor a few

paces behind, & asked my pardon for his 'many trespasses' against both me & the tarboys under my charge. He called himself a man emerging 'from a nightmare that has lasted longer than you've known my name'. I think he wanted to shake hands, & busied mine with a greasy wheelblock. 'Glad you're mending,' was the best I could do, & I dare say it came out less than heartfelt. Why I could find sympathy for the man when he was raving, but feel only contempt at the sight of him dressed & decent is a matter for philosophers. I only know that I do not like him, & never expect to. Perhaps this is my failing, for are we not told to answer trust with trust, humility with respect? Uskins shuffled off with the doctor's hand on his shoulder. To this very hour I feel like a cur.

Wednesday, 13 Halar. There has a been a knife fight on the orlop, & a Plapp's Pier man is fighting for his life. No witnesses, but there was deathsmoke in the air when the Turachs arrived. Before Chadfallow put him under the ether, the lad swore he'd been jumped. This is likely a fib: a number of lads on the deck above heard *two* men shouting at each other well before the thumps & crashes began.

The Burnscove Boys swagger about like new fathers, unable to hide their joy. The victim is particularly hated for some deed back in Etherhorde involving the Imperial police & a shipment of ivory. Rose is livid. Haddismal is both angry & concerned. There has been a shaky truce since Masalym, but it is clearly breaking down. And that is in no one's interest: the balance of power on the *Chathrand* is just too fine.

I've long known that Rose depends on the gangs' mutual hatred to ensure that the crew never comes together to oppose him. But last night I learned another thing. It was that boozy smuggler Mr Druffle, of all people, who opened my eyes.

I'd set Druffle & Teggatz at work together on a comprehensive food inventory: part of my report to the captain on our readiness to brave the Ruling Sea. It was a poor partnership: between Druffle's laziness & Teggatz's incoherence, the inventory had simply ground to a halt. I had knocked their heads together rather roughly, then felt mean about it & joined in the effort, thinking it could not take long.

We finished near sunrise. Poor Teggatz had to go right into his morning ritual of stoking the galley stove. Druffle & I watched him, too tired to crawl away. Then our beloved cook produced a jug of good rum from some cubbyhole in the galley & poured us each a dram.

Druffle's eyes grew moist. 'That's some fine nectar, Teggatz. Oh, for the sweet things in life! Have you never tasted island honey? A gentle soul like me could kill for it, die for it.'

'Let's have no talk of dying,' I said.

We sat on the floor & talked awhile – or rather Druffle & I talked, & Teggatz made his usual blurts & interjections. But the rum loosened his lips (he should drink more often) & when I began talking about the gangs he shook his head.

'Ain't you curious?' he said.

'Well now, Rexstam, I don't think of myself as such.'

'As to why they don't recruit? Eh, eh?' He poked me in the chest. 'The gangs. They don't recruit. Why not, why not?'

'But of course they recruit,' I said.

Teggatz shook his head. 'Not for serious. Not like Etherhorde.'

'He's right,' said Druffle. 'There's a lot of scare-talk here. But in the capital, Pitfire! Say no and it's choppy-choppy, off-with-his-private-parts-into-the-soup.'

I drank, meditating on the matter. They had a point. Nearly forty per cent of our boys remained neutral, outside of either gang. In the dockyards that situation wouldn't have lasted a week. Invitations to join up were not really invitations: they were orders. The ones who said *Bugger off* showed up floating in the marshes, if they showed up at all.

Why had the gangs taken it so easy? The more I thought about it, the stranger it seemed. 'All right, you've stumped me,' I said at last. 'Explain it to me if you can.'

Teggatz rubbed his apron sorrowfully: he could not explain.

But Mr Druffle had a gleam in his drunken eye. He beckoned me closer. He winked.

'I have a suppository.'

'Do you now?'

He nodded proudly. 'Want me to share it?'

Fortunately he didn't wait for an answer. 'Listen, Graff: on most ships, you have your Plapps or your Burnscovers – but just the *lads*, just the membership. The two kingpins never used to sign on with nobody. They'd sit home in Etherhorde, plotting to kill each other, getting richer by the year. And they didn't care what their lads had to do to win new recruits. But this time Rose changed the game. He made your Emperor stick Kruno and Darius aboard *personally*. Was that easy, I ask you?'

'Bah ha,' said Teggatz.

'Not likely,' I said.

'Likely!' said Druffle. 'It was a pig's business, and you know it! But Rose got it done, and now what do we have?' He held up both index fingers. 'Balance. Order. And if one of 'em tries too hard to tip the balance, Rose can do something no other captain ever could.'

He folded away one finger.

'Kill him?' I said, appalled. 'Kill a ganglord?'

'Who's to stop him?'

'But my dear Druffle, that would bring the house down! Boss or no boss, the gang would explode!'

'BOOM!' shouted Teggatz, flinging his arms & spilling precious rum.

'Boom is right,' said Mr Druffle, 'but boom don't help a dead man. I'll bet you a bottle Rose warned each gang not to use their old, bloody methods to boost their numbers – not to rock the boat, see? And if one of 'em does anyway – well, our captain knows what to do.'

Druffle sat back & drank. There was nothing more to his 'suppository', but he had made his point. The gangs were actually weaker with their bosses aboard. If there was anyone the members feared more than a ship's captain, it was their bosses back home. This time the bosses had been dragged along – and they were the ones who had to be afraid.

Teggatz, in his halting way, put the cap on the discussion. 'Plapp, Burnscove – is it bad to have them aboard? Too bad! Nasty, icky, wash your hands. Only one thing could be worse.'

'And that would be, Mr Teggatz?'

'Not having them,' he said.

Thursday, 14 Halar. A spot of embarrassment & confusion. The dlömic woman who spit the seeds that day caught me looking at her. She was kneeling beside a bucket, bathing her face & arms. I think it was the way her half-webbed hands held the sponge that made me stare. I'm sure I did not know I was doing it, though, until those sly silver eyes caught my own & held me like a predator for a moment. I turned away, reddening, & she mumbled something caustic that made her fellow dlömu laugh. Their eyes tracked me too, until I invented a reason to march swiftly amidships. She is lovely. Also hideous. Black skin & silver hair & bright eyes that can't ever be read.

Friday, 15 Halar. Of the two ganglords, Darius Plapp has generally distinguished himself as the stupider (a remarkable achievement). In a bar in Etherhorde, I watched him drop a fat purse before a stunning, green-eyed girl seated alone at a table for two.

'It's a blary crime, love,' he said, 'a peach like you, sittin' there all neglected-like. Tuck that gold away, now, and come upstairs. I'll tickle your sweet spot. Might even make you laugh a bit.'

The room fell suddenly silent. Plapp went on leering at her, a tomcat watching a bird. At last the girl did indeed tuck his gold away, gazing at him with disbelief. And then he found out why she was 'all neglected-like', when Sergeant Drellarek ('the Throatcutter') returned from the privy. Plapp's departure was so fast it was almost a magic trick. I expect he gave her more laughs than he'd counted on.

As I say, no titan of intellect. Yet lately Kruno Burnscove's been vying for his dullard's crown. Tonight he & two of his heavies caught a Plapp sailor on the No. 4 ladderway. With the thugs keeping an eye out for officers above & below, Kruno backed the lad up against the wall & set his knife casually to his throat. He wanted to know what Darius Plapp had in mind once we were back safely north of the Nelluroq. Did Plapp mean to go on cooperating with Rose & Sandor Ott, even though they were leading us to Gurishal on a mission of no return? Or was he maybe thinking someone other than Rose might be better suited to taking the wheel?

I have this on good authority: Kruno Burnscove wanted to know if his rival was plotting mutiny. But did he truly imagine he'd get an answer? Of course the lad swore his ignorance backwards & forward. Burnscove pressed the knife harder against his flesh.

'I know there's an endgame coming, boy. What's more, Darius *knows* I know. He expects someone to spill the gravy sooner or later, see? By talking now you'll just be living up to his expectations.'

No use: the Plapp boy had no gravy to spill. His resistance must have irritated Burnscove. 'You think I'm fooling with you?' he said. 'You suppose I'd think twice about gutting you like a fish? Don't throw your life away, lad. Nothing old Darius might do to you compares with what you're risking here and now.'

At that moment his goon on the lower stair gave a whistle that meant 'officer approaching'. Kruno sheathed his knife, but he struck the lad a parting blow to the stomach that left him writhing on the stair. 'You know what I think, boys?' he said, as they hurried away. 'I think that if these Plapps keep turning into monkeys, we're going to have to chain the bastards up and keep 'em as pets!'

The second warning, from his man above, came too late. Burnscove rounded the corner, laughing at his own witticism. There, with folded arms, stood Captain Rose. For a moment no one moved, & in the silence Rose heard the wheezing of the injured man.

Burnscove is the captain's equal in size & ten years younger, but that did not stop Rose from charging down the stairs at him with a roar. The ganglord should have committed decisively to some action: running like a coward, say, or fighting for his very life. I suppose he did neither, for when I arrived moments later (I was the 'officer approaching' from below) the captain was beating him with fists like wooden mallets, the blows knocking Burnscove against the wall with such force that he toppled forward again into the next piece of punishment, & the next. In desperation Burnscove pulled his knife again. Seeing it, Rose hit a new threshold of rage. Most men put distance from a knife by sheer (sane) instinct. Rose just smacked it from Burnscove's hand. Then he seized the ganglord's forearm near wrist & elbow & snapped the arm like a stick over his knee.

Burnscove fainted dead away. One of his underlings had fled already; the other vomited on the stairs. I was close to doing the same: Burnscove's forearm made a right angle halfway down its length, & from the torn skin a bone protruded obscenely.

Still swearing like a Volpek, Rose dragged the man by his hair onto the lower deck & ordered the Turachs to throw his 'worthless carcass' in the brig. That is where Chadfallow straightened & splinted his arm, & that is where he remains. It is the first time either ganglord has been harmed or jailed since the journey began (save by the ixchel, who locked them up together, sensibly) & it is a deep humiliation for the Burnscove Boys. That, I suppose, is why Rose attacked the man himself. He, Ott & Haddismal are the only men aboard the ganglords fear. And blast me if Druffle's 'suppository' isn't turning out to be true. However maimed, Kruno Burnscove is still alive. He is trapped here, with nothing but thin cabin doors between him & a hundred Turach spearpoints. He cannot act against the captain, & neither can Darius Plapp. While the ganglords live, Rose has nothing to fear from the gangs.

Sunday, 17 Halar. Felthrup has been stabbed. It was a light wound to his shoulder & he will certainly live; already he is hobbling around the stateroom, reminding us all that he has been through worse. More troubling is that his attackers were ixchel. They had secreted themselves inside a cannon on the lower gun deck. When Felthrup passed this evening they leaped down, crushing Felthrup to the deck & pinning him there beneath their swords.

'Who have you told of our whereabouts, vermin?' they demanded. 'Speak quickly or die on our blades!'

Felthrup's first response was to cover his eyes with his paws & beg the men to leave. 'You're in terrible danger,' he said. 'Trust me, run away!' When this tactic failed, he began to chatter wildly about the difference between *telling* & *implying*. Still they pressed him, leaning into their swords. Felthrup then announced that he had come to the conclusion that time was ephemeral, & that no one could predict the shape tomorrow would take, or even the shape *one would take on the morrow*, by which he referred not only to one's physical body ('lest we forget the lesson of the caterpillar') but also the values that define us, the ideas that will outlive us, the philosophies that pass like a germ from one mind to another, didn't they think so, & how he had read incidentally that the philosopher who first argued that moral conviction was the signature of the soul had also called for an end to the persecution of ixchel, as well as a vegetarian diet, though he did in fact ask for pork on the night of his execution, but had to settle for lamb chops as a certain parasite had decimated the local hogs, & then one of the ixchel stabbed Ratty in the haunches just to make him shut up.

That was when Sniraga pounced. The great red creature had been trailing Felthrup at a distance, slinking in & out of shadows as cats will. Lady Oggosk has made her Felthrup's guardian, & she never shirks that duty. But Felthrup too has made his wishes known these many weeks, talking to the red cat, scolding her, imploring her to be 'peaceful and loving'. It's a wonder the beast has not gone mad trying to square that circle. Fortunately for Ratty, his request only delayed her but so long.

The attack was lethally precise. The ixchel who had used his sword was bitten through the head & neck & died at once. The other one stabbed at her bravely. He was a better fighter by half than his kinsman, but all the same Sniraga hooked him with a claw

& flung him high into the air. He came down fighting, but she rolled on her back & met him with four paws this time & mauled him badly. He only just managed to fight out of her grasp. Then he must have realised that his kinsman was dead, for he began to fight a blazing retreat. Sniraga let him go, crouching & hissing beside Felthrup, looking for further attackers.

None came, but Marila did. She had been expecting Felthrup, & came out at last to look for him. She took one look at rat, cat & ixchel body & let out a cry. Felthrup squealed that she must hurry & hide the corpse, but it was too late. Sniraga, knowing her guardianship was done for the time, took the ixchel in her jaws & sprang away.

What will she do with the body? Deliver it to Oggosk? Devour it? Toy with it awhile & leave the remains in plain sight? If the latter occurs there will be a new fear stalking the *Chathrand*, & Marila & I will be questioned savagely, perhaps even by Ott.

As for Felthrup, he has promised us that he will not budge from the stateroom. 'They meant to kill me as soon as I complied with their demands,' he said, 'and then they'd have tried to kill the ones I named – kill you, Mr Fiffengurt, and dear Marila, expectant mother though she is! So terrible, so mean! And we do not even know what they will do when we reach Stath Bálfyr.'

'You were brave, there, Ratty,' I said. 'And brave to go to them, in their stronghold, on a mission of peace.'

He gazed up at me from his little basket, puzzled. 'They have never believed me,' he said. 'All I ever wanted was a good conversation.'

12

Loyalty Tests

Eberzam Isiq awoke to the laughter of the witch. She was in the next cabin, Gregory's cabin, and so was Gregory himself. Isiq could hear them plainly; the interior walls on the *Dancer* were as flimsy as the rest of the boat.

Twilight, the Gulf flat and still. They stood becalmed off the Haunted Coast; the last stage in their journey to the Empress would happen in the dark. Isiq was obeying an old dictum of the Service: *When there is no task before you, your task is sleep.* He'd been a champion napper since his tarboy days; he could sleep through combat drills. So why had Suthinia Pathkendle's laugh woken him so easily, cutting through his sleep like a knife through muslin? She was laughing at her husband's yarn, something about a dog and a dairy maid. At Isiq's bedside, the dog from Simjalla City gave a low, offended growl.

'Did you hear that? "Lazy cur", indeed! Lazy notions about all things canine, more like.'

Suthinia laughed again, and Isiq experienced a moment of ridiculous jealousy. They were sounding very much like a couple, that former couple. And now they had apparently retreated to the captain's tiny chamber to wait for nightfall.

The dog stared in the direction of the voices. 'Every time he speaks of someone low or despicable, it's "The dog!" or "That stinking dog!" Well you're no rose garden yourself, Captain. You smell like old socks, dead fish and someone's nappy shaken together in a bag.'

'He doesn't mean it,' said the little tailor bird, standing in the open porthole. 'In fact I think he's fond of you. He beamed when you told him you wanted to come aboard. Only don't expect too much of him. He's not an educated man like our friend Isiq.'

The dog scratched behind an ear. 'If he says "lazy cur" once more. I'll give him a mouthful of education.'

Isiq sat up and groped for his boots. 'Dog,' he said quietly, 'you know human nature, and how to survive on human streets. That is fine knowledge, and hard-earned to be sure. But you know nothing of life at sea. There is a code we must keep here, because it governs our own survival. Respect the captain, even a captain you hate – and *never* speak idly of rebellion. It will be no idle day if ever you are forced to stand by such words. Now let's get above.'

Nothing had changed on the topdeck save the light, which was failing fast. The clipper was surrounded, as before, by mist: great rafts of white mist, so thick in places that one could imagine parting them like curtains. They were famous, these mists of the Haunted Coast: *ambulatory* mists, Gregory had called them. And it was true that they seemed to wander this part of the Gulf like flocks of sheep, independent of the winds and one another, capricious in what they obscured or revealed.

Just as well that they had anchored six miles out. For when the mists did part, one could catch a glimpse of the sprawling grave-yard between the *Dancer* and the shore. Men had perished here in untold numbers – upon the jagged reefs, the shifting sandbars, the countless rocky islets that loomed suddenly out of the mists. The rumours were many and fantastical: rip tides so powerful they could tear a ship free of its chains. A black mould in the seaweed that turned one's flesh to grey slime that sloughed off the bone. And sea-murths, naturally, directing all these calamities, and more.

He looked down at the grey-green waters. Sea-murths, right below them? Half-spirits, elementals, a people of the depths? Could *they* have provided the 'help' Thasha had spoken of, when Pazel and the other tarboys probed these waters for the Nilstone? Were they the guardians of the Coast?

Isiq believed in murths, but only in the way he believed in the monstrous sloths and lizards whose skeletons graced the museums of Etherhorde: creatures from long ago, creatures who had made way for the advance of humankind. Yes, strange beasts remained in Alifros; he had seen a few in the Service, in the more distant stretches of sea. But *here*, sandwiched between the Empires, so close to the world's busy heart? He didn't like to think so. It made civilisation appear fragile, like a scrim that might fall at any time. But something kept sinking those ships. Something more than wide reefs and poor seamanship.

He stood and watched the dying light. He could still hear the booming of guns, distant and sporadic; the massive engagement had concluded one way or another. He thought of the wreckage and the death behind them, the corpses in the water, the poor sod or two (or ten or twenty) lost overboard, still breathing at this minute, still clutching at a fragment of his ship.

So familiar, so shamefully comforting. War was a state of affairs he understood — a state he liked, admit it, for the razor it took to social pretence: minced words, delicate non-promises, games of maybe and speak-with-me-tomorrow. Not in wartime, not for soldiers. You lived or died by your good word, by the trust you generated, by aspects of character that could not easily be faked.

But did he have the character of a peacemaker? When this righteous fire burned out, would he be emptied, useless as an old gunner, the kind who retired with weak eyes and weaker hearing and any number of fingers blown off over the years? Before the *Chathrand* sailed, he had told Thasha that even old men could change. That he had become an ambassador and would work for a better Alifros. That he had, once and for ever, hung up his sword. He had underscored the point by thumping the table and turning red in the face.

'Peaceful out here, ain't it?'

Gods of death, there was a boat alongside! A slender thing shaped like a bean pod. A canoe. Just two men aboard her, large ruffians, grinning like boys. They had glided out of the fog in perfect silence.

'Bosun!' snapped Isiq.

'Don't shout, Uncle,' said the second man. 'Didn't Captain Gregory make that clear?'

He had, of course: no shouting, no loud noises of any kind. In short order Gregory himself appeared, still buttoning his shirt. The newcomers touched their caps, and Gregory answered with a nod and his wolfish grin.

'You rascals. Not dead yet?'

'Can't die when we owe you forty cockles, can we, sir?' said the man in front.

'Forty-two,' said Gregory. 'Interest.'

'What's moving today, Captain?' asked the other.

'No goods,' said Gregory, 'but there's a package for you about here somewhere, I expect.' He twinkled at them, then turned to Isiq. 'Get your things, old man, and be quick. You're going with Fishy and Swishy here.' He pointed at the men. 'Fishy here's a Simjan, rescued from a felonious past by our brotherhood. Swishy's a halfwit from Talturi.'

'Those aren't our real names,' said the Simjan.

'And your passenger here *has* no name, see, so don't ask him,' said Gregory. 'Keep calling him "Uncle", that will do. And see that he stays out of trouble all the way to the Hermitage. Your word as gentlemen, if you please.'

Hermitage? thought Isiq.

The newcomers looked him over dubiously, but they gave their word. Then Gregory smiled and declared that their 'Uncle' had just paid off their debt, and Mr Tull came forward with a bundle of tobacco for each.

Isiq turned aside and muttered in Gregory's ear: 'Are we truly to visit the Empress in a hollow log, like savages?'

'Savages!' said Gregory. 'That's blary perfect. We depend on such ignorance from Arqualis, don't we lads? Now grab your things, duffer! I won't tell you again.'

Isiq had few things to grab. His weapons from Oshiram, his boots and jacket, the purse of gold that was presumably forty-two cockles lighter than when he came aboard. The dog and the bird watched him anxiously.

'I would welcome your companionship,' he told them, 'but I do not know what is to come. If you go with me now there may be no chance of your returning to Simja for a very long time. Nor can I be sure that the ones who will receive me are – how did you put it, Tinder? – educated. They may not know how to relate to woken beasts.'

His words added greatly to their distress. 'I will go with you regardless, friend Isiq,' said the tailor bird at last. 'My brainless darling has forgotten me, as she does every spring. Let her nest with someone else, someone better suited to matrimony. I have other things on my mind.'

'And I will stay on the *Dancer*,' said the dog, 'if you will ask Captain Foulmouth to return me to the city at his earliest convenience. The witch has said enough about your cause to make me want to help. But Simjalla is the place I know. Her streets, her smells, her gossip. That is where I can be of use to you, if anywhere.'

'Then go well,' said Isiq, scratching his muzzle, 'and see that you don't bite the captain.'

'No promises,' said the dog.

On deck again, Isiq faced the great indignity of needing to be helped into the canoe. His knee did not want to support him on the rope ladder, and the crew had to improvise a sling and ease him down the *Dancer*'s side. Isiq knew he was scarlet. He thanked the Gods that Suthinia had stayed below, and then felt perfectly desolate because she had. Apparently he was unworthy of a goodbye.

Gregory leaned down the side, trying not to smile. 'You're a force of nature, Uncle,' he said. 'We'll meet again, I'm sure of it.'

'On the battlefield,' said Isiq, 'if we live that long. Today I can only thank you for your deeds. They were strange but well executed.'

Gregory humbly dipped his head. 'Need a job done, call a freebooter,' he said.

On an impulse, Isiq tossed the purse of gold back up onto the *Dancer*. 'Take what you need to rebuild your house,' he said.

Gregory looked abruptly chagrined. 'Oh, as for that—'

'He took it already.'

Suthinia was there, bending to snatch the purse from the deck. She was wearing her sea cloak, and a headscarf of fine black lace, and before Isiq's startled eyes she threw one leg over the rail. Astride it like a jockey, she looked her husband in the eye. Isiq knew he should turn away, but didn't. Suthinia moistened her lips.

'Hopeless,' she said.

The captain grinned. 'We figured that out a long time ago, didn't we?'

'Not *us*, Gregory. Just you.'

'Now that *is* unfair. From a woman in your position.'

'There's only one position you care about.'

She leaned nearer, eyes half-closed; she placed a hand on his chest. 'Brush your teeth, next time, darling,' said Gregory. Suthinia turned away, furious, groping for the ladder with her heel.

They sat like cargo in the bottom of the canoe, the witch and the admiral, enemies and allies. Suthinia, in front, gazed fixedly at the Talturin in the bow. Isiq's knee ached. He wondered if he could ask her to soothe it with a touch, as she had done the night they met.

Then he heard her spitting oaths, soft and venomous. *Perhaps later,* he mused. *Perhaps in a week.*

The young men paddled in silence. They did not aim for shore but zigzagged in the growing darkness, as though pursuing a wayward thought. The Gulf was still remarkably flat. It was very weird, to be gliding soundless among the fog-blanketed shipwrecks, the coral knobs and giant fist-like rocks. The men showed no fear of the shipwrecks, and threaded a course so close among them that Isiq could have leaned out and touched the rotting hulls.

'We're no closer to shore than when we started,' said Suthinia, breaking her silence at last. 'Are you lost, or is this a tour of the Haunted Coast?'

The young men glanced at each other, suddenly uneasy. 'We're not lost,' said the Simjan, who sat aft. 'Just waitin' on the signal.'

'Whose signal?'

The men shuffled uneasily. 'I imagine they have more secrets to guard than the one Gregory asked for, Lady Suthinia,' offered Isiq.

'How *piercingly* clever you are.'

She had a knack for asphyxiating conversation. They glided on. A crescent moon began to wink at them between the clouds. Isiq put a hand to his vest pocket, felt the trembling of the tailor bird. The distant cannon had stopped booming at last.

They were passing between a reef and the black shell of an Arquali frigate when Suthinia asked suddenly, 'Will you start again with the deathsmoke?'

At the bow, the Talturin fumbled his paddle. Furious, Isiq gripped the sides of the canoe. *How dare she. In front of strangers.* If she knew what the fight had been like! The months of terror, the racking pain, the mind squeezed in a tourniquet, squeezed like bread in a fist ... And to think that this poisonous witch had inspired fancies in him. Longings. That he had imagined them together, someday, when the fighting was done. He should tell her to go rot in the Pits.

'No deathsmoker ever *intends* to start again,' he said through clenched teeth.

'That's right, Uncle!' said the Simjan. 'But to answer your question, Lady Suthinia: I don't know. I look for the Tree of Heaven every night, and send my prayers up to Rin. Two good months I've had, but you know I've kept off the drug this long before.'

Isiq stared into the darkness, abashed. The witch had not even been speaking to him.

'You must stay strong for your little ones,' said Suthinia to the addict. 'Come see me at the Hermitage, as you did last year.'

'Oh, Lady—'

'Don't thank me yet; the charm may not help. And it *will* not, unless you fight on.' She twisted about now, pulling the headscarf back to let her see the Simjan. 'You will fight on, I'm certain. You'll make us all proud, and what's more you'll win your own pride back – with interest, as Gregory would say.'

Isiq wished someone would strike him in the face. He had nearly exploded at this beautiful witch. Even now she had the courtesy not to notice, not to mock his error; why had he imagined her cruel? She had not been cruel, she had been honest. As bluntly honest as any warrior, any man.

'Oppo, m'lady,' said the Simjan, his voice close to breaking.

By the Gods, thought the admiral, *I want this woman in my life.*

Then he saw the child on the reef.

It was a boy, and it was sitting on the just-submerged coral, staring at them. When the next swell came it rose to its feet. It stood no taller than a man's knee. It had arms and legs and eyes and fingers, yet nothing could have been less human. In the moonlight its flesh was the colour of old pewter. Its face, so much like an infant's, sported a mouth full of pointed teeth. The boy-creature's limbs flexed in ways no human limbs could, as though they were not jointed but ribbed like snakes.

Suthinia made a small sound of fright.

'Don't worry, m'lady,' said the Simjan, 'that's what we were waiting for.'

'It's a murth!' she said.

'Of course. A sea-murth. They're in charge here, you know.'

The little creature made a clicking sound in its throat. Isiq thought it looked angry, and then thought that he was a fool even to speculate on its emotions. Suddenly the murth bent at the spine and flipped backwards, otter-like, into the waves.

The bowman pointed. Fifty yards away, two figures sat crouched on the wave-washed deck of the frigate, serpentine arms hugging knees. They were elders, a man and a woman. Just beyond them, Isiq saw delicate hands rise to grasp the timbers. A young murth-girl pulled herself up beside the other two. A strange beauty, Isiq thought, as she stared at the humans with wide green eyes.

'Put one hand in the water,' said the Simjan.

Isiq and Suthinia gaped at him. 'Are you quite cracked?' said the admiral.

'No, Uncle, it's the way,' said the other, plunging in his hand. 'Do it quickly, or they won't let us ashore.'

Suthinia leaned away, terrified. 'This is what Gregory was teasing me about. *Jathod*, I hate that man! No wonder he's not here.'

The two elder murths slipped back into the water and vanished, but the young girl remained, watching them sorrowfully. Isiq muttered a curse, then put his hand in the water. 'Come, Suthinia,' he said.

'You don't know these creatures,' she said. 'You've never crossed the Ruling Sea. They're a race of orphaned spirits. They're the stepchildren of the Gods.'

'They're fussy, too,' said the Talturin. 'Put your hand in, lady. We've got nowhere else to go, unless we paddle out to sea.'

Isiq leaned forward and touched her shoulder with his free hand. She stiffened but did not pull away. She put her hand in the Gulf.

The four of them sat there, awkwardly balanced, and the canoe bobbed like a cork. Suthinia was trembling. Isiq felt like a fool. What did Emperor Magad have to fear from them, exactly?

Nothing happened for a time: the lone murth-girl stared across the water. Then it came: a touch, cold and otherworldly and electric. Small hands were gripping his own, turning them, feeling his swollen knuckles through the flesh. Suthinia jumped; they had touched her too. She started to shake and Isiq tightened his grip on her shoulder. *What in Pitfire happened to her on the Nelluroq?*

The murth-hands withdrew. 'Done!' said the Simjan, and Suthinia jerked her hand from the water and cringed. 'No fear, Lady S, that's all that's required of us. A bit like signin' for your pay, says Captain Gregory, or askin' permission to board a boat. And the beauty of it is that the murths don't let no one cross their territory but us freebooters. Captain Gregory struck a bargain, the wily old – *Uch!*'

A murth-man breached like a seal, right beside Suthinia. The witch did not cry out but flung herself away, and came close to overturning the canoe. The murth showed its teeth. It had a snow-white beard and solemn eyes, and shells adorned the raiment on its shoulders.

Suthinia was still flailing. Isiq threw his arms about her. 'Be still! He's not attacking!' But even the smugglers were aghast; this was no part of the routine. The murth placed a glistening hand upon the gunwale, and spoke.

Everyone winced. The voice was part wooden ratchet, part shrieking albatross. The murth watched Suthinia expectantly, but the terrified witch just shook her head. Frowning now, the murth raised a finger to point at the sky.

'*Baaa* ... ' The creature's mouth and neck strained with effort. Now vaguely human, the sounds it produced came from deep in its stomach. ' ... *b-baaaaaa—*'

'Back?' whispered the Simjan.

'*Baaaaaad. Baaaaaaad reeepestreeeeee.*' The murth raised his finger higher, still looking at Suthinia.

'Bad *what*?' asked the Talturin.

'*Yoooo...helllp ... weeee ... helllp ... or alllll ... m-m-muhh—*'

'Muh—?'

'*Muh-murrrrrrrrrr.*'

'Murth? Sea-murth?'

'*Murrrrrd! MUUURRRRRRRRRRRRRRRRD!*'

'Murdered,' said Isiq.

The sea-murth pointed at him. Then he turned the pointing finger on himself, the others in the canoe, and finally swept his hand in a wide, encompassing arc.

'Everyone,' said Suthinia. 'Everyone murdered together, by something from the sky.'

The creature nodded. '*Yoooo helllllp,*' it repeated, and this time the words sounded like a plea. It submerged, and they saw no more of it. But as they paddled off, the young murth-girl still sat watching them upon the wreck, and now Isiq thought her green eyes were sad.

250

Isiq smacked his forehead, and bloodied his fingers by the deed. The Crab Fens. A mystery hell-hole, unexplored by Arqual's navy, hidden behind the death-trap of the Haunted Coast. Isiq had imagined a short journey up a tidal stream, then a hidden deep-water vessel with the Empress in the stateroom, surrounded by Tholjassan guards. But as they rode the swell in among the bulrushes and black trees, the Simjan remarked casually that he hoped they'd arrive in time for dinner. 'No one dines this late, surely?' said Isiq. The man looked back at him, confused. Then he smiled. 'I meant dinner *tomorrow* night, Uncle. And that's if we hurry, and there's not a squall.'

Isiq feared it would be a torturous trip. His knee was on fire and he could not straighten it, and the night was frigid, and he had nothing to do with his hands. But things turned out much better than he expected. The canoe had impressed him already among the corals and shipwrecks; here in the Fens it proved a revelation. It cut water like a knife, turned like a damselfish, skimmed through shallows where a rowboat would have run aground. And when the stream narrowed and the insects found them, the two men sprang into action, rearranging their cargo and urging the passengers to lie flat. Blessed relief! His leg was straight at last! He passed the tailor bird to the Simjan; the creature was fond of any man who, like 'friend Isiq', had done battle with deathsmoke. Then the young men stretched a kind of cheesecloth over the top of the canoe and secured it at both ends, leaving themselves exposed but protecting Isiq and Suthinia from the insects, or the bulk of them.

To call it undignified was an understatement: Isiq had to rest his face on the canoe's damp and grimy floor. Suthinia's back was to him. When he turned over and brushed her foot by accident, she kicked.

'Stay clear of me, you old mucking lizard!'

'Madam Suthinia!'

'Go to sleep! This night's going to be rotten enough without any of *that*!'

Isiq almost laughed. Sleep was out of the question. His mind was galloping, intoxicated. They had probably gone ten miles already, and would cover fifty or sixty more at this rate. Sixty miles into the Fens! That meant the Empress wasn't underestimating the threat posed by Sandor Ott. It meant she had some grasp of what it took to stay alive.

'He visits whores,' said Suthinia, apropos of nothing.

Isiq made a sound of polite surprise.

'These days he scarcely bothers to hide it. Maybe that's better than expecting me to say nothing, to pretend not to notice what he does. Still, I hate him. I've hated him since the day we married.'

Isiq's heart was hammering. He said, 'What I saw did not look like hate.'

'He's a lecher and a pig,' said Suthinia. 'But it's something, you have to admit – making peace with the sea-murths, enjoying their protection, winning free movement through this land.'

'*He* made the peace? Gregory, personally?'

'On behalf of his beloved freebooters, of course. Little by little, year after year. He went about it like a child, but somehow it worked. He would toss sacks of gold among the shipwrecks, and glass jewellery, and beads. He'd put his face close to the water and shout, "Presents for the maneaters! Go ahead, play dress-up! None of us will laugh. And we're not thieves, or colonists, or even fishermen. We're just orphans like you." And he'd walk, Eberzam – walk from Cape Córistel, thirteen days up the beach, and then just sit in the shallows and call out to the murths, *sing* to them.'

'Sing?'

'Love songs and praise songs, drinking songs, and he'd say how much more he respected them than human beings. He didn't even see one for the first four years. And if they heard him they surely didn't understand. They didn't speak a mucking *word* of any human tongue.'

'But they do now?'

'Gregory taught them. He taught Arquali to the mucking sea-murths, that man.'

She fell briefly silent, then added, 'I never believed him, until tonight. I thought this sea-murth business was another lie, one he invented because he knows I fear them. It kept me out of his hair, kept me away from his real family here in the Fens.'

'But why such extraordinary fear?' asked Isiq. 'Courage blazes from you like heat from a bonfire.'

'Very pretty. I'll tell you why. It was during our crossing of the Nelluroq, twenty years ago. One freezing night we lay becalmed, and they surrounded us and swept aboard, and all our lamps went out together. They moved among us silently, inspecting us, touching our clothes and faces, and no one on deck breathed a word. And there was a lord among them, a very ancient murth. When the moon sailed out from behind the clouds I found him staring at me. He hobbled near and touched my hand, and it burned. Then all of them slipped back into the sea.'

'A bad burn, was it?'

'Not at all,' said Suthinia. 'But when we had the lamps burning again I saw that there were faint lines on my palm. Symbols. They were already fading, so I copied them out on paper before they disappeared. And years later Gregory showed them to these murths, here at the Haunted Coast.'

To Isiq's almost unbearable joy, Suthinia reached back and took his hand tight in her own. 'I'd garbled the words a bit,' she said, 'but the murths took a guess at their meaning. It seems they meant, "This one will descend among us and remain."'

'Oh, rubbish,' said Isiq.

'Yes, well. That's what most everyone says about their blary existence. And Gregory, he grinned when he brought me the translation. Like I said, I thought he was lying, just trying to scare me. He loves my weaknesses, the cur.'

'Do you truly hate him?'

'I hate most men, most of the time. When I dream of a better world it has no room for you. The horrid mess you make of everything, the wars.'

'I was born into war,' said Isiq. 'I could have walked away from the Service, pretended that Arqual was not threatened with annihilation. But that would not have made the threat disappear.'

For the first time he heard amusement in her voice. 'Walked away like me? Gregory told you, didn't he? How he charmed me right into his bedroom? How I quit magecraft to be with him?'

'He hinted,' said Isiq.

'Well it's true: you can have magic, or a life and family. Not both, never both. But it's also true that if I hadn't walked away from magecraft, Arunis would have found me, and killed me, as he did almost all of us. So I burned my spell-scrolls, poured my potions into the sea. And I managed to be a mother and a wife. Until a certain doctor came to Ormael, that is.'

Isiq had wondered if she would ever mention the doctor. 'Chadfallow reveres you above all women in Alifros,' he heard himself say.

'We were lovers for years,' she said. 'Pazel always talks about the day Gregory *introduced* us. But that only happened because Ignus had finally struck up a friendship with Gregory, down on the waterfront. By then, *credek*, I'd been with him almost seven years. I was trying to leave him, not for the first time. I could have killed him for approaching Gregory like that.'

'Why did he?'

'Why do you think? So that he could cross my threshold. I'd never brought Ignus around the Orch'dury. I didn't want the children to know about him, although Neda suspected I had someone. A lot of sailors' wives do, you know.'

'You can't mean it.'

'Go ahead and laugh, but Neda was furious; she wanted me dead.' Suthinia paused. 'And then there was Pazel. He idolised Gregory, the man who tossed him in the air when he came home, who tossed gold around like a sultan; the man who captained a ship. Of course Gregory forgot about him as soon as he walked out the door, but I couldn't tell Pazel that. Any more than I could tell him who his real father was.'

'Chadfallow.'

'What if he'd known?' asked Suthinia defiantly. 'He'd only have begun to doubt Gregory's love for him, and Rin knows there was reason to doubt. He'd have learned that Neda was only his half-sister. And Ignus – he could have been recalled to Etherhorde at any time. He *threatened* to go often enough. To wash his hands of the whole "sordid Ormali chapter in my life", as he put it. To go back to something familiar and safe.'

Suthinia drew a long breath. 'I was fighting for a normal life, too. For Pazel, Neda, myself. I should have known it would come apart in my hands.'

'Because of me,' said Isiq gruffly. Then, correcting himself: 'Because of the invasion.'

'And because the choice was never truly before me. I was still a mage in my heart.'

'And now?'

'Now it's not just my heart. It's everything. I'll never be much of a mage, probably. But while this fight continues I can't be anything else. I was saying goodbye to Gregory, tonight on the *Dancer*. It was the first time I had touched him in years. And the last.'

She withdrew her hand, and they both lay still and silent. There was, finally, perfect understanding between them. He could not argue with her, could not tell her she was killing him with her beauty, with her flood of simple trust. He would not chatter, would not remark on her honesty, or his amazement (face to face with honesty now) that he could have failed to notice the honesty's absence during all his years with Syrarys. They would never be lovers, that dream was gone. But as he lay there he sensed with awe that a new being had appeared beside him, a sister maybe, even though she came from the far side of the world.

'Our children,' he said at last, 'my daughter, your son—'

'Yes,' said the witch, 'isn't that the strangest thing?'

Twenty hours later the Simjan toed him gently in the ribs. 'Wake up, Uncle,' he said.

He rose stiffly, blinking. The sun was once more going down, but now it was setting over a vast lake, dotted with hummocks of greenery and flocks of waterbirds, and bordered on all sides by the Fens.

In the centre of the lake was an enormous building made entirely of logs. At first Isiq thought that it stood on giant stilts. But no, it was afloat, built atop a number of conjoined barges. It was square and plain and four stories tall, with rows of windows on the two upper floors. It reminded Isiq of a warehouse in Etherhorde, complete with the lookout towers at the corners by which the bosses could keep an eye on the stevedores. A number of vessels – sailboats, rowboats, pole barges, canoes – milled about it; others were scattered over the lake.

Suthinia was kneeling; the wind tossed her sable hair. 'The Hermitage,' she said. 'It's been two years for me.'

'How did you manage to visit, without ever laying eyes on a murth?' asked Isiq.

She smiled at him. 'There are many paths to this lake,' she said, 'though none is easy to find. I used to come here from the Trothe of Chereste, before my children were born.'

'Was there a … hermit in residence, even then?'

Suthinia raised an eyebrow. 'We brought the Hermit here, Gregory and I. Fourteen years ago, that was.'

As they drew nearer, Isiq caught the sparkle of glass from one of the towers. A telescope lens. *Someone's taking a good look at us.*

They rounded a corner. On the western side of the great structure a wide gate stood raised, its iron teeth catching the last of the evening sun. 'I hear music!' said the tailor bird. 'It is coming from that arch!'

The structure was open at the centre, Isiq saw now: the barges formed a great floating square, like a villa with a watery courtyard. They neared the arch. Festive noises, a piano banging drunkenly, the scent of onion and frying fish. They passed under the iron gate, and the Talturin said, 'We're home.'

Sweet Tree of Heaven.

It was like stepping into a bustling town on market day. The inner walls were entirely made up of balconies: four unbroken balconies running around the structure, and crowded with people of all kinds. There were many rough-looking freebooter men and women, to be sure, but also children, mothers with babies on their hips, toothless elders leaning over the rails. The crowd spilled out onto docks and tethered boats. There were streamers of laundry, buckets raised and lowered for water; tankards lifted in welcome as the paddlers were recognised. Everyone was poor, that was certain: the children's clothes were made of neatly stitched rags. But winter was ending, and the day had been fair, and there appeared to be plenty to eat.

'Where'd you find the fish-head?' shouted a portly man nibbling a sausage, looking down on Isiq.

'He's a friend of Captain Gregory,' shouted the Talturin. 'Be civil, you! He's here for some peace and relaxation.'

'So naturally Gregory sends his witch along,' quipped another.

Suthinia's glance cut the laughter short, but even in her eyes there was a flicker of amusement. 'Nobody *sends* me anywhere, as you people know well,' she said, 'but if Old Lumpy has any crab cakes left, tell him to send them to our chambers, with some bread and ale.'

'Lots of ale, lots of bread!' bellowed their guides. 'And cheese, and butter, and marmalade!'

It was all arranged by shouting, here, apparently. The paddlers shouted to their sweethearts; the children shouted questions about the murths; the old women shouted to Suthinia, complaining of their toothaches and gout. *Pure anarchy*, thought the admiral. *Maisa can't possibly be here.*

When they docked, the mob pressed close around them, and Isiq feared they would be trapped and chattering until dawn. But somehow in short order he found himself in a damp, plain, utterly delightful cabin on the east side of the enclosure, slicing bread with his dagger while Suthinia bathed in the washroom at the end of the hall.

The bird pecked at fallen crumbs. 'Bread is good,' he said, 'but insects are better. I will go to the roof and feed properly.'

'Go then, but be careful,' said Isiq. 'I will leave the window open.'

The bird vanished into the night. When Suthinia returned they pounced on the food, and talked easily of their children. They even laughed a bit – though surely that was a mask for fear. Isiq was flabbergasted when she told him that Neda had become a *sfvantskor*. But Suthinia only shrugged.

'It makes a kind of sense. Neda used to scorn me for not committing. "You're half-mage, half-mother. Who wins, if you're living half a life?" Well, she's found something to commit to, that's certain.'

She looked at him very seriously. 'You must stay close, Eberzam. These are good people overall. As Gregory's friend you'll not be harmed or robbed. But they are wild, and not always wise. They will try to sell you ten thousand things, and to borrow money; they will offer services you don't need. They will send girls to your bedchamber, and failing that, boys. They will try to sell you deathsmoke.'

He nodded. 'I expected that. But the drug is everywhere, Suthinia. I can't avoid it unless you keep me in a cage.'

'Turn to me when the craving starts. I may be able to stop you in time.'

'A bull elephant could not stop me, if I am ever brought so low as to reach for deathsmoke again.'

'Will you let me try?'

He sat there, trembling with the memory of pain. 'I will,' he said at last.

She smiled and squeezed his hand. Then a strange look came over her face.

'What is it?' he asked.

She blinked at him. 'In the South, there is a thing called the *nuhzat*. A kind of dream-state in which we lose our minds a little, but gain something else – insight, second-sight, other powers now and again. Few humans experience the *nuhzat*, but I used to. It happened even after I came north, even after Neda and Pazel were born. They were frightened of me. It can be terrifying, the *nuhzat*. In my case it usually was.

'But in one of those *nuhzat*-visions I saw this moment. A strange, hard man, a former enemy, alone with me in a small room, eating crab cakes, laughing with me about our children. I knew that I had long hated him; that I blamed him for the course of my latter life – at least for all the parts that went wrong. And I knew that just the night before I had refused him as a lover.'

Isiq dropped his eyes, colouring.

'I knew also,' she said, 'that I would have to hurry to tell him, even before the meal was over, that he must believe in himself as never before. That he must trust not only in his wisdom and martial skills, but in his heart. Trust your own heart, Eberzam, remember. I am glad the memory came back to me in time.'

'In time for what?'

She turned and looked at the door. Isiq put down his plate. There were footsteps, then a loud, impatient knock.

When Suthinia opened the door Isiq thought for a moment that he had lost his mind. Before him stood a man slightly older than the admiral himself, with a face that was intensely, eerily familiar. Two younger men with light halberds stood behind him.

'Leave your weapons,' said the older man. 'Wipe the crumbs from your beard. Close your mouth. Leave the hat.'

Military.

'Stand up; you're expected at once.' The man glanced briefly at Suthinia. 'He's to go alone, Mrs Pathkendle.'

Not just a soldier, but an Arquali soldier. His Dremland accent was a giveaway.

'Don't I know you?' asked Isiq.

The man hesitated, biting back some retort. 'Irrelevant,' he said at last, and turned on his heel.

Isiq looked at Suthinia; she nodded. Impulsively he took her hand and kissed it. Then he followed the old soldier down the corridor, with the guards walking behind. They passed the washroom, a busy kitchen, open doorways where cards and wrestling matches were underway, a little booth where a cobbler sat hammering nails into a well-worn sole. The old soldier rocked a little to the left as he walked, and that too was somehow familiar. *Who in the Nine Pits is he?*

At last they came to a temple chamber where a few elders were bent at evening prayers. They slipped around the dais into the sacristy, and a young monk stood up from his desk and welcomed them, smiling. He shut the door, then turned to a heavy rack of vestments and parted them like curtains. Beyond it was a plain wooden wall, but when the monk pressed the wall it swung inward. The old soldier stepped through the gap without a word.

Now they were climbing a staircase, very narrow and dark. Isiq was perplexed by the heavy carpet. Then he thought: *To deaden our footfalls. Good, very good.*

After three flights the staircase ended before another door, this one heavily padded. The old soldier gave a precise series of taps, and Isiq heard the sliding of bolts.

They stepped directly into a barracks. Forty soldiers in varying states of dress turned and stared at Isiq. 'That's him!' they murmured. 'By the hairy devils below, that's *him!*'

Isiq was looking at a medley of Imperial faces. There were some Etherhorders and other men of inner Arqual, but many more Ipulians, Opaltines, and folk of the Outer Isles. All of them decades his junior. There were also a great number of Tholjassans – their slender features were unmistakable. All of them stared in fascination.

The old soldier shut the door. 'Yes,' he said. 'This is Admiral Isiq. Now stop staring like a gopher pack.'

But the one who was staring now was Isiq. *A gopher pack.* The phrase unlocked his memory at last. This old man, incredibly, had been his drill sergeant on his first deployment. *Gods of death, that was fifty years ago!* When he was just a midshipman, not yet eighteen.

When Maisa was still on the throne.

'Bachari!' he cried, astonished. 'Sergeant Bachari! You went with her into exile!'

'And you,' said the old man, unsmiling, 'did not.'

The complex occupied the entire northern third of the Hermitage: a great warren sealed off from the freebooter's floating village, except for a few well-hidden passages like the one they had just used. 'Of course they all know something strange is afoot here,' said Bachari gruffly, 'and a few have perhaps guessed its nature. But only a very few. It is the best compromise we have been able to manage, but I do not like it, not at all. I am in charge of her personal security.'

The men looked fit and well fed, but their bearing worried Isiq: the salutes they gave Bachari came too slowly for his liking. They wore uniforms of a sort – plain trousers and ill-fitting shirts, canvas jackets stained at the wrists, patched at the elbows. Only the officers wore proper Arquali attire, and even theirs was faded.

'We have three hundred men within these walls,' Bachari told him, 'and twice that many on vessels secreted about the lake's periphery.'

'Nine hundred?' asked Isiq, his heart sinking to his shoes.

Bachari looked at him sharply. 'That is twice the force we had a year ago. But I did not say that was all Her Majesty could call upon. Do you think I should tell you everything, Isiq? By what merit, pray? Thus far you have only proven your need of a refuge from the Secret Fist.'

His words stung – what words did not, from a man's first drill sergeant? – but Isiq could not refute them. 'Turachs?' he asked dubiously.

Bachari was growing irritated. 'Why ask such a question? You know as well as I do that the Turach Legion never splintered when Her Majesty fled. As it happens we have one Turach, a recent addition to our number. But I do not have full confidence in the man. He admits to having fled his unit on the eve of a deployment.'

Isiq sighed. 'Just take me to the Empress,' he said.

They passed through the rest of the meagre barracks, a gymnasium, a humble officers' club. Isiq felt despair circling him like a tiger, hidden but inexorable, waiting for its moment to pounce. *Nine hundred men at arms! Less than the complement on four Arquali warships!* And the navy boasted some five hundred vessels. *They'll be mucking exterminated. Unless this man truly is hiding much from me. Gods, let it be so.*

They came at last to a heavy wooden door, guarded by six more halberd-wielders, who stood aside for Bachari. As he opened the door the old man put a finger to his lips.

The room they entered was the largest he had yet seen in the complex. It was also profoundly elegant – but no, that word did not suffice. The walls were draped in rich red tapestries: Arquali tapestries, clearly of ancient workmanship, depicting hunts in primeval forests. The furnishings too were splendid relics. A table on doe's legs, its surface a mosaic of ivory and rosewood and mother-of-pearl. A small golden harp on a marble pedestal. Twin bronze statues of the Martyrs of Etherhorde.* Portraits in gilded frames, men whose faces swam up dimly from the murk of memory: the first kings, the heroes of Unification.

The word you're seeking, Isiq told himself, *is* Imperial.

At the back of the chamber, an Arquali flag hung from the ceiling. It was huge: the golden fish was nearly man-sized, and the golden dagger pointed straight down at the one plain object in the

---

*The legend is, in the strictest sense of the word, pathetic. A lame and sickly peasant girl from the Northwest Province (later Chitai) received a midnight visit from an angel. This burning spirit declared that Etherhorde would be invaded by Sikand mercenaries in six days' time; and further, that she would not be believed unless she told the Emperor personally, to his face. The girl's father said that she was mad, and would not lend her their horse or hear of riding out on such an errand. But her brother believed the story, and set the girl upon his shoulders, and ran afoot through the Empire, day and night without rest. They reached the foot of Castle Maag on the evening of the sixth day, just as the Emperor was descending to the city for a meal. They waved and shouted by the roadside, but the king did not heed them, for he had many petitioners. Then before his eyes the girl's brother dropped dead of exhaustion. Moved, the king halted his train and approached the girl, and when she told him of the angel's message he believed her, and alerted the army, and brought the people of Etherhorde within the walls before the Sikands arrived. But the girl did not live an hour after her brother's fall. The sun had withered her; she died of thirst. - EDITOR

room: a wooden chair. It stood alone upon a dais. Other chairs, far more sumptuous, were arranged beneath it in a semicircle.

Upon that simple chair sat Maisa, Empress of Arqual. She was straight and proud and bright of eye. And old, very old. Isiq felt stabbed to the heart. *She was not yet thirty when you saw her last.*

She had visitors seated before her, and did not glance up at Isiq. Bachari stabbed a finger at the spot where they stood: *Do not move.* He was to wait on her pleasure. Fair enough; he only wished that he'd bathed.

Bachari left without a sound. Isiq could hear Maisa's voice but did not recognize it. How could he? Only once in his life had he stood this close to her, and on that occasion she had not said a word.

The image returned with arresting force: a hooded figure exiting the Keep of Five Domes, holding the hands of two small and frightened boys. The mass of soldiers around them, looking fearfully over their shoulders, urging them on. The harsh wind as they rounded the fountain, its spray blowing out over the Plaza of the Palmeries, striking the cobbles like a hard rain. Striking the dead bodies that lay at her feet.

There were four of them, slain at a distance by archers dispatched by Sandor Ott: the first casualties among Maisa's loyalists. Isiq had watched her from the edge of the Plaza, standing with a group of astonished, off-duty navy men who had just wandered in from the port. He was nineteen, which meant he was a man – childhood ended when one left for the Junior Academy at thirteen. He came from wealth; he was officer material. He thought he knew something of the politics of the Imperial family. But he could make no show of comprehending this. Staring, abashed and mute, he wondered if his Empress would walk left or right around the bodies. She had done neither; she had stopped and knelt before each one, studying their faces, touching their hands. Then she had thrown back her hood and swept her eyes across the gawkers in the Plaza; and Isiq, thirty feet away, had marvelled at her striking intelligence, her magnificent calm.

263

Thundering hooves: a cortège of nine carriages swept into the Plaza, almost at a gallop, and Maisa and her sons climbed into one of them, and the cortège raced out of the square. Isiq had never seen the monarch again.

Until tonight. *Look at her. Fifty years in the shadows. Fifty years hunted by the ones who stole her crown.* And yet if anything she looked prouder than before.

The conversation at the dais concluded with a peal of laughter from the Empress. The guests stood and bowed, and the old woman rose to her feet and raised her voice: 'You must dine with us, gentlemen, and forgive the menu's shortcomings, this once. They will be amended when we receive you at Castle Maag.'

An escort appeared and led the visitors out by another door. Isiq studied them as they passed: two black men, young and lithe and wary, and behind them a much older man wearing a monk's round travelling cap. Isiq straightened his jacket. Empress Maisa was descending the dais. Still she did not look at him, but walked instead to an ornate secretary desk near the statue of the martyrs, and scribbled something. Two servants approached her, and she glanced distractedly at the men.

'White goose, I think. And the doors, Hectyr. That is all.'

The servants withdrew, and Maisa went on scribbling. Isiq glanced about the chamber and saw that they were entirely alone.

His eyes snapped forward, she was approaching quickly. Trying to hide his pain, he sank to one knee.

She slapped him, hard. '*That* is for your unwavering loyalty to the usurper, Admiral Isiq. Not as a young naval cadet half a century ago. As a decorated officer, a hero, who has surely known for the past several decades that his Empress was alive and well. Oh get up, will you, and look me in the eye.'

Isiq rose stiffly to his feet. And slapped her with equal force.

'*That*,' he said, 'is for embroiling a young girl in your deadly plan without ever informing her father. I do not yet know how Thasha factors in your schemes, but I know that you have been elaborating them with Ramachni and Hercól Stanapeth since her infancy, if not her birth. As for my loyalties, of course I knew you were still alive. All Etherhorde knew it. Stanapeth himself spoke of you, as did Chadfallow. They praised you often – but they never breathed a word about your activities. Restoration! The idea never crossed my mind! I thought you'd found sanctuary in Tholjassa and would remain there until you died. If you wanted me to join this campaign, you might have started by letting me know it existed.'

Empress Maisa's hand was on her cheek. She was gaping at him, speechless with rage. Isiq met her eyes, unflinching. There was no hope without perfect honesty. Not at this hour. Not in this life.

Then Maisa laughed. 'I will benefit from this exchange. No one has dared lay a hand on me since my mother passed, when I was twelve. It is a very long time since I was twelve.'

'I did not come here to serve you,' said Isiq.

'What then? To strangle me? You had better do it now, don't you think? I have made it very easy for you.'

'I will never be your pawn, Empress. Never your unthinking tool. I was long a tool for Magad the Fourth, and even longer for his son. I committed atrocities because I did not let myself think. My beloved wife was killed, murdered by Sandor Ott, because I could not imagine that I was merely a device, a puppet worked by unseen hands.'

'Neither could they,' she said. 'I mean our enemies, yours and mine. That is the greater tragedy. Ott has been the unwitting tool of Arunis, and worked tirelessly to undermine the very Empire he thinks he defends. Magad agreed to a war conspiracy centred on the Shaggat Ness and your daughter, never dreaming that he too was dancing on a string. A failure of imagination, partly. And yes, you were guilty of the same.'

She laughed again, turned away, ran her fingers over the exquisite table. 'So was I, Admiral. Fifty years ago. The barons and the warlords and the great men of Arqual – they were jackals, hyenas. Next to them you're a cultured philosopher. They only let my father crown me because we were losing the war. That was still a great secret. We were going to lose, we were going to be routed, our children would all speak Mzithrini. But soon, they knew, it would burst out onto the streets of Etherhorde. And when it did the hyenas did not want the blame. Let the street think it was a woman's incompetence. Let them hang *her* when the Black Rags close in for the kill.'

'But you did not lose the war.'

'No, the Shaggat saved us then. His rise crippled the Mzithrin when they could least afford it, and gave us time to rebuild our forces. I did not fail – how they hated me for that! And even more so for not wishing to stab the wounded Mzithrin Empire through the heart when it was down. *My* peace emissaries were real, Isiq. Chadfallow's mission to Babqri City was real. This half-century of madness need not have happened, this world need not today be so blighted and burned – if only *thinking* had been valued over tribalism and blind allegiances. Over unthinking service, as you say.'

She gazed up at the great flag over her chair. 'I accept your declaration, Admiral. It is what I hoped for. But I could not possibly have let you know about my enterprise.'

'Why not?'

'Because if you had not joined that enterprise I would have fallen. One word from you to the Emperor would have sealed my fate. Magad has never ignored your warnings, Eberzam Isiq.'

'And now that I am disgraced?'

'But you are not disgraced,' said Maisa. 'You are presumed dead, and that is altogether different. As everyone in Alifros knows, you were last seen following the bearers of your daughter's corpse through the streets of Simjalla, on Treaty Day. All was terror and confusion. Perhaps you were picked up and tortured by the Mzithrinis.'

'I was tortured by *Ott*.'

'Ah, but that is no tale to warm the hearts of Magad's subjects. No, yours was a tragic death. If the Black Rags did not get you, then surely you collapsed of a broken heart, and were stripped of your wedding finery by a mob, and buried with the many beggars and tramps who perished that day. Or you returned to the

Chathrand in secret, to accompany your beloved daughter to her final rest in Etherhorde, only to go down with the ship off Talturi. Such are the rumours in the capital.'

'Ott said he would poison my name.'

'Ott said whatever he thought would break you. But here is where fate has sided with us at long last. *The Secret Fist truly believes that you are dead.* How that miracle was accomplished I would very much like to know. I gather it has something to do with that plague of rats?'

Isiq closed his eyes a moment.

'Never mind, never mind. Why would the Secret Fist pillory a dead man whom the Empire adores? Why waste a hero, when his death can provoke such a frenzy of patriotism? Magad did quite the opposite: he lionised you. He sent his own son, blind Prince Misoq, to the temple to pray for your soul. There is a bust of you already in the Naval Academy—'

Isiq looked up. *She has a spy in the Academy!*

'—and when they open the little garden commemorating the wreck of the *Chathrand*, there is to be a tribute to you engraved in stone. You are still their tool, Isiq. You cannot escape them even in death.'

Isiq's breath had grown shorter as she spoke. He was slipping. He should have foreseen everything Maisa had just told him. Great heroes like Magad needed the shoulders of lesser heroes to lift them up.

'As for involving your daughter in my plans, that is quite absurd,' said the Empress. 'Sandor Ott and Arunis manipulated your family, Isiq. Ott selected Thasha to be the sacrificial bride; Arunis turned the plot to his favour.'

'Ramachni does not serve you?'

'Oh for Rin's sake. His mistress was the great Erithusmé, and none other. I haven't the least idea what your daughter is to him. Mages guard their secrets as fiercely as monarchs, it appears. Ramachni came to me a decade ago and begged for help in guarding her. "I need a man of flawless honesty," he told me, "but a fighter, too, and a thinker." "Why not ask for a demigod and be done with it," I said. All the same I gave him my right arm: Hercól of Tholjassa, and sorely have I missed the man.'

'You must have suspected that there was more at stake than the life of one girl.'

'Of course I did. And now I'm sure of it: Suthinia Pathkendle has been able to verify that much merely by watching her children's dreams. Your daughter is somehow extraordinary, Isiq. Erithusmé herself was the first to notice.'

Isiq looked at her dubiously.

'I know,' said the Empress. 'You thought Erithusmé was a figure out of fairy tales. But she was as real as Arunis, and indeed more powerful. Suthinia tells me she owned the *Chathrand* outright, long before the ship passed into Arquali hands. What's more, the mage came to Etherhorde less than a year before Thasha's birth. Don't ask why: Suthinia doesn't know, and Ramachni never breathed a word about it.'

'You *never* had plans for her? For Thasha, I mean?'

Maisa shook her head. 'None at all. Though I was practically the only one in Alifros without them.'

'And now?'

Maisa looked at him a moment, then stepped to the wall and pulled on a rope. Isiq heard no bell, but moments later a servant appeared. 'Rum,' said the Empress. 'Two glasses. The better stuff, the Opaltine.'

When the servant was gone she looked back at Isiq. 'This is a special occasion. I have a small fortune in liquors, here, for my guests. One must try to keep up appearances. But I almost never drink. This will be the first time since early Umbrin.'

'I am flattered that Your Imperial Majesty chooses to make an exception for me – with me.'

'And were you impressed with Gregory and his freebooters?'

'I have never been more masterfully smuggled.'

She gave a sudden laugh. 'He is good at what he does. His buffoonery is an act, and so is his selfishness. He may not much care for Arqual or its fate, but he cares very much about his own beloved Ormael – so near at hand, and yet closed to him for ever. *That* is true patriotism: to go on loving the land that spits you out, reviled. They still call him Gregory the Traitor there, you know. But Gregory Pathkendle is also a man of vision. He married Suthinia, and he knew when to leave her. I began to court his help at Suthinia's urging, and little by little I gave him my trust. Of course that culminated with Treaty Day.'

'And your visit to Simja,' said the admiral. 'I remain astounded that you hazarded so much, merely to show your face to a handful of princes.'

'Can you really believe that was all?'

When Isiq said nothing, she waved a dismissive hand. 'Soon enough, soon enough. Gregory came through brilliantly, that's what counts. And yet there was still a chance that he was helping us for purposes strictly his own: revenge, maybe? Revenge on the Empire that had burned Ormael? Even after he returned me safely to these Fens, I thought that might be the case. Now of course we may dispense with that particular theory.'

'Why is that, Your Highness?'

'Because he had you under his thumb for a week. If he wanted revenge for that bloody massacre he would have started with you.'

Isiq flushed. Perhaps he always would at the mention of Ormael.

'Gregory is of course just one of my operatives. As this is just one of my strongholds. It has all been excruciatingly slow. How could it be otherwise, when a single betrayal would end it?' She looked at him, chin high, and her gaze was bright and steady. 'We are almost there, Isiq. Almost ready to strike.'

The admiral nodded, but his eyes flicked away. *Nine hundred soldiers.* Perhaps this was all a great vanity, an old queen's way of jeering at death.

'Your Majesty,' he said (for one had to say something, before the silence did), 'when did you learn that I was alive?'

'Nine or ten weeks ago,' she said. 'King Oshiram informed me, of course.'

And was that, Isiq wondered, *when you had your last drink?*

'I decided then and there to give my trust to Oshiram,' she said. 'I have not rued the decision. He was a fool to let himself be played so long by the Secret Fist, but it was hope for peace that tempted him, and to that temptation only the noblest yield. Besides, he will not be played again. As with you, his pride has been deeply stung.'

Maisa paused again, considering. Then she said, 'He did it, you know. He put Syrarys in jail.'

'Thank Rin for that,' said Isiq quickly.

'He is not thanking Rin. I am told he fell very hard for that creature, and struggles with despair.' She smiled darkly. 'Perhaps that is why he does not mind entangling his fate with my own.'

'He has joined the cause, then?'

'Not officially, not as King of Simja. But yes, I believe he has. And he knows more of how I shall achieve my aims than any other monarch alive.'

'Then I am sure he knows more than I do. Will you tell me, Empress?'

'Of course not. But here's our rum.'

The servant was advancing with a silver tray, which he placed on the table. Maisa poured, then handed Isiq a glass. He smiled his thanks (the good stuff, if she only knew how he needed it) but the Empress did not smile in return. They stood silent until the door closed again.

'Forgive me,' said Isiq. 'My loyalty has yet to be sufficiently tested, isn't that so?'

'Correct. I am impatient to confide in you, as it happens – but I have conquered nothing in my exile if not impatience. No one learns my plans until they prove themselves, and you are not yet on par with those freebooters out there, gobbling clams on the balconies.'

He bowed his head. He deserved this much censure, it was true.

'Tell me, Isiq: has Magad kept up the gardens in Etherhorde? Do the flying foxes still roost in the silk trees?'

'I have heard that they do.'

'And the arch of roses still shades the Pilgrims' Esplanade?'

Isiq hesitated, then shook his head. 'No, Empress. The arch collapsed under its own weight, five or six years ago.'

She looked stricken. He tried to imagine her as a young girl, arms spread wide, running the length of that bee-busy tunnel of flame. But the girl his mind was showing him was Thasha, always Thasha. He cleared his throat.

'May I at least know if your plans have gone beyond the theoretical?'

Maisa nodded slowly. 'Yes, you may know that much. They have gone far beyond it – to a point from which there is no return.'

Nothing could have pleased him more.

'I will be blunt, Isiq,' she said. 'I do need a tool. If you will not be that tool I expect my campaign to fall to pieces. It is not blind obedience I ask for. But you may be certain that I wish to use you, terribly and cruelly, in the pursuit of a better world.'

'And how can I prove myself worthy of your confidence?'

The Empress gazed at him sternly. There was a resolve in her that put his own suddenly to shame. 'To begin with,' she said, 'you can marry me.'

With that she threw back her rum.

13

A Task by Moonlight

~~~

Pazel's leg grew worse in their first hours in Uláramyth. He took to
bed, much to everyone's relief, but the pain did not abate. The selk
doctors frowned and whispered: the spittle of the flame troll had
burned deep into his flesh, and even penetrated the bone. To fight
it they had to probe deeply themselves, extracting tiny particles of
filth and sand, cutting the dead flesh away. For Pazel the ordeal
was very strange. He was in agony; at times he could not keep
from screaming aloud. And yet somehow the pain was a distant
thing. He observed his own suffering as though from a mountaintop, where a part of him remained at peace. Was it the magic
of Uláramyth, or had the selk given him some rare draught that
divided body from mind?

The next stage of his recovery was terrible, however. Chills and
fevers raced through him, and his wounded leg became too heavy
to move. He slept, but in his dreams he saw the Swarm of Night
moving among the clouds over Alifros: huge and hideous. Where
its shadow passed over the land, colours faded, growing things
turned sickly, backs bent with weariness and care. And the Swarm
grew larger even as he watched.

Then a morning came when he woke to the sound of shutters
opening, and sunlight bathed his face. Neeps was at the window,
dressed in fine new clothes, a boy prince on holiday. When Pazel
sat up he turned, beaming, then rushed to Pazel's side.

'Well, mate, you look like you recognize me, and that's an

improvement. How's that blary leg?'

'Fine. Marvellous, actually. What do you mean, recognize you?'

Neeps said that in Pazel's delirium he would wake but appear not to see anyone, or to know where he was. 'You were peaceful, fortunately – no mad capers like Felthrup. And the selk told me that faraway look was a good sign. They said it meant you were busy, fighting back to strength.'

'They were right,' said Pazel, kicking away the bedclothes. 'Is there anything to eat? I'm famished.'

'You should be,' said Neeps. 'Four days you've lain in that bed. There's food in the common room – if you're sure that leg is steady.'

'Steady!' Pazel laughed and sprang to his feet. 'I feel as if I could run.'

'Try it and I'll smack you,' said Thasha from the doorway.

She was dressed with simple elegance, like Neeps, and her golden hair was braided in a style he had never seen before. She came to him slowly, eyes thoughtful and serene. Pazel could feel her health when he embraced her.

Neeps looked away, instantly unsettled. 'She wouldn't budge from your side,' he said stiffly. 'We were thinking of tying her to a tree.'

Thasha stared hard at Neeps a moment. Then she flung an arm around his neck and pulled him close, and kissed both boys' foreheads until they laughed and squirmed.

When Pazel had dressed they stepped out into the sunny courtyard. The white dog Shilu rose to greet them, but there was no one else about. Neeps handed Pazel a bowl of rice and vegetables, and Pazel attacked it, not bothering to take a seat at the table.

'Where is everyone?' he asked between mouthfuls.

'Exploring,' said Neeps, 'except for Hercól and Ramachni, who will be studying the Nilstone and discussing the Swarm with the elders. And Cayer Vispek, of course. He'll be crouched in some little room, praying or contemplating death.'

'Neeps!' cried Thasha.

'I'm not blary exaggerating. The man even makes Neda

uncomfortable, and she half-worships him. Sorry, mate, but it's true. And if you ask me, it's real work to be unhappy in this place. It's been just four days, but I feel as if I've rested four *weeks*, at home on Sollochstol, with my Gran fussing over me.'

'It's the food,' said Thasha, 'and the water, and the air. It's richer, somehow.' She looked around. 'That's strange. Bolutu and Lunja were here a moment ago. I wonder why they ran off so quickly.'

'Because we're here,' said Neeps, 'and soon enough we'll all wake up and find ourselves back on some stony trail, cold and damp and surrounded by wolves. Finish eating, piglet; there's glory awaiting.'

Pazel finished, and they walked out into Uláramyth with Shilu at their heels. Thasha and Neeps had not done much exploring (Pazel suspected that they had both been watching him night and day, but they had seen something of the immediate area. The township was called Thehel Urred, and tiny though it was, it brimmed with hidden gardens and waterways and strange alleys tucked just out of sight. They showed Pazel a fountain where marble cranes strutted in glittering spray; a woken tortoise who dozed beneath a brysorwood tree, mumbling in his sleep; a pool from which a water spirit was said to emerge in the hour before dawn; a hedge maze where Bolutu had gotten lost chasing beetles and dragonflies, until Big Skip went in after him, unwinding a string.

The selk stopped them often, always with good cheer. They gave the youths small cups of wine or cider, and showed them places Thasha and Neeps had yet to discover. An amphitheatre, a gold smithy, a stone table where gems lay unguarded among scattered leaves, a glasshouse full of silkworms, an archery range where Nólcindar was practising, landing arrows in a spiral shape upon her target, neat as a tailor stitching a sleeve.

'You're getting tired,' said Thasha, watching Pazel's laboured breath. 'One more stop, then it's back to bed with you.'

The last stop was a little hill on the edge of the township. It was round and solitary, and a steep staircase led to its peak. At the summit, benches formed a circle about a strange hole fringed with ashes, from which steam puffed like a handkerchief shaken in the wind. It was a fumarole, a volcanic steam vent, like the ones they had seen on the lava field called the Black Tongue.

'No flame-trolls,' said Thasha, 'but plenty of fire underground. You can find these all over Uláramyth. Nólcindar brought us here yesterday, and showed us a thing or two.'

They turned Pazel this way and that. To the west, high on the crater's rim, stood the landing with the willow trees where they had arrived. On the north rim, higher still, a dark triangular doorway opened in the rock: that led to the Nine Peaks Road, an ancient trail over the mountaintops, by which no one journeyed any more. To the south the floor of the crater was all forest, moist and dark, with white mists drifting over the trees. And a mile east lay the great lake they had spotted from the landing, with its tall and solitary island.

'We're not allowed there,' said Thasha. 'In fact we're barred from three places in Uláramyth: the tunnels leading out of the city, a certain temple guarded by wolves like Valgrif – and that lake, which they call Osir Delhin.'

Pazel started. 'Do you know what that name means?'

'"Lake of Death",' said Thasha. 'Ramachni told us. But the selk won't talk about it at all.'

They sat down together on the turf, outside the ring of benches; the dog dropped down beside them with a contented whine.

'I don't understand the selk yet,' said Pazel. 'There's something different – *really* different – about them. Something you can't just *see*, like the strangeness of their eyebrows.'

'I feel it too,' said Neeps, 'every time they glance at me. And here's something else you can't tell by looking: Ramachni says there are just five thousand of them.'

'Five thousand in Uláramyth?'

'Five thousand in all the world.'

Pazel froze.

'A lot of them are here, in Uláramyth and the surrounding mountains,' said Thasha. 'The rest are scattered over Alifros. In the Northern world there are hardly any – maybe a few dozen all told.'

'*Five thousand*,' said Pazel again. The idea shocked him profoundly. There were more humans in little Ormael City than selk in the whole of Alifros. 'Where are their children?' he said. 'I haven't seen a single one.'

'I've seen a few,' said Thasha. 'But they're very quiet about their children, and seem to want to keep them out of sight.'

'Who knows when they *stop* being children,' said Neeps. 'At age twenty, or two hundred?' He looked out wistfully at the green landscape. 'I wish Marila were here. She would love this. I don't think she's ever known much peace.'

A silence fell. Pazel wished he'd never mentioned children. 'You shouldn't have clung to my bedside, you two,' he said at last.

Neeps and Thasha exchanged an awkward glance. 'It wasn't just for you, mate,' said Neeps. 'The doctors have been poking and prodding me around the clock. Weird treatments. They gave me mare's milk. And they asked Lunja to sit and stare into my eyes – which she did very reluctantly, I might add. None of those tricks changed anything, as far as I can tell. But Uláramyth has. The truth is, I felt my head clearing as soon as we stepped out of that tunnel. It's no cure; I can still feel something's wrong up here—' he rapped on his forehead '—but I think it may be buying me some time.'

Pazel could find no words for his friend. He was trying to imagine Neeps staying here, safe in Uláramyth but cut off from everyone he knew, from Marila, from their child …

He glanced nervously at Thasha. *What about you?* he thought. But he could not bring himself to ask, not yet. Instead he linked arms with both of them.

'Do you know why I wouldn't let them carry me?' he said. 'Because if we live – if some of us do – I want us to have this. A memory of seeing this place for the first time, together. Because right now we're alive, and I'm blary grateful for that – and, well, that's all, really—'

Thasha squeezed his hand. Neeps looked him up and down. 'Pitfire, now *he's* going to start with the blary kissing.'

Pazel tackled him, and Thasha joined in, besting them both, and they were still laughing and rolling when they heard a sharp canine *woof.*

Valgrif stood over them, looking amused, if that were possible in a gigantic white wolf. 'You look as healthy as cubs,' he said, 'but come quickly, Master Undrabust, for the doctors have been waiting to see you this hour and more.'

Neeps jumped up. '*Credek*, is it time already?'

'We'll come with you,' said Pazel, rising.

Neeps shook his head. 'Don't bother, mate. No others allowed when I'm being tested. No other humans, at least. Bolutu's often there, and Lunja. Devil take these tests, anyway! What good are they doing?'

'Go on,' said Thasha firmly. 'You told me this morning that they were almost finished. Don't quit now.'

Still grumbling, Neeps followed the wolf down the stairs. When he was gone Pazel looked at Thasha quickly. 'Have they said *any-thing* else to you? Privately, I mean?'

Thasha nodded. 'That there's hope. Real hope, but nothing certain.' She leaned into him, looking stunned. 'We were sitting here yesterday at this time, and a dozen *tol-chenni* shuffled by. They live here safely, like the birds and the deer. Some of them were chewing bones. The selk feed them, Ramachni says. And Neeps made a joke about how if he became one of them at least he'd never have to mend his socks.'

She gazed at him, as if asking how the world had ever produced so singular a creature as his friend. Pazel found himself laughing, and soon Thasha was laughing too, and it went on until she was limp and winded in his arms. 'We're supposed to keep him happy and relaxed,' she said. 'Of course the second part's impossible, since it's Neeps we're talking about. Still, that's our job.'

'Could be worse,' he said, and kissed her. It was an impulsive kiss more than a passionate one, but Thasha returned it desperately, clutching him about the neck. When he stopped to breathe she whispered *I found a place,* and he let her help him down the

277

stairs, giggling at his clumsy urgency. She led him south, by foot-paths and alleys, through the scattered buildings at the town's edge, across a meadow, over a stile, and at last deep into a field of green grass that rose higher than their shoulders. On they went for hundreds of yards, and the warm grass smell was shot through with richer scents, lavender and sage, and Thasha turned to him with burrs clinging to her hair and put a hand under his shirt. He felt the edge of her nails, a warning.

'You keep it away from me this time, or it's going to bleed.'

'Right,' he said at once, repressing a gesture of self-protection.

'You think I'm kidding. That I'm going to let you, no matter what I say.'

'Actually, I don't.'

'You'd better not. Because later we won't be able to do even this much. It's what I told you before. Later we'll have to think of other things.'

'I know that. And Thasha, listen: what I said on that island, in the river—'

Thasha shook her head. Beneath his shirt her hand began to move. He touched her cheek; she was trembling. There were tears at the corners of her eyes.

Time passed like a dream in Uláramyth: a dream of peace and heal-ing. It was the very end of summer, here in the Southern world, but the cold of the coming season had yet to arrive. Even at midnight (and Pazel was often awake at midnight, listening to selk music, or trading tales with them, or simply walking under the stars) there was as yet no chill, and by day the sun filled the crater-realm like liquid amber.

He thought: *The Swarm is out there, growing, gorging on death.* He knew that was the truth, but part of him was working hard to deny it. No world that held Uláramyth could hold *that* as well. And yet they themselves had brought a thing into Uláramyth that gave the Swarm all its power. A black sphere, a little flaw in the world's fabric, a tiny leak in the ship. Give it time and it would sink the ship, every last compartment, even one this small and secretive and blessed.

Often Pazel found himself thinking of Chadfallow. The man was not his father by blood: Pazel had finally forced him to answer that question definitively. But what was blood? Nothing more than an illusion, a lie. Captain Gregory Pathkendle was his blood, but Gregory had abandoned his family and never looked back. If anyone had earned the right to call himself Pazel's father, it was Ignus Chadfallow.

And how he would have loved Uláramyth! How he would have begged the selk to show him its wonders, to open their libraries, clinics, laboratories, to teach him *everything*. Chadfallow might have found peace in the Vale. And perhaps the two of them could have made up a little for all the wasted years.

We'll start that the day I get back to the Chathrand, *Ignus. The very minute. I swear.*

The others in their party had found pursuits of their own. Big Skip had befriended smiths and carpenters among the selk. Corporal Mandric was fascinated by their weaponry. Myett had travelled the forests with Valgrif, and Ensyl had been invited underground, and returned speaking of wondrous chambers of fire and ice. Hercól and Ramachni walked often with Lord Arim and Nólcindar and other leaders of the selk, but they were never long away, and stayed particularly close to the youths.

Only Cayer Vispek held himself apart. He was courteous, and showed true joy at the speed with which their wounds were healing. But he was not enraptured by Uláramyth, and he kept a stern eye on Pazel's sister. Neda herself was obedient to her master and dutiful in her prayers. Yet when Vispek allowed it she sought Pazel out, and no *sfvantskor* discipline could keep her from grinning at him, with that rare Neda grin he had almost forgotten. It had vanished so long ago, that grin. It had sailed with Gregory Pathkendle.

No one spoke yet of leaving Uláramyth. Thasha said that she thought the reason was probably simple: they had nowhere to go. The wilderness was vast, but beyond it lay the Bali Adro coast and the forces of the Ravens. Other reasons for the delay occurred to Pazel, however. Neeps, for starters. But he, Pazel, had not healed fully either, despite how good he felt. Walking was one thing, but if he ran or climbed any distance his leg began to burn. Each day the feeling lessened, but it never quite disappeared.

And then there was Thasha. Her body was healed, and by day her spirits were as bright as the late-summer skies. One morning she even challenged Hercól to a wrestling match, and laughed when he pinned her to the ground: 'What an old man you are! I remember when you could do that in half the time!' But at other moments, at night especially, a wall of strangeness descended. Pazel had seen it before: the chilliness in her eyes. The bleeding away of all recognition of those around her. The fierce awareness of something no one could see.

One night Pazel's sister shook him awake and led him to a window in the common room. Over the streets of Thehel Urred, the Southern moon hung like a pale blue fish egg – and beneath it, in her nightdress, stood Thasha, arms raised as if to pull it down from the sky.

'You know what's happening, don't you?' said Neda in Mzithrini. 'The wizardess is stirring inside her.'

'Of course,' said Pazel.

'My master says that Erithusmé took a part of her own soul and wiped it clean of memories, and let it grow for seventeen years, into Thasha. Is he right, Pazel? Is she living with just part of a soul?'

'No,' said Pazel. 'There's nothing partial about her. She's a whole person, the same as any of us.'

Neda glanced over her shoulder, as if afraid someone else might see her. Then she took Pazel's hand. 'Thasha is my sister. I swore as much on the battlefield, and even my master cannot say that I was wrong. But Pazel, there is a martyr's look in her eyes. We call it *kol-veyna*, the gaze into darkness. Cayer Vispek says—'

'Neda, don't.'

She saw it then, how hard he was fighting for control. They both fell silent. But when Thasha began to drift away from the square, Neda herself walked out into the moonlight, woke her with a touch, and led her back inside.

It was hard for Pazel to remember such moments when Thasha was in his arms, or when she and Neeps bickered contentedly, as they'd been doing since their first encounter on the *Chathrand*. Together the three youths ranged further across Uláramyth, exploring woods and keeps, caves and towers; and they guarded the memories of those joys for the rest of their days, like windows on a sunlit land.

Early one evening they heard shouting in the street, and left the house to investigate. From all the doors of Thehel Urred, selk were emerging, running and all in the same direction. The youths watched, mystified, until a selk man paused and looked up at them.

'Join us, citizens!' he cried. 'Join us at the Armoured Chamber! The elders have spoken: Thaulinin your benefactor will go free!'

He ran on without a word. Overjoyed, the three friends made to follow at once. 'As a matter of fact, you two should run,' said Pazel. 'Try to get there before he's released. I'll come as quickly as I can. Well go on, hurry!'

For once neither argued with him, but merely raced off. Pazel followed impatiently; most of the selk were drawing away. He broke into a cautious run, and had to smile. He could have kept pace with them after all: his leg was finally healed.

A selk man crossed the path ahead of him. Pazel glanced at the figure – and nearly stumbled in amazement.

'Kirishgán!'

For once again it was he. Pazel's friend from Vasparhaven was running like the other selk, but in a completely different direction. 'Wait!' cried Pazel. 'By the Tree, Kirishgán, can't you just stay a moment?'

Kirishgán stopped. He turned back to look at Pazel – but as before, appeared to do so with reluctance or difficulty. Their eyes met. Pazel stepped nearer, and a smile appeared on the face of the selk. But the next instant he turned, as though hearing a summons he could not ignore. Then he sprinted down the path and vanished among a stand of apple trees.

Pazel was confused and saddened. Kirishgán had never acted so strange in Vasparhaven Temple. Why on earth did he refuse even to speak? But there was no hope of catching up with him. Pazel went on his way.

In the square of the Armoured Chamber a crowd had gathered – and there on a platform stood Thaulinin, a free selk once again. The selk did not cheer, as humans might have done at such a time, but hundreds of them pressed close to the platform, obviously delighted. Only a few, at the edges of the square, looked on with unease.

Neeps and Thasha had found Hercól, and Pazel made his way to them through the crowd. When he arrived he saw that Ramachni was there as well, curled like a cat in Thasha's arms. Pazel had barely greeted them when a hush fell over the crowd. Thaulinin was about to speak.

'I have little to tell you,' he said. 'You all know my heart. But my freedom is a small matter, beside all that we face. Change is upon us. The earth trembles, the Swarm is loosed and spreading its dark cloak over Alifros. The return of human beings is one sign; if you would have another I can provide it. Our pilgrims are coming home, as they always have before a crisis. Some, like great Nólcindar, bring us joy and song. Others pass in silence. Among these is our brother Kirishgán. I saw him through my window this morning, running the silent race.'

A sorrowful murmur rippled through the crowd. 'I saw him running as well,' said Nólcindar. A few others spoke up then, saying much the same. Confused and unsettled, Pazel raised a hand.

'I saw him tonight,' he said, as hundreds of blue selk eyes turned his way. 'He was in a great hurry, I think.'

His words caused a stir. 'Could you not have been mistaken, Pazel?' asked Thaulinin. 'You met Kirishgán in Vasparhaven, but this is a very different matter. And no doubt we selk look rather alike to you.'

'No you don't,' said Pazel. 'and it *was* Kirishgán. I called his name, and he turned to look at me, and smiled.'

The sounds of amazement grew. 'Whatever's the matter?' asked Thasha. 'Isn't this Kirishgán welcome in Uláramyth?'

'As much as any selk who breathes,' said Thaulinin, 'but perhaps we should speak of this later. Night comes soon, and there is much to decide.'

The selk began to disperse, glancing thoughtfully at the humans as they went. 'You never fail to surprise me, Pazel,' said Ramachni, 'but I should have told you about the selk. You befriended one weeks ago, after all.'

'Told him what?' Neeps demanded.

'I will let Thaulinin answer that question, now,' said Ramachni. 'And others, perhaps. Let us go.'

Thaulinin was waiting by the edge of the square. Beckoning, he led them down a twisting staircase bordered by junipers, and then into a dark, moss-covered tunnel. Pazel thought it must lead to some forbidding place, but on the far side lay a pleasant, hidden yard tucked into the bend of a swiftly running stream. A cool breeze touched their faces, carrying smells of nectar and pine. Thaulinin sat down by the stream's edge, and the others followed his lead.

The selk looked grimly at Pazel. 'See here, don't be angry,' said Neeps. 'No one told Pazel to keep quiet.'

'Oh, I am not angry,' said Thaulinin. 'It is just that we are all saddened by these glimpses of Kirishgán, and stunned that he answered Pazel's call.' He closed his eyes, and the feathered eyebrows knitted. 'In many ways my people are unique in Alifros. We neither live nor die as you do.'

'Are you saying ... that you are immortal?' asked Pazel.

Thaulinin shook his head. 'Such beings exist, but we are not among them – nor aspire to be, like your enemy Arunis. But our difference is indeed a difference of the soul. Among humans, the soul remains with the flesh, or at least very near it. The souls of dlömu range further afield – much further, during the *nuhzat*

283

ecstasies. But for the selk, the soul is a distant brother or sister. It roams over Alifros, free and fetterless, and it is our life's work to seek it out. That is why we are nomads, you see. That is why even blessed Uláramyth is no home for long. Ten years one of us may dwell here, or fifty – even a hundred, in rare cases. But these are only brief pauses in the journeys of our lives.'

Leaning back, Thaulinin cupped a palmful of water from the stream and drank. Then he said, 'Death comes when at last we find our soul. It is a sacred moment, and no tragedy for the one whose life is complete. But it is sad for those left behind. Much changes in the lifetime of a selk: forests die; streams widen into rivers; kingdoms become entries in books. Our friends, however, witness all this change, and remember with us.'

The shadows were lengthening; far off at the crater's rim, Pazel saw the last rays of sunset glittering on an icy peak.

'During our lives, we see no more than hints of our soul: far-off shadows, images, flickers of movement in the corners of our eyes. Only at the very end do we see our souls face to face. Those who will survive us – our soul's witnesses – may see it somewhat earlier. In outward form the soul is identical to its owner, but it cannot speak, or tarry. We say that it is running the silent race. That is what you saw, Pazel: Kirishgán's soul. But it was your second revelation that amazed us: that his soul heeded you, and even turned. Except in rare cases, only dear friends and close kin may cause a soul to pause in its flight.'

'We're hardly close,' said Pazel. 'I mean, he was very kind, marvellous in fact – but for Rin's sake, we just met once, for a few hours in a temple. We're not old friends.'

'Some forms of friendship elude all definition,' said Ramachni.

'Yes,' said Thaulinin, 'but there is another group of persons to whom our souls must answer: though it happens far more rarely. I speak of those who kill a selk by their own hands.'

Pazel was appalled. 'This is getting crazier by the minute,' he said. 'I'm not going to kill him! I *like* him, for Rin's sake!'

'Something must explain his turning at your call,' said Thaulinin.

'Let us hope it is merely friendship,' said Ramachni. 'Pazel's is a most open heart.'

'But Kirishgán's not even here, is he?' said Thasha. 'Truly here, I mean, in the flesh?'

Thaulinin shook his head. 'Remember that our notion of *soon* is unlike yours. Kirishgán's death may be months away, or years. And when Pazel does meet him in the flesh, he may well be far from the Secret Vale.'

'But where can we go?' asked Neeps. 'Back to Masalym? Further down the Ansyndra?'

Thaulinin's blue eyes were starting to gleam in the darkness. 'Neither,' he said. 'Only a few reports from the wider Peninsula have reached us lately, but they were worse than our darkest fears. A retreat to Masalym is impossible. The Inner Dominion is held by two Plazic legions, and the pass at Ilvaspar is closed. Soldiers have been billeted in great numbers in all the towns of the northern coast. The Lower Ansyndra and her tributaries are swarming with Imperial troops, and upriver the hrathmogs are innumerable. There will be no escape that way either. And the sorceress has even infiltrated these mountains, vast as they are.'

'Is Uláramyth threatened, then?' asked Hercól.

'Not by Macadra,' said Ramachni. 'The mountains are too deep, and this haven is protected by a magic as old as the mountains themselves. Even her winged servants cannot see it.'

'What about Dastu?' asked Thasha. 'What if he's captured, and tells everything he knows?'

'Dastu might indeed say much to our disadvantage,' said Thaulinin. 'He could tell Macadra that we bear the Nilstone, if she has not guessed already. But he cannot help her find Uláramyth. Your companion was far from here when he deserted, and we would have known if he tried to follow us. No, two things alone could bring ruin on this land: the Nilstone wielded by an enemy, or the Swarm of Night as it completes its killing work. But beyond Uláramyth nothing protects us at all, and I fear the Ravens will have spies at every crossroads.'

'What's left to us, if we can't go back, or follow the rivers to the coast?' asked Pazel.

Before Thaulinin could answer, something splashed in the stream. It was Bolutu, dressed in some kind of swimming trousers. He climbed up onto the bank, laughing at their surprise; evidently he had covered some distance underwater. Bolutu had been swimming every day in Uláramyth, and had already shared many a story of rainbow-hued fish, flooded ruins, green river dolphins that nipped his toes. But this time he told no tales.

'Mr Undrabust, why are you not at the house? The doctors are waiting. I have been seeking you high and low.'

'You are *such* a donkey,' said Thasha, socking Neeps in the arm.

'Ouch! Not fair! I didn't forget; they had at me first thing this morning. They never do it twice in one day.'

All the same he leaped up and ran for the communal house. Bolutu watched him go, then turned and looked at Ramachni. His look of elation was gone. 'Have you told them?' he asked.

His words struck Pazel cold. 'What's happened now?' he asked.

'I do have *good* things to tell you, on occasion, Pazel,' said the mage. 'This is one such occasion. There is new hope for your friend.'

Joy welled up in Pazel's chest. Thasha's eyes lit with happiness, and even Hercól's face brightened. But Ramachni quickly raised his paw. 'I did not say that we had found a cure, for there is no cure for the mind-plague, until the Nilstone is cast out of Alifros. But Neeps has suffered no real damage yet, and we have devised a plan that could – if all goes well – delay the advance of the plague by several years. By that time our struggle with the Nilstone will have ended one way or another.'

'What plan?' said Thasha. 'Tell us, for Rin's sake!'

'And say how we may help,' added Ensyl.

'The latter is easier by far,' said Bolutu. 'You may help by not minding any strange behaviour on Undrabust's part, and never letting on that he is being … treated at all.'

He turned and looked away upstream. And Pazel saw that another figure was swimming towards them, dark and swift. With a splash the figure broke the surface: it was Lunja. She stood with the water about her calves, her soldier's arms crossed before her and her silver eyes bright and wary.

'Well?' she said.

'The elders have spoken,' said Ramachni. 'If you are willing it may begin tonight.'

'I've told you already that I am willing, if there is truly no other way,' said Lunja, 'but I do not do this gladly. The notion repels me. I wish that you could promise success.'

'No one can, woman of Masalym,' said a voice from their right.

It was Lord Arim, standing by the tunnel's mouth. He walked slowly into the yard, and behind him came Valgrif the wolf.

'From the first ragged militias in their stand against the Chaldryl Argosies, Bali Adro soldiers have been courageous,' he said. 'Now you must show courage of a different sort, if you are to help your friend.'

'Friend?' said Lunja. 'Is that what he is?'

She stepped out of the stream. To Pazel's great surprise it was to him that she came – haltingly, looking him up and down. Only when she stood right before him, lovely and alien and severe, did Pazel realise the extent of her unease. Her face was rigid. Forcing herself, she reached out and placed a wet, webbed hand upon his cheek. She held it there, silently, studying his face. Just when Pazel was about to demand that someone explain, Lunja turned and marched swiftly past Lord Arim and into the tunnel. There she paused, and spoke without turning back.

'Forgive my selfishness. He is my comrade too, and I will do what I can to save him. Only do not force me to speak of this idly. I will tell you when it is done.'

She vanished, a shadow among shadows. Pazel and Thasha looked at the others, amazed. 'What in the bubbling Pits was *that* all about?' said Thasha. 'What does she have to do with Neeps' cure?'

'As Sergeant Lunja is one of just two dlömu in Uláramyth, she has *everything* to do with it,' said Thaulinin. 'But you will see soon enough. Come, my lord Arim: would you sit with us?'

'There is no time,' said the old selk. 'We make the crossing tonight.'

Ramachni nodded, but Thaulinin looked gravely concerned. 'Tonight!' he said. 'My lord, I fear the youths are not ready.'

Arim came slowly forward, gazing at Pazel and Thasha in turn. 'Pazel Pathkendle is stronger than you know, and Lady Thasha will not benefit from delay. In any case it must be tonight.' He raised a trembling hand and pointed. Nearly invisible (for there was light yet in the evening sky), the little Southern moon gleamed over the mountains. 'The Candle passes through the horns of its mother-moon, and will not do so again for ten years. I must prepare, and you should rest while you can. After your meal we will find you.'

That evening the youths had little appetite, but others in their party were eager to talk. Myett had spent two days on the far fringes of Uláramyth, riding Valgrif's broad shoulders. Big Skip, traces of sawdust in his beard, described the skills he was learning from his artisan friends. Neda and Cayer Vispek were in foul spirits, however, and ate apart. Lunja and Neeps did not come to dinner at all.

When Pazel, Thasha and Hercól stepped outside, the night was distinctly cold. Above was a sky full of brilliant stars, and a sliver of the yellow moon. A selk in dark robes was waiting for them beside a carriage. The two horses were black and solid as rhinos, but their eyes were the shining blue of the selk.

They set off. The roads of Uláramyth were empty, and for three dark miles no one spoke. Pazel was afraid for Thasha: the distance was back in her eyes. He glanced at her now, gazing from the carriage window, breath puffing white as smoke through her lips. A haunted face. He thought suddenly of the girl who had climbed atop another carriage, in the bedlam of the Etherhorde waterfront, to gape at him with a child's mischief. The admiral's daughter. He had never expected to so much as speak to her.

The driver spoke softly to the horses. The carriage stopped, and the three humans climbed out upon the barren shores of Osir Delhin, the Lake of Death.

It was a chilling place. The wind moaned like a voice from a melancholy dream. Both moons had cleared the horizon, and by their light Pazel saw driftwood and black stones, and small waves lapping the shore. The island too was dark. *What are we doing here?* he thought.

'We have to wait here,' said Thasha.

'Yes,' said the driver, climbing down from the carriage. 'A boat will come for you. If you like you may wait in the carriage, out of the wind.'

Thasha began to walk towards the water. 'Beware!' called the driver. 'The lake has a curious property: it cannot be swum. If you try, you will sink to the bottom as though wrapped in chains.'

Thasha kept moving, and Hercól and Pazel rushed after her. Pazel had a growing sense that the night held something terrible for Thasha. She had been distant so many times, but this would be something else, something altogether more drastic. There was no telling what she might do – or what might be done to her.

A few yards from the water they seized her arms. 'Far enough,' said Hercól gently. To Pazel's immense relief she made no objection, but merely folded her legs and sat. Pazel and Hercól did the same on either side of her. Thasha laid her head on Hercól's shoulder, and put her arms around her chest. She did not glance at Pazel at all.

'I could do it,' she said. 'I could walk right into that lake.'

'I doubt that you are immune, Thasha,' said Hercól. 'There is magic here as old as Alifros itself.'

Thasha closed her eyes and smiled. 'Of course I'm not immune. I'd drown like anyone. Otherwise, what would be the point?'

'Don't talk that way!' hissed Pazel. But Thasha just clung tighter to Hercól. 'The boat is coming,' she said. 'You have to stay here.'

She hadn't looked, but it was true: a small, lightless craft was approaching from the island. Pazel could see neither oars nor sail. Strangest of all, the boat appeared to be empty. But as it drew

nearer he saw that that was not quite true. Ramachni stood upon
the bow, like a dark figurehead. When at last the boat struck
ground he flicked his tail.

'Come,' he said.

They were on their feet now. Hercól took Thasha's hands in
his own. 'Be strong, Thasha Isiq,' he said. 'I will be here when you
return.'

She raised her head and kissed him briefly on the lips. 'Someone
will return,' she said.

Pazel watched her climb into the boat. He raised a hand as if
to touch her, then let it fall to his side. He couldn't speak, couldn't
choose among the thousands of words he needed to say. 'Thasha,
wait!' he managed to croak at last.

Only then did she look at him. In her face he saw alarm for the
first time, indeed shock, to find him still ashore.

'We *are* waiting, lad,' said Ramachni. 'Get in, and be quick.'

Speechless, Pazel scrambled into the boat. Thasha had been telling Hercól goodbye, but not him. Not yet. 'What a fool I've fallen
in love with,' she said, touching his arm. Her voice ethereal, a distant echo of the one he knew.

The crossing was swift and frigid. Ramachni stood at the bow as
before, and Pazel wondered if the force that moved them was his
doing or some magic of the selk. Thasha's mind cleared briefly: she
looked at Pazel and told him plainly that Erithusmé's memories
were trickling into her mind.

'A drop here, a drop there. Like a leaky tap.' Thasha tried to
smile.

'What does that mean? Is she waking up?'

Thasha considered the question, then shook her head. 'I don't
think she's ever been asleep.'

The island drew near. It was stark and forbidding, and larger
than Pazel had supposed. Ancient trees, vast of girth but bent low
to the ground and twisted into writhing dragon-shapes, stood scattered over the dry earth, their roots clawing among paving stones
and broken columns and the remains of tumbled walls. The wind

was tearing the first leaves of autumn from their boughs, hurling them like playing cards into the night.

The boat ground ashore. Ramachni leaped out, and the youths followed, and soon they were marching up a dusty trail onto higher ground. They had not gone far when Thaulinin appeared, running sure-footed and soundless.

'You're here!' he said. 'Very good, it is time.' He took a wine skin from his shoulder and filled a cup. 'Have a sip to warm you – and then follow quickly. We dare not arrive too late.'

Pazel drank when his turn came, and felt the night's chill retreating to his fingertips. Thaulinin led them on, over hills, up staircases of shattered stone, among the shells of ancient halls and towers. The trees cast twin shadows in the double moonlight. A great number of them, he saw now, were dead.

'Why is this place so miserable?' Pazel asked Thaulinin. 'When did your people abandon it?'

'You ask questions that would take all night to answer,' said Thaulinin. 'The selk never dwelt here, and the fall of those who did was a great tragedy, which some name as the moment this world lost her innocence. They were defeated in a war before the Dawn War, and Uláramyth became the seat of a demonic power. *Wauldryl*, it was called: the Place of Despair. If ever a land was hated, it was this one that we love. Its king dwelt on this island, in a secret chamber no one shall ever see again. Over the ages we have healed most of Uláramyth, but our successes here have been smaller, for the damage was profound.'

He glanced quickly at Pazel. 'If Dastu had come here, all Uláramyth might have looked this way to him. Few persons have ever come to our realm against their will, but those who do find themselves in another place altogether – a deathly land, poisoned by the fumes of the volcano, where all that lives becomes rapacious and foul. It is always thus. We never spoke of Uláramyth in Dastu's hearing, but his heart must have sensed what he would find here, and turned from it. May it find peace somewhere in Alifros, or beyond.'

They were nearing the top of the longest staircase yet, winding up the side of a barren hill. Pazel wished Thaulinin would go on speaking, if only to distract him from the mournful wind. The stars were sharp as cut-crystal, and for a moment Pazel imagined that he saw them through as the selk did: mute witnesses, looking down in judgement or pity. *We are all young beneath the watchful stars.* Would he ever understand just what that meant to the selk?

On the hilltop they stepped into the full blast of the wind. There was a railed platform here; it was the highest point on the island. And looking down at the back of the hill, which had been hidden until this moment, Pazel saw an extraordinary thing.

He took it at first for a walled pond or water tank. It was fifty or sixty feet square, and surrounded by a number of the ancient trees. Black and lustrous, it reflected the moons and the stars with an uncanny brilliance, like a mirror polished to perfection. But a moment later Pazel saw that it was not liquid he was gazing at, but stone.

The trail descended from the hilltop to the edge of this strange black courtyard. Beside the latter stood Lord Arim, alone and still, his bright blue eyes gazing up at them.

'Go to him quickly,' said Thaulinin. 'I must remain here and keep watch. Farewell, Thasha Isiq!'

Thasha and Ramachni started down without a word. Pazel glanced at Thaulinin – why had he wished Thasha alone farewell? – but the selk only beckoned him on.

Arim did not move as they approached, but when they reached him the old selk turned and waved a hand over the square. 'The Demon's Court,' he said. 'Nothing older will you ever behold in Alifros. You are the first humans to stand here in many centuries, and you may well be the last. It was brought to this island in the dark times, for a dark purpose. But it is not evil in itself – not exactly.'

'Remove your shoes,' said Ramachni. 'You must walk unshod upon the stone.'

Lord Arim's feet were already bare. The old selk pointed up at the sky, and Pazel saw that the Polar Candle now stood precisely between the horns of the thin yellow moon.

'Follow me when you are ready,' said Lord Arim. With that he stepped up onto the stone, onto his own perfect reflection. Slowly he walked away from them. Pazel stared, transfixed. He was quite certain the stone was dry, and yet with each footfall its black surface *rippled* slightly, as though Lord Arim were walking on the surface of a pool.

Ramachni nudged Pazel's ankle. 'Crouch down, both of you. I want to see your faces.'

They obeyed, and Pazel saw stars reflected in Ramachni's great black eyes. 'Do you know why you are here?' asked the mage.

'Of course,' said Thasha. 'To bring Erithusmé back. So that she can fight for us. So that she can help us take the Nilstone out of Alifros, and defeat the Swarm. But before that can happen you need to get me out of the way.'

'That is about half right,' said Ramachni. 'We need her aid, and desperately, for without it we are hopelessly unmatched. And though many count me wise, since the death of Arunis I have not felt so, for I cannot explain what prevents Erithusmé's return. But with any luck that will change tonight.'

'Gods damn it all!' said Pazel, startling them both. He gripped Thasha's arm. 'What about *her*? You say they share a soul, but I can't believe that. Thasha is Thasha. She's seventeen. You can't flood her with *ten centuries* of memory—'

'Twelve,' said Ramachni.

'—and expect anything of her to be left intact. That's like—' he shook his hands desperately '—like pouring a cup of wine into a lake, and saying, "Don't worry, the wine's still there." Well it's not there, it's ruined.'

'Calm yourself,' said Ramachni. 'That is not how things stand.'

'You're a mage,' said Pazel. 'Seventeen years is nothing to you. But to Thasha it's everything. If you do this, her life will be *drowned*, do you hear? It will be just some little moment that Erithusmé recalls now and then. Like a fever, a time when she was not herself. You might as well kill her.'

'Right,' said Thasha. 'Kill me.'

'Over my dead body!'

'Pazel Pathkendle!' said Ramachni, his fur bristling. 'I will tell you this but once. You love Thasha. You are hardly alone in that distinction. There is great danger to her in what we do tonight, and that cannot be avoided. She may even die – or you may, or I myself. But she was never singled out for sacrifice. This is not Treaty Day on Simja, boy, and I am no Sandor Ott.'

'Ramachni,' said Thasha, 'where did Lord Arim go?'

Pazel started. The old selk had simply disappeared.

'No more talk,' said Ramachni. 'Follow, unless you would undo all that we have worked to achieve.' He stepped onto the stone of the courtyard, then looked back over his shoulder, waiting. Thasha groped for Pazel's hand. Together they stepped onto the stone.

Pitfire!

The sensation was like a plunge into frigid water. And yet the shock was far deeper than that: he felt it in his muscle, his blood, his very bones. It was a moment of total annihilation, of not existing. But he was still here, still holding Thasha's hand. Both of them were gasping, and their breath sounded oddly loud. Then he knew why: the wind had vanished, utterly. It was as if someone had just sealed a hatch.

'What's happening, Ramachni?' Thasha whispered.

'Look there,' said the mage, pointing with his eyes. Pazel turned and saw nothing at first. Then his eyes made out a brown autumn leaf just beyond the edge of the courtyard, one of countless leaves tumbled by the wind. It was five feet off the ground – and perfectly motionless, as though trapped in a pillar of glass.

'We have stepped outside of time,' said Ramachni. 'Once every ten years, when the moons conspire, anyone who enters the Demon's Court may escape time's dominion, for an hour or an age. When we depart, not a minute will have passed in the world outside. The old king of Wauldryl raised demons here, gaining servants overnight that would otherwise have needed centuries to mature. And there were other uses: prisoners who resisted interrogation saw their loved ones brought here, and made elderly in a heartbeat. Royal children were brought instantly to marriageable age. But the selk have turned even this place to the good.'

The mage crept forward, choosing each step. The perfect silence only added to Pazel's fear, his sense that Thasha was walking to her doom. Inwardly he raged at himself: *Trust Ramachni. Like you always have, like she's done all her life.* But at the same time a part of him recalled Thaulinin's words by the streamside: *I fear the youths are not ready.*

At the centre of the Court, Ramachni stopped and closed his eyes. 'Now, Thasha,' he said, 'lift me up.'

Thasha glanced quickly at Pazel, then bent and gathered the mage into her arms. 'Step forward!' barked Ramachni, and Thasha, startled, obeyed at once. Her bare foot came down upon the stone—

—and passed through, as smoothly as if she had stepped off the end of a pier. She fell, too amazed even to shout as her body vanished into blackness. Pazel cried out and lunged for her. Too late. Thasha and Ramachni had fallen through the stone. Pazel struck the glassy surface; it felt hard as steel. But within the stone he could still see them falling – Thasha reached for him, horrified – deeper, deeper, gone.

He beat the stone, howled their names, very close to despair. He looked around wildly for help. Death he could manage; death he had so often faced; but not survival without them, left alone with that last image of them sinking in the dark.

A mistake, he thought, sobbing uncontrollably. Ramachni had made them before. *Rin help them, bring them back or take me too.*

Something touched his shoulder. He leaped away in shock. Upon the stone before him stood a human woman, tall and tremendously old, dressed in a green woollen cloak. Her skin was translucent, her arms stick-thin. In her eyes was a fascinated gleam.

'You're the tarboy, aren't you? Pazel Pathkendle. The one who keeps trying to get her britches down.'

He stared. She stared back. She wore glass bangles and a blood-red scarf that looked for all the world as though it were made of fish scales. He felt a powerful urge to get away from her but did not move an inch.

'You're not going to fall through the stone, if that's what concerns you,' said the woman. 'Ramachni and Old Arim had to work to make it happen, just as I did to rise to the surface.'

Her accent was a bit like Cayer Vispek's. *Yes,* he thought. *Erithusmé was born in Nohirin, a Mzithrini land.*

She squinted at him, perplexed. 'Can't you talk?'

He was about to answer, but he stopped himself. Let her do the talking. Let her explain why he shouldn't hate the sight of her. But the woman only clicked her tongue and stomped towards him. Before he could decide whether to fight or flee she slapped one bony hand over his eyes, and when she lowered it the Demon's Court was changed.

There were columns, now, and a partial roof. There were heaps of sand and masonry. A wall with chains and shackles. Stone benches so old and worn they looked like waxworks left out in the sun.

'This is how the Court appeared in the days when I wielded the Stone,' she said. 'They kept prisoners in that corner, over there; if you look carefully you can still find their teeth. I am glad the selk cleared all this rubbish away.'

'Why did you bring it back, then?'

'I needed something to sit on. The ground may do for tarboys, but not respectable ladies like me.'

She laughed. Pazel did not. The woman shrugged and walked to a bench.

'Let us get down to business,' she said. 'Time has stopped outside the Court, but it is passing for you and me – and for them, especially for them. Watch out for the fire.'

'What do you mean? What fire?'

'The one directly behind you.'

He turned: not five feet away stood an iron cauldron on three stout legs. Within it a few small logs crackled spitefully. The smoke rose straight as a plumb line to the heavens.

'The fire is our timepiece,' she said. 'We may talk as long as it burns, and no longer. Come and sit beside me.'

Pazel stood his ground. The mage looked at him with some irritation.

'I am not some lurking spirit, boy. I have not spied on you two. A little of her knowledge and emotion reaches me, faintly, like noises through a wall. Otherwise I have had nothing to do with her.'

Liar, he thought. Aloud, he asked, 'Where are they?'

'Deep in the earth,' said Erithusmé, 'and you should be glad of that, because what we are doing would be impossible if they were anywhere else.'

'What *are* we doing, exactly?'

'Thasha is experiencing the anguish that results when a part of oneself leaves the flesh. Ramachni and Lord Arim are protecting her. And I – I am a soul without a body, a soul who has hidden in *Thasha*'s body for seventeen years, deaf and mute. I could not speak with Ramachni, or the selk, or the few other vital allies the Ravens have yet to kill. Not even, maddeningly, to Thasha. But tonight, and tonight alone, I am free to speak with you. To help our cause if I can.'

She pinched her arm. 'This flesh is illusion, of course. I can manage illusion even without a body, in this exceptional place.'

Pazel walked slowly to the bench. 'I don't believe you're a part of Thasha.'

'Nor am I.'

He felt a surge of relief – but then the mage tossed her head back, laughing like a crow.

'Ridiculous idea! Of course, Thasha is a part of *me*. And only a tiny part, a cutting from a sprawling vine. The fact that the girl has a body, and that I destroyed the one you're gaping at when I hid from my enemies within her – those are incidentals, nothing more.'

'You've been trying to steal Thasha's body,' said Pazel, hating her. 'I've watched the whole blary struggle. You've been clawing at her from the inside, trying to get out.'

'No, Pazel. Thasha has been begging me to come out.'

'What?'

'From a few hours after she slew Arunis. Waking and sleeping, in her thoughts and her dreams. She knows that I must rejoin the fight – and so do you, if you are honest with yourself.'

'We've managed without you. We killed Arunis without you.'

The mage looked at him silently. Pazel met her gaze, not at all sure if he were defending some vital truth or simply making a fool of himself. They had also let Arunis unleash the Swarm.

'The job must be done, boy,' she said, not unkindly. 'It is worth the sacrifice of a life. Any life.'

'Isn't that just what you've planned, you and Ramachni? For Thasha to *remember*, to welcome you back, with your twelve hundred years of memories? To die, in other words?'

Erithusmé laughed again, but now the laugh was bitter. 'A genius,' she said. 'He's seen right through our wicked hearts! Listen to me: Thasha Isiq was *never* meant to die – but I was.'

He stared at her, dumbfounded. The old woman sighed and rubbed the back of her neck. 'Thasha Isiq's mind has two chambers. The first is where her soul resides. It controls her body, her senses; it is entirely in charge. The second chamber is my deep refuge, my cave. I am free to leave it – but should I do so anywhere but here, where time is at a standstill, I should be dispersed like smoke on the wind: truly dead at last. Of course you'd like that.'

'I wouldn't,' he said.

'Just look at your face. Why, you'd break into song. You and Macadra, and the ghost of Arunis, and the Night Gods waiting to settle Alifros when the Swarm has done its work. I can read a face, boy. I know you wish me death.'

Pazel turned and walked to the cauldron. The fire was much lower, a shrinking blossom in a grey wreath of ash. 'You can't read *my* face,' he said. 'In fact I'm not sure what you can do, except talk and lie.'

The mage's eyes flashed, but Pazel found he truly wasn't afraid. She had her plans. She'd keep to them. Tossing insults back at her wouldn't change things.

After a moment Erithusmé dropped her eyes. 'We should not quarrel. We are allies in the greatest fight since the Dawn War. The fight I was thrust into twelve hundred years ago, when I was little older than you. Before I ever suspected I might be a mage. No, I cannot die just yet. And neither can Thasha Isiq.'

She jabbed a bony finger at him. 'Watch her. She is tempted to destroy herself. She thinks that if she drowns or suffocates it might let me return, but that is not true. It would be the end of us both.

'And it would indeed kill Thasha if we attempted to share one consciousness – to merge into a single, undivided being. As you guessed, her soul would simply drown in mine. She is indeed a little cutting from my ancient stem, you see. But that cutting has grown roots and leaves and branches. It came from me, but ultimately you're quite right, boy: it is *not* part of me any longer. Her soul is tiny, but complete in itself. How did you know?'

A silence. The mage looked him up and down. 'Never mind that,' she said. 'Just listen, for the love of Rin: Thasha's soul and my own must dwell in separate chambers, always. *But we can still pass in the hall.*'

'The hall?'

'Between the two chambers of her mind. Between the seat of consciousness and my darkened cave.' She spread her hands. 'There, now you have it. The great nefarious plan came down to this, boy: that our souls would trade places, until this damnable fight is won. Sit down, will you?'

Pazel just looked at her. 'Trade places, until we deal with the Nilstone?'

'Until *I* deal with it.'

'And what then?'

Erithusmé looked away, gazing at the suspended leaves, the

frozen figure of Thaulinin on the hilltop, the untwinkling stars. 'Then,' she said heavily, 'I concede the truth of what her mother told me at the start: that it is time for my long life to end. Then I leave both chambers to Thasha Isiq, and let the wind take my soul where it will.'

'You promise that?'

She shot him a startled look. 'I promised to let Thasha choose freely.'

An awkward silence fell. *Something's missing*, Pazel thought. *Is she lying, or just holding something back?*

'If what you say is true,' he asked, 'if Thasha wants to go into hiding, and let you return, if she's *begging* for it – then why in Pitfire hasn't it happened?'

The mage leaned forward, eyes bright with rage. 'Because,' she said, 'someone or something has walled off Thasha's chamber, with her soul inside it, and that wall is harder than this demon's rock under our feet. I cannot get in. Thasha cannot get out. And it is entirely possible that the girl herself has raised that wall, to enclose herself like a nautilus or a snail.'

Pazel felt a surge of panic. He knew suddenly what would come next. She was going to ask him to help her break down that wall. To overpower Thasha. She would say that it all came down to him, that their quest would fail if he refused. This was why she had asked for him – for 'the one who keeps trying to get her britches down'.

Because Thasha would trust him with her soul.

He went to the cauldron: only embers remained. He lowered his hand and felt no heat. Their time was almost up.

'I can't do it,' he whispered.

'I dare say,' sighed the mage.

He blinked. 'Weren't you – that is, don't you want me to convince her?'

'Are you thick, Mr Pathkendle? She is *already* convinced. She wants me to return. The trouble is that none of us know quite what is preventing me. Learn the nature of that wall – that is what I am asking. Between you and Thasha and Ramachni and the selk, you *must* learn how it formed, and how in Rin's name we can destroy it.'

A thought struck Pazel suddenly. 'I have one Master-Word left.'

'And a great one; I can feel it from here. A word that "blinds to give new sight". There might be something in that. When the wall crumbles, Thasha will feel some pain, and your word could blind her to it. But fear of pain alone could not have made the wall so infernally strong.'

'What if it wasn't Thasha? What if that wall was put there by an enemy – by Arunis, before he died?'

'Then we must find the flaw in the spell that made it. There is always a flaw, be it only a hairline crack.'

She patted the bench beside her. Pazel shook his head. 'I still don't trust you,' he said.

'Heavens, what a surprise.'

'You used the Nilstone for all sorts of spells. And made a right blary mess of things too.'

She waited.

'You cast the Waking Spell,' said Pazel. 'You made creatures like Felthrup and Master Mugstur.'

'I tapped the potential in their souls, to be precise.'

'And killed every human in Bali Adro through the mind-plague. To be precise.'

'That is true. Sit down.'

'I'll be damned if I will. You're a monster. That spell is killing my best friend, right now. It's done more harm than all the blary atrocities Arunis managed to pull off in two thousand years.'

She pursed her lips, considering. 'Hard to say.'

Her calm was hideous. *This,* he thought, *is the mage who lives in Thasha's head.*

'You should know one thing, however,' she went on. 'The Waking Spell was not some idle joke I chose to play on Alifros. It was a final tactic in a long war between mages. Perhaps you've heard of Sathek?'

'Yes,' said Pazel. 'The one who built that sceptre. The founder of the Mzithrin, although they hate him now. Arunis called up his spirit when we were docked in Simja Bay.'

Her eyes widened. 'Did he indeed? That *is* interesting … But what you may not know is that Sathek and Arunis were after the same prize.'

'Godhood,' said Pazel.

Erithusmé nodded. 'So Ramachni has told you something. Godhood, yes. And it is our great misfortune that the Night Gods, the high lords of annihilation, long ago chose Alifros as a kind of proving ground for their students.'

'Then that part's true as well,' said Pazel. 'Arunis was a student. He didn't care about Alifros, he just had to destroy it—'

'As an examination, a test. Sathek too tried to pass that test. It is the Night Gods' standing challenge: scour Alifros of life, and we will make you one of us, deathless and divine. But after Sathek's failure they made a concession. If one of their students sets the holocaust in motion but dies before it is complete, he may linger in Agaroth, death's Border-Kingdom, and still take the prize if the world perishes within a century. That is what Arunis is doing: sitting in escrow, watching the growth of the Swarm he unleashed, praying that it kills us all.

'Sathek's approach was somewhat less efficient: he thought to start by eliminating animal life – all animal life, including rational beasts like humans and dlömu. To that end he launched a series of Plague Ships from his fastness in the Mang-Mzn. The Book of the Old Faith tells the story well: how those vessels dispersed across Alifros, loaded with hides and woollen goods and cured meat and grains; and how embedded like a tasteless venom in each of them was the germ of a pestilence. Each of those ships was a kind of black-powder bomb of disease, and many did their work quite well. Some lands have never recovered. But the most insidious cargo of the Plague Ships was its living animals. Rats, bats, birds, feral dogs. These were simply released in port after port – and Sathek in his cunning had crafted *their* disease not to start killing its hosts for several years – not until they had multiplied, and passed the dormant seed of the plague down to their offspring. Had that seed ever sprouted, it would have spread like a lethal, wildfire rabies – and *no* creature would have been immune. The whole web of life in Alifros could have been destroyed in a summer. Indeed it almost was.

'By providence, I detected the plague in time – *barely* in time. There was no hope of a medical response. I had to fight it magically, with a single, monstrous spell: the greatest I ever attempted.'

'The Waking Spell?'

'Of course. Sathek's disease attacked the mind, so my spell had to reach those minds first – thousands of them, across the whole of Alifros, *without a single exception.*' She looked at him with sudden ferocity. 'I am a great mage in my own right – greater than Arunis, greater than Macadra – but such a spell was beyond me. Or would have been, without the Nilstone. I had to use it, though I knew better than anyone how it twists all good intentions. That is just what happened, of course. Every infected animal was changed. Total ruin was averted, and the birth of woken animals was a side effect. So was the destruction of every human mind in the South.'

'And it's still going on.'

'Obviously. The spell does not answer to me. Until someone casts the Nilstone from Alifros, it will continue.'

Pazel sat down on the bench. It was a struggle to find his voice. 'You saved the world ... and killed half the human beings in the world.'

Erithusmé nodded. 'It was a single act.'

Wonder, horror, vertigo. Pazel thought of the *tol-chenni* in their cages in Masalym, their huddled forest packs, the stinking mob in the village by the sea. The last Southern humans, mindless and doomed. How could he be talking to the woman responsible for *that*?

How could he possibly condemn her?

'I thought you were just mucking about,' he said. 'Experimenting. Ramachni could have blary mentioned why you cast the spell.'

'Not without breaking his promise. I swore him to secrecy on that point.'

'Well what in Pitfire did you do *that* for?'

She ignored his tone, this time. A strangely gentle look had come over her. 'I got to know a few of them, the woken animals I'd created. I called a falcon down from the clouds once, sensing the mind awake in him, and he befriended me, and travelled with me until he died. There were others, too: a spiny anteater, a snake.' She looked at him sharply. 'I was almost perfectly fearless: a freak of nature in my own way, like them. But they lived with a vast, gnawing fear, a fear in the souls. Who had made them? Why were they here, scattered minds in random bodies, hunted and abused and exhibited in circuses by the humans and the dlömu who surrounded them? It was hard enough for them to stay alive, and stay sane. They needed to believe there might be a purpose behind it, a grand design. I couldn't give them that purpose, but I let them hope. I wasn't about to steal that away.'

Pazel looked off into the night, and thought of Felthrup. That choice, at least, was something he could understand.

Erithusmé sighed. 'The Red Storm, incidentally, has stopped the mind-plague from spreading north. That is the Storm's whole purpose, as perhaps you've surmised. If your ship should eventually pass through it, you will all be cleansed.'

'And propelled into the future. Another unfortunate side effect.' She nodded.

'Better to lose all our friends and loved ones than to lose everything. That's how you see it.'

The mage appeared puzzled. 'Is there another way to see it?'

Pazel looked at her with immense dislike. 'Anyway,' he said, 'the Red Storm is dying. Or so Prince Olik told us.'

'Your prince is quite right. Not all spells are for ever. Within a decade or two it will give no protection at all. But it doesn't matter. The Swarm of Night will kill us all long before the mind-plague reaches any Northern land. And listen to me, boy: *we cannot fight the Swarm.*'

She seized his hand with her cold, thin fingers. 'All our effort must be to rid the world of the Stone. Nothing else. Take the Nilstone from this world, and all the forces it compels – the Red Storm, the mind-plague, above all the Swarm of Night – will falter and die. The Nilstone is the air that feeds those fires. To snuff the fires we must cut off the air. Nothing else we do will long matter if we fail in that.'

He nodded, leaning back heavily against the bench. He had understood the power of the Nilstone for a long time, but getting rid of it felt more impossible than ever.

'Tomorrow we'll do the impossible again,' he murmured.

'What's that?'

'Something Ramachni said. Just before we burned Arunis.' He turned to face her, nose to nose. 'If we win,' he said, 'Thasha gets to go on living – just like that? No tricks, no complications? You'll depart and leave her in peace?'

'I stand amazed,' she said, 'at the ill luck of your desire for that girl. You bear my mark. You were chosen. And here you sit brooding, like a child who doesn't want to share his candy.'

Another silence. Her avoidance of his question dangled between them like a corpse. Erithusmé glanced up at the moons. 'Well,' she said at last. 'I'm going to tell you. And Rin save Alifros if I err in doing so.'

'Tell me what?'

'How to use the Nilstone.'

Pazel's breath caught in his throat. The mage nodded at him solemnly. 'Any of you can do it. Any who bear my mark. You need only be touching one another – six of you at least – and concentrate on fearlessness. Then one of you may set his hand on the Stone, and whatever fear is in that one will flow out into the others. The one emptied of fear can command the Stone as I did – very briefly, perhaps only for a matter of seconds, but it might be long enough to kill Macadra, say, or blast a hole in a pursuing ship. You should try it here in Uláramyth, first, with the guidance of the selk.'

Pazel's mind was reeling. 'Six of us?' he said.

'Yes, six. The Red Wolf marked seven, in case one of you should be killed. Whatever's the matter now, boy? I know that the ixchel woman died – but six of you still breathe, I think?'

He nodded, wondering if he'd be ill.

'Out with it!'

'Five of us are here,' he said. 'The sixth is Captain Rose.'

'*Rose?*'

'He talked about coming with us.'

'*Nilus Rose?*'

'I almost believed him, but when it came time to leave the *Chathrand* he went into his cabin and didn't come out.'

'Get up. Move away from me.'

'What?'

She shot to her feet. The light around her changed. She clenched her fists, muscles straining, face contorting, and then she screamed with a fury that grew and grew and the sound was like the breaking of a mountain. Pazel crouched behind the stone bench. Light was pouring from her; the air convulsed with shock waves like the recoil of a cannon; his chest was imploding; the stone of the bench began to crack.

Illusion?

Then it was gone. Erithusmé stood there, breathless. The fury still throbbed in her, but it had changed, transmuted into something soundless and cold.

'With six of you, and the Nilstone's aid,' she said, 'you could have removed that wall in Thasha Isiq, no matter what its origin. You could have let me return.'

Pazel stared at her. *That's why she gave us the power to use the Stone.*

Erithusmé looked at the motionless trees, bending in an arrested gust of wind. 'The *Chathrand* has sailed without you, hasn't she?'

'They had no choice,' said Pazel, 'Macadra was bearing down on them. But we can still catch up. They haven't crossed the Ruling Sea.'

Erithusmé nodded distantly. Then she said, 'The fire is nearly out. Goodbye, Mr Pathkendle. In spite of everything, we *will* meet again. On that you may bet your precious little life.'

Pazel jumped. He had been holding in his own questions, overwhelmed by her non-stop talk. 'Wait,' he said, 'Ramachni told me something else I'll never forget: *"The world is not a music box, built to grind out the same song for ever. Any song may come from this world – and any future."'*

The mage turned him a faint, ironic smile. 'Ramachni was ever the romantic.'

She moved towards the fire cauldron. Pazel ran to her and seized her arm. He was more afraid of her departure now than anything she might do to him.

'Diadrelu wasn't supposed to die,' he said, 'Rose wasn't meant to stay with the ship. And Thasha wasn't supposed to have a wall inside her to stop you from trading places. But those things happened. Nothing's guaranteed. And if nothing's guaranteed, maybe you won't be able to return after all. What then?'

'What if the sun explodes?'

'Oh, stop that. You must have thought about it at least. What if this is the end? What if it's your last chance to do *anything* to help us win the fight?'

'Then we are doomed.'

'That's not blary good enough!'

'It's how things stand. Now take your hand off my arm, tarboy, or I will set it afire.'

Pazel tightened his grip. 'You *want* it to be true,' he said. 'You want to believe that you're the only one who matters. That there's no point even trying, unless we bring you back to save us all. But be honest, for Rin's sake! You're twelve hundred years old. Isn't there anything else in that mind of yours that we should know about, that could help us do this thing without you, if we must?'

Erithusmé flung her arm, and there was a Turach's strength behind the gesture. Pazel reeled and fell. When he looked up the mage was bending over the cauldron.

'Arrogant brat!' she said. 'I did not stumble unprepared into this

Court! Seventeen years I have been preparing for nothing else but this battle, this last task of my life. You could sit here thinking for a decade and not come up with a question I have failed to consider. I am on top of things, boy. I *have* determined how to rid Alifros of the Stone! I set thousands labouring at the task, though none of them ever knew the cause they truly served. The drug-addled Emperor of Arqual reunited me with my ship. Sandor Ott devised a scheme to take that ship to Gurishal, to the very door of the kingdom of death. And you and Arunis, together: you raised the Stone from the seabed and brought it onto the *Chathrand*, where I waited in disguise. I left out *nothing*. It is a master plan.'

'It's failing,' said Pazel.

For a moment her look was so deadly that he feared she would attack him. But Erithusmé was gripping the cauldron, now, and did not appear to want to release it. 'Destroy that wall!' she snarled. You can't beat them without me. You'll die under Plazic cannon, or the knives of Macadra's torturers. You'll die the first time the Swarm descends from the clouds, and in that black hell you'll curse your own stupid waywardness, that has cost Alifros its life.'

'Erithusmé,' said Pazel, 'I can see right through you.'

'The Pits you can, you imp.'

'I mean literally,' said Pazel.

The mage raised a hand before her eyes: it was transparent. She sighed. But it was not only the mage whose time had come. The entire court was fading. He could see the hillside through the ruins, the dry earth through Erithusmé's chest. The mage growled and plunged a hand into the cauldron, digging furiously. At last she straightened, and in her soot-covered hand lay a last, softly glowing coal.

'I am coming back,' she said, 'and you, Thasha's lover: you are going to make it possible. I know this. I have known it since I first heard your name. But I said I would answer your question, and I shall. If all seem lost – and *only* if it does – then take Thasha to the berth deck. Show her where you used to sleep, where you first dreamed of her. When she is standing there she will know what to do.' A wry smile appeared on the ancient face. 'And if that day comes, and you find new reasons to hate me – well, remember that you insisted.'

Her hand closed. He saw smoke through her fingers.

She was gone.

Thaulinin beckoned to him from the hilltop: apparently he was still forbidden to descend. The Demon's Court had vanished, and in its place lay nothing more than a barren slope. Pazel shivered as he climbed; the wind was unrelenting.

Clouds had appeared, pursuing one another across the sky, swallowing and disgorging the moons. He was exhausted, suddenly. The dead earth, so unlike any other place in Uláramyth, spoke to him of the endless brutality of the road ahead. *Do not forget the world outside*, Thaulinin had warned them. As if one could, even in a land of dreams.

The selk greeted him with a sombre nod. 'Were you successful?' he asked.

Pazel leaned on the iron fence. 'I don't know. I'm not even sure what that means any more.'

Thaulinin looked at him strangely. 'That is unfortunate. Your quest is bringing greater losses to my people than anyone foresaw. I hope they are not all in vain.'

Pazel jerked upright. 'What are you talking about, Thaulinin?'

'Come, I will show you.' He led Pazel to the opposite side of the hilltop, facing the side of the lake they had crossed. 'Wait for the cloud to pass … there.'

As if a curtain had been thrown open, moonlight flooded over Uláramyth. And there on the lower slopes of the island, near the shore, a crowd was running fast. They were selk, sixty or eighty of them, and they ran like contestants in a race, bunched close together; but in their hands were spears and daggers and long selk swords. Over a small rise they passed, fluid as horses, then down onto the rocky beach and—

'No!' Pazel shouted. 'Oh Pitfire, no!'

—straight into the lake, one after another, without slowing or appearing to mind when the water closed greedily over their heads.

'They will emerge again,' said Thaulinin softly, 'but you are right to ache. I counted seventy-six. Tomorrow the tears will flow in Uláramyth: we are so few, and when those souls find their owners we will be fewer yet. If any doubted that battle lay before us we have our proof tonight. Something was decided here that will also decide the fate of the selk.'

Noises behind them: Thasha was racing up the slope. Ramachni and Lord Arim walked behind. Pazel dashed through the gate to meet her, caught her in his arms. She was tear-streaked and shaking, and her hands trembled violently.

Like an old woman's. Pazel pulled sharply back from her, studying her face.

'Don't,' said Thasha, flinching.

'What happened? What did you do?'

'I didn't do anything,' she said. 'I just fell through the rock, down and down and down. We never reached bottom, we just stopped and hung there. It was so black, Pazel, and so *ancient*. I thought we were dead, and then I thought we'd died a million years ago, and our souls were caught in the demon's rock, caught like flies in honey. But then something burst out of me and flew off, and left me in pieces. I was broken, Pazel. Ramachni and Lord Arim held me together until I healed.'

Pazel stared deep into those frightened eyes. *You're back in there, aren't you? Back in your cave where you belong.*

'Pazel?'

He pulled her close again. 'I'm on your side,' he said. 'No one else's. Do you hear me?'

She kissed his ear, weeping freely. 'They broke me open. So that she could come out and talk to you. They had to, I know that—'

'Did they?'

She blinked at him, her look accusing – no, self-accusing. She swabbed her face with her sleeve.

'I didn't think I'd be so *scared*.'

Her voice came out tiny, a little girl's, a voice he knew gave her shame. He kissed her, undone by love; no force in Rin's heaven could challenge this one; they could try anything they liked.

'I'm with you, Thasha. I'll always be with you. No matter what happens I'll keep you safe.'

Thasha shook her head, adamant, trembling like a leaf. 'Promise,' she said, weeping again. 'Promise you won't.'

14

—ᴖᴖ—

Wednesday, 20 Halar 942. The wolves have finally pounced.

As I write this, I feel how lucky we are to be alive. Whether luck & life will still be with us much longer is uncertain. For now all credit goes to Captain Rose. People change; ships grow faster, arms more diabolical. But nothing beats a seasoned skipper, no matter his moods or eccentricities.

Five bells. Lunch still heavy in my stomach. A shout from the crow's nest: Ship dead astern! I happened to be right there at the wheel with Elkstem, & we rushed to the spankermast speaking-tube to hear the man properly.

'She was hid by the island, it's not my fault!' he shouted. That told us next to nothing: there were islands all about us, great & small, settled & unsettled (though with each day north we saw fewer signs of habitation), sandy & stony, lush & bone-dry. We'd been winding among them for a week.

'A monster of a boat!' the lookout was shouting. 'Ugly, huge! She's five times our measure if she's a yard.'

'Five times our blary length?' cried the sailmaster. 'Gather your wits, man, that's impossible! Distance! Heading!'

'Maybe *longer*, Mr Elkstem! I can't be sure; she's forty miles astern. And Rin slay me if she don't have a halo of fire above her. Devil-fire, I mean! Something foul beyond foul.'

'What *heading* is she on, damn you?' I bellowed.

'East, Mr Fiffengurt, or east-by-southeast. They're under full sail, sir, and—'

Silence. We both screamed at the poor lad, & then he answered shrilly: 'Correction, correction! Vessel tacking northwards! They've spied us, they've spied us!'

Not just spied, but fingered us for dinner, it appeared. I blew the whistle; the lieutenants started bellowing like hounds. In seconds we were preparing for war.

From the hatches men were spilling like ants, the dlömu answering the call as quickly as the humans, if not more so. Mr Leef finally brought me a telescope. I raised it, but shut my eyes before I looked. *Don't show the lads any fear; they're watching*, I thought.

The vessel was a horror. It was a Plazic invention to be sure, one of the foul things sustained by the magic the dlömu had drawn from the bones of the lizard-creatures called eguar. Prince Olik had told us a little, & the dlömic sailors a little more. Eguar-magic was the power behind the Bali Adro throne, & its doom. It had made her armies invincible – but their commanders depraved & self-destroying. It is a frightful state of affairs, & one that reminds me uncomfortably of dear old Arqual.

We'd seen monster-vessels before, in the terrible armada that passed so close to us just after we reached the Southern main. But this was something else altogether. Impossibly large & shapeless, it was like a giant, shabby fortress or cluster of warehouses that had somehow gone to sea. How did it *move*? There were sails, but they were preposterous: ribbed things that jutted out like the fins of a spiny rockfish. It should have been dead in the water, but the blue gap between it & the island was growing. It was under way.

Captain Rose bounded up the Silver Stair. Without a glance at me he climbed the quarterdeck ladder, & kept going to the mizzen yard, where he trained his own scope on the vessel. He held still a long time (what's a long time when your heart's in your throat?) as Elkstem & I gazed up at him. When he turned to us, his look was sober & direct.

'Gentlemen,' he said, 'you are distinguished seamen: use your skills. This foe we cannot fight. We must elude it until nightfall or we shall lose the *Chathrand*.'

The captain's rages are frightful, but his compliments simply terrify: he saves them for the worst of moments. In such times a mysterious calm descends on him; it is deeply unsettling to observe. He hung there, face unreadable within that red beard, one elbow hitched around a backstay. He examined the skies: blue above us, thick clouds to windward. Islands on all sides, of course. Rose looked over each of them in turn.

His eyes narrowed suddenly. He pointed at a dark, mountainous island, some forty miles off the starboard bow. 'That one. What is it called?'

Elkstem, who knew Prince Olik's map better than I, told him that it was Phyreis, one of the last charted islands in the Wilderness. 'And a big one, Captain. Half the size of Bramian, maybe,' he said.

'It appears to sharpen to a point.'

'The chart attests to it, sir: a long southwest headland.'

Rose nodded. 'Listen well, then. We must be fifteen miles off that point at nightfall. That will be at seven bells plus twenty minutes. Until then we are to stay as far as possible ahead of the enemy, without ever allowing him to cut us off from Phyreis. Is that perfectly clear?'

'By nightfall—' I began.

'Fiffengurt.' He cut me off, suddenly wrathful. 'You have just disgraced your very uniform. Did I say *by* nightfall? No, Quartermaster: my command was *at* nightfall. Earlier is unacceptable, later equally so. If these orders are beyond your comprehension I will appoint someone fit to carry them out.'

'Oppo, sir,' I said hastily. '*At* nightfall, fifteen miles off the point.'

Rose nodded, his eyes still on me. 'The precise course I leave to your combined discretion. The canvas likewise. That is all.'

And that was all. Rose sent word that he required Tarsel the blacksmith & six carpenters to join him on the upper gun deck, & lumbered off towards the No. 3 hatch, shouting at his ghosts: 'Clear out, stand aside. Don't touch me, you stinking shade! I know what a barometer is. *Damn you all, stop talking and let me think!*'

Elkstem & I put the men to spreading all the canvas we could think of; the winds were that sluggish. I even sent a team down to the orlop, digging for the moonrakers that hadn't been touched since Arunis calmed the winds off the Straits of Simja. Then we dived into our assignment: plotting, calculating, fighting over the maths. It is no easy job to ensure that one arrives at a distant spot *neither early nor late*, above all when one must seem to be fleeing. And to make matters worse, we were fleeing. There was the open question of just how fast that unnatural behemoth could move. One thing was clear, though: far more than wind propelled it over the seas.

The *Chathrand*, however, remains a beauty of a sailing ship. Despite the torpid day she was making thirteen knots by the time we ran out the studding sails. I was proud of her: she'd weathered a great deal & come through. But the Behemoth was still gaining. As it crept nearer I studied it again. A monstrosity. Great furnaces along her length, belching fire & soot. Black towers & catapults & cannon in unimaginable numbers, giving the whole thing the look of a sick, spiny animal. Hundreds, maybe a few *thousand*, crowded onto her topdeck. What possible use for so many?

'Traitor!'

I ducked with a curse. It was Ott's falcon, Niriviel. The bird screamed low over my head, shrieking, & alighted on the roof of the wheelhouse. It was the fourth time this week.

'Bird!' I sputtered. 'I swear on the Blessed Tree, if you *ever* come at me like that again—'

'My master orders me to announce my mission!' it shrilled. 'I go on reconnaissance. My master requires you to inform me of the distance between the ships.'

'The distance? About thirty miles, currently, but see here—'

'I hate you. You're a mutineer, a friend of Pathkendle and the Isiq girl. Why aren't you in chains?'

On the deck below, Darius Plapp looked up & grinned. The ganglord was working the mizzen halyards, along with twenty of his lackeys. The dispirited Burnscovers were far forward at the jiggermast. I had separated the gangs after a warning from Sergeant Haddismal that they were itching for a fight.

'Captain Rose finds me more useful here than in the brig,' I told the falcon. 'Now listen, bird, stay well above that ship, we don't know what sort of weapons they—'

'Some enemies sail over the horizon, coveting our land and gold,' cried the falcon, 'but worse are the sons of Arqual whom the Emperor has showered with love, and who do not love him in return.'

'Showered with love! Oh flap off, you blary simpleton!'

Niriviel stepped from the roof, beat his wings, & shot away southwards. The bird's abuses make me livid, but I can't manage to hate him for long. The poor beast was lost for a month after the Red Storm, & Ott seemed almost human in the way he nursed him back to strength – feeding him bite after bite of raw, fresh chicken, along with ample fibs about the greatness of Arqual & the vileness of her enemies. I think often of Hercól's assessment: 'Niriviel is a child soldier: trained in fanaticism, more a believer than those who taught him to believe.' In other words, a simpleton. But a useful one: he might well come back with knowledge that would save the ship.

'Why in Pitfire are we still tackin' north?' grunted Darius Plapp. 'This is blary suicide. We should be runnin' downwind.'

'If we need tactical advice we'll inform you, Plapp,' I said.

'Oppo, Mr Fiffengurt, sir.'

I could have had him sent to the brig for that sneering tone, but instead I pretended not to notice. Lately I am tempted to indulge the ganglords (the one who walks free, and the other who controls his little kingdom from the brig) so long as they don't set the lads on one another like so many dogs.

Once again there is peace between them: a seething, hate-heavy peace. Rose too has taken certain steps to foster it, despite making a savage example of Kruno Burnscove. A month ago, when the Burnscove Boys turned in that deathsmoke-addicted Plapp, I'd expected the poor wretch to be hanged. Rose had promised no less, & Rin knows he's bloody-minded enough. But instead he shackled the man to the rail near the left-handed stinkpots.* Four times a day, a Turach lit a deathsmoke cigar & left it burning in a steel bowl some five yards away. It was clearly torture. He could catch whiffs of the drug when the wind allowed: just enough to whet the knife of his craving. His howls were like those of a man awake during the amputation of his legs. What's more, every last hand saw the wretch when they came to void their bladders: saw how he pulled at the shackles until his wrists bled, thrashed against the deck until his face was one black bruise. It may even have scared a few lads away from the drug. Whether this one will survive the ordeal I cannot guess.

We went on tacking north. Clouds rolled in, their grey bellies heavy with rain, although for now it refused to fall. The wind freshened as well: soon we were at fifteen knots. Elkstem & I watched the Behemoth, & after a bit we exchanged a smile. The gap between us was no longer shrinking: indeed it was, ever so slightly, growing. The Behemoth was falling behind.

'Give me an honest wind over magecraft any day of the week,' said Elkstem. In a voice meant just for me, he added: 'Tree of Heaven, Graff, I thought we were dead.'

Marila, bless her, brought tea & biscuits to the quarterdeck. Her own belly is showing now, a little fruit bowl tucked under her shirt. In her arms was Felthrup, squirming with impatience to move: it was his first venture beyond the stateroom since the attempt on his life. As soon as his feet touched the boards, he raced the length of the quarterdeck and back again, then dashed excitedly about our heels.

'Prince Olik spoke the truth!' he squeaked. 'That ship is a mutant thing, a mishmash held together by spells alone! The Plazic forces are in decline. The power they seized has devoured them like termites from within, and turned them senseless and savage. But not

*Fiffengurt refers to the portside heads (toilets). As on most vessels, the *Chathrand*'s heads are located in the extreme forward section of the bow, where the wind (always somewhat faster than the ship) carries their stench away. – EDITOR

317

for long! Olik said they were melting, those Plazic weapons, and that Bali Adro cannot make any more.'

'Not without the bones of them croco-demons, is it?' said Elkstem.

'Very good, Mr Elkstem! Not without the bones of the eguar – and they have no more, for they have plundered the last of the eguar grave-pits. They are drunkards, taking the last sips from the bottle of power, and reeling already from withdrawal.'

'Godsforsaken rat on the quarterdeck,' muttered Darius Plapp.

'I believe you, Ratty,' I said, 'but it's no real comfort at the moment. Their last sips of power may blary well kill us.'

'Do you really think so?'

As if the Behemoth wished greatly to convince one little rat, something massive boomed on her deck. I snapped my scope up, hoping that one of those furnaces had exploded & torn her apart. No luck: it was rather the opening of a tremendous metal door. At first I couldn't see what lay beyond that door. But after several minutes I made out what looked like a bowsprit, & then a battery of guns. Something was detaching itself from the Behemoth & gliding out upon the waves.

'Graff,' Elkstem murmured to me, gazing through his more powerful scope. 'Do you know what that is? A sailing vessel, that's what. I mean a regular ship like our own. And blast me if she ain't got four masts!'

'You must be wrong,' I said. 'The monster can't be that big.'

But it was not long before I saw for myself that it was true. My hands went icy. 'That colossus,' I said, 'is a naval base. A *moveable* naval base. We're being pursued by a mucking shipyard.'

'It's the daughter ship that worries me,' said Elkstem.

The daughter ship, the four-master, was narrow & sleek. She might have been a pretty vessel once, but now her lines were ruined by great sheets of armour welded to her hull. All the same she would be faster than the Behemoth.

Her crew began spreading canvas. Elkstem growled. 'They're clever bastards. That four-master will catch us, sooner or later,

unless the wind decides to double. We could outfight her, maybe –
but so what? All she needs to do is nip our heels, hobble us with a
few shots to the rigging. Once we're slowed, the monster can catch
up and finish us.'

'I tell you we should run downwind,' said Darius Plapp.

'They would only do the same, Mr Plapp,' cried Felthrup,
through the rungs of the quarterdeck.

'The blary rodent gimp wants to be a sailor, now,' muttered
Plapp.

'Wrong again,' said Felthrup, 'and may I say that against that
particular desire you, sir, provide a fine inoculation?'

Plapp scowled. 'I ain't never provided you with nothin',' he said.

'Mr Fiffengurt,' said Marila, who had taken my telescope, 'what
if they don't catch us by nightfall?'

'Why, then our chances improve,' I said, 'so long as we keep the
lights out on the *Chathrand*. They could very well lose us in the
dark. Of course we won't know until morning. We could even wake
up & find 'em right on top of us.'

Marila started. 'Something's happening on the big ship,' she
said. 'They're moving something closer to the rail.'

Before I could take back the telescope there came a new explosion. From the deck of the Behemoth, a thing of flame was blasting skyward on a rooster-tail of orange sparks. A rocket, or a
burning cannon-shot. Its banshee howl caught up with us, but the
shot itself was not approaching, only climbing higher & higher.
Suddenly it burst. Five lesser fireballs spread from the core like the
spokes of a wheel: beautiful, terrible.

'Maybe they're trying to be friendly?' said a lad at the mizzen.

Then, in unison, the fireballs swerved, came together again, &
began to scream across the water in our direction.

Terror gripped us all. I bolted from the wheelhouse, shouting:
'Fire stations! Third and fourth watch to the pumps! Hoses to the
topdeck! Run, lads, run to save the ship!'

Marila had scooped up Felthrup & was racing for the ladderway. The fireballs had twenty miles to cover, & from the look of

it they would do so in the next three minutes. But what sort of projectile could change course in mid-air?

'Drop the mains, drop the topsails!' Elkstem was shouting. And that of course should have been my first command: those ten giant canvasses made for a target twice the size of the hull, & they would burn far more easily too. Someone (Rose?) at the bow had given the same order; already the sails were slinking down the masts.

By the grace of Rin we got the big sails down, & even furled the jibs & topgallants. All in about two minutes flat. I was by now down on deck & heading for the mainmast. I saw the first fire-team near the Holy Stair, wrestling with a hose that was already gushing salt water. But there were none close to me. I leaned over the tonnage hatch, screaming: 'Where's your team, Tanner, you boil-arsed dog?' When I turned, the men on deck were staring skyward. I whirled. A fireball was plummeting straight for us.

'Cover! Take cover!'

Everyone ran. I threw myself behind the No. 4 hatch coam. But I had to look – my ship was about to be massacred! – so at the last second I raised my eyes.

What I saw was a nightmare from the Pits. The fireball was no shot, no chunk of phosphorous or glob of burning tar. It was a creature: vaguely wasp-like, its great segmented body blazing like a torch, & it struck the deck & splattered flame in all directions like a dog shaking water from its fur.

I dropped, horrified. My hair caught fire but I snuffed it quick. A blizzard of sparks blew past me; without the hatch I'd have been roasted on the spot. When I looked up & down the length of the ship I thought our doom had come, for all I saw was fire. *Get up*, I thought, *move and fight while you can!* There were screams from fifty men, a gigantic howling & thumping from the creature itself. I don't know how I made myself stand & face the thing, but I did.

Heat struck me like a blow. The creature had smashed halfway through the deck & was lodged there, dying. It had made a suicide plunge, & when it struck its body had burst open like a melon. As it writhed & heaved, flame gushed from it like blood. Where was the rain? Where was our mucking skipper? I looked the ship up & down, & thought we were finished. Right in front of me a man caught fire: who he was I could not tell. He was running, screaming, & the flames wrapped him like a flag.

Then a mighty spray of water hit the man, knocking him clean off his feet. Rose & five Turachs were there behind me with a fire hose. They had wrestled it up the No. 4 & were blasting the poor wretch with all the force sixty men at the chain pumps could deliver. Thank Rin, it worked: he was doused, & two mates seized him & bore him away. Then Rose turned the spray around to the creature. It screamed & twitched & vomited fire, but it could not flee the blast. Very soon it was sputtering out.

Fire was still everywhere, though. At least four of the five creatures had exploded in like fashion. One had torn through the standing rigging, causing the entire mizzenmast to sway. The battle-nets were burning, the port skiff was burning, halyards were burning on the deck in coils. Beside me, Jervik Lank threw a younger tarboy into the life-saving spray, & I swear I heard the hiss as his burning clothes were extinguished. At the forecastle, Lady Oggosk opened her door, shrieked aghast & slammed it again.

Suddenly Rose exploded: 'Mizzenmast! Belay hauling! Belay! Damnation! BELAY!'

The men aloft could not hear him. Rose left the Turachs & ran straight through the fire, then swung out onto the mainmast shrouds, over the water, waving his hat & screaming for all he was worth. I saw the danger: high on the mizzenmast, the brave lads were trying to save their mainsail by lifting it clear of the smouldering deck. But a line was fouled in the sail – a burning line. They couldn't see it for the smoke, but they were about to spread the fire to the upper sails.

Captain Rose got their attention at last, & you may be sure they BELAYED. I looked around me, & by Rin, there was hope. All the creatures had been snuffed, the hoses were still blasting, & save for the mizzenmast the rigging was remarkably intact.

'Two of them mucking animals burned up 'fore they could reach us,' said Jervik Lank, popping up beside me again. 'And when their fire died they just fell into the sea.'

So we were at the edge of their range. That answered one question: maybe they preferred to take us alive, but failing that they didn't want us to escape. They'd waited as long as they dared to hurl those obscene fire-insects at us, then let loose before we could slip away.

The hose-teams went on blasting, & it began to look as though we'd won a round. The *Chathrand* had lost her jib sail, one minor lifeboat, some rigging about her stern. It was an unholy mess, & work for the carpenters for a fortnight. But the daughter-ship was still miles off, & the day was ending, & they hadn't sunk us yet. Best of all there was no sign of another volley like the first.

'Captain Rose, you've done it – *Aya Rin! Captain!*'

His left arm was on fire. 'Nothing, pah!' he said, calmly stripping off his coat. But the Turachs were taking no chances. They still had hold of that writhing dragon of a fire hose, & with a cry they swung around & aimed it at their burning captain – and blew him right off the shrouds & into the sea.

A fall like that (backwards, sixty or seventy feet) is a brutal thing for a young & strapping lad. Our captain is ox-strong, but also ox-heavy & far from young. We ran screaming to the rail, tearing life preservers from their hooks. I feared the marines had just written the last line in the tale of Captain Nilus Rotheby Rose.

It would have been so, surely, but for the hero that stepped forward. A dlömic sailor, barefoot already, tore off his shirt & leaped to the shrouds, just where Rose had been standing. He balanced there a moment, a jet black figure searching the waves. Then he saw what he was looking for, let go & dived.

It was a breathtaking sight: he sliced the waves like a black dagger thrown point down. Rose was unconscious, & already sinking, but the man surfaced beneath him & got his head above the waves, & swam easily enough (considering the great bearded bulk on his shoulder) to the nearest preserver, & held on there until we tossed him a sling.

Rose did not move as we hauled him up. Chadfallow & Rain were waiting – and so, on the other side of the hauling team, was Sandor Ott.

'That's a corpse you're lifting,' said the spymaster. 'Fiffengurt, are we fifteen miles off that headland, as he requested?'

'Nearly,' I replied, not looking at him.

'What was his plan?' Ott persisted. 'What was he building, with the blacksmith and the carpenters?'

No one knew, so no one answered. 'Night Gods!' Ott shouted. 'The sun is going down, gentlemen! He must have told *one* of you how he meant to escape?'

'Shut up, shut up 'til we revive him!' said Dr Rain.

'The man is dead, imbecile,' said Ott.

We bent the captain over the rail. Water – quarts it seemed – gushed from his mouth. We laid him out, grey & cold upon the deck.

'He is not breathing,' said Chadfallow. 'Rain, stand by to compress his heart. You know the procedure, I trust?'

Dr Rain blinked at him. 'The procedure? Yes, of course! The procedure. He's rather large, though.'

Chadfallow knitted his eyebrows, but there was no time for talk. He tilted the captain's bushy head, pinched his nose, & sealed his lips to Rose's own. He blew; Rose's chest lifted like a balloon. Again the doctor breathed, & again. The crowd grew. Men were praying, quite a few upon their knees. Without Rose there would be panic; without Rose we'd be at the utter mercy of an assassin. Chadfallow delivered a tenth breath, then glanced up at Rain.

'Now.'

The old fellow turned, took aim, & fell on his bottom in the centre of Rose's chest. He began to bounce, vigorously.

'Onesie! Twosie! Threesie – *erch!*'

Sandor Ott shoved him aside. He knelt over Rose's chest & started pressing down with both hands. 'Just twice!' said Chadfallow, & at once started breathing again. We waited. The captain lay limp. The dlömu who had rescued him was hauled over the rail in turn.

'Press harder this time, Ott,' said Chadfallow, & the process went on.

I heard an old woman mumbling beside me: Lady Oggosk. She too was praying softly, leaning on her stick, tears caught in the wrinkles of her ancient face.

Ott and Chadfallow worked on. From above came an eerie sound: the beat of wings. Niriviel had just alighted on the fighting top.

The rain began at last. Then Sandor Ott ceased his efforts and stepped away. 'It is over,' he said. 'Rose served his part well enough. And your skills are needed elsewhere, Doctor.'

Chadfallow ignored him, delivered the compressions himself. No one spoke save Ott & Niriviel, discussing what the bird had seen of the Behemoth's weaponry. 'A glass cube?' said Ott, sounding almost delighted. 'How intriguing. But are you certain it had no entrance, no doors?'

The rain strengthened. The light sank low. Finally, ashen, Chadfallow sat up. He licked a finger & held it to Rose's parted lips. Then he shook his head. 'Now it is over,' he said.

Lady Oggosk shrieked.

From the look of agony she wore, I thought her heart had burst. Nothing of the kind: she raised her stick high & swung it like a club, narrowly missing the doctor's chin. 'Backstabbers! Parasites!' she cried. 'You've sucked his blood every day he's been on this ship!' We retreated. Oggosk swung her stick over & over, as though fighting wolves in the night. 'I dare you! I dare you to stand there and watch him die!'

'Duchess,' said Chadfallow, 'he has passed on. If I had any remedy—'

'Silence, bastard, or I'll kill you!' She threw her stick away, dropped on her knees by Rose's head. 'I will drive you from the ship! Chamber by chamber, deck by deck! I'll uproot you, tear you out with these hands, watch you blow away like dust!' She curled her old fingers in Rose's beard. 'Are you listening? After all this time do you doubt my word?'

It was too sad. I knew she cared for the skipper, but this was beyond anything. It wasn't just her heart that was broken but her mind.

Then Rose bolted upright.

He gave a horrendous, moaning gasp. His mouth was open & his eyes were bugging from his head. We stood transfixed. There were no cries of joy, only staggered silence. Lady Oggosk had raised the dead.

But wasn't there something changed in Rose? Not just his pallor, which was still that of the drowned. No, it was something less tangible, but undeniably there. Like the charge in a cat's fur: you could feel it, even before the spark that made you jump.

'Captain,' I whispered, 'd'ye hear me?'

'CLEAR THE DECK!'

The cry was in his old, storm-shattering voice. All at once he was scrambling to his feet, bellowing the command again as he did so, waving & gesticulating.

There were quite a few gawkers to be sure. 'You heard the captain!' I cried. 'Clear out, there, give him some breathing room! Topmen, back to your—'

Rose leaped on me, smacked his hand over my mouth. 'I SAID *CLEAR THE DECK*! ABANDON MASTS, ABANDON RIGGING! ALL HANDS BELOWDECKS! THE LAST MAN BELOW GETS HIS BUTTOCKS WHIPPED TO BLARY RIBBONS!' He released me & waved his arms. 'Officers! See them below in ninety seconds or I'll have your hides! Run!'

There was of course no room for argument. We carried out his orders as though we had not just seen him lying dead at our feet. Even as we did so, a cry of dismay rang out: the men aloft had spotted something heading our way. 'Down, down!' we screamed, & down they came like troops of monkeys, some of them from three hundred feet above the deck. What had they seen, though? I heard 'shiny' & 'spinning' on a few lips, but nothing I could make sense of.

I ran as far the forecastle house & back again, & in that time all but a few dozen sailors had made it safely to the deck. But there was trouble at the hatches. The previous attack had brought men to the topdeck in their hundreds – perhaps twice as many as could be sensibly used to fight the fires – and now they'd been joined by two hundred more from the rigging. Many were wounded; some were in stretchers. Add to this the hoses, buckets, fire brooms, fallen cables, scorched canvas & other debris in & around the hatches & it made for awful bottle-necks. Rose was nearby again, howling & kicking men down the ladderways. Somehow, in a solid shoving mass, they went. But it was not fast enough for Rose. He drew his sword & jabbed the descending men with the point, between the shoulders. A few more seconds & the last men were squeezing down.

'Back from the hatches! Stand clear!' Rose whirled around & looked at the sky once more. 'Great flaming Gods!' he howled. 'Fiffengurt, you mucking fool!'

I caught a glimpse of the missile – a cube of glass the size of a house, plummeting from above. Then Rose slammed into me like a stampeding rhino, & he bore me backwards into the tonnage hatch.

There was battle-netting over it, of course, but the nets were scorched, & we narrowly missed a hole that would have meant the death of us both. The captain seized me in a bear hug & rolled, three or four times, & when we stopped he was above me, & the dark mass of the longboat on its sling loomed over us like an umbrella. And then came the blast.

It was not as loud as I expected & no conflagration followed. Instead I heard a sound like fine furious hail, & the sky around the longboat filled with glass. The cube had exploded in mid-air, showering the *Chathrand* in a million needle-thin slivers of death. Screams erupted from the ladderways: not everyone had made it safely below.

'Gods, what a weapon!' Ott's voiced echoed up through the tonnage shaft. I turned my head: there he was, one deck below, displaying a handful of sharp, shattered crystals. 'It could kill an entire ship's company, and leave the vessel perfectly sound!' he cried, delighted.

'Captain,' I said, 'you saved my life.'

Rose looked at me somewhat hatefully, as if I'd accused him of a crime. Then he heaved himself over so that we lay side by side. 'Bedour spoke the truth,' he said. 'Captain Bedour. He'd seen it used, that weapon. He knew what was coming at us out of the sky.' Rose stared up at the belly of the longboat. 'I was dead, Fiffengurt. The ghosts were thick over the water, clawing at me, biting.' He raised a hand to his face, remembering. 'They were trying to tear my soul away from this flesh. Your time's come, they said. You're one of us now. Let go. Give in.'

'You were lifeless on the deck,' I said. 'We did everything we could to revive you. Chadfallow finally gave up.'

'Yes,' said Rose, 'but I didn't. They were going to have to rip me away. And they were getting down to it too. Oggosk's threats scared them off at first. They need this ship to carry them to their final rest, and don't fancy being cast to the winds. But the eldest ghosts are so tired of being trapped aboard *Chathrand* that they have ceased to care. They kept at me, even on the deck. My grip on this flesh was breaking. In the end it was the bird that saved me.'

'The b-b—?'

'Ott's falcon. It spoke of that cube, & Bedour overheard. He recognised the cube, somehow, and knew it would be the end of the *Chathrand*.* And there was only one man aboard who could do something about it. That was when they understood that they had

---

*Velamprukut Bedour was captain of the *Chathrand* in the years 427-436, before the sundering of ties between North and South. A great lover of military history, he may have learned of the glass cube from a notoriously grizzly painting at the Oceanic Museum in Bali Adro City. The weapon is of ancient design, perhaps dating to the Maduracha Siege (-1174). It was resurrected by the Plazic generals, one of whom may have drawn his own inspiration from the painting. - EDITOR

no choice. The ghosts shocked my heart back into service, so that I could save this ship.'

His eyes drifted skyward. 'You see, Fiffengurt? Everyone, even the dead, ultimately depend on Nilus Rose.' Then he looked at me & barked: 'Off your back, Quartermaster! Did some other commander grant you a holiday? Get the men to their blary stations! We shall tack west, a close reach around that island! Now, Fiffengurt. I want immediate headway, is that clear?'

He was alive, all right. And in the next few minutes, as the light failed, he showed us what he'd been building those many hours. It was a barge made of barrels, with a sturdy platform atop it, & a steel tripod mounted on the latter. Dangling from the tripod was a big emergency signal lantern: one of our spares. Coiled beneath it, in a kind of metal chimney, was a long braid of tobacco leaves. The end of the braid was tucked into the lamp's ignition chamber.

'A tobacco fuse,' said Sandor Ott, inspecting the contraption with a smile. 'Very good, Captain. How long do you imagine it will burn?'

'Longer than my patience with your insolent questions.' He picked up a fine hand-drill & set about boring a tiny hole near the top of one of the barrels. This action he repeated on every second barrel, until he had worked his way completely around the barge. Then he lifted an oil canister & soaked the lamp's wick, but poured none at all into the tank beneath it.

Ott looked at me; his eyes said, *Your skipper's a madman*. The lamp would light, sure enough, but with an empty tank it would not shine for more than a minute.

I had a prior worry, though. 'Captain, you do realise that it's only *just* gotten dark?'

'Since I am neither blind nor witless, yes, I do.'

'Oppo, Captain. What I mean is, they may have been able to see us, when we made our turn for westward.'

'May have? Your imprecision wears on me today, Fiffengurt. They *did* see us; the point is not open to question. Tanner! Get this barge above, along with the deadweights. Fiffengurt, see that no

328

one comes anywhere near us with a source of light – douse *every* light on the topdeck, in fact. And close the gunports. And see that the gallery windows stay dark. And bring me four cables, six fathoms long apiece. Use the fallen rigging, there is more than enough.'

We all scrambled. Tanner's men hoisted the barge by cargo-crane to the topdeck, which was by now quite dark. The *Chathrand* was on her new heading already, drawing away west of the island's rocky point. Behind us, the Behemoth glowed like a weird, pale gaslamp, & the daughter-ship had gained another several miles. At this rate it would catch us by morning.

Rose stood by his invention for some fifteen minutes in silence, as we dragged the four lines he wanted into position, & secured them to Mr Tarsel's 200-pound deadweights. Then Rose ordered the barge lifted a few feet in the air. On her underside we found four iron rings, & to these we tied the other ends of the cables. Then Rose struck a match & eased it into the metal chimney. The odour of sweet tobacco wafted over us.

'Get her afloat,' he said.

We raised the barge & swung it over the rail. Deadweights dangling, the whole assemblage descended into the lightless sea. When it was safely afloat Rose gave the order to cut it loose.

'Now, Officers,' he said, looking at us all, 'hard about, and brace up fore and aft. We are going *east* around that headland. As we did off Talturi: silent and invisible. Go to.'

It was vintage Rose. The turn was sharp but not perilous, & the wind from the south was as friendly to our new course as it had been to our old. The men stepped lively, too: they knew Rose was trying to bluff death once again, somehow, even if they couldn't guess the particulars.

The daughter-ship, in no fear of us apparently, still had her running lights ablaze. She had not turned to intercept us, but was coming on straight at the point. For nearly two hours she kept that course, as we made east under the cover of those blessed clouds. Once the Behemoth fired another round of living fireballs, & we braced ourselves for the worst. Two went east, three west, but they all burned out well before they neared us, & no one was the wiser of our position, I'm sure.

Suddenly, miles behind us to the east, a light flared up bright & fitful. It was the signal-lamp, of course, & it sputtered & winked & died in thirty seconds, just as Rose had intended. And not three minutes later his gamble paid off: the daughter-ship broke westwards round the point.

What could I do but smile? The ruse was brilliant. We'd had to break left or right around sprawling Phyreis, & had waited to choose until the darkness was almost upon us. But under that barrage of hellish weapons we'd seemed to panic, turning west before the light was truly gone. A feint? Well maybe. The daughter-ship had taken no chances & kept straight on, hoping for some sign, some giveaway. And that's what Rose's decoy had provided. It would seem an accident: a carelessly opened gunport, a lamp carried above deck by some foolish lad & quickly smothered. And the beauty of it was that they would never spot the barge & learn that they'd been tricked, for all this while the sea had been trickling in through the holes Rose had drilled in the barrels. Soon the weight of lamp & tripod would sink the barge like a stone. They'd sail west all night, trying to catch up with a ship that wasn't there.

'You're a prodigy, Nilus,' said Lady Oggosk, clinging with both scrawny hands to his arm. 'And to think how they scorned you back in Arqual: *a low-born smuggler with the arrogance of a king.* But there were some who meant that as a compliment, you know.'

Friday, 22 Halar. Left Phyreis behind this morning. No pursuit, no sails. For two days we've been alone on the seas. Five men & one dlömu dead of their burns. And I escaped with no more than a hair-scorching, & a little spot behind my left ear that crackles at the touch.

Winds steady & growing, as though the South were anxious to be rid of us. One or two charted isles left ahead of us, then what I must assume is barbarous territory all the way to the edge of the Ruling Sea.

Rescued that fool Druffle from a suicidal binge. I smelled only rum on him, but his behaviour suggests some fouler liquor: grebel, maybe. He thought I was his father, & he begged, weeping, for some bread & honey – 'island honey,' he is on about it again.

But Mr Uskins continues to improve. He is consigned to quarters now rather than sickbay, for there are no spare beds in the latter. He is shy, and eats alone, and perhaps suffers from some difficulty swallowing, for his hand is often at his neck.

Saturday, 23 Halar. No pursuit. We are rid of both vessels, it would appear. Lest we enjoy the briefest lessening of our dread, however, a terrible vision came tonight. I was far below & did not see it, but those who did can speak of nothing else. They say it was a cloud that moved. That it raced over us with the speed of birds on the wings but paused over our quarterdeck, & even lowered a little, & that it was black as pitch, & though it boiled & writhed it was thicker than any mist, seeming almost like a black growth or tumour, half as big as the *Chathrand.* Off it flew northwards, & vanished into the thunderheads that broke above us shortly thereafter. Felthrup saw it & has since been impossible to calm: he declares it is the Swarm of Night. Rose saw it too – from the height of the mizzen topgallants, where he'd pulled himself for a last scan of the seas behind us. After the cloud had passed he stayed there, motionless, & when I climbed up to consult him I found his eyes distracted & his face deathly pale.

'My life has been all wrong,' he said.

Sunday, 24 Halar. Star of Rin, grant me courage. The nightmare we have all feared is upon us. Two men have gone mad. I am not speaking of an attack of nerves or a delusion. They have lost speech, reason, everything. They scream and run in panic; they bite and claw and fling their limbs about like monkeys. One is young Midshipman Bravun, of Besq; the other a passenger from Uturphe.

I have ordered the dlömu not to breathe the word *tol-chenni*, but in truth the precaution comes too late. The lads all know about the

331

mind-plague. They are afraid as never before.

Chadfallow too is mortified, and hiding his fear behind an exhaustive medical inquiry. The two men were not acquainted, did not frequent the same parts of the ship, did not even eat on the same deck. Both, however, were Plapps: the midshipman had been recruited to the gang just days ago, I'm told.

There has already been some trouble on this score: Plapps are whispering that the outbreak was engineered somehow by Kruno Burnscove, maimed & imprisoned though he be. At five bells this morning a Burnscove lad was found in the bottom of the hold – gagged & tied up in his hammock & dangling by his feet. He was positioned over the bilge well, at a height that required him to arch his back & neck to keep his head out of the bilge. He'd done just that through the night, and was found at dawn just as the last of his strength was giving out. Luckily, Rose is the sort of captain who expects to wake up to a statistical report on his vessel, written out & slipped under his door by the officer of the day. Such reports naturally include the depth of water in the well.

If nothing else, Chadfallow's investigation should help to stamp out such noxious stupidity. The Burnscove Boys did not inflict the mind-plague on the Plapps. We know from Prince Olik that the disease is not transmissible from person to person, that it struck Bali Adro like a snowfall – meaning slowly, uniformly, everywhere at once.

Mr Uskins' symptoms were of course very similar to those of the new victims – and Uskins recovered in a fortnight. That recovery bewilders us all. Prince Olik claimed, and our dlömic crew confirms, that *no one ever recovers from the plague.* 'Once you burn down a house, it's gone,' says Commander Spoon-Ears. 'That's how it was with human minds. You can't repair something that no longer exists.'

So what happened to Uskins? Spoon-Ears can't tell me, and neither can Chadfallow. Least of all can Uskins himself account for his recovery. 'I was a long time afflicted, but the illness passed,' he says. 'I was warned that madness would come, and that it would be a fate worse than death. But I was spared. I am a new and happy man. Please forgive me for what I did to the tarboys.'

What he did to the tarboys! That's a subject I can't bear to explore with Uskins, yet, though perhaps the lads themselves can enlighten me. If he means that he was cruel to them, I know it already. If he means something more, I may just turn him over to the Turach they call the Bloody Son. Either that, or find someone (Chadfallow, Sandor Ott, old onesie-twosie Rain) to attempt a little corrective surgery. I have crossed half the world without murdering Uskins, but Rin knows I'm still prepared.

Of course that is in awful taste. One should not make a joke of murder, not on this ship at any rate. When I told the captain about the Burnscove Boy who had nearly drowned, I expected a detonation: something on the order of what had happened the day he assaulted Burnscove himself. To my surprise Rose's reaction was quite the opposite. He listened in perfect stillness, then walked slowly to his desk, where he sat down & played with a pencil. Finally, almost sorrowfully, he told me to start naming members of the Plapp gang – just off the top of my head. I didn't know them all, I told him.

'Never mind,' said Rose heavily. 'Name all that you can.'

I complied. The names rolled off my tongue, & he sat there with eyes closed, so still that I began to wonder if he was asleep. I must have named thirty or forty when his eyes suddenly snapped open. 'Him,' he said. 'Bring him to me at once.'

'Skipper, with my utmost respect—'

'Bring him,' said Rose quietly. Then he looked up at me, his face strained & sad. 'Or send the Turachs for him, if you prefer.'

Of course I went myself. The man I'd named was a tall, skinny, red-nosed Etherhorder who'd been with us from the start. He was also a personal favourite of Darius Plapp. He delivered the ganglord's messages, brought food to his bedside & for aught I know tasted it for poison. I found him seated next to Plapp on the berth deck, grinning & whispering in his ear. He came along with a shrug, snickering at me behind my back.

'Did you know, sir, there's men call you Old Fool Fiffengurt, and Rat-Fancier Fiffengurt, and nastier things? Much as we try to keep 'em in line, of course.'

I did not even glance back at him. This was an old game, insulting officers with a veneer of respect. The lad was playing it crudely. On another day I'd have put him in the stocks.

'Personally,' he said, 'I don't hold with makin' sport of a man's life back in Arqual – do you, sir? I mean, say a dry old geezer falls in love with a brewer's lass & wants to give up the sailing life—'

I stopped dead.

'No one should laugh at 'im. Good luck to the geezer! Maybe he *will* keep her satisfied, keep her cute little eyes from roaming. There's odder things in this world – not many, but some.'

It went on like this all the way to the captain's door. I thought the man's nastiness would make what was to come a little easier, but it did not. When we arrived, Rose was on his knees, unfolding a dusty oilskin over the polished floor.

'Come here,' he said immediately. 'Not you, Fiffengurt.'

The man stepped uncertainly onto the tarp. 'Shall I help you up, Captain?' he said. There was no hint of a snicker any more.

Rose raised his busy head & stared at the man. 'You are close to Darius Plapp?' he asked.

'Mr Plapp's been very good to me, sir, yes indeed! I try to do what's expected of me – that is, always assumin' it don't get in the way of orders – of my duties, I mean, sir, my duties.'

Rose climbed laboriously to his feet. 'Do not be alarmed,' he said. 'I am going to feel your muscles.'

'What for, sir?' asked the Plapp, as Rose squeezed his arms experimentally.

'To be certain I do not need a blade,' said Rose. He walked back to his deck & picked up a coiled leather cord. Turning, he held it out, as though for the man's inspection.

The man shot me a beseeching glance. 'What's this all about, Captain?'

'Order,' said Rose, & struck him hard in the stomach. The man bent double, & Rose whipped the cord around his neck. It was over quickly. The steward & I wrapped the oilskin around the body & carried it below.

Darius Plapp went berserk, & had to be restrained by his own thugs, lest he hurt himself. Kruno Burnscove too was shocked at Rose's escalation. He issued a startling order from the brig: not one of his men was to gloat, or laugh, or be anything short of professional seamen, until further notice. Rose himself carried on as if nothing had changed.

Druffle is correct: the gangs dare not touch him while their leaders are aboard. Besides, since the day we faced the Behemoth, there is a new air of mystery & fear about the captain. Fifty men saw him laid out on the topdeck, pronounced dead by Chadfallow, grey & motionless for a quarter-hour. And fifty men had seen him bolt to his feet & resume command. Even Sandor Ott has been put in his place, they are saying, because Nilus Rose simply cannot be killed.

Monday, 25 Halar. Maybe not. But if he is immortal, Rose is alone in that distinction. The whole ship is rising; there is talk of a gang war. Kruno Burnscove has been stabbed to death in his cell.

15

The Editor Takes Certain Precautions

I am sorry to have denied you the pleasure of my insights. There has been a spot of difficulty with the chancellor, and it became needful to barricade myself in the library, and to write without pause. I scarcely need to mention that doing so is harder with each passing day. My hands are changing shape, my thumb resists bending like a thumb. I have broken two quills, spoiled countless sheets of linen paper. I have experimented with other arrangements, tying the quill to an outstretched finger. It works, after a fashion: I scratch fitfully at the page, like the cat who begs at my kitchen door.

I must send someone around to feed that animal, for I have not been home in a week. The day before my tactical relocation, the chancellor sent a messenger to my door. Reading from a scroll, the boy declared that I was to visit the head office 'without hesitation' (did he mean *delay*?) and to account for the 'irregular conduct' of which I had 'made an unfortunate habit'.

Naturally I laughed. But I could not coax so much as a smile from the flat-faced boy. 'Irregular conduct *cannot* be habitual – surely you see that?' The lad only fidgeted, trying not to stare at me. I tipped him. He fled for his life.

That night I received a second message – this time from the Greysan Fulbreech Self-Improvement Society (of Delusional Imbeciles) – and tied to a brick that shattered a window. I slept through the assault (face down on my manuscript). The geniuses had chosen to attack my bathroom, and the brick landed squarely in the tub, and yesterday's bathwater. Finding it the next morning, I dried the threatening note, and read what I could:

PROFESSOR: IF YOU DO NOT ▬▬▬▬▬ WE WILL ▬▬▬▬▬ WITH A MIGHTY ◆ OF TRUTH & JUSTICE!

Not much of a narrative, to be sure, but far better than the alternate endings they continued to send me for *The Chathrand Voyage*.

I packed my notes, stuffed a bag with clothes, whistled up Jorl. The Young Scholars were waiting in the library tower, as on any morning, and we worked in peace for two days. Then I caught one of them – my favourite, as it happened – stuffing a copy of chapter sixteen into his underwear. An interrogation followed, and the sobbing Scholar at last confessed that the Fulbreech freaks were paying him handsomely for every page he smuggled out.

I dismissed them all. The next day I sent out messengers of my own, and interviewed several copyists from the village. The one I have retained is a mendicant preacher, whose faith decrees that he wear nothing but a loincloth. He stinks, but then so do I.

I have hired guards, too, and had no end of trouble with them. They are flikkermen, you understand. They took a week to find my residence, and then demanded payment in advance. We came to terms in the end, but they are disgruntled, and like to revisit the argument between themselves, with peevishness and poor diction, just outside my chamber. Nor were they happy to promise not to subject the library patrons to electrical shocks. They wish to see the long hair of the girl students standing up like quills on a porcupine.

No matter. Their weird physiognomy had the desired effect: I am free of visitors at last. The terrified cook leaves my meals on the staircase. The flikkermen bring them to me, and empty my chamber pots. I think my food offends their nostrils more than my bodily wastes, and given the declining standards at this Academy I begin to concur.

Since taking to the tower I have had no visits from the Fulbreech Society. I can see them from the window, though: huddling, conspiring. For a day they pressed leaflets into the hands of students, professors, groundskeepers, but the confused indifference these evoked must have demoralised them; now they sit and sulk. But they are not harmless. A few come from wealth. The society's president, Mr My-Name-is-Not-Important, is one such child: his mother gave the school a courtyard full of statuary. Great marble heroes, chests jutting, weapons raised, regal faces spangled with sparrow droppings. The wretch's passion runs in the family.

Did he truly wish to kill me, with that knife? I think not. If he wished for anything besides a release of fury, it was to punish me with a scratch. He and his fellow cuckoos need me to finish the tale – to their liking, of course. And they need my singular credentials to see that it is taken seriously. My name on their version of *The Chathrand Voyage*: that is how they think all this will end.

Irritatingly enough, I need them too.

The society, after all, detests one figure above myself – and I am not speaking of Passive Pathkendle. I mean the chancellor, the man who quipped that he would burn the *Voyage* if it contained any affront to 'national pride' (ask him what the phrase means; you will come away bewildered). He is a cowardly soul in almost every respect, but cowards with authority are more dangerous than crocodiles. Above all he fears embarrassment. Certainly a mad (not to say lycanthropic) professor emeritus who seizes a library tower and defends it with the humanoid equivalent of electric eels could prove embarrassing. Especially if said professor remained in said tower during a Donors' Conference, such as the one that begins next week.

What could be worse? Many things occur to the imagination. The professor leaping from the tower in broad daylight. Or setting it ablaze. Or a siege by the Academy Police, and the chancellor's name tied evermore to visions of slaughtered flikkermen, their bloody hands still sparking, their frog tongues lolling on the stairs; and the weird old prof curled in death around his manuscript.

Or worse yet: forbearance. The chancellor waits the madman out. The madman finishes his book and sees it published, and the *incontrovertible verity* of its claims is recognised by all thinking creatures. The donors, falling largely outside this category, rise up in savage denial. Talking rats! Dlömic atrocities! The towers of Bali Adro built by slaves! It will never do! Flag-fondling simpletons, they would prefer no history at all to one that complicates Our Glorious Past.

You see the chancellor's dilemma. I have laid a banquet of embarrassments before him, and he must choose his seat and dine.

But I do not wish him to choose assault – not yet. I need eight days and nights. By the eve of the Donors' Conference my book will be complete, and the allies to whom I wrote in desperation will have come in force – if they are coming at all. Until then I need my guards to protect me from the Fulbreech freaks, and the freaks and their rich mums to hold off the chancellor.

And so today I have lied. I sent the mendicant with a message for the freaks under my window:

Dear Sirs: Perhaps I have, indeed, been unfair in my treatment of Greysan Fulbreech. I am reading your proposed endings with an open mind, and find much to my liking. I will give them full and favourable consideration – provided, of course, that the chancellor does not put an UNTIMELY END to this MOST SACRED EFFORT to recount the HEROIC STORY of OUR FOREFATHERS.

Merely a precaution: I shall of course give their scribbles no consideration at all. How loathsome, this manoeuvre. And how fitting. The survivors of the voyage were saved as often by enemies as loved ones. We needed them, they needed us; we stained our hands scarlet together. The chancellor is quite right to fear for his school; when my book is published many donors will abandon us, and weeds will grow high about these halls. But I am right to fight him, to not let him falsify the past. On my desk at home,

Sandor Ott's skull grins in the shadows; I can almost hear his taunts: *We cannot help it, we ambitious men. We make common cause with fiends.*

16

Nine Matches

6 Halar 942
265th day from Etherhorde

Neda sat cross-legged in the unfurnished room. Upon her lap a smooth board, and on the board a sheet of linen paper. In her hand the most exquisite pen she had ever touched, with a nib of pure gold and a body carved from the deep red root of a mountain cypress.

It was a gift of the selk. They hoped she would keep it; they hoped a love for Alifros would imbue the words she wrote with it and that those words would touch many hearts.

On the floor in front of her were two smooth stones. One weighed down the stack of blank sheets the selk had given her. The other lay atop the pages she had already filled with transcriptions from the Book of the Old Faith. Over the three days she had been writing, the second stack had grown to nearly five inches. The stack of empty pages shrank each day but the selk always brought more.

Cayer Vispek had not yet seen the marvellous pen. Neda had found a simpler one in the common room and used that when he came near. If he saw the pen he would tell her to leave it behind.

She wrung the stiffness from her hand and started again. Her arm raced across the sheet, the words spilling out in a shape that declared her mongrel heart: angular Mzithrini characters ever so slightly distorted by the rounded, flowing style of an Ormali schoolgirl.

Then will you know thy calling: for the Dragon seeketh naught but the Dragon's prey, and never dines on base creatures of the barnyard, in their own filth confined.

Memory was a weapon, memory was a curse. As Neda wrote the phrase she could see the face of her first master, the high priest known as the Babqri Father, reciting it on the day of her induction. The Father had rarely smiled, but that day he had glowed. Neda was his discovery. He had plucked her from a bleak life of concubinage and made her an aspirant to the order of the *sfvantskors*, the first non-Mzithrini ever to receive such a singular honour. That day she would begin the training, renounce her former life, devote herself for ever to the Gods. She remembered the mischief in his eyes: the choice of her had already become a scandal. Being Neda, she could also recall his smells (green onions, sweat), his silk robe (a long thread had trailed down his back from the golden collar, as though he were being unravelled by imps), his ailments (a toothache, a wheeze when he rose from a chair, a fresh scratch on his left wrist given to him by his favourite alley cat, whom he called Shadow and the village boys called Smoky and the half-blind cook in the refectory called Dirty Thief).

So will thy purpose seize you: in jaws of iron and enduring flame.

Being Neda, memory-blessed, she could hold up that long-lost day for inspection as a jeweller might a ring. There was the colossal edifice of the shrine, its dark interior still cold though the city itself was steaming. There was the pitcher of sacramental milk (small chip in base of handle), the golden cups (two dented, but the dents had noble histories), the basin where the aspirants would wash their hands. There were the lonely candles (twenty-four green and burning two green and not burning sixteen white and burning five white and not burning one white fallen sideways abandoned dust-covered forgotten for ever by everyone but Neda, mongrel monster prodigy freak).

The way of the sfvantskor *is perfection. Thy soul will make a slave of the flesh, whereas in lesser men the flesh takes mastery of the soul.*

And there were the other youths come for training (Sparro Suridín Adel Ommet Ingri Jalantri Tujinor Kat'jil Perek Fynn Ushatai Mendhur Malabron), all but six of whom would fail the initial tests. All but six of whom would go home to devastated families, to start the long, loud complaint that a foreign girl had been given what they themselves were denied.

The way of the sfvantskor *is perfection.*

Weapon, curse. Neda had understood the connection between the two for a very long time. Memory (the weapon) gave her power over others, reminded her of their weaknesses, the word or notion or name that brought them to tears, to fury, to a readiness to do as she wished. Memory (the curse) flooded her with proof that she was stumbling on her chosen path.

The young *sfvantskor*'s mind had to be nurtured by the elders, cleansed of distraction, pruned of idle curiosity, disciplined in the service of the Unseen. Above all, it had to be equipped with a vision of Alifros and its heavens, its hells, its mystic byways; a vision that told the *sfvantskor*s where they stood and why they were suffered to live and breathe and consume the bounty of the world.

It was a beautiful vision. The world was one family: rocks, trees, people, white monkeys, black crocodiles, birds, bacteria, dust. All one. The wind its breath, the waters its blood. The night simply the closing of one great, shared, polyfaceted eye. But Alifros was also a family adrift, a ragtag entity wandering a savage universe. The *sfvantskors* were its defenders, the guards who passed the night awake.

And she, Neda, meant to abandon her post.

A spasm went through her, making her ruin a word. *You don't just mean to,* she thought, *you've done it already.* For belief did not

343

end with a public renunciation, a moment when one's brethren called one a heretic, and damned. Belief ended in solitude and silence, the same way it began.

She had opened her eyes this morning and known it was over. The room was still dark; Uláramyth was quiet and still. A bird was singing outside the window, each phrase like an urgent but reasonable question, which hung unanswered in the silence until the bird could no longer stand it, and asked the question again. Finished, gone. She no longer believed. She lay there in stark terror between Lunja and Thasha, afraid to move, afraid to think. When the tears came she did not understand them. She thought: *I love the Book, I love the Book more than ever.* She loved her master and the Father who had trained her, and her brother *sfvantskors* who had fallen in battle. And she had no doubt that the Old Faith had been a gift to this world from the divine.

Long ago. Too long. In a form that no one could extract from the bowels of the creature that had swallowed it, the corrupt thing that prayed and shambled and made war and hated happiness, the modern Old Faith, the beast she had tried so hard to love.

She had stared at the ceiling, wondering if this was madness, if she would presently start to scream. Why now? What had happened? Was it Cayer Vispek's command four days ago – just that and nothing more?

Her master had caught her laughing and sharing a melon with two selk warriors in the village square. He had asked her coldly to return to the house. Later he made her tell everything, how she had run with them (for the joy of running, climbing, sweating in the midday sun) almost to the top of the crater wall, then lain back beside them on the snowdrift there, so hot her skin almost sizzled, wildly happy in a way that bewildered her, until she realised with a start that it was only because *they* were happy. Because beings thousands of years old could still exult in mere sun and tired muscles, and the cool shocking snow.

She told Vispek they had asked her to wait while they looked over the rim: like all the travellers she knew she was forbidden to gaze beyond Uláramyth, lest she gain some clue as to its location. She had waited for them, studying the tiny starburst flowers that grew between the rocks, wondering if today or tomorrow would be their last in this strange haven, or their last alive.

When the selk returned their faces had changed. 'What is wrong?' asked Neda. 'Did you see Macadra's forces? Are they near?'

'We saw them, but they did not see us,' said the selk. 'Uláramyth remains hidden from all enemies, for now at least. But we also saw something much worse: a black cloud, racing. It was the Swarm of Night, Death's hunting-cloud, and it chilled our souls to see it, even from afar.'

They descended in silence. At the bottom of the hill they went together to Lord Arim and Ramachni and explained what they saw. She stayed with her selk friends for a time after that, and slowly their spirits revived. While they were sharing the melon the selk performed silent impressions of her friends. A straight, serene posture and a piercing stare: that could only be Hercól. A wild-eyed figure grabbing at imaginary tools: Big Skip. The selk were clever mimes. Neda laughed until she ached.

Cayer Vispek had listened to all this without saying a word. Then he had gone away into his chamber awhile. When he returned he said that she must avoid the selk whenever possible, share nothing but brief pleasantries, excuse herself if they became familiar. 'You were trained for a purpose, and that purpose is not to sit and laugh with men of any race.'

'I was not beguiled by them, Cayer,' she said. 'I thought they might tell me something to our advantage.'

'Then why did you look shamed when I chanced upon you?'

Before she could recover enough to answer he shook his head and went on: 'I have been careless with you, Neda Ygraël. All my thought was of survival until we came here, but threats to the body are not the only kind. Your mind is growing distracted by pleasure, your instincts dulled by the ease of this place. As your elder and teacher I am to blame.'

'But master, I have said my prayers, performed my meditations—'

'You see?' he broke in. 'You feel a need to defend yourself. That feeling is your soul crying out for order, for a return to what is real.'

'But what harm has befallen me?'

At that Vispek had become truly angry. One objection he had tolerated; two bordered on rebellion. He did not rage or shout. He merely dropped his eyes, as though he could not bear to look at her. Neda quailed. She felt unclothed. Vispek asked her in a distant voice if she might write some passages from the Book.

'Which verses, master?' she asked.

Vispek started for the door. 'Anything you remember,' he said.

She had taken him at his word. This morning she had written seven hundred and fifty verses from memory, filling sixty sheets. Her Gift was cooperating; it liked these manic feats of memory better than anything measured or practical. As long as she kept writing like a madwoman the Gift would no doubt carry on as well, feeding the holy text into her consciousness like coal into a stove.

When a band of *sfvantskors* became separated from the Book it was the task of the eldest student to speak or write long passages from memory, to be shared by all. That student had been her faith-brother Jalantri until he died in the Infernal Forest. Consequently Neda had never written any passages for Vispek's approval. He knew she had a special memory, but did not begin to guess just how special it was. Neda's transcriptions were more accurate than his own. Would he rejoice in her knowledge or consider it a mockery, a magical cheat? Was learning the Book by heart still a holy act if one did it by accident, if one had not even tried?

The twelve core chapters every aspirant had to memorise simply to become a *sfvantskor*. A much larger section, known as the Inner Path, might require decades, if it was learned at all. The whole of the Book's ninety-seven chapters had been memorised only by certain heroes of the Faith, high priests and mystics scattered through its history. And Neda, of course.

In the seventh chapter the Book laid out the duties of a

sfvantskor. They were many and complex. The sixth verse of the chapter was Neda's favourite:

> *Recall as well that man's wisdom is a fair crystal, but Fact the blade of diamond that cuts the crystal, a blade created by no man but hidden in the earth from the beginning. Shield not man's certainties from the diamond knife, but know that with each cut their shape is lovelier and more true.*

No command could be clearer. Use your mind. Use your eyes. Do not prop up old ideas like a shack in a windstorm. Accept what you see, even if it shatters what you're told is true. Don't substitute a story of Creation for Creation itself.

Of all the commandments in the Book it was the one least favoured by her masters, the one they never invoked, the one Neda suspected they would like all believers to forget. Most of them could only wish, of course. But the Father, her beloved teacher, had the power to make that desire come true, for he alone placed his chosen aspirants in trance.

Almost nightly, they had surrendered to his control. Trance was the only proper state in which to receive the holy mysteries. And while in trance the Father could order his *sfvantskors* to forget any inconvenient fact or notion, and they would forget. It was a terrible, tempting power, and he had held it alone for half a century.

But it had failed with Neda. Her Gift brought everything back. Usually it happened the instant he released her from the trance: she would wake in the full, scarlet shame of remembering. But at other times the forgetting would linger for days, or longer. She had once passed the burned-out shell of a mansion in Babqri City and suddenly remembered standing guard there a few nights before, at a great feast honouring one of the Five Kings of the Mzithrin. Halfway through the meal some terrible insult had been uttered or implied; the King had departed hastily, and late that night the elder *sfvantskors* had returned to the shrine with spots of blood upon their sleeves.

On another occasion she had gone to meditate in the Hall of Relics, before a small clay cup. Many centuries ago the angels had filled that cup with milk in the desert, thereby saving the life of the prophet Mathan, an early champion of the Faith. She had gazed at the humble cup and suddenly known that it was an imitation, a fake. The true cup had been stolen by the Shaggat Ness, in the same raid that took the Red Wolf and other wonders: she remembered the lecture clearly. But some weeks ago the Father had decided that the Faith still needed the cup. He commanded them to forget the lecture, and to recall instead that the cup had resided in the Hall of Relics for hundreds of years.

So many things she wasn't supposed to remember. So many certainties protected from the diamond knife.

Neda raised her eyes from the sheet. Amber light filled the window, making the green leaves blaze. The Gods had left her. The Unseen was becoming unfelt. If she had felt its presence at all it had been in that moment of abandon, spreadeagled in the snow beside two gasping strangers.

She rose and carried the stack of pages to her master's room. His door stood open, and in the centre of the room she saw him motionless, stripped to the waist, and balanced on one hand. Neda's breath caught in her throat. His body was straight and rigid, his eyes gently shut, his skin aglow. The way of the *sfvantskor* is perfection. She set the pages down outside the door with the stone atop them and crept back to her room.

Her heart was pounding. She had been thinking about her stolen memories because another was trying to come back. The sight of those two beautiful selk, and now of Vispek, was bringing it nearer. She wanted to run again; she wanted to steal from the house unseen. There were voices in the outer chamber: her brother was asking if anyone had seen Neeps, and whether Neda was still hiding in her room.

Neda slipped out of the window and crossed the little garden and pulled herself easily over the wall. There was a shaded lane here. She looked left and right and saw that she was alone, then leaned back against the wall and closed her eyes.

Thy soul will make a slave of the flesh, whereas in lesser men—

She slid down the wall, and the thing she'd been commanded to forget came back to her. It had happened two years ago, in one of the darkened chambers where the Father often left his children in a trance until sunrise. Neda had been in deep, dreamless trance, all volition gone. Someone had stepped into the room and touched her. It was not the Father himself: she knew the rattle of his ancient hands. Two fingers had caressed her hair, grazed her lips, touched her briefly on the throat. Then the man had drawn back, sighing, struggling with himself. At last, surrendering, he had kissed her hand over and over, weeping a little and murmuring *Neda, Neda, my phoenix, my dream.* The voice was faint even now. She'd been commanded very firmly to forget.

Who could have dared? One of the other aspirants? Malabron, whose sanity she had always doubted? Or poor Jalantri? Neda thought he had probably loved her, though he had never admitted the truth even to himself. How could he? The *sfvantskors* were commanded to love things eternal. To pursue carnal love was a grave sin; to pursue one's faith-sister, unthinkable. No wonder Vispek had warned Jalantri to keep his distance from Neda at the first slight sign of his temptation.

Neda covered her eyes, digging for the memory, for clues. The man had said he loved her. He'd said it many times through his tears.

She thought again of Vispek. Neda had known him in Babqri: he was their weapons trainer; he had stood behind her and guided her arms through fluid sword-strokes. Impossible to think, sinful even to imagine, that it could have been him.

She hugged herself and felt debauched. She did not know who had come to her that night and feared that she would never know. But she knew this much: it had taken so long to remember not because of the strength of the Father's command, but because she herself had wished so desperately to forget. And she had wished to forget not out of horror but shame.

For when the man had left the chamber she'd been sorry. She wished he had stayed there, bathing her hand with tears and kisses; until the dawn broke her trance and she could move again, touch him maybe, see the eyes of the one who had told her she was loved.

That night, for the first time in years, Neda dreamed of her mother.

They were in the kitchen of the Orch'dury, the family home on the hillside above Ormael City. Suthinia was chopping vegetables with a will. Leeks, carrots, turnips, chives. She scooped them up on the big knife's edge and tossed them into a steaming vessel, never looking at her daughter who stood six feet away.

'Mother,' said Neda. 'Who are you cooking for?'

'Oh, oh,' said Suthinia breezily, turning to the rack of spices.

Neda told her mother that she was not in the mood for visitors. Her mother hummed and went on cooking, like some kind of strange machine. Neda walked through her beloved house and saw the floor littered with children's toys. The beautiful pen from the selk was among them, just lying there on the floor waiting to be trampled. Irritated, she retrieved it and slipped it into the folds of her cloak. She was startled to find that she was naked beneath the robe.

'Out of matches,' said Suthinia. 'Shit, shit, shit.'

Neda ran a hand surreptitiously over her own body. All her battle scars were there. And glancing up at the mirror above the fireplace, she caught a glimpse of her red Mzithrini tattoos.

'Finish up, do you hear me?' her mother shouted. 'Pazel has to bathe before we eat.'

Neda looked at her. 'Are you talking to me?'

Her mother started, knocking over the bottle of cooking wine.

On the kitchen wall hung an old map of the city before the shattering of the wall. *Ormael: Womb of Morning.* That was what the name meant, in some ancient tongue; she'd not thought of it in years. She looked in the mirror again. She had been born here, born of that womb, and the womb of that impossible woman behind the stove. Before her rebirth as Neda Ygraël, Phoenix-Flame, servant of the Unseen.

She walked to the back door and opened it. At the table in the garden sat her brother, just nine or ten years old, and Dr Chadfallow. They were puzzling over a text in Mzithrini together.

'That's Father's shirt,' said Neda. 'Your mucking lover is wearing his shirt.'

Suthinia poked at the fire in the stove.

Neda stepped outside. The sun was fierce; the colours bled to white. She stood right next to the boy and the man and wondered if anyone could sense her presence at all. Bees were buzzing in the orange tree she'd planted as a small girl. Dr Chadfallow was conjugating the verb *kethak*: to forgive.

'There is no passive voice in the Mzithrin tongue,' he told Pazel. 'You cannot say, "The sin was forgiven." You must declare who is doing the forgiving, see? You cannot play fast and loose.'

He went on talking, pointing at lines in the weighty tome. Through the garden gate Neda could see the edge of the plum orchard. It was harvest time; there were the harvesters with their hoop-baskets tied to their wastes. But instead of the old procedure where someone would climb a rickety ladder and try not to fall, the men also had smaller baskets on poles that they were hoisting high into the trees. Shielding her eyes, Neda saw that there were ixchel in the treetops, selecting the ripest fruit and dropping them into these baskets as they passed.

'*Deketha*, I forgive. *Troketha*, you forgive—'

Suddenly Pazel looked straight up into her eyes.

'This is *your* dream,' he said. 'You have to give Mother permission to enter it. She's afraid to interfere.'

'But she's already here!'

'That's what you think,' said her brother, and lowered his eyes again to the book.

Neda returned to the kitchen. Her mother was mincing onion, blinking back tears. Neda watched her work. Sometimes her hands closed on an object that had not been there a moment before.

'Mother?'

'Hmm-hmm ...'

'Stop that and look at me. I want you to. I want you to come into this dream.'

Her mother cried out. Neda was sure she had cut herself. But no, she had dropped the knife and pressed both hands to her face. She was looking straight at Neda and weeping with joy.

Dream tears are like nothing else in human experience: a plunge into total feeling, a ripping away of words, lies, excuses, of the bandages we have been winding about ourselves since we first learned to speak. Holding Suthinia, Neda wept for the years wasted, for the pain she had both caused and received, for the distance that had suddenly been bridged and the vast distance that would not be.

We must stop, said her mother, pressing Neda's head to her breast. *The tears will wake us if we don't.*

But neither woke. When the tears ended Neda felt herself changed, and knew the change would persist when she emerged from the dream.

'I don't believe any more,' she said, wiping her eyes. 'It's like dying. I don't know what I'm going to do.'

Suthinia just looked at her and held her hand.

'Cayer Vispek is going to kill me.'

'You mean this never happens to *sfvantskors*?'

'If it does no one admits it. The elders probably kill them, quickly and quietly. And blame the death on Arquali spies, or the Shaggat, or devils. Who knows.'

'We're almost strangers, aren't we?' said Suthinia.

Neda said nothing. Her mother squeezed her hand tighter.

'I will never ask you to forgive me,' she said, 'for failing to protect you, for harming you with that spell.'

'You're talking nonsense,' said Neda. 'The spell didn't kill me. Probably it saved my life a few times. Pazel has it worse. I can pretend to be normal, but he can't hide those fits.'

'You sound so …'

'Foreign?' said Neda. 'Religious?'

'Old, I was going to say. Much older than twenty-two.'

'The last six years were longer than the first sixteen. They were my second life.'

'The first one ended when you took your vows?'

Neda didn't know how to respond. It was certainly what she'd told her masters, and herself.

The sunlight flickered: shapes were passing the windows. Suthinia got to her feet.

'Come with me,' she said.

'Where are we going?'

'I can't say exactly. Shopping?'

'Mother, I'm a *sfvantskor*. I don't want to go shopping.'

Suthinia bent and pulled on her shoes. 'Neither do I, love, but don't you know how this works? You're still dreaming. What happens here is not under my control, or yours. And if you don't keep moving the dream changes the world around you. Radically, sometimes. Trust me, it's better just to take to your feet.'

In the garden, Chadfallow was sitting alone with drooping shoulders. 'Where is Pazel?' Suthinia asked.

'Gone swimming,' said the doctor. 'A murth-girl came and took his hand, and they went off together to the Haunted Coast.'

'Well then,' said Suthinia. 'Why don't you stop moping and come with us?'

Chadfallow shook his head sadly. 'Because that is not my fate.'

They left him there in the garden, and stared downhill towards the city. The houses rippled in the blazing sun. 'Ormael is *so* much better with ixchel about,' Suthinia declared. 'Once we passed the sanctuary law they started coming here on any boat with a hold to hide in. You wouldn't believe how quickly they've rid us of rats.'

'Mother,' said Neda, 'we have to concentrate. Is there any way you can get a message to the *Chathrand* for us? They don't even know that we're alive.'

'A message to the *Chathrand*! I don't know if I have the power, darling. Yes, I warned Pazel about Macadra, but I played only a small part in that chain. The message began with your ally Felthrup, who has apparently learned to swim the River of Shadows better than most beings alive. He passed the message to my old teacher, Pazel Doldur, for whom your brother is named. Doldur is long dead; he visited me as a ghost. All I had to do was pass the warning on to Pazel, the same way I'm speaking to you today. I can't summon the dead.'

'Then go into the River yourself. Don't you know how to swim?'

Suthinia laughed. 'I'm from Bali Adro, Neda. Half my school mates were dlömu.' She waved her hand over Ormael. 'I can swim rings around these people. But that's hardly the point. Look, I'll show you.'

At their feet there was a sewer drain set in the road. It had not been there a moment before. The two women crouched beside it, and Suthinia placed her hand upon the iron grille. Neda could hear water flowing beneath them. But as she listened the sound grew strange: deeper, wilder, and less like water than a roaring wind. As with certain moments during their journey on the Ansyndra, she had a terrifying sensation of bottomless depths under their feet. But this was much more close and fierce. Whatever fell into that raging torrent would be swept away like a leaf.

Suthinia pulled. The grille rose on creaking hinges. Neda gripped her arm and leaned away.

'Felthrup Stargraven,' said her mother. 'Maybe he's down there, somewhere, in one of the public houses on the riverbanks. I could climb in and search.'

Neda shook her head vehemently. 'Let's go,' she said. 'Don't make that sort of thing happen again.'

They passed the crossroads where one could turn east to the Cinderling, or west towards the flikkermen's hovels on the edges of the Crab Fens. On their left, men were cutting hay with fluid sweeps of their scythes.

'I've cast just two major spells in my lifetime,' said Suthinia. 'The first let me collect your dream-essence, which I'm still using to this day. That was a success; neither of you suffered, or even noticed what I'd done. The second—'

354

'Created our Gifts,' said Neda.

Suthinia looked at her. 'It's kind of you not to call them curses. But remember, darling: *your Gifts were already there.* The charm only strengthened them. You had a splendid memory to begin with, just as Pazel had a way with languages.'

There was a market just inside the gate. They milled quickly through the familiar Ormali crowds, buying bread, wine, candles, matches, flowers.

'I wish we could have brought Pazel along,' said Neda. 'But that wasn't really him I saw, was it? Just a fake, a dream-dummy.'

'That boy was no fake,' said her mother, squeezing a pear, 'but he was not the whole boy, either. That was the part of Pazel who lives in your mind. He might have come along with us, I suppose, but he couldn't tell us anything we don't already know.'

'I must do some telling,' said Neda, 'before one of us wakes.'

'Please do,' said Suthinia. 'For the past two weeks neither of you has done much dreaming. And when you do it's *never* about where you are at the moment. Normally a few things appear in your dreams *and* Pazel's, more or less the same. A face, a river, the shape of a hill. Those things, I guess, are what you're really seeing. But lately you've been almost invisible. I could feel that you were safe and sleeping deeply, but no more. Where are you?'

Neda stopped short. Confused, she raised a hand and touched her lips. She had been about to say the word *Uláramyth*, but could not. Her mouth simply disobeyed her, refused to form the words.

'What's wrong, my dear?' said her mother.

'There something—'

Once again she got no further. She had meant to say *something about the place where we are,* but the words would not come. The Secret Vale was not to be spoken of, apparently. Not even in dreams.

'Never mind,' said Suthinia, touching her arm. 'Tell me what you want your friends on the *Chathrand* to know.'

'We have the Nilstone,' said Neda.

Suthinia nodded. 'Yes, I could sense that. Oh Neda, I'm so proud of you, and afraid for you. I hope you don't have to keep it long.'

'We're with the selk,' said Neda.

Her mother beamed. 'I thought so. I heard their music in your heads. And I saw Ramachni speaking to one of them, from a tree. Hold these flowers for me, while I pay the man.'

'And Arunis is dead.'

As soon as Neda spoke, the world went mad. Suthinia turned, screaming like a banshee, letting her purchases fall from her arms. The crowd drew away from her, then fell away, the market melting and swirling like a kaleidoscope, with only the two of them still and clear. Suthinia grabbed Neda's shoulders, her nails biting through the robe, and several seconds passed before Neda understood that her mother had not lost her mind.

'You!' she was screaming. 'You, you!'

Or had she? Neda had lost her faith and it felt like dying. Suthinia had crossed the Ruling Sea and lost everything. Her family, her people, her language, the whole Southern world. She had even lost her century: the Red Storm had taken that. All to fight a mage who had slipped through their fingers. A mage who had hunted down and killed nearly everyone who came with her from the South. Arunis had been the torture of her life. And the reason, the cause. *'My children!'* she screamed for the whole world's hearing. *'My children got you, you horror, you walking piece of hell!'*

Suddenly her mother's eyes darted. Neda tried to hold her but could not. Suthinia made a quick, unnatural lunge past Neda's shoulder, and when Neda turned she found herself alone by the city gate.

She shook her head. Suthinia had woken herself up.

For Neda, however, it remained the most lucid dream of her life. 'Are you still able to listen?' she said aloud, thinking of her mother with her dream-vials. 'If I talk to you, can you hear?'

She started walking – her mother was right, you had to move or bad things would happen, Neda could somehow feel it in her bones. She entered by the gate and walked the upper city, past Pazel's school, the textile mill, the humble museum closed for lack of funds.

She told her mother about the Swarm of Night. When she spoke the name all twenty or thirty people around her fell silent and glanced upwards, but nothing passed in the sky except a crow.

Neda left the city by the same gate and started the climb back to their house. Something kept forcing her to the right, however, and as the light faded (too quick for any sunset) Neda decided she knew what it was. Something had to explain why she still carried one of their purchases.

The barn belonged to a neighbour called Cranz. One of many who hadn't helped her. Not that she could truly blame them: if any had tried to free a girl from the hands of the Arquali marines they would simply have been killed. She understood that now, but she hadn't at the time. The absence of those people who had always smiled at her, of Farmer Cranz with his big square fists and his son who used to carve wooden figurines and the strapping farmhands who made eyes at her when no one was watching: it had been part of the horror of that day, Invasion Day, when she was just sixteen.

Neda slid open the door. There had been horses. She went forward until she found them: two old plough-pullers, grey and brown, their long tails swishing flies. Neda led them outside and well away from the barn, then stepped back inside. She walked the length of the building, tall and straight, a *sfvantskor* disbeliever, a new creature on the face of Alifros. A native come home.

The last time she had passed this way they had been dragging her, screaming.

She stood a while looking at the hay mound, which was broad and tall and dry. She dropped her cloak and stood naked, then stepped into it, wading, until the hay reached her thighs.

'No,' she told her mother, 'my first life didn't end with my vows. I believed that when I said it, but I was wrong. I hope you're listening. I never did blame you.'

She took a match from the box in her hand and struck it, and tossed it burning into the hay.

'It ended here,' she said.

An eager crackling began at her feet. She struck another match, and another. Nine in all, one for each of the soldiers. Thanks to her Gift she could remember them quite well. She had never lain with a man before that day. Afterwards it was unthinkable. The *sfvantskor* order with its law of total abstinence had brought her a welcome safety. But the Book also warned the faithful that to live was to hazard something, 'for only the dead are safe from all harm'.

The flames raged, tall as men. She lifted her arms above her head and dared them to touch her.

Time accelerated, as it had been wanting to, and the barn became a torch, and all Ormael saw it blazing over the city, and even a few eyes on boats in the Straits of Simja caught the glow.

The roof collapsed, and the walls followed, and then she walked forward naked among her people, common Ormalis come to gawk and stare, and wonder at this apparition stepping unharmed from the fire.

'Don't be afraid,' she told them. 'I'm one of you. My name is Neda Pathkendle, and now I think I can wake up.'

17

At the Temple of the Wolves

On their last day in Uláramyth the summer warmth still held.

At least it did here, low in the crater on a sunny morning. Clover and phlox and mistflower were blooming; a dragonfly landed on Thasha's arm. But when she raised her eyes to the mountains she saw fresh snow on the peaks. Autumn was advancing; the Swarm was loose and growing by the day; and the *Chathrand* was still sailing northwards, leaving them ever further behind.

For several days Lord Arim's scouts had been returning to Uláramyth, and all their talk was of enemies: hrathmogs, Plazic soldiers, worse creatures they were reluctant to name. Thasha had a feeling that the path to the sea would be hacked through the bodies of many foes.

Hercól had asked Corporal Mandric to oversee their physical readiness, and he'd been at it as only a Turach could: inspecting their limbs, the digits of their hands, the soles of their feet. He'd made them get haircuts and start the day with sprints. He'd forced them to double their meal size and sleep ten hours a night and climb the crater walls twice daily with heavy packs. Whatever lay ahead they would face it strong.

But Thasha had a more immediate concern. She was in the northeast quarter of Uláramyth, a mile or two from the shores of Osir Delhin. She had climbed a little ridge overlooking a forest of bamboo, which seethed in the wind like an emerald surf. From where she stood, the path snaked down the ridge to a shady clearing. There on the moist grass lay Neeps and Sergeant Lunja, asleep. The small boy was curled like a child. Shirtless, he lay with his back to Lunja and his head on her arm. His face serene, his skin unearthly pale against her midnight black. Lunja's other arm held him close, her half-webbed hand spread open on his chest. She was a magnificent soldier, muscled like Neda, tall as Hercól.

Thasha had been sent to find them. She'd been warned what to expect. This was the heart of the treatment, Neeps' only chance. To hold off the mind-plague he had to pass into *nuhzat* at least once. Mr Bolutu said that only one human in a thousand had been able to enter *nuhzat* in the old days. The selk doctors agreed. 'It was not the yearnings of the body that mattered,' one of them had explained. 'Dlömic prostitutes never brought their human clients to *nuhzat*, however much they pleased them otherwise. Bali Adro investigations of the plague made that much very clear. Only trust could occasion the *nuhzat*. The deepest trust, the most intimate.'

He'd meant love, of course. Neeps had to feel love for a dlömu. And how could anyone make that happen? Spells and potions were useless, Ramachni had told them: infatuation could be generated, and certainly lust. But the *nuhzat* was mysterious and very personal. It could not be induced like a reaction of the nerves. If it came at all, it came with sincere emotion, a thing no spell could force.

Pazel had objected. 'I happen to know that love *can* be ... induced. By magic. I've seen it happen.'

'You are speaking of murths,' said Ramachni, 'but the divers enchanted by murth-girls are not really in love, only confused long enough for the murths to kill them.'

Pazel had shaken his head, blushing, and Thasha had come to his aid. 'He's not talking about the divers, Ramachni. He means Klyst, the murth-girl whose spell backfired, so that she fell in love with him.'

Ramachni had looked at Pazel in fascinated surprise. 'It lasted,' sputtered Pazel, 'a long, long time. She followed me, followed the *Chathrand*.' He raised his hand to touch his collarbone, where Klyst's tiny shell lay beneath his skin.

Ramachni gazed at him another moment, then shook his head.

'The murth-world is a place beyond your knowledge, or mine. But I know this much, Pazel Pathkendle: a façade can sometimes grow into true feelings, if the potential was there all along.'

Neeps turned over, reached for Lunja without opening his eyes, lay still again with a hand in her hair. It was hard for Thasha to accept that no magic had brought them to this point. Lunja had agreed that day when she rose up from the stream, and set to work, and the work had led here. *They're lovers, probably. What does it matter. I hope they are. Even Marila would want it if she knew.*

She walked down the ridge the way she had come, then called out for Neeps as though trying to locate him. After a moment Neeps replied with a befuddled shout.

Thasha walked to the clearing. Lunja was gone; Neeps was pulling on his shirt. No one would question them; no one would ask them to explain. But when Neeps approached her his eyes were not hiding a thing.

'You know,' he said, scowling. 'Don't pretend, for Rin's sake. You know.'

What was she to say? 'They told me you'd be here. The two of you, I mean.'

He was very angry. Did he think she was laughing at him?

'They tried *everything* before resorting to this. They had me drink something that made my gums bleed. It didn't work. Lord Arim tried selk-magic and that didn't work. Ramachni put me in the healing sleep. By the next morning he knew it was useless.'

'We were there, Neeps. We saw.'

'Prince Olik said the *nuhzat* isn't dangerous, or even unpleasant. But *this* is mucking terrible for her. Not because humans are so strange. Oh no, it's because we're not strange enough. She's seen us all her life, you know. In cages, zoos, sometimes in the bush. When her family went for picnics her mother used to let her toss carrots, bits of bread. Later we weren't around so much. The wild ones are mostly dead and gone. They're rotten hunters, and fragile, and so mucking stupid. When the dlömu stop feeding them they just starve.'

He was raving, but he couldn't stop. 'Then one day some of these pale animals show up and *Pitfire*, they can talk. And what happens? Straight away her prince asks Lunja to march off with these animals into the wilderness, and she goes. Right to the Black Tongue and the flame-trolls and the Infernal Forest, which is to say right to the blary Pits. Her friends get slaughtered one by one. Then she finds out that she can't even go home, because now her prince is an outlaw, and she'll be punished for helping him, helping us, and she has a brother in that city, Thasha, and two nieces, and a normal dlömic man who might have married her. And when she's already given everything to protect these crazy, ugly animals, it turns out that one of them needs—'

He paused; he was gasping for breath. Thasha reached for him but he jerked sharply away. He gazed at her as though expecting the worst.

'You think Lunja's been complaining, don't you? Well forget it. Not one word. It's just me thinking, putting the pieces together, and how am I supposed to thank her, Thasha, she's so mucking kind, and inside I know she's disgusted, she *has* to be—'

'But you're not,' she said.

Neeps swung at her. Thasha ducked the blow; she had guessed where this was heading. He swung again; she jumped back out of range. The third time his fist grazed her cheek. Then she tripped him easily and threw him flat on his back.

'I love you,' she said, feeling a fool.

He stared: that had caught him off guard. He lay on the turf for a moment, winded, dabbing at his eyes with his sleeve. Then Thasha helped him to his feet.

'It isn't working,' he said at last. 'She watches me, watches my eyes for the change. It hasn't happened. What if it never does?'

Thasha pulled him close and held him until she felt his breath start to slow, and the rigidness leave his muscles. 'Do you know what Hercól would tell you?' she said. 'You've found your path—'

'Now close your mouth and walk it.'

Neeps let her go. He was smiling, a forced smile if Thasha had ever seen one. Then the smile vanished and he looked her straight in the eye.

'You'll tell Marila what this was about, won't you? I mean if something happens and I don't get the chance? You have to. Oh Thasha, if she ever heard a rumour, or some nasty joke … Will you do that for me? Promise?'

'Cross that one off your list, you fool. I'll tell her. I promise.'

Neeps' eyes pinched shut. He nodded. Thasha took his arm, and together they went looking for their friends.

The meeting was to occur in Thehel Bledd, the Temple of the Wolves, a place forbidden to them until today. Pazel was hurrying towards it along a trail through the oak grove when he met Hercól and Ramachni.

'I've been lost for an hour,' he said. 'There are three or four ways to get everywhere in this land, and twice as many to get nowhere you've seen before. Aren't we running late?'

'Not at all,' said Ramachni. 'The temple is quite near. Save your strength for tomorrow and walk with us. As it happens we very much need to talk.'

Pazel looked up. 'This is about Thasha, isn't it?'

'Yes,' said Hercól. 'Along with Neeps, we are her closest friends. And you of course are more than a friend.'

Pazel said nothing to that. He loved these two, but he had become wary of them both. In the bitter end he feared they might be capable of sacrificing Thasha. That did not make them evil; it might even make them what Alifros needed to survive. Rin knew Thasha was capable of sacrificing herself. But he, Pazel, could not sacrifice her. Not unless he could go with her, into whatever death or transformation she faced.

'This wall inside Thasha—' Ramachni began.

'I've told you what Erithusmé said five times over,' said Pazel. 'It's between them, and it won't let them trade places. It won't let Thasha hide in that "cave" in her mind, or let Erithusmé take control of her body and come fully back to life. And that's all.

Thasha can barely feel the thing; Erithusmé can't find out what it is. Maybe Thasha built it herself, unconsciously. Or maybe Arunis put it inside her somehow, before he died.'

'I do not know if he ever had such power,' said Ramachni, 'and even if he did, to implant such a spell would have required him to touch her, and for rather longer than an instant.' The mage looked at each of them. 'Has he ever done so?'

Hercól shook his head. 'Never.'

Pazel agreed. 'And he could have, when we were locked up in Masalym. He never tried.'

'When we fought him on the *Chathrand*, he summoned darkness, just before he fled the ship,' said Hercól. 'He might have touched Thasha then. But the darkness was brief, and he was desperate, fighting for his life against us all.'

'The spell could have reached Thasha by means of an object, if she kept it on her person long enough,' said Ramachni. 'That was his approach with her mother's necklace. But when he cursed the necklace Arunis did not know of the connection between Thasha and Erithusmé. You witnessed his shock on Dhola's Rib, when he glimpsed the truth at last. Think carefully: has she been given *anything* else that might have come from the sorcerer?'

'No,' said Pazel.

'No,' agreed Hercól. 'Since the incident with the necklace, Thasha has been wary of gifts from any quarter, I am glad to say. However—' He paused, glancing uneasily at Pazel.

'Go on, say it.'

'What if the object was Fulbreech?'

'Fulbreech?' cried Pazel.

'He was, after all, the sorcerer's tool,' said Hercól.

And he touched her, thought Pazel, feeling suddenly ill. *Many times. For longer than an instant.*

'If Arunis had the power to infect her mind at all, Fulbreech could indeed have been the agent,' said Ramachni. 'Pazel, have you spoken to her of those encounters?'

'No!'

'She would have felt the magical intrusion, for a moment at least. One of us must ask her.'

Pazel took a deep breath. 'She's ashamed of the whole business,' he said. 'Of course she *shouldn't* be; she was brilliant. But playing along with his lies, pretending to want him, to be under his spell – honestly, Hercól, it's about the nastiest thing you could have asked her to do.'

'And you and she both know why I did so,' said Hercól.

Pazel nodded, reluctantly. By playing Fulbreech, they had almost succeeded in killing Arunis back on the *Chathrand*. And would have, he recalled bitterly, if he, Pazel, had not interfered.

'I will speak to Thasha,' said Hercól. 'Pazel is right: I put her up to the foul game.'

Ramachni shook his head. 'On second thought, I think it must be me. This is a matter of spells, and my questions to her may be more precise. Besides, I will not shame her. There are some advantages to not being human.'

They passed on through the trees, through the rich smell of loam and the flutter of unseen wings. 'Ramachni,' said Pazel at last, 'do you trust her, completely?'

'What a question!' said the mage. 'Thasha has proven herself beyond my wildest hopes. I would place the fate of all the worlds in her hand without a moment's hesitation, if I could.'

Pazel looked at him keenly. 'I was talking about Erithusmé,' he said. 'Can you say as much about her?'

Ramachni stopped walking.

'Because I just remembered,' said Pazel, 'how you didn't know who had created the magic wall around the *Chathrand*'s stateroom. And it was Erithusmé; she told me so. It's a bit odd that she kept something like that from you, don't you think?'

Ramachni's deep black eyes fixed on him. 'Listen to me, lad,' he said. 'Since the dawn of woken life on Alifros, in days so ancient even the selk have forgotten them, only a handful of beings have ever been born with utter mastery of magic inscribed in their souls. Erithusmé is one. She did not know the power latent in her until the Nilstone awakened it – that is true. But what matters is that she never let the Stone enslave her. What matters is that she was noble enough to be satisfied with greatness and spurn omnipotence. A lesser being would have clung to the Nilstone even as it killed her, built keeps and castles, raised enfortressed islands in which to guard the cursed thing. Erithusmé gave it up. She knew its rightful place was not Alifros but the land of the dead, and tried to send it there. What further proof of her intentions do you require?'

Pazel had no answer. He did require more, but how to ask for it? Even Ramachni might have a blind spot, and if he did it was surely for his mistress, the one who trained him as a mage.

'Some day,' he said, 'I'd like to hear the story of your childhood, Ramachni.'

'I shall be glad to tell you, at the appropriate time,' said Ramachni. 'Perhaps if we rejoin the ship, and start the crossing, and lie becalmed for half a year upon the Ruling Sea.'

Pazel smiled, but could not laugh. He was uneasy still. Then he heard footfalls behind him. To his surprise it was Neda, running to catch up with them, and for once unescorted. When she arrived she amazed him further by kissing him on both cheeks, and then looking at him with the plain, frank, critical eye of an older sister, rather than that of a warrior, or a priest.

He studied her, alarmed. There was something in her face that was liberated, or unhinged. 'Neda,' he said, 'what in Pitfire's happened to you?'

'I spoke with our mother,' she said.

Thasha and Neeps saw the wolves before they saw the temple. They were still in the bamboo grove. A pair of the regal animals, coal-black and chalk-white, bounded onto the trail.

'Welcome, rare birds of the North,' said the white wolf. 'Valgrif spoke of you, but we have only seen the little ones – the women so small our cubs try to pounce on them. Come quickly: Lord Arim awaits.'

Thehel Bledd was a large complex with several halls, and many long rectangular pools that mirrored the surrounding mountains, and marble terraces of differing heights that stood open to the sky. Parts of the temple grounds were half lost in vines and creepers and the ubiquitous bamboo; others, swept clean, appeared to enjoy more frequent use. Many wolves padded through the temple, watching them with bright, intelligent eyes.

Rounding the corner of a large hall they came suddenly on Pazel and Neda. 'Thasha!' Pazel cried. 'Come here, listen to Neda! You won't believe your ears!'

Neda was changed – there was a directness to her look that Thasha had never seen before – and what she told them changed Thasha too, or at least made her weep with joy and longing. She asked Neda to repeat it again and again, in her poor Arquali, until Pazel could not stand it and rattled it all off in one breath.

'Is true, sister,' said Neda, aglow. 'Your father being fine.'

'But – friends?' said Neeps, looking at them dubiously. 'Her dad, and your witch-mum?'

'Why not?' said Pazel. 'Mom's a little crazy—'

'Very crazy,' said Neda.

'—but she's never been a fool. And the admiral, why, he's capable of anything.'

'Is what mother saying, too,' said Neda.

'And Maisa,' said Thasha, 'hiding out in the blary Fens. It's a blary miracle. Pazel, we have to tell Hercól.'

'I am telling,' said Neda.

'She means she told him already,' said Pazel.

Neda looked at Thasha curiously. 'When I am saying "Empress Maisa" I think Hercól getting cry. But no, no tears.'

'What did he do?' said Thasha.

Neda looked unsettled. 'He being quiet; then praying little bit. Then saying if I not *sfvantskor* he kissing me like no woman ever before his life.'

They might have talked a great deal longer, but the wolves urged them on. A moment later Valgrif himself bounded into view. 'Good!' he said. 'Now you are all accounted for, save Sergeant Lunja. Come, we are about to begin.'

'Valgrif, you're hurt,' said Neeps. And so he was: a white bandage had been tied about his ankle, and his ear was torn.

'I have killed five servants of the Raven Society,' said the wolf. 'Four fell quickly, but the last was a terrible dog, an *athymar*. That battle was ugly, but I prevailed, and the bodies will never be found. Lord Arim sent many wolves to the mountains. They are all back now, save my sons – and all with evil news I fear.'

The wolves led them through a few more twists and turns, and at last through a stone gate. Beyond, a crumbling stair led down to what Thasha presumed was the temple's innermost terrace. Here a round stone table awaited them, upon which fruit and bread and decanters of selk wine had been set. The other travellers, except for Lunja, were here already. There were also some half-dozen selk, among them Thaulinin and Lord Arim. Nólcindar was not present; in fact Thasha realised that she had not seen the warrior for many days.

'Citizens,' said Lord Arim, 'you deserve full honours and a splendid farewell. Indeed, I had hoped to show you something of the esteem we hold you in – you who felled Arunis, and recovered the Stone from his keeping. But that cannot be. We must have a war-council, and a brief one at that. One of you is missing, but we dare not wait for her. Come and drink a cup with us, and let us begin.'

'What's keeping Lunja?' Neeps murmured to Thasha. 'She only meant to go and bathe in the stream. She shouldn't be this late.'

The selk poured everyone a cup of dark wine – even the wolves drank a little, from a brass bowl on the terrace. Then Thaulinin helped Lord Arim to a chair, and the others sat down as well. Ramachni leaped onto the table and sat between Thasha and Hercól. The ixchel settled beside the mage.

'You have heard,' said Lord Arim, 'that we sent scouts into the world beyond. Now they have spoken: Uláramyth is all but surrounded. Macadra may have learned that the Nilstone came inland with the sorcerer, or she may still be uncertain whether it did so or was taken from Masalym aboard your ship. But either way she has landed forces in the Peninsula on a scale never seen before. No, they will not find the Secret Vale, but there can hardly be a path between here and the coast that her forces are not watching. No great legions of soldiers await us: the land is too extensive for that. Macadra has rather spread her forces thin, like the strands of a spider web – and therein lies the danger. Is it not so, Ambrimar's son?'

'It is, Lord,' said Thaulinin, 'for while there are many paths to the sea, Macadra too has her riders, and they are swift. And should they spot us on any of those paths, those riders will fly before us, sounding the alarm, and her forces will converge between us and the path we have chosen. And remember that those paths are long. We might kill any number of her servants, but we will not kill unnoticed for sixteen days running, all the way to the Ilidron Coves. If we disturb Macadra's web but once, we will never reach the sea.'

'And we do not have sixteen days,' said Hercól. 'For after the march there is a great sea journey we must somehow accomplish. And with every hour that passes the Great Ship moves a bit further north.'

'I told you, swordsman,' said Cayer Vispek, looking sternly at Hercól. 'We have lingered too long in this place of soft beds and sweet music! It has lulled us to sleep, or into pastimes unworthy of us. And now the length of the road dismays you? Thaulinin warned us of it when we met him on Sirafstöran Torr.'

'I do not speak in dismay,' said Hercól, 'only in observance of fact. Sixteen days is too long.'

'If you would blame someone for the length of our stay, Cayer, blame me,' said Ramachni. 'I counselled against moving in ignorance, and nothing else could we have done before the return of Lord Arim's scouts. But it is true that we have run out of time. The *Chathrand*'s northward progress is one reason. Another is the growth of the Swarm of Night.'

He looked at the assembled faces. 'You know what the Swarm is, and you know Arunis dredged the River of Shadows until he found it, and used the power of the Nilstone to bring it forth. Some of you know as well that our hosts have seen it from the mountaintops in recent days. Now I will tell you how it kills – and why.

'The Swarm was created to patrol the border of death's kingdom, to stop the dead from spilling out into Agaroth, and attempting to migrate back in the direction of the living lands. Whenever a breach in the border wall appears, the Swarm falls upon any of the dead who pass through it, and drives them back to their proper place. The larger the breach, the stronger the Swarm grows in order to contain it. But in the living world all of this goes awry. Death still attracts the Swarm, and death's dark energy can still feed it and make it grow. Small or scattered deaths will pass unnoticed: their energy will still leave Alifros in the natural way, along with the spirits of the deceased. But a great catastrophe – a war, a famine, an earthquake – is quite different. The Swarm flies to such horrors, and if they are still unfolding, it drops upon them and makes them complete.'

'Complete?' said Big Skip. 'You mean it kills everyone that hasn't yet been killed?'

'Everyone and everything within its compass,' said Ramachni. 'Trees, grass, insects, people. And then, like a sated vulture, it rises again into the clouds and moves on.'

'It has already happened at least once,' said Thaulinin. 'Our scouts listened to the fireside grumblings of the enemy. Several times they spoke of a "cloud of death" that had ended the fighting in Karysk, along with most of Bali Adro's terrible armada.'

'This Swarm sounds almost like a peacemaker,' said Corporal Mandric.

'It could have that effect for a time,' said Ramachni, 'if all the warlords in Alifros somehow learned of their peril. But I fear we would not be safe for long. There is no way to be certain, but my guess is that the Swarm only ignores the little deaths because the larger call to it so loudly. If wars ceased, it would begin to harvest death from smaller conflicts, minor plagues. And in time darkness itself will become the killer, as crops and forest die in its shadow.'

'Watchers above!' said Bolutu. 'Surely it will never grow *that* large!'

'Will it not?' Ramachni glanced about the table, his eyes settling at last on the bowls of fruit. 'Consider those grapes, Mr Bolutu: how many would it take to cover the table?'

'Entirely?' said Bolutu. 'That's hard to guess, Ramachni. Thousands, surely.'

'Let us say ten thousand. And let us imagine we start with one grape, and double the number each day. Think back to your early arithmetic: how long will it take?'

'Fourteen days,' said Neda. There were startled glances, but Neda shrugged. 'Very simple problem. Only double and double: two, four, eight, sixteen—'

'And so on,' said Ramachni. 'Fortunately even this scale is deceptive: if the table stands for Alifros, the Swarm today is still no larger than a grain of sand. And on many days it will feed on nothing, but merely fly toward the next battle or site of pestilence. We need not measure our time in days, just yet – but we dare not measure it in years. Six months from now, Arunis will have joined the Night Gods, and this world will be a black and lifeless grave.'

There were sighs and looks of horror, as though the mage had stabbed them with his words. Pazel thought of all the quiet days in Uláramyth and felt a pang of guilt. He had not wanted to hasten their passing. He had not wanted to think about the Swarm.

'At the very least, our task is clear,' said Hercól. 'We must make haste to Gurishal, and give the Nilstone back to death.'

'This might be a good moment to tell us *how*,' said Thasha, 'or at least how we're to reach the coast.'

'Mr Pathkendle is quite correct,' said Lord Arim, 'and here is the best answer we have found: it is true that Macadra is watching every sensible path. But there remains one, rather less sensible, that she may have forgotten.'

He rose stiffly from his chair and pointed northwards. High on the crater's rim, Thasha could just make out the dark triangular doorway in the mountain's wall.

'The Nine Peaks Road,' said Lord Arim, 'or as we call it, Alet Ithar, the Sky Road. It is a remote and treacherous path, though part of it follows the Royal Highway that linked the halls of the Mountain Kings. Ages have passed since those kingdoms fell. The Highway is lost in many places: bridges have fallen, forests regrown; earthquakes have changed the shape of the peaks. Today only the selk continue to speak of a road at all. Yet with skill and daring one can still pass that way – at least until the deep snows drape the mountains. And that is a third and final reason to hurry: as you can see, the snows have already begun.'

'The path is certainly treacherous,' said Ramachni, 'but it is also a shortcut. By that path, and the wild lowlands beyond, we may come to the Gulf of Ilidron in a mere nine or ten days.'

Ensyl was gazing up at the distant doorway. 'I thought we were forbidden to learn the way out of the Vale, Lord Arim,' she said.

Arim nodded. 'You are indeed. But that door above you does not mark the start of the Nine Peaks: it is but a final shelter and waystation for those leaving Uláramyth. You will climb to that station at midnight tonight, and I will go that far at your side.'

Ramachni looked startled. 'That is very good of you, my lord, but need you tire yourself?'

Arim smiled. 'There is power yet in this old selk, Arpathwin: even a spark of that fire we wielded at the Battle of Luhmor, should it come to that. Yes, I must make that climb, for not even you may pass the guardian we keep at that door, without my intercession.'

'Our plan is not without risk,' said Thaulinin. 'Countless travellers have met their deaths in the Nine Peaks. It is even possible that Macadra has set watchers upon the high road after all. If so we must fight and kill them, and let none escape to sound the alarm. We will also, of course, bear the danger of the Nilstone.'

'That danger at least we have tried to reduce,' said Hercól. 'Go ahead, Sunderling: tell us of your work.'

Big Skip nodded. 'Time was, the Stone was encased in explosive glass, you know, and the glass embedded in the Red Wolf. Not very practical for travelling. Still, we don't want any accidents – not when one little touch can kill a man. So Bolutu and I got to talking with the selk, and in the end we gave the Stone a new, thick skin of glass. Selk glass, made from sand drawn from the bottom of that dark lake of theirs. It quiets the Stone down, you might say. You can touch it, although it still burns like a potato fresh from the oven. So we've fashioned a box for the Nilstone as well, out of solid steel. The top half screws down and locks against the bottom – and nothing short of Rin's own hammer and tongs will get to it—' Skip held up a heavy key '—without this.'

'Needless to say,' added Bolutu, 'the key and the Nilstone will be carried separately.'

'Always,' said Big Skip, 'and just in case we need to take the Stone out of the box, the selk blacksmiths gave us a a pair of their own gauntlets. I lifted the Stone myself, wearing 'em. It wasn't pleasant, but it didn't kill me either.'

'That is fine work,' said Hercól, 'but let us return to the journey itself, now.'

'I shall be your guide in the mountains,' said Thaulinin, 'and if the stars are willing, I will see you all the way to the Ilidron Coves. There we have a secret harbour, a place of last flight, which long ago we prepared against the day when the selk might be forced to flee like hunted game. The world has changed since we hid those vessels; there are no more selk homelands to be reached by sea. And yet one ship remains: the *Promise* we call her. She is too small to brave the fury of the Nelluroq, but she can bring you to a rendezvous with the *Chathrand*, if the latter still awaits you.'

'And if the Empire's warships do not sink us first,' said Cayer Vispek.

'Five years ago, escape from Ilidron would have been unthinkable,' said Lord Arim, 'but today the door stands open a crack. In the *Platazcra* madness, Bali Adro has slain Bali Adro, and most of her remaining ships have been sent east in the armada, to face the delusional threat from Karysk. Of course terrible forces remain, especially the Floating Fortresses along the Sandwall, but the little *Promise* may slip away unseen, if only you can reach her.'

'Lord Arim, how can you give us your escape vessel?' asked Thasha in distress. 'Even if your homelands are gone, you might need to flee somewhere.'

Lord Arim shook his head. 'Not over the waves – not that way, ever again. Nor can we go on risking the lives of those who guard the *Promise* away in the west. Bali Adro's star grows dim, Thasha Isiq, but the assault on this peninsula has just begun. New people are coming: refugees from the war, and from the doomed cities of the Imperial heartland. Rogue armies, splinters of the great legions, warlords for whom the only rule is plunder. They will come afoot, or creeping along the shoreline in anything that floats. I cannot say if they will penetrate these inner mountains, but before the tide turns they will almost certainly devour the coast. Our harbour has waited many centuries, but it will not be a secret much longer.'

'Yet today we still depend on secrecy – and *perfect* secrecy at that,' said Ramachni. 'Macadra cannot guard every port and cove in the Peninsula, but should she learn the path we have taken, she will throw more enemies at us than we can possibly defeat.'

'We must be nimble and swift,' said Thaulinin. 'Just ten selk warriors will accompany us, and we shall all wear white, the better to hide against the snow. We also have some plans for Macadra's forces. Even now, bands of selk are leaving Uláramyth by several roads. They will try to draw the enemy astray. Nólcindar herself left three days ago, to see what trouble she might stir along the banks of the Ansyndra. If the Ravens and their sometimes-servants the hrathmogs come to blows, so much the better.'

'My two sons are with her,' said Valgrif. 'If their work goes well they may even join us on the Nine Peaks Road.'

'Us?' said Myett, looking startled. 'Then you are going too, Valgrif?'

'As far as the low country, little sister,' he said. 'But I must turn back when I smell salt in the air, for I was born with blood-terror of the sea.'

Then a wolf appeared at the stone gate atop the stairs, holding a leather pouch in his teeth. 'Ah,' said Lord Arim, 'here is something I put aside a long time ago, for just such an expedition.'

The wolf descended, and Arim took the pouch and opened it upon the table. Pazel jumped. Within the pouch were a dozen or more scarlet beetles, dry and dead, each one the size of a mussel shell. '*Zudikrin*,' said Arim, 'fire beetles from the deep caves under Uláramyth. You must each carry one in your coat, and guard it well. It is a last defence against freezing.'

'*Zudikrin* make dangerous gifts, Lord Arim,' said Thaulinin.

'So they are,' said the elder. 'Use them only in the face of death: if the cold is winning, and your life ebbing away. If that time should come, bite down on the insect, break the carapace – and spit the beetle out. You will be warmed, I promise you.

'Now,' Arim went on, 'there is a custom we must observe. If you would honour your time here, then honour this custom too, even if you cannot see its worth. The matter is simple: for thousands of years we have tried to make a haven of this place. When any living soul comes here in friendship, we name that one a citizen. And we recognize no one's right to force that citizen to leave, for any cause whatsoever. Therefore I must ask if any one of you feels bound in your heart to remain here and abandon the quest. Silence, silence! Remember my entreaty! And remember too that every trial and hardship you left behind in this vale may come again in the outer world. Fear no shame or censure. Only if you would stay here, for a week or a year, or to the end of your short life, bid your comrades farewell upon this terrace, in the sight of all.'

His words left a silence. Thasha glanced in wonder about the table. It was a strange custom, but a noble one perhaps. All the same it was rather unthinkable that—

'I will stay,' said Myett.

There were loud crics. Ensyl, grief-stricken, began to shout in the ixchel tongue the humans could not hear. Arim raised his hands high.

'No more! The choice is hers alone, and it is for no one to gainsay.'

'May I speak, my lord?' asked Myett.

'If such is your wish,' said Arim sternly, 'but you who listen must do so in silence: that is my command, and I will not repeat it.'

Myett looked at her companions with a kind of misery. 'I would stay, first because I found so few ways to be of use to this expedition. I am not as strong or swift as Ensyl. I can fight, but I was never trained like her, as a battle-dancer. I have been a burden, a thing to be carried, more often than a help. And I would stay because nothing awaits me in the North but solitude. Even if we somehow found the ship, the clan will not have me back. Even if we reach Stath Bálfyr, and find it still a homeland for the ixchel, Lord Talag will poison my name.'

How can you be so certain? Thasha wanted to scream.

Now Myett dropped her eyes, as though too shamed to look at them. 'On the *Chathrand* I tried to take my own life,' she said. 'I almost succeeded. Since then I have tried to be stronger, to turn my eyes to the sun. But I was failing. I could feel the sadness closing over me again like black water. Until I came here.'

She's not acting on impulse, Thasha realised. *She's been thinking this over a long time.*

'That is all,' said Myett, 'save that—' She made a gesture of confusion. 'Lord Taliktrum. He abandoned me without a thought, without even a spiteful goodbye. If I am to live I must forget that. Please try to forgive me, Ensyl. You will be the last of our people I shall ever see. I will live among the wolves, if they will have me. I do not think I can forget anywhere but here.'

Now Myett forced herself to look each of her comrades in the eyes. 'You will be stronger without me,' she said. 'Farewell.'

'Come, sister,' said one of the wolves. Myett leaped to his back. In three bounds the wolf ascended the stair and vanished through the gate. Once again that morning Thasha found herself fighting tears.

'Guard her spirit if you can, Lord Arim,' said Ramachni. 'Your realm's power is very great, but I do not know if it will pierce the darkness within her.'

'She will be cared for,' said the selk, 'and now we must conclude the business of this council, and you must return to Thehel Urred and rest. Would any of you speak?'

'Yes,' said Cayer Vispek. 'I wish to know if Macadra herself is patrolling the seas off this peninsula.'

'That we cannot know, without some sighting of her,' said Thaulinin, 'but we have told you already that with stealth we hope to reach the Sandwall unmolested. The Island Wilderness beyond is uncharted by the dlömu, but we selk still recall the way to Stath Bálfyr.'

'And that is priceless knowledge,' said Ramachni, 'and our best chance of catching the *Chathrand* before she vanishes into the Ruling Sea. For while our friends on the Great Ship blunder about in search of that island, we will be sailing straight.'

Cayer Vispek laughed darkly. 'Through what gauntlet we know not. After what carnage in the mountains we know not.'

Thasha glanced at him surreptitiously. *What's wrong with him today?* Then she saw his eyes dart in Neda's direction – and Neda look quickly away. *Vispek's part of it. Whatever's happened to Neda is affecting him too.*

'Lord Arim,' said Ensyl, still drying her eyes, 'do my people truly reign on Stath Bálfyr? Do you know?'

'It has been theirs since my father's day,' said Arim, 'and that was before the first dlömic ships were built, when only selk went to sea, and the Bali Adro were a wild clan upon the Doámm Steppe. But two centuries have passed since any selk made landfall there. I cannot say who rules the island now.'

'Let us go together and find out, Lady Ensyl.'

The voice came from the stone gate above them, and even before she placed it Thasha felt a thrill of recognition. Everyone rose; shouts of joy and wonder on their lips. Descending the staircase, escorted by four wolves and a joyous Sergeant Lunja, was a tall and beaming dlömic man.

'Prince Olik! Prince Olik!'

Chairs were overturned in the rush to greet him. And Prince Olik Bali Adro laughed and spread his arms in delight.

'How by all the roads of twilight did you find your way *here*?'

For some minutes the war-council collapsed into a joyous re-union. Olik had saved all their lives back in Masalym, and to most of the travellers he had become a cherished friend. He was leaner and harder-looking than Thasha recalled, but his eyes still held that hint of merriment she had first noticed on the deck of the *Chathrand*. A grey dog walked at his heels, looking as strong and weathered as the prince himself. Behind it, with somewhat less dignity, came Shilu, sniffing and prancing in delight.

'Welcome, citizen-prince,' said Lord Arim. 'I have long been hoping you would return, for your last visit brought hope and song to the Vale, yet you departed in great haste. Do you remember what we were speaking of?'

'Less well than you, *alpurbehn*,' said Olik, 'for that was twenty years ago. But I swear to you, that neither my first home nor the fairest estates of my family have I yearned for as I have this place. Alas, yearning alone cannot bring one back to Uláramyth. Perhaps nothing can save dire need.' Then, noticing Ramachni, he said, 'What is this, friends? You have lost a rat but gained a weasel.'

'Mink,' said Ramachni.

'Mage,' said Hercól. 'Sire, this is our leader and our guiding star, Ramachni Fremken, whom the elders of the South call—'

'Arpathwin?'

Thasha could scarcely believe it: Prince Olik had dropped to his knees. His voice had come out a whisper, and it was scarcely louder when he continued. 'Arpathwin! You came to us when I was but a child. To our house, to our table, when my cousin the Emperor turned you away. But you were not a mink, in that time. You looked like a human man.'

'That body perished,' said Ramachni, 'but yes, I recall. Your father was far more hospitable than the Emperor himself.'

'And I was a brat, with no interest in the world beyond myself. But even I could sense that what you spoke of was of the gravest importance. Of course it was the rise of the Raven Society, and the danger it posed to all the South. If only we had heeded that warning!'

'Your father understood me,' said Ramachni, 'but I think the shock of what I told him – the deep decay in the Bali Adro Empire, the lateness of the hour – was more than he could face. A pity: the world might indeed be a very different place today.'

'But how did you find us, Sire?'

'My only accomplishment has been to stay alive, and for that I am indebted to Nyrex here—' he scratched the grey dog's chin '—and to the selk who found us, lost in the forests of the lower Sarimayat.'

'Your Highness!' blurted Big Skip. 'You helped us plan this expedition! How could you stay so blary quiet about wonderful Uláramyth?'

'You great buffoon, Skip,' said Bolutu, laughing. 'It's the rule of the house; you know that.'

'Hmmph!' said Skip. 'Yes, I know. But one little whisper, in private like? It would have made things so much simpler.'

'It would have made Uláramyth a wasteland, centuries ago, if that rule had been less than absolute,' said the prince. 'Yes, silence is the rule of the house, and the selk have many ways of enforcing it. I should like to think that honour sealed my lips, but there are other seals in place as well.'

He swept his gaze over them again. 'So many fallen! Seven dlömic warriors, two of your Turach marines. And where is my faithful Ibjen?'

When they told him that the dlömic boy had vanished into the River of Shadows, Olik's pain was clear to all. 'He was a brave lad, with a clear-thinking mind; there are not many like him. In another time I would have sent him to university, or to Castle Buriav to become a Defender of the Realm. But I have broken up your meeting. Forgive this weary castaway, Lord Arim.'

'It is for you to pardon us, for bringing you to a war-council within an hour of your arrival,' said the old selk.

'Even more to be regretted, Sire,' said Hercól, 'is that we must part with you on the morrow, for we dare not delay.'

Prince Olik sighed. 'I do not doubt you, though it wounds my heart.'

'We'll be stronger just for having seen you, Prince,' said Thasha. 'If you can escape Macadra all alone, surely we can do it with Thaulinin's help.'

'You misunderstand me, lady,' said Olik. 'I will be going with you, and will share whatever fate is yours.'

Now there were more cries of joy and amazement. 'Olik Ipandracon!' said Thaulinin. 'We could hope for no better addition to our party than yourself.'

'But are you rested?' asked Hercól with concern. 'Are you ready for the trial of the mountains?'

'I can fight, and I can march,' said Olik, 'but I must beg you to endure my melancholy. Twenty years have I dreamed of stepping once more within these mountain walls, and now I am fleeing them at once. Ah well! I must hope to return before another twenty passes, and I become too old and stiff to make the journey. But as for rest, that I do not want for.'

'The selk kept His Highness in a safe house, a place like Sirafstöran Torr,' said Lunja. 'He was there for a week, until they found a way to come here unobserved.'

'And then of course, I was carried,' said the prince.

'There are no safe houses on the Nine Peaks Road,' said Thaulinin. 'Rested or not, you must all – but what is this?'

He was gazing at the staircase once more. There, abashed and until this moment unnoticed, stood Myett. Ensyl ran towards her, then stopped. The two women exchanged words that Thasha could not hear; then Ensyl leaped up the stairs and embraced her kinswoman.

'The lady has changed her mind,' said Prince Olik. 'Indeed the words I brought her from Lord Taliktrum would change the mind of anyone whose heart still loved.'

'But where *is* Taliktrum, Sire?' asked Thasha.

Olik inclined his head. 'Somewhere beyond our help,' he said. 'We parted on the banks of the Sarimayat, not two days out of Masalym. He told me he had a plan for survival should I be forced to flee downstream, but I never learned what it was.'

With his last remark the prince cast a pensive gaze over the assembly. Thasha looked at him, imagining his calculations, his doubts. *A plan of survival*, she thought. *We left Masalym with one of those. And no one was hunting us then.*

The council adjourned, and for the first time since their arrival the entire party returned as a group to the house in Thehel Urred. Thasha realised that she had begun to love it, in the same way that she had come to love the stateroom on the Great Ship: for an exile nothing is more seductive than the idea of home. 'All these books,' said Pazel, gazing at the glass cases with longing, 'I barely touched them.'

'We barely touched Uláramyth,' said Hercól. 'I could read this country for a lifetime and never tire. But that is not our fate.'

Then he bent low beside Myett, and offered his hand like a platform. When she stood upon it he raised her to the level of his eyes.

'Never hide your darkness from us, sister,' he said. 'We will meet it with whatever light we can. There is no shame in sadness. But also, there is no sadness that may claim us as its rightful prey. This lesson I myself struggle to remember. We dwell in pain, and journey from loss to loss, but there is also love and wonder about us, and bright sunlight on the peaks. For today I am merely glad that you choose to carry on at our side.'

Thasha saw that Neda was watching Hercól and Myett with a curious intensity. How much of what Hercól was saying could she understand?

'My choice scares me,' said Myett, 'but not because of the dangers ahead. No, I fear that I shall seek what I cannot find. Or perhaps the opposite: that I shall find something I do not seek at all.

But none of that matters now. It is the heart that chooses for us—'

'And who may ask it to explain?' said Hercól with a smile. 'Diadrelu taught me that.'

'In the world's last hour, the Unseen shall demand explanations from us all,' said Cayer Vispek sternly. Neda, as if startled from a dream, turned and rushed from the chamber.

'Could be,' said Mandric, 'but meanwhile, have a look at what the selk have brought us.'

Ranged neatly along the back wall of the chamber was a large assortment of knives, bows, baldrics, leather jerkins, warm furs, gauntlets, arm-guards, throat mail of fine steel chain. There were snow-picks and grapples and other climbing implements, a tent, a light telescope – and a fine selk sword for each. Cayer Vispek lifted one of the sheer blades, twirled it, tossed it from hand to hand.

'Exquisite,' he said, 'and very old, though the edge on them is new, and lethal. I wonder how long these blades have slumbered here.'

'Find the sword that fits you,' said Ramachni. 'Then try on your snow garb, ready your belongings, fill your packs. We must all try to slumber a little before our midnight climb.'

The preparations took longer than Thasha had expected. When they were done at last, many of the travellers did try to sleep. Thasha tried as well, and failed: she had never been able to sleep when the sun was high. She wanted to take Pazel back to their green field one last time, but he was deeply asleep; she did not have the heart to wake him. She took a swim with Bolutu instead, and he showed her river eels that flashed golden in the sunlight, and clouds of freshwater squid no larger than coins. Across the river she saw Lunja and Neeps walking close together among the trees. They were talking quickly, gesturing, and for the first time Thasha heard the soldier laugh.

At sundown they ate a light meal and returned to their beds. This time Thasha dropped into sleep as though falling into a well. She dreamed of stone breaking, a crack that spread like ivy on a granite wall. She pressed her fingers to the crack and sensed a hand on the far side doing the same, heard a woman's voice berating her, *Let me out, selfish girl, you claim to love them, when will you prove it, who will save them if not me?* and then a ghost passed through the fissure and her hand caught fire. She examined it: that blazing hand, that power. The flames were bright and sulphuric and she could not feel a thing. She was invulnerable; she had ceased to be herself.

18

Blood Upon the Snow

At midnight the party filed out of the snug little house, packs on shoulders and the dog Shilu at their heels. Pazel had expected a lonely walk through a sleeping Uláramyth, but what he found was quite different. Some two dozen selk had gathered outside. Each one carried a staff that curved at one end like a shepherd's stick, and at the end of each hook dangled a pale blue lamp. The light danced in the sharper blue of the selks' eyes. There was no other light from any quarter, save the heavy brilliance of the stars. But Pazel could see a line of the blue lamps, marking the path through the village and beyond.

As the travellers emerged the selk began to sing, their voices so soft that they merged with the night wind. As before the words defied Pazel's understanding, but it did not matter; the feeling in them was clear. A nomadic people had come to witness another departure, another leave-taking, the very stuff of their lives.

When they started walking the crowd of selk went with them. They passed the workshop where Skip had become so enthralled with selk craftsmanship, the tree where the tortoise slumbered in his burrow, the little volcanic hill. Each selk they came upon fell in with the rest, taking up the melancholy song. But when they reached the great hall the singing ceased. Lord Arim stood among the pillars with his hand on Valgrif's shoulder. Thaulinin too stepped from the shadows, and the three figures approached without a word.

Now the procession walked in silence, so that Pazel could hear the night birds, the autumn crickets, the gurgle of the streams. In this way the miles passed, and the hours. Lord Arim walked as swiftly as any, though now and then a look of pain creased his face.

They reached the end of the crater floor and began to climb. There were by now several hundred selk with them, and the lamps swayed close together like a school of deep-sea fish. Up they went, by stair and switchback. Pazel walked beside Thasha, now and then touching her arm, or holding her hand for a few paces. He noticed that both Neeps and Lunja, though they walked some distance apart, looked often for the other, as thought to be certain the distance between them had not changed.

By the time they reached the North Door it was very cold. Here the path broadened into a great stone shelf, large enough for all the selk who had joined the climb: and surely almost the whole thousand were here, Pazel thought. The black triangle was just what it had seemed from below: a tunnel mouth, framed with great blocks of stone, and richly carved with both figures and words. An icy wind issued from it, much colder than the air about them. Pazel squinted at the carved words, but it was still too dark to read them. There was also a smaller door at one end of the shelf, and several windows carved into the stone: the Way-House, Pazel guessed.

Thaulinin called the travellers together and presented the ten warriors who were to join them. He told a little of their deeds and life-stories (a very little; the youngest was two thousand years old) and voices in the crowd called out with contributions of their own. Then the selk gave each traveller a folded cloth, silver in colour but woven of some rough, sturdy fabric.

'Tie back your hair with these,' said Thaulinin, 'or wash your face, or bundle them about something you do not wish to lose. They do not look like much, but they were woven by Arim's mother, Irehi, before the journey from whence she never returned. And this week they have been soaked in the five sacred springs, and touched and blessed by every selk in Uláramyth. Still you need not handle them like relics: they are strong, and meant for use.'

Then Pazel felt a hand on his shoulder. Lord Arim himself stood beside him, and his old lips formed a smile.

'You tried to read the words above the threshold,' he said, 'and well you should: they are a parting wish for travellers. Shall I recite them for you?'

He spoke then in Sabdel, and Pazel was moved by the beauty and simplicity of the verse. Then Arim repeated the lines in the language of Bali Adro, for all to hear:

Behind you dieth a dreamland, ahead is the blinding day.
Still thy song is in all tongues and on all voices lifts,
And even the white range declares it to the skies.
Never but by you is it forsaken, no silence but thine own is its
  decay.
Go not mourning what is ended.
Go not with winter in your eyes.

'That is our hope for you all,' he said. 'But come: we must rest in the Way-House. Your true journey begins at sunrise.'

Then the selk came forward in groups, touching their arms, whispering words of farewell. Pazel had come to know some by name, and dozens by sight, and felt a great sadness at this leave-taking. Very soon it was done, however, and Arim led the travellers into the Way-House, and a simple room where they could sleep.

Most did so quickly, but once more Pazel found himself wide awake, and unable to be otherwise. *This is crazy,* he told himself. *Sleep, fool, or you'll be useless at dawn.* At last he gave up, as he had done on Sirafstöran Torr, and found his way back outside. He crossed the wide shelf, and saw a ribbon of blue lamps snaking down into the darkened Vale, and dispersing by many paths along the crater floor.

An hour later the party was on its feet, and the sun was gleaming on the crater wall. They glanced a last time at Uláramyth, and Prince Olik knelt on the trail where it began its descent into the crater, and kissed the earth. Then they all turned away, and followed Lord Arim into the tunnel, and not one of those travellers ever again set foot in the Secret Vale.

It was dark in the tunnel, but the selk still had their lamps. Pazel tightened his coat against the biting wind. Very soon he saw ice slicking the walls, felt his boot crunching a thin crust of snow. Every five or ten minutes they would climb a long, steep staircase. They were still ascending the mountain, only this time from within.

After an hour's march they reached a gate very much like the one in the tunnel by which they had entered Uláramyth. Thaulinin opened it with the same key he had used before, and when they had passed through he locked it behind them. Shortly thereafter Neda remarked that the air was growing *warmer*, and so it was: decidedly warmer, until they were all loosening their coats. Walking beside Valgrif, Pazel asked what was happening, but the wolf said only that he would see soon enough.

Then the tunnel widened abruptly, the walls falling away left and right, and Pazel realised that they had stepped into a natural cave. The air here was dry and hot. By the dim lamplight he could just make out the ceiling, where stalactites hung like rows of teeth. Fifty feet or so ahead, a staircase climbed the left-hand wall. As they moved nearer he saw that it led to a large, round archway overlooking the cave below.

'Now,' said Lord Arim, 'I must speak to the guardian of the North Door. You may come with me, Arpathwin; but the rest of you must wait for us to return. Do not approach, no matter what you see or hear! You cannot go on without the guardian's consent.'

He started off at once, and Ramachni went with him. Pazel studied the archway. There was something about it he did not like at all. He glanced at the others and saw that they did not feel it. They were curious, and perhaps slightly worried by the mystery, but none were suffering from the dread he felt, the sense that something terrible was near.

Arim and Ramachni climbed the stair, and stepped before the archway – rather cautiously, Pazel thought. Then they walked inside. 'Valgrif,' Pazel murmured, 'what sort of creature is this guardian? Why was Lord Arim so concerned that we not approach?'

'Because we could not help, only imperil ourselves,' said the wolf. 'Let us speak no more of it. They will return at any moment.'

But the selk and the mage were gone much longer than Valgrif predicted. Through the stone, Pazel thought he felt a low, angry rumble, as though thunder were shaking the earth. At last the two figures emerged from the opening and started back. Ramachni walked straight to Pazel, and in his black eyes was a look of concern.

'My lad,' he said, 'the guardian is an eguar.'

'An eguar!' cried Pazel. 'Oh *credek,* no!' Of all their party, he alone had ever faced one of the demonic reptiles – and it had savaged him, burned him, and dug like a mole into his mind. Worst of all, his Gift had forced him to learn its language, and it was the weirdest and most painful tongue Pazel had ever heard before that of the demon in the Infernal Forest.

'Ramachni,' he said, 'I don't want to see an eguar. Kirishgán told me the selk sometimes talked to them, but I didn't know they used them as blary border guards.'

'The creature will not harm you,' said Ramachni. 'Arim and I had words with it. They have an accord of long standing: the selk permit the beast to live on the doorstep of Uláramyth, hidden from enemy eyes by the same spells that hide the Vale itself. And in return the eguar keeps watch on the North Door.'

'It is a task well suited to the eguar's stillness,' said Lord Arim. 'Forty years have passed since last a traveller came to us by way of the Sky Road. But each door must have its watch, and this eguar has been a friend to Uláramyth for centuries. I am sorry, Pazel: I did not know that you had faced an eguar before. They are deadly, of course. But as a rule they are not evil – not given to killing for its own sake, or to mindless hatreds. The creature you met on Bramian is an exception. I know him: Ma'tathgryl, a wounded and embittered beast. This one is also an exception, but of the opposite sort. He has given us many timely warnings of the enemy's deeds, and has even descended into the Vale, and bathed in the waters of Osir Delhin. He discarded his birth-name in favour of the one we gave him: Sitroth, which means Faithful. We selk revere him for his wisdom, and his guardianship.'

'But you protect him as well?' asked Bolutu. 'What threatens him?'

'In the past, nothing,' said Arim. 'But today the Platazcra madness has brought death to the eguar as it has to many others. You know that the Plazic weapons were made from their ancient bones and hides, dug from eguar grave-pits by the alchemists of Bali Adro. In time those pits were emptied, and the warlords faced an end to their power. They tried to leach that power from other materials, such as the bones of dragons and the teeth of the Nelluroq serpent. None of these efforts succeeded. At last, in desperation, they sought out *living* eguar to butcher and exploit – at a terrible cost in dlömic lives, needless to say. And these experiments too were failures.'

'But not perfect failures,' added Ramachni.

'No,' said Arim, 'and for an addict, even the smallest whiff of one's chosen poison can be irresistible. To our knowledge, fifty-one eguar were sought out and killed to provide such whiffs: a sword that splintered on its third use, a siege engine that exploded on the battlefield, a helm that gave the wearer titanic strength, then burned through flesh and skull like some horrible acid. Fifty-one eguar: and to our knowledge that leaves but eighteen alive in all the world.'

Corporal Mandric hissed. Pazel looked up, and terror seized his heart: from the archway a sea-green light had begun to shine. It grew stronger even as he watched, and so did the heat.

The dog growled. Pazel was struggling to breathe. *I don't want to see it, I don't want to* hear *it*. He stepped backwards, and would have tripped if Neeps had not caught him.

'Rin's blood, Ramachni!' said Thasha. 'That mucking thing's language is a torture to Pazel, you know that!'

'Peace, Thasha,' said the mage. 'The creature has pledged not to speak in his native tongue.'

'But what a splendid gift, Pazel Pathkendle!' said Thaulinin. 'Not even the selk have ever learned to speak the language of the eguar.'

Pazel was shaking all over. 'Never ... try,' he said.

At that moment a shimmering vapour began to pour from the archway. It was exactly the same vapour that had engulfed Pazel on Bramian – and there, there was the smell: rank, acidic, burning his nostrils. Out it came: the sliding, slouching black creature, lizard-shaped, elephant-huge, hotter than the depths of a furnace. The row of spines along its back scraped the top of the archway, and above the black crocodile jaws its eyes glowed white-hot.

The creature emerged only halfway from the arch, then settled on its belly at the top of the stairs, with one great clawed foot dangling over the ledge. Within the cloud of vapours it was hard to look at steadily. But its eyes drilled down at them with an intensity that was almost physically painful.

'Humans!' it said, and its voice was like a boulder shifting. 'Woken humans! Come forward, and do not fear me. It brings me joy to see you.'

'Why is that, old father?' said Ramachni.

'So many reasons,' said the eguar. 'Because their form is fair. Because I sense friendship, even love, between them and their dlömic comrades, although the dlömu enslaved and killed them. Because to see the proof that their race is not extinguished gives me hope for my own.'

With each breath, the creature threw off waves of some great force; Pazel could not see anything, but felt them pulsing through his body. His mind was thrown into confusion: the eguar had spoken with undeniable courtesy, and yet it was so much like that other, a creature that had swallowed a man whole before his eyes.

'They must pass swiftly on, Sitroth,' said Lord Arim, 'but I shall return within the hour, and will count myself blessed if you will talk with me awhile.'

'You honour me, my lord,' said the eguar, 'but can they not tarry a little while? Since I cast my lot with the selk my blood is thinned. I crave company, and speech, although my kind would call me weak if they heard of it.'

'Our kind calls you friend,' said Arim. 'But no, they cannot wait. The humans are castaways, and the one ship that can bear them home is drawing away even now. They must hurry to catch up with it while they can.'

The eguar lowered its head onto its forelegs. 'That need I understand. The fate of the castaway is hard. Go, then, humans, and seek your ship.'

Pazel dared another glance at those burning eyes. Dumbfounded, he realised that the terrifying creature was lonely, starved for companionship of its own kind or any other. It had allied with the selk, and been changed – as they themselves had, perhaps. For just an instant he felt tempted to speak to the creature in its own tongue. But no, that was impossible: eguar put whole speeches into single, unimaginably complicated words. On Bramian, just hearing *one* of them had felt like being screamed at for an hour by a mob. Trying to form such words might just drive him mad.

But he could speak to it in the common tongue.

'I wish—' he said aloud, sputtering (what in Pitfire did he wish?). 'Oh, *credek* – that is, I wish you could be happy.'

Happy? Neda and Neeps were both staring at him, incredulous. The selk warriors looked simply astonished. Slowly, the eguar turned its enormous head in Pazel's direction. Black lids closed slowly over the searing eyes, opened again. It spoke.

'When my grandfather first took this spire in his claws, little eel, the world beneath it was still a tomb of ice. He lived in the long, terrible ages before any creature with hands yet walked the earth. In his day the Gorgonoths still crawled, who ground the bones of the earth in their teeth, and cut the chasms of the sea. And then in my father's day the world caught fire, and ashes rained from heaven for a century; but he waited, and new trees grew, and Urmesu the Bear emerged from her cave and prowled the forests of the South.

'I can see through their eyes: I can examine the world that was. Even now I look, and see that cold star falling in Siebr Shidorno that carried you to brutal Alifios   that slow-falling star that set the plain alight, as though in tribute to your birth. And in all that time not one of you has wished us happiness. If you speak the truth you are a stranger being than you seem.'

'He's pretty strange,' murmured Neeps.

Thasha elbowed him. Then she in turn looked at the eguar, and Pazel knew that she too was aware of its loneliness. 'When our work is finished,' she said, 'I will gather your people together in one land, if you wish. There's room enough in Alifros.'

'Gather us, child?' said the creature. 'By what unearthly power?'

Thasha looked as though she might speak again, but then Hercól touched her arm, a gentle warning. 'You cannot have forgotten our love of fantasy, great one,' he said. 'Forgive our chatter; we will leave you now.'

'I will be with you anon, Sitroth,' said Arim. 'Come, travellers; the road ahead is long.'

One by one they passed the staircase, right under the beast, coughing as they touched the vapour cloud. Pazel feared the waves of force surging out of the creature would make him stumble, but he kept his feet. When they were all passed he felt an immense relief. Some distance ahead the cave narrowed once more into a tunnel. But they still had to get there, and Pazel could still feel those blazing eyes.

'Happy,' whispered Neeps, shaking his head. '"I wish you could be happy." Has it occurred to you, Pazel, that you're raving mad?' Then he jumped and cast a guilty look at Lunja. '*Aya Rin*, sorry—'

The dlömic woman brushed against him deliberately. 'You *will* be sorry,' she murmured, mock-severe. 'Mad this, crazy that—'

'Yes, yes, I know,' said Neeps, hushing her in turn.

So blary intimate, thought Pazel. Like lovers, Neeps and Lunja were starting to talk in a style no one else could quite understand. *It's the only way*, he reminded himself. *We asked her to do this, and she's trying. They both are, magnificently.*

To their right, Olik was coughing badly; the fumes seemed to have affected him more harshly than the others. Bolutu took him by the arm.

'A few more steps, Prince Olik. When we reach the tunnel you'll feel just—'

Lunja howled. A warning. Pazel clutched his temples: the waves of force had surged a hundredfold. Instinct took over: he turned and dived on Thasha, whose hand was already on her sword. The eguar was smashing through them like a cannonball. Thaulinin had been knocked aside; another selk was in the creature's teeth. Pazel tried not to breathe, while the others fell around him, writhing in pain. This close the vapours were like a mule-kick to the chest.

Olik! The eguar's white-hot eyes were locked on the prince. Olik had his sword out and was holding his ground – but then Hercól lunged before him, whirled with blinding speed, and stabbed.

The eguar gave a deafening roar: Ildraquin had pierced its flesh behind the jaw. The beast threw its head, wrenching Hercól from the ground and hurling him away. The eguar spat out the fallen selk and lunged once more at Olik – and then a searing light filled the cave. The beast twisted, and its roar grew louder still, shaking the cave and bringing stalactites down like hail. Then it turned and fled. In three heartbeats it had flown up the stairs and vanished through the arch. They could still hear its bellows of pain.

'Lord Arim!' cried Thaulinin. *'Eyache,* master of masters, are you burned?'

Arim had fallen on his side. 'I am burned,' he gasped, 'but by my own spell merely. It is long since I called down the lightning, and this body is too old to be a lightning-rod. Never mind, Thaulinin! What of the others?'

The answer to his question was plain to see: the selk that the eguar had bitten was dead, his body horribly torn and scalded. Another warrior had also been burned by the spittle of the creature, and Hercól was bruised and shaken, but both were on their feet.

'Arpathwin, you matched my spell, as in elder times,' said Lord Arim. 'How do you fare?'

'I have felt better,' said Ramachni, shaking the dust from his fur, 'but also much worse. You took the better part of the shock, my lord.'

'Betrayed,' said Thaulinin, kneeling by his kinsman's corpse. 'After all these centuries, Sitroth has turned on us. How could this happen?'

'Could he be under another's spell?' asked Pazel.

Lord Arim shook his head. 'No spell to control the mind of an eguar has been cast in Alifros since the Dawn War, and even then it was a great undertaking. No, something terrible has occurred in the heart of Sitroth, to bring him to this pass.'

Ramachni looked up at the prince. 'You were his target, Olik Ipandracon. He attacked the moment Bolutu mentioned your name. No, Doctor, the fault does not lie with you—' for Bolutu had bowed his head in shame '—nor with any of us. This was a disaster no one could have foreseen.'

'And it leaves an entrance to the Vale unguarded,' said Thaulinin.

'Yes,' said Arim, 'for we cannot let Sitroth remain here. The faithful one was not faithful.' He sighed. 'I must do a thing while the power is in me. Go, all of you, into the tunnel ahead, and await me there.'

Thaulinin protested, but Arim waved for silence. 'You must remove every bit of clothing that the eguar touched. Leave it here; I will send our people back to collect and burn it. Then wash your hands and faces, and clean any wound with utmost care: first with water, then with our good wine. Do it quickly! There is poison to rot flesh and weaken hearts in an eguar's mouth.'

He made for the staircase, and the others reluctantly obeyed him, leaving the cave for the narrower tunnel. The selk had the worst of it, but Hercól and Olik too had to discard their coats and gloves, and Thaulinin personally scrubbed out a wound on the back of Hercól's hand.

'Aya!' said Hercól, gritting his teeth. 'So that is eguar spittle! It is far worse than the slobber of the flame-trolls.'

Suddenly there came a great *boom* and a blast of air and dust. Thaulinin dashed into the cave, and returned supporting Arim, who looked exhausted and frail.

'I have collapsed the tunnel behind Sitroth,' said the old selk. 'He has another exit to the mountains, but he will not soon be returning to Uláramyth. And now I must rest, and return with our fallen comrade's body, when I can.' He looked at the travellers sadly. 'I have failed you, here in this first moment of your journey. If I had the strength I would go with you to the Sky Road. But that strength is fled. I called, and it came a final time. I do not think it will dwell in me again.'

'You failed us in nothing, Arim,' said Ramachni. 'Go to your rest, and be certain that a part of us goes with you.'

Thaulinin commanded two selk to escort him, and to carry the body. 'We will make do with your seven comrades,' he said. 'But you two: leave your coats and gloves for Hercól and the prince. Their road will be far longer than yours.'

Lord Arim looked up at Thasha. 'You are trying to breach the wall inside you,' he said. 'You must persist in that struggle, but do not overlook its cost. A battle in the mind will tax the body, and in the High Country your body will need all its strength. At all costs you must reach the sea alive. Once aboard the *Promise* you will be warm and fed, and have long days to seek a path to Erithusmé.'

Then his gaze swept them all. 'Farewell, citizens. Your quest is our own, though we did not foresee its coming. It is not likely that we shall meet again in your short time in Alifros. But there are worlds beyond Alifros, and minds that reach out to us from them, and in that reaching there is hope for us all.'

With that he started back towards Uláramyth, and the selk warriors lifted the body of their companion and followed after.

'Quickly, now,' said Thaulinin. 'The portal is just ahead.'

He led them on, and very soon it proved so: the tunnel ended in a pair of tall and curious doors. They appeared to be carved from two enormous pieces of jade, and on each was carved a staring eye.

'The Gates of Cihael the Explorer,' said Thaulinin. 'He was the greatest mountaineer of all our people, and he fell here, defending Uláramyth from the ogres of the Thrandaal Caves. Shield your eyes when I open the door, or the sun will dazzle you.'

He strode forward and set a shoulder to one of the doors. He pushed, then looked back with a sad smile. 'Blocked with snow. Ah well; perhaps we had better remain.'

The prince actually laughed, and went forward to help him. Together they pushed, and the door moved slightly, and a blade of sunlight appeared in the crack—

—Pazel was swaying, stumbling on his feet, and then he fell. His knees met snow. Wind-driven snow tapped at his face. Everything was white. A hand gripped his shoulder.

'You're confused,' said Hercól. 'Don't worry. You will not be for long.'

They were on a narrow ridgetop covered in snow. The sun was high, and the others were all here, ten white-clad figures against the whiter snow. Pazel was exceptionally tired, as though he'd been walking for days. All around them, close and savage, towered the peaks.

'What – how—'

'You can't remember coming here,' said Hercól.

'Of course I can, I—'

Pazel looked back over his shoulder. The ridge ran straight behind them for a mile, then twisted down and to the left. There was no door of jade. There was no opening of any kind to be seen.

'It is happening to us one by one. I myself came out of the memory-fog just minutes ago.'

'Memory-fog?'

'The doorway set a spell in motion,' said Bolutu, coming up beside them. 'We have been walking a long time, Pazel. We have descended into valleys, and climbed again to saddles like this one, and turned at many forks and crossroads. It has all been stunningly lovely, and quiet. And now as the spell breaks it is carrying away all our memories, from when we passed through the door of jade – to this very moment. Thus is Uláramyth protected: we cannot find our way back there, or tell another soul just where it lies.'

'Why do *you* remember?' Pazel demanded.

'Because the spell has yet to break for Belesar, of course,' said

Ramachni, picking his way through the trampled snow. 'In time his memory will vanish, too – and you may be explaining all this to him, or to Lunja, or your sister. Those three are the last holdouts.'

'How long have we walked?' said Pazel.

Bolutu flashed him a smile. 'I'd rather not say.'

'Ah. Right.' Pazel struggled to his feet. 'You mustn't tell me. That's the whole idea, isn't it?'

'The rule of the house,' said Big Skip, laughing. 'And an irritating one, to be sure. I'd like to know how long I've been on my feet.'

'Days,' said Thaulinin, 'but more than that we cannot tell you. We have our oaths. But this much I will gladly tell: we are at last upon the Nine Peaks Road. Do not imagine that we will be climbing nine of these grandfather-mountains from the base – not at all. Rather we shall climb once, and never fully descend until we pass the ninth. A massive ridge runs through Efaroc, like a wall of the Gods. The peaks are like turrets along that wall – and the Road is like a set of daredevil catwalks leaping between them.'

'I thought it was supposed to be a grand highway,' said Pazel.

'We have not yet reached the Royal Highway,' said Thaulinin, 'nor will we always be upon it, for we must take every shortcut we can.' He pointed at a huge, crooked, ice-sheathed summit in the distance. 'There stands the first of the Nine Peaks, which we call Isarak. A shelter awaits us on its western slopes. And that is fortunate, for I sense that tonight will be colder by far than any other night this year. Our tent will not suffice. We must reach Isarak by nightfall, or freeze upon this ridge. And it is already past noon.'

He started walking – or resumed walking – and the others fell in behind him. Pazel winced: his shoulders were sore and his muscles ached. *Of course they do. You have been walking for days!* Just how many? It unsettled him to think that he would never know. But his selk boots were dry and comfortable, and the pack, which they had made for him, rode snugly.

Nor was the snow as pervasive as he had thought at first. They were passing through a long drift, but just ahead the ridge was bare, and there were even tufts of ice-withered greenery along the trailside. The peaks themselves were deeply snow-clad, but the slopes beneath them less so. They were not too late, it seemed. Even the light snowfall of a moment ago soon ended, and ahead was bright blue sky.

When they were out of the snowdrift and marching over frozen soil, Hercól approached him again. 'You're a lowlander,' he said. 'Those bumps above Ormael you call Highlands do not count. Listen to one who came of age in the wicked Tsördons, and take no chances on the trail.'

'Don't worry about that,' said Pazel.

'I worry with reason,' said Hercól. 'Thaulinin says that the way will soon grow treacherous. Besides, the air is thin, and will grow thinner as we ascend. You may feel dizzy and careless, but you cannot afford to be.'

Pazel shivered. Still ascending. He wondered how cold it would get. Then he felt a stinging blow to his cheek: Hercól had cuffed him, not at all gently.

'Even now your mind wanders!' Hercól aimed a finger at the peaks ahead. 'We are going *through* those, Pathkendle, do you hear? Stay sharp, if you would stay alive. One careless footfall and your journey will have a pitiful conclusion.'

They marched on. Big Skip came and walked by Pazel's side. 'He's had the same talk with all of us "lowlanders" as we pop out of the spell. He didn't have to smack you, though.'

Pazel looked at the mountains before them: huge, cold, insanely steep. 'I think maybe he did, Skip. But thanks all the same.'

The path was now climbing steadily, but the mountain did not seem to grow any nearer. In the middle of a rough scramble Pazel saw Lunja stop in her tracks, staring without recognition at the world around her. It was Neeps who went to her and took her hand.

Pazel watched them furtively. *She doesn't look as though she finds him unbearable.* But even as the thought came to him, Lunja took her hand from Neeps' own, and held it strangely, as though repressing an urge to wipe it clean.

Bolutu's release from the spell came shortly thereafter. As he re-covered, Thasha hurried to Pazel's side. 'What's the matter with you? Go walk with your sister! She's the last one.'

'I thought she'd rather be with Cayer Vispek,' he said.

'With Vispek? Didn't you – oh, Pitfire, that was before *your* spell broke. Pazel, he spat at her. I thought he was going to hit her.'

'What?'

'Nobody knows what it was about. Hercól started forward, and Vispek shouted at him to stay out of their affairs, and stalked off ahead. Go on, will you? Make her talk to you. Once her memory breaks she won't even remember fighting with him.'

Pazel moved carefully past Hercól and Bolutu. Cayer Vispek walked twenty feet ahead, with Prince Olik and the selk. Neda marched grim and soldier-straight. But her eyes softened a little at the sight of Pazel.

'When the spell breaks you don't feel a thing,' he said in Mzithrini.

Neda looked at Cayer Vispek's back, and glowered. 'Speak Ormali,' she said. 'I don't want him listening.'

'What happened, Neda?' he said.

His sister drew a deep breath. 'He wanted me to tell him … everything. The length of our journey, and the turns, and everything that happened after we passed through the gate. He wanted me to cheat the spell, before my memory goes. I asked him why he would wish to do such a thing. And he was furious. Of course I already knew. He is afraid. Cayer Vispek, the war hero, the *sfvantskor* master, is afraid of any spell that affects his thoughts.'

'So am I, if you care to know.'

Neda shot him an irritated glance. 'Don't you understand? *I asked him why*. Instead of simply obeying. That is not something a *sfvantskor* is allowed to do. I placed Uláramyth above my vow of obedience.' Neda paused, eyes straight ahead. Then she said, 'I am no longer of the Faith.'

'What!'

'Pazel, don't tell.'

'Because you blary asked him *why*?'

Again she was silent. 'Because I don't believe any more,' she said at last. 'In the Path of the Seraphim, in the divine blood of kings, in persecution by devils, in the Unseen.'

Tears glittered in her eyelashes. They crunched forward over the frozen ground. 'Or maybe I still believe in the Unseen,' she said, 'but I don't believe we know anything about it. Whether it's good or evil, or distracted, or insane.'

Pazel did not know quite what Mzithrinis meant by the Unseen. But he thought of the Night Gods, setting the murder of a world as a challenge on a school exam. 'My money's on insane,' he said.

Once more she looked at him askance. 'Don't make jokes,' she said.

'I wasn't.'

She stomped on, and he feared she was too angry to talk any longer. The path narrowed, until he could no longer walk at her side. 'Neda,' he said, 'is there anything you want to remember, about the … words that passed between you and Vispek? Something you want me to remind you of later on?'

Neda looked back at him, startled. 'Pazel, I came out of the spell hours ago.'

For a moment Pazel was at a perfect loss. Then he saw it, and wondered that he had not before. 'Your Gift,' he said.

She nodded. 'The door-charm worked. I did lose my memory – for a heartbeat or two. Then everything came back. It happened even faster than it used to in Babqri, when the Father put me in a trance. And that's not the worst part. I remember *everything*, Pazel. Every turn, every trail, and how long we spent on each, and twenty, thirty landmarks. I could draw you a map.'

'Pitfire, Neda.'

'I can't help it. There's no way to make it stop.'

Pazel looked at the selk ahead, and lowered his voice. 'Didn't they know about your Gift? I thought Ramachni talked about it.'

'We both did. I even showed them what I could do. But they still didn't imagine it would prove stronger than the magic of the gate.'

Pazel was shaken. 'People underestimate our mother,' he said.

Neda's hands were in fists. 'I swear on her life,' she said, 'that I will not be the one to betray that place. Never.'

'Oh, for Rin's sake,' said Pazel. 'You're not going to betray anyone. Just keep your mouth shut about Uláramyth, that's all.'

'And what if I'm captured? I might be able to withstand torture – we are trained to resist the methods of the Secret Fist – but what could I do against a spell? What if they use magic to dig the secret from my mind?'

'You tell me. What then?'

This time Neda stopped and leaned over him, the way she used to in the days when he only came up to her waist. He could not really look at her; he was facing into the sun.

'Then I'll claim the privilege of an unbeliever,' she said, 'and cut my throat.'

By mid-afternoon they had climbed much higher: the path behind them dwindled to a thread. For a long time they walked in the mountain's shadow, and the air grew cold indeed. At length they joined a wider, flatter trail. Pazel could see old paving stones poking out here and there from beneath the frozen soil. 'Those are fragments of the Royal Highway,' said Thaulinin, 'by which travellers could once walk or ride, or even hire a carriage, from these slopes all the way to the city of Isima, and beyond it to the Weeping Glen. It was from Isima that the greatest of the Mountain Kings ruled: Urakán he was called, him for whom the tallest peak is named, and great-grandfather to Valridith the suicide. In Urakán's day the high country bustled with merchants and peddlers and herdsman, passing from one fastness to the next.'

As they marched on, Pazel saw other hints of the glory of those lost days: a great limbless statue on a ridgetop, its boulder-sized head cracked open like an egg beside the trail; square holes that might have been the foundations of houses; rock walls enclosing barren fields – former pastures, maybe, or cemeteries.

Round one steep knoll they came suddenly upon a chasm,

spanned by a stone bridge. It was a narrow crevasse; Pazel might easily have thrown a stone across it, but the bridge was less than four feet wide, and frighteningly unrailed, and the wind came in blasting gusts between the cliff walls. Here for the first time they bound themselves together with rope. Even Shilu was tied to the rest, although Valgrif crossed untethered, crouching low on his belly. Creeping over the arch, boots skidding on tiny patches of ice, Pazel felt dizziness assault him suddenly. His head was light. The wind pushed, pulled, teased. He could almost *see* it, snapping and coiling in the gorge ...

A hand touched his shoulder. It was Cayer Vispek, who had been tied into the line behind him. The *sfvantskor's* voice was low and calm.

'The bridge is two lines painted on solid ground. Fear not: you could walk between them in twice this wind. You have that level of control. Think of walking, nothing else.'

Pazel took a deep breath, and tried to obey. Two lines on solid ground. He stepped forward, and found to his surprise that the dizziness was almost gone. *He knows what he's doing*, Pazel thought, *in some matters at least*.

Just beyond the bridge there stood a dense clump of pines. The selk, heavily burdened as they were, dropped their packs and began snatching up armfuls of dry, dead limbs. The rest of the party joined the effort. The limbs they tied up in bundles and strapped atop their packs, and into any spaces left over they stuffed pine cones. *Brilliant*, thought Pazel. *We're going to need these when we reach that shelter*. But when he felt the extra weight on his back he wondered if they ever would.

Now Thaulinin set a faster pace, for the sun was low in the sky. They even ran where the trail was level. In this way they came at last to the base of the first peak, Isarak – and saw before them a disaster.

The road ahead was carved into the mountainside, its outer shoulder a cliff that fell away to terrible depths. And covering it, burying it, was snow: deep, powdery snow, in a wind-sculpted drift that followed the trail for a mile or more. Pazel thought: *Impossible. We can't go through that. We're not blary miners, or moles.*

'Sheer cliffs above and below,' said Ensyl, shielding her eyes. 'We may be spending the night in that tent after all.'

Thaulinin turned and looked at her sharply. 'We cannot,' he said. 'The cold that is coming is too great. We need stone around us, and a fire.'

'That is not fresh snowfall,' said Hercól, raising his eyes. 'It must have broken away from the summit on a warm day, and settled here.'

'Who cares where it came from?' said Big Skip. 'There's no muckin' way we can—'

'Dig!' said Thaulinin. 'Dig or perish! In an hour's time this trail will be black!'

Straight into the white mass they dived. The snow was light, but piled to depths of twelve feet or more. They were digging a tunnel, and each time they advanced a yard it collapsed. Their new coats were tight at sleeve and collar, yet it trickled in all the same. The selk had the worst of the job, cutting the initial trail, mindful always of the savage drop-off nearby. But for everyone the labour was exhausting. The snow toppled; they scooped it away and wriggled forward. It was like an odd sort of swimming: half dog-paddle, half treading water. But how long could you do that before you grew tired and sank? Ahead, behind, above: there was nothing to see but snow – that and an occasional, stomach-churning glimpse of the distant lowlands, when they strayed close to the precipice.

Dusk fell. Pazel rubbed his eyes, struggling to distinguish snow from air. Ramachni and the ixchel, walking atop the drift, shouted down encouragement. But they had been doing that for ages. If they all curled up here, close together beneath the snow, would they keep each other warm? Or would they die in their sleep, frozen, fused together like an unfinished sculpture, and be found by crows in the springtime?

Even as he mused on the question he heard glad cries from the selk: they had reached the far side of the drift at last. One by one the party stumbled out, shaking snow from their clothes and hair. The sun was gone: only a dull red glow remained in the sky. Now, as he felt the knife of the wind, Pazel had his answer: they *would* freeze to death if they stayed here. The snow melted by the heat of their bodies had soaked them through.

'I feared as much,' said Thaulinin. 'We have taken too long. The shelter is still three miles away.'

'Then let us tie ourselves together and run,' said Hercól. 'Not quickly, but steadily, wherever the trail permits.'

'Locate your fire beetles,' said Thaulinin, 'but I beg you: *do not use them* unless you feel death itself tugging at your sleeves. The heat they contain is terribly potent, but it will not last long.'

Once more they bound themselves together. Then they ran, limbs shaking, teeth chattering uncontrollably. The light dimmed further, the trail narrowed and grew steep. Bolutu slipped on a patch of ice and skidded wildly; the rope stopped him only when his torso was already over the precipice. They raised him, clapped him on the back – and shuffled on, half-frozen, dogged as the chain gang they resembled.

When the way was too steep, they walked; when the light was gone they lit torches. Hercól shouted at them over the wind: 'Move your fingers, wiggle your toes inside your boots! Let them seize up and they'll snap like carrots!' Pazel felt the fire beetle in his coat, and fought the urge to put the thing into his mouth. *Not yet.* Somehow they kept going, right around the peak, and came at last to Isarak Tower.

It was a grander shelter than Pazel had expected: a soaring ruin two hundred feet tall, though its crown was shorn off like an old forest snag. The great doors were long gone, and snow had filled the bottom floor, but a stone staircase hugged the inner wall, and when they dragged themselves to the second floor they found it windowless and dry. By now the humans and the dlömu were so cold they could barely speak. They rushed about in the dark, swearing in many tongues, brushing the snow from the firewood. *Aya Rin, please let it burn*, Pazel thought, maniacally wiggling his toes.

Neda and Big Skip appeared with two more armloads of sticks: Pazel had no idea where they had come from. They mounded all the wood together, lit pine cones by the torches and nudged the cones under the pile. Hercól bent and blew. There was a glimmer, then a tongue of flame; then the dead wood roared to life. Soon everyone was crowding around the blaze, stripping off their wet clothes and putting on dry: men, women, human, ixchel, dlömu, selk. Only Cayer Vispek changed alone, far from light or warmth.

The selk passed a skin about, and they all took a sip of the smoky selk wine. For a few minutes even Pazel's fingertips were warm. In the dimming light he looked around for his friends. There was Thasha, still dressing: her bare legs pale and strong, her wind-chapped lips finding his own for a haphazard kiss. There were Ensyl and Myett, laughing among the embers, drying each other frantically with Hercól's gift-cloth from Uláramyth. And Neeps? Pazel turned in a circle. His friend was nowhere in sight. He asked the others: no one knew where he had gone.

'He *was* acting a bit strange after we got out of the snow,' said Thasha. 'Holding his hands up in front of him as we went. I thought he was afraid of his fingers breaking off.'

'Neeps!' Pazel shouted. 'Speak up, mate, where are you?' Only his own voice, echoing; then a silence that chilled his blood.

And then, very faintly, a moan. Pazel froze. The sound came again: from somewhere overhead. With Thasha beside him he ran to the staircase and climbed headlong, feeling out the steps in the dark. The third floor was windowless like the first, but the voice – no, voices – were coming from higher still.

The fourth floor had a large pair of windows. Through one, the little Southern moon was shining on a snow-dusted floor; and Pazel saw fresh footprints, and clothes discarded in haste. Before the other, darker window, two figures were embracing, their voices low and urgent, their bodies a study in contrasts: tall and short, jet black and almost-white. Unaware of the intrusion, they moved together, holding on so tightly they seemed scarcely able to breathe; and yet their limbs struggled to tighten further, as though the lack of any distance between them were still too much distance, and must somehow be overcome.

Thasha tugged Pazel away.

On the third floor steps they sat in darkness, stunned. Neeps cried out. Thasha held Pazel's hand, and he remembered what it felt like, when the hand was webbed, when the woman who touched you was not human but this other thing, this cousin-creature, with skin like a dolphin's or a seal's.

They were about to go down to the others when Lunja suddenly crashed into their midst, still fastening the buckle on her belt.

'You!' she snapped at them. 'You keep him away from me now! Do you both hear me plainly? My work is done!'

She shoved past them, a hand covering her mouth. Thasha went after her, but Pazel climbed the stairs again to find Neeps standing barefoot in the snow, his trousers pulled on hastily – by Lunja? – and his hands in fists. He was staring vacantly at the floor, and singing under his breath: a weird, wordless tune. Pazel led him to the moonlit window and raised his chin: Neeps' eyes were solid black.

'You mucking impossible Gods-damned—'

Pazel broke off, glad that no one was there to see his own eyes stream with tears. Neeps stood insensate, like a deathsmoker, like a stump. But it was all right, all right at last. He was in *nuhzat*. Pazel embraced him, and smelled the sweat and grime of that endless day. There was no smell of lemons at all.

'One down,' said Thasha, gazing out through the gap in the wall, 'and all those mountains still to go, by the Tree.'

'Warmer air is coming from the east,' said Thaulinin. 'Winter does not yet reign supreme, last night's cold notwithstanding.'

Pazel stepped up beside them. It was early, most of the others were just beginning to stir. He and Thasha had found Thaulinin here on the highest (remaining) floor of the tower. Warm air might be coming, but it was not here yet. The wind gnawed at any bit of Pazel's skin it found uncovered. Beads of ice had formed in Thasha's hair.

Thaulinin passed him a selk telescope, and showed him the slide-whistle manner of its focusing. 'I saw hrathmogs at sunrise,' he said. 'A great host of the creatures, marching along a lesser road there in the south. And dlömic riders along that stretch of river, further yet. Neither of them was bound for the high country, however. And from this vantage I can see the road ahead in some dozen places. Not much of it, to be sure – a bend here, a short stretch there. I had hoped for better: when last I came this way, this tower had five more stories, and one could see all the way to the aqueduct on Mount Urakán, greatest of the Nine Peaks.'

'How many centuries ago was that?' asked Thasha.

Thaulinin smiled. 'Just two. But there has been an earthquake since. We are fortunate: no man or beast appears to be moving on the Nine Peaks Road. The high country is empty, except for foxes and mountain goats. Perhaps Macadra has forgotten its existence altogether, or merely decided the way was too treacherous for anyone to use. If the latter, we must make haste to prove her wrong.'

Soon the party was back on the trail. At first it threaded a path between towering boulders, but Pazel could see bright sun ahead, and his spirits rose. Just before the trail emerged from the rocks Thaulinin called them together.

'We are stepping up onto the spine of the mountains, and a long stretch of the Royal Highway. This means we shall often be visible from afar. That cannot be helped, but there are measures we should take to aid our chances. Do not shout: echoes travel for miles if the wind is right. Your shields are wrapped in leather, and your scabbards, buckles and the like are all dulled with paint. But your blades will reflect the sun, so think carefully when you draw them.'

'And the dlömu must remember their eyes, which outshine silver,' added Valgrif.

Out they stepped onto the Highway. It was a relic, of course: the broad stones cracked and heaving, and ice and scree burying them in many places. Still it was pleasanter walking, for the Highway neither climbed nor descended much, and here at least it hugged no frightening cliffs. The snows had yet to claim this open land. Sinewy bushes and low, storm-blasted trees grew alongside ruined walls and broken colonnades. There were even patches of late wildflowers, yellow and scarlet, lifting their tiny heads among the stones.

Pazel and Thasha walked with Neeps, and Pazel found himself smiling. His friend was his old, cheeky self, teasing Thasha about the way she'd tried to blackmail him on the *Chathrand*, a lifetime ago it seemed, by promising to accuse him of stealing her necklace.

'If only I blary *had*,' he said. 'Imagine if you'd never put that cursed thing around your neck again, never let Arunis get that power over you.'

'Don't even start with the *if*'s,' said Thasha, smiling in turn. 'If, if, if.'

He was healed, at least for the present. But when he thought Pazel and Thasha were looking elsewhere he shot glances over his shoulder. Pazel knew why: Lunja was behind them, walking with Mandric and Neda. She had not said a word to any of them since dawn.

They rounded the second peak, just a few miles from the first, before the sun was halfway to its zenith. Nor did the third appear too distant. But now the destruction caused by the old earthquake grew more severe. In one place the ground had been forced up nearly twenty feet, road and ruins and all, only to drop again a quarter-mile on. At another they were forced to leave the road and walk for miles around a gigantic fissure that had opened across their path. When at last they returned to the road Hercól looked back over the fissure and shook his head.

'Two hours to advance a hundred feet,' he said.

They were nearing the third peak when something odd happened to Pazel. For no reason he could think of he felt briefly, intensely unhappy, as though he had just thought of something dismal that for a time he had managed to forget. He looked down the ridge on his left, miles and miles, to lesser slopes dark with forest. The thought or feeling had something to do with that land.

He listened, and thought he heard a faint rumble echoing through the mountains. The feeling returned, stronger than before. Pazel shielded his eyes, but his eyes caught nothing unusual in the landscape. Then Ramachni appeared at his side.

'You heard it, did you not?' asked the mage.

'I thought I heard something,' said Pazel. 'What was it? Thunder?'

'No,' said Ramachni, 'it is the eguar, Sitroth.'

Pazel jumped. 'How do you know?'

'The same way you know a brig from a barquentine when you see one on the horizon, Pazel. Because it is your business to know. So it is with mages and magic, except that we feel better than we see. An eguar's magic is unlike any other sort in Alifros. Sitroth is down among those pines, somewhere, trying to commune with others of its kind. There was a time when all the eguars in this world, North and South, could link minds and share their knowledge. But this linkage was a collective effort, and as the eguars' numbers dwindled it became much harder. After the massacres Lord Arim spoke of, I would not be surprised if Sitroth is struggling to reach even the nearest of his seventeen remaining kin.'

'What do you suppose he wants to say?'

'My lad, how should I know? Perhaps he hopes one of them can offer him refuge, or tell him where best to hide from Macadra. Perhaps he is still venting whatever fury led to his betrayal. Perhaps he is asking advice.'

'I've seen two of them,' said Pazel, 'and both of them killed before my eyes. I hope I never see another. But it's horrible what's happened to them, all the same. Ramachni, do you know why Sitroth wanted to kill Prince Olik?'

The mage looked over his shoulder at the prince. 'No,' he said, 'but I think His Highness does.'

The second night was even colder than the first, but they faced no tunnelling, and were still dry when they took shelter. This time there was no roof above them, merely rough cold stone, the foundation of some long-ago ruined castle or keep. The travellers pressed tight into the chilly corner. Pazel fell asleep sitting up, back to back with the prince.

For the next two days the road was utterly abandoned. Of the eguar there was no further sign, and only once did they spot the enemy: a plume of dust revealed itself to be some twenty dlömic riders, galloping along a distant track, and vanished almost as soon as seen. They were alone here in these heights, in this wreckage of a perished kingdom.

On the sixth day the character of the road changed again. The Royal Highway turned north to begin its descent to the ruins of Isima, city of the Mountain Kings; but the travellers kept to the Nine Peaks Road, west by southwest, even as the Road dwindled to a narrow, death-defying trail. Gone was the solid spine of the mountains. Everything became jagged and steep, and far more treacherous than the worst moments of the previous days. The path hugged spires that rose like crooked tombstones. It leaped between them on bridges as astonishing to look at as they were terrible to cross: ancient stone bridges, where the wind sighed through top-to-bottom cracks; hunchbacked bridges of impossible workmanship; bridges squeezed into canyons or wedged between eroding cliffs; bridges the Gods might have lowered from the sky. And when had the party climbed to such altitudes? There were clouds drifting eight and nine hundred feet below them, and entire ranges that reached away like fingers into the distance, their highest peaks a mile or more below the travellers' feet.

The path twisted and meandered so greatly that they scarcely seemed to be advancing. Thaulinin swore that it was by far the quickest way through the mountains, however, and promised that they would be out of the maze by the next afternoon.

As if to spite him, a savage wind chose that moment to blow up from the south. Minutes later a driving sleet began. The treacherous path became quickly, obviously deadly. Stung by the downpour, the party huddled to confer.

Thaulinin had hoped that they would camp that night on Mount

Urakán. 'It cannot be much further – two hours at the most. There are hidden caves on its eastern face, where the selk keep firewood and other stores. Nólcindar's troop may have passed that way, with Valgrif's sons, and left us some word. But to reach Urakán one must cross the bridge over the Parsua Gorge, and that is not a thing to be attempted in bad weather. The Gorge is a terrible abyss, and that bridge is wind-plagued at the best of times.'

'Let us choose quickly, ere we are soaked through again,' said the prince. 'Dry clothes are not a luxury here: they are the difference between life and death.'

To this everyone was agreed, and it was swiftly decided that they would retreat to the last structure they had passed, just a few minutes back along the trail. Pazel had taken it for a kind of stone silo, but this did not prove to be the case. Stepping through the doorway, they found the floor several feet below ground level, and when they dropped upon it they found themselves on smooth, solid ice.

'A cistern,' said Thaulinin. 'Of course: there are ruined water-works all about the summit of Urakán. Well, it must do. At least the roof is sound.'

Bolutu stamped his heel against the ice and laughed. 'A hard bed's nicer than no bed at all. Let us go no further today.'

'That I cannot promise,' said Thaulinin. 'Dusk is still hours away. If the sleet relents we should press on, at least to the old customs-house at the foot of the bridge.'

'What, go on up that mad path today?' said Big Skip, appalled. 'We'll end up at the bottom of a cliff!'

'If we don't hurry,' said Thasha, 'we'll end up in Macadra's hands.'

'That's better than dead, Missy.'

'No, Skip, it is not,' said Ramachni, 'but there is still hope of avoiding either fate. In any event we cannot cross the Parsua in sleet *or* darkness. If we can safely reach the foot of the bridge tonight, we shall. For the moment, rest, and eat some of the bounty of Uláramyth. I believe there are persimmons left.'

To Pazel's surprise, sleeping on the ice was not unpleasant. It was flat and smooth, and the cold did not penetrate their bedrolls, which were made of the same marvellous wool as their coats. As he nodded off, Pazel gazed at the sleet lancing past the doorway and hoped, selfishly, that it would last until dark.

For better or worse, it did not: an hour before nightfall the sleet ended and the sun peeked out. Cautiously they ventured outside – and Corporal Mandric fell flat on his back.

'Pitfire! The mucking trail's a sheet of ice!'

It was no exaggeration: Pazel too had to struggle at every step. 'We selk can walk this path,' said Thaulinin, 'and I dare say Hercól and the *sfvantskors* could follow me. But for the rest it is too dangerous. I fear we must remain here after all.'

Valgrif padded confidently forward. 'I was *raised* on such trails, and can manage them even in the dark,' he said. 'Give me leave to scout ahead, Thaulinin, and we shall be that much better prepared for the morning.'

Thaulinin nodded. 'Go a little distance,' he said, 'but do *not* try your luck in the dark: that I cannot sanction. And I must forbid you to set foot on the bridge, should you go that far.'

Valgrif bowed his head, then turned and looked at Myett. 'Will you come with me, little sister? Your gaze is even sharper than my own.' Myett agreed at once, taking her familiar place on Valgrif's shoulders, and with careful steps the wolf moved down the trail.

For the others there was nothing to do but wait. They had no dry wood to burn, but in the shelter of the cistern's wall the late sun warmed them a little. Thaulinin told them further stories of the Mountain Kings, and of the terrible overthrow of Isima by ogres from the south. But Ramachni said one should not make too much of the invasion.

'The city was doomed before the first foe lumbered from the Thrandaal,' he said. 'King Urakán's people starved themselves. They cut the forests that slowed the spring meltwater, and their croplands vanished in floods. They drained the marshes downriver that fed the game birds, and dragged nets across the lakes with such efficiency that not a fish remained to be caught. They were weakened; their unpaid army devolved into gangs; their famished peasants fled westwards before they could be drafted to the city's defence. The avalanche was coming; the Thrandaal ogres were merely the stone that set it off.'

'Were you there?' asked Thasha.

Ramachni shook his head. 'I saw Isima only in smoking ruin, with Lord Arim at my side. It was the first and last time I ever saw him shed tears. He had tried to warn the city, and when that failed, to defend it. But it was too late: the ogres had already conquered the southern mountains, and were advancing on Urakán. Still Arim worked a mighty spell, at great cost to himself, diverting a blizzard that would have closed the Royal Highway. By his deed the city's children were evacuated and saved. To this day the descendants of those children inhabit the Ilidron Coves, and bless themselves in Arim's name.'

Night fell, but Valgrif and Myett did not return. Thaulinin gazed anxiously down the trail. 'I consented too easily,' he said. 'Who knows how treacherous the path becomes when one approaches the Gorge?'

'Valgrif is a wise beast,' said one of his men. 'I watched him train his sons to respect the dangers of the ice. He will come to no harm.'

But when another hour had passed they all felt the same anxiety. Then Thaulinin lit a torch and called his men together. 'Bring rope, and your spikes and mallets,' he said. 'We may find them clinging to some ledge.'

Hercól and Vispek wished to go along, but Thaulinin refused. 'You are mountain-trained to be sure, but even the best human feet cannot move as swiftly as our own.'

Then Ensyl laughed. 'Wolf feet are another matter, it seems. Look there!'

She pointed not down the trail, but above them, on the icy ridge over the cistern. Pazel squinted, and at last made out Valgrif cutting a zigzag path towards them downhill. Moments later he slid to a halt at their feet, Myett still clinging to his shoulders. The wolf was exhausted and panting.

'Enemies!' he gasped, dropping on his stomach. 'And the bridge—'

'The bridge has fallen,' said Myett. 'We came to its foot: there are only fragments arching out over that terrible gorge. And Valgrif smelled dlömu on the far side, when the wind gusted towards us.'

'You didn't see anyone, then?' asked Pazel.

Myett looked from face to face. 'We saw one figure only,' she said. 'We saw Dastu.'

'Dastu! Here!' cried the others.

'He was among the trees on the far side of the gorge,' said Myett. 'We did not let him see us. He was pacing back and forth.'

'What in the devil-thick Pits can that rotter be doing here?' said Neeps.

'Nothing good,' said Prince Olik. 'I remember that one: he followed your spymaster about like a dog, but he also had a cunning of his own.'

'That he should have come *here* from where he ran from us strikes me as all but impossible – without help at any rate,' said Thaulinin. 'Perhaps Nólcindar found him and took pity. She might be there right now, along with Valgrif's sons.'

'I smelled neither selk nor wolves,' said Valgrif, 'and the scent of the dlömu came faintly, from the far side of the gorge. We waited, and once there came an echo of a voice – not a dlömic voice – from above us.'

Myett pointed at the ice-slick path. 'This trail ends at the fallen bridge, but when we heard that echo I climbed the cliff above us, and saw another bridge around a bend in the chasm. It was high above me still, and oddly built, with the far side higher than the near.'

'The Water Bridge,' said Thaulinin. 'So one span at least survived the earthquake. That bridge is part of the King's Aqueduct, which ran for nearly two hundred miles, carrying snowmelt from the high peaks to the farmlands below. Alas, it was built too late to save them.' He looked at Ramachni. 'The Water Bridge is not a pleasant way to cross the Parsua. But cross there we must, unless we would retrace our steps all the way to Isarak.'

'That we cannot do,' said Ramachni, 'but there is another explanation for Dastu's presence, is there not?'

'Yes,' said Neda. 'Selk not bringing him. Macadra bringing, as the trap.'

'As *a* trap,' corrected Mandric automatically, 'but I was thinking just the same. Rin's gizzard, that's all we need: another young pup helping the enemy.'

'It does seem the likeliest explanation,' said Hercól, 'but if Dastu is helping Macadra, I am sure he does not do so willingly. Dastu is flawlessly loyal: both to his master and his master's religion, which is Arqual. He is not Greysan Fulbreech.'

'There is something very strange about him,' said Valgrif. 'I cannot explain it even to myself. I wish I had caught his scent.'

'One thing is certain,' said Cayer Vispek. 'His presence at that bridge is no coincidence. He is waiting for someone, and who could that someone be but us?'

Thaulinin squatted down beside Valgrif and put his chin on his hands. 'We have been fortunate, and I have been rash. We should have sent you out ahead of us each day, Valgrif: the enemy would not know you for a woken animal, let alone the citizen that you are. If Macadra *has* sent Dastu here, then she has not overlooked the Nine Peaks at all.'

'And we've lost already,' said Big Skip.

'No, not yet,' said the selk, 'for she has many roads to watch, and on some of them my brethren will have harried her forces and led them astray. If she is trying to watch *every* road, then she cannot dedicate too many servants to each. And what better place for a small number to guard the high country than at the bridge over the highest gorge of all?'

'So she sends a team of soldiers here to wait for us, along with Dastu,' said Pazel, 'and finds the bridge destroyed. What then?'

'Then she waits to see if we come blundering up to the Gorge, as I would have led us to do,' said Thaulinin. 'A fall of sleet may well have saved us, this day.'

'They'll be watching the aqueduct, too,' said Thasha.

'Presumably,' said Hercól. 'We must approach in stealth.'

They passed a night of great unease, and Hercól roused them all before sunrise. 'Now more than ever, take care with the metal on your persons, lest it be seen or heard,' he said. 'Remember the council at Thehel Bledd: we could doom our quest just by being seen, if one of Macadra's servants flees the mountains and sounds the alarm.'

The selk had been out already, and chosen their path up the ridge. It was a rough, cold climb under frigid stars; and a very long one, as they struggled up one sharp rise after another, winding among sheer falls of rock. Pazel thought of Bolutu, struggling with the weight of the Nilstone on his back. He had asked no one else to carry it since Uláramyth.

After nearly three hours they broke suddenly onto a jagged ridgetop. It was not the very summit of the ridge but rather a broad, irregular shoulder that curved away towards the chasm, studded with boulders and small shrubs and rounded, ice-glazed drifts of snow. By now the sun was beginning to glow behind the eastern mountains. Thaulinin made them all crouch low. 'I can hear the wind in the canyon,' he hissed. 'We are very close.'

Like a band of thieves they crept across that flattened ridge. Pazel could see what looked like a gap ahead, and soon he too heard the change in the wind, as though it were moaning through a narrowly cracked door. Pazel tried to keep his teeth from chattering. He could hear his every footfall on the icy ground.

The wind rose, and so did the light. And suddenly before them lay the aqueduct. It was an astonishing relic: a stone chute some twelve feet wide and half as deep, built right into the ancient rock. The chute was pitched gradually downhill, and when he looked to his right Pazel saw that where the ridge fell away the chute emerged from the ground and was held aloft by columns, so that the angle of descent never changed. Straight as an arrow it raced away across the mountainside, until at last, very far away to the east, it made a sharp turn and set off northwards.

Pazel was awed. *Two hundred miles.* How many years, how many decades, did the Mountain Kings' people give to the building of the waterway? Even now there was a little ice-fringed water flowing along the bottom of the chute.

Thaulinin beckoned them all to drop back, and then led them west, parallel to the aqueduct but on lower ground. It was a sheltered area, crowded with boulders and small, dense firs. After a few minutes they found themselves on a narrow trail.

Hercól flung out his arm, stopping the party in its tracks. The aqueduct loomed before them, suspended on its stone arches. But that was not what concerned Hercól. There was a clearing before the structure where no trees grew, and beside the clearing was an abyss. It was the chasm, of course: perhaps two hundred feet wide, and far too deep for them to dream of seeing the bottom from where they stood. The aqueduct leaped over the chasm in a single span, with no arch to support it, and as it crossed it rose much more steeply than elsewhere along its length, joining the opposite cliff some fifty feet higher than it began. The Water Bridge. Clearly ancient, it might once have been beautifully carved. Now the knobby protrusions along its sides were blurred and indistinct: dragons or leopards, serpents or vines. At its foot, across the chasm, rose a crumbling tower. On the tower's battlements sat a large, black bird.

Right at its centre the bridge was mortally cracked. The fissure stretched halfway across the water chute, and where it began whole stones had fallen away, leaving a gap some eight feet wide. Above the crack the chute was filled with rushing water to a depth of several feet, but nearly all the water passed out through it, gushing straight down into the gorge and fringed by immense beards of ice.

Thaulinin was correct: the structure was built for water, not people. But beneath the water chute there did, in fact, run a kind of footbridge, accessed by a staircase leading down from the edge of the cliff. Pazel felt ill at the very sight of that footbridge. It was about two feet wide and suspended between V-shaped struts that descended from the underside of the water chute. No rails ran between the struts. The water gushing through the crack poured right over the footbridge, and from that point all the way back to the travellers' side of the chasm the narrow platform lay sheathed in ice.

Sudden movement along the opposite cliff. Pazel jumped: it was Dastu. The older youth had been sitting on a rock, so still that Pazel's gaze had swept right past him. Now he walked slowly, idly along the edge of the chasm. Then he shot a glance at the bird.

The party fell back. The faces of the others were ashen. 'Two watchers, Thaulinin,' said one of the selk. 'The eagle cocked its head at the human youth, just as the youth looked up at the eagle. They are in league.'

'And surely not alone,' said Valgrif. 'What is the matter with that boy? I tell you I do not like how he behaves.'

'You don't know the half of it,' said Neeps. 'So that was an eagle? I've never heard of black ones.'

'They have long been my family's playthings,' said Prince Olik. 'They are hunters, bred for strength and endurance – and keenness of eye.'

'Ramachni,' said Pazel. 'What if that mucking bird's woken? What if it sees us and flies right to Macadra?'

'Then your quest fails, and your world soon after,' said Ramachni. He looked at Hercól and seemed about to say more, but something in the swordsman's gaze made him save his breath. Hercól understood, and Pazel felt he did too. The bridge was held against them. Possibly by unseen enemies. At the very least by one that could flee and sound the alarm.

Realizing that they had to get out of sight at once, the party retreated to the nearest cistern, which was also filled with ice. The roof was partly collapsed, and to keep out of sight from the air they had to huddle in the shadows by the opposite wall.

'Now,' said Ensyl, 'you must let the ixchel earn their keep. Valgrif might pass for a common wolf at other moments, but any creature seen approaching that chasm is sure to raise suspicions. Myett and

I will not be seen, however. Let us go and watch the bridge awhile, and see what else we may discover.'

'My lady,' said Prince Olik, 'those eagles spot creatures your size from a thousand feet.'

'But not ixchel,' said Myett. 'We have been hiding from birds of prey as long as we have from humans, if not longer. Besides, the deadliest foe is the one whose face you never see. If that eagle takes to the air we will bury ourselves beneath the pine needles, or the snow. I was unforgivably careless when I let the eagle from Uláramyth catch me in its talons. That will not happen again.'

Hercól sighed. 'We cannot go back, and we dare not go on before we learn just what we are up against. I do not like it, my ladies, but I think we must accept your offer. Go then, and take twice the care as ever you did in the streets of Etherhorde.'

'Note everything you see, however trivial it appears,' said Ramachni. 'Above all, heed the fine instincts of your people. If they tell you to flee, do so at once, even if you think yourselves perfectly hidden. Some means of detection require neither eyes nor ears.'

'We have no wish to die,' said Ensyl. Then she looked at Myett and winced, as though regretting her choice of words. But Myett just smiled grimly. 'No,' she said, 'not even I wish for death any longer. Let us go.'

They took a long look at the sky, and then darted back along the trail towards the chasm, moving like a pair of swift white spiders from one snowbank to the next.

This time Pazel found the waiting almost unbearable. He could not even pace: the ice was too slippery, and the cistern too small. An hour passed, possibly longer. Neda looked at him and tried to smile. Thasha's eyes were distant, in that worrying way he knew.

Then suddenly Ensyl and Myett burst back into the cistern, and the news spilled out. 'Hrathmogs!' said Ensyl. 'At least six of the creatures, maybe more. And three dlömic warriors with the Bali Adro sun and leopard upon their shields.'

'Their leader is one of the dlömu,' said Myett. 'He wears a fell knife at his waist. It is a Plazic blade, like the one Vadu used against us on the Black Tongue. The dlömu and the hrathmogs came out of the rocks and spoke together, then slipped back out of sight.'

'So it *is* an ambush,' said Big Skip.

'And a Plazic warrior in command,' said Thaulinin grimly. 'I should have known Macadra would send one of them. They are dying very quickly, and she no longer trusts them with command of her armies. Some have turned on her – on the Ravens, and even your family, Prince Olik – but the lesser blade-keepers she still controls, and uses for special tasks.'

'Such as searching for Uláramyth,' said one of his men.

Thaulinin nodded. 'We must beware of that man. If he has come this far, then the blade has not yet crippled him. He may still be able to draw on its power.'

'There are dogs with them,' said Myett. 'Great red animals that slavered and growled. Their jaws looked as powerful as those of horses, but full of canine teeth.'

'Worse and worse,' said Prince Olik. 'Those are *athymar* eight-fangs, the same creatures that chased me west of Masalym.'

'They are abominations,' said Valgrif, his lip curling back with rage. 'They were bred for killing and rending, and have no minds for anything but death.'

'Is there more to tell?' asked Lunja.

'Yes,' said Ensyl. 'We think there is something inside the tower. The door faces away from the cliffs, so we could not see inside. But they all glance at it oddly, and approach the door with caution. And the black eagle *is* woken, or the cleverest bird I ever saw. It sat upon the battlements listening to their speech, as though it understood every word.'

'And the boy?' asked Ramachni.

'Dastu is one of them – or that at least is what anyone would think, to see how they look at one another. He does not cringe before them, or show any special deference, although he keeps his distance from the dlömu with the Plazic knife. He is still there, and so is the eagle.'

Now the debate began in earnest. No one suggested turning back: that would be to abandon the *Chathrand* for ever, along with any hope of crossing the Ruling Sea. But how to go forward? Pazel thought of how they had charged Arunis in the Infernal Forest, armed mostly with sticks. That had been terrifying but comprehensible: the mage had been their only foe, and they had simply crossed the ground to him at a run. Now they were facing many foes – and the worst of them might be the bridge itself.

'We have to fell that bird, right?' said Mandric. 'So why not start with a good spray of arrows?'

'We would be hazarding the whole of the quest on those shafts,' said Prince Olik. 'and I do not like the odds, my good man. We would be shooting a great distance, at a small, swift target, and worst of all, through the blasting winds over that chasm. Still, I do not see a better choice.'

'What of your powers, mage?' said Cayer Vispek, his tone almost accusing. 'You could kill the bird with a single charm, could you not?'

'I might,' said Ramachni, 'and indeed I will try, if there is no other choice. But to kill with a word is no small spell, Cayer, and you might wish that I had saved my strength for other uses, if that Plazic warlord draws his knife. And remember that we may not have seen all our foes.'

'We could wait for nightfall,' said Neeps.

'Hear the fool,' said Lunja. 'If we try to cross that bridge in darkness we will die.'

'I fear the sergeant is right, Neeps,' said Hercól, 'and we can ill afford to lose even one more day.'

'What about Nólcindar and her company?' asked Thasha.

'It was never certain that they would come this way,' said Valgrif, 'and with hrathmogs on the mountain it is less likely still. But if she has come and gone she would leave a tiny mark upon the bridge itself – upon both bridges, probably.'

'What if them dogs are woken too?' said Big Skip.

'What if the mucking bridge falls?' snapped Mandric. 'Think

too much and you'll soil your leggings. Get your blood up for butchery, and stop hoping someone else will do it for you. That's my strategic advice.'

'*They* will do it for us, if we are careless,' said Thaulinin.

The bickering went on. Pazel could taste his fear mounting with every word. *Not now*, he thought furiously. *Be afraid when it's over.* He touched the pommel of his selk sword; and in his pocket, the reassuring weight of Fiffengurt's blackjack. He glanced at Neeps and Thasha: he could read them like the pages of a cherished book. Neeps was looking fierce and defiant. And while Thasha's eyes brightened a little at his look, she was really gazing inwards, searching for the power that could save them, at whatever the cost to herself. Searching for a gap in the wall.

And not finding it. Pazel could see that too, by the deep frown of guilt that was gathering in her lips, her eyebrows. *She's taking it all on her shoulders*, he thought. *She's wondering who's going to die because of that wall.*

He reached for her hand, but she pulled it quickly away. 'Ramachni,' she said, 'what did it cost you to fight the eguar? Are you empty inside, the way you were in Simja?'

The mage stepped close to her. 'No, not like that,' he said. 'Lord Arim shouldered most of the burden of the lightning strike. I have been stronger, but I am still quite strong.'

'You said once that the quest had no hope without Erithusmé,' said Thasha. 'Was it because you foresaw a moment like this?'

Ramachni's dark eyes looked at her with compassion. 'This moment was foreseen by no one, my champion. Not by us, nor by those across the bridge, nor by the sorceress who set them in our path. How it will end is not predestined. We must remember that, and seek the ending without fear.'

An hour later the party launched its assault.

Once more the ixchel led the way. It was their awful task to cross the bridge unseen and slay the eagle – silently if they could, but in the end by any means whatsoever. The two women had decided against the footbridge beneath the water chute: neither had much confidence that they could pass through the falling torrent at the bridge's centre and not be swept away. They had also seen the dlömic soldiers des-cending the staircase beneath the aqueduct to have a look at the footbridge.

That left only the main bridge to consider. There was a foot-wide rim on either side of the watercourse, and the sun had kept both free of ice. But for a stealth attack, the upper surface of the bridge was out of the question, for it was in plain view of both Dastu and the eagle. At last the ixchel had chosen a more har-rowing course: along the side of the bridge, clinging vertically to those ancient carvings. Dastu was keeping largely to the near side of the aqueduct, and the eagle's perch on the tower gave it a view of the clearing and the open top of the watercourse, but not the side. Unless one of them (or some other enemy) moved to the northern edge of the clearing, Ensyl and Myett would be hidden. They would also, of course, be exposed to that monstrous wind, with nothing to hold on to save the faint, time-smoothed shapes of animals and men. And what if they encountered ice?

'Do not let the wind take you, little sisters,' said Valgrif as the two women set out.

Ensyl and Myett looked back at the party. 'Human beings named us *crawlies*,' Ensyl said. 'Judge us today by our crawling.'

'If you can feel these eyes upon you,' said Hercól, 'then you will know that they watch not with judgement but with love.'

The two women gazed at him in silence a moment. Then they crawled forward on their stomachs, with infinite care, until they could just see the eagle on its perch.

The rest of the party crouched among the boulders, watching with the deepest anxiety. Pazel could still see Dastu meandering back and forth. What was he doing with them? How had he been treated? The telescope revealed no obvious wounds or signs of tor-ture. Despite what Hercól had said about his loyalty to Arqual, Pazel found himself wondering if Dastu might not have quickly agreed to help Macadra any way he could.

'Now,' whispered Ensyl.

The two ixchel sprinted for the pines, and froze as one behind a trunk. Pazel held his breath: the eagle did not move. It had seen nothing, and the ixchel were now halfway to the cliff.

Bows at the ready, Hercól and three selk warriors crept into position behind the boulder nearest the pines. They had no clear shot of the bird from here, but could at least rush forward and fire from the chasm's edge. If Myett and Ensyl failed, their shots would give the quest another chance.

The ixchel sprinted again. This time they made for a rock in the centre of the clearing. It was utterly exposed, and barely large enough to hide them both: they came to rest on hands and knees, with Myett folded over Ensyl's body and their heads curled down. Once more they stayed hidden, this time by a finger's width. Another pause, then they ran for the third and final time, and reached the shelter of the stairwell. Ensyl looked back and gave a wry salute. Then they slipped under the aqueduct, making for the blind side of the bridge.

Aya Rin, thought Pazel, *let them do that well above the gorge.*

Now all eyes turned to Ramachni. They could see him by looking under the aqueduct; he was at the opposite side of the clearing, lying flat behind a fallen pine. It had taken him a long time to squirm down the ridge to that position, but it had a singular advantage: from there he could see both the party and the ixchel as they climbed. For the others, Ensyl and Myett would be invisible until the moment they attacked.

They would need at least thirty minutes for the crossing, Ensyl had said. Pazel wiggled his toes. He thought, *The waiting will be the worst part.* Then he thought how unlikely that was to be true.

Looking at those crouched beside him, Thaulinin tapped his vest pocket meaningfully. The fire beetles. On Isarak he had warned them that biting into the creatures might prove more dangerous than the cold itself. But digging through a snow drift was one thing, and wading uphill against a three-foot-deep flood of meltwater quite another.

Pazel's knees were growing stiff. On the far side of the chasm the eagle stretched its wings. Dastu climbed the stairs to the top of the watercourse and sat upon the rim.

Pazel looked back over his shoulder. Neda and Cayer Vispek were mouthing silent words to each other, sketching movements on their palms. Vispek's eyes were fierce and hard. In recent days he had barely spoken to Neda, and Pazel knew that her master's coldness had wounded her. But they had trained together, and Vispek had insisted that they would fight side by side.

The others looked about as bad as Pazel felt. Big Skip caught his eye, smiled with some effort, made the sign of the Tree. Lunja glanced savagely at Neeps and motioned for him to button his coat.

Then at last Ramachni raised his head. Everyone grew still. Through the pine limbs Pazel could just see the tower battlements where the eagle perched. Ramachni lifted one paw from the ground: *Steady, steady—*

The eagle shot into the air.

Instantly everyone was in motion. Ramachni bolted for the bridge. Hercól and the selk archers erupted from behind their boulder and flew towards the cliff. Behind them, the rest of the party sprinted forward as well.

The eagle, veering erratically, was already soaring away from the bridge. The archers let fly, but the surging wind over the chasm blew their arrows wildly off-target. Dastu turned to them, waving and shouting: 'You're here! Don't shoot! Ramachni, let me explain! Don't shoot that bird!'

Ramachni had bounded onto the lip of the water chute and was charging up the bridge's steep incline. He ignored Dastu's shouts.

Pazel surged up the stairs, gasping at the force of the wind. For an instant he gazed down into the gorge – hideously deep, the bottom so far away it was like gazing at another world – and then jumped into the chute beside Prince Olik, and felt the icy water close about his feet. The archers fired again and again, but the shot was hopeless now: the eagle still flew erratically, but it was disappearing fast.

'You fools!' cried Dastu. 'Thank the Gods you missed! That bird's on *our* side!'

'Whose side is that, boy?' shouted Cayer Vispek.

'Yours and mine! Come across and I'll tell you everything! What's happened to you? Did the selk let you keep the Nilstone?'

The question swept the last doubt from Pazel's mind. Dastu had betrayed them a second time – was betraying them even now.

'Tell me something, mate,' he shouted on an impulse, 'are you doing this for Arqual?'

Dastu's response caught Pazel quite off guard. He did not sneer or shake his head or frown with anger. He simply looked at Pazel with no comprehension whatsoever.

Now Pazel was mystified. Had Dastu been so changed and tormented that he had forgotten even his beloved Empire?

Then Thasha cried out and pointed west. Pazel looked up and saw the eagle fall like a stone from the sky.

The ixchel! Pazel thought. *One of them was on its back all along!*

One of them had just fallen with that corpse.

Dastu had also turned at Thasha's shout. When the bird fell he reached for it, clawing at the air. Then he screeched. It was the ugliest sounds Pazel ever heard from human lips.

From the trees on the far side of the chasm, figures erupted: hrathmogs, dlömu, *athymars*. All of them raced towards the bridge. More hrathmogs burst onto the roof of the tower, bows in hand.

Ramachni was far ahead of the others; he had already passed the great crack at the centre of the bridge. The hrathmogs targeted him first, and Hercól bellowed at the mage to take cover. But as the archers drew, Ramachni fixed them all with a stare, and suddenly three of the creatures turned and fired on their comrades. Those who were not slain leaped on those who had attacked them, and the tower descended into chaos.

The diversion gave the attackers the chance they needed. They gathered into a tight column, huddling beneath the shields of the fighting men, and charged. Ramachni, meanwhile, leaped onto the bridge's stone foot, and then onto the snow. He was making for Dastu, and the youth was retreating, shrieking and gesturing for aid. The hrathmogs with their great axes were too slow to strike at him, but the dogs came on like furies. When their fangs were inches from him the tiny mage whirled and made a sweeping motion with one paw. The dogs were tossed backwards away from him like so many dice. Ramachni turned to Dastu. The youth was at the edge of the chasm, still screeching like a lunatic.

Suddenly he turned to face the cliff.

Credek, no!

He leaped. The wind cupped him and spun him as he fell and thrashed his body against the cliff. Pazel watched, sickened, torn. *Rotter! Quitter! Piss-ignorant fool! You didn't have to do that, you—*

'Oh Gods,' said Thasha, 'he's changing.'

It happened so quickly Pazel almost doubted what he saw. Dastu's body blurred, then grew suddenly enormous, and solidified once more. Below them now was a nightmare beast: humanoid body, long snake-like neck, leathery wings, whiplash tail. It was the *maukslar*: foulest servant of Macadra, the very demon that had hunted them in the forest. Its wings filled. As the party turned the creature rose before them, yellow runes burning on its forehead, and then that snake's head struck with blinding speed, and Big Skip's arm was in its jaws.

Skip howled. Pazel saw his face for an instant, transformed by pain and the imminence of death, and then the *maukslar*'s neck jerked back, and Skip was wrenched from his feet and hurled into the abyss.

Gone. Even his scream swallowed instantly by the wind. Pazel thought he would go mad with the horror of it. But he did not go mad, and he did not freeze, and neither did anyone else. They flew at the demon, and Hercól was out ahead of them all, swinging Ildraquin in a killing arc. But the *maukslar* was too quick: just in time it flung its head back, and the sword only grazed its jaw. Then the creature dropped beneath the bridge. The party turned at bay: it was directly under them, screaming. One clawed hand rose above the rim on the bridge's north side – and while their eyes were turned that way, its tail whipped up from the south, caught a selk guard by the neck, and hurled him after Skip into the gorge. Pazel whirled. His will was strong and his sword raised, but there was nothing to strike at, nothing he could reach. Then a hideous cry, and the *maukslar* rose, wings beating hard, neck retracted like a cobra preparing to strike.

But it did not strike. As Pazel watched, the demon began to tremble, then to writhe with great violence, beating itself against the bridge. The party fell back, for the very bridge was shuddering. It was worse than any seizure – worse than what the creature's own body should be capable of, Pazel thought.

He cast his eyes about for an explanation – and found it. Ramachni had come back to them. His fur stood on end, and he was shaking, shaking in wild fury, snapping his tiny head back and forth as minks do when they mean to kill the prey in their teeth. The demon was twenty times Ramachni's size, but was caught in his spell all the same, and Ramachni meant to shake it to death.

The *maukslar* screamed and flailed. It clawed at the bridge, ripping stones away. It tried to fold its wings before they were crushed but could not turn its body to do so. The others lunged and stabbed, and Neda's sword pierced its side. Even as she did so, however, the beast knocked another stone free with a swing of its arm. The stone ricocheted off the wall of the chute, narrowly missed Neda's head, and struck Ramachni on the flank.

The mage was briefly stunned – and in that instant the *maukslar* was free. With a croak of pain it released the bridge and fell into the chasm.

'Arpathwin, it can still fly!' cried Thaulinin, gazing over the rim. 'It is departing! It is going to Macadra!'

Ramachni stood and shook his fur. 'That disguise,' he said. 'I should have guessed. Once upon a time I would have guessed. And now there is only one way to proceed.'

He leaped deftly onto the rim once more. Then he looked back at them, a tiny creature buffeted by the wind. 'You know what you must do,' he shouted. 'Fight on, stop for nothing. Find and kill them all.'

'Ramachni?' said Thasha.

'I hoped never again to leave your side,' he said, and jumped.

Thasha screamed. Pazel grabbed at her, irrationally fearful that she would try to follow the mage. 'Where is he, where did he go?' shouted Neeps, leaning over the rim.

Pazel heaved himself up and looked into the abyss. He could not see Ramachni, but he could see the *maukslar*: the demon was soaring away, following the contours of the Parsua like a great bird. Then came the ghastly thought: Ramachni's magic had failed, the demon had blocked it somehow; he had stepped off the bridge and fallen straight down to his death.

Then Thasha pointed.

Far below the bridge, yet still hundreds of feet above the *maukslar*, soared an owl. It was no creature of the mountaintops; it looked very small and out of place. Yet its wings churned the thin air powerfully, and when the demon turned, so did the owl.

'That's him,' shouted Neeps. 'He took that same shape exactly in the forest. But what will he do if he catches that thing?'

No time for further talk. The enemy had regrouped, and five or six hrathmog archers were firing from the tower. The three dlömu, including their fell-looking commander with his Plazic knife, waited by the foot of the bridge, with the *athymars* circling and baying at their heels.

'Assemble, assemble!' Thaulinin was shouting. 'Shield-bearers, forward!'

Clenching his teeth, Pazel stepped back into the frigid water. The column reformed; they scrambled on and up. It was hard to climb in a crouch, and harder still when one's feet were numb with cold. The floor of the water-chute was very slick. But between the shields and the walls of the chute the hrathmog archers could find nowhere to sink a shaft. Beside Pazel, Bolutu's eyes were streaming.

He and Big Skip had become fast friends.

Finally they reached the great crack. There were hisses and oaths, for it was even wider than they had imagined, and the gushing torrent made it difficult to tell just where the edges lay. Still lofting the shields they tried to squeeze past it, two by two, feeling out the stones with their feet. Pazel's head was reeling: a few inches to his left there was nothing: air, spray, sucking wind. He felt a stone shift under his foot.

Think of walking, nothing else. Others had done it, somehow. He stilled his heart, and inched forward, and he was through.

But things only grew worse. Above the crack they were right in the flood, wading uphill against a ripping current that splashed to their thighs. Pazel wanted to scream: the cold was agonizing, like long-nailed fingers stripping the flesh from his bones.

Now, he thought. *Wait any longer and you'll fall down dead.*

With clumsy fingers he tugged the beetle from his vest pocket and put the frozen, scaly thing into his mouth. But he could not bite; his teeth were chattering like some strange machine. At last he used his hands to force his jaws together, until the beetle's shell cracked like a nut.

Oh Gods.

The heat passed through him in a scalding wave. His mouth was a furnace; his head was on fire, and even his vision changed, as though he were seeing the world through pale red wine. He half expected to see steam rising from his body.

Remembering Arim's warning, he spat the beetle out, along with a fair amount of blood: the insect had literally burned his tongue. Other beetles floated past him: he was not the only one who had decided the time had come. But what of Valgrif and Shilu? The wolf was almost swimming, and Lunja was even now struggling to tie a harness around the neck and shoulders of the dog. *They should have waited on the cliff*, thought Pazel. *They'll die if this takes too long.*

Hercól stood up suddenly from beneath his shield. He fired the selk bow twice in rapid succession, and two archers fell. How many did that leave? Hrathmogs were still firing from atop the tower, several more from the foot of the bridge. A selk cried out: he had raised his bow as Hercól had done, but this time one of the hrathmogs sank a shaft deep in his side. Thaulinin lifted the wounded man, trying to guard them both with his shield. Hercól fired again, and another hrathmog fell.

The dlömic commander turned and ran for the tower. Pazel was close enough now to see that a massive archway opened in its wall on the northern side. The commander stopped at the threshold and shouted into the tower, pointing imperiously at the bridge as he did so.

There was a rumbling sound, and the archers on the towers swayed, as though the building had just rocked beneath their feet. Those still firing from the bridge turned and fled. Only the ravenous dogs held their ground.

Through the tower arch something huge and pale was crawling. At first Pazel could only see its face: an old woman's face, bloated, pock-marked, with protruding eyes and a mouth full of black and rotting teeth. An iron crown, spiked and bloody, sat upon her head, and from beneath it yards of grey, matted hair hung like sheets of bog-moss. Then the creature rose to its feet.

'*Miyanthur*, save us!' shouted the selk. 'That is a Thrandaal broodmother, an ogress of the race that conquered the Mountain Kings!'

She towered over them, dressed in rotting leather from which a few shells, bones, glass beads and other trinkets still dangled. A sack tied to her waist leaked a soot-like powder that stained the snow. A mighty chain dragged from a manacle at her wrist.

The creature's first act was to pounce on one of the fleeing hrathmogs. It tore the beast's armour away, then stuffed the hrathmog head first into its mouth. The hrathmog's legs still protruded, still kicked; then the ogress bit down and the kicking ceased.

'Fear no devils!' bellowed Cayer Vispek. 'Forward, while yet we may!'

They tried to climb faster, but the current was too fierce, the ascent too steep. The ogress was chewing thoughtfully, an old grandmother with a mouthful. It was slow to notice the Plazic commander, who was howling with fury: 'Not them! The bridge! Kill the creatures on the bridge!'

The ogress trained a lazy eye in the party's direction. It spat a bone at the commander, and began to turn away. The dlömu leaped into its path.

'By the curse I carry, animal, you *will* obey!'

The commander gripped the handle of his Plazic knife. The ogress hesitated, suddenly wary. Then with a gesture of agony (like one ripping stitches from a wound) the commander jerked his arm upwards. In his hand shone a ghost-knife, the pale image of a blade that had once been long and cruel, but was now corroded down to a few blunt inches of bone. The commander himself gazed at it with hatred. But with that stump of a blade he struck fear into the monster: it recoiled, shielding its eyes from the weapon. Then it groaned and rushed the bridge.

The party had sixty feet to go when the ogress climbed atop the aqueduct. It stared at them with dull hate, then it raised its manacled arm and swung the chain over its head. The chain came down with thunder, and the last iron link struck the wounded selk leaning on Thaulinin's arm. Thaulinin himself was not touched, but the man was torn from him, and Pazel watched with horror as the flood bore the lifeless body away. The ogress hauled in the chain for a second swing.

'Back, back!' cried Hercól. 'That chain will be the end of us!'

But backing up was not something they had tried; it was hard enough to keep one's feet when climbing forward. Warning shouts; then the chain struck again. There was a great splash: this time everyone had managed to dive to one side or the other. But in so doing many had lost their feet. They clawed at the stone, the ice, each other: anything to stop themselves from sliding headlong into the crack. Pazel, luckier than most, managed to lock an arm over the bridge's rim. Prince Olik, nearly submerged, reached out wildly and caught his other hand. With a single furious tug Pazel hauled him from the water, and then saw with amazement that he had somehow found the strength to lift Thasha too: the prince had hold of her belt.

As he struggled to gain his feet again Pazel looked back along the bridge.

Neda!

His sister was whirling down the chute. She was limp, barely conscious; he thought she must have fallen and struck her head. *So fast.* Pazel had barely time to scream, to feel a part of him dying, to wish for death for the first time in his life. One moment his sister was there in the sunlit water; the next her body folded down through the crack and was gone.

He howled, the world blurring with tears. He let go of the bridge and tried to follow her, and Olik and Thasha had to fight him with all their strength. Then came the next ghastly shock, as a second body reached the crack and was sucked away to oblivion: Cayer Vispek. But the elder *sfvantskor* had not gone helplessly. He had been wide awake. He had aimed his body for the hole.

Crash. The chain fell again, splitting stone, but for the moment the party had slid beyond its reach. The ogress screamed at them from the edge of the watercourse; clearly she had no wish to climb out over the abyss itself. Plunging a hand into the sack at her waist, she drew out a fistful of black powder. Thaulinin bellowed a warning, but it was too late: the ogress blew the powder from her hand, and as she did so it burst into flames.

A plume of orange fire billowed towards them. Above the rim of the chute it was soon dispersed by the wind, but just over the water's surface it slithered on until it broke against the warriors' shields. Pazel saw their faces: some of them were burned. Already the ogress was raising another fistful to her lips.

Hercól's bow sang again. The ogress gave a murderous scream, dropping the powder and clawing at her face. The shaft was buried in her eye.

The monster's scream went on and on. She tore the shaft away, along with much of her eyeball. She whirled and swung the chain blindly, and the remaining archers were swept from the tower. When she managed to strike the bridge again the chain passed inches from Thaulinin's face.

Then the selk leader did an amazing thing: he dived upon the chain. The ogress had fallen to her knees, one hand over her bloody eye socket. With each jerk of her arm Thaulinin was pulled further up the chute.

The dlömic commander saw what was happening and cried out. Two *athymars* burst onto the bridge and were crushed when the ogress rolled on them in her agony. As she struggled to hands and knees Thaulinin released the chain and drew his selk sword. Then he reeled. A hrathmog arrow had pierced his leg below the knee.

The ogress saw Thaulinin then, and fumbled for him. But Thaulinin was not bested yet: he leaped sidelong into her blind spot, then reached up and caught a handful of her matted hair. The ogress whirled around, swinging him through the air, and Thaulinin drew his blade in a precise, slashing motion across her jugular.

Blood exploded from the creature's neck. Thaulinin was tossed high and landed in the clearing. The ogress fell forward into the chute, and for a few seconds they all felt the warmth as the torrent around them turned crimson. Then the flow stopped altogether. The body of the ogress was blocking the chute, and the water was spilling over the sides.

Like some crazed band of cannibals, blood-splattered from feet to faces, the survivors charged. Pazel heard the savagery in his own voice and did not recognize himself. He was changed; he had lost his sister. He climbed the body of the still-quivering ogress and plunged his sword into her stomach. Only killing could blot out the death inside him. He leaped down into the clearing, howling for more.

It came. The hrathmogs were returning, now that the ogress was slain. The party outnumbered them, but the creatures were tall and ox-strong, and they were better with both axes and teeth than they had been with their bows. Still Pazel felt no fear. And as he attacked he felt the rage and grief diminish also. There was no room for them; in his mind there could only be deeds. He danced through axes, judging, voracious, calm, and then he feinted left and whirled about to the right beneath an axe-blow and cut a hrath-mog's throat to the bone.

He did not kill again that day, although he helped Corporal Mandric do so, distracting one of the creatures with his charge long enough for the Turach to drive his blade through the creature's back. Pazel was not tired, he was not cold. Through his mind all the practice and the forms and the earlier battles of the voyage danced like lightning, and he followed without a conscious thought. Hercól had said it: *In the battle you make choices; when it is over you find out what they were.*

A time came at last when there were no more hrathmogs to kill. Pazel turned in a circle. A selk was hacking the last of the creatures to the ground. One dlömic soldier lay twitching feebly. Another selk had died upon a heap of snow, an axe still buried in his chest.

Then Pazel saw Thaulinin.

The selk leader was near the edge of the clearing, the two remaining *athymars* had him in their teeth. One dog had sunk its fangs into his thigh, the other his opposite forearm. Behind them, the dlömic commander stood with his back to a tree and his ghost-knife pointing skyward. Thaulinin was awake but not resisting. Within two yards of him, Valgrif lay still.

Lunja was racing to Thaulinin's aid, and Hercól was not far behind. Pazel sprinted after them, but even as he ran he saw Lunja fall forward, helpless and stunned. Hercól tried to stop as well, but it was too late: he dropped beside Lunja and lay still.

Pazel skidded to a halt. All three warriors had rushed into a trap, a spell-field created by the Plazic blade. Valgrif was another victim: Pazel saw now that the wolf was awake.

'Disarm!' screamed the commander. 'Throw your weapons into the gorge, or I will kill him here and now!'

'You muckin' bastard!' cried Mandric. 'We'll chuck *you* over that cliff, one little piece at a time.'

The dlömu shouted a word of command. At once the dogs released Thaulinin's limbs and pounced on his unguarded face and throat. Pazel closed his eyes – too late; he had seen it and could not unsee. He turned away and vomited. Thaulinin was dead.

When he looked again the dogs were standing over Lunja. The dlömic commander pointed at the gorge. 'Every last weapon!' he shouted. 'Or do you wish her to die next?'

There were no taunts this time. Thasha had thrown her arms around Neeps, who was staring at Lunja like a man deranged. Everyone was still. Pazel heard the distant cry of some mountain bird. He noted with a stab of disappointment that Prince Olik had fled somewhere; indeed he realised now that the monarch had skipped the fight altogether.

The dlömic leader, calmer suddenly, turned them a ghastly smile. 'I will not be counting to three,' he said.

Deep inside, Pazel felt his decision: the decision he would understand only when it was over; when everyone who was going to die had died. He walked to the cliff and threw his sword into the depths. Then he went to Bolutu and took his sword, and asked for his backpack as well.

Bolutu shed his pack, dumbfounded. Pazel tried to lift it from the ground, and failed. The pack was suddenly unnaturally heavy. Since the fight with the hrathmogs began Pazel had thought his strength inexhaustible, but it was deserting him quickly.

Not yet, he told himself. But he had to settle for dragging the backpack to the cliff.

When he was as close as he dared, he tossed Bolutu's sword over the edge. The commander watched him, increasingly confused. 'Why is the boy the only one who obeys? You wish the dogs to kill her? Very well, watch them, if you have the stomach for it.'

With great difficulty Pazel lifted the pack from the ground. '*All* the weapons, Commander?' he said.

'All of them! Is your whole company deaf?'

Pazel heaved the pack over the cliff.

'What did you have in there, boy? Stones?'

Pazel gazed at him, winded. 'Just one,' he said.

The commander froze. A look of terror came over his face. He sprinted for the bridge and dashed up the stairs, bounding onto the corpse of the ogress. Looking down into the chasm, he lowered his knife and shouted: '*Valixra!*'

The magic was evidently something unpractised, for he tried again and again, stabbing at the abyss and screaming '*Valixra! Eidic!* Rise, rise!'

At last he held still, and it appeared to Pazel that a painful energy was coursing through him. Pazel sighed and turned his back, staggering away from the cliff. He was feeling every wound now. At least every wound to the body.

The commander was shaking. His free hand made a grasping motion at the air. Then his eyes lit with triumph. Seconds later Bolutu's pack shot past the clearing and high into the air. The commander guided it with the point of his blade, in a long descending arc towards the clearing, where it landed with a resounding boom.

Then Pazel hurled the axe.

The hrathmog weapon was long for him, and very heavy, but he had swung it like a mallet, both hands over his head. It flew straight, and struck the commander squarely in the chest. The Plazic knife flew from his hand, and the commander fell backwards off the bridge, never crying out, and was gone.

Snarling erupted behind him: the paralysis spell had broken. Lunja had stabbed the *athymar* nearest her face, and the others attacked it from the sides. The last dog turned and fled, and Valgrif, his face already scarlet, pursued it into the trees.

Pazel knelt in the bloodied snow. The survivors crowded to him, praising him; Mandric called him a genius, but Neeps and Thasha just held his arms and said nothing, and Pazel was grateful for that. No hiding behind the danger now. The real pain was just beginning.

But there are kind fates as well as cruel in Alifros. Even as his friends embraced him, a shout came from the direction of the chasm. It was Olik. He was on the footbridge beneath the main structure, one hand braced against the chute above him, and the other holding a body to his chest.

'Help me, damn you all!'

It was Neda. She was drenched, and her skin was a ghastly blue, and her open eyes did not see them. But she was breathing, and in her mouth they found the shattered remains of a fire beetle. And when ten minutes later a fire blazed (dry wood in the tower, matches on their foes) she woke and asked for Cayer Vispek, and then remembered, and broke into loud, un-*sfvantskor*-like tears.

'My coat snagged on the ice,' she told Pazel in their mother tongue, when she could speak again. 'I was hanging there in the falling water. He came through and caught one of the struts, but the force of it dislocated his arm. He was bleeding too, but with his good arm he pulled me out of the water and onto the footbridge. Then—' She put a hand to her lips. She could not go on.

'He kissed you?' said Pazel.

'No. Yes.' Neda stared helplessly at her brother. 'He gave me his fire beetle. He pulled it from his coat pocket with his teeth. I tried to share it with him, but he shut his mouth and turned away. Then he held me against him, gave me all the warmth he had left in his body. Why would he do that, Pazel? For a damned soul? I was dead to him, wasn't I? Wasn't I?'

Cayer Vispek's body remained beneath the Water Bridge, and with great care they extracted it and brought it to solid ground. An hour later Valgrif emerged limping from the forest. He had chased the dog far across Urakán, but slain it at last, then staunched his bleeding foot in the snow. On the way back he had found Ensyl and Myett upon the trail. Neither woman was scratched. They had jumped the eagle together, and killed it with their swords, and when it had crashed into the pines they had leaped together and fallen through a lattice of needles and thin branches, which had slowed them so gradually that they had actually come to rest a yard above the earth. They had dropped lightly to their feet, and Myett had sheathed her sword and remarked how good it was to be alive.

19

Forgotten Prisoners

—◦◦◦—

1 Fuinar 942
289th day from Etherhorde

Captain Rose looked at the body of the man he had killed.

Darius Plapp was hanging by a rope strung over the main yard. There was a fair swell this morning: the body swung like a pendulum, and the cloud of flies about him kept getting left behind.

'Fetch a boathook, Mr Uskins,' Rose said to the first mate, who was loitering behind him.

'Oppo, sir. Justice is done.'

As he fell, Darius Plapp had jammed his fingers into the noose. The deed ran contrary to Rose's frank advice to the man. It had delayed his death, of course, but only prolonged his suffering thereby. The hands were still there, tucked under the rope, as though Plapp were trying to button his collar. His mouth was wide open, as it had been during his final week of life, tirelessly proclaiming his innocence in the death of Kruno Burnscove.

The hapless fool. As though his fate had hinged on the question of innocence or guilt. All that had mattered here was prejudice, the story the crew could bring itself to believe. That, and the swift elimination of any possible rival to Rose himself. As rivals, the ganglords had neutralised each other. Alone, either one could have grown into a threat.

Uskins returned with the boathook, and Rose fished the hanged man near. Then he drew his sword with his free hand and raised it high. 'Thus do we bury murderers and rebels,' he shouted to the tense little crowd. 'No prayers, no ceremony for a man who wished evil on us all.'

The rope parted at the first swing, and one more Etherhorder departed the *Chathrand*, far from home.

'Have this line down from the yardarm, Uskins.'

'I shall do it with my own hands, sir,' said the first mate.

Rose turned and looked at him squarely, for the first time in a week. Uskins stood contrite, calm, well-groomed. He had not looked so well since Sorrophran, before his conflict with Pazel Pathkendle brought about his first disgrace.

Rose detested Uskins, counterfeit seaman and transparent bootlicker that he was. But what to make of this picture of health? Chadfallow could not explain it, though he literally followed Uskins about with a notebook, hoping for some clue, any clue, to help him fight the plague. Since their escape from the Behemoth nine men and two women had succumbed.

Eleven *tol-chenni* lunatics, eleven reasons for panic and revolt. The brig was half full of gibbering ape-men, and every time a messenger approached, the captain feared that someone else had succumbed.

Uskins might just hold the key to their survival; therefore Uskins would be tolerated.

'Stay out of the rigging,' he said, turning his back on the man. 'Just have the mucking thing removed. Tell Fiffengurt to meet me portside. And send a boy with my telescope.'

Rose crossed the ship to the portside rail. When the telescope came he studied the island again. Dark, lush, horsehead-shaped. Some highlands, some sand, and plenty of fresh water giving life to those trees. More than that he did not know, although they had been in the island's orbit for two days: it was extraordinarily difficult to approach. On its southern flank there were reefs within reefs; on the north there were offshore rocks, and rollers that began in shallows eight miles out.

The waves: Rose could hear the long thunder of their breaking even here, twenty miles away. That sound told Rose everything he needed to know. The waves were monsters. Beyond those rocks there were no more islands – only the endless, pitiless Ruling Sea, all the way home to Arqual, that fading memory, that dream. Stath Bálfyr marked the end of the South.

There was but one possible landing: a bay on the eastern side. From a distance it appeared promising. The mouth of the bay might be rather narrow, but the colour suggested depth enough, at least along the southern cliffs. And once inside they could tack close to the south shore, and be hidden from the sea while the smaller craft went ashore. They could also put a look-out on the clifftops, where the view would be immense and unobstructed. If a vessel approached from almost any direction, save out of the Ruling Sea itself, they would have a minimum of eight hours' warning.

All very straightforward. Yet something made Rose hesitate to send the *Chathrand* into that bay. He ordered a longitudinal run along the island's southern shore, with every telescope in their possession trained on the island. The survey yielded few surprises. The woods were dense. The birds were many. A small shipwreck on a western beach might have been any two-master out of Bali Adro or Karysk or some other land; it was clearly ancient. There were no other signs of visitation.

Sandor Ott had been enraged by the delay, which came to nearly twenty hours. But when they at last returned to the mouth of the bay and Rose ordered a second, closer pass, the spymaster exploded. He barged into Rose's quarters without knocking, and even appeared on the verge of lifting a hand against him, a thing that for all his bluster and threats he had never done.

'It is Stath Bálfyr, Rose!' Ott roared. 'The location is precisely as we expected, and Prince Olik confirmed. The shape of the bay is perfect. We have arrived. What is there to do but plot the course and set sail?'

Idiotic question. They would have to land, if only to cut silage for the animals and refill their water casks. And they needed to take a compass ashore to calibrate the binnacles,* a task they had put off far too long.

'Binnacles be damned!' cried Ott. 'You're making excuses. You're conspiring with Chadfallow and your treasonous quartermaster to keep us here as long as possible.'

Rose had taken offence. He could delay perfectly well without the aid of any man.

'We found this island as much by chart and dead-reckoning as by the compass,' he had conceded to explain (how his father would have raged: explanations, to a non-sailor and a spy!). 'But there are neither charts nor landmarks on the Ruling Sea. If something we took on in Masalym has altered the pull of the compass needle by a mere half-degree, we could arrive many hundreds of miles off course – in the ice of the Nelu Ghila, for example, or in the centre of the Mzithrini naval exclusion zone. That would complicate your plans for the Shaggat rather more than an extra day or two of preparations.'

Ott had been right on a few counts, however. The island was Stath Bálfyt, and Rose did wish to delay. But it would never do to admit to that wish, to Ott or anyone else aboard. For even if the spymaster were blind to it, the fact remained that the *Chathrand* was more imperilled now than when the Behemoth attacked.

The unthinkable had happened: both ganglords dead within a fortnight. Rose had played his only card in hanging Darius Plapp. Although they did not realise it yet, the gesture marked the end of his control of either gang. They could run riot, slaughter each other, take revenge for generations of bloodshed on other vessels, on this vessel, on the Etherhorde waterfront. And then there was the plague, from which no one could deliver them, and the fear that their enemies might yet catch up. The one thing that still could generate hope and cooperation was the prospect of a journey home. If the idea ever took hold that Rose was delaying that journey, not only his captaincy but his very life would be in danger.

*The main, installed compasses of the ship. – EDITOR

Rose jumped. Sniraga was rubbing at his ankles. He bellowed at her, and the cat shot a few yards away and began to lick. That sound. How he hated it. Aloud, to no one, certainly not to the cat, he said, 'Where the devil is Mr Fiffengurt?'

But of course the cat had nothing to do with the quartermaster. Her job was to escort the rodent, Felthrup, who even now was sidling up to Rose.

'A delightful morning to you, Captain,' he said, 'and if I may, the Lady Oggosk entreats you to call on her at your earliest convenience.'

'Call on her? In her *cabin*?'

'She begs leave to inform you that she is hoping for a family communiqué.'

The rat was often nervous in his presence. Rose had no idea why, but it upset him like anything unreasonable. 'Speak plainly or be gone,' he said.

The rat squirmed. 'She is pregnant—'

'You're deranged.'

'Pregnant with anticipation, sir. Concerning the aforementioned epistle.'

Rose's hands became fists. 'I still have no idea what you are saying, and I forbid you to say it again. We are about to enter the port of Stath Bálfyr. Tell Oggosk I am unavailable before this evening, six bells at the earliest.'

'As you please, Captain. It is curious, however, that Lady Oggosk could be so grossly mistaken.'

'Mistaken?'

'She was certain you would take interest in this ... how shall I put it ... this *necropaternal missive*. But I shall not speak, I shall not! For it's quite likely that I should fail to capture the ardour with which the duchess spoke. The exigency, in a word. Yes, the exigency.'

'I would like to stomp you flat,' said Rose.

Felthrup discovered an urgent need to be elsewhere. Rose watched him flee, thinking: *necropaternal missive*. A letter. From his father. Another lashing from beyond the grave.

'Fiffengurt!' he bellowed. 'By the black Pits, where can the man be hiding?'

In fact the quartermaster stood just a yard to his left, waiting to be recognised. By his doleful expression Rose knew he brought bad news. 'What has happened?' he demanded. 'Tell me at once!'

Fiffengurt took a slip of paper from his vest pocket, and passed it to the captain. Upon it were written three names. Two were sailors, Burnscove Boys. The third was a tarboy by the name of Durst. From the Kepperies, like Rose himself. He knew of that family, the Dursts. Utter indigents, for generations. Rose's father had owned the land where they built their shanties.

'The men were strangled,' muttered Fiffengurt under his breath. 'The lad's still with us ... in a manner of speaking.'

Another plague victim. Rose crushed the paper in his hand. 'Where were the murders done?'

'No telling, sir. The bodies were stuffed in the forepeak. Old Gangrüne found blood seeping under the door.'

Rose stood very still. Something else was the matter with Fiffengurt, but he had yet to grasp it. The man was normally transparent. During their first crossing of the Nelluroq, this quality had made Fiffengurt's stab at organising a mutiny as obvious as a sandwich board hung about his neck. But there was a certain duplicity about him now. Something he was both itching to reveal and frightened even to think about.

Rose determined to have it out of him. He stared mercilessly, until Fiffengurt began to fidget and blink. Every one of his officers produced a background hum just by standing and thinking; they were the telltale noises of inferior minds. Rose leaned closer, cocked his ear. Fiffengurt leaned ever so slightly away.

'Which is it?' asked Rose.

'Which is what, Captain!' Fiffengurt all but screamed.

'I want your opinion. Do we enter the bay at this time, or not?'

The quartermaster swallowed. 'We don't know if there's seaway, Captain. The reefs—'

'Blast the reefs. Assume that an approach is possible. Should we enter, should we attempt a landing there?'

Fiffengurt was sweating. He chewed his lips, preparing to mouth some idiocy. Rose lifted a warning finger.

'I have you, sir. I do not wish to hear lies. You will come to a decision about what you wish to share with your captain, knowing his sacred responsibility to guard the life of this crew. No hiding, Fiffengurt. You will decide, and shortly. Agreed?'

The man was flabbergasted. He had prepared himself to withstand threats or violence, but not this. 'Agreed, agreed, Captain. Thank you, sir.'

Rose nodded slowly. Then he passed Fiffengurt the telescope. 'What are your thoughts on the Storm?' he said.

Far to the north, a band of scarlet ran along the ocean's rim. It stood about three fingers' widths high and was paler than an old wine-stain on a linen tablecloth. But it did not vanish with the sunset, and at night it grew starkly visible, and filled the crew with fear. They had faced it once before, except for the dlömic newcomers. It was the Red Storm, Erithusmé's great spell of containment. A magic-dampening, curse-breaking barrier that had protected the North from the ravages of the plague for centuries, if Prince Olik was to be believed. It had not harmed them when they passed through it from the North: indeed it had saved them, by dispersing the Nelluroq Vortex, the whirlpool the size of a city. But now—

'I've told you what I think, Captain,' said Fiffengurt. 'It's still there. And that's a wee problem for us.'

'You trust Olik? Even in this preposterous business?'

Fiffengurt took a deep breath. 'I might not have,' he said, 'if what he claimed about the Storm didn't match so well with Mr Bolutu's ... experience. They'd never met, Captain. They didn't get together and conspire. Mad? Well certainly they could be. But neither one of them had a whiff of madness about 'em. And why would their stories match? Pitfire, they ain't even two stories. They're one.'

Rose stared at the red ribbon. A single story, but mad all the same.

'One more thing's clear to me, sir,' said Fiffengurt. 'The Storm's much weaker than before.'

Rose looked at him sharply. 'You noticed as well,' he said.

Fiffengurt nodded. 'Captain, you were still a prisoner when we came upon it the first time. But I watched it night and day. It burned like Rin's own brushfire, sir. I tell you it's a pale, frail thing compared to what it was.'

'But not gone,' said the captain.

Fiffengurt stared at the distant light as if wishing he could blow it out, snuff it like a candle, disperse it like smoke with his hands. 'No sir, not yet,' he said.

'I will tell you something, Fiffengurt,' said Rose, gripping the rail, 'and may the Pit Fiends roast me for eternity if I speak false. This is my last voyage, my last ship, my last foray into any water deeper than my testicles. Should I somehow live through this I will commission a home in the high desert, on the edge of the Slevran Steppe, of the kind the savages make of mud bricks and straw. I will dwell there with a peasant woman to cook for me until I die.'

Fiffengurt nodded. 'The desert will still be there, Captain.'

But precious little else, he might have added. For if they sailed into the Red Storm they would be carried into the future: that was the spell's unavoidable side effect, the cost of protecting the North from the plague. Bolutu and his shipmates had been hurled two centuries forward. Their fate might not be so extreme: just one century, perhaps. Or eighty years, or forty. Long enough for every last person who knew them to die.

Rose glanced at Fiffengurt. Long enough for his Annabel to become a crone, if not a corpse. Long enough for their child to have passed through life without a father.

And what evil, in forty or eighty or a hundred years, would the Nilstone have worked, in Macadra's hands or someone else's? What if, as the ghosts insinuated and Oggosk feared, some terrible process had already been set in motion by the power of that Stone? That horror that had passed overhead, the thing they were calling the Swarm: what if the talking rat was correct, and it grew over

Alifros like mould upon an orange? Would the Red Storm propel them into a dead future, a murdered world? If he yielded to Ott, would they sail straight into the very apocalypse that he, Nilus Rose, had been chosen to prevent?

Rose touched the scar on his forearm. It was that mark that bound him to the rebels – to Pathkendle, Undrabust, the Isiq girl, Hercól Stanapeth, Bolutu. He shook his head. Two tarboys, a girl in britches, a pig doctor, and a swordsman trained by Ott himself. There was no escaping fate. The Red Wolf had declared Rose one of that misbegotten number. Of course it was insulting company. And yet—

All his life Rose had known that he possessed a fate. For lack of anything better he had long assumed that fate was wealth, a business empire that would dwarf his father's nasty little fiefdom in the Kepperies. Rose had pursued that destiny with single-minded efficiency, become notorious and indispensable, the captain who would stoop to anything for a price. He had moved Volpek mercenaries and secret militias, deathsmoke and weaponry and the contents of plundered estates. Emperor Magad had employed him thirty times without ever knowing his name. Once Rose had actually paid a huge sum to one of Magad's toadies, merely so that the man would point him out to His Supremacy at a ceremony in honour of the Merchant Service. No list of his many deeds, no flattery: just a pointed finger, and his name in the Imperial ear. The man had done it, and as it happened Rose was standing near enough to catch the Emperor's casual rejoinder:

'Yes, yes, our delivery boy.'

To stand still and indifferent as the royal bastard sauntered on, and the snickers of his fellow captains began, was one of the harder moments of Rose's life. Not long afterwards he had faltered, stumbling in the darkness of his father's shadow. Too little graft and larceny and you were beneath notice, a sap, unfit to sit at table with the mighty. Too much and they would wash their hands of you, forget they had ever needed you, throw you to the pack of lawyers they kept kennelled behind the manse. When His Supremacy had taken away the *Chathrand* Rose had almost stopped believing in his fate.

Then Ott had come to speak to him about a possible mission in the east, and his world had expanded as the old killer talked. *I did this*, he thought. *I made the Emperor take notice, and this is the result. They will give me back the Great Ship and I will use it to make them pay.*

At the same time the voice of reason had told him that Ott was a lunatic, and any monarch who relied on him doubly so, and for a time that voice had prevailed. Rose had fled, but the lunatics had caught up with him and placed him in command. Soon thereafter the intimations of destiny returned with a vengeance.

Somewhere between Etherhorde and Bramian, however, a second change had begun. Rose had found himself infected with a strange notion. At first it had been a mere tease in the throes of sleeplessness: a shred of a dream, the whisper of a ghost. Later it became harder to ignore, and now it throbbed like a blister. What if his destiny was not power, nor even wealth? The idea was so foreign to him that it was hard even to contemplate.

Power, wealth: he had known both. And lost both. And won them again. Even now they were at his fingertips – and slipping through them, as though greased. The *Chathrand* was his, but could be snatched away by mutiny or enemy fire. In her walls were hidden millions in gold and precious stones; but out here they were useless, so much ill-stowed ballast, chunks of metal and rock.

What if his fate was somehow not primarily about him, but others? What if the name of Nilus Rose lived for ever because he chose (late but not too late) to use his power to alter the world? To redeem it, in a word.

Preposterous. A vanity of the first order. By the Pits, he had just hanged a man to keep up appearances! Still, the notion would not leave him. There was a wound in the world, a sinkhole into which all life would eventually be drawn. That wound was the Nilstone, and anyone who helped defeat it would never be forgotten. It was a pragmatic path to greatness – and the only one, probably, given the time he had left.

'Delivery boy,' he murmured.

'Beg your pardon, Captain?'

Rose jumped. Fiffengurt was standing right beside him – and improperly near at that.

'Quartermaster! What in the Nine smoking slag-furnace Pits are you doing here? Is it your function to lurk at my elbow like a catatonic? Say nothing! Go and alert the men: we will enter that bay at the tide's turning. That is at one bell past noon, as you may possibly recall.'

Felthrup raced along the starboard rail with Sniraga creeping behind. His destination was Oggosk's cabin, but first he planned to seek Marila at the chicken coops. They were once more full of birds: not the round, plump Arquali chickens, those indefatigable egg machines; but small, sturdy Bali Adro wood-hens, gifts from Masalym, with eggs the colour of a cloudless sky. Marila had taken to caring for the birds, and was not above pocketing an occasional egg (so very cool, sweet, viscous, gummy, sublime) for Felthrup himself. But the rat was not after eggs this morning.

The door was closed, but Sniraga's caterwauls brought Mr Tarsel from his smithy to see what was the matter. Tarsel struggled with the outer door (knobs had vexed him since the day he allowed Greysan Fulbreech to treat his dislocated thumb) but opened it at last, and the rat leaped through before he could close it again. Tarsel cursed and shouted at him, but he had nothing to throw, and Felthrup did not stop to thank him, as he might have another day. Sniraga was left outside, wailing and scratching.

Felthrup hated the coops. They reeked like no other part of the ship. They had taken on some ducks, too, and even a few stranger fowl with swanlike necks and wattles below their beaks like globs of dough. These latter pecked at him, and their beaks were hard as hooves. All the birds grew hysterical whenever he drew near.

'Marila! Hurry, hurry, I need you!'

But Marila was not here. Felthrup leaped onto the grain bin. He rubbed his paws together nervously. Better to wait. Lady Oggosk could not silence two as easily as one.

They had at last decided: Marila, Fiffengurt and he. They would break their silence about the ixchel and Stath Bálfyr, tell the captain how he and Ott and the whole Empire of Arqual had been deceived. They might not believe it, and what could they offer as proof? But to do nothing as the ship glided into that bay – no, that was impossible. At Felthrup's urging they had held out for peace as long as they possibly could. But that time was over. Talag had sent no emissary. He was, however, sending ixchel in ever greater numbers back to the Great Ship, with orders to kill him.

Felthrup had never seen one, but he had caught their scent. It was reason enough to put up with Sniraga. He was, after all, the only being on the *Chathrand* who could swear that he had seen an ixchel since the day Rose ordered their massacre. And he was the only one who knew the exact location of the magic doorway, leading to the island wreck.

The stink of this place, the miasma. It hurt his head, clouded his thoughts. He rehearsed his confession, before Rose and Ott: *You were fooled. This island is the ixchel homeland. Your course headings are useless, a document forged with more care than ever you lavished on a forgery. You know nothing of where we will emerge when we sail north. Regardless of what the Red Storm does to us, we are blind and marooned.*

He could imagine the explosion. One or both men would likely commit murder on the spot, and feel it was their right. Violence first; then reason of a sort, twisted and mangled to explain their deeds. And fury, always fury: that most sacred emotion in the human range. How to restrain that pair of bulls? Rose had proved willing to subdue the spymaster from time to time, but who would subdue Rose?

Only Oggosk. She would have to be there when they spoke. If they could not bring the captain to the witch, they would have to make the witch seek the captain. And soon. If they waited until

Rose ordered a landing on Stath Bálfyr it would be too late.

'Bother the girl!' Felthrup squeaked aloud. 'Bother these birds and their mingled effluents! I will go alone!'

Then he saw it. Right there on the wall, between the ducks and the wattle-swans. Where moments before there had been nothing at all.

The Green Door.

Felthrup's heart raced. *So it is my turn at last.*

Most of his friends had seen it already: that ancient, half-height door, with an opening lever so corroded one feared to seize hold of it at all, lest it break. The patch of wall it occupied was the only place in the chamber not blocked by a birdcage. Convenient, that. And even more convenient was the nearness of the three-legged stool. A few nudges and Felthrup would be able to reach that rusty lever, if he chose.

Felthrup stepped in front of the door and sat down. He could feel his pulse racing. *Think. Do not panic. Do not be a rodent now.* Enchanted, perhaps cursed, the door appeared in odd places throughout the ship, vanished quickly, and did not appear again for weeks. Most of the crew had never glimpsed it; a few, like Thasha and Chadfallow, had seen it multiple times, and the doctor even logged the sightings in a notebook. Ramachni had warned Thasha to keep her distance. But oddly enough, the mage had also told Chadfallow that the door *must* be opened, sooner or later. That to do so could mean the difference between triumph and defeat.

Which story to believe?

Felthrup pushed the stool close to the door. He leaped up. The door was so old that cracks had opened wide enough for him to insert a paw. He bent his eye to a crack but could see nothing. Apparently the space beyond was dark.

Then Felthrup heard the voice.

'Help me!'

A chill passed over him. The voice belonged to a young man. It was shouting, but Felthrup heard it faintly, as though from a great distance.

'Help me! For the love of Rin, don't turn away!'

Should he answer? Should he run? Chadfallow had never mentioned hearing voices, and neither had any of his friends. Why was he, Felthrup, being singled out? Was it because he had already passed through the ixchel's magic portal? Or because of where he ventured in his dreams?

'Who are you?' he shouted into the crack. But his voice set all the birds to squawking so loudly that he could hear no answer, if answer there was. Felthrup whirled and hissed at the birds, then realised he was making matters worse. *Aya Rin! This will be the death of me.* He leaned his weight on the handle.

It moved. Old hinges shrieked, and dust lifted around the edges of the door. Now Felthrup heard the voice more plainly. *'Is someone there? Don't leave me, I beg you! I'm a prisoner in the dark!'*

Felthrup leaped down and pushed away the stool. He sniffed: the air from beyond the door was close, like a vault opened after centuries. Or a tomb.

He shouted his question again. When the birds quieted he listened. The man's voice came again: *'Save me! In Erithusmé's name I implore you!'*

Erithusmé's name! Felthrup rubbed his paws together in a whirl. *Don't listen! Don't be fooled, rodent! Go and find Marila and warn the captain of the ixchel threat.*

In Erithusmé's name?

Felthrup wriggled inside.

Marila chased after the captain, fuming.

'Listen to me, sir! Lady Oggosk is throwing a fit! Throwing other things, too. Cups and books and ink bottles and little glass figures. You've got to talk to her before she kills somebody.'

'She has my blessing, provided she starts with you,' said Rose, plunging down the No. 3 ladderway.

Marila pursued him down the stair. 'That's not all, Captain. Didn't you see Mr Fiffengurt? Didn't he *explain*?'

'Fiffengurt has nothing to teach me about that woman's hysteria,' he shouted. 'Be gone, girl! I have no time for urchins, married or not.'

He charged across the upper gun deck, and Marila saw that two figures were waiting for him ahead: one was the leader of the dlömic sailors, whom Mr Fiffengurt called Spoon-Ears. The other was Dr Chadfallow. Both men looked worried and confused.

Rose barrelled past them, beckoning. They followed him past the forward cannon to the door of the little room called the Saltbox, which Rose had given the dlömic officer to make what use of he would. All three men rushed inside. The door slammed. Marila stood a yard away and stared at it, hands in fists. Men and dlömu passed her with nervous glances. She felt very small and primitive and pregnant.

The door flew open; Rose stormed out. Or rather he tried to, but found Marila blocking his exit, a furious, dishevelled, black-haired little demon staring straight up into his eyes. 'I have to speak with you,' she said.

Rose lifted her like a straw and moved her aside. Then he rushed off across the deck.

Marila shot a glance at the two men in the chamber. The dlömu was leaning on the table, shaking his head as though overwhelmed by something he had learned. Chadfallow looked almost physically ill. He snatched up his medical bag and ran out of the Saltbox.

'What's wrong, Dr Chadfallow?' demanded Marila.

'What isn't?' he replied, not looking back.

Marila ran to catch up with Rose. He was talking to himself, rubbing his hands against his shirt as though he had touched something loathsome. He even sniffed them as he reached the Silver Stair and began to climb. To her pleas for attention he made no response at all. When they emerged into the hot sun again he made straight for his own chamber beneath the quarterdeck.

Rose hurled open the door and walked through.

'Keep her out!' he bellowed to his steward. The man was reeling; the door had struck him in the face. Hobbling forward, he made a gesture for scaring pigeons.

'Get on. You're a nuisance. Always have been. Go make trouble for somebody else.'

'You think there's trouble *now*,' said Marila. She turned on her heel and began the long march back to the forecastle.

At the mizzenmast she intercepted Fiffengurt, who was rushing aft. The quartermaster too looked as though he might prefer to avoid her.

'You didn't tell him,' she said, accusing.

'Tell who?'

Marila just stared.

'Ah, no, that I didn't,' said Fiffengurt. 'Captain Rose – well I couldn't, you see. The timing wasn't right.'

'We're out of blary time. We've been here for nearly two days. How long do you think *they're* going to wait?'

Fiffengurt looked sheepish. 'He was confiding in me, lass. He's never done that before.'

Marila shook her head in disbelief. 'You and I are going to Oggosk,' she said. 'We'll bring Felthrup; he should be waiting for me at the bird coops. We can't put this off any longer.'

But Fiffengurt said he could not possibly go with her until the ship was safely inside the bay.

'How can you use the word *safely*?' asked Marila, struggling to keep her voice down.

Fiffengurt too spoke in a strained undertone. 'We'll be no more blary vulnerable inside the bay than out. It ain't the same as *landing*, my dear.'

'I know the difference,' said Marila.

"Course you do. Well, the main thing is, we'll be hidden from any Bali Adro vessels, see? Give me thirty minutes; then you and I can have our little chat with the duchess.'

'What if Rose orders you to put a landing craft in the water *right away*?'

'That ain't likely. Now go stand over there.'

Marila planted herself near the quarterdeck ladder, arms crossed, as Fiffengurt shouted at the sailors and Mr Elkstem worked the helm. The manoeuvre did not look challenging. The mouth of the bay was a mile wide. The *Chathrand* had come around in a gentle arc from the south, close to the southern headland, and once past it they could see the bay's white, sheltered beaches, and stands of majestic palms.

But as they drew closer the forward lookouts sounded an alarm: whitecaps, which meant shallows, or perhaps another reef. 'Topsails down!' bellowed Fiffengurt, and very soon the *Chathrand* slowed to a crawl. A lieutenant came running from the forecastle: there was a reef, he reported, but it did not close off the whole of the bay. The southern third of the mouth appeared wide open. They would have to skirt nearer to the cliffs, but they should still be able to pass inside with ease.

Fiffengurt so ordered. They sailed on, but the reports kept coming: reef outcroppings to starboard, deep clear water along the cliffs. With each report they nudged closer. Elkstem and Fiffengurt exchanged a look.

'There's no drift to speak of,' said Elkstem. 'We can tiptoe right in along the cliffs, if that's what you want. She's a beauty of a bay on the inside, that's plain to see.'

'Yes,' said Fiffengurt, pulling savagely at his beard, 'all the room in the world, once we're past the cliffs. Not more than a half-mile to go.'

'Only if you *don't* mean to take us in, speak now,' added Elkstem. 'There's still room to come about, but who knows for how long? What d'ye say, Graf? Steady on?'

Marila shook her head emphatically, but Fiffengurt did not see her. Or chose not to see her. 'The captain's word stands, Mr Elkstem. Take us in, and round off mid-bay with her ladyship facing the mouth once again. Then we'll await Rose's pleasure.'

On a single topsail they crept on, until the cliffs were sliding past them a mere sixty feet from the portside rail. Marila looked up. It was strange to be in the shadow of *anything*, here on the top-deck, but the rocky clifftops loomed four hundred feet above the height of the deck. Even the lookout high on the mainmast was staring up at them, not down. There were great boulders poised at the tops of the cliffs. *Where they've been for thousands of years,* she told herself. *Pitfire, girl. It's not as if the ixchel are going to throw them.*

Nor did they. The half-mile passed, and soon they found themselves in as lovely a bay as one could ask for, holding steady on topgallants a mile or more from any point of land. Fiffengurt turned and smiled at Marila. She did not smile back. Together they went in search of Felthrup and Oggosk.

The rat was nowhere to be found. In the chicken coops, however, the birds were in a state of severe agitation. 'Someone's been here; the stool's been moved,' said Marila. 'Egg thieves again, probably. Fine, we'll go and see her alone.'

'Marila, dear, d'ye really think that's wise?'

'If you don't want to tell her, I will.'

Fiffengurt shook his head firmly. 'Ah, lass, there's no cause to be that way. I'll tell her, don't you worry.' But there was a tremor in his voice.

They could hear Oggosk screaming from twenty yards, though they could make no sense of the string of names, dates, cities, ships and bodily fluids, all punctuated by crashes and wordless shrieks. 'What's the matter with her?' whispered Fiffengurt.

'Something about a letter,' said Marila. 'One of those crazy letters to Rose that she says come from his dead father. Usually she just tosses them off, but this one's different somehow. Felthrup knows more than I do.'

Glass shattered against the inside of her cabin door. 'Dead!' screamed Oggosk, within. 'Caught by fishermen, washed up on beaches, stranded by the tide!'

Marila took a firm grip on Mr Fiffengurt's arm.

'Ninety-three years of bloated crab-nibbled corpses!'

Marila pounded on the door. Oggosk fell silent. After two minutes Fiffengurt said, 'She ain't going to let us in. We'd best try another time.'

He was smiling. Marila just waited. Very soon the door opened a crack, and one milky blue eye stared up at the quartermaster.

'Well?' she croaked. 'What have you done now, you old piece of gristle?'

Fiffengurt cleared his throat. 'Duchess,' he said, 'perhaps you've heard some of the debate concerning the name of this here island?'

'It is Stath Bálfyr,' said Oggosk.

Fiffengurt smiled, fidgeting terribly. 'Well now, m'lady, that's quite correct. Only it happens that things are just a trifle more complicated than we hoped. It's no cause for alarm, but—'

'The island's useless,' said Marila. 'Ott's papers were forged by the ixchel. Stath Bálfyr is where they came from, centuries ago, and they've tricked us into bringing them home. We don't have course headings from here – they're all fake. If we cross the Ruling Sea from this island we could come out anywhere in the North.'

Now she could see a bit of Oggosk's mouth, which hung open like an eel's. 'What?' said the old woman.

'Oh, and the whole clan's still aboard,' said Marila, 'the ones that we didn't kill in Masalym, anyway. They're going to do something and it will probably be terrible. Stath Bálfyr is the only reason they ever came aboard.'

Oggosk closed the door again. Fiffengurt looked at Marila awkwardly. 'I was about to say that, Missy. You beat me to it, is all. Well now, we'd best leave the duchess to mull this over, don't you think?'

Before Marila could tell him that she thought nothing of the kind, the door flew open, and Oggosk emerged with her walking stick, which she swung with great force at Fiffengurt.

'Traitor!' she screamed. 'Crawly lover! You've known about this for months, haven't you? That's why you look like you've swallowed a poison toad every time we mention Stath Bálfyr!'

Fiffengurt backed away, shielding his head. 'Duchess, please—'

'Don't speak to me ever again! Don't *look* at me, you lying, worm-laden bag of excrement! Move! Walk! We're going to the captain, and I hope he skins you alive!'

The corridor was wide and black. Felthrup looked up at the cargo stacked to either side of him: musty crates, huge casks for spirits or wine, clay amphorae nestled in rotting burlap, secured with ancient ropes. The air was chill, and the only light came from the chamber at the end of the passage, fifty feet ahead, where a single lamp dangled on a chain. The brightness of the lamp was slowly, steadily increasing.

'Sweet heaven's mercy! You're here!'

The man's voice also came from the chamber ahead, but Felthrup could see no sign of movement. He did not answer the voice, but crept forward along the edge of the cargo, keeping out of the light. The voice implored him to hurry, but he did not. Every instinct told him that he was in a place of unspeakable danger.

'Where are you? Why don't you say anything?'

Felthrup reached the chamber and drew a sharp breath. He was looking at a jail. Thick iron bars divided the room into cells: four cells, two on either side of the dangling lamp. He saw now that the lamp was an odd specimen of ancient brass, although it burned as brightly as any modern fengas lamp. The two cells on the left stood wide open, but the right-hand cells were closed. And in the nearest of these stood a young man in rags.

He saw Felthrup and put a hand through the bars: a gesture of joy or excitement, maybe, but Felthrup responded by leaping backwards.

'No! No!' cried the man. 'Don't be frightened! Please don't run away!'

In the cell next to the ragged man there lay a corpse. It was curled on its side like a sleeper, its face turned to the wall. Indeed Felthrup might have *taken* it for a sleeper, if not for a glimpse of one hand, where bones protruded through a translucent layer of rotten skin. The rest of the figure was completely clothed: heavy coat, trousers, headscarf. Felthrup had no idea whether the thing before him had been a man or a woman.

'It is too late for Captain Kurlstaff,' said the man, 'but not for me. Oh, please, come here and nudge open the door! There is no latch; enchantment alone prevents me from swinging it wide.'

Demonstrating, he took the door in both hand and shook it violently. When Felthrup jumped again he checked himself and smiled.

'Forgive me. This is not my real nature. It's just that I have been so long alone – Tree of Heaven, you don't know how long!'

'Tell me,' said Felthrup, glad to hear that his voice did not crack. He was examining the man's feet, for he had already discovered that he did not much care to look at his eyes.

'My dear friend, you won't believe it. This is the Vanishing Brig of the I.M.S. *Chathrand*, and I am its forgotten prisoner. It is a cunning and merciless invention: set but a foot inside one of these cells, and the door slams behind you, and cannot be opened from within – not ever. I have been locked in here since the days of the Black Tyrant, Hurgasc, who took the Great Ship and used her for plunder. My family opposed Hurgasc more bitterly than any others in the Kingdom of Valahren.' The man lowered his voice, and his eyes. 'He slew my brothers one by one and cast their bodies out upon the plain, where the jackals gnawed their bones. I wish he had done the same with me. Instead I was brought to this cell, in which no man may ever age, and left for all eternity.'

'You do not age?' asked Felthrup.

'Nor sleep, nor tire, nor feel anything but a dull hunger that never abates. I lie still for years at a time. The lamp springs to life for visitors; otherwise I lie in perfect darkness. For centuries, my friend. No one comes here any more.'

'But someone used to?'

'Oh, very rarely – and when they come, fear masters them, and they flee like cockroaches. But you, woken rat! You're braver than any human ever was!'

Or more foolish, thought Felthrup.

'But open the door, open the door!' cried the man. 'I will tell you my whole sorry tale, and show you other secrets of the *Chathrand*. Did you know that there was *gold* aboard, hidden in many places?'

Felthrup knew it perfectly well. He gazed back along the

corridor. The Green Door stood ajar, but the light of the lamp was so bright that he could barely see it.

'You don't trust me,' said the man, his voice taking on an air of desperation. 'Gods below, it is almost funny! Little rat-friend, do you know why my family ran afoul of Hurgasc? Because we sheltered woken animals like yourself. The Tyrant had a wild superstition that they were his defeated enemies, returned to life in bestial form. Madness, but that did not stop him from killing every woken animal he could. We gave refuge to scores of them in our family estate. I was *raised* by such creatures! But for every good man there are five who burn with jealousy merely because he is loving, and they are not. One day some mucking dog informed on us, and Hurgasc stormed the estate, and we fled to the wilderness to begin our life as rebels.'

'And this Vanishing Brig, who made it? What is it for?'

'The shipwright-mages of Bali Adro made it, sir – dlömu and human beings and selk, all working together in those days. No doubt they intended it for noble purposes, but they are all gone, and the ship has had so many lives and owners since. There is no escape from these cells save death – and that is what most choose.' He gestured at the corpse. 'Kurlstaff there broke his pocketwatch, and swallowed the pieces, glass and all, and so made his escape. Others did so before him, and their bodies were at last removed. Now then: will you not be bold, and free a friend of your kind? I tell you I was imprisoned for nothing. Why, I was never even accused!'

'That has just changed,' said Felthrup. 'I accuse you of lying.'

The man looked up sharply. Felthrup's nose twitched with irritation.

'Some of "our kind" read,' he said, 'and among those few, one at least reads history. The *Chathrand* was built five hundred years *after* the slaying of Hurgasc. To be precise, five hundred and three. And Valahren – well, really. In Hurgasc's time the name did not exist; it was *Valhyrin*, and would remain so for centuries, I believe. And when Hurgasc ruled in *Valhyrin*, "our kind" did not exist at all, for the Waking Spell that created us had yet to be cast.* But if woken animals had existed then, and your family had loved them so keenly, you might possibly have lost the habit of referring to those you despise as *mucking dogs*. And now good day.'

He would have liked to walk with dignity from the chamber, after such a speech. But in fact he was still terrified, and so he ran. The prisoner watched him, statue-still. Felthrup was halfway back to the chicken coops before he broke his silence.

'Your quest is doomed, Felthrup Stargraven.'

Felthrup skidded to a halt.

'The *Polylex* has taught you a little. But it yields its wisdom slowly, does it not? Too slowly to help you save this world. I can do better, for a price.'

Felthrup turned and looked back into the chamber. The voice had not changed, and the lamp burned on as before, but the figure he saw by its glow was not a man.

Nilus Rose sat at his desk with the curtains drawn. Propped before him was a small, ornate picture frame, which he had just rummaged from the bottom of a drawer. It was a portrait of three young women: the two eldest seated, the youngest standing before them. All three beautiful, distracted, docile as sheep. They wore identical gowns: the straight and formless gowns in which wealthy Arqualis draped their daughters, before sending them to temple, or to bridal interviews.

They were quite obviously sisters. Behind them stood a man with a broad chest and choleric expression; a man old enough to be their father; a man any casual observer would have identified as Rose himself. In this the observer would have been deceived, but not entirely wrong: the figure was Captain Theimat Rose. He was indeed a father – but to Nilus, not these women. They were his concubines, his slaves. His father had not bothered to conceal his

*Mr Stargraven's historical claims are, as usual, precisely correct and verifiable. – EDITOR

intention to wear them out, one after another, until their useful-ness as childbearers and his pleasure in them were alike exhausted, and then to find some other place, far from his sight, where they could age.

The eldest, Yelinda, had ruined the lives of all three. Poor island women, they had nonetheless had freedom of a limited sort, until Yelinda fell under the sway of a sweet-voiced, gentle-faced man from Ballytween, who promised all three sisters jobs in a wealthy household in the Crownless Lands, and instead deposited them in the Slave School on Nurth. They were spared the long tutelage in servitude meted out at the school, however. A young captain by the name of Theimat Rose, having just come into money by some swindle or other, grew excited at the thought of possessing sisters, something none of his peers could boast of. He had bargained for all three, and the price he settled on became another boast, though he tended to lie about their pedigree.

Before they reached Mereldín Island and the Rose estate, Theimat informed them all of the shape of their future. Yelinda would be shown to the world as his wife, though he had no inten-tion of actually marrying her or otherwise bestowing any sem-blance of rights; the younger sisters were henceforth mere cousins that he had taken into his household out of charity. They were never to leave the estate, nor to speak to anyone save the peasants who worked it; they were to bear him sons, one apiece, and to spare him even the sight of any girl-child who might be born into the household. During his absences at sea they were to dedicate them-selves to prayer, and later the raising of his children. He would not tolerate noise, sloth, disagreeable odours, despondency, laughter, tears, the presence of cats or imperfect table manners. He prom-ised to sell them separately, and 'into households that will make you appreciate what you have lost', if they should displease him.

Upon arrival he showed them a weedy spot outside the garden wall. It was where his own father had buried the bodies of two slaves. 'They tried to run,' said Theimat. 'Very foolish, on so small an island.'

Mereldín Island had some eight thousand inhabitants, and most of them appeared to owe money to Theimat Rose, including the Imperial governor and the Templar monks. His estate sprawled over a quarter of the island; his web of trade stretched over the whole of the Narrow Sea. Those who did not fear him found him useful. For the daughters there was simply nowhere to turn.

Nor did he soften with the years. Once he beat Yelinda for setting his evening rum on his desk without a coaster. After Nilus was born the man found the child's eating habits revolting, saying that he did not properly chew his food. But the more Nilus attempted to focus on the task the less he managed to please his father, who grew infuriated by the boy's cowed expression and stolid, terrified chewing.

One morning, when his son was four, the captain set a fist-sized mass of raw *xhila*-tree rubber in a dish in front of Nilus and told him to put it in his mouth. The boy obeyed, with some difficulty. The rubber was acrid and burned his gums. 'Now,' said the captain, 'you may practise chewing to your heart's content. But it will go very badly for you, Nilus, if you dribble or spit before I give you leave.'

He emphasised the point by placing a claw hammer on the table. Nilus began to chew, and found at once that the evil taste was mostly beneath the rubber's surface; very soon his mouth was aflame. His father sat at the far end of the table, doing his weekly accounts. The rubber stiffened the harder Nilus bit down, but if he stopped chewing for a moment his father looked up with fire in his eyes. Nilus knew that weeping would bring greater punishment than dribbling or spitting, and so he chewed, and swallowed when he could no longer avoid it, and sat very straight in his chair.

When the sisters noticed the boy's distress Theimat ordered them all to the outdoor kitchen, which is where they were usually banished when he did not wish to see them. After twenty minutes the boy's stomach began to hurt and his thoughts became wild and confused. After sixty his jaw hurt so badly that he tried to distract himself by driving a fork into his leg. Sometime thereafter he began to fight down vomit. That was when his father's looks began to show some interest. At length the man put down his pencil, lifted the hammer and drew near. He watched Nilus begin to choke, raised the hammer when it appeared he might spit. Nilus did not spit but tried to swallow the whole mass of rubber, and failed. He fell to the ground, the world darkening around him, and then his father took another fork and pried the sticky mass out of his throat.

'You will henceforth confine yourself to proper etiquette,' said the captain, wiping his hands on a linen napkin and departing.

When he was gone the middle sister burst into the chamber and carried the boy away. She alone had disobeyed Theimat and snuck back into the house. This was not her first rebellion. Indeed for over a year she had been defying him in two respects: by attempting to get pregnant by one of the farm workers, lest he sell them off as defective childbearers;* and by studying witchcraft with the same man's mother, crippled and nearly blind but still famous for what went by the name of 'the Devil's Calling' among the island folk. Whenever Theimat was away at sea, this middle sister would make her way through the plantation to that verminous shack among the fever trees, where a nearly hairless monkey crouched in the shadows munching sugar cane, and the wind that sighed through the cracked walls and rotting floorboards spoke now and again in words. Sometimes she would bring Nilus, and ask the blind woman to speak about his future, which she learned by feeling the contours of his skull. To this day Rose could close his eyes and feel those rough hands, smell the woodsmoke and rancid butter on them, wince as they squeezed his temples.

The middle sister learned very quickly, and became very strange. Her name was Gosmeíl. Three marriages and as many decades later

---

*A disease of the bordello had by this time rendered Captain Theimat Rose infertile, a condition he may well have passed on to one or more of the sisters. – EDITOR

she would become Lady Gosmel Pothrena Oggosk, Eighteenth Duchess of Tirsoshi.

The day Nilus was tortured at the dinner table, Gosmel resolved to murder Theimat Rose. She confided first in Biyatra ('the Baby'), the youngest sister of the three. Biyatra too wished him dead, but she was fearful by nature and demurred. And when Gosmel went to Yelinda, the eldest daughter not only refused to participate but swore to denounce them if they ever again hinted at such an act. Yelinda had played the part of 'wife' in public a very long time, and as Theimat's fortunes grew her own stature in the society of the island had increased as well. It grew awkward to beat her or terrorise her into perfect incoherence; he had even to dance with her at the Governor's Ball. In the end Yelinda had come to believe in the lie herself, and to treat her sisters more like the impoverished cousins they were supposed to be.

Nilus believed as well. He had long since begun to call Yelinda 'Mother', and firmly believed that he had sprung from her womb. This certainty lasted well up into his fifties, when Oggosk punctured it with her usual tact:

'She was *supposed* to be your mother, wasn't she? Because you were the first-born, and she was the eldest. Theimat wanted things that way: orderly, shipshape. He took each of us whenever he liked, but he intended to dispose of us in order of age. Therefore Yelinda had a job to do. Therefore she's your mother.'

'But he was there, Oggosk,' Rose had protested. 'You all were.'

'Pah. Your father left on a sea voyage before the pregnancy was two months old, and barely made it home by your first birthday. He never saw anyone's belly grow fat, except his own. As for the rest of us, we let the story stand. If Theimat believed one of us had coughed up a son, out of order – well, poor Yelinda would have been shown up as useless, and sold in a fortnight.'

'Then who was it, damn you? Which of you is my mother?'

Oggosk had cackled. 'All of us. None of us. You'll never find out from me.'

Whether or not Yelinda was truly Nilus' mother, she had grown obsessed with being his father's wife, and would never agree to murder. The stand-off lasted for years. In that time Gosmel's powers as a witch increased. Very early she learned to hoard that power, rarely casting so much as a spell to keep the milk from turning. All the while, however, she was plotting another end for Theimat Rose.

By the time Nilus was ten, Gosmel was almost ready to act on her plan. Then a day came when Theimat raped the bride-to-be of a peasant who worked his land. The captain pronounced himself within his rights, claiming that the (illiterate) man had signed an agreement stating that his debts could be collected in a variety of forms, one of them being carnal. Biyatra had been friendly with the girl, and that evening she herself went to the barn for rat poison. Her courage began to desert her before she reached the house again, but Gosmel was ready for that. 'I'll do it,' she said, taking the jar of lethal powder. 'Just keep Yelinda out of the way.'

But the Baby failed even in this. She did send for her eldest sister at the appropriate time, but when confronted by Yelinda she froze in terror at her own complicity, and could not make conversation or explain why she had called. Yelinda presently laughed and went her way – which happened to be to the liquor cabinet in the den. She poured Theimat's evening cup of rum and took it to him in the library. Then, exercising the privilege of a wife, she returned to the den and poured a second glass for herself. Moments later Gosmel heard the violent choking sounds she had wanted to hear – but from two chambers, and two throats. She ran screaming for the den, and arrived just in time to watch Yelinda die with foamy spittle on her lips.

It was at this point that Nilus himself heard the noises and raced down the stairs in his pyjamas. His first sight was his father, in the hall outside the library, lying in an odd position with a hand on his throat. Frightened by this apparition, he turned away from the corpse and ran towards the other voices in the den. There lay his dead Aunt Yelinda, better known to him simply as Mother. Over her stood Aunt Gosmel, howling with tears. Then Biyatra appeared in the doorway behind Nilus, and Gosmel pointed at her and screamed that she had killed their sister.

'I?' shot back the Baby. 'You bloody-minded witch! The only murderer in this house is you!'

Aunt Gosmel's face had twisted in a spasm of hate. She raised her hand as though gathering some force, and then flung it at Biyatra, and with it the curse she had saved six years for their tormentor.

Rose laid the portrait flat. He heard Oggosk's screaming long before she reached his outer door. There was little hope that the steward would turn her aside, and he did not. The greater surprise was that Fiffengurt and the girl Marila entered with her. No surprise at all of course was the red animal that snuck in with them: Sniraga, whose name meant 'Cowardly'. Sniraga, who had once been Biyatra, the Baby. Who had become a cat three feet away from him, the worst fright so far in the life of a child who had already suffered fears aplenty. Who was first a sister, then a pet to this unbearable banshee of a woman standing before his desk and screaming *ixchel, ixchel,* of all absurdities. This repugnant crone who was as likely to be his mother as the one she had cursed, or the one they poisoned alongside his father.

'I am not listening to you, Oggosk,' he said wearily.

'You mucking well should! You think their claim is so fantastic, so impossible?'

'I think nothing one way or the other.'

'It fits, Nilus, can't you see? They came aboard for a reason. They're not ignorant and they don't ride *any* ship without a purpose. I told them – *Glaya*, I *ordered* this ugly swamp-rat of a girl to bring me the book! Stath Bálfyr! It's certain to be in the thirteenth *Polylex*! We needn't ever have gotten ourselves into this unforgivable fix! And your afflicted quartermaster has kept the secret for months!'

'I am the one who is afflicted '

'Hang them, Nilus! Give them to Ott!'

467

'Snakes and devils, woman, can't you be *quiet!*'

Oggosk struck the desk with her walking stick. The captain shot to his feet and leaned towards her, and the bellowing began to look dangerous. Fiffengurt and Marila backed away.

Then the adversaries stopped together, gaping.

'What did you say, hag?'

'I said that anyone who sets foot on shore will be killed. By crawlies, or some crawly trap. What did *you* say?'

'That I have the plague,' said Rose. 'Chadfallow has confirmed the symptoms. In a matter of weeks my mind will be gone.'

Oggosk's screams began again, but they were short-lived. She collapsed, and the two men carried her to Rose's bed, while Marila ran for Chadfallow.

The creature in the cell was still looking at Felthrup, still waiting. Its head was as round and podgy as a newborn baby's, and from the fat cheeks two small, deep-set eyes twinkled in sudden flashes of gold. Large ears like withered yams stuck out from its head. The creature wore nothing but a winding-cloth belted at the waist and tossed over one shoulder: that and many rings with enormous, multicoloured stones on its podgy fingers. The body too was fat, but powerful, like some wrestler who has endlessly indulged. But below its knees the creature's legs became those of a monstrous bird, and ended in talons that rasped against the floorboards. Upon its back a pair of great black wings lay folded.

'You are a demon,' said Felthrup.

'And what is a demon, pray?'

Felthrup said nothing. More than ever he wished to run, to leap out among the friendly chickens and ducks and wattle-swans, to slam the Green Door and never look for it again. The creature smiled. 'Come here, and I shall tell you how you will die.'

'No thank you,' said Felthrup.

'Your ship may well be sunk here at Stath Bálfyr, and all of you drowned or murdered. If that does not come to pass you must either sail south into the death-throes of Bali Adro and the clutches of the White Raven, whom you call Macadra. Or you must continue north into the Red Storm, and be hurled into the future.'

'But the storm is weak,' said Felthrup.

'Oh, very weak, compared to the maelstrom it was,' said the creature. 'But you are forgetting something far more powerful. You are forgetting the Swarm of Night. *I* cannot forget it, however. I was here when last it burst into Alifros. I saw it, fled from it, barely outraced it with my lungs bursting and my wings so strained I feared they would be torn from my back. That was at the height of a war more terrible than you can imagine, and the Swarm had grown monstrous, bloated with death. Today it is still an infant, no larger than the *Chathrand*. If you had lingered in the open sea another day or two you would have seen it.'

'Again?'

'It is prowling along the edge of the Red Storm,' said the creature. 'There is more killing in the Northern world than the Southern, currently, and like a moth the Swarm flies to the brightest candle. But it cannot yet cross the Storm without great harm to itself. And so it prowls, impatient, waiting for a gap to open. When that happens it will speed to the battlefields of the North, and feed, and grow enormous, blotting out the sun, and plunging the world beneath it into a perpetual, starless night. There will be no stopping it then.'

'There is no stopping it *at all*, unless we get rid of the Nilstone!' wailed Felthrup, throwing himself on the ground. His fear of the creature was subsiding as he thought of the greater doom facing them all. 'We do not even *have* the Stone, and if we did we should not know what to do with it, and Macadra is using all that remains of her Empire's might to find it. She may already have found it. She may have killed Lady Thasha and Pazel and all my friends! What do you say to that, you lying thing? What hope can you possibly give me?'

'The only worthwhile kind,' said the creature. 'The kind that comes with knowledge. And here is some knowledge I will give you for nothing, as a token of my good faith. Macadra does not have the Stone. Your beloved Erithusmé has it – or someone she travels with.'

'My Erithusmé?'

'You call her Thasha Isiq.'

Felthrup sat up slowly, blinking. 'Thasha is a girl of seventeen years.'

'She is a mage of twenty centuries. The girl is a mere façade, like the one I showed you. But it is true that she has lost her powers. Otherwise she surely would have used the Nilstone, while she and it were still aboard.'

'How is it you know of Thasha's deeds? How do you know my name, and which island we have reached, and so much else?'

The creature gazed at him for a moment. Then he looked up, sweeping his golden eyes across the ceiling, and at the same time spreading his corpulent arms. The lamp darkened, but the walls grew bright – and then, with a brief shimmer, they became glass. Felthrup crouched in fear and astonishment: the floor beneath him was transparent, and the walls of the chamber, *and all the walls beyond as well*. The *Chathrand* surrounded them, but it was a *Chathrand* of flawless crystal. He could see through deck after deck, right up to the topdeck and the glass spider-webs of the rigging, the gleaming spires of the masts. He could look down all the way to the hold, and gaze through the crystal cargo and ballast into the waters of the bay. Only the people remained unchanged. He could see them in their hundreds, figures displayed in a jeweller's shop: crossing invisible floors, climbing transparent ladderways, lifting glass spoons to their mouths in the dining hall.

The creature lowered his hands. The vision was gone. 'You are correct, Felthrup Stargraven. I am a demon, though *maukslar* is a fairer term. And although I am a prisoner here, I am not helpless. Indeed I have powers that could be of great use to you.'

'I know what comes of that sort of help,' said Felthrup.

'No, you know only what comes of helping sorcerers, though of course you never meant to help Arunis. But consider what will come of *refusing* help, when it is offered: of standing on purity to the bitterest, bleak end. Not only death. Not only a lost world – and what a jewel is Alifros yet, despite the wounds she has suffered – not just these, I say, but the knowledge that you might have acted, but chose fear instead.'

'Was it Erithusmé who imprisoned you?' asked Felthrup.

The demon held very still. 'Some things you will *not* learn for nothing,' he said.

'Can you strike others from that cell? If I turned to go, could you stop me?'

No answer. The creature was no longer smiling, but his eyes still twinkled gold.

'If I were to bring you an egg from the chicken coop and roll it through the bars, could you make it float in the air?'

'I could make it float, or hatch, or turn to silver, or glow like the sun. But none of those would help you.'

'How would you help us, then?'

'Free me from this cage, and I will tell you where the Nilstone must be taken, if you would expel it from Alifros.'

'But we do not have the Stone. Can you bring it to us across the seas?'

'Certainly I could. Let me out and I will fetch it.'

'Along with all our friends?'

The demon laughed. 'What do you imagine, rat? That I will fly here all the way from the Efaroc Peninsula with that party dangling beneath me in a blanket? No, you must finish the task without them. Hold them in your memory, but go on while you still may.'

'So that is your counsel,' said Felthrup. 'To trust you, and abandon my friends.'

The demon shook his head. 'You abandoned them when you sailed from Masalym,' it said. 'My counsel is that you face the truth. You are outmatched. Upon this ship you are a tiny minority, protected from execution by the whim of that lunatic Rose. You need new allies, for the old will not be returning.'

'Liar!' cried the rat. 'You tell me Thasha lives, that they have re-covered the Stone from Arunis, and that after this miracle, a smaller one cannot be achieved? I will not abandon them! I will not set you free to steal it from them! I have sound reason to doubt you and none at all to give you my trust! I do not even know your name!'

Resolved this time, he raced away down the passage. He could almost feel the glittering eyes upon the back of his head. At the threshold he nudged the Green Door open and smelled the blessed, natural stink from the coops. Then the demon shouted behind him:

'Tulor.'

Felthrup looked back once more. 'Tulor? Your name is Tulor?'

'Another gift,' shouted the demon, 'and my last, to one who gives nothing in return. Go, and think of your choices – but do not think too long. Alifros is nothing to me. But for the likes of you it is everything. Where will you run on the night of the Swarm, Felthrup? Where do you think you can hide?'

20

Nipping the Tiger

On 11 Halar 942, as the *Chathrand* crept north between scattered islets, and Pazel and his friends neared the bridge over the Parsua, Empress Maisa of Arqual declared herself to the world.

She did it through simultaneous letters to her peers on fourteen thrones, from the Crownless Lands to Noonfirth, from Tholjassa to Bodendell and Auxlei City. She did it also through anonymous placards erected overnight in every town and city of the Empire she meant to reclaim. The announcements were explicit, describing the circumstances of her overthrow, the defamation of her character, the purging of her loyal subjects, the murder of her sons. And very significantly, it announced her marriage to 'Arqual's proudest native son', Fleet Admiral Eberzam Isiq.

But Maisa declared herself most clearly in the cries of the two thousand lean fighters who coalesced out of the still-snowy Highlands and swept down into Ormael City, and in the cannon-fire of the twenty ships that took the harbour at dawn.

She had timed the attack with exceptional care. Arqual had held little Ormael for almost six years, and its forces were entrenched. But in early spring the Empire found it necessary, or perhaps merely comfortable, to adjust its grip on the city-state. The new war with the Mzithrin was going its way: Commodore Darabik had led a second incursion into the Gulf of Thól – far larger than the one Isiq had witnessed on his way to the Crab Fens – and had lost far fewer ships and men than anticipated. In Etherhorde this was seen as proof of Mzithrini weakness* and a reason to accelerate their plans for conquest.

Thus, late in the month of Modobrin, six thousand Turachs were withdrawn from Ormael to Ipulia for training in mountain warfare. Most were soon dispatched for hidden bases in the Tsördons, on the very margin of the Mzithrini heartland. Others were placed on war vessels and sent south to the Baerrid Archipelago. The White Fleet had been spotted conducting exercises north of the angry volcanic island called Serpent's Head. There were even reports of Mzithrini vessels slipping east into the Nelu Rekere. Arqual feared nothing so much as an assault from the Rekere, which was too long and rough to guard completely. It was in the Rekere that the White Fleet had crushed Arqual's navy in the last war. Never again would Emperor Magad be caught unprepared.

But the first assault came from the mountains, not the sea. Maisa's foot soldiers, trained over a decade in the Crab Fens, had been moving into the sparsely patrolled Chereste Highlands for more than three years. They looked like peasants, not soldiers; and they had entered the Highlands by the rudest of Highland paths. Threadbare and shuffling, they had taken up not arms but agriculture, blending in with the mountain folk. Year after year Maisa's emissaries had moved among these villagers: boys in rags, girls leading scrawny goats, women bent under bundles of sticks. Every one an operative, passing the Arquali checkpoints with blank faces, fearful stares. Every one with a message for the dormant fighting-force: *The lake is filling, but it is not yet full. When the lake is full the dam will burst. Some will drown in the flood, but we will ride it. Listen, listen, for the bursting of the dam.*

On that decisive morning, Maisa's forces swarmed over the city's northern wall. Ormael had faced no Highland enemies in three

---

*A low standard of proof to be sure. In fact Darabik called for ceasefire after ceasefire during the second incursion, and the warring fleets spent more time studying one another through telescopes than pressing the attack. For the troops, who had faced horrors in the first incursion, this restraint may have cemented his popularity. - EDITOR

hundred years, and the occupiers had gradually relaxed their guard on the sleepy northern quarter. Even when the attack came the Imperial governor felt more embarrassed than afraid. Two thousand peasants? What sense did it make? Even after the redeployments of the previous month, he still had three thousand trained Arquali soldiers, including several hundred Turachs, who were each as good as five. The simpletons had not even slowed down to contest the wall itself, but had pushed deep into the northern quarter – looking for meat pies and brandy, no doubt. They were trapped. They would be slaughtered. Why had Emperor Magad condemned him to rule a land of dunces and suicides?

But the dunces fared better than expected. They were not seeking meat pies but the northern armoury, which they seized and raided; and the gates between the city's third and fourth quarters, which they lowered and jammed, thus delaying the arrival of reinforcements. They were also joined by a number of regular Ormalis, labourers from the tanneries and the docks. This was not quite, the governor conceded, a spontaneous raid. But surely it did not amount to a revolt?

Fortune smiled on him, then: twenty ships, the bulk of Commodore Darabik's squadron, were entering the bay in splendour – unexpected, but more than welcome under the circumstances. They were cheered by the nine other Arquali vessels still in port, and urged to land as many men as could be spared to aid in the city's defence.

The vessels did indeed land a great number of men – but they did not leave the port. Rather, they seized the cannon placements along the waterfront, and trained them on the vessels not under their command. At the same time, Darabik's vessels ran out their guns.

The resistance was bloody but short-lived. Of the nine vessels, seven were at anchor, with no chance whatsoever of running. The *Glave* and the *Vengeance*, two proud Arquali sloops on manoeuvres in the bay, prepared to fire on the new arrivals and were buried in ordnance. The *Vengeance* sank outright; the *Glave* listed, her stern filling fast. Out of the palls of smoke men came swimming for their lives, and the rebels were as fierce in their rescue efforts as they had been moments before in their attack. Nearly two hundred perished in that horrible exchange, the first time Arquali had fired on Arquali in forty years. But twice as many lived, and the other vessels surrendered without a fight.

In the city, men were rising, joining the tanners and stevedores. There was some hesitation: six years earlier, Turachs had swarmed into the streets like bees, wave after killing wave, and those who had resisted were summarily executed. But when word reached the city that *Arquali rebels* held the bay and all its ships, doors flew open by the hundreds, and soon nearly every able-bodied Ormali fell in with Maisa's troops. Here too the Empress had her partisans; here too there were those who stood ready to create diversions, wave the Arqualis into ambushes, lead Maisa's forces to the jails, which were bursting with political prisoners. By midday the governor knew that the half-restored Palace of Ormael would fall, and sent out emissaries to arrange for a peaceful surrender. By mid-afternoon the last Arquali soldiers laid down their arms.

It was a cool spring day. At the old Slave Terrace (where Pazel had begun his life as a tarboy six years before) the defeated soldiers were herded together in a mob. They had a look of desperation, although only the Turachs were chained. Some had heard that they would be handed over to the Mzithrinis, others that they would be run through with spears.

All that followed for good or ill (Admiral Isiq would later muse) had hinged upon a confrontation on Commodore Darabik's flagship, the *Nighthawk*, two evenings before the raid.

Darabik had spent the last six years gathering his most trusted officers into his squadron. Patiently, he had probed them, learned their gripes and sympathies, and slowly stacked the deck in his favour. To a very few of these men, his soul-brothers, he had even spoken of Maisa, and the rebellion to come.

Then a fortnight ago he had taken the boldest step of all,

dismissing the officers he knew would never side with Maisa, on trumped-up charges of malfeasance and graft. The charges would never survive review by the Lord Admiral; indeed, they would explode in Darabik's face, and very likely end his career. But for the present it was ideal: the officers were recalled to Etherhorde, and their commands passed to underlings promoted by Darabik himself.

The present was all that mattered now.

On the evening in question, the *Nighthawk* had veered a little away from the squadron, edging closer than was strictly necessary to the perils of the Haunted Coast. There the commodore had made them linger an hour, until at last a little skiff had tacked out of the darkness and come alongside. They hoisted up the tiny vessel. She was sailed by a crew of three ruffians, but there were two passengers aboard as well: an old warrior, whose face was immediately familiar to most of Darabik's crew; and an even older woman, whose profile struck a disturbing, dream-like note in their recollections. Forbidden portraits, fading memories of picture-books too dangerous not to burn.

The warrior, of course, was Isiq himself. He swung down from the skiff onto the deck, and scores of men cried his name – amazed, frightened, confused. Then he and Darabik helped the lady descend.

Silence fell, though no one called for it. The oldest sailors made the sign of the Tree. The woman freed her hands from the two men and looked the crew over sharply, carefully, before she spoke.

'You are not deceived,' she said. 'Your Empress has returned, and she will fight for you. Not for your glory – that is a chalice filled with brine – but for your well-being, and your children's. And for justice, which alone can bring them to you. You do not understand me yet: never mind, you will. For now, you must think on one matter alone, and try to face it.

'The usurper in Etherhorde does not love you, men of Arqual. Magad the Fifth has never learned love, though he demands it everywhere. Once he tried to love me, the aunt who raised him as her own. But his father was the Rake, the beast who tried to drown his mother, while she still carried Magad in her womb. The Rake, who through slander and mutiny drove me, his sister, away into exile, killed my husband and my sons. The Rake, who through his hatred at last drove Magad's mother to walk into a smithy in Etherhorde and procure a bowl of bubbling lead and gulp it down.'

Maisa raised her hands as if to demonstrate. Long fleshless fingers, swollen knuckles, veins. But her gaze was hawklike as she studied them, and not a man aboard drew breath.

'Hear me now. It is hate that has poisoned our lives. Magad is evil, yes, but his evil began as a canker, and that canker was born of hate. My brother taught his son to hate. When they drove me from Arqual, Magad was still a boy, too frightened and confused to know lies when he heard them. And years later, when he understood his father's betrayal, Magad was still too weak and frightened to reform himself. But he lashed out, and slew his father, and so doubled the hatred he felt for himself. He squats now upon my throne in a deathsmoke-stupor of self-loathing, and lets the Secret Fist decide the fate of Arqual. Decide *your* fate, my soldiers, and the fate of those who would bear your name, if only you were there to raise them. And there are those at work in this world for whom even the Secret Fist is but a tool, and Arqual a chip to be wagered in a larger game. I speak of sorcerers. This is *their* war, not Arqual's. They seek victories more scorched and savage than the vilest dreams of Sandor Ott. To them, each of you is but a pinch of black powder. You exist only to be burned. They are very clever, these plotters. But none of them was clever enough to kill Maisa of Arqual, and now their chance is gone.

'I am an old woman,' she went on. 'I am sick to death of pride and status and deceit. But I would fight for your children, who will love you as children should. Who in peacetime will sit upon your knee and adore you – parents, providers, builders of a world worth living in.

'Home, family, the bounty of love: they have all been denied you through hate. We need not fight the Mzithrin again. We need not seize the Crownless Lands. This war was sparked by Arqual's smallest minds, in loathing of an enemy that no longer matters. An enemy that is only sailing against us because we have played cruelly on its fears.'

She paused, coughed, swallowed. Perhaps she was having trouble with her voice. But when she spoke again it was as clear as before.

'I have been trying to convince you, of course. I am finished now.' Then she reached for Isiq's hand, and raised it high, and all who looked saw the lamplight dancing on a great bloodstone ring on the admiral's finger.

'This man I did *not* have to convince,' said Maisa. 'He came to me with the same purpose, the same fire. They betrayed him too, finest soldier of the finest navy in all the world. They tried to kill him and his only child – the Treaty Bride, Thasha Isiq. He has taken up my banner again. And I have taken him as my prince.'

There was an involuntary roar. Then Isiq spoke for the first time, booming, 'Silence in the ranks!'

Maisa dropped Isiq's hand. She stepped forward, unguarded, and gazed at them with neither fear nor hope.

'That was well done: you have just obeyed an order from your Fleet Admiral. But look again: he has no power, unless you choose to give it. And I am the same: without your pledge I am nothing. If you stand with me, you stand with the Arqual we were all taught to cherish, and one day this fragile world will thank you. Have no doubt: it may be our only reward this side of heaven. I cannot promise victory, but I can promise my soul. I am Maisa, your Empress, and in no thing shall I ever deceive you. But you must decide whether or not to believe me – and you must decide *here and now*. Choose well, men of Arqual. You hold the very world in your hands.'

With that the Empress dropped her eyes. The crew held so still that Isiq heard the waves sucking and sloshing among the fog-hidden reefs. Then a young lad stuttered: 'M Maisa!' and the dam burst, all of them taking up her name and cause and not a soul holding back. In the men's eyes Isiq saw a brilliant excitement, a hunger, an alertness to hope. *By the Tree*, he thought, *they've been waiting for her all these years.*

On the Slave Terrace, the crowd grew massive and disorderly. A few youths lobbed stones into the stockade where the Arquali soldiers were waiting to die. No one was quite in charge, but word leaked out that a boat had been dispatched from the *Nighthawk* with the rebel leadership aboard. The citizens of Ormael waited, grumbling.

Nothing could have prepared them for that moment, however. For it was left to Isiq himself, the most hated man in Ormali history, to declare the city not reconquered, but free.

He spoke from atop a fish crate. Sturdy enough, but it teetered underfoot.

'Six years ago I burned this city,' he shouted over the mob. 'Do not forgive me. I do not want forgiveness I have yet to earn. But with what days are left to me I shall right all the wrongs I can, and fight the villains who led me to that crime. I was a fool to follow them – a fool and a coward. It was a son of Ormael who proved this to me at last, when he refused to bow before me. I punished that boy. I hated him for speaking the truth. He told it anyway, and in his courage my own liberation began.

'Your freedom, people of Ormael, is no man's to give. But in the name of Arqual and my Empress, I bow to that freedom, now and for evermore.'

The cheers were not for him, but they were deafening all the same. Isiq waited grimly for them to subside, then spoke to them once more.

'Magad the Fifth will never bow to your freedom,' he said. 'He will try to steal it back, as he stole the Ametrine Throne from Empress Maisa. He will send great forces westwards to destroy this rebellion. Some will abandon him and join us. Most will not. Today we are like the little dog who nips the tiger. If the tiger turns and catches us, we die. We must be swifter. We must dodge and bay – bay loud and long, for all Alifros to hear. We must call a pack out of the forest, and stay alive until it comes.

'How long must we run? I do not know. But I know this: we cannot protect you, not yet. If we stay we will only bring about your certain destruction. The best favour we can do for you now is to leave, to draw Arqual's fire away from Ormael, and to harry the tiger from the bush. I do not ask for your aid. That is not my right—'

He broke off, abashed, and struggled down from the crate. This time the cheers did not come. Isiq marched stiffly away through their staring eyes, feeling less a liberator than a cheat. The little dog was running. Ormael knew better than most what to expect from the tiger.

At the back of the crowd, Suthinia waited for him. She was hooded and veiled, lest anyone recognize the wife of the second most hated man in Ormael, Captain Gregory. She bowed at the waist, but her dark eyes stayed on him.

'Well done, Prince Eberzam.'

'I hear your irony, vixen,' he muttered.

'By now I should hope so.'

She was laughing at him, behind that scrap of silk. Oh, but he wanted her. Day by day his wanting grew, and her utter unreachability did nothing to cool the fire. It had grown so unbearable that he had nearly asked Maisa to send her back to Gregory, or to King Oshiram's court in Simja. How could he, though, when Suthinia had become his most trusted friend?

How could he, for that matter, when her mage-craft brought him visions of Thasha? True, they came only through the dreams of Neda Pathkendle, and were clouded and cluttered and rarely about Thasha at all. But Suthinia *walked* in those dreams, and Neda was sensitive to her presence, and would even answer questions, now and again. Once Suthinia had sought him out at dawn, half-dreaming still, and placed a bomb in his hands:

'It was your daughter who killed him, killed Arunis. She beheaded him with Hercól's sword.'

Of course he'd had no choice but to marry the Empress. Tactically, it was a master stroke: now the restoration of Maisa, instead of fracturing the military, could be seen as a chance to exalt it as never before, by giving it a foothold in the royal family itself. And unlike a widow, a married couple could make any willing Arquali their child in the eyes of the law. They could reach into the populace and pluck out heirs.

And if his daughter was restored to him? *It could happen, by all the Gods. Thasha herself could one day follow Maisa to the throne.*

Yes, he'd had to marry. And Suthinia Pathkendle had to go on being a mage, in love with nothing but the mysteries of her calling. She did not have to keep watching him in that maddening way, though, or smiling furtively when he and Maisa departed for the same chambers at night.

Like the marriage itself, those departures were for show. Her tiny army, her foetal court: apparently they thought quite a lot about the old woman's need for a mate. 'They must think us conjugal,' Maisa had told him, that first evening in the Fens. 'They must never for an instant fancy that we might be divided. Be ready to perform, Isiq. A show of love inspires men like nothing else.'

But they were not in love, and they never removed more than a coat or shawl in each other's presence, and within their chambers they had separate bedrooms, always.

'Sleep with no one for half a year,' the Empress had said, 'and then confine yourself to servants until the war is won. And see that they're gone before daybreak, always. That's family tradition.'

His knee was aching. Suthinia helped him down the stairs onto the docks.

Now, in a fit of recklessness, Isiq shared those words with Suthinia. She gaped at him, then stopped to lean against a wall, shaking with silent laughter. 'What's so blary amusing?' he'd demanded. But Suthinia just shook her head, and dried the tears before they wet her veil.

That afternoon she slipped away into the city, alone. Maisa raged, and Isiq too was fearful: Suthinia's disguise was hardly foolproof. But she returned before nightfall, and bowed her head while Maisa shouted that no one in her company was to run off like a wayward child. When Isiq caught up with her on the deck of the *Nighthawk,* she told him merely that she had visted her old house above the city, and that the plum trees were budding in the snow.

He heard the misery in her voice. What had she found there, he wondered? A ruin, a burned-out shell of the house she called the Orch'dury? It was, after all, where her happiest years of exile had been spent. The years when exile had become belonging, when lead had transmuted into gold awhile, for this lonely woman from across the Ruling Sea.

Suthinia had looked him up and down. 'You're exhausted,' she said. He rubbed his face, wondering why she had to state the obvious.

'I defied your Empress today,' she said. 'If you wish to defy her too I can meet you below. It would be an act of the body only, not an act of love. You know my limits.'

'But you do not know mine,' he snapped. 'Out of the question.'

To imagine touching her when she did not want it. A kind of charity. Not in this lifetime, witch. But to his surprise he saw her eyes were moist. She was nodding, head lowered, accepting his rebuke. 'I meant no insult, Eberzam,' she said.

What did it mean to befriend a woman? Could he ever hope to understand?

Suddenly she looked up at him, challenge in her gaze. 'Is this lunacy? Is Arqual going to massacre us, and everyone who fights at our side? Don't tell me what you say to the men. Tell me the blary truth.'

Now he was the one who had to look away. 'We're vulnerable,' he said. 'By my count we have twenty-eight ships, including Maisa's hidden half-dozen. Arqual has five hundred.'

'And they'll chase us.'

'Pitfire, they'll live for nothing else. They'll pull ships in from the Rekere, they'll dispatch forces that would have sailed on the

Mzithrin. And they'll never quit while a single boat lofts Maisa's flag.'

'She has a plan, though? And alliances? All those dignitaries she smuggled into the Fens throughout the years? Some of them will help us, won't they?' When Isiq said nothing, Suthinia leaned closer, her face suddenly alarmed. 'Hasn't she confided in you *yet*? Pitfire, you're her mucking husband!'

'Lower your voice,' he growled. *And of course she's confided in me, witch. But if she hasn't told you, what in Alifros makes you think I'd dare?*

'It would be safer to disperse,' he said, just to fill the silence. 'Make them struggle to guess where our commanders are. To say nothing of Maisa herself. But if we disperse it may be impossible to regroup.'

'And if we don't?'

'They may box us in – sometime, somewhere – and crush us with a single, massive blow. It's as I said before: nip and run, nip and run, for ever.'

'For ever?'

'Are you deaf, woman? Those were my words.'

She turned on her heel, leaving him alone on the forecastle. Angry at her for nothing. For making him face the truth.

Isiq was shaking. Across the bay Ormael glowed in the red light of dusk. *Some will abandon him and join us. Most will not.* Freedom had returned to the city under the shadow of a second death. He turned away. The deck was in shadow; Suthinia was gone. Darkness had crept up behind him like a cut-throat. Darkness was coming for them all.

But hours later Empress Maisa asked permission (permission!) to set foot on the sovereign territory of Ormael, and when it was granted she took Isiq and Suthinia with her and went ashore. She left her guards at the docks, over the sputtering objections of Sergeant Bachari, and walked out into the throng unguarded, holding the elbows of her admiral-husband and her witch. The crowd swallowed them. It surged and grumbled, stinking of blood and alcohol and sweat. There were some hisses, no cheers. Maisa ploughed forward like a soldier through a swamp.

She took a cup of plum wine in a waterfront tavern, for that is Ormael's drink, and dabbed a little on her forehead, and her ankle above her satin shoe, for that (who had told her? Suthinia?) was the region's beloved pagan prayer: *Let this sweetness anoint me, head to foot; let me age not as vinegar but as wine.*

Word of Maisa's gesture rippled out from the tavern into the growing throng. Then she asked which neighborhood was the roughest in the city. When they replied that it was surely Tanners' Row, Maisa set out for it afoot. Laughing and amazed, the crowd moved with her. Block by block Isiq watched it grow, fast as word and feet could travel, until it seemed there could hardly be anyone in Ormael who was not making for the Row.

The squalor here was frightful. Blocks of rubble, homes built of scrap. Children watching from broken windows, thinner than castaways. Ashamed of what the Empress was seeing, the crowd kicked garbage out of her path, broomed away puddles of filth that nonetheless rushed back and soaked her shoes. Isiq looked at Suthinia, who walked a pace behind Maisa. There was fear in her eyes.

When they reached the poorest, shabbiest streetcorner, Maisa asked for a platform. A crate was produced from somewhere, and she let herself be helped atop it. When she was certain she had her balance she gazed around her sadly, and shook her head.

'Tomorrow it will be six years,' she said suddenly, in a voice that shocked them with its power. 'Six years that you have lived under the boot of the Usurper. You know what has happened to Ormael in that time. Slavery for some of you, starvation for others. A lean, bare, scraping survival for the lucky ones. Your wine stolen, your fisheries plundered, your shops strangled for want of goods. In just six years. Now here's an ugly thought: what will it be like in sixty?'

Then she looked over the mob and declared that if anyone thought Ormael would gain more by her death than by the war she had declared on the Usurper, that man should strike her dead.

Here. Tonight. A chance to do what was right for your homeland, she shouted, taunting them. Perhaps the best chance you'll have.

The throng shifted nervously. Isiq gazed out at the harbour. The woman was mad to provoke them; she didn't know the depth of their pain. He experienced a frigid stab of premonition: not fear, but awareness that this moment, like that one on the deck of the *Nighthawk*, was a fulcrum. They might well kill her, and thrust all Alifros onto a trail of blood and ashes. But if they did not: what new lands, what strange vistas would open before them, sweeping away into the future from this place of despair?

The silence deepened. The city of Ormael stood transfixed, a single mind contemplating an old, grey woman on a crate. Finally, slowly, Maisa raised her arm, as if to grasp a piece of the night. Her voice rang out in the darkness like a siren's call.

'Ormael does not choose to slay me, because Ormael is rightly named. The people of the Womb of Morning cannot be kept for ever cowering in the dark. I will have my throne. I will see a world where thieves and murderers are brought to heel – and you, and this night, will never in a thousand years be forgotten.'

By the next morning, her forces from the mountains had doubled in size, and there were more volunteers ready to join the rebel fleet than boats to carry them.

21

Out of the High Country

12 Halar 942

The soil of Mount Urakán was frozen hard as oak; the travellers could not bury their dead. They took the bodies to a level place south of the Water Bridge, and there built rock cairns over Cayer Vispek, Thaulinin and the other three fallen selk.

Before she covered her master's face, Neda set her finger in the blood that still oozed from his forehead, then dabbed the finger with her tongue. Pazel stood near her, helpless to ease her pain. If Vispek had died at home, there would have been a cup of milk in which to mix that drop of blood, and any Mzithrini present would have tasted it.

A hand on his arm: Hercól. The swordsman beckoned, then crouched beside Neda, who looked up astonished. Hercól pressed his thumb to the bleeding spot on Vispek's forehead, then licked his thumb clean. He glanced at Pazel expectantly.

Pazel made himself do it. He was disgusted, but then it came to him that he was honouring the man who had given him back his sister, and gratitude welled up in him anew. *For this the Arqualis called them savages,* he thought. *For this the Arqualis said they should be killed.* Pazel looked up to find that Thasha and Neeps had joined them. Without hesitation they tasted Vispek's blood, and Neda said calmly that she would die for any of them, and then they rose and finished building the cairn.

At the cliffside, Bolutu knelt and said a prayer to Lord Rin for the safe keeping of his friend Big Skip Sunderling, and the selk sang for the comrade that the *maukslar* had slain. Pazel looked down into the gorge a last time. *Ramachni, what's happened to you?* It had been hours since he took owl-form and went in pursuit of the *maukslar*. Had he slain the demon, or been slain? Had he prevented the creature from sounding the alarm?

Thasha and Hercól were looking at the body of the ogress, still lying in the aqueduct's flowing water.

'She was a miserable creature,' Thasha said. 'You could see it in her eyes.'

'Nothing but pain has ever issued from the Thrandaal,' said one of the selk. 'But the ogres had a hand in their own misery. I have heard it said that their leaders found fear and murder so useful in conquest that they came to think of little else, and at last fell into a strange worship of pain, even inflicting it on themselves. In time this practise dulled their senses and their minds, until they were left with nothing but an impulse to do harm, and a few grey memories of elder times.'

'Let us try to move the body,' said Prince Olik. 'It is too foul a thing to leave rotting in the aqueduct.'

Working together, the six humans, three dlömu and four selk just managed to heave the vast corpse onto the rim of the bridge, where it balanced for a moment before toppling into the gorge. As it fell, the cruel iron crown slipped from the creature's head and caught upon a jagged spire thirty feet below, where it hung like a sinister wreath.

'There's a message for the sorceress, when next she sends her creatures here,' said Lunja.

'Yes,' said Hercól, 'but we must be far away before she does. If Ramachni prevailed against the *maukslar* we may yet be undetected, but other enemies will be waiting for these dead ones to report, and sooner or later their silence will be noticed.'

He turned to the four selk. 'Which of you will guide us now? For to my eyes the mountains are still a labyrinth, and the sea is still far off.'

One of the selk, darker-haired than his comrades, shook his

head. 'It is not so far off now. But Thaulinin knew the roads best, and Tomid, whom the ogress killed, was second to him in that lore. I myself have been as far as the Weeping Glen, but that was centuries ago in my youth. All the same we may set out: there is but one trail that leads away from the Parsua.'

They rose and pulled their equipment together; Pazel and Bolutu armed themselves with the swords of the fallen. Then they turned their backs on the Water Bridge and started west, following the narrow path among the trees.

The sun blazed fiercely on the white mass of Urakán, rising above them like a great blunt horn. The cold was retreating; drops of melt-water glistened on the pine needles.

'I hate to mention this,' said Neeps, 'but we've lost our tent. Big Skip was carrying it.'

The dark-haired selk turned and looked at Neeps with concern. 'In that case we should make for the Urakán Caverns,' he said. 'There are supplies hidden in their depths, and we need only turn aside for a few miles to reach them.'

'Any detour worries me now,' said Bolutu. 'Hercól is right: we dare not linger in this place. Is there no shelter along the downward trek?'

'I have never heard of any,' said the selk, 'but I can tell you this much: if you hope to escape the high country today, you must move faster than you have done since we left the Secret Vale. Urakán is the last of the Nine, but even the lesser peaks beyond her are severe. We have no tent, and no fire beetles – and bad weather is coming; don't you feel it?'

Hercól shook his head. 'At home in the Tsördons I might be able to read clues in the wind, but not here. Lead on; the rest of us will try to match your speed. But remember that we must aim for stealth also. The foe that sees us is a foe that must be killed.'

They set off through the twisted pines, jogging along the narrow westward trail where Valgrif had pursued the *athymar*. The snow was deeper here, but it had clearly melted and refrozen many times, so that now it bound the land in a smooth crust that snapped like eggshell underfoot. Their slain enemies had broken a path, but their footprints were hard and icy. For several hours they struggled west, rounding Urakán, and in all that time they descended no more than a hundred yards. Pazel grew frustrated: the day was passing, and they were still almost as high in the mountains as they had been on waking that morning. But whenever there was a break in the trees he saw the reason for this roundabout course: the vast gorge was still beneath them, and until it diverged they could not dream of descending.

The divergence came in late afternoon, when from a rock outcropping they saw the gorge twisting away to the south. 'This is good news and bad,' said the dark-haired selk. 'The trail will soon start its descent into the valley, but we have not been fast enough. Tonight we must dig a snow-shelter, unless we chance upon some ruin or cave.'

They carried on another hour, with the lowering sun in their eyes. Then, a short distance ahead, they saw that the pine forest ended, and that the snow was mounded high.

'That's a funny sort of drift,' said Neeps.

'There speaks a son of the tropics,' said Hercól. 'That is no drift, Undrabust. It is the remains of an avalanche.'

They approached, and Pazel gasped at the spectacle. Across the trail, and stretching up and down the mountain for as far as he could see, lay a huge battlement of snow. It had obliterated the trees, and was indeed several yards taller than their highest tips. Looking up at the peak, he could see the vast hollow cavity from which the snow had collapsed.

'Our enemies scampered right up,' said Corporal Mandric, pointing out a line of footprints on the slope. 'I guess we'll be doin' the same then, won't we?'

'No trees to hide behind, up there,' said Ensyl.

'And no other path,' said Hercól. 'We must cross quickly and hope for the best. Keep your hoods up, and your blades out of the sun.'

They donned their white hoods and climbed the rugged

snowbank. At the top they could see that the avalanche was at least a mile wide, and ran straight down the mountain for many miles. It was like the line a finger leaves when dragged across a dusty chalkboard. Nothing stood in its path.

'Look there, in the next valley,' said one of the selk, pointing. 'Can you see two roads converging, and four standing stones? That is the Isima Crossroads, where we are bound.'

Pazel could just make out the four stones, which were grouped together in a square. Then the selk hissed and drew everyone down. 'Soldiers!' they said. 'Dlömic soldiers! They were hidden by the stones.'

'I cannot see them,' said Lunja. 'I can barely see the stones themselves.'

'Selk eyes are sharper than our own,' said Bolutu, 'and that is a good thing today, if it means that they will not be able to spot us either.'

'Unless one of them produces a telescope,' said Hercól. 'Move along.'

'Just a moment,' said Thasha. She pointed down the length of the avalanche. 'Is *that* our trail, by any luck?'

Pazel shielded his eyes. Far down the slope, a second line of foot-prints crossed the ribbon of snow. The dark-haired selk shielded his eyes. 'Yes,' he said at last, 'that is the second switchback, and there is a third below it, much further, which perhaps you cannot see. Eventually there must be a fourth.'

'A shortcut?' said Lunja dubiously.

'It would be that,' said the selk, studying the slope. 'There are some small snow-ledges, eight- or ten-foot drops at the most. That is probably why our enemies did not climb it themselves. But they would not hinder our descent. We could save a day's march by that path.'

'And get spotted, and killed,' said Pazel. 'Nice idea, Thasha, but we're better off under the trees,'

'Some days you're thick as cold porridge, mate,' said Neeps. He pointed back down the slope they had just ascended. 'We can walk along the edge of the avalanche, and stay hidden from anyone in that valley. And after sunset we can climb up here and carry on.'

'What, in the *dark*?' cried Mandric.

'In the dark,' said Olik, nodding. 'Yes, by damn, that's a fine idea. This snow is packed: that will make for better footing than this trail.'

'And that bad weather you say is coming?' demanded the Turach.

'All the more reason to descend quickly,' said Hercól, 'and along the path of the snowslide we can at least be confident of not losing our way. But you are right to be wary, Mandric. Tonight we must tie ourselves together as before.'

It was decided. They retreated halfway down the snow mass, until its bulk hid them from the valley, and started straight down the mountain. The angle of the snow made walking difficult, but they were heartened by the thought of escaping the mountains sooner, and even the approach of nightfall did not dampen their spirits. *Better to walk through the night than to try bedding down in this cold,* Pazel thought. But the wind was rising, and the selk looked anxiously over their shoulders at Urakán.

As darkness fell they climbed the snow ridge again. Once tied together they began to feel their way downhill, with the sharp-eyed ixchel on the shoulders of the selk leading the way. While a little light remained they made steady progress, never straying far from the edge of the avalanche, and before long they crossed the first switchback. The moons were hidden by the peaks, but the starlight helped Pazel find his footing, and now and then a selk would look back at him with a glowing blue eye. They dropped from several ten-foot ledges without incident, although letting himself fall into darkness frightened Pazel more than he cared to admit. *Enough!* he thought, after landing hard for the third time. *Someone can blary well strike a match at the bottom next time, so that we know how far we're going to fall.*

They reached the second switchback and pressed on. But shortly thereafter the wind surged, cold and brutal, and snow began to fall. Pazel was appalled at the speed of the storm's arrival. Before any of them could speak they were staggering and shielding their eyes from the driven snow.

'Down, down to the trees!' roared Hercól. 'Hold fast to the ixchel! Valgrif, keep that dog beside you!'

They fled the open surface of the avalanche and began to burrow into its side. They used their picks, their scabbards, their bare hands. It was much harder than digging into the fresh powder on Isarak: this was old, dense snow, and many a broken pine lay buried within it, and there was no light at all. Meanwhile the storm became a blizzard, the snow slashing horizontally, the brittle pines crashing around them and the wind like a throng of tortured souls.

Finally they were all out of the blast. They had dug a cramped burrow, mounding the excavated snow into a wall and propping branches against the opening to block at least part of the wind. But they were blind and soaked. The selk wine went around, but when Pazel's turn came he found that he was shaking uncontrollably, and he spilled more down his chin than he managed to swallow. 'Dry yourselves!' said Hercól. 'Use the cloths from the selk. Use anything you like, but do it now.' Pazel's cloth was at his neck. The outer layer was damp, but within its folds it was, amazingly, dry. He rubbed it frantically over his limbs, and a little feeling came back into them.

'I have spread a canvas on the snow,' said Hercól. 'Squeeze onto it, the closer the better.'

'Night Gods!' shouted Corporal Mandric. 'Mr Bolutu, your pack is hot! The blary Nilstone's giving off heat!'

'Do not warm yourselves by the Nilstone!' said the selk. 'Its heat is illusory; the old stories tell of just such a snare. It cannot warm you; it can only scald and kill. If Arpathwin were here he would explain.'

'Well he ain't here,' growled the Turach, squirming, 'and I don't need a mage to tell me hot from cold. Give your pack here, Bolutu; let me move it to the centre. We'll see who don't warm his hands.'

'*Stay away from the Stone!*'

It was Thasha – and it was not. Her voice had come out with

493

more ferocity than ever Valgrif put into a snarl. Mandric froze, and neither he nor anyone reached in Bolutu's direction again.

Pazel had been cold before, but now he understood that it had only been a tease. This was agony, and they were all in it together, moaning, blind. Even the selk were quietly shaking. Hercól made them report one by one: were their toes dry? Were their heads covered tightly? Were they all sharply awake?

'I've been more so,' said Myett.

'Then sleep – if you never mean to wake,' snapped Hercól. 'Where are you, crawlies? Come here.'

In the ixchel tongue, Pazel heard the women laugh grimly. 'He's only trying to provoke us, to keep us alert and alive,' said Ensyl.

'Of course,' said Myett. 'Do you know, sister, I could almost love this man.'

'But I do not love his armpit,' Ensyl replied.

Then Hercól passed out dried fruit and seed cakes and hazel-nuts and hard black bread. 'Eat!' he said. 'The food is coal, your stomach is a furnace; you will see how fast it burns away.'

'How long until daylight?' asked Thasha.

'Long enough. Chew your food.'

'Pitfire, now he thinks he's Captain Rose,' muttered Neeps.

It hurt to laugh. It hurt to breathe, to move, to refrain from moving. Someone (who cared who) had taken Pazel in a bear hug; Pazel himself held tight to Thasha, and found that she in turn had wrapped herself around Valgrif, who had curled into a ball. Pazel heard Neeps and Lunja whispering together – insults, surly apologies, then softer words he tried not to hear. Time slowed, as if they were trapped in some diabolical ceremony, sustained for cruelty's sake and nothing more. They held one another. Little by little the howling of the storm died away.

When the selk declared that dawn had arrived Pazel did not believe them: it was still dark as pitch. But then the nest of limbs and bodies broke apart (cramped muscles, fresh cries of pain) and light poured in suddenly from one side. The storm had piled another eight feet of powder against the side of the avalanche.

They crawled out, dazzled, into bright sun and crisp, still air.

The storm had left its mark. The humans had cold blisters on their hands and feet, and some of them were bleeding. For the dlömu matters were worse: their skin had cracked in places, and the blood in the wounds had frozen into tiny crystals that fell out when they moved, like pink salt.

'The caves would have protected us,' said Hercól. 'I was wrong to insist on this course of action.'

'No, swordsman,' said Prince Olik. 'If we had lingered on the mountaintop, we would still be facing the whole descent, and under a much greater depth of snow. All this day we should have spent ploughing through it, hip-deep or deeper, only to reach the spot where we stand now.'

Hercól nodded, but he did not seem much inclined to look at the bright side. 'We have won back a little time. We must win back more. Let us walk for an hour before we breakfast; it will do us good to move.'

They struggled down along the side of the avalanche, wading through the fresh snow like bathers in the surf. The trail's third switchback was of course quite lost to sight, but the selk found it anyway by the ever-so-slightly wider spacing between the trees. They followed it away from the peak, steeply downhill. The air warmed, their limbs warmed, and gradually the depth of snow decreased.

Much of that day they walked in silence – around the edge of a frozen lake, through a forest of strange evergreens that smelled of ginger, along the edge of an ancient wall that ran for miles through the foothills: one more defence breached by the ogres of the Thrandaal. Again and again Pazel found himself scanning the skies. He saw any number of vultures, crows and woodpeckers, but no owl, no Ramachni.

The old wall became still more ruined, and the travellers picked their way between the tumbled stones. At one point Pazel found himself and Neeps walking a little apart from the others. He glanced around surreptitiously. Then he whispered in Sollochi, Neeps' mother tongue.

'Listen, mate, I need to tell you something. You, and no one else.'

Neeps blinked. 'Pitfire. What?'

'That night at the Demon's Court, when I spoke to Erithusmé. I told you most of what she said. But just before she vanished she told me something strange: that there's another ... power, hidden on the *Chathrand*. The mage didn't want to tell me. I had to badger her something fierce.'

'What kind of power?' said Neeps. 'Do you mean another way to bring her back?'

'No, she'd have been more keen on that,' said Pazel, 'and besides, she was obsessed with Thasha breaking through that wall inside her. As far as Erithusmé's concerned, that's the *only* right way now. This other power is something dangerous, something mad. You remember the spot on the berth deck, where I used to sling my hammock?'

'The stanchion with the copper nails.'

Pazel nodded. 'She told me to bring Thasha to that very spot. And nothing more. "*When Thasha is standing there she will know what to do.*" That's it. A moment later she was gone.'

Neeps was clearly struggling for calm. 'You mean,' he said, 'that you've not told *anyone*? Not Ramachni, not Hercól?'

'Just you,' said Pazel. 'Maybe we should tell them. But what if they say something to Thasha? She's the problem, don't you see? If Thasha knew, she'd want to use this thing as soon as we set foot on the *Chathrand*. Even if it killed her.'

'She is stubborn. Like a blue-blooded mule. And Pitfire, those copper nails? She must have seen 'em before.'

Pazel looked at him sidelong. 'Don't be dense, mate. The compartment's always full of bare-assed tarboys.'

They almost laughed. Pazel needed a laugh. But he wouldn't let himself, not now. The laughter could too easily spill into tears.

'If something happens to me—'

'Nothing's going to happen to you, Pazel.'

'—and you take her there alone, please – make her be careful.

Erithusmé was very clear on that point: whatever's hidden there is a last resort.'

Neeps gave his promise, and they trudged on into the lengthening day. The ruins ended; the land grew flat, and the forest rose about them tall and ancient and seemingly at peace. Suddenly Valgrif stopped, rigid. He lowered his muzzle and sniffed, then showed his fangs.

'Dogs,' he said. '*Athymars.* They passed here in the night, or very early this morning.'

'Many?' asked Neda.

'Many,' said the wolf. 'A large hunting pack, twenty or more. But they must be far away now, or well hidden; otherwise I should be able to catch their scent on the wind, not just here where their flanks rubbed against trees.'

Pazel felt as if someone had just broken a cane across his back. *Twenty of those mucking creatures!* 'So what now?' he said.

'Eat,' said Valgrif.

'I beg your pardon?'

The wolf looked at them urgently. 'Eat, eat for several hours' marching. Then wash your faces and hands, and wash your mouths out with snow, and bury the place where you spit. And you dlömu, change the dressing on your bandages. You must bury the old ones here, along with anything soiled or food-stained.'

'What's all this about?' asked Corporal Mandric.

'Staying alive,' said the wolf. 'A pack that size is far more dangerous than what we faced at the bridge. If they find us, they will kill us – and they *will* find us, if they catch our scent. They would pay no heed to a single wolf, but they will know the smell of dlömic blood. And your food's reek is unlike anything in this forest. You must remove any trace of it – and wash your hair, too, if you can stand the cold.'

'We can stand it,' said Lunja firmly. 'We saw what the *athymars* can do with those fangs.'

They ate, and scrubbed with snow, and buried what Valgrif had told them to bury. Then they set off, more guarded than ever. The air beneath the giant trees was still and quiet. Valgrif ranged far ahead, and the noiseless selk followed, just near enough to keep the party in sight.

For nearly an hour they crept without incident through the forest, and heard no sound but the cawing of crows. Then Valgrif loped back among them. 'Something is wrong,' he said. 'I can smell the dogs: they are much nearer than before, but the scent is weak, as though some of them had disappeared. Perhaps the pack has divided.'

'Or dug in?' suggested Pazel. 'To ambush us?'

'Twenty *athymars* would not wait for an ambush,' said the wolf. 'They would simply tear us to pieces. We must bear north, away from their scent.'

He moved on, out of sight, and the party followed as before. Hercól and the selk archers held their bows at the ready; the others walked with their hands upon their swords. The snow cover was by now quite thin, and they could hear the crackle of leaves and sticks beneath their feet.

Pazel winced at every sound. He glanced up at the tall pines around them. The lowest branches were twenty feet above their heads.

Then Valgrif snarled. Pazel turned and saw a dog's shape flashing towards the wolf between the dark trunks. A second followed. Hercól whirled around, drawing his bow as he did so. The selk too were taking aim.

'Don't fire!'

It was a selk's voice, shouting from far off in the trees. The archers paused, and for an instant Pazel feared some trick, for the dogs had just closed on Valgrif. But they were not dogs, they were ash-grey wolves, and they greeted the black creature with whimpers of joy.

'Kallan! Rimkal!' barked Valgrif. 'Comrades, these are my sons!'

The wolves ran in circles, yipping and prancing. They were woken, like the creatures at the temple in Uláramyth, and they greeted the travellers with great courtesy. Then Pazel heard the four selk in their party crying out with joy.

'Kirishgán!' they shouted. 'Fire's child! Kinsman!'

For it was he. Pazel almost cried out as well – but a dark thought made him hold his tongue. Everything Thaulinin had told him about the selk way of death rose suddenly in his mind. Kirishgán, meanwhile, rushed forward and embraced his fellow selk, then turned and looked at the other travellers with delight.

'Hail, Olik, prince and brother! I feared for you, when I heard that you had defied the sorceress.' Kirishgán's eyes moved to Pazel. '*Smythídor*,' he said, 'how I hoped we would meet again.'

'Then it's you?' said Pazel. 'The ... *whole* you?'

'We selk are whole but once,' said Kirishgán, 'and for me that time is yet to come. But yes, Pazel, I am flesh and blood. And here are your family! Sister Neda, brothers Neeps and Hercól, Thasha Isiq, who has palmed your heart.'

Pazel blushed. He had spoken of them all to Kirishgán, over tea in Vasparhaven Temple. And of course the selk remembered. *Brothers:* that was exactly right, of course, and so was what he said of Thasha. So right that Pazel couldn't face her, in fact. 'Where have you been, Kirishgán?' he asked.

'Among Nólcindar's people, whom I met in the West Dells of the Ansyndra. For eight days and nights we have led the Ravens on a merry chase, away from Uláramyth and the Nine Peaks. Hundreds there were, but we have reduced the count.'

'And the *athymars*?' asked Valgrif.

'Slain, father,' said one of the wolves. 'They were scouting this valley from Urakán to the Weeping Glen, and letting no creature pass. But at nightfall they always congregated here, and last night we fell upon them during the storm. Rimkal and I tore six between us, and the selk killed the rest. We buried the pack not far from here, but by the smell I think some scavenger has found the grave and dug them out again.'

'Where has Nólcindar gone?' asked Thasha.

'To the Ilidron Coves,' said Kirishgán. 'When we saw the extent of the forces arrayed against you, we knew that someone had to run ahead and ready the *Promise* for the open sea. There will be no time to waste when you arrive with the Nilstone. We three stayed behind, and sought you in the mountains, for we guessed that you would cross the Parsua by the Water Bridge. We were still far south of Urakán, though, and you crossed before we could come to your aid. There are still many hrathmogs in the southern peaks. And when at last we came to the last mountain before the Nine, we looked down on a terrible sight: an eguar fighting a demonic creature, a *maukslar* probably. More worrying still, the eguar was our loyal Sitroth, who had sworn never to leave the North Door of the Vale unguarded.'

The others told him at once of their own battle with the creature. 'Sitroth attacks me,' said Prince Olik . 'Then a demon attacks us all, and is driven off by Ramachni. And now Sitroth and the demon fight each other. How to make sense of it all?'

'But saw you nothing of our mage?' said Bolutu. 'No owl, no mink, no sign of spellcraft?'

'We surely missed a great deal,' said Kirishgán. 'The battle was scorching trees and melting snow, great clouds of steam were rising. We could see the path of destruction leading back along the Parsua Gorge. The *maukslar* lashed out with teeth and claws and fire: it was the faster of the two. Many times it struck like a snake, and recoiled out of reach. But Sitroth's fire burned hotter than the demon's, and its bite was deadly. Every blow it landed did terrible damage. At last the *maukslar* rose into the air and fled. Its wings were burned, however. It could not fly far, nor reach the clifftops, and Sitroth pursued it below. I would have hailed the eguar, then, had our own secrecy not been so vital.'

Suddenly Valgrif and his sons went rigid, their eyes and ears turned westwards. After a moment Pazel heard a distant rumbling sound, and the echo of a hunting horn.

'That is part of the Ravens' host,' said Kirishgán. He glanced at Prince Olik. 'Common Bali Adro soldiers, for the most part. You could ride out and greet them, Prince, but I do not think they would bow to you.'

'They would not bow,' said Olik. 'Macadra has made a slave of the Emperor, but the generals still march under his flag, and no minor prince's command may outweigh that of the Resplendent One. We would be seized – with mumblings of regret perhaps – and then delivered to torture and death.'

'What of the Crossroads?' asked Valgrif. 'From the peaks we saw enemies stationed there.'

'The Standing Stones are always watched,' said Kirishgán. 'We must keep to the woods and fields if we are to have any chance. We will cross the Mitrath, north of the Crossroads, and the Isima Road further west. But we go swiftly. When the dogs do not return at nightfall, Macadra's riders will know something grave has happened, and converge here. They are still scattered, chasing false leads. But gathered together they could watch every inch of both roads, and cut us off from the sea.'

'We would travel faster without our mountain gear,' said Lunja.

'Leave it, then,' said the selk, 'There will be no more climbing, until you scale the boarding-ladder of the *Promise*.'

They dropped their tarps, picks, and grapples in a heap, and covered them hastily with snow. Then they set off running, west by northwest. The forests here were beautiful, with columns of golden sun stabbing down through the moist, moss-heavy trees. Pazel, however, was in too much pain to enjoy them: his blisters were leaking blood into his shoes. When they jumped over streams he imagined ripping off his boots and plunging his feet into the clear water. But much worse than the pain was the awareness that he might – somehow, unthinkably – be fated to kill the friend who had joined them.

Time passed. The snow stretched thinner and at last disappeared. Here and there the forest gave way to patches of soggy meadow. Then the wolves came bounding back to the party and announced that the first road, the North–South Mitrath, lay just ahead.

They crept on until it opened before them, broad and dusty and stretching away straight as a ribbon to north and south. All was still. From where he crouched Pazel could see hoofprints and the marks of wagon-wheels. Far off to the south rose the four Standing Stones of the Crossroads. To the north the road climbed into grey, forbidding hills, studded with the ruins of old homesteads and keeps.

'Many riders have passed here today,' said Hercól.

'Soldiers of Macadra,' said Kirishgán. 'No one lives here any longer. These were the outer settlements of Isima. And deep in those hills lies the fairest spring in all the Efaroc Peninsula, where the first selk queen, Miyanthur, gathered wild strawberries as a courting-gift to her betrothed. I used to swim there as a child, thousands of years after Miyanthur's time, but still centuries before the rise of King Urakán. We asked him to build his road elsewhere and leave the hills untouched, but he was a king and had no time for talk of strawberries. The land is healing slowly, however. And the berries are still there.'

'Unlike the king,' said Hercól. 'Well, we are fortunate: the road is empty, and the Crossroads are distant enough, unless there is a telescope trained on this spot. We must chance that. Come swiftly.'

They stepped out upon the high, hard-packed road. Pazel felt very exposed, here in the bright light of a sprawling sky. Hercól came last, frowning at the hoofprints to either side of them, and sweeping a pine limb lightly over their own tracks like a broom.

It was a relief to plunge back under the trees. They ran on, west by southwest, racing the setting sun. Now and then the wolves paused and cocked their heads, but Pazel heard nothing but their own pounding feet. An hour passed, and then the forest came to a sudden end. They were at the second crossing.

They crouched down in the grass. This road, the Isima Road, was wider and clearly more travelled. To the east, Pazel saw the four Standing Stones once again. They had rounded the crossroads unseen.

'Clear again,' said Neeps.

'For the moment,' whispered Neda in Ormali. 'But we'll be in plain sight even after we cross the road, unless we crawl that is. Tell them, Pazel.'

She was quite right: the trees had been cleared for at least two miles on the far side of the road, and the grass was merely elbow-height. Still, they had no other choice, and so on the count of three they dashed across the road and into the grass. Once more Hercól brought up the rear, sweeping their tracks away. But as he reached the edge of the road he suddenly raised his head like a startled animal, then sprinted towards them, waving his hands and hissing.

'There are soldiers riding hard out of the east! Scatter, scatter and lie low! And be still as death, unless you would meet your own!'

They obeyed him, racing away into the grass. Pazel found himself near Kirishgán and no one else. They threw themselves down and waited. Moments later Pazel heard the sound of horses on the road. It was no small contingent: the host was surely hundreds strong. Then a man's voice barked a command. The pounding hooves slowed, then stopped altogether.

Now there were several voices, murmuring impatiently. 'Ride in, then, have a look,' shouted the one who had halted the company. 'But be quick – you know how she deals with latecomers.'

Pazel heard a swishing sound. One of the riders had spurred his horse into the grass.

With infinite care, Kirishgán moved his hand to the pommel of his sword. The rider drew nearer still. Pazel saw a helmet gleam through the grass-tips, and sunlight on a dark dlömic face. Kirishgán met Pazel's eye. *Don't do it, don't move!* Pazel wanted to shout. But he could do not more than slightly shake his head.

Five yards from where they lay, the rider turned his horse and looked back in the direction of the road. 'Nothing here,' he shouted. 'You saw a dust-devil, Captain, if you want my guess.'

'Don't speak to me of devils!' shouted a second voice, from closer to the road. 'We'd be out of these wastes by now if the *maukslar* hadn't smelled something odd in the mountains. Well, get out of there! We have that cursed dog-pack to locate yet.'

The rider spurred his horse back towards the road. Kirishgán took his hand from his sword, and Pazel let himself breathe. *Not today, thank Rin in his heaven.* At a shout from their captain, the host galloped on into the east.

The travellers regrouped. 'Four hundred horsemen, and fifty more on *sicuñas*,' said Prince Olik. 'An Imperial battalion, no less.'

'And the *maukslar* was with them,' said Thasha. 'I wonder if it had taken Dastu's form already.' Her eyes were bright. 'The mucking idiot. I expect they've killed him.'

'That is one possibility,' said Kirishgán. 'Let us not speculate on the others. But it is the fate of your mage that worries me now.'

A heavy silence descended, and it fell to Hercól to break it. 'We must try to keep our spirits up, as Ramachni would no doubt implore. Well, Kirishgán, what shall we do? Crawl?'

'Yes,' said the selk, 'crawl. And that is not a bad thing, for very soon we shall bid this good land farewell. It is fitting to touch it with our hands, to breathe the air closest to its skin. The wicked have many servants – even the selk have been corrupted now and again, to our shame. But stone, snow, grass, forest: these are ever willing to help us, in their humble ways. I shall ache for this land when we depart. It is an ache that can only end when I find my way back here, or my errant soul finds me.'

So they crawled, knees aching but sore feet relieved, and passed slowly across those miles of open grass. An hour later, the host of riders swept back westwards along the road, sounding horns for the pack of *athymars* that lay dead at the foot of Urakán.

Finally the trees resumed, and the travellers stood and continued their painful run. The ground rose and fell; sharp rocks pierced the earth among the roots and leaves. The forest was pathless, dense. They scrambled down into ravines, pushed through walls of savage thorns, forded rivers with the icy spray about their hips. But that night Kirishgán brought them to the shelter of a cave, and the fire they built in its mouth warmed them all. There the selk told them a tale about Lord Arim and Ramachni, and their battle with Droth the *Maukslar*-Prince. It was a harrowing tale, and the others listened, rapt. All save the wolves: they paced uneasily in and out

504

of the cave, and raised their muzzles often, appraising something on the breeze.

'What do you smell, Valgrif?' Myett asked, rising and touching his flank.

The wolf looked down at her. 'Nothing, little sister,' he said at last. 'The enemy is far away.'

That night Pazel slept deep, his fingers and Thasha's interlaced. He did not dream, except for a single, phantom moment, when he thought a dog's tongue licked his chin. But at daybreak Myett was sitting cold and apart, and the three wolves were gone without a trace. Then Pazel knew. Valgrif had smelled salt. He feared no living thing, but waves and surf filled his heart with dread. Waves and surf, and farewells perhaps.

They nibbled some seed-cakes, sipped wine against the morning chill. Hercól and Kirishgán swept out the cave, hiding every trace of their visit. Then the travellers set off through the last of that dense wood. In time they came out upon a windy plateau and crossed it running, scattering a herd of spotted deer. From the plateau's rim they saw a silvery tongue of water below them, twisting among dark cliffs, and tracing it with their eyes for several intricate miles, the sea.

22

Practical Men

—◌◦◌—

No man can know his deliverer, nor yet the thief of his soul.
Their faces are covered; they swirl in the mob at the mas-
querade ball. Wine flows, and dance follows dance, and we
are never certain of their names until that Midnight when all
masks are removed.
– *Embers of Ixphir House* by Hercól Ensyriken ap Ixhxchr.

1 Fuinar 942

For Ignus Chadfallow, Mr Uskins had become an obsession. Not
only had the first mate achieved something no other human ever
had – recovery from the madness produced by the plague – but
he had actually rebounded into a state of clear and lucid thought
greater than any he had previously enjoyed. He was a smarter, saner
man. And today Dr Chadfallow was no closer to discovering what
had cured him than on the day his investigation began.

Now the captain himself had the plague. All the signs were
clear – the lemon sweat, so easily overlooked; the wild swings of
emotion, the slowly mounting struggle to think clearly. It had cost
Rose a great deal to admit the latter, but in the end he had done
so: right there in front of Fiffengurt, Marila and Chadfallow (Lady
Oggosk had yet to awaken from her faint).

'Need I describe what would follow should my condition become
known to the crew?' Rose had asked them. 'Have no doubt: it would
be anarchy and death. There is no one else around whom to rally.

Fiffengurt is easily the most capable sailor—' the quartermaster looked stunned by the compliment '—but he is tainted by mutiny, and he lacks the fire and rage of a commander. Elkstem is pathologically quiet, and thinks only of things mechanical. Coote is too old, Fegin and Bindhammer too stupid. That leaves no one; that leaves a deadly void. Ott and Haddismal will attempt to fill that void. They'll try to run the ship like an army camp, at spearpoint. The gang loyalists will conspire against them, and each other. The dlömu will withdraw; there will be murders, riots, suicides. And all this at a standstill in a protected bay: on the open sea matters will be infinitely worse. Do you doubt these predictions, any of you?'

They had all stayed silent. 'Very well,' said Rose. 'Chadfallow tells me to expect a few more weeks of life. I wish to use them efficiently, provided the crawlies do not manage to overwhelm us somehow.'

'You're not even angry!' Marila had blurted. 'That we kept the truth about Stath Bálfyr from you, I mean.'

Rose's eyes had smouldered at that. He appeared to struggle for words, breathing heavily, staring her down like a bull. At last he said, 'I have been anger's slave for sixty years. I will not die a slave. I will die trying to save this ship, and if that means cooperating with fools and mutineers, I will do so. But understand this: if you hide anything from me, ever again, I shall treat you to a death more slow and excruciating than ever Ott devised for a traitor to the Crown.'

After his words there fell a silence, in which they all heard Oggosk snoring in the captain's bed.

'Fiffengurt is quite correct, all the same,' grumbled Rose. 'Knowledge of the crawlies' deception would only have led to our abandoning the South that much sooner. And I know we must not do that without the Nilstone. I too have seen the Swarm.'

'Then what shall we do presently, sir?' asked Fiffengurt. 'The duchess has it right, I'm afraid: we're better off not trying for a landing, easy as it seems to drop a boat over the side.'

Rose had stalked slowly away from his desk, around the formal dining table and the admiral's chairs, to the smaller, round meeting table near the stern windows. He had placed his hand on its dark surface.

'What shall we do? Wait for the tide to turn again, and then slide back out of this bay before sunset. We will not spend the night here, even though a mile of deep water lies between us and the closest beach. Never again will I underestimate the crawlies.'

He raised his eyes, but they were closed; he was looking at something held tight in memory.

'The nearest islands are small and dead. But forty miles to the east stands one with greenery: we will find fresh water there, and silage for the animals. I saw no good landing spot, but we will manage.' He opened his eyes. 'There remains an overriding danger, however.'

'Macadra?' Chadfallow offered.

Rose shook his head. 'Sandor Ott. He will move against me if I give such orders without explanation. And if he learns the truth about Stath Bálfyr, he will kill everyone who knew and said nothing. I do not know if Haddismal's men will side with him or with me, but the odds are in his favour. As he told me once, treason nullifies a captain's powers. He will cry treason, and the Turachs may choose to believe him.'

'We'd have to hide in the stateroom,' said Marila.

'Yes,' said Fiffengurt, 'until he starved us out.'

'We will have to come up with another reason for leaving,' said Chadfallow.

Rose gave him a withering look. 'In this whole, enormous Southern world, Ott has taken an interest in just one place: Stath Bálfyr. He believes this island to be his gateway for attacking the Mzithrin, for stabbing Arqual's enemy from behind. Nothing else interests him. Tell me: what reason for abandoning it will he accept?'

'Perhaps if he thought we were mistaken,' said Chadfallow, 'if he believed that Stath Bálfyr were really that island to the southeast—'

'He has studied the same charts and drawings that I have, and he is no fool,' said Rose. 'He knows where he is. And he will skewer anyone who tells him a less-than-perfect lie. Now be quiet.'

He still leaned on the table, head cocked to one side, brooding. Finally he stood and walked to the wine cabinet and drew out something that did not look like wine. It was a large glass jar of the sort that Mr Teggatz had once used for lime pickle and other condiments. Rose brought it back to the desk and slammed it down before them.

Marila screamed. Fiffengurt and Chadfallow turned away, quite sickened. Inside the jar, floating in a red-tinted liquid, was the mangled body of an ixchel man. The left arm and both legs had been torn away, leaving only shreds of skin. The abdomen too was torn open, and the head was a ruined mass of hair, skin and fractured bones.

'Sniraga brought this one to Oggosk a fortnight ago,' said Rose. 'I hoped it was a rebel from the clan, one who had stayed aboard when the others deserted us in Masalym.'

'Sniraga killed one of the ixchel who attacked Felthrup,' said Marila, with tears on her brown cheeks.

'Belay that snivelling,' said the captain. 'I have moved beyond sparing your lives and am trying to save them. When Ott asks me how I learned the truth about Stath Bálfyr I shall display this crawly. He will be angry that I did not let him take part in the supposed interrogation – but not as angry as he would be to learn that the real source was you, and that you hid the truth for months. If he should learn that, I will be unable to protect you. Throw yourselves over the rail, or take poison if the doctor can provide it. Anything quick and certain. Do not fall into his hands.'

From the bed, Oggosk was moaning: 'Nilus, Nilus, my boy—'

'We are finished here,' said Rose. 'Quartermaster, you will begin preparing a landing party, just to keep up appearances. My countermanding order will reach you in a few hours' time. As for you, Doctor, I hope your investigations may yet save a few of us from dying like beasts.'

A fine hope, thought Chadfallow now, but very possibly in vain.

For the hundredth time he tried to focus his thoughts on Uskins. What stone had he left unturned? Diet? Impossible; the man ate the same food as any officer. Habits? What habits? If needling others and gloating at their misfortune counted as habits, well, the man had broken them at last. Sleep? Average. Drink? Only to impress his betters, when they too were drinking. Lineage? A peasant, from a crevasse of a town on the Dremland coast, though he had claimed noble birth until an old friend of the family exposed his charade. Abnormalities of blood, urine, faeces, hair follicles, ocular secretions, bunions, breath? No, no, no. The man had been remarkable only for his malice and ineptitude. Remove those and he was painfully normal.

As the victims mounted, Chadfallow had started going without sleep. He questioned Uskins repeatedly about his interactions with Arunis, whom Rose had commanded him to observe for some weeks. The first mate recalled no telling moments. Arunis had never touched him, never tried to give him anything, only grunted when Uskins delivered his meals: 'I was beneath his notice, Doctor,' he'd said, 'and for that I shall always be grateful.'

And their capture in Masalym? Uskins had been sent to that awful human zoo, but so had eight others from the ship, including Chadfallow himself. They were never separated in those three days, which Uskins had spent largely hidden in a patch of weeds. He was mentally frail before the plague struck, certainly. But on the *Chathrand* that was hardly a distinguishing trait.

At his wit's end, Chadfallow even turned to Dr Rain. The old quack at least let him talk without interruption, and this helped Chadfallow sort his observations into mental drawers and cabinets. Rain took it all in gravely, and then sat quietly doodling in the corner of sickbay, face to the wall: the living emblem of a doctor's pledge to do no harm.

Hours passed. Chadfallow heard the order go out: *To your posts, lads: the captain don't like this bay after all.* So it was dusk already; they were leaving with the tide. He stared at Uskins' answers to his questionnaire, the words swimming before his eyes.

'I know!' Rain shrieked from his corner (Chadfallow gasped; he had forgotten the man was there). 'Uskins was already a dunce! You've said so, you called him a puffed-up buffoon. Well, what if intelligence is the trigger, and the first mate didn't have enough? What if the plague couldn't sense any mind in there to attack?'

Chadfallow's mind leaped, clutching at the idea. He wondered if he had not voiced it to Rain himself, and forgotten it in the fog of exhaustion. Then the flaws in the theory began to pop like gophers from their holes.

'The plague *did* attack him, Claudius,' he said. 'Uskins did lose his mind; he simply got it back again. And the plague has claimed others of dubious intelligence. Thad Pollok of Uturphe answered to "Dummy", according to his friends. He lost a finger by placing it in the mouth of a moray eel. Just to see if he could.'

Rain looked thoughtful. 'I would never do that,' he said.

A sound at the doorway: Mr Fegin was hovering there, hat in hand. 'Another victim, Doctor,' he said. 'A lad from Opalt. He was ninety feet up the mainmast, and he started howlin' like a blary baboon. They had a time of it, getting him down in one piece. He bit a lieutenant on the ear.'

'Off we go!' said Rain, reaching for his grubby medical bag. They examined each and every new victim, of course. Or rather Chadfallow did, while Rain mumbled trivialities.

Chadfallow massaged his eyelids. 'Might I ask you to take a first look?' he said. 'I might just be getting somewhere with Uskins, and want to read a while longer.'

It was a bald lie, but Rain did not argue. He glanced at the papers spread across Chadfallow's desk. 'We could draw a little of his blood, and inject a drop into everyone aboard.'

'I'll consider it,' said Chadfallow.

'Or take away his scarf.' Rain slouched out the door. Chadfallow sighed, staring at a vial of the first mate's urine and wondering what else he could do to it.

Then he turned in his chair, blinking.

Scarf?

He stood up and went after Rain, who had only reached the next compartment. 'What the devil are you talking about? What scarf?'

'Haven't you seen it?' said Rain. 'That old white rag of his. Threadbare, filthy. He keeps it under his shirt, but it's always there. He clings to that scarf.'

Rain chuckled and moved on, but Chadfallow stayed where he was, transfixed. A white scarf. He fetched his own bag from sick-bay and made for Uskins' cabin.

The *Chathrand* was once more nearing the mouth of the bay: out-bound, this time, with the reefs to portside and the cliffs towering high over the starboard bow. Fiffengurt had relieved Elkstem at the wheel; the sailmaster had gone to the chart room to consult Prince Olik's sketches and notes. It was easy sailing once again: if ever a bay were made for smooth ingress and egress, it was this one at Stath Bálfyr.

Nonetheless Fiffengurt was sweating profusely. Sandor Ott was at his side.

'A crawly in a pickle jar,' he said. 'Preposterous. This is all a sham, Fiffengurt. Another delaying tactic, in the service of your insane devotion to the Pathkendle crowd.'

'It ain't my order,' said Fiffengurt. 'Aloft there, mizzen-men! Is that a close-reefed sail, by Rin? Look sharp, or I'll send a tarboy up to teach you your trade!'

'Tell me what is really happening,' said Ott.

'We're preparing to thread a needle between reefs and rocks, that's what. And you're making it blary difficult.'

'It is not difficult. You're putting on a performance. Like a circus bear, only much clumsier.' He turned and spat. 'I tell you I will tolerate this no longer.'

'Take it up with the captain, Mr Ott. Unless you mean to drag me away from the – *Great Gods of Perdition!*'

Straight ahead, boulders were raining down from the clifftop.

The ship erupted in howls. Fiffengurt threw all his weight

on the wheel. 'Help me, you useless blary butcher!' he screamed. Ott seized the wheel beside Fiffengurt, and together they spun it hard.

The *Chathrand* heeled wildly to port, bow rising, stern digging deep. Up and down the ship men stumbled, grabbing for handholds. 'Furl topgallants, fore and aft!' bellowed Fiffengurt. 'Standby anchor! Rin's gizzard, something up there is *hurling* those stones!'

Even as he spoke a particularly enormous boulder struck the water, some fifty yards from the ship. 'Did you see that?' cried Fiffengurt. 'That stone was bigger than the wheelhouse! A rock like that could stave us in!'

Rose burst from his cabin and raced to the starboard rail, unfolding his telescope as he went. But there was nothing to look at: for the moment, the onslaught had ceased. The ship levelled, motionless on the bay.

Fiffengurt looked at the spymaster. 'Preposterous?' he said.

'You cannot believe that crawlies were responsible for *that*,' said Ott.

Fiffengurt said nothing. He certainly did have his doubts, but he'd be damned if he'd give Ott another stick to beat him with.

'Come around and try again,' said the spymaster, 'but further from the cliffs, this time, out of range.'

The quartermaster turned to face him. 'Mr Ott. When those rocks began to fly we were still edging *nearer* the cliffs. There's no mucking way we can sail any *further* from 'em, unless you want to tear the bottom out of this boat. Have a look at the reefs, away there to starboard. With the sun behind us you can see 'em with the naked eye.'

Ott did not walk to starboard, or look at the reefs. He stared up at the high, broken clifftop. 'A bombardment like that could finish us in minutes,' he said.

'Less, if a couple of those big bastards found their mark,' said Fiffengurt. 'I think the first time was a warning.'

'Quartermaster, that cliff is half a mile long. The enemy could get off *dozens* of shots before we cleared it.'

Fiffengurt nodded. 'You're getting the idea. We're trapped in this bay.'

'That is correct,' shouted a voice from above them.

They jumped, searching, shading their eyes. Twenty feet overhead, seated at his ease on the main spankermast yard, was Lord Talag.

'Crawly, crawly aloft!' shouted someone, causing a general stir. Lord Talag paid no attention. The swallow-suit hung loose upon his shoulders.

'You are trapped again,' he said, 'but not by us, this time. We took some of you prisoner once, by necessity. The deed gave us no joy. To cage any living creature is a deed that sickens the heart. We struggled to keep you alive and comfortable. When you escaped you killed as many of us as you could.'

'And we're not done yet,' said Sandor Ott.

'Be silent, you wretched man!' hissed Fiffengurt.

Captain Rose appeared on the quarterdeck ladder. He climbed up stiffly and walked up to the wheelhouse, his eyes never leaving the ixchel.

'On this day,' Talag continued, 'my island brethren have made prisoners of you all. Be glad that you did not kill me in Masalym, Sandor Ott. If I had not flown ashore and greeted them, they would have sunk you as you tried to enter this bay.'

'How do they move the rocks?' asked Fiffengurt.

Lord Talag smiled strangely. 'I haven't the faintest idea.'

'Your brethren kept it to themselves, did they?'

Talag frowned at him. 'We are not a sentimental race. We do not spill our secrets at a first encounter, not even with our long-lost kin.'

'We're a mile from shore,' said Sandor Ott. 'How do you plan to leave us, exactly?'

'That is not your concern,' said Lord Talag.

'What if I make it my concern?'

Talag got to his feet, eyes locked on the spymaster. 'My people watched you for years, Sandor Ott. In the Keep of Five Domes,

514

in the tunnels under Etherhorde, in the blue chambers of Castle Maag. I myself heard you planning deaths, from Thasha Isiq's mother to guards of the castle you deemed too inquisitive. I saw you mate with that whore, Syrarys, never guessing that years before you made her a spy in Isiq's household, Arunis had picked her out to be a spy in yours. I saw you cackle with glee over the charts we forged. You are a failure, Ott. Like all giants, you confuse brute power with absolute power. And now it is time to pay for that mistake. Oppose our exodus, and we will wait you out. How long can you survive without fresh water? Two months? Three, if you kill off the sickly? But we can wait a year, Ott, or longer. We will not even be thirsty when the last of you falls dead.'

'And if we do not oppose you?' said Rose.

Talag turned his burning eyes on the captain. 'I would give a great deal to know what you truly expect of me,' he said. 'What does a crawly do with his eight hundred tormentors, when he has them at last beneath his heel? Eight hundred sadists, bigots, butchers? I know what a giant would do. Make the crawly beg. Increase the pressure, slowly. Watch him suffer, fascinated; pretend to consider his pleas. Then step down hard and crush his skull.'

Talag's body had gone rigid. 'I know,' he said. 'I saw it done to my father when I was ten. He was as close to me as you are now, but I was in hiding, I was safe, and even as the giant screamed at him, told him to beg for his life, my father was speaking to me in the tongue your kind cannot hear, ordering me to live, to fight on, to serve our people.

'It was five years later that I first heard the legend of Stath Bálfyr, the island from whence you took us in jars and cages. I swore then and there that I would lead any of my father's house who would follow me home to this place, and today I fulfill that oath. You ask what will I do with you?'

He took a deep breath. 'Nothing. Live out my life endeavouring to forget your very existence. And if you are cooperative, and do not hinder our departure from the *Chathrand*, I shall go one step further, and waive the right of vengeance.'

'Meaning what?' asked Rose.

'That you shall be dealt with as my island brethren see fit. They would surely extend me the courtesy of deciding your fate: that is fitting and customary. But vengeance was never the purpose of this mission – and today that purpose is all but achieved. I will not seek your executions.'

'But you will not ask for clemency?'

Talag turned to him, bristling. 'You kept one of us in a birdcage, in filth, and made him taste your food for poison. Your command triggered the massacre. Your first bosun wore a necklace of our skulls. Blood-red monster! This *is* clemency, beyond anything you giants deserve.'

With a sharp motion he turned away, smoothing the feathers of his coat. 'You are trespassers in Stath Bálfyr,' he said. 'The island's rulers will make their own decisions. For myself the end has finally come. I shall grow old here, among my people and my books. You no longer matter.'

Dr Chadfallow had just reached Uskins' door when the bombardment commenced. He stumbled when the ship lurched, half expecting the passage to explode in a swarm of attacking ixchel. But none came. Whatever had just happened, the clan was still lying low. He considered putting off his investigation, then reprimanded himself: *Put off until when? Until how many more succumb?* He cleared his throat, straightened his sleeves with their silver cufflinks, and knocked.

The door rattled, as though Uskins was struggling with it. At last the first mate shouldered it open. 'The latch,' he explained with a smile. 'I tried to fix it and have only made things worse. Do come in, Doctor.'

Chadfallow stepped into the little cabin. 'I was napping,' said Uskins. 'Did something happen above?'

'I'm not sure,' said Chadfallow quietly. 'Nothing important, in any case.'

'I tire more easily now that my duties are so light,' said Uskins.

'Is that not strange? I wash dishes, carry messages, feed the men in the brig, and suddenly I am fatigued. May I ask if you have made any progress?'

'Not really,' Chadfallow admitted, studying him. The man's shirt was buttoned to the neck. It was, thought the doctor, *always* buttoned to the neck.

Uskins had begun to notice the doctor's peculiar manner. 'You have an idea, though, don't you? Something to build on?'

'Perhaps,' said Chadfallow, barely conscious of his words. 'But it's … rather complicated. I'm afraid I need to examine you once more.'

'Anything to help, Doctor. But I can tell you right now that I'm unchanged.'

'I'll be the judge of that,' said Chadfallow, trying to evoke his usual, peremptory tone. 'Sit down, sir. Take off your shirt and breathe deep.'

Uskins consented amiably enough for someone who had been examined almost ceaselessly for a fortnight. He sat in the room's one chair with his back to Chadfallow, unbuttoned the top two buttons of his shirt, and pulled it over his head. There it was: the tail end of the scarf. Uskins had removed it along with the shirt, and was now holding both in his hands.

As he did each time before, thought Chadfallow. *How under Heaven's Tree did I fail to notice?*

He placed the stethoscope on Uskins' back, went through the motions of listening.

'I'm feeling truly fine today,' said Uskins. 'My appetite is immense.'

'Arms out to either side, if you please,' said Chadfallow.

Uskins tucked the shirt under his leg before he obeyed. Now Chadfallow could see the scarf's tasseled edge: just two inches, but that was enough. His skin went cold. His hand trembled on the stethoscope.

Captain Rose had named himself a slave to anger. He, Chadfallow, had been a slave to pride. He was intelligent; he knew

517

that. But for the first time in his life he understood with perfect clarity that he was also a fool.

'I must … step out,' he heard himself say. 'I left an instrument in the surgery.'

'What instrument?' asked Uskins. His voice was abruptly cold.

Chadfallow's mind seized. 'A spirometer,' he managed to blurt. 'Also known as a plethysmograph. It measures a patient's lung capacity.'

'I don't think you care about my lung capacity,' said Uskins.

'Now you're being foolish,' said the doctor, all but lunging for the door.

But the door would not open. Chadfallow heaved at it, wrenching at the knob. The door held fast. Slowly he turned to face Uskins. The first mate had put the white scarf back around his neck.

'No more games,' said Chadfallow.

'Oh no,' said the other, 'I quite tire of them myself.'

'What happened to you, Uskins?'

The man smiled: a wide, toothy, ear-to-ear grin, unlike any smile the doctor had ever seen on his face. 'Your first mate is not available for questioning,' he said.

Chadfallow did not even see the knife, but by the force of the blow, the white blaze of pain-beyond-pain, the rich smell in his nostrils and the dysfunctional lurch of the organ in his chest, he had his diagnosis at once. So fascinating. The left ventricle. If only he had time to make some notes.

These thoughts were lightning-flashes. Others followed. He had a son; his son might yet be alive; his son would never embrace him and say *Father*. He should have been more reckless in love. He should have noticed that life was but a heartbeat, maybe two heartbeats, nothing guaranteed.

'Arunis?' he whispered.

'Of course.'

Show him no fear. He could manage that much; he always cut a good figure; he was dying without Suthinia; everything he loved he misplaced.

'Dead … ?' he whispered.

The man raised his eyebrows. 'Who do you mean? You, me, Uskins? Never mind; the answer is yes.'

'How.'

'How did I win control of this body? Just as you'd go about such a task. I reasoned with Uskins. He had the plague. I reminded him that a continent full of doctors had failed to cure it, and persuaded him that his one chance was to let me into his mind. To sign over the house, as it were, and let me see what I could do about the termites. He hated the idea, but saw the logic in the end.'

The doctor's strength was gone, his vision going. Arunis lowered him quietly to the floor. 'Our Imperial surgeon,' he said. 'A scientist, a practical man. It was you who ended the stand off that day in the Straits of Simja. You threw me the rope ladder, let me climb aboard. I might have failed that day, but you couldn't bear to let me strangle Admiral Isiq's little bitch. Astonishing weakness, I thought. And do you know, nothing angers me so much as weakness? Even here in Agaroth, on death's doorstep, it enrages me. I had hoped to keep you alive. I wanted you there on the night of the Swarm, so that you would know what your weakness had made possible. You will have to use your imagination instead. The nothingness before you, the blackness closing in: that is the future of Alifros, Doctor. That is the world that you shall never see.'

23

Gifts and Curses

———◦◦◦———

A silent canyon, blanketed in early snow. The chilly Parsua dances, gurgling, between cliffs that soar above two thousand feet. Black boulders stand in the river, pines struggle along the shore; further from the water rise old oaks and ironwoods. Upriver there are waterfalls, where the gorge descends in jagged steps. High overhead, wisps of cloud scud across a narrow slab of sky the colour of a robin's egg.

Stillness, sunlight, cold. A finch alights and vanishes again; a pinch of snow tumbles from a branch. The wind above the Parsua can scarcely be heard. Straining, one might fancy it carries sounds of violence, of horror, from some unthinkably distant land: sounds all but dissolved in the vast, consoling indifference of the air.

Then a noise cuts through the morning: a desperate, clumsy sound like rough shears through wool. It grows nearer, louder. It is the sound of feet in snow.

From upriver he appears: a youth, bloodied and in rags, his white breath puffing like smoke through his lips. He is running for his life, tumbling over snow-hidden rocks, careening through drifts. His gaze swings left and right, studying the cliffs that offer no cave or crevice, no place to hide. When he glances back over his shoulder it is with naked fear.

He passes the tree where the finch rested, catching his sleeve on a branch. Two or three steps later he has blundered onto the thin ice that girds the riverbanks, and falls on hands and knees into the water. He bites back a howl. As he drags himself onto solid ground his pursuer erupts into view.

It is an eguar. Black, burning, elephantine. It roars at him from atop the last set of falls, over a mile back along the canyon. Then it hurls itself from the cliff into the river below.

Flailing, the youth doubles his speed. He cannot see the eguar now, but the vapour above it forms a white flag, racing towards him along the bottom of the gorge. Trees crack; steam hisses where the burning flanks of the creature slide through snow. Before it has closed half the distance the youth knows he will not escape.

He turns. His body is shaking uncontrollably; his eyes have a sheen like fogged glass. Suddenly he throws back his head and screeches at the sky. As it was on the Water Bridge, the transformation is swift: the head flattens into the neck; the neck elongates; the limbs become massive; the jaw stretches to reveal enormous fangs. But the *maukslar* has paid a cost for returning to its natural form: between the shoulder blades, its fleshy wings hang broken and torn. Dark blood pours from them, staining the snow.

The *maukslar* shields its lamp-like eyes. Born in the infernal regions, it does not care for snow, and less for naked sunlight. When its foe thrashes into view, it spits blindly in the creature's direction. A great viscous mass of fire blossoms from its mouth and flies up the canyon, exploding spectacularly before the eguar. Pines go up like torches; snow vaporises; the edges of the river boil. The eguar rushes straight on, unscathed, shaking off the fire like globs of mud.

The demon turns to run. But what has happened? In that brief moment of stillness, ice has closed around its ankles. Spellcraft. The demon wrenches, claws at the glassy ice. When it finally breaks free it has bloodied both feet, and allowed the eguar to close half the distance.

Now the gorge jackknifes to the left. Once around the bend the demon wrenches a barrel-sized stone from the frozen earth, and screeches with delight when the blow connects. Stunned, the eguar drops on its side. Once again the demon flees.

And once again meets with a strange barrier: this time the very trees have somehow thickened around it, and their criss-crossed branches thwart it at every step. The more it fights, the more entangling they become, until at last in desperation it vomits more fire, scouring out a path through which to flee.

Hard ground beneath its feet: the fire has burned all the way to bedrock. And there, there ahead is the split in the Parsua that means the gorge is near its end. Beyond that, open fields and forests. And beyond the latter, Macadra's forces in their thousands, waiting only for someone to tell them where to strike.

'Hold!'

The demon stops dead. Before it, on the branch of a tall pine, sits a large, black owl. It is this creature who has spoken. The *maukslar* knows this new enemy at a glance, and screams in terror and rage. Then its nostrils catch that telltale reek of sulphur, and it whirls about: the eguar stands twenty feet upstream, its body a hot iron, its great tail thrashing among the stones.

'You are bleeding to death,' says the owl. 'Moreover you are cornered by two foes greater than yourself. Behind you waits Sitroth, the Ancient, who killed the hound of Toltirek. I am Ramachni, servant of Erithusmé and ward of the selk. You have felt my grip once; if you feel it again it will be too late to beg for mercy. Depart this world if you would live.'

The demon speaks in a voice like boiling pitch. 'I beg no mage's mercy. I dwell in those places where you scarcely dare to wet your feet. One alone dared call me forth. I serve the White Raven, while it pleases me to do so. The White Raven, who outlived your Northern hag.'

'Erithusmé the Great is alive,' says the owl. 'Macadra fears her, and with good reason. But I warn you, try no spell of your own. If you do we shall kill you swiftly. Where is Dastu, the boy whose shape you mimic?'

'In the stomach of the ogress,' says the demon. 'The hrathmogs live in fear of her appetite.'

The owl falls silent. When it speaks again its voice has hardened.

'Go, demon. Return to the *Duirmaulc* while you can. Your days in Alifros are through.'

The *maukslar*'s yellow eyes are fixed on the owl. 'We shall see whose time is through, when Macadra takes the Nilstone in her hand.'

'There is a pattern jewel in the creature's gut,' says the eguar suddenly. The *maukslar* jumps, glancing at the beast with scalding hate.

'A pattern jewel?' says the owl. 'That is a crime in itself. Why do you carry such a thing, *maukslar*, when you know it belongs with others?'

'My mistress gave it me,' hisses the demon.

'Then she took it from a murdered selk,' says the owl. 'You must cough it out before you leave this world. It would prevent your departure anyway.'

The *maukslar*'s eyes dart, scanning the ground for a weapon.

'If you refuse,' says the owl, 'we will simply wait for you to die, and then remove it from your corpse. Hear me for the last time: go back to the Nine Pits, back among the damned. If you do so we will prevent Macadra from binding you to service again. If you will not go, we will scatter your ashes when you die and prevent your resurrection. The choice remains yours, for a moment longer.'

The *maukslar* looks from one to the other. It stands now in a pool of its own blood.

'Do not slay me,' it says at last. 'I yield. Take the jewel, and let me take my leave.'

The creature drops on all fours. It retches, back arching like a dog's. Four or five times its body heaves. Then, painfully, it crawls to a fallen pine and lies over it. At last its snake-like neck convulses, and a great red ruby drops from its mouth into its waiting palm.

'Leave it there!' screeches the owl. But the *maukslar* pays no heed. On its forehead the fell runes blaze. 'Magic! Beware!' bellows the eguar. But as it rears up, the fallen pine tree rises, flies with all the force of the demon's curse, and pierces the eguar's chest like a stake.

The eguar falls without a sound. But the demon howls in agony.

On the high branch, the owl has become a small black mink. Its jaws flex, biting hard at empty air. In the body of the *maukslar*, bones begin to crack.

Then the *maukslar* vanishes, so suddenly that drops of its spilling blood seem for a moment to hang suspended in the air. Thrown by his own spell's sudden release of power, the mage nearly falls from the tree. Exhausted, he flies down the trunk and races towards the eguar.

'Stay!'

The eguar's warning comes out like thunder, but it is followed by a rattling wheeze. The mink stops in his tracks. The tree has shattered the creature's chest.

'I spew poisons enough when my skin is whole,' says the eguar. 'Now that I bleed even you dare not approach.'

'I may help you,' says the mage.

'My body is beyond help,' says Sitroth. 'But we may still speak; the eguar are slow even in death. Tell me, Arpathwin, is honour restored?'

'Yours was never truly lost,' says the mage, bowing his head. 'Only wisdom deserted you, briefly. And whom has it not, at some point in life's long march? The two princes look alike, they say. And since Olik the father passed through the Red Storm, he is no older than his grandson.'

'No hatchling would err as I did,' says the eguar. 'The selk gave me sanctuary and purpose and a feast of bright thoughts, wafting nectar-scented from Uláramyth. I betrayed them. I killed one of their number, and left the North Door without a guard.'

'You sought vengeance against a murderer of your people,' says Ramachni. 'The wisest of us all still have our passions, Sitroth, and as long as living blood runs in our veins they will sometimes prevail. Not even the Gods are immune.'

'The *maukslar* has departed?'

Ramachni nods. 'It has fled Alifros, and cannot return without some aid.'

'It cast the pattern jewel away into the river,' the eguar wheezes.

'I am sorry we did not recover that stone. I would have liked to lay it at Lord Arim's feet.'

'One day I shall bring the selk here to find it, and take it home to Uláramyth,' says Ramachni. 'There is time.'

As if to belie his words, the twin points of seering light that are the eguar's eyes wink out. But the creature still draws breath. 'Arpathwin,' it says, 'could you truly name me friend?'

'What else could I name you?' says Ramachni. 'Have we not both seen the centuries pass, the plagues and rebirths, the wonders forgotten in a fleeting year by men? Besides, you are beloved of the selk, and I am their ward and kinsman.'

'Then you must come near after all. For not all my wisdom is gone. I have remembered something. I have remembered the nature of your Gift.'

The creature's blood is pooling, sizzling on the stone.

'Ramachni *Fremken*,' it murmurs. '"He who steals the form of his friends." Arim himself mentioned it once, so many centuries ago. You can take many shapes—'

'Not so many,' says Ramachni quickly.

'—but only the shapes of those you have befriended, and slain. An orphaned owl. A mink caught in a hunter's trap. A great bear rescued from a life of torment in the arena.'

'They were woken animals,' says Ramachni. 'And they were all ill, or hopelessly wounded. They understood what they gave. Yes, that is my Gift-curse. I add their shapes to my collection as I kill them, kill my friends.'

'Then let me give the same gift, while I can.'

'Sitroth!'

'Your fight goes on. With an eguar's strength few enemies will stand against you.'

'My change is not like that of the *maukslar*, not a mockery of the host. You do not know what you offer, Sitroth.'

'Would you deny me this?' snaps the eguar, suddenly fierce, its blind eyes swinging towards the mage. 'Step close; you will need great strength. Use the charm you placed on the demon, but use it to still my heart. And when you assume my form in future years, think of me.'

'Your own body will turn to dust. There will be no burial-pit, no bones to honour.'

'Or to carve into Plazic blades. Arpathwin, hurry. I am near the end of my strength.'

Ramachni looks into the blind black eyes. He does not tell the eguar that to assimilate his body will be as hard a deed as the fight they have just waged. Nor does he explain the deeper price his Gift exacts: how each new form he collects pushes a little more of his original self aside, erases another page of memory of what he was, before magic, before the shadow-war that never ends. He only thanks Sitroth, and draws on his power, and stops the eguar's heart.

The feeling is familiar. As with the mink, the owl, the bear, the Dafvni gardener: there is that sense of a mirror flipped, a mirror stepped through; now the reflection is looking at its source. But the source – the body of a great primordial monster – is already gone. Even the vapours, even the acidic blood. Upon the stone and shattered tree is a patina of fine silver dust.

Afterwards he lies stunned, nearly comatose, his body flickering through its forms. He cannot remember the one he feels at home in, here in Alifros. The birds creep back. A fox sniffs at him, but cannot understand why it has smelled a bird and found a bear, and flees unsettled. Fresh snow falls and covers him. Each time he becomes an eguar it turns to steam.

Late in the night his head clears a little, and he rises, man-shaped, to drink from the Parsua – but the water burns his lips. Sitroth's acids are in the river, the snow. Sitroth's, or his own. At dawn, still aching, he takes weary flight as the owl.

Once more peace reigns in the canyon. The day passes like any other; except for a few scorched trees there is no sign of what has happened here. The next day is warmer; rain falls instead of snow.

Late on the third day the silence breaks again. This time hoof-beats echo in the canyon: iron shoes on stone. The riders come in force, fifty dlömu on swift chargers, their shields emblazoned with the sun-and-leopard ensign of Bali Adro. At the heart of the band are two dlömu with the red sashes and aiguillettes of generals. And behind this pair rides an apparition of a woman, tall and gaunt and bone-white, with spectral eyes that rake the canyon as though hunting for food. She wears a dark riding coat, but from beneath it trail the ends of ancient satin and lace. Her dry lips are parted; her hands seem poised to snatch something from the air.

As they reach the shattered pine the woman screams the band to a halt, and slides to the ground before the generals can offer their aid. Four strides bring her to the river's edge. Twitching, she looks upstream and down.

'It was here. I can smell its stench. It reached this point and fell.'

'Fell, my lady?' says one of the generals. 'What enemy do we face that could kill a *maukslar*?'

The sorceress looks up at him sharply. The general cringes, begs her pardon in abject terms.

'Stand back from me, and keep your bastards silent,' shouts the woman. 'I must think.'

The dlömu turn their steeds quickly away. They know too well what happens when Macadra declares that she must think. The mage stalks along the riverbank, first upstream, then down. Several times she pauses, holding very still. Then she curses aloud and plunges into the river.

'She *is* mad, isn't she?'

The words are spoken in a whisper, by one dlömu at the rear of the band. Only his nearest comrades hear a word. His comrades, that is, and Lord Taliktrum, looking out through the slit his knife has opened in a saddlebag, where he has ridden for a day and a night. He smiles grimly. He knows what will come next.

'Quiet, fool!' hisses another rider. 'She hears *everything*, don't you know that yet?'

They are both right, Taliktrum thinks: Macadra does have an uncanny ability to know when her officers breathe a word against her. In the month that he has hidden in her entourage, Taliktrum has seen her pluck half a dozen men from the ranks and send them to the noose. It might well be enchanted hearing. But it could just as well be natural intuition. Many leaders have it. A few (his father springs to mind) come to trust in nothing else.

She is, however, unquestionably mad. Look at her, plunging waist-deep in that ice water, eager as a bear after fish. The sight makes Taliktrum boil with frustration. When he lost Prince Olik in the wilds above Masalym, Taliktrum had known exactly what to do. It was what his people had always done: stay close to the enemy, infiltrate their strongholds, ride their ships. He had smuggled himself back to Istolym, riding one of the dogs Prince Olik had been forced to abandon (it took two days, for its feet were very sore), and then, with great care, rode a cargo shipment out to the *Death's Head*.

Taliktrum does not think much of his own intuition. Not after his disastrous spell as clan leader, and his unforgivable abandonment of them all. Not after spurning Myett, torturing her heart, failing to notice that she loved him, alone of all beings alive.

But while he stands self-condemned, he cannot deny that his choices have been better since coming ashore. Helping the prince: that was well done. Olik Bali Adro is both a thinker and a barb in the side of the slaughtering Empire that bears his name.

Or was. Odds are the prince is dead, now – drowned in that river, or starved in the sprawling wilds he spoke of. Still, Taliktrum has chosen the right friend, the right allegiances at last.

Boarding the *Death's Head*: even better. He'd known the sorceress craved the Nilstone, and was deploying every surviving asset of Bali Adro in the hunt for it. What he'd only suspected, though, was that she trusted none of her lackeys – these Plazic generals with their stumps of eguar-bone weaponry, diseased and desperate men – to bring her the Stone. No, she had to chase it herself, follow every lead, swoop down on whichever of her servants found it before they knew what they held.

Stowing away was horribly dangerous at first. Macadra had not travelled in decades, and despite her ferocity, feared almost every-thing – magical assault, treason, seepage in the hold, foul weather, flies. Her vessel crawled with every manner of guard and inspector. Her cabin was a fortress, and those who entered were searched like criminals brought to plead before a queen.

Which is, he supposes, *precisely how she sees the matter.*

But she was not on guard against ixchel. The prince had told him bluntly: there *were* no ixchel, not on the mainland at any rate. Not even the rats aboard knew his smell. He was utterly alone: a tactical advantage, certainly. Also a sentence of living death.

Once they sailed from Masalym he discovered his second advantage: knowledge of the *Chathrand*. For it was exactly as he had thought on the headland, when he and Olik first glimpsed Macadra's vessel: except for the armour and ghastly weapons of the *Death's Head*, the ships were twins. Seven decks. Five masts. An inner hull and sealed forepeak. And the ladderways, hatches, light shafts, speaking tubes, pumps and drains: so familiar he had nearly laughed aloud. Before the first day was out he had found not one but two refuges, places he could sleep without the least fear of discovery. By the third day he was crawling under Macadra's floorboards, and catching some of her words.

'Watchers Above, she's soaked to her elbows!' says the first dlömu. 'She'll freeze to death!'

'Don't count on it,' says the other.

After a fortnight the *Death's Head* had rendezvoused with a small Bali Adro sloop, fresh from the Island Wilderness. It was then that he (and Macadra) learned of the *Chathrand*'s escape from Imperial waters, despite a spectacular bombardment. Macadra's wrath had certainly been spectacular, but she'd had no one to punish: the sloop had not even been present for the engagement. And she had brightened considerably when the vessel's commander reported that the *Chathrand* had used no magic of any kind.

'No spells at all? Then they are not my quarry. Our prey has fled inland, as I always suspected.'

She believes they'd have used the Nilstone against her if they had it, Taliktrum had realised. *Why? Not even Arunis could control that deadly thing.*

The *Death's Head* had touched land at the naval bases called Fandural Edge and Sibar Light, where Macadra had dispatched more teams to the interior. Finally, three weeks out of Masalym, they had docked at the great smoke-lidded, soot-blackened city of Orbilesc.

He'd flown ashore that first night under cover of darkness. But there was no true darkness in Orbilesc, only shadows and blinding smoke. The city stretched on and on, over hills and around the slopes of mountains, along both banks of a river the colour of diluted blood. Parts of it appeared to be on fire: they throbbed in the distance like open sores, their orange glow reflecting dully on the filth-laden sky. The city was a point of convergence for great roads leading deep into the continent, to Bali Adro City and Kistav and other centres of Imperial might. Dlömu by the thousands thronged its squares, encamped in its denuded gardens and gutted shops. They were mostly poor and filthy, huddling with their scrawny dogs beside illicit fires that the rain was always putting out. It appeared that they had come to work the hellish factories, but whether voluntarily or at spearpoint he could not ascertain. There were other races too in those shabby streets, mystifying creatures that fascinated and repelled him. All of these strange beings, dlömu included, spoke Imperial Common, but in such a variety of forms and accents that Taliktrum doubted everything he heard.

Worst of all were the shipyards. He hardly dared approach those grim towers and black belching mills, from which great plumes of fire erupted, and cold shimmerings of yellow light, and noises loud as the maiming of Gods. Carrion birds wheeled above them; titantic sea-serpents of the sort that had threatened the *Chathrand* off Naribyr writhed in the polluted bay, flailing at their chains. Huge gears and moving cables brought steel and lumber and lead and brass into the open jaws of the shipworks. Taliktrum flew nearer, alighting on one of the countless outbuildings surrounding the mill. Creeping to the edge of the roof, he found himself looking down on corpses, mangled corpses impaled on hooks, being cabled away towards a mountain of smoking rubbish to the south. Prisoners? Criminals? Aghast, he realised that they were neither: they were workers, slain and discarded by the monstrous industry they served. And for every dlömu killed there were surely five or six lined up at the doors.

The city generated a kind of fear Taliktrum had never before im-agined. *Great Mother,* he'd thought, *don't let me die in such a place. Send me to sea again quickly, far from this nightmare world.*

But the ship had lingered, day after day. Macadra kept to herself, awaiting word from her inland scouts. For five days she did not stir from her cabin. Then one morning she had stormed out on deck, screaming for horses. A vision had come to her in the night: battle in a wintry gorge, the *maukslar* killed or driven from Alifros, and another creature of great power slain as well. Macadra had been certain that the Nilstone was involved.

Taliktrum frowns at the sorceress, wading like a rapacious bird. He still does not know what a *maukslar* is. But he knows somehow that he must stay near this vile mage. If he is to fight her, that is. If he is to have any chance of mattering in this world, after so much error and cowardice.

'Look at her now!' hisses someone. The riders grow still. Macadra has drawn a knife, and bared her bone-white arm to the elbow. With a swift motion she slices her own forearm: a deep, cruel cut. But she does not bleed: the wound gapes red, but dry.

The sight is too much for the dlömu. 'No blood!' they whisper. 'Macadra has no blood in her veins!' Cursing, Macadra works her hand, in a motion like squeezing a ball. At last Taliktrum sees it: a slow, dark trickle on the too-white flesh. She lets it drip into the river: five drops, and then the wound runs dry.

From out of the Parsua, something leaps into her palm: a red ruby, glittering in the sun. Macadra encloses it in her wounded hand.

Her eyes shut. Then she screeches, with more lunacy and rage then ever Taliktrum has heard on giant's tongue.

'*Miña Scaraba Urifica!* We ride, we ride! They have passed over the Water Bridge and descended Urakán! They are west of us and making for the sea!'

She is flailing for shore, knife still in hand, snarling: 'Assist me, you dogs!'

One of the generals plunges in and wades towards her, extending his hand. 'My lady,' he shouts, 'the horses are nearly spent.'

'Did you not hear me? We ride at once!'

'Yes, lady,' says the general, 'but what of your demon? Is that not why we came here?'

Macadra grasps his hand, pulls hard, and with a speed that even Taliktrum finds startling, cuts the general's throat. The man's mouth opens with hideous silence. He drops face-first; his coat balloons with trapped air. The sorceress presses down upon his neck as though feeding him to the river.

'It lives, dog,' she says. 'It will heal, with time and blood.'

24

━━◆━━

Monday, 2 Fuinar 942. It is truly extraordinary: our ixchel have charmed the birds of the air. One sort of bird, anyway – the swallows of Stath Bálfyr – and in truth just one ixchel appears to have the knack. He is Myett's granddad, the old duffer they call the Pachet Ghali. At six bells today he pulls out a tiny flute & sets to playing on the forecastle, & in they swarm from the island, skimming low over the bay. Lord Talag stands among them in his swallow-suit, pointing & shouting, & thirty more of the little people materialize out of their hiding places, laughing at the birds with delight. Who's in control, I wonder: the musician or the feathered lord? But how they do keep coming, until they outnumber the ixchel four to one.

Suddenly they descend in a jabbering mass. Grown men fall back, protecting their faces, but the birds have no interest in humans. They seize the ixchel in their claws & rise, bearing them away towards the island & its steamy woods. Only the Pachet is left behind.

This, then, has been their plan since Etherhorde: to bring us all the way here from Etherhorde, & then depart on swallows' wings. They mean to repeat this trick again & again, until their whole clan is on dry land. And what then? Ott declares for a certainty that they'll not let us go, & this time I fear the old snake is right. What if we talked about this place? What if we came back with catapults & fire-missiles, & burned Stath Bálfyr to a crisp? What if we came back with a navy?

But there are surely hundreds of ixchel hidden on the *Chathrand* yet, & thus far only thirty have departed. When the first group vanishes from sight the old Pachet (the word's his title, not his name) sets the flute aside & talks to us quite reasonably. He invokes Diadrelu, 'our lord's dear departed sister', & compliments Marila & Felthrup & myself for befriending her.

'She would have wished us to part without illusions, and without hate,' he says. 'You are guilty of many crimes, but hating you has served us ill. Lady Dri understood this and would not pretend otherwise. She would not lie to us, or to herself. But the cost of seeing that truth was death.'

I suppose I'm in the mood for a fight. 'It ain't just that she *saw*, old man,' I say. 'It's that the rest of you refused to.'

'Not all of us,' he replies.

I tell him he's a mucking hypocrite. 'If you think so much of her, why d'ye still serve the bastards who stabbed her in the throat?'

The old man looks at me, untroubled. 'I serve the clan,' he says, 'as she did, to the end.'

Some hours later the birds return. With them are just three ixchel: Lord Talag & two strangers, hard-faced sorts dressed only in breeches & weaponry. They are the first proof we have that ixchel really live on Stath Bálfyr. They're outlandish, too: they have fantastic, elephant-like creatures tattooed on their chests, & their hands & forearms are painted red as though dipped in blood. They flank Talag & nod to him courteously, but Talag is all business as he speaks with the Pachet in that tongue we humans cannot hear. Now the old man looks surprised & uneasy. The birds have settled along the bowsprit, spattering the Goose Girl with their droppings, but when he starts to play again they rise up twittering & excited. This time they bear the Pachet away with the rest.

It is hard not to stare at the spot on the island where they disappeared. Sometimes I think I see the treetops moving, as if a wind were trapped there, or some big hand riffling the crowns. But there are other urgencies. The gangs have exploded yet again: there are two dead & twenty wounded. And a deathsmoker who lost his mind & threw himself at the augrongs, who panicked a little & squeezed him to death. And a plague of horrible green flies from the island. They have settled in the heads & bite our arses, & give us great goose-egg boils.

And there is a last thing, so terrible my hand is shaking as I write. About a week ago someone nicked a goat from the animals' compartment. This was strange but not catastrophic: somewhere a confused & frightened sailor was hoarding goat-flesh, maybe, & no doubt the flies would soon give him away. But last night Mr Teggatz noticed a change in the stench around the water casks, & had the good sense to pry the lid open before he sipped. He howled. The goat's head & viscera were floating there, half-decayed. The whole cask was poisoned, & so were four others beside it. The cook's nose has saved lives – hundreds of lives, maybe; for he was about to boil up the evening broth. Is *this* the work of gangsters? Could they possibly have gone so far?

Whoever the culprit, we are now once again low on fresh water. All this, & Dr Chadfallow nowhere to be found. I have put eight tarboys on the hunt for him, & will have to watch my temper if I learn that he is poking about the lower decks yet again in search of his green mucking door.

Tuesday, 3 Fuinar 942. I cannot sleep, & fear the visions that would plague me if I did. My heart is pounding. My shoes reek so badly of blood I have had to tie them up in a sack.

Last night Rose summoned us to a secret council in the galley – me, Ott, Uskins, Sergeant Haddismal, even Marila & Felthrup. Mr Teggatz was instructed to make a great deal of noise with pots & boilers. In this way Rose hoped the ixchel would not catch our words, if they still bothered to spy on us.

The meeting was a failure. It was clear to all of us that the ship would never be permitted out of the bay. Rose ordered Haddismal & Ott to pull together plans for a night assault on the island, & for once all three were in complete agreement. 'They can throw boulders,' said Ott, 'but that will be of little use against Turachs dispersed among the trees. They are still just crawlies, and we are men.'

'We have enough small craft to put two hundred on the shore at once,' said Haddismal. Then he frowned and glanced at the spy-master. 'Of course, that would leave us with no means to evacuate the ship.'

'Timbers, then,' said Ott. 'The bay is calm, and the water warm enough. Lower some mastwood under cover of darkness, and let the men swim ashore on either side.'

The rest of us objected desperately. Marila said we should be sending gifts, not soldiers. Felthrup squeaked about shark fins in the bay.

'And my officers have nothing to contribute?' Rose demanded with a snarl. Uskins shook his head sorrowfully, but I cleared my throat. Our best hope was to find the ixchel stronghold on the *Chathrand*, I said, & to seize their food & water, along with a good number of hostages. Then we could bargain our way out of this trap.

But at this Felthrup only wailed: 'You can't, you can't!'

'Be quiet, Felthrup!' hissed Marila. But it was too late. Rose loomed over him like a mountain, ordered him to reveal all he knew. Felthrup only shook his head & muttered, 'Impossible, don't try.'

Then Rose exploded. He seized Felthrup & stormed across the galley, making for the oven. Marila screamed, Teggatz sputtered & waved a spoon. And I – I drew my knife & went for the captain. I do believe I would have stabbed him in the back. Ott moved like a panther, however. I caught a glimpse of his face (grinning) before something struck my skull. Then darkness swallowed me up.

When I woke I was alone with Teggatz in the galley. 'Out cold!' he said, helping me up with a grin. 'It's Monday. Like every Monday. Every one is the same.'

'Felthrup—'

Teggatz pointed proudly at the oven.

'Gods of Death – no!'

I shoved him aside & flew across the room & threw down the

iron door. Felthrup was in there, all right – blinking, terrified, unharmed. The oven was stone cold.

'No plum duff,' said Teggatz. 'No baking on Monday. Bah hah.'

A few minutes later Marila appeared & carried Felthrup back to the stateroom. I sat there hoping Teggatz would produce his jug of rum, but he was all business tonight, readying the galley for lock-up so that he might snatch a few hours' sleep. I'd rarely felt more wretched. The boils in my trousers were as sore as my head. 'Where in the shade of the Blessed Tree is Dr Chadfallow?' I asked aloud.

Teggatz closed the door behind me. I turned away & found myself facing Uskins, of all people. He was strangely lucid, & nervous in the extreme. 'Thank Rin you're awake,' he said, glancing nervously about. 'I came looking for you, Fiffengurt. I have the most terrible news.'

I felt my heart skip a beat. 'What is it? The doctor?'

Uskins started, then shook his head. 'I know nothing of Chadfallow.' Then he lowered his voice to a whisper. 'It's the crawlies, Fiffengurt. They're going to sink us for certain. I've found the proof.'

I stared at him. 'What sort of proof?'

'Can't you guess?' he hissed sharply. 'You know this ship as well as Rose. You tell me: how could a man sabotage her from within? Swiftly, irrevocably, leaving no time for the damage to be stopped?'

'There ain't no certain way.'

'But the most likely. Think, Fiffengurt: how would *you* do it?'

I shook my head. 'Maybe ... the way Old Captain Ingle sank the *Blaze* in Rukmast Harbour.' He looked at me blankly. 'Where were you in '26, man? They say he braced a cargo jack against the keelson, and cranked it hard against the hull until a wale popped its screws.'

'A wale.'

I pressed a hand to my throbbing head. 'A facing timber, Uskins. A blary plank. You know what a wale is, by damn. Now what's this news?'

He was silent for a moment, as though lost in thought. Then he looked up at me sharply. 'What you're describing is almost exactly what's going to occur.'

'Going to?' I cried. 'Are you bent full sideways? What did you find, and why haven't you been shouting your daft dirty head off about it? Flaming toads, Stukey—'

He thumped me in the stomach, then clapped a hand over my mouth. He pressed his lips close to my ear.

'Maggot,' he said. 'I have your peasant girl in my cabin with a death scarab on her forehead. If she screams, or moves, or I but think the command, that scarab will burn down through her skull like magma. You will not shout. You will show me this cargo jack, and help me position it. And you will deflect any questions, and send crewmembers out of our way.'

'Who—?'

'Not a word, not a word but to my purpose. I will give her agony before she dies. I warned her not to cry out even if it burned. I told her to think of her child.'

'Arunis!' I gasped.

He gave me a little frown. 'The scarab has just burned through her skin. Next will come her skull, if you do not heed me. The cargo jack. Take me to it. I will not ask again.'

I started marching. Nightmare, nightmare. Arunis in Uskins' body, intending to sink us at last. Arunis torturing Marila, disfiguring her. And damn him to the Pits, but she was strong enough to keep silent as her flesh burned. She could do that. He had chosen well.

'You ruined our water, too, I suppose. With the goat innards.'

'Be silent,' he snarled.

My legs were wobbly. We crept down the No. 3 ladderway, then crossed to the narrow scuttle by the cable tiers. Uskins (Arunis) walked naturally at my side. He'd told me to deflect questions, but there wouldn't be any. Nobody but Rose would question either of us; we were officers.

At the mercy deck I lit a lamp. There were cargo jacks down

in the hold, where the sabotage would have to be done. But why make it easy for him? I started aft towards the Abandoned House, that loneliest part of the ship, where the youths & I hatched our doomed plans for mutiny. There was a jack here, in a crawlspace. But there were many crawlspaces, & they all looked the same. A man could get confused.

The halls were narrow & black. Arunis (Uskins) grew twitchy. 'What are you doing, maggot? This is not the hold.'

'The jack,' I whispered. 'Just ahead.'

'What was that noise? Who is down here?'

'There's *nobody* here,' I told him. 'But look: that's the one.'

Except that it wasn't. In fact I wasn't exactly sure what was behind the crawlspace door at our feet, but I was blary sure it wasn't a cargo jack. I was stalling, of course. I'd remembered that this particular door was triple-bolted, & the bolts stiff & rusted. But now I was seized with fear for Marila. Helping to sink the *Chathrand* wouldn't save her, but how could I let him maim the girl?

'Open it!' Arunuskins hissed. 'Any tricks and that little whore will know pain beyond reason, I swear it.'

I set the lamp down & knelt. The first bolt slid free easily (I cursed inside) but the second put up a fight. My hands were shaking. Marila's face, Marila's tears—

'Chadfallow guessed,' said Arunuskins.

I started, twisting about, & he cuffed me on the cheek. I turned back to the bolt.

'Mr Uskins died of nerves,' said the voice behind me. 'Despite the plague, he tried to refuse my services. But before I left the ship I persuaded him to keep my scarf, just in case. It was my voice in his ear, that scarf. It stoked his terror as the plague advanced, until he could think of nothing else. And then he let me in, and I took over the house.'

'And his soul?' I asked, shaking. 'Where are you keeping it?'

'Nowhere,' said the voice. 'That coward's mind was of no use to me. I forced it out through the window, and let the breeze carry it away. You should thank me, Fiffengurt. You despised the man. Didn't everyone?'

The second bolt slid free, & I moved on to the third. Slowly.

'I too am dead,' said the voice. 'Dead to this world, that is. But when the Swarm has lain it waste I shall inherit the universe. Then I shall need no more puppets. I will never stoop so low again.'

I popped the third bolt. The door fell open – on a thoroughly empty crawlspace. I winced, expecting to feel him cuff me again. But instead I heard the sorcerer lurch violently away. I whirled. He was writhing, both hands at his neck. Behind him, holding tight to a garrotting wire, stood Sandor Ott.

'Don't do it!' I howled. 'He'll kill Marila!'

'Unluckily for him, I could not care less,' said Ott. 'Keep still, monster! I can drop your head on these boards with a twitch of the wrist.'

A ghastly wheeze escaped Arunuskins' throat. His eyes were locked on me. 'But Ott!' I pleaded, 'He's put some some vile thing on Marila's forehead, he's torturing her—'

'Shut up. And stand clear, unless you want to be soaked.'

The mage's cheeks had hollowed out; his eyes were bulging like grapes. The wire had already drawn a little blood. A thin sound, like steam from a kettle, came from Uskin's throat.

Ott grinned. 'You have some comment on the precedings? In fact I think we've heard quite enough from you. But if you care to bargain for this stolen body, you may try. Let me spare you some effort: we know already that Macadra has taken the Nilstone.'

Arunuskins twitched violently. The wire bit deeper into his flesh.

'Careful!' said Ott. 'Yes, we have that on good authority. Your old sparring partner learned it, dream-walking. I'm speaking of Felthrup of course. Macadra has taken the Nilstone, and slain Pathkendle's gang. And she is halfway here.'

Once again Arunuskins jumped. His face contorted with pain.

'Beyond that, have you anything of consequence to say?' demanded Ott. 'If so, just raise a finger.'

Arunuskins hesitated, beady eyes swivelling. Ott clicked his tongue. 'I thought not,' he said.

His arm jerked fiercely. The wire slashed, the flesh parted. I slipped in the blood as I shoved past Ott & the gushing corpse, blinded by my tears. Ott called after me casually, as if to say, Don't bother. I flew to the upper decks, smashed into sailors, incoherent with grief—

Marila was standing on the lower gun deck, unharmed. 'What is it?' she cried. 'Why are you bloody? Mr Fiffengurt, are you *all right?*'

I fell on my knees, hugged her, weeping like a child. All lies. They were so good at it, these spies & sorcerers. And I am hopeless & always will be. I couldn't seem to release her. I felt her heartbeat, & I felt that wee babe kick.

Wednesday, 4 Fuinar 942. We found Dr Chadfallow in Uskins' cabin, under a shroud of flies. I have no heart to write of my friend just yet. Not a word more, or I shall be unable to continue.

Let me write instead of the scarf. Captain Rose soaked it in lamp oil, applied a torch, and held it out over the sea on the end of a boathook. A crowd gathered for the grim little ceremony: the ones who had outlived the sorcerer. No one said much. It felt good just to stand there. As the cloth burned, Thasha's dogs whined and pricked up their ears, and Felthrup asked if we didn't hear someone moaning, very far, very faint?

Now in bed I am thinking of Sandor Ott. Did he have a spy watching Uskins – or watching me? It hardly matters any more. What does matter is this: that whore's bastard *didn't know that Arunis was lying*. About Marila, that is. He simply didn't care. He'd lost a few hands of poker against the mage before, & wasn't going to lose this one. Come what may.

Later, in Rose's cabin, he all but crowed. 'I enjoyed spilling that blood. There was no reason to question Arunis further. He was dead, and you can't threaten the dead: there's a lesson every prince ought to learn. Nor can you bribe a man who wants nothing you possess. All we could hope for was to learn what the mage *didn't* know.'

'You lied to him,' I said.

'Of course. Felthrup does not know if Macadra has the Nilstone, or that she is chasing us. But now we know that Arunis *hated* both ideas. The two mages were not in league; or if they were, Arunis was only pretending, and planning to betray Macadra. In either case he is unlikely to have been guiding her towards the *Chathrand*.'

'But why did he try to sink us?' growled Sergeant Haddsimal, enraged. 'We've got the Shaggat Ness on board! Didn't he want that fiend delivered to his worshippers? *Ain't that the whole mucking idea?*'

'Fool!' snapped Lady Oggosk. 'It was *your* idea. Which is to say Arqual's. Which is to say Ott's.'

'It was the sorcerer's wish as well, for a time,' said Rose. 'But we all know better now. The Shaggat was a tool. So was the war between Arqual and the Mzithrin. Even the Nilstone, ultimately, was a tool. The end was something blacker and more immense.'

'And maybe Arunis found another means to that end,' I said. 'Maybe the Shaggat just ain't necessary no longer. But sinking the *Chathrand* is.'

'Or prudent, at the least,' said Ott. 'But why prudent, I ask you? What can we do with this ship that worries him? Nothing that a thousand other ships cannot do – except cross the Ruling Sea. In the North that makes the *Chathrand* unique. And even here such ships are exceedingly few.'

'That is so,' said the captain. 'The Behemoth that chased us was vast, but any tarboy could tell you it wasn't seaworthy. The waves on the Nelluroq would have sunk it in a matter of hours. Macadra's ship is rumoured to be a *Segral* like the *Chathrand*, but the prince made it clear that she was just one of a handful of such vessels left afloat.'

'And only one of them is *making* for the North,' added Ott. 'That is what distinguished us, gentlemen. There was certainly a time when Arunis wished us to take the Nilstone to Gurishal. But now, in death, he has learned something that makes him fear what once he craved.'

All this was in the wee hours of that horrid night. Despite our exhaustion we were all on our feet save Lady Oggosk, who was slumped at the dining table, chewing cow-like on a lump of *mül*. But at Ott's words she grew still, & her milk-blue eyes gazed up at us with wonder.

'A tool,' she said. 'By the Night Gods, Nilus, the loathsome spy may be right. We know that Arunis made tools of everyone he touched. But in another's hands *he himself may have been a tool*. And for what?'

She straightened up in her chair. 'Not for the death of the world. He wanted that himself, needed it, worked like a lunatic to achieve it. No, Arunis feared nothing but the world's salvation. And after death, he's learned that this very mission stands a chance of bringing it about.'

The room fell silent. On Rose's desk, Sniraga watched us, purring. Finally the captain spoke: 'Arunis, a tool of the Gods?'

Lady Oggosk shook her head firmly. But Sandor Ott began a slow, loud clap. At first I thought him jesting, but then I looked at his face. He had never looked so blissful, so moved. He squeezed the witch's hands (Oggosk recoiled with a scowl), & even gazed fondly at the rest of us. His eyes, I swear to Rin, were moist.

'So,' he said, 'the truth appears at last. Despite ourselves, we are on the same side.'

We waited. No one had any idea what he meant.

'Your duchess is most wise,' he continued. 'And let no one doubt it further: we *shall* be this world's deliverance. The return of the Shaggat will be the Mzithrin's death-knell, and the dawn of the Arquali age. In my darkest hours I have asked myself: why? Why did we ever cross that horrid sea? Why so vast a journey, into such unknowns? Now I understand: it was that we might learn of Arqual's greater task.'

'Greater?' rumbled the captain.

The spymaster nodded, enraptured. 'The Black Rags will fall.

The Crownless Lands we will harvest like grapes on the vine. And when the banner of His Supremacy waves over all lands north of the Nelluroq, then it will be time to plan a reckoning with the South. Don't you see? Bali Adro is imploding, ruining itself. Their sun is setting; ours has just begun to rise. Arqual is the best hope for this poor, bludgeoned world. You know that. Everyone does, in his heart. And now at last we see the guiding hand. This bay will not hold us. *Nothing* can hold us, nothing ever stops this boat for long. Storms, thirst, whirlpools, crawly infestations, magical armies, mutant rats. We pass through them, straight and certain as the mind of Rin. And behold, this final proof: a devil risen from the Pits to try and thwart us. But he could not. The Emperor's cause has the mandate of heaven.'

'I didn't say that!' shrieked Oggosk. But the spymaster was already making for the door.

Thursday, 5 Fuinar 942. Fegin is our first mate, now; old Coote has replaced him as bosun. Jervik Lank, Chadfallow's last assistant, is caring for twenty-four men in the sickbay, with help (of a sort) from Dr Rain, who is indefatigable, but cannot be left alone with the patients. I am told he recently brought them soup in a bedpan.

This morning Lank showed me a note he discovered in Chadfallow's desk. It is written in the late doctor's hand:

> *Let it be known that it is my wish to be buried in the heart of the Ruling Sea, not in waters claimed by any power in Alifros, for it was only when I cast off belief in nations that I perceived something of my soul.*
>
> *However if circumstances allow, I should like my son, Pazel Pathkendle, to light a candle for me in the Physicians' Temple at 17 Reka Street, Etherhorde. This is an amendment to my Last Testament of 5 Vaqrin 941, which in all other particulars remains in force.*

Five Vaqrin! It appears that just days before the *Chathrand* sailed from Etherhorde, old Chadfallow made a will. I have asked Lank to search for that testament, even if he had to dig through every one of Chadfallow's twenty-two crates of documents & scrolls. Lank was more than willing when he understood that by finding it he might be doing Pazel a good turn.

Felthrup, too, has taken an interest in Chadfallow's papers, or at least one set of them: his log of the times & places where the Green Door appeared. Fascination with the door has passed like a germ from the doctor's mind to the rat's. Marila says that he read the logbook straight through six times, and then began to beg her to race about the decks with him to see if Chadfallow really had found a pattern. I gather they believe he has.

As for the doctor himself, we have embalmed him after the mariner's fashion until we somehow escape this bay.* And how long do we have for that little job? Today at five bells the swallows returned (along with Lord Talag & his frowning escorts) & carried off more ixchel, and at seven bells they did the same. At least a hundred have fled the *Chathrand* already. Most did not spare her a backward glance, but a few did, their copper eyes softening with affection. The worst of boats still tries to save us from the sea.

At eight bells, Felthrup made an odd request – an audience with poor Captain Magritte, the whaler we picked up in the Nelu Rekere, & his Quezan spearmen. Of course Magritte is blind – was *blinded*, rather, during the carnage at Masalym. An ixchel dropped on his head from above, and that was that. Two knives, tok-tok. Chadfallow told us he was lucky to have lived through it. I often wonder if Magritte concurs.

'What d'ye want to go bothering him about?' I asked Felthrup.

---

*The 'mariner's fashion' refers to a solution of vinegar and potash, to which any of the following may be added, in any concentration: alum, arsenic, germanium, fluid styrax, ambergris, flowers of sulphur, cedria, wood aloe, xanath gum, sapwort, capsicum, turpentine, walrus oil. Results, to no educated person's surprise, are at best erratic - EDITOR

'The world's salvation!' he squeaked. I had to bite my lips to keep from shouting *Not you as well!* I tried to put him off until evening, but to my surprise he grew quite fierce with me.

'What favours have I ever asked of you, you white-whiskery man? Or have I not earned even one? You think me talkative, excitable, custodian of a vacillating mind. You think my worries are dander in the wind.'

'Now, Ratty—'

'Our doom is near, Mr Fiffengurt! The Swarm of Night is growing, growing. He did not lie about that!'

'Who didn't?'

'Who! Who! That is my question exactly! His name is *not* Tulor, he lies! But if I guess his true name I shall *have* him!'

A man can face but so much jibberish. I roused Magritte & led him & Ratty to the compartment on the main deck where the Quezans sleep. For whalers & reformed cannibals they are an amazingly pacific bunch. All four stand over six feet & have long horizontal scars on their chests for every harpoon kill. But they fear sorcery more than death itself, & have never truly recovered from the battle with the monster rats. At the sight of Felthrup (who rushed at them, babbling) they exploded to their feet & fled by the opposite door. We had to hobble after them, across the deck & down the No. 4 to the berth deck. It took a great deal of soothing before they'd consent to listen to a talking rodent.

I was most irritated with Felthrup; I daresay Chadfallow's murder oppressed us both more than we knew. Luckily he wanted just one thing from the whalers. It was the meaning of a word, 'Kazizarag', which I gather he found in his blessed *Polylex*. He'd somehow deduced that it had its roots in the native Quezan tongue, & that Magritte was the only one aboard who might effect a translation.

In fact he was right on all counts. 'Kazizarag' means 'greed' or 'gluttony'. But the word sparked nervous laughter among the Quezans, & after some hesitation they told Magritte that it was also a word attached to many a devil or villainous God in their stories: *Uchudidu Kazizarag* is 'the Greedy Pig-Devil' who steals from the poor man's hut while he's out fishing the reefs.

'Of course he is!' shrilled Felthrup, hopping with delight. Then he turned & looked up at me. 'I must have gold, Mr Fiffengurt! A great deal, and quickly!'

I took him from the chamber & lowered my voice. 'Come now, Ratty; why do you say such silly things?'

'Oh, am I *silly* now?' he shot back. 'You have done no research. You have enjoyed fresh air and pleasant company while I sat alone on Thasha's bed, turning pages with my teeth. And all the while *he* is screaming, screaming behind those iron bars.'

'Iron bars? Are you talkin' about someone in the brig?'

Felthrup shook his head. 'Tell me quickly: do you know where the hoard is? The great hoard from the Emperor's coffers?'

I was startled. 'It ain't in one place. They broke it up into smaller caches. I've a pretty good guess where one of 'em is, though.'

'You must raid it. You must bring me gleaming treasure.'

'But why?'

'Why!' shouted Felthrup. 'Why, why, why, why! Of all puerile words in the Arquali tongue! Of all vacant, gnawed-off, insipid, animal-mews—'

'Never mind yer commentaries!' I barked.

'So you refuse.'

'No I don't mucking refuse! I'd walk barefoot in a bed of razor clams for you, if you care to know. But Rin's gizzard, just tell me what it's about!'

'I would rather face him alone. He is vile and tricky.'

'Black Pits of Damnation, Felthrup! Are you sayin' Arunis has his claws in *another* man?'

'Not Arunis. The Glutton. The Glutton is far more dangerous now.'

'You can't mean the Shaggat Ness?'

'*Of course not!*' He ran six times around my feet. Then he stopped, rubbed his face with terrible anxiety, & told me of the demon in the cage.

Friday, 6 Fuinar 942. It was a suspicious box. No latches, no screws, and its lid glued down fast & for ever. It was mounted on the underside of the floor planks of the portside afterhold, about ten feet above the noxious, sloshing bilge well.* You could easily miss it, even if you had cause to creep down inside that watery space, as few men did. I had noticed the box during the removal of the rat carcasses in Masalym. But I'd never breathed a word, for it could only be one of the treasure chests brought aboard in secret back in Arqual, and would only bring evil and infighting down upon us if its existence became known to the crew.

I'd put it quite out of my mind until my talk with Ratty yesterday. And when I arrived and stuck my head through the little bilge-hatch, I cursed.

'What's the matter?' whispered Marila. I'd brought her with me to hold the hurricane lamp, which we'd only just dared to light. It had taken us the better part of an hour to find this spot, feeling our way down lightless passages. I'd made Felthrup stay behind in the stateroom: if the ixchel found him here there'd be no protection we could give.

But it was all in vain: someone had beaten us to the gold. I reached in and felt the hatcheted remains of the box, still dangling from the boards. I cursed again: Felthrup would be apoplectic. Then Marila lowered her face to the hatch and *she* cursed.

'Well ain't that the devil's pancake,' I said. 'And that gold ain't no use to anybody while we're on this ship. Including Felthrup's own greedy devil, if it exists.'

'Demon,' she said, 'and Felthrup's only going by—'

She broke off, squinting at the darkness. Then she lowered the lamp into the bilge-well on its chain. 'Look down there,' she said, 'at the very bottom. Aren't those coins?'

Sure as Rin makes rain, there were gold cockles winking up at us, under twenty feet of frigid, ship-filthy water. The raiders had

---

*And within a few yards of the spot where Myett attempted suicide, after Lord Taliktrum abandoned her and the *Chathrand*. - EDITOR been sloppy. They'd spilled a part of their takings into the bilge.

'How much does Felthrup need?' Marila asked.

I shrugged. 'As much as we can lay our hands on. But it doesn't matter, does it? We ain't collecting those.'

'Of course we are. Go on, empty the pouch.'

'See here,' I said firmly, 'if you think I'm about to go diving into that slime just because Ratty's been dream-debating some pot-bellied spook—'

'I don't think anything of the kind.'

Before I quite knew what was happening, Marila had stripped down to her dainties and was getting set to leap into the bilge. She was a pearl diver, as I'd nearly forgotten. I told her no, no – get away from there – we'll find a tarboy, we'll scoop 'em up somehow – sit down, you're too fat, you're a mother-in-the-making—

She jumped. I was so frightened I nearly dropped the lamp chain. Marila struck the bilious water, gasped once, then turned head-down and kicked for the bottom. I must record here that she was lovely, graceful as a murth-girl, for all that her belly was round as a harvest moon. After a few strokes she'd churned up so much flotsam that I could barely see her. But when she surfaced (two long minutes later) there was gold in her purse.

She dived twice more. Then I unhooked the lamp & dropped her the chain. The first tug nearly broke my back – that babe will surely be a giant, parents notwithstanding – but there was no choice, I was going to haul her out or die trying. I fought for inches. There was no good footing; the chain snagged on the edge of the hatch. Just when I feared to disgrace myself by dropping her back into the bilge, out she came: a stinking, beautiful seal. I wrapped my coat around her. In the sack were forty gold cockles & a silver Heaven's Tree with gems for fruit.

[Two hours later]

Something is amiss with the little people. This afternoon Lord Talag & the two islanders returned once again, & as usual there was a crowd of ixchel waiting to depart. But as the swallows descended Talag suddenly began barking orders. We couldn't hear the words of course – it was all in ixchel-speak – & I daresay his native escorts didn't fully understand them either. But his own clan did. At Talag's first word they scattered in all directions, & in a matter of seconds they were gone below.

Talag brought the birds swooping down, but his gestures were different this time, more erratic, & the flock surged about in confusion. The islanders were suddenly outraged, screaming & threatening; one even waved a knife. Talag appeared to be protesting his helplessness. But after a moment he reassembled the flock, & the three flew back across the bay.

At my elbow, Sergeant Haddismal turned & gave me an accusing look. 'What are yer little darlings up to *now*?'

'Talag's no friend to me and never has been,' I snapped. 'But Stath Bálfyr's not workin' out like he planned.'

'Oh ho,' said Haddismal. 'And how do you know *that*?'

'By that scene, of course. By his blary face.'

'You can't read a crawly's face. And what's this plan you're talking about?'

'I'm *not* talking about any plan! What I mean is, they're fighting, or arguing at least. So maybe these islanders didn't greet their brothers with wide-open arms.'

Haddismal cracked the knuckles of his enormous hands. 'If they're fighting, let 'em fight on. Let 'em bleed! I'd step on 'em one by one if I could.'

'Gods damn it, tinshirt, they ain't all the same! Talag's a lunatic, and his son's a fool, but Lady Dri was—'

'Scum!'

I jumped a foot in the air. It was Sandor Ott. The snake had slithered up behind me.

'What is happening?' he hissed. 'What message did Talag pass to his clansmen, just now?'

'How should I know? Do I have crawly ears?'

'Tell us of their plan, Fiffengurt.'

At that my self-control just snapped, & I raised my eyes to heaven: 'I DO NOT *KNOW* THEIR PLAN. I DO NOT KNOW THAT THEY EVEN *POSSESS* A PLAN. I AM NO BETTER INFORMED THAN YOU, YOU OLD—'

His arm moved in a blur. I felt a sharp sting beneath my good eye & recoiled. He had drawn his white knife & cut me, with a surgeon's precision, just deep enough to break the skin.

'If I learn that you have conspired with the crawlies again, I will kill you, and slaughter that whore Marila like a pig. Do not imagine my threat is as empty as the sorcerer's. It will be done.'

Saturday, 7 Fuinar 942. All day there is eerie silence from Stath Bálfyr. Then at dusk a man on the foremast reports hearing a strange echo: maybe a trumpet, maybe the bellow of some forest beast. Ott's own beastly instincts are surely triggered, for he persuades Rose to roll out the guns & flood the deck with Turachs. The drums sound, the officers scream; the men & tarboys fall terrified into their practised roles.

And nothing happens. The night grows dark & chill. Hours pass, the gunnery crews crouch drowsy by their weapons. Rose paces, stem to stern. I too am on deck & waiting, for what I cannot say.

It comes at six bells, three o'clock in Rin's blessed morning. But it is not the attack we fear. No, it is only the swallows again, swooping down for another group of ixchel. This time the exodus begins on the quarterdeck, not the forecastle. Men start to race there, who knows why. I hear bellows from the soldiers in the lead.

I'm halfway to the bow but make a run for it. I see Ott far ahead. *'Alive!'* he's shouting. *'Take them alive! Catch them, sweep them up, you slow-arsed dogs!'*

When I draw near I see that Talag has come from ashore without his minders, & with a much larger flock of birds. On the quarterdeck, hundreds of ixchel are waiting to leap into their claws. They are earnest & grim. No sense of victory here. Every last man & woman is armed to the teeth.

The Turachs have nets. Someone – Ott, Rose? – has commanded

them to prevent this exodus, lest we find ourselves holding no hostages, & thus no cards. But the ixchel have mostly slipped through our fingers. Maybe a dozen get nabbed, or crushed underfoot,* but the bulk of the clan flows straight up the rails & rigging, like beads of oil drawn magically skyward, & the urgent swallows pluck them & make off across the bay, with Talag circling, shouting them on.

Ere they vanish I catch one glimpse of his face. For an instant I think he is disfigured: something (an ear, an eye?) has surely been ripped away. Then I realise it's nothing physical. It's his confidence that has ruptured, his certainty. And that is a thousand times crueller in Lord Talag, that colossus of pride. He is still fighting, still leading his people somewhere, & furiously, but the reason behind it is gone.

Monday, 9 Fuinar 942. Marila has come running. The Green Door has appeared on the mercy deck, & Felthrup's mind cannot be changed. We are to meet there at once, to bargain with a creature of the Pits.

---

*Here Fiffengurt scribbles in the margin: *Remember it, the savagery of your own kind, a woman crushed beneath a soldier's boot-heel, the crackle of bones & the woman protruding only from the waist up, screaming, screaming until she faints or dies, & not the least whisper of her agony could my human ears discern. Is this silence why we find them so easy to kill?* - EDITOR

25

The Flight of the *Promise*

—◦◦◦—

Her figurehead was a white horse, and its flowing mane swept back in delicate whorls along the prow. Thasha sat beneath it on the little platform that fronted the keel. Dawn light on her face, salt stinging her eyes. Before her was a spread of countless islets, drops of wax on the vast blue cloth of ocean. Thasha was murmuring a song that had come to her in a dream. *Leheda mori che gathri gel, leheda mori arú.* A melancholy song, she imagined. A song of farewell.

The *Promise* was a swift, sleek three-master. Like the selk who built her, she somehow conveyed the presence of another world, or perhaps a version of this world governed by subtly different laws. There was a stillness about her, even as she rose and plunged on the waves. Her sides were painted silver, her masts and spars of a pale white wood such as Thasha had never seen. Her crescent sails were the blue-white of the mountain peaks behind them. Yet all these colours shifted slightly with the changing sun or clouds, as if the *Promise* were trying to blend in, to vanish against the sea and sky.

You know what we're facing, don't you? Thasha asked the ship in silence. *You know we're a rabbit among wolves.*

She was far too small for the Ruling Sea. But Nólcindar, who captained her, had assured the travellers that she was ready for any waves to be found here in the Island Wilderness – and as fast as any boat in Bali Adro.

Just as well, Thasha had reflected, for the *Promise* was no fighter.

There were gunports, but no guns: the selk had long ago chosen lightness over force. But the crew looked forceful enough: twenty selk and twenty dlömu, the former from Nólcindar's band, the latter fishermen from the tiny villages that were all the barren coast could support.

The fishermen were a restrained, self-conscious lot: Thasha had yet to see one smile. The presence of Prince Olik left many speechless with awe, but the selk affected them even more profoundly. They were indebted to the people of Uláramyth for some deed long ago. Thasha gathered that it was this debt that had saved them, for when they looked at the humans the fishermen's looks grew dark.

'They are what they seem,' Prince Olik had explained. 'They are human beings, such as the oldest among you may recall from childhood. You need not fear them.'

'We do not fear them,' said the leader of the fishermen. 'But two days ago the *Platazcra* was here, with a warship many times larger than the *Promise*. This was no surprise: they often snatch our ablest sons for crew, or for darker work in Orbilesc. But this time they had another purpose. They spoke of *tol-chenni* who had recovered from the plague: human beings who could think and talk, like men. They swore they were unnatural, and aided by criminals and traitors from Masalym.'

'Such names the mighty have always given their enemies, and always will,' said Kirishgán.

The fishermen went on staring. 'Tell them the rest, Jannar,' growled a voice from the back of the crowd.

Their leader's face was grim. 'We were told,' he said, 'that should we aid the *tol-chenni,* or even fail to keep them here, that we would all be killed, after seeing our children burned alive.'

Silence fell. Prince Olik and Lunja bowed their heads in shame.

'Those prepared to issue such threats will also be prepared to act on them,' said Nólcindar. 'I am sorry we came to you in this way. Of course, you must try to keep us, and we must fight and flee you, who have been our brothers so long.'

The dlömic fishermen had bristled.

'You do not understand,' said their leader. 'They have tortured us already, robbed us of our children, poisoned the very fish we eat. But things were different once. We came here starving, out of the Wastes of Siralaç, and food appeared at the margins of our camps, and medicines that saved our children. We settled here, and in two years there were nut-trees sprouting in the clefts of the headlands, and fruiting vines. Whose gifts were those, Nólcindar? And when we were besieged, who came to us with blue steel burning, and put our enemies to flight? We are poor, and our numbers have dwindled, but we will never break faith with the selk. Your boat is waiting as it ever has been, in that cove no Imperial eyes have ever seen.'

Their plan, it appeared, was to abandon their villages before Macadra's forces could return. Thasha did not know how they would flee – by land, by boat? – or what havens they might find when they arrived. Nor did the fishermen themselves know where the *Promise* was bound.

Safer that way, Thasha mused. *Any of us could end up in Macadra's hands.*

It had not been easy to escape the Coves. The fishermen had sent out scouting vessels, and placed lookouts on the headlands, peering into the darkness of the Gulf. For six hours the *Promise* had stood ready, every soul aboard waiting tensely for the all-clear signal. When at last it came they raced to their stations, and the ghostly vessel glided out from the dark cliffs and swept north by starlight.

The Gulf was not actually empty; it was never empty, this close to the Imperial heartland. There were large vessels to the south, and beyond them a light fell over the shore, as of a bonfire of poisonous things. Another pool of light, due west, was so large that Thasha took it at first for an army encamped on an island. Then (her stomach lurched) she saw that the island was moving, crawling southwards like a monstrous centipede over the waves. Glowing shapes wheeled above it, and sudden flares like heat lightning illuminated its flanks. She did not know it then, but she was looking at the same Behemoth that had attacked the *Chathrand*, groping its way back to Orbilesc to fill its maw again with coal and slaves and sailors.

Eleven days had passed since their depature from Ilidron. Behind them lay the charted islands, claimed by Bali Adro and heavily patrolled, no longer a true wilderness at all. Ahead lay the sprawling, uncharted northern archipelagos – and the *Chathrand*, as Ildraquin's whispers to Hercól still confirmed. For a week they had been skipping and sneaking through these little foggy isles, their beaches crowded with nesting birds, or seals that lay in the sunshine like cast-off coats. Eleven days, and dangers aplenty. Hardly had they left the Coves when a fierce squall tried to dash them on the lee shore. They had scraped off with the sand showing yellow between the breakers, and the wives and children of the fishermen in plain sight atop the cliffs, near enough to wave, but too horrified to do so. Two days later a warship had risen up suddenly from the east, flashing an order to hold position. Of course Nólcindar had declined the invitation: the *Promise* had fled, and been chased as far as the Redvane before losing their pursuers in a fog bank.

'We escaped,' Prince Olik had murmured to the youths, 'but this is a disaster all the same. For they were close enough to see us – to see selk and dlömu working the ship together. Macadra will hear of this in no time.'

Nólcindar appeared to be of the same opinion, for that night they played a desperate trick: sailing the *Promise* through the narrowest gap in the Sandwall. The long barrier islands were breached in many spots, but the Empire kept close watch on all the larger, permanent inlets. That left only the shifting channels, washed open by one storm or cyclone and closed by the next.

'And even these may be guarded,' Prince Olik warned. 'It would be a simple matter of dispatching a few more boats from Masalym, or Fandural Edge.'

So it had proved. The waterway was tiny and twisting, barely wide enough for the *Promise* to make her turns. And yet a dozen soldiers were encamped there, and two had enormous, feline mounts.

'Sand cats,' Bulutu declared, frowning into the telescope. '*Sicuñas* bred for desert work. They'll run fast along the beach.'

'To some larger outpost, maybe,' said Prince Olik, 'or to a signal-point. Either way we cannot let them go.'

The fishermen were in clear distress. 'What do you mean to do, Prince?' asked their leader.

But it was Hercól who answered, not at all proudly: 'We shall ambush them,' he said, 'like thieves in the night.'

When darkness fell they brought the *Promise* to within three miles of the Sandwall. They tied swords and knives up in canvas, and the canvas to floats made of cork. Then some twenty selk and dlömic fighters began to undress and slip down ropes into the waves. Prince Olik and Lunja went with them, and so did Neda and Hercól.

Thasha too prepared for the assault, tying back her hair and starting to undress. But when Hercól took notice he caught her roughly by the arm.

'What is this?' he demanded. 'Have you forgotten everything? Have the tarboys and I been talking to thin air?'

'You blary well know I can fight.'

'Irrelevant,' he snapped. 'If we lose you we shall very probably lose this whole endeavour. Cover yourself, girl, and step back.'

'Girl, am I?'

'You will stay aboard, Thasha Isiq. We need another sort of strength from you.'

He was trying to avert his eyes. Thasha knew with sudden certainty that she had aroused him, and that the distraction made him furious. She crossed her arms over her chest. Hercól was right, this was unforgivable, what in Pitfire was *wrong* with her?

'I'm sorry,' she stammered. 'It's just – fighting feels easier than—'

'Than freeing Erithusmé? I'm not surprised.'

He still would not look at her. He had scars on his torso that she had never seen.

'Do you recall what Ramachni said at the Temple of the Wolves?' he asked suddenly. 'About how quickly the Swarm is gaining strength? How long do we have before it covers Alifros, do you suppose? How many nights, before the night that never ends?'

He climbed over the rail, naked but for Ildraquin and a cloth about his hips. 'We can't lose you, either,' she stammered. 'I mean I can't. You know that, don't you?'

He made no reply, not even a smile or a frown. He just dived. Thasha stood there with her shirt open, watching the swimmers vanish in the dark. When she was barely of age she had dreamed that Hercól would touch her, take her, in the study or the garden or the little scrub room where she changed before their fighting lessons. Gently or furiously, silently or with whispers of love. She had never quite renounced those dreams, but they had fled somewhere so distant as to become almost chaste, part of the love she felt for the man, a love that was nothing at all like her love for Pazel, which could blind and devour her. *To lose either of them* – how could she survive that? And what if no one else survived? What if she were left alone?

It could happen. Erithusmé might give her a way out that was closed to everyone else. Could the world be so cruel as to force her to take it?

But Hercól had not fallen that night, and neither had Lunja or Neda. The Bali Adrons, surprised and outnumbered and bewildered at the sight of Prince Olik, mostly obeyed his call to surrender, and those who did not were quickly subdued. The *sicuña*-riders sped to their mounts and tried to flee westwards, but Neda and Lunja were ready and waiting. Racing down from the dunetops, they leaped and tackled the riders, battling both men to the ground.

Only two died in the operation: Neda's rider, who fought to the death; and one of the dlömic fishermen, who was bringing up the rear as the raiders swam back to the *Promise*. The man simply disappeared. The captured warriors spoke of sharks, hunting along the inside of the Sandwall. Hercól nodded grimly. 'We have met with them before. And this time there was blood in the water.'

There was one other casualty: Lunja's cheek, raked by the claws of the *sicuña*. The beast had whirled on her in fright when she tackled its rider, before the selk arrived and calmed the creature with a touch. Thasha winced at the sight: the wounds were pale and livid on her blacker-than-black dlömic skin. Later, as the *Promise* moved cautiously through the gap, Thasha heard Neeps and Lunja talking in the shadows.

'What are you holding against your face?'

'My cloth from Uláramyth. Kirishgán says I should cover the wounds with it until dawn.'

'You must be tired of holding it. Give it here.'

'I am not tired, boy.'

A silence. Then Neeps asked, 'Your people can grow back fingers and toes. Can you grow fresh skin as well?'

Thasha saw the fierce gleam in Lunja's eye. 'Will I be scarred, do you mean? Will I be ugly? What is that to you?'

Thasha moved away from them, not wanting to hear more. She took a turn at the halyards, in a line of selk, their blue eyes shining in the darkness like living sapphires. An hour later, as they cleared the Sandwall and emerged into the high, thrashing seas beyond, she saw Neeps and Lunja seated side by side against the hatch coaming. The dlömic woman was asleep with her head on his shoulder, and Neeps was still pressing the cloth to her cheek.

That night Thasha held Pazel close, and he murmured a song into her ear. It was in the selk language he had learned on Sirafstöran Torr, but he himself could not say where he had learned the tune.

'Someone must have been singing it in Uláramyth,' he said. 'There are times when I feel as if we spent years in that place. As if a whole stage of our lives passed there in safety.'

They slept, and Thasha dreamed they made love, and in the dream Pazel changed many times. He was a selk, and then he was Hercól, and then a dlömu with the voice of Ramachni, singing *Allaley heda Miraval, ni starinath asam*, and then he was a sea-murth with sinuous limbs, and he sang a murth-song, and when she woke there were tears in Pazel's eyes.

The shadow of a bird swept over her face. Starting from her reverie, Thasha reached up and grasped the carved mane of the horse above her, and stood. It was very early; only a handful of selk were about, and none were near. She had spent an hour on this platform already, puzzling over the erotic dream and the song that came to her in such detail, *Leheda mori*, was that *Goodbye in this lifetime, goodbye in this world*?

Idle fool. What impulse had brought her here? She had meant to rise and go straight to the struggle, that inner assault at the wall between herself and Erithusmé. It was how she had begun every day on the *Promise*: seeking desperately for any fissure, any hidden latch or keyhole. Smashing, flailing. And finding nothing. *You're out of time, out of time*, chided a voice in her head, and every day it rang more true. If they were caught on the high seas, pincered between warships or snared by some *Platazcra* devilry, what then? The selk and nineteen fishermen could not fight off a host, or shield the *Promise* from withering cannon-fire. No one could help – save possibly Erithusmé, furious and caged. And every day she feared Hercól would draw Ildraquin and learn the dreaded news: that the *Chathrand* was leaving, setting off into the Ruling Sea, waiting no longer.

The others felt the same urgency, now. Hercól had questioned her about every moment in the last year when she had noticed any trace of that other being inside her, however remote. She answered his questions dutifully, but they brought no breakthrough. Then Lunja and Neda had taken her off to a little cabin in the stern and asked other questions, mortifying questions, about Greysan Fulbreech. It seemed the builder of the wall might be Arunis himself, and Greysan the tool he used to put it in place. But Ramachni had said that to do so would have required some force, and that Thasha would have felt it – unless greatly distracted. Were there such moments? Scarlet, Thasha admitted that there had been: two times, before her suspicions of Fulbreech became acute. No, she'd not let him go too far. But yes, Rin help her, she'd been distracted, aware of nothing but his kisses, his hands.

A soft sound from the deck above. Someone was waiting for her: Hercól or Pazel or Neda or Neeps. Waiting and hoping: had she found the key at last? Thasha closed her eyes. One more day of disappointment. One more day when they would cheer her, warm her, salute her for the fight she was waging.

She turned and ducked under the bowsprit, seized the top of the rail, pulled herself to the height of the topdeck. And froze.

A few yards from her lay an ungainly brown bird. A pelican. It was splayed on its side, one black eye gazing skyward. It was so still Thasha feared it was dead.

She slid over the rail. Nólcindar and several dlömic crewmembers had also noticed the bird. The dlömu stared with wonder, and Thasha realised with a start that she had not seen one pelican south of the Ruling Sea. The dlömu were edging nearer, but when Nólcindar saw Thasha she waved for them to be still. Thasha stepped closer. A muscle twitched in the pelican's wing, but otherwise it did not move.

Thasha knelt. The pelican was breathing, but only just; its eye had begun to glaze over. The moment felt unreal and yet absolutely vital: she was kneeling beside a bird and the bird was half dead of exhaustion and the fate of their whole struggle was in that failing eye. She stared: the orb was dreadfully parched. Once more bowing to impulse, she breathed on the eye, and saw the fog of her breath upon its surface.

Then the eye blinked. The two halves of the yellow-orange beak parted minutely, and a sound emerged. It was not that of any bird. It was a voice, huge and deep but extremely distant, like an echo in a canyon far away. She could catch no words, but there was an awesome complexity to the sound, thunder within thunder, lava boiling in the earth. And Thasha knew she had heard the voice before.

'Bring Pazel,' she said aloud. 'Someone fetch him, please. And hurry.'

Pazel must have been already on his way, for seconds later he and Neeps were beside her. Thasha took Pazel's hand and drew him down.

Neeps stared with wonder at the pelican. 'Where did that come from? Is it dead?'

The strange voice was fading. Thasha pressed Pazel's head closer. 'Listen! Can't you hear it?'

He strained to hear – and then he did hear, and looked up in horror.

'What's the matter?' said Neeps. 'What in Pitfire's going on here?'

Thasha just shook her head. 'Get ready,' was all she managed to say.

Pazel was shaking. 'Oh *credek*. Help me, help me. Gods.'

His lips began to work. Thasha had no idea how to help, so she embraced him, and Neeps wrapped his arms around them both. The three were bent over the pelican like a trio of witches, but only Pazel was caught in the spell. His mouth opened and closed; his tongue writhed, his face twisted and he clung to them savagely. A soft rasping noise came from his throat.

'What's he doing?' cried Neeps. 'Is that the demon's language? The one he learned in the Forest?'

'No,' said Thasha, 'it's worse.'

A convulsion struck Pazel like a lightning bolt, the spasm so violent that they were all three hurled backwards. He kicked and flailed, and Thasha shouted at Neeps to hold on.

The sound exploded from Pazel's chest, an impossible roar that seemed to lift him with its power, that shook the deck of the *Promise* and trembled her sails and made the selk recoil in frightened recognition. Then it stopped, cut off at a stroke. Pazel gasped, restored to himself but coughing, gagging on blood – his own blood; he had bitten his tongue. But he didn't care about that. He was trying desperately to pull them to their feet.

'Away, get away!'

The bird was twitching. They dived away from it as from a

bomb. Out of the corner of her eye Thasha saw the transformation, the small form expanding with the suddenness of cannon-fire, and then across the bow of the *Promise* sprawled an eguar, forty feet long, shimmering, blazing, black. Its crocodilian head punched straight through the portside rail. Flames licked at shattered timbers. The creature's fumes rolled over the deck in a noxious cloud; everyone in sight had begun to choke.

The eguar pulled its head back through the rail and stood. Rigging blazed and snapped; the foremast listed. 'Nólcindar, Nólcindar!' the dlömic fishermen were crying. 'We are finished! What have the humans done?'

The creature's white-hot eyes swept over them. Beneath its stomach the deck was smoking. Then its eyes found the youths and remained there. Its jaws spread wide. Thasha heard Pazel groaning beside her, 'No more, please—'

The jaws snapped – and the eguar vanished. The fumes immediately thinned. There at the centre of the devastation stood Ramachni, the black mink.

'Hail, Nólcindar,' he said. 'Permission to come aboard?'

Then he fell. Thasha ran and lifted him in her arms. The mage's tiny form was limp. 'Water,' he said. 'Pumps, hoses. Tell them, Thasha: they must scour the vessel clean.'

Nólcindar was already shouting orders: eguar poisons were no mystery to the selk. Thasha pressed Ramachni to her cheek and wept. 'Oh you dear,' she babbled. 'You mad, dear disaster.'

The other travellers crowded near them. 'Ramachni, master and guide!' cried Bolutu.

'And friend,' said Hercól. 'Once again we have been lost without you. Heaven smiles on us today.'

'I was the one lost,' said the mage. 'Sitroth gave me his form, and gave up his life so doing, but his life was just a part of the cost. Oh, I am weary. But have I hurt you, Thasha? Hurt anyone?'

There were no injuries – save for Pazel, who had bruised himself badly. Neeps was still gripping his shoulders. 'Something's wrong,' he said. 'He won't talk.'

'His tongue is bleeding, fool,' said Lunja.

'It's not just that,' said Neeps. 'Look at him. There's something wild in his face.'

Pazel sat gripping himself, as though chilled, but there was sweat on his brow, and his eyes darted fitfully. Behind the bloody lips his teeth were chattering.

Ramachni leaned out, and Thasha held him close enough to touch Pazel's cheek. The tarboy flinched, then gazed at Ramachni as if seeing him for the first time, and his look of fear lessened slightly.

'Pazel called me back,' said Ramachni, 'in the last tongue I could hear in this world. Sitroth and I fought the *maukslar* together, and made it flee to the Pits. The fight was terrible, but it was the journey that nearly finished me. Twelve days have I sought you, and that is too long for me to take any shape but this, my prime form in Alifros. But there was no trace of you, so each day I went on as owl or pelican. And each day it grew harder to remember who I was, or the path back to myself. At last in despair I flew the length of the Sandwall, until I came to a tiny inlet with an abandoned outpost, and signs of a fight. It was my one chance. Blindly, I set out north over the open sea, driving myself to death's door with the effort. By the time I saw the boat I had lost speech, reason – almost every part of my thinking self.'

'The one spark that remained was eguar-fire: deep within me, I could still howl in the eguar's tongue. And Pazel heard me, and responded in kind. But in doing so, he did what he always feared: set his mind to forming words in that language, which no human mind is meant to encompass.'

Neeps took off his coat and slipped it over Pazel's shoulders: his friend had curled into a shivering ball. Thasha could read the anger and confusion in his face. What right had Ramachni to use Pazel in this way?

Ramachni must have sensed Neeps' feelings as well. 'I did not ask this of him, Neeparvasi. I was beyond asking. He simply heard me crying out in the darkness, and answered. But I do not think he has taken lasting harm. Probably he will suffer one of his mind-fits as soon as he regains a little strength. Later we must try not to speak of eguar, for it will be harder now to keep his thoughts from shaping words in that tongue.'

'For long?' asked Neda, touching her brother's head.

'Yes, Neda, for long,' said Ramachni. 'For the rest of his life, unless a merciful forgetting should strip him of the language. We mages have an old rule: that every act of enchantment takes pre-cisely as much from the world as it gives back, though we rarely grasp the whole of the exchange. You should help him to a quiet place before the fits begin.'

'We'll have to carry him,' said Thasha.

'Then do so. And carry me to my rest as well. But first you must be warned.' He raised his head and looked at Nólcindar. 'The *Kirisang*, the *Death's Head*, is coming. She was the last thing I saw before my reason fled. And she was already north of the Sandwall, flying fast over the seas – much faster than the wind should have allowed for. She has called up a false wind, somehow, and har-nessed it.'

'She is flogging the last drops of power from her Plazic generals, maybe,' said Olik, 'or else the pact that gave her a *maukslar* servant has given her other powers, too. I wonder what the price will be in her case.'

'What matters now is that she is on our trail,' said Nólcindar. 'Go to your rest, Arpathwin, for I fear we will need you again before long. And I must see that foremast braced anew, if not better than before. We must outrun the *Death's Head*, and the mistress of death at her helm.'

Ramachni's sudden return lifted all spirits. But within the hour a sail emerged from the morning haze, fifty miles southwest. It was not one of the Behemoths, but it was a huge ship: the size of the *Chathrand*, probably. The keen-eyed selk soon confirmed it: the ship was the *Death's Head*. The terrible news was allayed by one fact alone: that the larger vessel's course paralleled their own without converging. Macadra had not spied them yet.

At once Nólcindar turned the *Promise* away, east by northeast, so that their narrow stern faced the *Death's Head*, rather than their flank and sails. The crew hooded the lamps and draped the stern windows in sailcloth, lest any glass catch the sun. There were islands ahead, and for a time it appeared the little *Promise* might just reach them, and slip away into a maze. But a cry from the lookout dashed their hopes:

'*Death's Head* changing course. Two points to starboard, Captain Nólcindar. She means to intercept.'

'*Daram*, let us see that she fails. Aloft, selk and dlömu! The white horse must gallop on the wind!'

In scant minutes the crew had spread topgallants and skysails, and were bending curious, ribbed wing-sails to the lower yardarms. But before they had even finished the job Nólcindar was giving orders for them to brace the main sails anew. The wind had turned suddenly fitful. They were slowing – even as Macadra's ship some-how gained speed.

Faces darkened: the gap between the ships was starting to close. 'She has spoken to the wind,' said Kirishgán quietly. 'It does not obey her happily, but it concedes her something. I have not seen such a spell deployed in many hundreds of years.'

Soon thereafter Pazel began to howl. It had all the hallmarks of his regular mind-fits (pain in his skull, babble from his lips, agony in the presence of voices), but it was far more punishing than any Thasha had witnessed before. His shaking grew so violent that he could not be left alone. They sat with him in shifts, trying not to make a sound.

Thasha found it hard to leave his side. After her third shift she began to wave the others away: she wasn't tired, her lover needed her; surely it was almost through.

Then the explosions started: the *Death's Head* had opened up with her long-range guns. Now everyone was shouting, hatches slammed and boots pounded, and beyond the hull the iron missiles began to scream. Thasha listened, transfixed, her arms enclosing

Pazel's head. Fifty yards to starboard. Now eighty or ninety to port. Twenty to port! A deep, sickening *boom* near the stern.

Neeps came and gave her a scrap of paper: *Macadra can't seem to close: when she draws near her own wind-charm speeds us up. But we can't shake her, either. Maybe at sundown, if we last.*

But sundown was still hours away. The barrage went on and on, and so did Pazel's agony.

Mid-afternoon there came a rending, shattering noise. A direct hit, probably to a mast or spar. Crash of falling timbers. Soft, sickening *thumps* of bodies dropping to the boards. Pazel shook and twisted and made impossible sounds, jackal, steam-pipe, wildcat, wounded horse, his body drenched in frigid sweat. Thasha wrapped him in blankets, kissed his clammy cheeks, appalled at her own impotence. Erithusmé could help him. Erithusmé could turn those missiles around in mid-air.

Thasha did not notice when darkness came. She locked her arms about Pazel, trying to control his shaking, biting her lips to be sure she never spoke. In lucid moments he would smile at her, but the smile always cracked into a spasm of pain.

The cannon-fire ended. Pazel's fit did not. Long into the night it raged. He vomited, wept from sheer fatigue. But at last it too was over, and he slept curled on his side with Thasha draped over and around him like a blanket. She let herself doze, then, and when she woke it was to his grateful kisses on her hands.

26

Good Sailing

~~~

Moments come in the life of any world when the forces shaping its future, however disparate they appear, begin inexorably to converge. In Alifros such a moment arrived in Halar, Western Solar Year 942. The month began with Empress Maisa's secret mobilisation in the hills above Ormael, and ended with the collapse of the Red Storm. Between these events, however, were thousands of others, simultaneous but unglimpsed from one region to the next.

On the foggy morning of 6 Halar, fate handed Arqual a substantial victory over the White Fleet, when a Mzithrini commander on the Nelu Rekere mistook his position, and led his eighteen warships to disaster on the Rukmast Shoals. A lesser number of Arquali ships had shadowed the Mzithrinis for days; now they closed and raked the hapless vessels at their leisure. In a few hours they sank all eighteen without suffering a scratch.

Aboard the Arquali flagship, Sandor Ott's regional lieutenant observed the carnage with satisfaction. The Black Rags were floundering, not just here but everywhere. One battlefield report after another confirmed their fragility. They had vast forces, but no steadiness of purpose, no unity. The latest dispatch even spoke of Turach raids *below the Tsördon Mountains*, in the very heart of Mzithrini territory. An almost unimaginable advance.

As he watched the enemy drown, the lieutenant came to a decision. They were off balance. It was time to unbalance them further. That night he dispatched a small clipper to Bramian with a message: *The day has come. Push the fledglings out of the nest.*

On Bramian the message had long been expected. As Pazel had

learned first-hand, the huge island contained many surprises, one of which was a secret colony of religious fanatics. It was the world's only community of Nessarim, worshippers of the Shaggat Ness, outside of Gurishal itself. They were just three thousand strong, but what they lacked in numbers they made up for in eagerness and rage.

For thirty years they had waited here, in exile. Thirty years of fever and snakebite; thirty years of raids by tribals with gauntlets of leopard claws, who ripped their victims open, chin to groin; thirty years dreaming of revenge. But not just dreaming. With Arqual's help, the Nessarim had also built ships.

Now the vessels stood crowded together on the sluggish river, bows pointing seaward. Forty ships – all armed to the teeth, at monstrous expense, by the heretic Emperor of Arqual. What of it? The worst heretics were the Mzithrin kings themselves, who had slaughtered their families, and denied the divinity of the Shaggat Ness. Even now those kings ruled over the Shaggat's rightful empire. Now, when all the prophecies bespoke His return; now, when his Glorious Son walked among them once more.

The Shaggat's son. Five months ago, Pazel himself had been present when Sandor Ott brought Erthalon Ness back to the Nessarim. The man was clearly insane. He had spent his life tormented by the Arqualis, by Arunis, and above all by his lunatic father. He could not grasp his present circumstances. Pazel had tried to tell him the truth: that Sandor Ott had nurtured the whole colony merely as one gear in the machine that would topple the Mzithrin. That all their 'prophecies' had been composed in the chambers of the Secret Fist, and spread by infiltrators. That their small fleet was meant only to discredit and demoralize the enemy before it was pulverised.

Erthalon Ness had listened to Pazel, but in the end he had gone to his father's worshippers all the same. And now he was leading that throng – shouting, screaming that the time of victory had come. The clipper's message was greeted with a war-chant that frightened the tribal people in the hills. The Nessarim were raised for martyrdom, and martyrdom can only so long be delayed.

By the time the clipper reached Bramian, Maisa's forces had liberated Ormael, and her partisans had spread her message over the whole of Arqual. Suddenly the news was everywhere. The Empress lived. Admiral Isiq lived. They had married, condemned the war, declared Emperor Magad an usurper. Some claimed that part of the Western Fleet had already gone over to her side. If the true scale of the rebellion was minimal, the people's imagination was not. And with every traveller who landed or set sail from Arqual the story grew.

The Secret Fist rounded up a great number of Maisa's allies (together with many who knew nothing of her), and what became of those unfortunates hardly needs to be told. But they did not catch everyone. The next placards to appear in the streets denounced the spy guild itself as 'an empire with the Empire, ruled by a depraved cadre of professional killers'. This was not a revelation; everyone knew the Fist was depraved. But very few had heard the next claim: that the organisation

... FOR REASONS OF BASE INTRIGUE, ENGINEERED THE GREAT SHAME AND BETRAYAL OF TREATY DAY, WHEREUPON THEY SOWED THE SEEDS OF THIS, THEIR LATEST, VILE WAR.

The spy guild panicked. Sandor Ott had never trusted his underlings: not since Hercól Stanapeth's defection, at any rate. Since then he had concentrated power in his own hands, with the result that when the *Chathrand* sailed he had felt that no one could be trusted aboard her but himself. Etherhorde, consequently, was left in the hands of spies who were technically capable but unprepared to address a calamity. And the rebellion was a calamity, now: the daily harvest of hearsay was too enormous to be fought by propaganda alone. Ambassadors were grumbling. Youths were tossing stones through barracks windows. Emperor Magad using more deathsmoke by the day, and screaming for someone's, everyone's, head.

Those who live in shadows are not immune to striking at them. Soon loyal ministers began to disappear, rock-solid generals were clumsily vilified, a Turach commander was snatched before the eyes of his troops in Ulsprit, who later received an anonymous tip as to his location, stormed the safe house, and found their leader dead from torture.

None of this directly hobbled the armed forces. They knew their duty, and right now duty saw them being redirected in vast numbers to the Crownless Lands, with orders to eradicate the rebels and leave no living trace. But on 19 Halar a bomb changed everything.

The Lord Admiral answered only to the crown. He had never warmed personally to Isiq, but his respect for the Fleet Admiral, second in command of Arqual's maritime forces, was boundless. Isiq had never lost a campaign, never questioned a deployment, never received orders from the Admiralty with anything but resolve to see them through. It was the Lord Admiral's misfortune to have reminded Etherhorde of these facts, somewhat publically, when the rumours began. He did not believe the rumours for an instant. Admiral Isiq was dead. Maisa was surely dead, or else confined to some shelter for the aged in Tholjassa. All this was hogwash, and he'd be damned if he'd vilify a hero of Arqual because of hogwash. This too he declared rather too loudly, and too often.

The Secret Fist only wanted him to close his mouth. They might have achieved this in any number of ways, but chose the expedient of a black-powder bomb. The device was planted in the outdoor kitchen of the Lord Admiral's residence on Maj Hill. The agents involved used the very finest of materials, including a smokeless fuse of Sandor Ott's own invention, and a timer set for well after midnight. But in their haste to frighten the Lord Admiral, the agents overlooked the fact that his fifteen-year-old son and certain friends met in the kitchen many nights with cigars and brandy and other forbidden things. Four boys (all from military families) were present when the bomb exploded. The building filled with fire, and the Lord Admiral, hearing the screams, lost his mind and ran into the blaze himself. Thirty seconds later he emerged, carrying the still-burning corpse of his son.

None of the youths survived, and the Lord Admiral himself succumbed to his burns within the hour. But as he staggered from the inferno, his screams of grief and hatred, his denunciations, were heard all over Maj Hill. By dawn they had become the chisel that would split the greatest navy in the Northern world.

On the Island of Simja, King Oshiram II had spent the month flirting secretly with suicide.

He put on a brave face, for it was vital that no one suspect. His people knew what mattered already: that he was the great royal fool of his times. He had been used shamelessly by Arqual, an Empire that any son of the Crownless Lands should have known better than to trust. Like a fish, like a mindless tuna, he had swallowed the Arquali bait. An end to war. A marriage to tie enemies together. A treaty to unfang Arqual and the Mzithrin alike, before they could send their armies raging again over the bloodied soil of the Crownless Lands.

Oshiram had wanted to believe it, and in his eagerness he'd made others believe. He had summoned them, his peers from twenty lands. He had committed the unforgivable sin of making fools of them as well. Some of them had travelled months. Who could resist? Who didn't dream of an end to war? And all Oshiram had shown them was another fiasco, a new upwelling of hatred between the Empires, and a young girl strangled before their royal eyes.

No, they would never forgive him. Indeed the other six rulers of the Crownless Lands had just met on Talturi: Oshiram still had enough gossips in his pay to keep him aware of such momentous gatherings. Even if his fellow princes no longer wanted him joining the conversation.

Then again, perhaps he *was* the subject of conversation. Perhaps they'd agreed to censure him, to dump Simjan goods into the Nelu Rekere, to punish his people along with their naïve king. Those parting looks at the gates of Simjalla City, those heads shaking in disbelief, the long silence when the last ships had left the harbour ....

Oshiram had come through all that. He had found a new purpose in the rescue and healing of Eberzam Isiq. And shortly thereafter had come a miracle: he was in love, for the first time in his stilted, ceremony-clogged life. A former slave, a dancer, a beauty to stop the heart. She watched him like a frightened child, at first; no doubt she'd heard that all kings gobbled their women like sweets from a platter. She'd expected to be raped. Oshiram had treated her with gentleness and dignity, assigned her light chores and spacious rooms, sent her flowers and invitations – not summonses – to dine with him quietly if she would. He had wooed her: that was what it was called. And when at last she came to him, and loved him, he knew a joy beyond all telling. He forgot about intrigues and rat infestations and the duplicity of Arqual. He lived for this woman, lay awake longing for the morrow beside her, or slept and dreamed of her voice. He gave her rings, dresses, dogs, excursions to the hills, mad promises. His heart.

Isiq had broken that heart with a word.

The woman's real name was Syrarys – formerly Syrarys *Isiq* – and she had been sent to him by none other than the Arquali spy-master, Sandor Ott. Years earlier, Ott had dispatched her to Isiq's own household, and Isiq's bed. Syrarys had poisoned the admiral for years, plotted both his death and his daughter's, who she had helped to raise. And if Isiq could be believed, she had even betrayed that serpent of a spymaster. Her true allegiance, he insisted, was to the Blood Mage, Arunis.

If he killed himself, he would do it cleverly. He was not so self-ish as to add a monarch's self-inflicted death to the woes of his people. He must go sailing and fall overboard, or go riding and be thrown into a ravine. Yes, that was better. There were always

573

moments alone on a hunt. A blameless death, and the crown to his younger brother, a man unburdened by shame. It could happen. These nights of misery could end.

On 20 Halar, as quiet hands lit a fuse in the kitchen of the Lord Admiral of Arqual, King Oshiram send a page to inform his huntsman that they would be riding at dawn. He lay alone that night, sleepless. At ten that evening he sent his chamberlain by coach to a certain notorious address, with orders to bring back a courtesan; it had been decades since such women had lived in the palace. She arrived by eleven, and he took her to his bedroom and undressed her beside a roaring fireplace. She was very beautiful. When he touched her, he cried.

His weeping terrified the girl. Rising, he told her to dress. At the doorway he handed her a note for the chamberlain: she would be handsomely paid. Alone again, the king went to the window overlooking the little pond where in summer (legend had it) the frogs spoke in the voices of his ancestors. He stood there until he was chilled. Then he pulled off his remaining rings, the ones not given to Syrarys, and threw them into the pond.

At daybreak he ate standing up in the stables with the hunting party, as was his custom before such outings. It was perfect, this smelly, sweaty, anonymous end. Bitter tea, foul tobacco. Surrounded by horses and dogs and brutes who cared only that he rode well, and followed their lead in the woods.

Almost perfect, that is: the chamberlain had infiltrated the stables. There were papers to sign before a day of leisure. And a message that had come the night before, when His Majesty had insisted on no interruptions of any kind.

The king nodded, wolfing sausages: 'Give it here, then.' He took the parchment, wiped his hands on his leggings, broke the oxblood seal.

It was from the Archduke of Talturi. Oshiram smiled: a last sting before the drop of the curtain. He scanned the letter indifferently. Then he froze, and started over, reading this time with care.

Beloved Oshiram: I have just left a conference from which Your Majesty was, by necessity, excluded. If by chance you have learned of this meeting, I beseech your forgiveness. The circumstances, and the matter under debate, were quite extraordinary....

He read on. Gods of death, they were ratifying the Simja Pact! He'd almost forgotten it existed: that framework for an alliance of the Crownless Lands against external aggressors. They'd dropped the initiative when peace between the two great Empires appeared to be achievable. Now the other kings had revived the pact – *and wished him to lead it.* They were asking him, begging him, to assume the role of Defender of the Crownless Lands.

They are not many, our forces – perhaps one hundred vessels, and twelve thousand men – if Your Majesty should see fit to contribute to its number. They cannot repel the invaders where they are already entrenched. But with skill and Rin's favour they may prevent the next entrenchment, or at least slow the bastards' progress across our lands.

All are in agreement: we must have you. Balan of Rukmast is losing his hearing, and brave Lord Iftan's people cannot spare him: a volcano is bubbling and oozing across Urnsfich. There were other contenders. We argued long. But when the shouting ended there was relief in every face. Because we know you, Oshiram. Because in this time of infinite deception there is one sovereign who never chose aught but truth and courage, and who saw before any of us that the world was changing, and that we must change as well. If you had not called Arqual's bluff, not let them bring their sham Treaty to your island, how else would the truth have emerged? And when word came that you, in secret, had harboured Admiral Isiq ...

Someone belched. Oshiram lowered the parchment and gazed at the hunters blankly. Then a small, quizzical smile appeared on his face.

'Gentlemen,' he said, 'it pains me to inform you that I cannot ride today. No, nor tomorrow either. Go and kill a buck without me. It seems the world has little intention of letting me go.'

Finally, to the rebels themselves. Maisa's land forces were paltry compared to the great legions of Arquali loyalists brought in from the east, but once back in the Chereste Highlands they were relatively safe. Officially, the Highlands had been annexed six years earlier, along with the city below; in practice, they were an afterthought. The Imperial Governor himself had never set foot in what he called 'those dull, drowsy hills'. And they *were* drowsy – until they exploded.

One effect of this drowsiness was that, over the years, the governor had shifted more and more of his troops out of the Highlands and back to Ormael City, where they grumbled less and could be more cheaply maintained. By the time of Maisa's declaration, the mountain checkpoints had become a form of punishment detail, and the total Imperial presence had dwindled to some five hundred men.

When the rebels stormed Ormael, those five hundred had no chance. A quarter were killed outright. Eighty or ninety defected to the rebels' side. The rest were stripped of their arms and driven down into the plum orchards, and left there to hobble barefoot to the city gate.

But at sea, matters were very different. Power in Alifros has always meant naval power, and in sheer numbers of men and ships the loyalists had an overwhelming advantage. The murder of the Lord Admiral and his son had cracked the navy's unity, but that crack would take long months to spread. Meanwhile, loyalist ships filled ports from Etrej to Opalt. The nearest squadrons were less than a day from Ormael.

Just three hours after Maisa's speech in Tanner's Row, a light sprang up across the Straits of Simja. It was a warning fire, lit by order of King Oshiram. Ships were making for Ormael from the east.

The scramble was chaotic. Men who had hoped for a day or two ashore were drummed back to the ships; food and water casks were all but tossed aboard. New recruits scoured the city for weapons, hammocks, sea coats, shoes. Romances just hours old fell to pieces, or were consecrated by marriages performed in Ormael's ruined temples, the monks too stunned by circumstance even to object when couples appeared before them still reeking of love. Isiq and Commodore Darabik aborted their inspection of the boats of the Ormali volunteers, most of which were not swift or seaworthy enough to join the fight. No one seemed to know where the Empress was. Her ministers responded to the question with glares.

Soon lookouts on the Chereste cliffs were able to spot the enemy: thirty warships in the vanguard alone. Some miles further, a second wave was advancing, larger than the first.

Isiq and Darabik received the news on the Slave Terrace, as they prepared to board their separate vessels. The two men exchanged a look. They had made but one move in this campaign; their second would be a desperate retreat.

'I should have married your sister, Purcy.'

'The hell you say, my prince. You were destined to take the hand of the Empress. One day soon I'll be kneeling before you both at Castle Maag.'

Isiq smiled and pressed his shoulders. One day soon.

Then he tightened his grip and looked Darabik in the eye. 'You must do something for me. Protect Suthinia, if and when you see her. Do your best to keep her alive.'

Darabik's black eyebrows climbed. 'My word on it, Prince.'

That was as much as either of them could say. Darabik knew that the Empress meant to keep Suthinia at her side. But not even he and Isiq could discuss Maisa's whereabouts. The Empress had a new task: to appear everywhere, to stir rebellion in port after port – and then disappear before the loyalists could seize her. To roar like a tigress and vanish like a ghost. The ship she chose to board at any moment was therefore the greatest secret of the whole campaign. Each man who knew where to find her was a man who might be taken and tortured into revealing the fact.

Maisa had shared just one point with Isiq: that she would not be leaving Ormael on his vessel. Isiq had all but revealed that fact to Darabik, with this talk of Suthinia. He did not, therefore, confess anything further: not his dark prognosis for the campaign, nor his terror of catching a whiff of deathsmoke, without Suthinia there to help him fight the urge. Nor his shameful inability to say goodbye to her, the witch he lusted for, and loved perhaps, the dreamer who saw Thasha in her dreams.

'You don't mind me taking over the *Nighthawk*?' Isiq asked.

'I suggested it,' said Darabik. 'She's our finest warship, and belongs with the Fleet Admiral. And you should have pleasant sailing, too. The old men say it will be fine for a week.'

'*We* are the old men, Purcy.'

'Almost, my prince. And we made a great mess of things, didn't we? All those years under Magad. Years of loyalty to a symbol, a moth-eaten banner. A rotted man.'

Isiq released him. 'A great mess,' he agreed. 'Nothing for it now but to start the clean-up.'

So it was that hours before dawn the tiny fleet that stood for Maisa of Arqual left the port of Ormael. At the harbour mouth they divided into three, saluted one another with roars and cannon-fire, and began their lives as hunted men.

Isiq took his squadron east, and was under fire by noon. A second squadron tacked west into the Nelu Gila: waters that no Empire but the Mzithrin had ever held. And Commodore Darabik took his forces south towards Locostri, and was caught by a task force of Arquali destroyers. The latter vessels had the wind, and closed quickly, and Darabik's entire squadron went down under a bright blue sky.

27

Souls Set Free

—◦⁓◦—

'By all that's holy, doubt your instincts!' my mother told me
when I came of age, 'and trust even less in those weak organs,
the eyes. Wait for the heart's eye to open. Then you'll know
how long you've lived in the dark.'
– *Embers of Ixphir House* by Hercól Ensyriken ap Ixhxchr

9 Fuinar 942
297th day from Etherhorde

'Ah, Master Stargraven! I knew you would be back.'

Felthrup led the way down the ancient passage with its rotting
wares. Ahead in the enchanted brig, the antique lamp burned on
its chain as before, and the light gleamed on the unlocked cells.
He was terrified, and elated. His scholarship was paying off – and
more importantly, he had friends beside him. Marila and Fiffengurt
would need his guidance. They had never faced a demon before.

This time the *maukslar* had not bothered with a disguise. It
stood at the centre of its cell looking just as Felthrup remembered:
talons, wings, bloated body, gleaming gold eyes. Its hands rested
lightly on the bars of the cell; lamplight glittered on its rings.

'Shall we bargain, rat?' it said.

'Oh yes,' said Felthrup. 'That is indeed why we came.'

The three humans remained silent, as he had hoped they
would. Marila and Fiffengurt each held a little pouch. The demon
studied them, allowing its eyes to linger pointedly on Marila's

belly. Unblinking, the Tholjassan girl met its gaze.

'Oho, little wife,' said the *maukslar*. 'Ferocity suits you. It will not protect you, however.'

The *maukslar* turned to the last figure in the brig. It smiled, fat cheeks folding in on themselves. 'Nilus Rose. Are you come to join your good friend Captain Kurlstaff? He was an amusing companion, while he lived.'

Rose's eyes betrayed nothing. His voice was low and deadly. 'Kurlstaff has spoken of you, monster.'

'Has he spoken of your death? It is very near. You will know shame, then agony; then the plague will simply melt your mind away. You will try to hold on, to remember yourself, to keep your human soul intact. But you will fail. It will pour from you in a rush, like bilge down a drain.'

Captain Rose stepped forward. A show of courage, but he did not truly feel it: Felthrup could smell the terror in the big man's sweat.

'Not too near, Captain!' he squeaked.

Even as he spoke the *maukslar* hurled itself against the bars with a snarl. Its reach was longer than anyone could have foreseen: one jewelled hand clawed the air just inches from the captain's face. Fiffengurt hauled Rose back by the arm.

The *maukslar* straightened, its calm suddenly restored. It held something red between two fingers: a bit of Rose's beard.

'I think I shall keep this,' it said.

'Abomination!' shrieked a voice from behind them. 'Fat toad of Slagarond! Drop that hair!'

It was Lady Oggosk, hobbling down the passage, brandishing her stick. Felthrup winced. He'd been wrong to tell the captain about this place. Neither he nor his witch could help them now.

'Drop it!' Oggosk shrieked again. But the *maukslar* did not obey. Instead it put the wisp of Rose's beard into its mouth, and swallowed. Oggosk's face twisted in horror. She struck the iron bars and snapped her stick in two. The *maukslar* held its vast belly and laughed.

'Enough, enough!' cried Felthrup. 'Duchess, you are not to inter-fere! Captain Rose, I thought we had an understanding, you and I.'

Rose took Oggosk's elbow, firmly. 'Go back to the door,' he told her, 'and see that no one approaches. That is my command.'

For once, Oggosk heeded him, though she wept and swore and as she departed, clutching half her stick.

'The ghosts are thick around you, Captain,' said the *maukslar*. 'They know when one is soon to join their number.'

Marila nudged Felthrup with her foot. She was right; it was for him to take charge.

'Tulor!' he said, inching nearer. 'I am ready for you today, but I warn you that I shall not tolerate behaviour unbecoming in a – that is, poor behaviour of any kind. You have knowledge to barter with? Very good, that is what I require. To begin with—'

'Free me.'

Mr Fiffengurt snorted. 'Now *there's* a laugh,' he said.

Felthrup suppressed an urge to bite his ankle. 'To begin with, I will ask you a simple thing. Is Arunis gone for ever, now that Mr Uskins is dead? Or is there still a man aboard who he has … infected, as it were?'

The *maukslar* spat.

'Hmmph!' said Felthrup. 'That is because you don't know.'

The creature bristled. 'I was perfectly clear with you, rodent. I will tell you nothing more until I am set free.'

'But I think you will. I think you will trade knowledge for food.'

'Food!' The creature looked at him with contempt. 'Little squirmer! You may keep your shipboard slops. I do not hunger here.'

'How ungracious!' said Felthrup. 'But you must offer him a taste all the same, Marila.'

Marila reached into her pouch and withdrew a gold coin. Taking care not to lean too close, she tossed it through the iron bars. The coin rolled in a half-circle and landed near the *maukslar*'s taloned feet.

The *maukslar* did not look at the coin, but it grew very still. *Wait,* thought Felthrup. The humans were looking at him, perplexed. In his thoughts he begged them to keep silent.

The *maukslar* crossed its arms. It glared, defiant, its vast chest rising and falling.

Wait.

The fat hands twitched. The golden eyes looked away. Then suddenly the creature threw itself down like a dog before the coin, and ate it. The demon moaned, as a spasm of wild pleasure crossed its face. Droplets of gold sparkled in its mouth, as if the coin had melted there. But the creature's joy lasted only seconds. It turned Felthrup a look of redoubled hate.

'Vermin.'

Felthrup sat back on his haunches. 'There is a great deal more, but you must earn it.'

'I shall skin you alive, each of you. I shall roast you on a spit.'

'You will answer my questions,' said Felthrup, 'or we will depart.'

The *maukslar* roared. It threw itself against the bars again, with even greater violence. The charmed door held fast. Twisting, screaming, the demon changed its body: suddenly a tall, savage-looking man with a red beard took its place, eyes fixed on Captain Rose.

'Nilus!' the man thundered. 'Free me at once!'

Rose's eyes went wide. The man in the cell bellowed again, and the captain flinched, as though expecting a blow. Then his eyes narrowed again, and he looked at the figure squarely. 'You are not my father,' he said.

'Worthless cretin! I order you to open this door!'

'But I wish you were,' Rose went on, 'that I might stand here before you, and lift not a finger on your behalf.'

The figure gaped at him – and then, in an eyeblink, it changed again. Within the cage there suddenly appeared Neeps Undrabust, dressed just as he had been the night before he left the *Chathrand*. The night Rose had married him to Marila. Neeps turned to his young wife, eyes brimming with emotion, and reached out a trembling hand.

'It's me,' he said. 'It's *truly* me. Come here, let me touch you. Let me touch our child.'

'Marila, leave at once!' cried Felthrup. But Marila's eyes remained fixed on her lover; she stood as though turned to stone. Fiffengurt closed one hand tightly on Marila's arm. She started and shook her head.

'I'm dying, you know,' said the thing that looked like Neeps. 'The same way Rose is dying. Of the plague. I don't want to die without touching you again.'

Tears streamed down Marila's face. Then she placed two fists over her eyes, and began to shout in Tholjassan. Felthrup could not understand the words, but he knew curses when he heard them, and so did the *maukslar*. The figure of Neeps disappeared, and was replaced by a perfect replica of Marila herself.

'Your man does not love you,' it said, in Marila's own voice. 'He's found another lover. A finer one, a beauty.'

'Liar,' said Marila calmly. 'You don't know him. I do. Besides, he's in a land without human beings.'

The false Marila laughed. 'And you think that has stopped him? *You* are the one who does not know the man, or the soul of men writ large. No depravity is beyond them.' The creature touched its bulging stomach. 'What do you think is growing, here? A healthy baby, from his seed? Shall I tell you the truth?'

At that Fiffengurt suddenly came to life. Spitting out a few choice curses of his own, he lifted Marila from the ground and ran with her down the passage. In the cell, the *maukslar* laughed and clawed at its belly. 'A grub, a flesh-eating grub! It is gnawing you, gnawing its way to the light!'

Felthrup heard the quartermaster's voice at the distant doorway, and a croaking reply from Oggosk. Moments later Fiffengurt returned alone. He had torn open his pouch. Before Felthrup could stop him he poured out a shower of golden coins upon the floor of the cell. The few that rolled in the *maukslar's* direction he stamped flat under his boot.

'Fiffengurt, Fiffengurt!' cried the rat. 'That is not the procedure!'

'It is now,' snarled Fiffengurt. 'Go on, bastard, eat your muckin' fill.'

The *maukslar* resumed its true form. Its small bright eyes fixed on the gold, and a moan came from its chest. It dropped to its knees and stretched out its jewelled hands as far as it could go. The nearest coin was barely an inch out of reach.

Crack. Mr Fiffengurt brought the broken end of Oggosk's staff down on the fat, squirming knuckles. The *maukslar*'s hand jerked back. It sat up, wings half-spread, its eyes flickering between their faces and the gold.

'Give me some,' it hissed.

'Answer the rat's blary question!'

'One coin first. Just one.'

Fiffengurt shook his head. 'Two, when you talk.'

The *maukslar* was gasping with want. Set free, it would tear them all to pieces; of that Felthrup had no doubt.

'Arunis is banished,' it said. 'He trapped Uskins through the white scarf, which was his soul's portal. Without it he cannot return, until the Swarm completes its work, and Alifros lies dead and cold.'

The quartermaster glanced at Felthrup. 'Well, Ratty?'

Felthrup shook his head. 'That answer does not merit two coins.'

Before the *maukslar* could howl again, he raised a paw. 'It merits twenty.' The *maukslar* started, eyes ablaze with doubt and hunger.

'Yes, twenty coins,' said Felthrup. 'If you will swear that what you say is true.'

'Wretched animal. I spoke no lie!'

Felthrup told Mr Fiffengurt to count the money out. The quartermaster looked dubious, but he bent to the floor and gathered twenty coins, and stacked them at Felthrup's side.

'Now swear,' said the rat.

The demon's eyes were locked on the coins. 'I swear that what I have said of Arunis is true.'

'And that everything you say to us henceforth shall be true.'

'Yes, yes – I so swear! Give me the gold!'

'Now repeat after me. "I shall speak no word of falsehood to those gathered here before me."'

'I shall speak no word of falsehood to those gathered here before me.'

'"Nor seek to harm them, or their friends, or their just interests."'

'Nor seek to harm them, or their friends, or their just interests.'

'"To this I swear by my name—"'

'To this I swear by my name—'

'"Kazizarag."'

The *maukslar*'s eyes snapped up. Then he exploded in horrible wrath, flying about his cage wreathed in yellow flame. Felthrup and the two men waited for a time, then gathered the coins and made to depart. Only then did the creature relent, and swear by his true name.

'Very good, thing of evil!' squeaked Felthrup. 'I knew you were no *Tulor*. And since a promise from your kind is binding only when witnessed by the living *and the dead*, I thank you for confirming the presence of ghosts in this chamber. Now feed him, by all means! We keep our promises too.'

Fiffengurt tossed the coins by twos and threes, and the *maukslar* snatched them up and devoured them like a starved zoo animal. When it had eaten all twenty it sat down in the middle of the cell, closed its eyes and crooned with pleasure.

'Kazizarag,' said Rose. 'The spirit of Avarice. How did you deduce this, Felthrup?'

Felthrup almost choked on his answer: the captain had never before used his name. 'I know more of the history of this ship than you might suppose, Captain,' he said. 'There are long passages in the *Polylex*, along with many words on the art of extracting oaths from things demonic. I even learned why Avarice here was imprisoned, and by whom.'

'Then you know I have served my time,' said the *maukslar*, still glowing with contentment.

'If that's a bid for freedom, you can choke on it, blubber-pot,' said Mr Fiffengurt. 'We'll never in a thousand years let you—'

'Fiffengurt!' shrieked Felthrup.

The *maukslar's* eyes opened wide. 'I should have known,' it hissed. 'You decided my fate in advance. Well, rat, I am sworn to speak nothing but truth. But I took no oath to speak at all. What is more, I can wait you out. That meal was my first taste of gold in centuries. It will hold me for … some time.'

'How long?' asked Rose. 'A day, a week?'

The *maukslar* grinned; flecks of gold shone in its teeth. 'Longer than you have, Captain,' it said.

Felthrup rubbed his paws together. *Blast Fiffengurt to the moon's cold backside!*

'I also did not swear to hold my tongue,' said the *maukslar*. 'Here is a dainty just for you, rat. You're a child of the plague. The same twisted spell that created you is killing Captain Rose, and others. And if the spell should ever end there will be no more woken creatures born. You will be alone in Alifros, and in a generation or two most will doubt that you existed at all.

'But in fact there will be no more generations. For here is another truth I am free to tell: Macadra is coming. She has staked her very soul on the winning of the Nilstone, and when she has it she will never give it up.'

'But why is she coming?' cried Felthrup. 'Does she believe we have the Nilstone? Or is she chasing someone who does? Is that it? Is *another* ship coming our way?'

The *maukslar* looked at him with loathing. 'Whether Macadra finds you first or the Nilstone does not matter. You will die at her hand, or die when the Swarm takes Alifros in its black embrace. Macadra may try to stop the Swarm, but she will fail. No sunrise will end that night, little rat. Life itself will perish, blind and frozen. Only we deathless ones will remain, feeding on the corpse.'

'Demon,' said Captain Rose, 'do you know where the Stone must be taken?'

'I know,' said the *maukslar*, smiling, 'but that is not all. I could tell you of the crawlies' secret power. I could plot a *true* course for you across the Nelluroq, since the one you have is nonsense. I could help you pass safely through the Red Storm. I could tell you the fate of those you left behind.'

'We are prepared to bargain further,' said Felthrup. 'We have another sixty coins—'

The creature made a sound of disdain.

A pause. Then Captain Rose said, 'We have more than sixty – far more. There is a great hoard secreted upon the *Chathrand*. We can bring you ten thousand.'

The *maukslar* rose on its bird-feet and pointed at Rose. 'You could bring me far more than that,' it hissed. 'I have seen the gold – and the pearls and gemstones – hidden all over this ship. Under the stone ballast, inside false stanchions on the mercy deck, sealed in iron shafts between the hulls. I saw you bring the hoard onto the ship in Arqual. I watched Sandor Ott remove a part of it for the son of the Shaggat Ness, saw another fraction discovered and seized by the shipwrights of Masalym. What remains you mean to give to the fanatics on Gurishal, to finance the Shaggat's uprising and destabilise the Mzithrin. I have seen them, Rose. They tortured me, shining there, just out of my reach.'

'We can still liberate a great many coins,' said Rose. 'if we take care not to alert Sandor Ott, or Sergeant Haddismal, or any of their informers. We can bring you gold by the sackful.'

'And taunt me as you have done today? I think not. You see, I had not eaten in decades – not since Captain Kurlstaff's day. I was starving. You fed me. Now my agonies have ceased.'

A rush of despair came for Felthrup, then. *He is not lying. We can no longer make him talk. And we learned almost nothing! Not even whether our friends are alive. You proud fool, Felthrup! To think you could match wits with such a beast!*

'Why speak of agonies?' he tried, desperate. 'We can feed you in the finest style. Gold and more gold! Why settle for enough, O Avarice, when you can be *replete*?'

'Replete, replete, that's the word!' said Fiffengurt.

'Shut up, Quartermaster! Demon, you were born to be – capacious. How long since you knew the satisfaction of gluttonous excess?'

The *maukslar*'s jewelled hands caressed its belly. 'I shall know it again without your help. Kazizarag was born to eat, not to suffer mockery and jibes. I shall wait out your doom. And your doom is coming, insects. Whether Macadra brings it, or the Nelluroq storms, or your own limitless folly. I need only wait for the *Chathrand's* spine to snap. When it does, every spell laid down by selk or mage or murth-lord will be sundered. These bars will melt away, and I shall be free to swallow that hoard, all of it, though it lie on the bottom of the sea.'

They filed back down the passage, watched by the silent denizen of the brig. Marila and Lady Oggosk were waiting outside the Green Door. When Felthrup and the two men had all clambered out into the mercy deck, the witch made a sound of disgust and prepared to slam the door.

'Wait!' said Marila. 'You haven't given up, have you? If you close that door the blary thing will vanish, and we'll have to start hunting it all over the ship again.'

'You're right, Marila!' said Felthrup. 'Dr Chadfallow's study of its comings and goings is not foolproof. It might be days before we find it again.'

'Days we don't have to spare,' put in Fiffengurt, 'and who knows? Maybe that tub of grease really can help the ship escape.'

Oggosk scowled at him. 'What, then? Leave it open? You saw that monster's cunning, Nilus. He knew just how to attack you.'

'He's not Arunis, though, is he?' said Fiffengurt. 'We had him furious enough to dice us up for soup. But he didn't use one charm that reached beyond his cell.'

'He cannot,' said Felthrup. 'If he could, that cell could not have held him for centuries.'

'He has a mind infernal,' said Oggosk, 'and he will use it against any guard we place here.'

Rose stared at the door. 'Find Tarsel, Quartermaster,' he said at last. 'The door swings outward. We will fasten a plate to the floor to prevent its closing fully. Also thick chains, and padlocks, so that it may not open more than a few inches. You yourself shall hold the keys.'

'Him? The idiot?' cried Oggosk. 'Why not keep them yourself? Or pass them to Gangrüne? Keys are the purser's duty.'

'Mr Gangrüne is somewhat addled of late,' said Fiffengurt.

'And you were *born* addled, you old salted sea-rat! Nilus, choose someone else, this cross-eyed bungler will only drop them down the heads, or throw them—'

'Oggosk, be *silent!*'

Something in his voice made Felthrup look up in alarm. Rose was pressing his temples. His eyes were closed and his face was clenched with an expression of painful effort – or perhaps simply pain. The others noticed as well. Mr Fiffengurt and Lady Oggosk exchanged a glance – the first without rancor that Felthrup had ever witnessed.

Then Rose opened his eyes, and he swept them all with a furious glance.

'That creature has knowledge that could save this ship. Get it out of him, you four. Nothing else concerns you. Quartermaster, your duties will pass to Mr Byrd. Consult your *Polylex*, consult the Quezan harpooners, consult the mucking stars if you like. But bring me something to try by sundown. That is all.'

But it was not all. Captain Rose was lumbering up the Silver Stair, brooding and stiff, when the shouting of his men pierced his thoughts. He raced up the ladderway, past the orlop and berth decks, bellowing for a report. *The crawlies, Skipper!* men were shouting. *The crawlies are coming back!*

'Beat to quarters, fools!' he shouted.

His command raced ahead of him. Drums sounded, the ship roared to life. When Rose burst out upon the main deck he found the crew staring up at the sky.

A flock of birds was winging towards them from the island: the same oversized swallows, bearing the little people in their claws. A large flock, but not as large as the one two days ago that had spirited Talag's fighting force off the *Chathrand*. Rose made a quick estimate: some two hundred crawlies were returning to the ship.

What in the Nine Pits for? Can they possibly mean to attack?

A voice at his ear whispered suddenly: 'There's been blood on the wind for days, Rose. Crawly blood. We've smelled it.'

The ghost of Captain Maulle, almost invisible in the crisp morning light.

'Turachs to the deck!' Rose howled. 'Bindhammer, Fegin, get your men aloft – don't concede the rigging to those mucking lice! Fire-teams to the chain pumps. Haddismal, send that sharpshooter of yours to the main top! The rest of you – stand by, stand by.'

Sandor Ott stood on the roof of the wheelhouse, bow in hand. The flock was swift approaching. Marines boiled from the hatches like armoured ants.

But this time the birds did not swoop down on the deck. Instead they flew straight and level across the *Chathrand*'s waist, parting around the top of the mainmast and flapping on, with the crawlies still held tight in their claws. A moment later the crew amidships was pelted with tiny objects, raining in their hundreds from above. 'Take cover, lads!' Fegin was shouting, but a moment later he added: 'Belay, belay. What in Pitfire, Captain Rose?'

The bombardment ceased. Rose gaped in wonder at the objects littering the deck: tiny swords, tinier knives, bows and arrows fit for dolls' hands. The ixchel had thrown down their arms.

'Stand by!' he shouted a second time, though no one would dare to move without his consent. The swallows turned eastwards, sailing out towards the mouth of the bay. They stayed far from the cliffs, as though the ixchel themselves feared assault from that quarter. Rose shouted for his telescope. By the time he had the birds in his sights they were descending again, upon one of the larger rocks beyond Stath Bálfyr. As he watched they came in for a gentle landing on the barren stone, just a few yards above the lashing of the sea.

'What's that about?' cried Sergeant Haddismal. 'What in Rin's name would make them want to come to rest out *there*?'

For several minutes nothing else happened, save that the dawn grew brighter, the air slightly less chill. Then the lookout cried that a single bird was flying back their way from the rock.

Rose found it with his telescope. The bird was carrying a crawly, and as it drew near he saw that it was none other than Lord Talag. As before, the swallow stayed high above the deck. But this time as they drew near, Talag shook himself free of the bird's claws and flew on his own, in the swallow-suit, in a circle about the ship. His flight was laboured, and brief: he flew only as far as the tip of the main topsail yard, some four hundred feet above the deck. There he landed, folded his legs, and sat. Now Rose could see that the swallow-suit was in tatters, and stained with dark blood.

Fiffengurt was right. They've been fighting the island crawlies. And those two hundred – are they all that remain of his clan?

Commotion aloft: Talag was shouting to the topmen. They relayed the message at once down the human chain. Rose made them say it twice, as he could scarcely believe his ears. Talag was asking Rose to climb the mainmast, near enough for a private talk, 'between men who care for their people'.

The gall! thought Rose. *As if listening to more lies and duplicity could help my crew.*

'If the crawly wants to talk he can descend to the quarterdeck,' he said aloud. 'Otherwise, let him rot there.'

'Better yet,' said Ott, approaching from aft, 'let me knock him off his perch with an arrow. You know he deserves it.'

There was a gleam in the spymaster's eye. Rose frowned. 'He has earned death,' he agreed. 'Very well, spymaster: bring the Turach sharpshooter as well. If the crawly does not explain himself in twenty minutes, you and he will have an archery contest, and the men may place bets.'

Ott looked at him, pleased. 'You surprise me, Captain. I had almost decided that you'd gone hopelessly soft.'

The men relayed the captain's answer to Lord Talag. The ixchel's reply came immediately. Talag claimed to know the secret of the boulder-throwers. He would share it, too, if only Rose would climb up and talk.

You cunning bastard, Rose thought. A chance to free the ship was the one hope he dared not spurn. Even to appear indifferent would demoralize the crew. And now a dozen men at least knew what Talag had promised.

'Clear the mast,' he shouted. 'I'll speak with the crawly alone.'

He expected rage from Ott, but the spymaster merely gazed at him, eyes bright with curiosity – a more disturbing response than anger. Rose climbed. It had been years since he had ventured as high as topgallants. The descending topmen eyed him with concern, but they knew better than to speak. Captain Cree, lounging at his ease in the fighting-top, had no such reticence: 'Take your time, old man! Nothing's more pathetic than a captain fallin' to his death on his own ship.'

Rose actually smiled at the ghost. Cree had done just that.

He was light-headed by the time he reached the topgallant spar. Lord Talag had risen and walked in along the heavy timber until he was a few yards from the captain. The two men were alone on the mast.

'Thank you for coming,' said Lord Talag.

Rose was gasping. He heaved one leg over the spar, hooked an elbow around a forestay, and leaned back against the mast. The sun was hot on his face.

'What do you want, crawly?'

'Death,' said Talag, 'but I have yet to earn that release.'

Rose shielded his eyes. Talag was seating himself on the mast, and though he tried not to show it, Rose knew he was in stabbing pain. The blood was not only on his swallow-suit: it had dried on his hands, his leggings, had congealed his hair into a sticky mass.

Talag spread his hands. A slight barren smile on his lips. 'Behold, your enemy. The Ninth Lord of Ixphir House, the master of his clan. Of what is left of his clan.'

'Why did you take your people out to that rock? They can't be safe out there.'

Talag looked at him. 'Safe,' he said. 'That is a fine word. Safe.'

'Don't start blary raving.'

'Forgive me,' said Talag. 'Only that is what the dream was about, you see. To be safe. That was what I promised them, years ago. That is why we brought the *Chathrand* to this isle.'

A ruined man, a broken man. At another time it would have angered Rose simply to be in his presence. Today what he felt was something darker: recognition, a likeness between them. Rose was chilled by the thought.

'You promised *me* some word about those boulder-tossers.'

Talag nodded. 'I will tell you everything I know of my ... brethren, on Stath Bálfyr. Indeed I'm prepared to tell you anything and everything I know, save the location of my people on your ship. My word on that. And no conditions.'

'You want nothing in return?'

Talag fixed his vanquished eyes on Rose. No anger in them, no hope for himself. And no pride, utterly none. It was as if the man before him had been skinned.

'I want something immense, Captain,' he said. 'But I know I cannot bargain for it. I am here to beg.'

Rose and Talag spoke for a surprisingly long time. Many on the deck below watched their conference for a while, before beginning to mill about in impatience. Only Sandor Ott stood like a statue, his telescope fixed on the pair from beginning to end.

The end was bellicose: Rose shaking his bushy head, the crawly pacing the spar and gesturing with increasing urgency, at last both of them shouting, and Lord Talag flying away from the *Chathrand* in a fury.

Scores of hands gathered by the mainmast, watching Rose slowly descend. When he reached the deck at last Sandor Ott handed him a glass of fresh water.

'From your steward.'

The captain drank like a horse, then wiped his beard and shouted: 'Clear out, you staring gulls! Have you not duties enough?'

The crew dispersed, leaving just Ott and Haddismal. Rose picked up his coat, drew out a clean kerchief and mopped his face.

'They're done for,' he said. 'The islanders are less like Talag's people than we're like the Black Rags. They're all crawlies, I don't mean that. They can understand each other's speech – or enough of it. But they have nothing else in common. Stath Bálfyr is religious, and divided. They treat the lower orders worse than dogs.'

'What do you mean, lower orders?' said Ott. 'The clans have different ranks, different privileges?'

'There are no clans any more,' said Rose. 'It's a theocracy. The nobles live like sultans, make the laws, talk to the Gods. The lower-downs just follow. And the lowest of the low—' Rose shook his head. 'Talag said he saw a man dangling from a noose by the trailside. He asked what the man's offence was, and they said, "He was caught uphill from his betters." Just *standing* uphill. Because water flows downhill, and he might have rendered that water unclean.'

'Gods of Death!' said Haddismal.

Sandor Ott gazed out at the mouth of the bay. 'Those two hundred, on the rock?'

'All that remain alive,' said Rose. 'The islanders were prepared to grant Talag a higher status, because of the magic of the swallows. But not his people – they were unclean. Any outsider, ixchel or otherwise, is unclean. And when they tried to herd them into work sheds, under lock and key—'

'Talag exploded.'

'Of course he did,' said Rose. 'That last mobilisation was a rescue party. And a great defeat. Talag's people are the better fighters, but there are tens of thousands of crawlies on that island. They rule every inch of her. That rock out there was the only place they could land.'

Ott gazed at him, unblinking. 'Besides this ship, you mean. That is what he asked you for, wasn't it? Safe return to the *Chathrand*, the ship they seized once, the ship they almost destroyed?'

'That was his request,' said Rose. 'He doubts the swallows are strong enough to bear them to another island. Even the nearest.'

'And in exchange, he told you how we might escape this Godsforsaken bay?'

Rose hesitated, and the other men saw his face darken. 'Nothing of the kind,' he said at last. 'That was only a ploy to make me hear him out.'

He drew a deep, brooding breath, then turned and started lumbering towards the stern.

'But Captain, what did you tell him?' asked Haddismal.

Rose paused, looking back over his shoulder. 'What did I tell him? That he had best hope the birds are stronger than they appear. Or else wait for a storm to wash them from that perch and end their suffering. That I would rot in the Pits before I'd welcome his ship-lice back aboard.'

Haddismal was speechless, caught between approval and horror. Sandor Ott too held very still, clutching the folded telescope and studying the captain minutely.

Once in his cabin Rose told the steward to pour him a generous snifter of brandy, then moved to his desk and began to write a letter. When he had his drink he set the steward to polishing the floor. But minutes later he glanced from the page and barked:

'What are you doing there? Off your knees, and bring me that lamp.'

The steward lowered the walrus-oil lamp from its chain and brought it to the captain. Rose blew on the letter, folded it twice. From a desk drawer he took a stick of sealing wax and a spoon. As he melted a bit of wax above the hot lamp he gazed at the other severely.

'How old are you?' he said.

'Forty-nine or fifty, sir. My parents weren't much for dates.'

'You are to leave the Merchant Service and learn a trade in Etherhorde. If you are not killed, that is. If you are killed, I submit that you must practise discretion in the afterlife. Tell no one you were a servant. You are well-spoken, and your table manners are fine. No one will guess your humble origins.'

'Oppo, Captain,' said the steward. He had been years in Rose's service and was incapable of surprise.

'This letter is for the duchess,' said Rose. 'Deliver it when she rises tomorrow. Until then keep it with you, safe and out of sight. Now go and eat.'

'But … your own dinner, sir—'

'Go, I say. Come back at sunrise with my tea.'

Alone, Rose sat with both hands flat upon his desk. Not a sound, not a scurry. The ghosts had all stayed outside his door. He nodded to himself: their reticence was a sign, a threshold passed. Now there was nothing to do but wait.

He was still there at midnight, wide awake, the brandy untouched. He seemed gifted tonight with exceptional hearing. All the sounds of his vessel, the pounding, stumbling, swearing human machine, reached his mind like an incantation known by heart. At two bells past midnight there was a scratch at his door. He stood and walked to the door and opened it, and the red cat with the maimed tail looked up at him, questioning.

'Come in, then,' he said, and the animal did.

For the last hour he sat with Sniraga on the desk before him, purring. Then he passed a hand over his face (dry, flat, pitted, a face like an abandoned pier), and blew out the lamp. Now the room was lit by the stars alone, filtering dimly through windows and skylight. He stood up and took the cat to his bedchamber, shutting it within. Then he walked to the gallery windows.

The ship was as peaceful as it would ever be. Rose unlatched the tall starboard window, pushed it wide, then crossed the chamber to port and did the same. The chill night breeze slithered into the cabin, bringing with it the slosh of the bay against the hull, the creak of the mizzenmast stays.

Very soon they arrived. Soundless, as Talag had sworn they would be. A black river of birds, flying in at one window and out by the opposite. They never landed, never slowed. But as they passed, the crawlies dropped from their claws, landing on soft cat-feet, running for cover even as they touched the ground.

Of course, they had nowhere much to go. His cabin had no cracks or crevices, no bolt-holes by which they could escape. Quite a few were too injured to run in any event. The crawlies formed a circle in the middle of his rug, backs to the core – unarmed, pitifully vulnerable. The strongest lifted the maimed onto their backs.

Lord Talag was the last to arrive. From the windowsill, he made his people count off, their mouths opening and closing as they silently shouted. Then Talag flew to the rug and turned to face Rose. He made a curious salute, raising the sword he no longer had, then sank to his knees and pressed his forehead to the ground.

Rose scowled. He had not thought Talag capable of such a gesture, or that he, Rose, could ever find it sincere. It was sincere. 'Get up,' he hissed under his breath. 'There's your conveyance. Will you fit?'

He pointed to a battered sea chest by the wall. Talag nodded. 'We will. There are breathing-holes, I trust?'

'You'll see them.' Rose walked to the chest and tipped it on its side, holding the lid ajar. 'Hurry, damn you,' he whispered.

The crawlies flowed like ants into the chest. When they were all inside Rose slowly tipped the chest upright and closed the lid. Then he tested the weight.

Bile of Rin.

Two hundred crawlies – and what, two pounds apiece? He flexed his hands, his shoulders. He walked to his cabin door and listened: no one about. He propped open the door and walked back to the chest, glaring at it like an enemy. In his youth he had carried a five-hundred-pound whisky barrel up a gangway on a dare. But his youth was a memory, a visitor who had come with dreams and promises. A visitor whose face he could no longer recall.

He lifted the chest. The crawlies shifted. He moved to the door, stagger-stepping like a draft animal. He pictured himself collapsing, spilling crawlies down the ladderway, found by Turachs with the stark evidence of madness and treason in his arms.

How he managed the descent he could not begin to say. Did the ghosts aid him; could they lend him bodily strength? Or was it merely his conviction that a path once chosen must be walked to the end?

On the threshold of the orlop deck he braced the chest against the wall and slid it to the ground. Pain like a knife in his back. Torn muscle. He raised the lid. Lord Talag, and the bleeding remnants of Ixphir House, looked up without a sound.

'Run, you little bastards,' he gasped. 'Run for your lives, and don't let me ever see your faces again.'

They vanished across the orlop, quiet as a sigh of wind through reeds. Not one of them failed to bow before they fled. Why had he done it? How had Talag compelled him to care?

Too late for such questions. Rose lifted the chest (so nearly weightless, now) and continued down to the mercy deck. His work not done. The greater test was waiting somewhere in the dark.

'Kurlstaff,' he whispered. 'Come along, you old pervert. Spengler. Levirac, Maulle. Why are you hiding, tonight of all mucking nights? Come out, I say. I need your witness.'

They came, stumping along in the darkness. They were reluctant, gazing at him with uneasy respect. Only Kurlstaff, with his lipstick and his bangles and his battleaxe, dared to speak. 'You're the maddest of us all,' he said.

Rose moved on, and the ghost-captains trailed in his wake. At last he stood before the Green Door, padlocked as he had ordered. He set down the chest and fumbled in his pocket. From the start of his career Rose had never once dispensed a key without retaining duplicates himself. He freed the locks and let the chains fall away.

The dangling lamp sputtered to life as he approached. Kazizarag stood as before in the centre of the room, his gold eyes seeking Rose. This time the demon was silent, as though he knew (and perhaps he did) that taunts were the last thing he needed tonight. But he grinned at the captain, a wide sly grin full of teeth.

Rose dropped the chest and stared him down.

'You can have the gold,' he said. 'All of it, and the other treasure as well. As Final Offshore Authority it is mine to dispense with. I give it to you.'

'If.'

'If you will swear not to seek it until the ship meets its death. A death you will not hasten.'

'You are not much of a bargainer tonight,' said the *maukslar*. 'I cannot leave the vessel until the *Chathrand*'s keel is cracked, and her blood spills, along with all the magic that courses through her. Only then will this prison release me.'

Rose glanced back at Kurlstaff, who stood uneasily at the threshold. The other ghosts had not dared to enter. 'What about *our* prison, Rose?' demanded Kurlstaff. 'When the ship sinks, will we go to our rest? Or will we rot for ever along with the carcass of the ship? Ask him, ask him!'

Rose faced the *maukslar* again. 'The woken rat,' he said, 'tells me you can look through the walls of this ship as though they were glass.'

The demon just waited, gazing at him.

'Everywhere, that is, save the stateroom. The latter, I assume, is guarded by a magic stronger than your own. Arunis could not pierce it either. The chamber is off limits to magical probes. We could even be hiding the Nilstone within it, could we not?'

'You could, but I know better.'

'The question is, does *she*?'

'What are you driving at, Captain?'

Rose ignored the question. 'The rat also said you claimed you could make a hen's egg glow like the sun.'

'Easily.'

'Could you make it burn, though? Burn with death-energy, throb with curses like an altar of the damned? Could you make it so black that it swallows light the way you swallow gold?'

The *maukslar* stared at him, fascinated and appalled. 'Lunatic. You are asking for a second Nilstone. Of course I cannot make such a thing, any more than I could lay new foundations under this world. And if I had such power, I should never offer the Nilstone as a gift. Not to you, not to Macadra. Not even to my mortal father, the Firelord who spawned me in his house of fear.'

Rose shook his head. 'I do not want another Nilstone. Only a counterfeit copy. Something Macadra will sense at a distance, and take for the real item.'

Once more the demon grinned. 'A decoy, you old wolf?'

'A lure,' said Captain Rose.

'For her, eh? For the White Raven. Nilus Rose, you *are* unpredictable, and that is the highest compliment I can give. A counterfeit: why not? But you would have to provide some solid artefact. I cannot anchor such a spell on thin air.'

Rose nodded. He put a hand into his coat and withdrew a small object that glittered in the lamplight. It was the glass eye of the Leopard of Masalym, the good luck charm on which he'd nearly choked.

The demon studied it appraisingly. 'That will serve,' he said. 'But now we come to it: what will you give me?'

'The gold is not enough?'

'I have answered that question already.'

'Your freedom, then,' said Rose.

'My freedom!' spat the creature, enraged. 'And what truth-telling oath will you take, king of swindlers? Do you know how many have come here through the ages – sailors, officers, tarboys, third-rate wizards, lovers seeking a trysting-place, assassins with bodies to hide? Do you know how many have promised me my freedom, Captain – sworn they would open the cell, right away, never fear – if only. If only I will grant them this, cure them of that, spread the secrets of eternity before their nibbling little minds. You are all the same. You strike poses. And when you have taken much from me, you walk out that door, and spend the rest of your lives not thinking about the prisoner you left in the dark.'

Still Rose's gaze was implacable. 'Do I look like them? Do I look as though I have time to waste?'

The *maukslar* blinked, conceding the point.

'I will free you, Avarice,' said Rose. 'The world is rife with demons, chained and unchained. The mischief you add will not be decisive.'

He waited. The *maukslar* gazed at him with the focus of a tiger watching its prey.

'Give me the bauble.'

'I will not accept a poor imitation,' said Rose. 'Do not forget that I have seen the Nilstone close at hand.'

'My arts will not disappoint you. Give it here.'

Rose held the eye closer, but not close enough. He asked several further, pointed questions, and the *maukslar*, hungry in an entirely new way, spat out the answers like seeds. Then he made the demon recite his oath, and his name, just as Felthrup had done. Kurlstaff was still here, death's witness: the bond would presumably hold. Rose tossed the glass eye through the bars—

The *maukslar* leaped like a dog, caught the glass eye in its teeth, and swallowed it.

'You stinking fiend!' cried Rose.

The *maukslar* threw its head back and moaned. Gnarled hands clawed at its stomach. Its body twisted like toffee; its head spun around upon its neck. Then the neck unwound with a snap, the belly heaved, and the monster vomited something onto the floor of the cell.

Rose hissed. Even Kurlstaff shielded his ghostly eyes. It was the Nilstone. Perfect in its blackness, horrible in the waves of power it flung out in all directions. It lay there, silently throbbing, an exact duplicate of that shard of death on which the fate of Alifros so strangely hung.

The *maukslar* nudged it with a taloned foot. 'It will not fool her, or any mage, if they summon the courage to touch it. Nor will it do anyone grievous harm. You may lift it and take it away.'

'But from a distance?'

'It would fool its very maker. And when Macadra draws near – within a few miles, say – it will call to her.'

'A few miles! Is that all?'

The demon shrugged. 'You did not ask me to *improve* on the Nilstone.'

Rose ran his fingers through his beard. 'No, I did not. And it is better this way. For perhaps she knows the true stone well.'

'She saw it wielded by Erithusmé,' said the *maukslar*, 'and since that day it has haunted her dreams.' Then the creature gripped the bars of the cell, and its voice grew soft and deadly.

'Rose ....'

The captain felt an unfamiliar kick inside his ribcage. His own heart. His tongue, too: all wrong, the way it cowered against the roof of his mouth. He looked for Kurlstaff. The ghost was fleeing down the passage with a swish of tattered skirt. The *maukslar*'s teeth were showing. Rose pulled open the door.

Not everyone heard it, and most who did thought that they dreamed. A strange dream, a dream that was pure sound. A whoop, a wild cry that made eyes snap open all over the ship. Was it man, dog, steam whistle? No one could be sure, for in the very act of opening their eyes the sound had gone. No one was moved to investigate. A few men whispered prayers, curled in their hammocks like babes in the womb.

In the secret brig, Rose climbed painfully to his feet. The *maukslar* was gone. It had become a whirlwind, knocked him flat on his back. The cell stood open. The false Nilstone lay in the centre of the floor.

Bastard. You might have kicked the mucking thing out of the cell.

Captain Kurlstaff had warned him about the cell doors, and Rose believed every word: the man had died here, after all. Rose walked to the cluttered passage, and combed through the detritus on hands and knees until he found a battered pike. He carried the weapon back into the brig, carefully avoiding the door, and teased the false Nilstone out through the bars, never letting so much as a finger cross the threshold.

So black! he thought. *You told the truth, creature: I am not disappointed.* The leopard's eye had become a well into which one could pour all the light in the world. It hurt to look at it: he struggled to focus on a thing that was all absence, a thing that was not there.

And this is just an imitation.

He picked it up. No, it did not kill at a touch. But it dizzied him, throbbing with enchantment, and it weighed a great deal. Once in his pocket, however, both weight and dizziness abated. He kicked the empty sea chest towards the cell, then finished the job with the pike, nudging it inside as far as he dared.

Outside the Green Door, he replaced the chains and padlocks. All was quiet: at least the *maukslar* had not roused the ship. He crossed the deck in darkness. Who needed a lamp? The *Chathrand*'s lines were etched for ever on his soul.

On the topdeck, a warm rain was starting, and a wind that gusted and died. He asked the duty officer for the status book, and scanned the entries as he had done four times a day for most of his life. When he was done he turned and saw that Fiffengurt had crept up behind him.

'You again,' he snapped. 'What is it? Have you something to report?'

'No, Captain,' said Fiffengurt. 'I ... couldn't sleep, sir. Just taking some air.'

Rose dismissed the duty officer, then turned and glared at Fiffengurt. In a low growl, he said, 'Your previous assignment: abandon it. That matter is closed.'

'Closed?'

'Thasha Isiq is alive. She is very near to the Nilstone, and they are both moving quickly.'

'Captain! Captain!'

'Do not shout, Fiffengurt. The creature knew no more than that.'

'You went to see that thing? Alone?'

'Listen to me,' said Rose. 'This is not a warship – not a *proper* warship – and the crew will never be as sharp as it was. They are weak in body and in spirit, and some of the best men with a cannon are dead.'

603

Fiffengurt began to mouth some reply, but Rose cut him off. 'A man is lost in the forest.'

'Who, sir?'

'It's a fable, you dullard. He is lost, and a tiger has his scent. He may be days, even weeks from the forest's edge. He has only a little knife; the tiger has claws and strength and cunning. It is circling him. It knows the forest better and can see in the dark. How does he escape the tiger?'

'I know!' said a voice from inside Fiffengurt's coat.

It was the rodent. Fiffengurt blushed, and squeezed the animal a little against his side. He had evidently told it to keep quiet.

'I'd say you take to a stream, sir. Hide your scent, and wait for the beasty to move off on his own.'

Rose shook his head. 'You're on the right track. But you cannot stay submerged for long in a chilly stream.'

'Carve a spear with that knife, then.'

'And trust your life to one jab with a crooked stick? This is a master killer, Fiffengurt. It will come at you out of the dark like a living cannonball. It will tear you to shreds.'

Fiffengurt closed his mouth and waited. Rose gave a snort of dismay. 'It is a wonder that you're still among the living,' he said. 'Well, that is your new assignment: save the man from the tiger. Now go to sleep. There is fighting ahead.'

With that Rose made for his cabin. Fiffengurt watched him go, bewildered as ever. Felthrup's head emerged from the fold of his coat.

'He should have asked me,' said Felthrup. 'I'd have told him: climb a tree.'

Rose slipped into his cabin, closed the door, leaned on it heavily – a gesture of fatigue he had not allowed himself in forty years. He was ready for that brandy now. Ready for this hellish night to end.

He had left the window open. The rain was gusting in from starboard. Rose stripped off his own coat and hung it by the door. The papers waited on his desk; the untouched dinner setting waited on the table. He closed the windows. From this one, here, he'd thrown a man to his death. A company tattle-tale, not one of his crew. Still, just another lost simpleton, another pawn. It was no good being the pawn of any man, king or commoner, living or dead.

He whirled.

The papers, yes: they were still there. But the glass of brandy was not.

Across the large room, in the corner reserved for informal visits, Sandor Ott was tipped back in a chair with his feet upon a small round table. His left hand cupped Rose's drink. His long white knife lay on the table, unsheathed.

'I think,' he said softly, 'that you had better give an account of yourself.'

Rose moved to the dining table, breath short, mind churning. Do not hurry. Ott was always ready for violence, never for superior calm. This was how you fought him: by making sure he needed you, and by drowning him in calm. Rose struck a match and held it to the fengas lamp, but the fuel was nearly gone, and the weak flame barely lit the room. He found the brandy and poured a half shot. His favourite, this one. But tonight it was foul, bile and bath-water. What had become of his will to drink?

When he faced Ott again the spy had risen, and was moving towards the door. Rose was shamed by his own relief, the cold sweat he was drenched in, the smack of his heart. Then he glanced at the little table and heard himself say, 'You've forgotten your knife.'

'Have I?' said Ott. 'Well, then, I suppose I'd better not leave, just yet.'

He hesitated, fiddling with the doorknob it appeared. Then he turned and put his hands in his coat pockets and walked to Rose. For a moment, despite his scars, he looked like an old homebody, some frail Arquali blue-blood about to whistle up a dog. Rose waited for the inevitable grin to break out across his face. But Ott was not grinning. He was waiting for Rose to speak.

'Did you pick the lock?'

'No need. You'd left the windows open. An easy climb from the wardroom below. Why did you open them, in the rain?'

'It wasn't raining when I left.'

'Then you've been a long time wandering your ship.'

'That is my prerogative. Now get out.'

'But Rose, I have suggested something better. Something *decidedly* better for you. If only you will heed me.'

Ott was staring up at him, and standing too close. Rose gazed at the white knife still lying on the table. He had his own, of course. Right there on his belt, just inches from his hand.

'I will receive you on the morrow,' he said. 'Come back then if you would speak.'

'The morrow is here, Captain Rose.'

As if to prove his point, the duty officer gave the bell seven strokes. A dark, wet dawn was breaking somewhere. Rose scowled and brushed past the spymaster, forcing himself to make contact with the man. Ott let himself be moved. Rose lumbered towards his bedchamber.

'Did the crawlies threaten you, or pay a bribe?'

Rose missed a step, and glanced back sharply. There, he'd botched it. He might as well have written a confession in scarlet ink.

'You let them reboard,' said Ott. 'You *aided* them. The creatures who poisoned our water supply, who took us both hostage. Who have imprisoned us all in this bay.'

'The crawlies are no longer our problem, Ott.'

'Indeed. They do not control Stath Bálfyr?'

'Not our crawlies, no.'

A knock at the door. Rose started, but Sandor Ott called without turning: 'Enter.'

The steward crept in, with Rose's morning papers and tea service. Ott turned and walked past the man and nudged the door shut with his toe. Then he slid the dead bolt. The steward glanced up, startled. Ott shrugged and smiled, as though he were improvising a game. The steward placed the tray on the dining table.

'Shall I fetch another cup, Captain Rose?'

Rose made no answer. Ott walked back to the table and poured himself tea in Rose's cup and sipped it. He drained the cup and set it back on the saucer. Then he grabbed the steward by the hair. In a blur of movement he hauled the man down, hooked his left arm around the steward's neck, moved his right hand to the man's chin, and pushed once, ferociously. The steward's head turned backwards, much too far. His gaze less shocked than saddened. The crack was audible. The man fell dead.

'What were we saying?' asked Ott. 'Something about "our crawlies", I believe?'

Rose found himself backed against the wall. Sandor Ott took a napkin and dried his lips. Less than six feet separated the men.

'You were seen on the mercy deck. Is that where you released them?'

'The mercy deck,' said Rose. 'Yes, it was there, forward of the tonnage shaft.'

'And they fled through this strange Green Door? The door that you have, oddly enough, both padlocked and wedged slightly open?'

Rose nodded. 'Perhaps they did at that.'

'Or perhaps not. Perhaps they are here under your mattress, or under the floorboards, or stuffed into speaking-tubes. How I wish there was trust between us, Captain. Our relations have been all wrong.'

What if he shouted? Just screamed for aid like a child? No, no: some things were forbidden him, forbidden any son of Theimat Rose.

He stepped away from the wall.

'Take your knife, and your insinuations, and your killing glee from my sight,' he growled. 'Prepare a defence for this murder. At nine bells I will send the Turachs to place you in chains.'

Ott finally allowed himself a smile. He walked to Rose's desk, tapped the papers there significantly.

'Mr Elkstem tells me you borrowed our charts. Our *crucial* charts. That you brought them to your chambers. But they are not on your desk, or in your cabinets there. Would you care to save me the trouble of ripping the place apart?'

Rose felt his heart quicken. His mind had never worked faster in all his years. His eyes flicked right and back again.

Ott raised an eyebrow. 'The washroom, Captain? What a curious hiding place. I do hope you've kept them dry.'

He stepped quickly to the door, passing very close to Rose again. Mocking him, daring him even to gesture at drawing that knife.

Ott pushed open the washroom door. He frowned: there were no charts in sight. He leaned in further to look behind the door.

A red whirlwind struck him full in the face. Sniraga had pounced from a shelf. Ott reeled backwards, tearing at the cat, and in that instant Rose drew his knife and stabbed.

The blade passed through Ott's upper arm. Roaring, the cat still affixed to his face, Ott spun on his heel and kicked Rose squarely in the groin. The pain like an explosion. Like pressing one's ear to the cannon as it fires. Rose staggered, swinging the knife before him, meeting only air.

Fall and die, fall and die. Rose slashed again, missed again. Ott tore the cat away and flung it with both hands at the wall. His face a ruin, his eyes blind with blood.

Blind. Rose charged the smaller man. He struck Ott like a bull, lifted him off the ground and crushed him against the wall. The spymaster's head struck the solid wood. His hands clawed; he was groaning, red bubbles on his lips. Rose grappled tighter, slamming Ott again.

Ott's teeth sank into his neck, tearing through flesh and muscle. Rose bellowed and lurched enormously. Then he slipped in the blood, and both men went down. Another crack. Ott's head striking the table.

They were on the floor, entwined like lovers, bleeding to death. Ott's torn mouth twitched, and he clawed feebly at Rose. The captain struck with his fists: two punishing blows, and Ott was still. Beyond the cabin men were shouting. He rolled away from

Ott and groped for the desk. Haddismal and his men were out there, pounding. Somehow Rose gained his feet.

Perhaps Ott was dead. Never mind: he would hang if he lived. Rose dragged himself to the door and freed the deadbolt, but there was still something amiss. The doorknob would not turn. And then a new agony reached him, shouting to be heard above the rest. It came from his palm. He released the knob and looked at it. The flesh looked oddly burned.

Poison.

With his next breath it struck him. Like standing naked in a blast of sleet. He was paralysed, his limbs stiff as boards. *The speed of it*. Even his eyes were affected. Even the filling of his lungs.

The pounding went on. Somewhere behind him, he heard Ott begin to move.

Fiffengurt was out there too. 'Get the rigging axe!' he was screaming. 'Those are siege-doors! You won't just kick 'em in!'

Ott was crawling nearer. Then climbing to his feet. When he moved into Rose's fixed angle of view he looked like a walking corpse. In one hand he held the shattered teacup by the handle, extending his little finger, ladylike. There it was, the grin. He turned the cup in his quivering hand, then drew the sharp edge once, swiftly, over the captain's jugular. Blood burst out in a torrent, but Rose himself stayed rigid as he died. After a moment, professionally curious, Ott nudged him slightly, and the captain fell like a tree.

Now Sandor Ott had very little time. He seized the linen tablecloth and tore it into strips. The first he tied, mercilessly tight, above the wound on his arm. The second he doused with gin from Rose's cabinet. Strong, antiseptic gin. He wiped his face with it, hissing with pain. He splashed more gin on his wound.

Crack. They were axing the doors. Ott cursed, and hurried back to Rose. He found the padlock key quickly enough, but what was that round thing in his vest pocket? He drew it out, and gasped at the weight in his hand. Then he saw what he held – and for the first time since childhood, experienced a moment of undeniable fear.

The Nilstone.

The Nilstone?

The black thing lay there in his hand, a pulsing orb, a tiny black sun. How was this possible? What had Arunis made off with, if not the Stone? Had the mage spirited it back aboard, somehow, through his control of Uskins? And why wasn't it killing him?

Crack!

No time. Leave it or take it. Decide.

Ott took it. Then he turned and staggered to the door.

'Leave off with that axe!' He wiped the knob with great care, then slid the bolt. Men poured into the room, Turachs, common sailors, Fiffengurt the traitor, Haddismal the loyal fool. All screaming like children. As if blood were something beyond their experience. As if murder were the exception, not the rule.

'The captain's dead! The captain's dead!'

'The madness came for him,' said Ott. 'Sergeant, where is your field kit? I need bandaging.'

Haddismal raised his eyes from the carnage. He stared at Ott. Everyone was staring at something.

'What's the matter?' said Ott. 'You can see what happened here.'

'Can we?'

'The mind-plague took him. I heard sounds of violence, and came in to find him thrashing his steward. The man was still breathing, and I tried to revive him. Rose stabbed me while my back was turned, yet I bested him. Two dead. Very simple. Get me those bandages, dullard! Why do you—'

He froze. Against the far wall of Rose's cabin lay a woman of some twenty-five years: naked, motionless, her hands and face soaked with blood.

Night Gods. The cat. The hag's horrible cat!

'Who is she?' said Haddismal. 'A passenger? I've never seen that woman before.'

'Did Rose kill her too?' said Fiffengurt. 'Why didn't you mention her, Ott? Mr Ott?'

But the spymaster was already running. Their shouts exploded behind him: *Commander Ott! What is it? Stop him, bring him back!* For the first time since childhood, Ott felt inadequate to the moment. He had looked at that gory beauty and found himself without his best and oldest weapon, the winning story, the necessary lie.

'She must have been mad as well,' said Haddismal. 'Look at her. Even her feet are soaked in blood.'

Fiffengurt just gazed at the carnage. Their captain dead, and stiffer than a week-old corpse. The steward with his head facing backwards. And a third victim, a naked woman no one could identify, though Fiffengurt began to think he had seen her before.

'I'm not sure anyone here was mad,' he said.

'You calling Sandor Ott a liar?'

Fiffengurt knew better than to answer. He brought a sheet from Rose's bed to drape over the woman. But when he drew near, she sprang to life, hissed at him, and scurried on all fours under the table.

28

Reunion

12 Fuinar 942
300th day from Etherhorde

'That, my dear selk, is a Bali Adro exclusion flag,' said Prince Olik, training the telescope on the bay, where the *Chathrand* sat at anchor. 'A warning, in other words: *Keep a safe distance.*'

'We shall do so,' said Nólcindar. 'Stath Bálfyr is unchanged, then. A lovely bay one must not enter, an island where no landing is allowed.'

The *Promise* was three miles offshore, sweeping north past the mouth of the bay. It was almost noon, but the east wind was frigid, and now it looked like rain. Thasha gazed at their beloved *Chathrand*, and felt a stab of irony: twenty-eight days racing to meet her, and now that they'd finally arrived she was warning them off.

'Not an ixchel in sight,' said Hercól, who had the only other telescope. 'Perhaps they have all gone ashore, somehow. In any case, Lord Talag has proved himself a genius – of a sort. He said he would bring the Great Ship here, and he has done it. However deranged, the plan was a strategic miracle.'

'But a heartless one,' said Ensyl, anger darkening her voice. 'All of us have paid dearly for his dream. I only hope our brethren find happiness there.'

'More flags,' said Hercól. 'One is white with two red bars. Another, blue with a white half-circle.'

'Arquali pennants,' said Pazel, taking a turn at the scope.

'Two red bars: that's *Enemies near.* And the other is – damn, I'm forgetting …'

Thasha cast her mind back – so very far back, almost another life – to her days sitting in the family library, poring over her father's books. *'Ambush,'* she said at last.

'Ambush! Right.' Pazel gave her a private smile. He had mocked her sailing-savvy once. That too was a lifetime ago.

He looked again through the telescope. 'She's been in a firefight. Look at the cathead. Scorched.'

'To the Pits with your cathead,' said Neeps, 'don't you see any *people?*'

'Yes,' said the prince. 'The deck is busy with sailors. Human beings, and a few dlömu – my loyal Masalym guardsmen, they must be. Have a look for yourself, Mr Undrabust. Perhaps you'll spot your wife.'

Neeps pounced on the telescope. Thasha watched his face, and knew in short order that Marila was not on the topdeck. She glanced at Pazel: he looked almost sick with frustration. To be stopped this close to the *Chathrand*!

Still, things were much better than they'd feared. Day after day, Ildraquin had whispered to Hercól that Rose was motionless, and what was more likely to account for that than a wreck? To find her whole and apparently seaworthy should count as a miracle. The ixchel, or some other 'enemies', might be holding them prisoner, but at least they were alive.

'There's that old rotter, Latzlo,' said Neeps, 'and Swift and Saroo, by the Tree! But where are the officers? Where's Captain Rose?'

'I still say we should circumnavigate the island,' said Corporal Mandric.

'There is no other harbour,' said Nólcindar, 'and by the time we return to the mouth of this bay we may find Macadra guarding it.' She raised her telescope again. 'They have not been boarded, unless those who boarded have come and gone. The men on deck are not starved or sickly. But I believe they are sick with fear. Shall we try mirror-signals? If there are real sailors among your guard, Prince, they will know the Maritime Code.'

'Look there!' cried Neda, pointing.

From the deck of the *Chathrand*, flashes of sunlight were leaping: short, measured, steady as a ticking clock. 'They are one step ahead of us,' said Kirishgán. 'Let us answer quickly.'

A silver platter was fetched from the pantry, and Nólcindar angled its polished face at a halfway angle between the zenith of the sky and the *Chathrand*. She adjusted the angle again and again, until a pause in the *Chathrand*'s signals told her that contact was established. She waited, and the flashes from the bay resumed. Now the pattern was more complicated. After a moment Nólcindar frowned.

'I know codes of Bali Adro, Thudryl, Nemmoc and beyond, but I do not know this one. I expect it is a human code out of the North.'

'It's the Turach cypher!' said Corporal Mandric, squinting. 'That's one of my mates! Here, give me that trinket, Captain. Rin help me, it's been so long—'

Mandric was indeed out of practice, and the roll of the ship did not help matters. Time and again he interrupted the *Chathrand* with flashes from the silver platter, muttering: 'Repeat, repeat, you jackass, that's not right, it can't be—'

Letter followed doubt-ridden letter. With excruciating slowness, words took shape.

BOULDERS – FROM – CLIFFS – REEFS – NORTH – NO – EXIT – NO – ENTRANCE – HELP

The flashes stopped. The travellers looked at one another. 'Strange, but useful,' said Hercól. 'At least we know something of the nature of the trap.'

Mandric pointed at the clifftops. 'There's your boulders.' Thasha saw that it was true: the cliffs were strewn with great loose stones, giving the whole ridge a shattered look.

'And *reefs north*,' said Pazel. 'Do you know, I think they mean the north side of the inlet to the bay. Look at all that choppy surf.'

'I fear you're right, Pazel,' said Ramachni, studying the waves. 'Well then: reefs on the north side, boulders from the south. Little wonder the ship cannot escape.'

'The *Chathrand* is ten times our size and draught,' said Nólcindar, 'but reefs are reefs, and the *Promise* will never clear them.'

'What about landing a boat on the north side, there beyond the inlet?' said Neeps. 'You can see that the island narrows down to a strip.'

'You may be on to something, lad,' said Prince Olik, looking again through his telescope. 'The spot is both low and narrow: those palms are barely above sea level.'

'We could run that strip in minutes,' said Neeps, 'and be swimming to the *Chathrand* before anyone knew.'

'We could swim from right here,' said Lunja. 'Three miles is nothing for a dlömu.'

'Nor a selk,' said Kirishgán, 'but rocks can sink swimmers as well as boats, and the north beach too may be guarded. And once we board the *Chathrand*, how do we help her escape?'

The others glanced furtively at Ramachni, and the mage saw their glances and sighed. 'My powers will not be enough to save the ship. One or two boulders I might turn aside, but not a hail of them. And I cannot lift the Great Ship into the air – not even my mistress in her prime could manage such a feat, save with the power of the Nilstone.'

'I could protect them, maybe,' said Thasha.

The others looked at her sharply. 'That is yet to be proven,' said Hercól, 'and besides, you are not aboard.'

'I can swim that far.'

'Don't be *daft*, Thasha,' muttered Pazel.

'I'm not,' said Thasha calmly. 'This isn't like that night at the Sandwall. There's something waiting for me on the *Chathrand*. Something Erithusmé knew could help us.'

Hercól and Pazel turned away, and Ramachni's eyes told her nothing. Thasha knew they would have to listen sooner or later. For months they had all been sheltering her, trying to shield her from outward danger, even as she struggled to set Erithusmé free. It was hard on Pazel, and all her friends. They were carrying her like a vase through the hailstorm; she was trying to shatter on the floor.

Then, two days ago, she had overheard Pazel and Neeps whispering about some 'other way'. She'd confronted them immediately. At last Pazel had yielded, and shared the mage's words:

Take Thasha to the berth deck, to the place where you used to sleep. When she is standing there she will know what to do.

Some hidden power, available to her alone. Thasha felt like smacking the tarboys for keeping quiet so long; but it was love, after all, that had sealed their tongues. Love, and fear. 'Erithusmé made it sound mucking *deadly*, Thasha,' Pazel had told her. 'She called it a last resort.'

Of course, that warning had not dissuaded her: it was high time for last resorts. Any doubt of that had vanished yesterday, when they woke to find themselves looking at the Swarm.

You could spend a lifetime struggling to forget the sight. A black mass the size of a township, high in the clouds, possessed of will and purpose. It appeared too solid to be airborne, and it *squirmed*, like a muscle or a clot of worms. It had been moving along the edge of the Red Storm, pausing, charging, doubling back again, an animal prowling a fence. Looking for a gap, said Ramachni. Hungering for death, for the greatest glut of death anywhere in Alifros. Hungering for the war in the North.

Is my father in the middle of that war?

Thasha left the others arguing by the mast. The Swarm had vanished eastwards yesterday, leaving a changed *Promise* in its wake: the humans and dlömu shocked and fumbling for words, the selk grim and philosophical. They had caught no sight of it today, but Thasha could still see the Red Storm, many miles to the north, a scarlet ribbon between sea and sky.

Time barrier, she thought. *We fight and fight on this side, but for what? A home we may not recognize when we get there. A future Arqual that's forgotten us, or a dead one. Unless we too find a gap.*

Walking to portside, she leaned on the rail and stared at the wooded island. Seabirds gyred above the north shore; waves shattered on the rocks. She willed the place to open to them, somehow, to let them take their ship and their people and be on their way.

You've won, Talag. You let your sister die and your only child go mad, but you've won. Your people are home. Don't be so proud that you end up killing them, killing all the world.

But her next thought was like a blow to the face: *Talag's not the problem, girl. You are.*

All the self-loathing that had assaulted her in the Infernal Forest, and at the Demon's Court in Uláramyth, welled to the surface once more. She was failing them, and her failure was bringing the house down upon their heads. They could not wait. Macadra was drawing closer; the Red Storm was weakening. Any day, any hour, the Swarm might slip through into the North. They could not wait, and yet they waited. For her.

All that month on the *Promise*, her friends had tried to help her. Oh, the things they'd tried! Ramachni, exhausted as he was, had undertaken a journey into her sleeping mind. It was a complex spell that had taken him days to prepare, but the journey itself had lasted only a single night. He had reached the wall, examined it – and declared on waking that it had nothing to do with Arunis.

'But it has *everything* to do with Thasha's will to live,' he had continued. 'It is built of the same stuff as the outer, permanent walls of her mind, and its foundation. For good or ill, Thasha, the creator of that wall is you.'

His words made her think again of what she had felt in the Demon's Court. That Erithusmé would return if she perished, and only then. She was ready to die. A part of her knew quite well that she had the courage. But Ramachni had sensed the direction of her thoughts, and intervened.

'Listen well to me, Thasha: your death is *not* the solution, on that point Erithusmé gave her word.' Pazel went even further, claiming that the mage had told him that Thasha's death would mean Erithusmé's as well. But the feeling persisted: only her death could break down the wall.

Nólcindar had also tried to help. She had sat with Thasha across the length of three cold, clear nights when the seas were calm. It had been a kind of selk meditation, Thasha supposed, but it had also felt like enchantment, for she had found herself transported to distant times and places in Alifros, walking green paths under ancient trees, or through deep caves where veins of crystal blazed in the lamplight, or down the avenues of cities that had fallen centuries ago to drought or pestilence or war. Sometimes Nólcindar was there at her side; often she was not. Alone or accompanied, Thasha had felt each of the places tug powerfully at her heart. When it was over Nólcindar said that she had merely been telling stories of certain lands Erithusmé was known to have travelled, in hopes of stirring memories that would open a crack in the wall. The memories had been stirred, maybe; but only distantly, and the wall remained sound.

Then it had been Hercól's turn. His efforts harkened back to their *Thojmélé* training, which placed clarity of mind and strength of purpose above all virtues. Late one night he took Thasha to a lower deck of the *Promise* and showed her a doorway blocked with sandbags. They were tightly fitted, reaching all the way to the top of the door frame. 'Sit alone beside this barrier,' he said, 'until it becomes the wall within your mind. Then pass through. Fear nothing, hope for nothing; do not dwell in emotion. This is a challenge, but not a judgement. If it is in you to do this, you will.'

Then he had taken the light away, and Thasha had put her hands on the black sandbags and calmed herself in the *Thojmélé* manner. For two hours she had not moved or spoken. Then Thasha stood, limbered her body, tightened her boots. She planted her shoulder against the wall of sandbags and pushed, and felt a shout of inner despair that made a mockery of her training. The bags might as well have been stone. She took a deep breath, steadying herself, reciting the codes Hercól had taught her across the years. *The task demanded of the body is welded to the task of the mind. Neither is a true accomplishment without the other. When you have mastered the* Thojmél *you will perceive but a single task, and know when you may achieve it, and when to forbear.*

Her training promised clarity, not success. It became very clear that she would not be passing through the door. When Hercól returned he showed her the wetted boards they had stacked between the sandbags. The wood had expanded with the moisture, creating a wall so tight they could only dismantle it by slitting the bags and letting the sand spill out. 'I made sure you had no knife,' he said. 'You were not to pass through without the mage's help.' For that, after all, was the whole point.

The tarboys had suggested no experiments, but they had helped more than anyone, simply by being near her, breaking her morbid silences, helping her think. Pazel still had a Master-Word: the word that would 'blind to give new sight'. For over a year he had known it, carried it about like an unexploded bomb, and he still didn't know what it would do.

'What if it doesn't cause real blindness?' Neeps had asked him. 'What if that just means forgetfulness or ignorance about some specific thing? Maybe Thasha needs to forget about Erithusmé altogether, before setting her free.'

Pazel looked at him thoughtfully. 'It could work that way. But I've no way to know. The Master-Words, they're like faces moving deep underwater. I can see them, but they're dark and blurry. I only know exactly what will happen when they surface. And they only surface at the bitter end, just before I speak. This last one, now: sometimes I think I could direct it at a single person, but other times I think it might change the whole world. Ibjen thought I should never use it at all. What if I start a blindness plague?'

'I think Ibjen was wrong, this time,' said Thasha.

'So do I,' said Neeps. 'The first two words shook you up, I know that. But in the end they didn't change anything beyond the ship, did they?'

Pazel hesitated. 'I don't know,' he said. 'But this wall inside you already exists, Thasha. If you forget about Erithusmé, you might not see any reason to tear it down.'

'I don't know that I'd even be able to *find* it, without her voice calling to me from the other side,' said Thasha. 'And not being able to find it, to feel it: that would be just as bad—'

'As not being able to tear it down,' said Pazel.

Thasha nodded, and the conversation had died. She could certainly feel the wall today, however. It was both real and unreal, a solid obstruction and the hazy symbol of her failure. Almost nightly she stood before it, the same stone wall she had dreamed of on their last night in Uláramyth. But now the cracks were closing, not widening; and the voice from the other side was growing faint. Rather than crumbling, the wall was growing stronger, more determined to stand.

Failure. Turn your mind in that direction and you'd find madness waiting, a vulture in a tree. Failure was darkness, death, a world devoured by the Swarm. Lifeless seas, barren hills, dead forests crumbling year by year into dust. No colours but the colours of stone. No spring renewal. No animals. No children.

She dreamed of children, now and then. She could close her eyes and almost see them: those angelic phantoms, impish and laughing, clumsy and perfect, blends of Pazel's features and her own. She wanted, with brute selfishness, to live on through them. Not her cheekbones or her eyes or nose but her cherished memories, the sweet story of the alliances they'd made, the trust they'd earned and given, the terrors that had proved less potent than love.

No children would learn any of that. No tales would be shared. No history could be written of a world that had died.

As she stared, helpless and angry, one of the seabirds lifted above the rest. It was making for the open water. Thasha stood up, frowning. The bird was flying very straight and swift – not *directly* towards them, but just a bit north.

An intercept course.

Thasha's heart was pounding. She walked back to the others and interrupted their talk. 'You can put down that platter, now,' she said.

The others just stared at her. Thasha couldn't help it, she laughed aloud. Then she turned and shouted a name into the wind, and the moon falcon answered with a shrill, savage cry.

Niriviel's report confirmed the earlier signals. The bay's entrance was a deathtrap: reefs to the north, flying boulders from the south. 'I can come and go as I please,' he said, 'but I am the only one.' And yet the travellers had no choice but to seek entrance somewhere. For Niriviel had also warned them that the *Chathrand*'s crew was nearing breaking point.

'Forty-three have succumbed to the plague. Forty-three locked in cages, reduced to mindless beasts. And Plapps and Burnscovers kill each other in the shadows, and the deathsmokers show their faces by daylight, and there is only the one fool doctor to treat them all. The traitor Fiffengurt has been made captain, and Sergeant Haddismal permits this, and submits to his will. Or pretends to. But this is only because there is no other leader the sailors trust. Not since Captain Rose was killed.'

'By a feral madwoman,' added Hercól, 'who appears out of nowhere, sneaks by night into his cabin, kills Rose and his steward, and succumbs instantly to the mind-plague. Quite a tale, is it not? My sword Ildraquin has led me to corpses before, but never to so mysterious a death.'

'I tell you only what others claim,' said the bird. 'Lady Oggosk says the woman is innocent, but she was found alone with the corpses, her mouth and hands dripping blood.'

'What does your master say?' asked Thasha.

'Ask him yourself, but do not expect an answer. I cannot even—' Niriviel stopped, as though aghast at his own words.

'Go on,' said Ramachni.

The falcon looked at him with one eye and then the other. 'We are thousands of miles from Emperor Magad,' he said at last. 'Arqual is mighty, but is it mightier than Bali Adro? Should it try to be, or will it only destroy itself, as Bali Adro has done? Master Ott says that Arqual will one day rule the world, that these corrupt lands of the South will implode, and we alone shall be left standing, the inheritors of all power. But Master Ott told me to tear Lord Talag from the sky.'

The bird flapped and fidgeted on the rail. 'I could have killed him. The crawly flies so slowly on his flimsy wings. But I have heard Talag myself begging the island crawlies to let the *Chathrand* go. What sense did it make to kill him? Was it merely because he embarrassed Master Ott? But Master Ott is not the Emperor, though he has been more than Emperor to me. I did *not* kill Talag. I let him go to the island, and Master Ott must know by now. Master Ott knows that I lied!'

Suddenly the bird screeched with anguish. 'Where has he gone, where has he gone? No one aboard will tell me. Has he died, or does he just refuse my service? How could he, when he says he trusts me like his own eyes? He said that, and more. He said I was the only thing of perfection that he has ever made.'

'Sandor Ott did not make you, Niriviel,' said Ramachni. 'I hope a day will come when you see that you are your own author, and that your tale may go on without him.'

'We are as good as brothers, falcon,' said Hercól. 'Your master said the same to me once, before sending me out to kill.'

'We are not brothers,' said the bird. 'I love my master and will fight for the Ametrine Throne. You are a traitor. You failed him, you lied—' The falcon broke off, confused. 'All the same we must be … sensible. We are woken creatures after all.'

'Sensible is quite good enough for today,' said Ramachni. 'Come, let us make a plan.'

Two bells: it was the hour before dawn. In the bay high tide was approaching, and the waters of the inlet were slowing almost to a standstill. Both moons had set, and while the Red Storm still pulsed and flickered, its light did not penetrate the bay. The *Chathrand*, trying to conserve lamp oil (along with everything else) stood in darkness. It was the twelfth night of the stand-off, and it would prove to be the last.

Atop the cliffs, the ixchel of Stath Bálfyr kept up their watch, looking for the selk ship that had sailed with obvious intent to the mouth of their island, and been warned away by the humans. The *Promise* had extinguished her running lights, but if she tried to enter the bay they would know it: their ixchel eyes could spot such a large ship even by starlight, even by the dimmest glow cast by the Red Storm, if that ship passed at their feet.

But they could not see the lifeboat.

Without sail or mast it went gliding, pulled by twenty dlömic swimmers who kept all but their heads submerged, and only raised the latter to gulp a little air at need. Over the submerged reefs they passed, among the dark schools of fish, the black shadows of larger creatures, guiding the boat through the coral maze. Only in the deepest troughs of the waves did the boat strike the coral, with a dull thump that carried a little distance, but not far enough.

In the boat, Thasha crouched between Ramachni and Hercól. Neeps and Pazel were behind them, and last of all came Bolutu, who had insisted. 'You heard Niriviel,' he'd told them. 'Ignus Chadfallow is being run off his feet. I may be an animal doctor, but I'm a blary good one. And the sooner I get aboard, the sooner I can help.'

He and Ramachni were the only ones Hercól had not smeared with soot. The boat too he had blackened, right down to the water-line. That line would have been higher but for the last item in the boat: the Nilstone, still safe within Big Skip's protective shells of glass and steel. Today the Stone felt heavier than lead. Wherever they moved it became the low spot in the boat.

The half-mile inlet felt excruciatingly long. Some reefs were shaped like walls, others like rocky hilltops. The dlömu had to flounder among them, feeling their way in the darkness, keeping the boat from any knobs or protrusions of coral, and never turning in the direction of the cliffs.

Lunja was out there in the water, leading the swimmers, for she was the strongest of them all. After the *Promise* launched the life boat, she had swum near them and rested a hand on the gunwale.

'We are nearly all in our harnesses,' she had said. 'And we have knives. If any of us should get entangled in the reefs we will cut ourselves free so that the others may go on, and tie on again when we can.'

'The spare ropes are already secured,' said Hercól. 'Take every care, Sergeant! The dangers may not all be from above.'

'Whatever happens to us,' said Ramachni, 'you *must* see the Nilstone aboard. Its power would continue to flow to the Swarm of Night from the floor of the bay, or for that matter the deepest trench in the Ruling Sea.'

'I understand,' said Lunja. 'Farewell for now.' Still she had hesitated. Then Thasha had realised that she was looking at Neeps. The tarboy was gazing at her wordlessly; his breath seemed caught in his throat. He leaned closer, but in that moment Lunja turned and vanished in the darkness. Only when she was gone had Neeps managed to speak her name.

Now a little light glowed behind them in the east. They were almost within the bay. Once there the dlömu could pull in a straight line for the *Chathrand* for one more unobstructed mile – and the guardians of Stath Bálfyr, with any luck, would be powerless to stop them.

There came a hard thump near the bow. '*Upa*, that was no reef,' hissed Pazel. 'Something just smacked into us, by Rin.'

'We are nearly out of the coral,' said Hercól. 'Stand by oars – let us give the swimmers all the help we can. Steady, steady … *now*.'

Two sets of oars plunged into the water. Neeps was left the job of holding the Nilstone, while Ramachni kept watch upon the bow. 'Pull!' he urged. 'The light is growing, and we are still too near the shore.'

Suddenly Lunja's head broke the surface next to them, along with those of two other dlömu. 'That reef was like a forest of blades,' she said. 'Many of us are bleeding, and some of the ropes have been cut. I fear we did not bring enough spares.'

It was then that the cry broke out: a strange trumpeting noise, strident and huge. It began on the clifftops, but was soon taken up on the north shore, which was much nearer the boat.

'Away, away!' cried Hercól. 'They have seen us!'

Lunja and her two companions seized the spare ropes coiled on the bow and vanished ahead. Thasha looked at the cliffs: the shadows of the boulders appeared to have multiplied.

The trumpeting grew louder. From the north shore there came a sound of crashing and breaking limbs, as though some great herd of animals was stampeding through the forest. Then a great concussive *boom* sounded on their left. Spray struck their faces, and a wave lifted and rolled the boat precariously. 'They've started with the rocks!' said Neeps. 'Say your prettiest prayers that we're out of range. *Upa!* Their aim's improving! Can't you blary row any faster?'

Thasha wanted to kick him, but she did row faster. Then she heard Bolutu gasp. He was looking at the northern shore.

In the half-light, a pale strip of sand glowed between the trees and the water, and crossing it were twenty or thirty of the largest animals Thasha had ever seen. They were shaped like buffalo, or bulls, and yet not quite like either, and they stood almost as tall as the trees themselves.

'Pull!' cried Ramachni. 'Pull for you lives! Those are *drachnars*, and they are the ones hurling the stones!'

The beasts were thundering into the water. Not buffalo: they were more like elephants, great shaggy elephants that would have dwarfed any specimen in a Northern zoo. The great ogress they had fought in the mountains would scarcely have reached the shoulder of one of these. But they were not elephants either – not quite. The mouths were like shovels, with great flat incisors on the lower jaw. The trunks were much thicker and stronger than elephant trunks, and strangest of all, they divided into three halfway down their length. *Yes*, she thought: *those trunks could grasp boulders, and hurl them. And if they could manage boulders, why not—*

'Look out! Look out!'

A palm tree struck the water like a spear, not five yards away. The boat rocked wildly. Thasha rowed with all her might. She could see now that many of the creatures were grasping logs or stones that they had dragged out of the forest, and some were already rearing up to hurl them. Others were still wading into the bay. They had come several hundreds yards already, and the water was not yet to their necks.

'Halfway!' said Ramachni. Pain seering Thasha's arms, her shoulders. On the ship, lamps blazed. Thasha could hear screeching – *Oggosk*'s screeching; had she ever imagined she could miss it? – and the rattle of davit-chains. The *drachnars* pelted them with whatever they could scavenge – old logs, young trees, even the remains of some other wreck. But the dlömu were swimming in formation, now, and pulling like a team, and soon the north shore fell behind them, and they were out of range.

Then Niriviel swept down out of the sky. 'I could not warn you,' he cried, hovering. 'Those creatures have never emerged by daylight. We did not know what we faced.'

'Never mind,' shouted Hercól. 'But tell us, brother, has Fiffengurt prepared the ship? Is she ready for the Ruling Sea?'

'The Ruling Sea!' cried Niriviel. 'You do not know what you are saying. The crawly lunatics will never let us depart. Can you not see them, riding on the heads of the monsters ashore?'

'Riding them!' said Ramachni. 'Well, there is the secret of Stath Bálfyr's defences: the ixchel have tamed the *drachnars*, or at least allied with them to fight intruders. No, falcon, our eyes cannot match your own. But hurry, now: back to the *Chathrand*. Tell Fiffengurt to start weighing anchor, if he has not begun already.'

'I will tell him,' said Niriviel, 'but there is no way out of this bay.'

The falcon departed. Pazel glanced over his shoulder at the *Chathrand*, caught Thasha's eye, and forced himself to smile. Whatever lay ahead, they were almost home.

Two of the dlömic swimmers returned to the boat. They were clearly weakened, and once aboard Thasha saw that they were bleeding from many spots. 'Bandages, Undrabust!' shouted Hercól. 'You two: are no others hurt?'

'How could we know?' they said. 'In dark water it is hard to judge your own wounds, let alone someone else's. But Lunja must have had the worst of it, for she led us through that coral maze.'

'Then she should come in!' cried Neeps.

'So we told her. But she paid no attention.'

'The *Chathrand* is lowering a skiff,' said Ramachni, gazing ahead. 'We must see the wounded aboard first – and then the Nilstone, and Thasha. Pazel, you must go too, since Erithusmé bid you escort her, and – Oh fiends beneath us, *no!*'

On either side of the boat, dark fins sliced the water. They were sharks: the same grey, man-sized creatures that had trailed the serpent off Cape Lasung. But these sharks were not following any serpent. They were following blood.

Everyone in the boat howled a warning. Someone among the swimmers must have heard, for they all broke formation, and then began to pull for their lives.

'They'll be slaughtered!' cried Neeps. Hercól stood and raised his bow.

'Put that away, are you mad?' cried Ramachni, leaping onto the prow. 'Cut the swimmers free, and row on!' With that the little mink launched himself from the prow, and took owl-form before his body could strike the waves.

Hercól drew his knife and slashed at the ropes. He was leaning far over the prow, and Thasha clung desperately to his belt, terrified that he too would fall among the sharks.

'Who's that one, what's he doing?' cried Pazel.

Thasha squinted: one of the dlömu was peeling away from the rest – and the sharks were following. As they had done off Lasung, the creatures hunted in a tight school that never divided. It seemed that terror had overcome one swimmer, who must have expected the sharks to follow the larger group. But who knew how that collective mind made its choices? The lead shark reached the swimmer, and Thasha saw the dlömu turn and open its arms – a gesture strangely like an embrace. Thasha closed her eyes for an instant; when she looked again the swimmer was gone.

Ramachni passed over the sharks, folded his wings, and dived.

The dlömu were making for the *Chathrand* with what remained of their strength. But now the sharks turned like a single body, resuming the attack. The lifeboat fell further behind. Neeps was almost sobbing as he cried Lunja's name.

Suddenly a change came over the water around the sharks. At first Thasha could not tell what it was. Then she knew: the water was boiling. Seconds later it was turning to lethal steam.

Oh, thank the Gods. Ramachni was surfacing, in eguar-form, and the unimaginable heat of his body was literally vaporising the sea. They could see him, a dark monstrosity suspended in foam; and they could smell the sulphuric fumes. The nearest sharks were killed instantly; those behind swam on, blood-maddened, to their deaths. Many scattered in confusion, but they never regrouped and pressed the attack. In another minute the first dlömu were hauling themselves into the skiff that bobbed by the *Chathrand*'s side.

The beast that was Ramachni kept its distance, but its white-hot eyes blazed at them out of the steam. 'Row on!' cried Hercól. 'Our mage himself is in some danger, I fear – else he would not turn those eyes upon us.'

At last they neared the ship. High above, men were labouring at the capstan, raising the skiff and the wounded dlömu to the deck. Then a high voice rang out over the water:

'Triumph! Triumph! Triumph! Triumph! Triumph!'

Thasha looked up and burst into tears of joy. Fiffengurt and Marila were waving from the rail, shouting their names over and over. The mastiffs were baying to raise the dead, their paws and faces appearing and vanishing again. Suddenly Fiffengurt turned and beckoned, and a mob, a throng rushed the rail, cheered them, bellowed at last without reservations, without divisions or doubt. And through it all she could still hear Felthrup, hysterical, squeaking *Triumph!* as though it were the only word he knew.

Ramachni, still in eguar-form, raced away from them at high speed. 'Where in the Nine Pits does he think he's going?' asked Pazel. But at that instant the great, black form of the eguar vanished, and the small, helpless form of the mink took its place.

'Gods of death, he is barely swimming!' said Bolutu. He stood and dived without another word, and swam powerfully towards the mage.

'Don't you understand?' said Thasha. 'Ramachni had to be moving fast when he changed back. If he let the water heat around him he'd have been killed just like the sharks.'

When Bolutu returned with his small burden, the mage was too exhausted even to stand. Thasha took him and tried to dry him with her shirt.

The cheering went on and on. Soon the lifeboat from the *Promise* was snug in the davit-chains and rising up the *Chathrand*'s side. 'That transformation has cost me,' said Ramachni. 'I may recover my strength before I leave this world – but then again, I may not. You must not depend on me if it comes to fighting again.'

'Just rest,' said Thasha. 'We'll do the fighting, next time.'

Ramachni let his head drop onto her knee. 'I believe you just might,' he said.

The moment they cleared the rail, Neeps jumped to the deck and threw his arms around Marila. She had watched them ascend, wild-haired, round-bellied, hands in fists. She had screwed her face up into a frown, struggling desperately not to cry. Now he kissed her and the struggle ceased. Her arms went around her husband, and her loud, nasal sobs made Thasha understand why she tried so hard to repress her feelings at other times. Neeps laid a gentle hand on her stomach, and a look of wonder came over his face.

Felthrup, for his part, had stopped shouting only because he too had been choked by tears. 'Thasha, Thasha, you have been gone a lifetime. You have brought goodness back to this ship and redeemed her!'

'Not yet, Felthrup dear.'

'And you have done it, you have taken the Nilstone back from Arunis, and killed him!'

'Felthrup! How did you know that?'

'Arunis,' said the rat. 'Oh dear, there are *volumes* to tell—'

'Rascals! Reprobates!' Fiffengurt was laughing, an arm around the neck of both tarboys, coating his uniform with soot. 'Lady

Thasha, how'd you manage to live so long with this pair of apes?'

'How did you manage to keep the ship afloat without us?' said Pazel. Neeps was about to make a quip of his own, but his smile vanished when he looked at the wounded dlömu, who were being treated a short distance away by the tonnage hatch. The youths had been making their way to the dlömu to give them their thanks, and to help bind their wounds if they could. Hercól and Bolutu were already among them.

Marila looked at Neeps' face. 'What is it?' she said.

Neeps pulled away from Fiffengurt and ran ahead. He pressed among the wounded, shouting. Then Hercól rose and took him by the shoulders.

Neeps cried out, his voice sharp as a child's, and covered his face with his hands. Marila turned to the others in a panic. 'Someone's died,' she said. 'Who was it? Tell me, Thasha, for Rin's sake!'

Bolutu came and spoke to them. It was Lunja who had peeled off from the other swimmers. Not with the hope of saving herself, but because she knew the sharks would follow her, bleeding profusely as she was from her cuts on the reef. 'That is the Bali Adro I remember, the way of love and sacrifice,' said Bolutu. 'My brethren owe their lives to Sergeant Lunja as surely as to Ramachni.'

'What about Neeps?' asked Marila. 'Did she save his life too?'

Yes, they told her, so swiftly that they sounded false. As though there were something to be ashamed of, some betrayal. Marila closed her eyes. 'Don't tell me,' she said. 'I want to hear it from him.'

Thasha looked at Pazel. 'The berth deck,' she said. 'Take me right now. Before anything else happens.'

'What could happen?'

'Oh *Pazel*, don't say that! Just take me there, you buffoon.'

'One thing first,' said Pazel. 'I won't be a minute, I swear.'

He ran forward, skipping through the well-wishers who tried to stop and cheer him, who slapped his back and shouted, 'Bravo, *Muketch*, you're a wonder, you're a man!' Then he raced down the Holy Stair and was gone.

Thasha smiled. 'He's heading for sickbay,' she said.

'Don't tell me he's ill,' said Marila.

Thasha shook her head and laughed. 'For once, he's not. There's nothing wrong with him at all.'

A look of understanding, and deep dismay, came over Marila. She glanced at Fiffengurt, whose face had also darkened. Then she raced after Pazel, shouting his name.

'Oh Missy,' said Fiffengurt. 'There ain't been time even to mention it yet. Dr Chadfallow was murdered.'

Tears, once more – how they could surprise one. She had never warmed to Chadfallow, but surely that would have changed. She knew Pazel loved the man, though he had spent half the voyage pretending otherwise.

'Niriviel told us that there was just one doctor aboard,' she said. 'I thought he meant that Dr Rain didn't count. Who killed him, Mr Fiffengurt? Was it Ott?'

'Oh, no,' said Fiffengurt. 'That bastard's in no position to hurt anybody. He's got himself in a fix, and I can't say I'm sorry.'

'Who did it, then? Who would kill a blary doctor?'

Fiffengurt drew a deep breath. The weight of all that had transpired seemed etched in his dry and weary face, and Thasha knew she would only ever grasp a part of it, that most of the tale would be lost.

'Arunis,' said Fiffengurt.

Shark bites were ragged, hideous things. Eleven dlömu had been attacked; one man was in danger of losing his arm. Neeps moved among them, his eyes red, cleaning wounds with an iodine solution someone had brought from the surgery. The survivors grinned morbidly, passing around a yellow, serrated tooth the size of a playing card. It had been extracted from a swimmer's leg.

At length Bolutu took the humans aside. 'Your help is a blessing,' he said, 'but another task awaits you. Go, and take the Nilstone, and do what my people fought and died to let you do. We have enough hands here.'

'We must find Pathkendle first,' said Hercól.

That was not hard: Pazel and Marila were seated in the passage outside sickbay, leaning against the wall. Pazel's eyes were very red; Marila held his hand.

Across from them, bearded now but otherwise unchanged, sat Jervik Lank. He jumped to his feet.

'I wanted to greet you up top,' he said, 'but the ward's a handful, m'lady, and there weren't nobody to cover for me.'

'It's horrible in there,' said Marila. 'The beds are full of death-smokers, strapped down so that they can't hurt themselves. And others who've been knifed or beaten up. The gangs don't have tactics any more. They just hate each other, and the marines, and anyone who tries to stay neutral.'

They too stood up, and Thasha put a hand on Pazel's cheek. He smiled sadly at her. 'It's all right,' he said. 'Ignus wasn't my father, you know. Although in the end he'd have made a pretty good one.'

'This ship's gone mad,' said Jervik. 'Until this morning, anyway. I could hear 'em cheering you, all the way down here. They did that for Rose, on New Year's Day. But there ain't been a blary moment since when the crew felt like a crew. You done a fine thing just by comin' back.'

'And you've helped save the ship we came back to,' said Thasha. 'I'll always be grateful for that. A lot of men would have just given up.'

'A lot of men did,' said Marila.

The older tarboy fairly glowed with their praise. 'When a Lank makes up his mind to do something, he does it.' Then all at once he looked abashed. 'No, no. That ain't the truth. You know what my life's been – the life of a great pig, eh, *Muketch*? I nearly killed you, once or twice.'

'Forget it, mate,' said Pazel, barely listening. 'We've all of us changed.'

'Have we?' said Jervik. 'You're all still clever. And me—' He shrugged. '*Ragweed don't make roses, and dullards don't grow wise.* That's me, ain't it? You don't have to pretend.'

Marila stepped close to Jervik. She reached up and took hold of the tarboy's jaw, which dropped in amazement. 'Promise me something,' she said.

'Wha?'

'That you will *never* say that again. You're not stupid. It's a lie somebody told you, because they couldn't mucking say you were weak. Spit it out.'

There was a silence. Jervik's eyes swivelled to the other tarboys.

'If you want your chin back, you'd better promise,' said Neeps.

Jervik blinked. 'No lady never asked me for my word on nothin',' he said. 'But since you want it, well – I promise, Mrs Undrabust. On my departed mother and the Blessed Tree.'

The tarboys' quarters were almost directly beneath sickbay. Neeps and Pazel slipped inside first. Thasha heard boys scrambling and swearing. 'All right,' Neeps shouted. 'Everyone's dressed, after a fashion.'

Within, the compartment was a maze of dark hammocks, dropped clothes, open footlockers, unwashed plates. Had inspections ceased, Thasha wondered, or just the consequences of failing them?

There were only a handful of tarboys about. Among them were the twins, Swift and Saroo, who had been cold to Pazel and Neeps since the massacre of the ixchel. They were cold now, too.

'Your whole gang's back, is it?' said Saroo. 'And your pal Mr Fiffengurt's in charge. You must be tickled pink.'

'Just what the *Chathrand* needs,' added Swift, 'another gang.'

'Ease up, mates, they're heroes, like,' said the freckle-faced Durbee, a tarboy from Besq.

'Fiffengurt will make a good skipper,' said Neeps.

'I suppose from now on you lot will decide what's good and what's bad,' said Swift.

'We didn't all make it, actually,' said Pazel. 'Big Skip was killed, and Dastu. And nearly all the marines. And Cayer Vispek and Jalantri.'

'The Mzithrinis,' said Neeps, when the tarboys looked blank.

'Oh, *them*,' said Saroo. 'Well now. I don't suppose even you cried much for a pair of blood-drinkers.'

'The stanchion's over here,' said Pazel, as if Saroo hadn't said a word. Despite the twins' hostility he had spoken with no rancour at all. Thasha felt an ache in her chest – just pride, just love for her friends. These tarboys were all roughly the same age, but how much older Pazel and Neeps seemed. *And no wonder*, she thought. *Tear your heart and your body to pieces, bleed and burn and freeze and make love and lose love and kill – and heal just partly, and hide what will never heal. Then try it. Try to stay innocent, try to pretend you're still the person you were.*

'That's my muckin' post!' said Saroo, when Pazel stopped before the stanchion with the eight copper nails. 'You can't just come back and swipe it. You ain't slept there in months.'

'What's the matter, Pathkendle?' said Swift. 'Fleas in your girl's brass bed?'

Pazel drew his knife.

'Pitfire, mate, there's no cause for that!' said Durbee, jumping between them. But Pazel only reached up and cut the hammock rope around the upper part of the stanchion. He sheathed the knife and glanced at Thasha.

'Erithusmé said you'd know what to do. Was she right?'

Thasha looked at the copper nails. They were arranged in a half-circle, with the open side facing the ceiling, like a cup or a bowl. She stepped nearer the rough wooden post, ran her fingers down its length. It felt like rock.

'Mr Fiffengurt says that's one of the oldest bits of wood on this vessel,' said Durbee cautiously. 'He says it was ancient when the boat was *built*. We all figured that's why you had such good luck, Pazel. Because there was some sort of charm on it. And that's why Saroo claimed it after you left.'

'Aught good it's done me, though,' grumbled Saroo.

Thasha closed her eyes. Trying with all her might to listen, to heed the voice behind the wall. Almost of its own accord, her left hand slid up to the nail-heads.

She hammered these herself. She laid power away for just such a moment.

Her hand passed through the wood as if nothing were there.

Swift and Saroo backed away in fright; Durbee made the sign of the Tree. Eyes still closed, Thasha found that the nails remained solid: she could feel them, suspended in the phantom wood. And just beyond them, more solid objects. Two of them. She closed her hand on the smaller and drew it out.

It was a short, tarnished silver rod. One half was quite plain, the other scored with a complex set of notches and grooves.

'What is it?' Pazel asked her. 'Do you know?'

Thasha stared at the little rod. She should know, she *almost* knew. But if a memory lurked inside her it belonged to Erithusmé, and she could catch nothing more than its echo. She gave the rod to Marila. 'Hold this for me,' she said.

The larger object was rough and slightly top-heavy. She took a firm grip and lifted it out past the nails. There in her hand was a stout bottle made of clay. It was stoppered with a cork and sealed in thick red wax. The bottle was chipped, dust-darkened, unimaginably old. It was solid and rather heavy. She turned it: a slosh of liquid, deep inside.

Thasha blew away the dust. The bottle was painted in thin white lines. Prancing skeletons of men and horses, dragons and dogs. Bare trees with what looked like eyes. Thasha shifted the bottle to her right hand and gazed at her left. It felt rather cold.

'Thasha,' said Marila, 'do you know what you're holding?'

She turned her head with effort; her thoughts felt strangely slow. 'Do you?' she asked.

Marila hesitated. 'Put it back,' she said.

'Back inside the post?' said Neeps. 'That's plain crackers. What if she can't get it out again? Marila, tell us what you know.'

'Nothing, nothing, so put it back!'

'Marila,' said Pazel reluctantly, 'don't get mad, but you're a terrible liar.'

'That's because I'm *honest*.' Marila's hands were in fists. Then she saw their baffled looks and the fight went out of her. She sighed. 'I think I know what's in the bottle. Felthrup was reading the *Polylex*, or talking about what he'd read. It was wine.'

'Wine?' said Thasha.

'Yes,' said Ramachni, 'wine.'

The tarboys jumped. The mage stood there in the disordered gloom, with Felthrup squirming beside him. No one had heard them approach.

'The wine of Agaroth, to be precise,' said Ramachni. 'Now there is something I never thought to lay eyes on again, or hoped to. Be careful, Thasha: you are holding a relic more ancient than the Nilstone itself.'

'It feels sturdy enough,' she said.

'That is not what I meant,' said the mage. 'A spell is at work here. I cannot quite sniff it out, but it is a dangerous charm, perhaps even deadly. I think you feel it already, Thasha. And there is another matter: be careful how long you hold that bottle without shifting your hand, and warming it. Those figures were painted by the dead.'

Most of the tarboys turned and ran for the compartment door. But Felthrup was overjoyed. 'We are saved, we are saved! It is right there in the *Polylex*! The wine of Agaroth takes away all fear – and fear alone makes the Nilstone deadly to the touch! One gulp of that wine, and the Fell Princes could hold it in their naked hand.'

'Like Arunis' idiot, in the Infernal Forest,' said Pazel.

'If you like,' said Ramachni. 'Both knew freedom from fear: the idiot through total madness, the Fell Princes through the taste of this wine. But I do not think the wine's effect lasted long. No tales speak of the princes marching to war with the Nilstone in one hand and a bottle in the other. But drink they did, and wield the Nilstone they did – briefly, and to evil purpose. In the end they turned orgiastic, and gulped the wine like fiends. I never imagined that any bottle survived in Alifros.'

Thasha's right hand was cold. She shifted the bottle to the crook of her arm. *Brought here from death's border,* she thought. *Who could do such a thing? Who could even dream of trying?*

But inside her the wheels were turning faster and faster, and the answer came: *I could.*

Thirty minutes later she was on the quarterdeck with the bottle in hand. Ramachni and Hercól stood with her, the latter holding a canvas sack. Behind them, at the wheel, stood Captain Fiffengurt. Lady Oggosk had somehow argued her way onto the quarterdeck as well. The witch stood apart from the others, dressed in mourning black. It was the first time Thasha had seen her.

At Thasha's feet lay the Nilstone, in the steel box Big Skip had fashioned for it in Uláramyth. Hundreds watched them from the topdeck below. Between the crowd and the quarterdeck ladder stood forty armoured Turachs armed with spears. Haddismal's precaution, and a good one: if any man aboard were seized by evil thoughts, or evil spirits, or plain madness, he would have no hope of reaching the Nilstone today.

'Right, Lady Thasha,' said Fiffengurt. 'Both anchors secured; we're floating free. The tide's not with us, but somehow I think that's the least of our troubles.'

He trained his good eye at the cliffs, where the *drachnars* were waiting, quite openly now, for any move by the *Chathrand* to flee the bay. A hundred more waded along the north shore, gripping enormous logs in their trunks.

Thasha looked down at the deck. Every friend left alive was watching her. Pazel made himself smile at her for an instant; Neeps and Marila wore looks of deep concern. In Marila's arms, Felthrup gazed at Thasha and never seemed to blink.

'Go on, Hercól,' said Thasha.

With a last look at Thasha, Hercól crouched beside the Nilstone. First he laid a hammer and chisel on the deck. Then he removed a key from the sack and unlocked Big Skip's box. Reaching into the bag once more, he removed a pair of fine metal gauntlets and slipped them on. Next he gripped the steel box in both hands and

637

twisted. His muscles strained. The box split in two.

Boom. The plum-sized sphere of glass fell to the deck with a sound like a dropped cannonball. Hercól stopped its rolling with his hand, then whipped the hand away and used his boot.

'It burns,' he said, 'through selk glass and selk gauntlets, it still burns a little.'

'It won't burn me,' said Thasha. 'Break the glass, Hercól.'

The task was easier said than done: the selk glass was amazingly sturdy. Watching Hercól's great overhand blows, Thasha couldn't help but think of that other ceremony, when Arunis had assembled the crew to witness his triumph. But this time was different. They knew exactly what the Nilstone would do to anyone unlucky enough to touch it. And they were drawing on its power only to help them get rid of it. Not to annihilate the world as a proof of one's powers, but to save it. For that reason, and that reason alone.

At last the chisel cracked the polished surface. Hercól struck again, and the crack widened. On the third blow the glass split like an eggshell, and the Nilstone slithered between the shards onto the deck.

Ramachni's fur stood on end. Thasha had not looked plainly at the Stone since that day in the Infernal Forest, after she beheaded Arunis, when it had fallen inches from her leg. She stared into its depths. Hideous, fascinating, beautiful. Too dark for this world; so dark that its blackness would stand out within a sealed cave, a cave under miles of earth, a cave sealed for ever. Thasha had the strange idea that she could put her hand right through it, as she had with the stanchion, but that this time she would be reaching into another world. Another Alifros, maybe a better one, where deep wounds had yet to be inflicted, hard curses never cast.

Ramachni clicked his teeth.

Thasha blinked, and wrenched her gaze from the Nilstone. Beside her, Hercól too looked shaken from a dream. How many had been seduced by the Stone and its mysteries, before it killed them?

A hand touched her arm: Lady Oggosk. Hercól tensed, ready to intervene. But Oggosk merely looked at Thasha and murmured. 'I will do this thing, if you wish.'

Thasha looked at her in amazement, and more than a little suspicion. 'The power won't last, you know,' she said, 'and it has limits. You can't use it to bring back Captain Rose. Not even Erithusmé could raise the dead.'

'I know all that, girl!' said Oggosk irritably. 'But there is some danger here that we have yet to identify.'

'She knows, Duchess,' said Ramachni. 'All the same this task falls to Thasha alone.'

'Why?' asked Oggosk. 'I am old, wretched. I cursed my sister. And I have outlived my son – yes, my son, I have every right to claim him!' Her old eyes flashed, as though someone might venture to object. If I fall, no matter. But her life is barely started. You don't have to—'

'Yes,' said Thasha, 'I do. Thank you, Lady Oggosk. I never dreamed you would make such an offer. But I can't accept.'

'For what it's worth, I received the same answer, Duchess,' said Hercól.

'No one but I would be standing before the Stone, had Erithusmé not been clear in her instructions,' said Ramachni. 'Stand aside, Duchess: the time for talk is past.'

Oggosk retreated to the wheelhouse. And Thasha, resisting the urge to look at Pazel one last time, broke the seal, uncorked the bottle, and drank.

When she tilted her head, the front of Thasha's pale neck shone in the mid-morning sun, and the crowd below could plainly see the scars left behind by the cursed necklace, almost a year ago. A stab of old pain leaped through Pazel at the memory. But it was nothing compared to the fear he felt when Thasha lowered her head.

Her eyes were wide open, and she did not blink. She was looking past them into the distance. Pazel saw one droplet at the corner of her mouth; then her tongue snaked out and licked it away.

Her throat seized. She was fighting not to vomit. She thrust the bottle into Hercól's grasp and fell to hands and knees, staring down at the deck. Her back arched and veins stood out livid on her arms. When she raised her head again her face was twisted, crazed.

'Pah! The wine is poisoned! It's going to mucking kill me!'

Eight hundred voices rose in cries. Pazel thought he would go mad. He made a run for the ladder, but the Turachs stood firm. Then Thasha shouted: 'Get away from the quarterdeck! Get back!'

She lurched away somewhere beyond his sight, and when she appeared again the Nilstone was there in her hand. Pazel's first thought was terrible: *She looks like the Shaggat.* For Thasha was unconsciously mimicking his gesture, lifting the Stone high in a single hand, as though pitting its darkness against the light of the sun.

'*Get back!*'

This time the voice exploded from her, an unearthly roar that swept the length of the *Chathrand.* Thasha wrenched her eyes from the Nilstone and gazed left and right, studying the water, the island, the sky. The crew did fall back, leaving only the Turachs and Thasha's closest friends looking up at the figures on the quarterdeck. The wind rose suddenly. Pazel felt a trembling in the planks beneath his feet. Thasha looked mad, and extraordinarily focused, but there was no hint of fear about her, none.

Then her eyes ceased roving, and fixed on one spot: the north shore. The thin arm of Stath Bálfyr, that half-mile of forest between ocean and bay. The *drachnars* were pacing there in the surf.

Thasha staggered into the wheelhouse. Oggosk and Fiffengurt shrank from her, clinging to the wheel. With no purpose, no thought at all but that she was in danger, Pazel shouted her name. Thasha turned as though whipped. A convulsion racked her, so violent she almost lost her feet.

But what occurred beyond the ship was on another scale altogether. From out of nowhere came a furious wind. Timber groaned, pennants filled and strained at their tethers; the rigging shrieked as if in memory of hurricanes. On the north shore, the surf withdrew, leaving the astonished *dranchnars* on bare sand.

Suddenly the *Chathrand* rocked. The surface of the bay was undulating, as though some great submerged mass were rushing towards the shore, lifting a bow wave before it. The wave grew and grew. The *drachnars* saw it coming and wheeled about, fleeing for their lives. The wave struck the beach and raced up it, surging through the legs of the stampeding creatures, combing at last through the palms beyond the sand.

Thasha convulsed again, and the surge increased tenfold. It was horrific: the bay was stabbing at the island like a sword. The palms, their roots stripped bare, let go of the ground and flew like battering rams against those behind, and the wind kept growing. Through it all the mid-morning sun looked gently down.

Once more Thasha's body shook. On Stath Bálfyr there was a titanic explosion of sand, water, trees. Pazel gasped: *the entire bay was shifting*, and then turmoil caught up with the *Chathrand* and he found himself thrown, sliding with scores of others across the deck. *Gods, she's sinking us.* But no, she was righting herself after all (good ship, sweet Rin what a darling) and the men locked arms like toy monkeys to save one another and Pazel was dragging himself to his feet.

The *Chathrand* was in motion, racing towards a huge wall of dust and sand that hung in the air over the north shore. They were not sailing; they were being hurled, leaning and pitching, helpless as a paper boat upon a stream. Pazel squinted at the oncoming wall, and perceived that a channel had been cut between the bay and the open sea: a second inlet, narrow as a village street, but widening even now.

Fiffengurt was roaring – 'Away from the rails, away!' – but few men saw or heard him. And suddenly the ship herself was in the channel, and there came an explosion of thumps and cracks and crashes: palm trees striking the hull. The ship careened, utterly out of control, rolling so far to starboard at one point that the torrent boiled over the rail, and Pazel looked up to see the tops of trees racing by at eye level. The deck was awash with foam, foliage, sand; and into that blinding slurry men tumbled and disappeared.

But Thasha had aimed her fury well, and before they knew it the tempest carried them out upon the sea, right through the humbled breakers, and left them revolving in an eddy that quickly died away to stillness. Away to the east stood the *Promise*, and to the north, the pale infernal glow of the Red Storm. Behind them, a great hole had been gouged through Stath Bálfyr, like something done to a sandcastle by the heel of an angry child.

Thasha was still standing: almost an act of magic in itself. Hercól got to his feet and stumbled towards her, but before he closed half the distance she waved him off. He stopped. Thasha lowered the Nilstone, caressed its blackness thoughtfully, then set it down upon the deck.

'That wasn't so hard,' she said.

29

Kiss of Death

————

Hercól and Bolutu left the topdeck at once, bearing the Nilstone and the wine of Agaroth. Thasha's other friends crowded near her, touching her as they might something exceptionally fragile. Men crept gingerly through the wreckage, inspecting the rigging, the masts. Whole palm trees were heaved over the rail. A stunned Captain Fiffengurt began to issue orders, salvaging his ship.

The disorder was massive, but the damage proved slight, and by two bells they were underway. A few hours later, Captain Rose's prediction was upheld: the little island east of Stath Bálfyr yielded both fresh water and forage. With dusk approaching, Sergeant Haddismal led a Turach squadron ashore with casks and heavy equipment. The pumping went on well into the night, lit by the glow of the Red Storm.

The *Promise* followed the *Chathrand* to the little isle, and even as the marines were landing, she dispatched a second lifeboat. Folding ladders were lowered from the *Chathrand*, and soon the last members of the inland expedition were climbing aboard: Mandric, saluting the new captain and the Arquali flag; Neda, her *sfvantskor* tattoos still uncovered but her expression somehow changed; Ensyl and Myett riding Neda's shoulders, scanning the deck for any sign of their people, and finding none. Next came Prince Olik. At the sight of him the *Chathrand*'s dlömu cheered and fell on their knees, and many wept with joy. They were all volunteers, the most loyal and loving of his subjects, and they had feared him dead at Macadra's hands.

Last aboard were Kirishgán and Nólcindar. Tall, olive-hued, eyes glowing like pale sapphires in the dimming light, they struck wonder into the crew of the *Chathrand*, not one of whom had ever seen a selk. They went to Fiffengurt and lay their bright straight swords at his feet, and bowed. 'Master of the Great Ship,' said Nólcindar. 'You carry the hope of the world upon your vessel. May the wisdom of the stars guide your choices.'

'It is our heads that should be bowed, m'lady,' said Fiffengurt.

'Let us have done with bowing altogether,' said Prince Olik. 'Rise, Bali Adrons – and you too, my good selk. Captain Nólcindar, Captain Fiffengurt—'

The introductions were mercifully brief. As soon as they were over, Neda turned to Thasha and pressed her hand. 'Sister,' she said, 'the Nilstone is not hurting you?'

'It didn't hurt me, no,' said Thasha. 'In fact I'm perfectly fine, at least as far as I can tell.'

'She didn't look fine,' said Pazel. 'She even shouted that the wine was poisoned.'

'I was wrong. It was only bitter – and *cold*. Terribly, magically cold. Maybe wine from Agaroth has to be kept that way. In any case, I have an idea that the bottle is enchanted too. Opening it was like opening the mariner's clock, and looking into another world – but not an inviting one like yours, Ramachni. It was a freezing, frightening land.'

'A land we all must visit, one day,' said Kirishgán.

'I was only scared until I drank, of course. After that nothing in the world could frighten me: the wine worked perfectly. But I thought it would last much longer – hours, or even days. No such luck: in minutes, the fearlessness was gone, and so was my control over the Nilstone. There was no warning, either: suddenly I just felt pain. It was as if someone were trying to strike a match down my side, and if the match lit I'd burn up like a scrap of paper.'

'As we have seen others do, who touched the Nilstone,' said Hercól. 'I was most relieved when you put it down, Thasha. You lingered, towards the end. I feared you were in a trance.'

Thasha turned and looked into the Red Storm's eerie glow. 'No, not that.' Something in her voice made Pazel uneasy.

'In any event, *we* cannot linger,' said Ramachni. 'What Macadra knows of our whereabouts is not yet clear. But if she has somehow learned our destination, she will not tarry. And we have already seen that she can harness the winds.'

'But how could she know about Stath Bálfyr?' asked Fiffengurt. 'Did she wring the name out of someone in Masalym Palace?'

'Impossible,' said Olik. 'No maid or manservant or palace guard was in earshot when we discussed the route ahead. Your destination was known only to me.' He paused, uncomfortable. 'Of course, there were those twenty of your crew. The ones who fled into the city, and were never found.'

'Stath Bálfyr was a secret from the crew as well,' said Pazel. 'They couldn't have told her. They'd never heard of it.'

'One of them had,' said Myett.

The others looked down at the ixchel. 'She means Taliktrum,' said Ensyl, 'but we do not know what became of him, sister. I doubt Macadra is even aware of his existence.'

'I wonder,' said Olik. 'He did not strike me as a man content to end his days in the shadows.'

'And some on this ship ain't content to end their days in the North,' said Fiffengurt. 'I mean your dlömic volunteers, Prince Olik. When they came aboard they thought we'd be sailing back to Masalym in a fortnight. Captain Nólcindar, will you take 'em home?'

'I will,' said Nólcindar, 'but first, Kirishgán and I would speak to you of the journey ahead. We have crossed the Ruling Sea, long ages ago, and remember something of the winds and the currents.'

'That would be a fine gift,' said Fiffengurt, 'and even finer if we knew we could start for home. The Red Storm's looking weaker off to the west, and we've sent our falcon scouting that way. But I won't sail us into that Storm, unless Ramachni here tells me it's the only choice. We need to find a gap.'

Pazel couldn't stop himself from scanning the horizon. Somewhere out there, the Swarm was also searching for that gap.

'The work ashore will last some hours,' said Nólcindar. 'If time permits, I would walk the decks of *Chathrand* a while, after we discuss your heading. To come aboard her has long been my dream. I remember the day I first saw the plans. I doubted such a ship could ever be built.'

Fiffengurt looked at her, puzzled. 'What can you mean, m'lady? The *Chathrand* is six hundred years old, and you—'

Nólcindar raised a feathered eyebrow.

'That is,' Fiffengurt stammered, 'I'm sure you're wise and strong and full of – benefits, or rather – I mean to say, you're young. A spring flower, or a sapling at the most.'

Nólcindar held his gaze sternly. Then she broke into a laugh of pure delight.

'A sapling! As a child, I *pruned* the saplings in my father's plot. That was far away to the west, in the green valley of Tarum Thün. A selk land, of such peace and stillness that a year might pass without words, and another when we chose to do nothing but make music, for the joy of it alone. From seeds to giants I watched those trees grow, and when they were very old and losing branches, we felled a few. Some went to ships, and the ships had long lives indeed. But today they are sleeping on the ocean floor, and some of us are still here, enjoying compliments.

'As for *Chathrand*, a few of her oldest timbers may have come from my father's wood. I always hoped to board her, and listen to them speak. But early in her life *Chathrand* went north, into service with the Becturian Viceroys. When she returned at last, Erithusmé was her mistress, and suffered no one to board her merely to appreciate her beauty, or because they loved the shipwright's art.'

'Love and beauty were never the concerns of Erithusmé the Great,' said Kirishgán.

Pazel smiled bitterly. *You knew her, all right.* But Ramachni looked up with sorrow in his eyes.

'*Never* is a place beyond our understanding, Kirishgán. Like the deepest chambers of the heart.'

While Fiffengurt escorted the selk through the *Chathrand*, the youths descended to their beloved stateroom. At first it seemed that nothing had changed. The invisible wall still sealed off the passage fifty feet from the door; Thasha could still permit or deny entry with a thought. The elegant furniture remained bolted down much as it had since Etherhorde. The enormous samovar still gleamed.

But at second glance Pazel saw damage aplenty. The escape from Stath Bálfyr had done more harm even than the assault by the Behemoth. Flying objects had smashed many windowpanes. Admiral Isiq's crystal bookcase had shattered, disgorging antique volumes in a heap. And where the heavy armchair should have been, two long, narrow holes gaped in the floorboards. The chair had ripped free of the boards and careened about the room, smashing lesser furniture, and lodging finally behind the table, like a stout skier upended in a snowdrift.

Felthrup apologised so profusely one might have thought he had personally ransacked the chamber. 'Oh fool! Never, never again will I ignore a squeaky floorboard! I tested every screw, twice daily when I could. But what good is a screw if the board needs replacing? Look at this place! And Marila worked so tirelessly – cleaning, repairing, fighting dust and mould. She wanted your homecoming to be splendid.'

Awkwardly, Marila took Neeps' hand. 'I just wanted you back,' she mumbled. It was the most affectionate thing Pazel had ever heard her say, but Neeps seemed not to be listening: his eyes were on the windows, and the cold water beyond.

They all fell to cleaning. 'Tomorrow we'll patch windows – there's plenty of spare glass laid away,' said Marila. 'Fiffengurt showed me how it's done – nothing difficult, but the cutting takes time. And I'll get my things out of your cabin, Thasha. I tried the master bedroom, but it was too huge and empty, with the three of you gone.'

'Stay where you are,' said Thasha, taking Pazel's hand. 'We'll sleep in my father's room, at least for tonight.'

Pazel was aware of the tightness of her grip. They had not made love since Uláramyth and he was not sure that they should do so now. She was fighting a battle inside, fighting for all of them, for the world. To turn her away from that in any way, to distract her: that couldn't be right.

'I wonder if there's any food in the galley,' he heard himself say.

Thasha looked at him as if he'd just spoken in the oddest language he possessed. She drew him into the master bedroom and closed the door. Backing him up against it, she put her hands over his eyes. He could feel her scars, healed and healing. When she kissed him he tasted the sea.

Her fingers parted. He looked between them, and laughed. Thasha looked over her shoulder, and she laughed too. One more casualty of their escape: Isiq's brass bed. The rear legs were cracked but still bolted to the floor; the front legs had snapped clean off. Pazel knew it had been her parents' marriage-bed: where the admiral and Clorisuela Isiq had tried and tried, failed and failed, to bring new life into their home. Only magic had let that good woman conceive. Erithusmé's magic. It had been there at the start of Thasha's life. No doubt it would be there at the end.

'Undress me,' said Thasha.

'What?'

It was not the reaction she'd hoped for. Thasha waited; Pazel didn't move. Something would happen if he surrendered; the task would grow harder, success further away. But in another moment he would not care about that. He let their fingers touch. He reached for the top button of her blouse. She was breathing like someone who had just run miles.

Voices in the outer stateroom: Hercól, Ramachni, Fiffengurt. Pazel began to kiss her wildly, nothing could prevent this, nothing, as long as he was left alive—

She stepped back, startled. 'Gods,' she said, 'that silver thing, that rod. I know what it is.'

What was she talking about? Why was she talking at all? He pulled her close again, but her hand was already on the doorknob. 'Let go,' she whispered, and slipped out of the chamber.

He stood there, gasping. He was ashamed of his weakness. The broken bed leaned towards him, plush and ruined, a sensuous ramp ending at a wall.

Hercól had brought the Nilstone and the wine of Agaroth. Mr Fiffengurt for his part had a bottle of Westfirth brandy. 'Compliments of Mr Teggatz, the devious lout. Where he hides his brandy is anyone's guess. He also begs to be told what delicacies you long for – if it's in the larder he'll cook it up for the returning heroes. But for now, what shall we drink to?'

'Too many choices,' said Pazel. 'Absent friends? Our own good luck? Thasha's deed with the Nilstone?'

'The *Chathrand*,' put in Thasha.

'Or the *Promise*, or Prince Olik.'

'Or the selk.'

'In Tholjassa, all toasts are silent,' said Hercól. 'Some things are better thought than said.'

The choice pleased everyone. They served the brandy in dented silver cups (none of the glassware survived) and drank it off without a word. Then Thasha asked Marila for the little rod from the stanchion. 'Come with me, all of you – and bring the Nilstone, Hercól.'

They filed into her cabin, which Marila had not changed in the slightest. Thasha rounded the bed and reached up to press a spot in the wall just above eye height. *Click* went a hidden latch, and a door unseen a moment earlier sprang open. Within was a small cabinet, empty save for a book, bound in dark leather and exceptionally thick.

Thasha smiled. 'Hello, old friend.'

She handed it to Marila: the *Polylex*, of course. But Thasha wasn't interested in the forbidden lore-book. She was looking at an iron plate set in the wall at the back of the cabinet. It was a rusty, formidable slab of metal, with a thick handle and a small round hole.

'Look close, you can see an outline of a drawer,' said Thasha. And so there was: a drawer some five inches tall and twice as wide, almost hidden by the rust. Thasha placed the notched end of the silver rod into the hole: a perfect fit. She turned it experimentally. 'Did you hear that?' she said. 'Something clicked.'

She gripped the handle and tugged, to no avail. She pressed the rod deeper into the hole and turned it again, pulling at the handle as she did so. She removed the rod and inserted it backwards. The drawer would not move.

'Gods damn it!' she said. 'I was so blary *certain*.'

Hercól set the steel box with the Nilstone carefully on Thasha's desk (which groaned a little at the weight). 'Make room, Thasha, there's a lass.' He stood square before the cabinet and seized the handle of the drawer in both hands. He drew a deep breath. Then he threw himself backwards with all his strength. There was a shriek of metal on metal, and the drawer slid open with a decisive *snap*.

'Locks were not your problem, Thasha – merely rust. Your key worked perfectly well.'

What had slid open was in fact no drawer at all, but a thick iron slab. It extended more than a foot into the room, and had but one feature: a cup-like hollow at the centre, about the size of a plum.

'I knew it!' cried Felthrup suddenly. 'This is Erithusmé's safe!'

Marila stared at him. 'What safe?'

'I told you, I told you! The safe they spoke of in the Orfuin Club!'

'I'm sure you're right, Felthrup,' said Ramachni. 'My mistress had various safes for the Nilstone in her dwellings ashore, though I never knew one had been installed on the *Chathrand*. They mask the power of the Stone, and make it harder – though not impossible – for enemies to detect. You won't need that box any longer, Hercól. I daresay no one will be able to steal the Nilstone from this spot.'

Hercól donned the selk gauntlets while Pazel unlocked Big Skip's box. With great care, Hercól tipped the Nilstone into his hand. '*Glaya*, it's heavy!' he wheezed. But the Stone fit snugly in the hollow of the slab.

Thasha gazed at the black orb, and it seemed to Pazel that she could not look away. Then Hercól pushed the drawer firmly shut, and Thasha blinked, as though starting from a dream.

They placed the wine of Agaroth in the outer cabinet, wrapped in scarves and braced by the *Polylex*. Thasha closed the outer door, and once again Pazel could see nothing but the wooden wall.

'Ramachni,' said Thasha, 'there's still wine in that bottle: two or three sips, anyway. I can use it. I can control the Nilstone.'

'Let us speak of that another time,' said Ramachni.

'I know what you're afraid of,' said Thasha. 'You think I'll hold the Stone too long, and let myself get killed. But I wouldn't risk that, I promise. I'll be safe.'

'Only my mistress could use the Nilstone safely,' said Ramachni. 'Keep striving to bring her back, and forget the wine for now. If we must turn to it, we will. But I would be happier if that bottle never again touched your lips.'

A faint *hoot* sounded from above: the bosun's wooden whistle. 'Ah, that's our sign,' said Mr Fiffengurt, rather sadly. 'Come quickly, all of you. The *Promise* is ready to depart.'

Pazel felt a sudden ache: he had not prepared himself for goodbyes. *But if Kirishgán only makes it back to that ship!* Then at last Pazel could stop fearing for him every time they spoke, every time the selk drew near.

Up they hurried to the topdeck. By the Red Storm's light they saw the *Promise* standing near, anchors up, sails loosed but not yet set. Her skiff was crossing the space between the vessels to collect any stragglers.

Hundreds of men had turned out on the *Chathrand*, but it was not hard to spot the few remaining selk and dlömu among them. Here were Kirishgán and Nólcindar, along with Bolutu, Prince Olik and a handful of the Masalym volunteers. The selk were talking with Neda and Corporal Mandric, while Myett and Ensyl looked down from the shrouds just a few feet above their heads. As the group from the stateroom drew near, Prince Olik turned to face them, and a hush fell over the crowd.

'Well, here we stand,' said the prince. 'The hunters of Arunis, together a final time. Do you remember the day I came aboard hidden in a water-cask, and Captain Rose bled me with his knife? I thought my end had come, but now I shall count that day as blessed. How else could I have met you?'

'You might have been better off if you hadn't, Your Highness,' said Pazel.

'No, lad,' said the prince. 'I should have been poorer, sadder, and most certainly lost. You saved me from that doom. You reminded me that however desperate my struggle for the soul of Bali Adro, it is but one battle in the larger war for Alifros. You let me feel the curve and compass of the world, beyond my darkening Empire. Alas, the wider world too is darkening swiftly. But look what has come from the darkness.' He spread his hands. 'You, friends, have been my candles and my hope. Allies undreamed of, allies I know I shall never see again.'

'A few of us may yet return to your country, Olik Ipandracon,' said Ramachni, 'if the darkness passes, and the world is renewed.'

'We will still fight the darkness together, even though we part,' said Kirishgán.

'Yes, brother, we will,' said Nólcindar. 'For just as I led Macadra astray in the mountains, so will we seek her now, and fool her again. When she spies us, we will seem to panic, and run down-wind. She will never catch us, but she may well give chase.'

'And now goodbye, and safe running,' said the prince. 'Whether we meet in this life or the next, you shall dwell for ever in my heart.'

They crowded near him, with words of praise, and not a few tears. Then the prince descended the folding ladder and was gone from sight. He was followed by most of the volunteers from Masalym, while the humans cheered them, and sang, and flint-hard old sailors stammered and wept. Some actually held the dlömu back by force, shaking their hands and plying them with brandy, trading hats, trading rings and trinkets. Secrets were told and pardons asked. Unsolicited confessions were heaped on the bewildered dlömu, and still the humans talked. They had never understood the dlömu, or quite ceased to fear them;* but the two races had fought and died together, and now it was finished, done.

Nólcindar took her leave next, and the survivors of the inland expedition struggled to find words for their gratitude. When his turn came before her, Pazel wished he could speak of Uláramyth, of the love that had filled him there and made him feel a foot taller and a century older and a match for any horrors from the Pits. He said none of it: the protective spell had sealed his tongue. Anguished, he gazed at this great woman of the selk, and something in Nólcindar's smile told him that she knew.

As she descended the ladder, Pazel turned to Bolutu. 'You've done so much for us,' he said. 'You saved my life on the bowsprit, that day Arunis left me to fall into the sea. More than that, you saved us from despair, by telling us the story of Bali Adro.'

Bolutu laughed. 'Even though it proved out of date.'

'Yes,' said Thasha, 'even though.'

Beside her, Neeps' mouth was frozen in a belligerent expression. It took Pazel a moment to realise he was fighting back tears. 'Pitfire, Mr Bolutu,' said Neeps, 'you've been fighting these bastards longer than any of us, except Ramachni. And you – you lost *everyone*, didn't you?'

'I lost my world, lad – my entire world.' Bolutu closed his eyes a moment, then smiled and opened them. 'I gained a new one, though. In time. It is only during this year away that I have come to understand how much it means to me. Human company, human food, the foul-smelling Etherhorde streets, Arquali music, the misfits of Empire who embraced me as one of their own. That

---

*The feeling was mutual, as the dlömic soldiers' letters and other testimony make clear. –EDITOR

world is mine, now, and I mean to keep it. That is why I shall remain on the *Chathrand*.'

His friends shouted with joy and surprise. 'But you'll be the only blary dlömu in Arqual!' said Pazel. 'They'll think you're a monster. Or will you try to become human again?'

'Never that!' said Bolutu. 'No, I shall depend on you to attest to my non-monstrous character. Daily, if necessary.'

'They'll hound you,' said Neeps. 'Even the *nice* ones.'

Bolutu nodded. 'Let us hope the world survives to inflict such minor miseries.'

Fegin blew two notes on his whistle. 'Time, gentlemen!' said Fiffengurt. 'To the ship you mean to sail on, double quick.'

There was a great rush to the starboard rail. The last of the Masalym volunteers descended, to cries of *Rin keep you!* and *Bakru waft you gently home!* Then the Arquali sailors broke down in messy grief, cursing and hanging on one another and bawling like calves: 'We won't forget 'em! Never! Who says we'll forget, damn the bastard? We love them old mucking fish-eyes!' It was not long before a Plapp swung at a Burnscover, or perhaps vice versa, and soon a dozen men were throwing fists. Captain Fiffengurt raged, looking for the first time like his predecessor. Fegin blew his whistle ineffectually; the dogs howled, and Mr Bolutu sat down atop a five-gallon bucket and laughed. But Pazel stood still, feeling a chill that had nothing to do with the night breeze. Kirishgán had not departed. He stood by the folding ladder, indifferent to the mayhem, watching the *Promise* as her ghostly sails bore her away.

Damn you, Kirishgán! Are you trying to get yourself killed?

Cooler heads dragged the fighters apart, and a kind of order returned to the topdeck. The *Promise* shrank away towards the southern horizon. Then Kirishgán turned his sapphire eyes on Pazel. Neither one of them had moved.

'Why?' said Pazel.

Kirishgán folded his hands upon the rail. 'My path had become a mystery to me,' he said. 'I was without purpose, and that is a fearful thing for any creature, young or old. The mists only began to clear when you arrived in Vasparhaven. The stories you told me of the North, that night over tea – they echo yet in my mind. Arqual, the Mzithrin, the Crownless Lands: they have forgotten the selk altogether. A great part of Alifros no longer knows that we exist. I must change that. I must look for my brethren, and find a way for them to speak once more to the peoples of the North. Or if I cannot find them – if they are all dead or departed – I must do what I can alone. If nothing else, I can remind your people that the story of Alifros is longer than the story of humankind.'

'Just by showing your face.'

'By doing as you have done,' said Kirishgán. 'By telling stories.'

'You're cracked, you and Bolutu both,' said Pazel. 'Have you forgotten what we're like? They'll panic, or throw stones. They'll lie to you, and take advantage of your honour. They won't listen to your stories.'

'They?'

'We. Human beings. Oh *credek*, Kirishgán, I don't know. I'm not sure I'm part of the *we* any more.'

Now the selk smiled. 'There is your answer, Pazel. I am going with you to encourage such doubts.'

Hard about, and due north. It was Fiffengurt's aim to sail as close to the Red Storm as they dared (some ten miles), and then tack west to meet Niriviel, keeping well clear of Stath Bálfyr and her shoals. Soon they were close enough to the Storm for Pazel to make out its texture: strands, snowflakes, rippling sheets of light. That storm had thrown his mother two hundred years forward in time. *No wonder she's so odd. She isn't just a foreigner in the North. She's a visitor from a world that no longer exists. And Bolutu's another. How have they been able to stand it? How have they done so well?*

He recalled what Erithusmé had said, how the Red Storm had stopped the plague from spreading north, how every human being in Arqual and the Mzithrin owed his life to that red ribbon of enchantment. Against all that, the time-exile of a few sailors counted for nothing. Unless you were one of them, of course. He looked again at the pulsing Storm. *The world's edge, that's what it is. We're ten miles from the end of everything we know.*

But the Storm did not tame the ocean. The minute the *Chathrand* cleared the shoals, every person aboard felt the huge, unbridled swells, and knew that they had at last returned to the Ruling Sea. There was almost no transition: suddenly the waves were gigantic, moving hills that barrelled towards them, tireless, infinite. The *Chathrand* rode them easily; she could stand much worse. Still, the sensation left men thoughtful. Worse was something everyone remembered.

They tacked west into a headwind, which they battled for the next six hours. It was hard work for the night watch; but then there was no true night this close to the Red Storm. The strange light caused some headaches, and a sense of unreality as men fumbled about in its saturating glow. But the urge to flee was strong. They left Stath Bálfyr behind (Myett and Ensyl watched it vanish, two women seeing the death of a dream) and at sunrise caught a favourable wind, upon which Kirishgán said he could taste the scent of honey-orchids in Nemmoc, and the dust of the Ibon Plain. But the human crew smelled nothing, and they caught no further glimpse, then or ever, of the lands of the South.

The day passed without incident, though the ship creaked and complained from spots Mr Fiffengurt had hoped were sound. Rain struck, benevolent and cool; when it passed on into the Red Storm it blazed like falling fire. Another bright night began. A pod of whales surrounded the *Chathrand*, and swam along with her for hours. Felthrup sat alone in a gunport and listened to their clicks, chirrups, rumbles, their pipe-organ breaths.

Deep in that night without darkness, someone screamed. It was not a sound anyone aboard had ever heard before. It was a selk's cry of anguish; it was Kirishgán. They found him near the bowsprit, crouching down as though praying. His body shook. When he raised his head there were tears in his brilliant eyes, and he told them that he had felt the death of kinsmen.

How many? they asked.

'Many,' he said. 'More than on any night since the Plazic generals began their exterminations.' But he could not say which of his people had fallen, or at whose hand.

Some hours later a different sort of cry – Niriviel's – woke Pazel for the second time that night. He tried to rouse Thasha, but she only groaned, so he left her sleeping and ran barefoot to the topdeck, pausing only to grab his coat. Hercól and Ramachni were there already, along with most of the dog watch. They were clustered around the ship's bell, and atop the latter stood Niriviel, exhausted, his cream-yellow chest heaving. When he could speak he confirmed the worst.

'I was far from both vessels, but I saw the *Death's Head* giving chase, and the *Promise* leading her away to the southwest. The *Promise* was faster, and drawing away. Then a shot from Macadra's vessel brought down her mainsail, and the *Death's Head* closed very fast. When she was within a half-mile, she fired again. But it was not a cannon she fired, this time. It was a ball of red fire, spit out from some foul weapon on her quarterdeck. It struck the *Promise* square on her hull.'

Pazel felt as though he himself had been struck, very hard in the stomach. This, of course, was what Kirishgán had felt. *Lunja. Prince Olik. Nólcindar.* They had led Macadra astray, given *Chathrand* time to flee. And for their courage they'd been killed.

'Macadra carries Plazic weapons, then,' said Hercól.

'Like the Behemoth's,' said Pazel, 'but why in the Pits didn't she use them before?'

'Perhaps because she feared to sink the Nilstone to the seabed,' said Ramachni, 'and this time, drawing near enough to sense its absence on the *Promise*, she did not hesitate to strike a lethal blow.'

'Do not think of aiding her,' said Niriviel. 'She is too far away, and the *Death's Head* would catch you first. Where is my master? Wake him! Macadra is still racing towards us.'

Pazel cast an involuntary glance over his shoulder. It was a good question: where was Sandor Ott? Why hadn't he shown his face even once since their return to the *Chathrand*?

'There is something else,' said Niriviel. 'The Red Storm is weaker ahead: with each mile it shone less brightly. I saw no gap, but I did not fly so far as I hoped. When the *Death's Head* turned in your direction, so did I.'

'And the Swarm?'

'That horror I did not see. I never wish to see it again.'

'Pazel,' said Hercól, 'go and wake the captain. And you, brother Niriviel—'

'Do not call me that.'

'Your pardon. Whatever else you wish to be called, I hope *strong* and *valiant* are permissible. Come, I will tell you of your master while you rest.'

Captain Fiffengurt had ordered a thorough cleaning and straightening of Rose's cabin, and conducted business there, but he still slept in his old quarters. Who could blame him? The stink of blood might be gone, but the memory of that carnage would take years to fade, if it ever did.

He woke like a startled cat at Pazel's knock, and dressed while Pazel related all that they had learned. 'Tree of Heaven, the *Promise* burned – and for our sake! And here we are running away from her. But we cannot help her, not from this distance. She'll have beaten that fire or succumbed to it long before we could arrive.'

Then Pazel asked him about the spymaster. 'Niriviel keeps asking for him. Wherever he is, can't someone take the bird there, even for a short visit?'

Fiffengurt stopped buttoning his uniform. 'No,' he said, 'the bird blary well cannot pay Ott a visit. Hasn't anyone told you?'

'Told me what?'

Fiffengurt leaned close to Pazel and lowered his voice. 'That monster's locked away.'

'In the *brig*?' said Pazel. 'You locked Sandor Ott in the brig?'

'Hush!' whispered Fiffengurt. 'No, not the regular brig. We couldn't do that; Ott has too much support among the Turachs, and a fight between soldiers and sailors would mean the end of this ship. No, Ott locked *himself* up. Do you mean Ratty hasn't told you about his great adventure? About what he found behind the Green Door?'

'Yes, yes, but I thought he was raving. He said there was a demon on the other side.'

'Not any more there ain't. Someone let it escape – probably Ott himself, though he swears otherwise. I say he's lying. Why else did he run straight there after he killed the captain?'

Pazel had to steady himself on the door frame. 'Sandor Ott killed Rose?'

''Course he did. You don't think that woman murdered our huge captain, and his steward, and very nearly Ott himself, all with her bare hands? And why was Ott there at all, before sunrise? And there was no blood on the steward – just a broken neck. A very *precisely* broken neck. No, Sandor Ott went to Rose's cabin with murder in mind, and found more than he bargained for in our skipper. There's one last proof, too: what *else* d'ye suppose is in the cell with the spymaster? Captain Rose's foot locker, that's what. Ott says he just found it there, and stepped into the cell to examine it, and the cell door slammed behind him. I've no doubt that last bit's true. But there's the Green Door too. You know it was wedged open with a metal plate.'

'Was?'

'I'm comin' to that. As it happened, Mr Druffle sauntered by, and saw that the chains had been loosed around the Green Door. He poked his head inside and saw Ott, fouled with dry blood and trapped in a cage with no lock. And the best bit of luck is that Druffle came to me straight away. I swore him to secrecy, and we'd all best hope he keeps his word. Then I paid Ott a courtesy call.

'He took one look at my face and knew I wasn't there to free him. He spat out all sorts of threats, but he was powerless, and I think the fact shocked him deeply. He tried to appeal to my love of Arqual. I told him no one could have done more to harm my love of Arqual than he. I'd brought a sack full of food and water and some medical supplies, and I tossed them all in through the bars of the cell. Then I just walked out. Back in the passage, I pried loose the metal plate with a crowbar and shut the Green Door. It vanished at once. Sandor Ott's in a cage he can't open, in a brig no one can find.'

Pazel shuddered. He was glad, relieved – but behind his loathing he felt a pity for the horrible old man. Pazel alone knew the bleak, savage story of Ott's life: the eguar on Bramian had shown it to him. Compared to Ott's, Pazel's own childhood had been a romp through fields of clover. Still it angered him, that pity. He wondered if the lack of it was what allowed beasts like Ott to rule the world.

'I won't breathe a word, Captain Fiffengurt,' he said.

Fiffengurt put a hand on Pazel's shoulder. 'You don't have to say "Captain" when we're alone, lad. Not to me.'

Pazel grinned at him. 'Oppo, sir,' he said.

It was the hour before dawn when he returned to the stateroom. The chamber was still; Jorl and Suzyt rose to greet him without barking; Felthrup twitched in his sleep upon the bearskin rug. Neeps, to his surprise, lay wrapped in a blanket in the corner, alone. Pazel winced. From the moment he saw Neeps and Lunja together on the Nine Peaks Road he had known pain lay ahead for both of them, and Marila. *It will fade*, he thought. *His heart's full of her now, but she's gone and not coming back. It will fade, and Marila will still be there.*

He crossed to the master bedroom and slipped inside. The air was close, stuffy. They had removed the bed's broken legs and nailed the frame directly to the floor. He smiled. Thasha had kicked away the blanket. She wore her father's shirt like a nightgown; there must have been twenty of them in the wardrobe. Pazel sat on the edge of the bed and touched her hand.

'Thasha? Oh Pitfire – *Thasha!*'

She was burning with fever. The shirt was soaked through, the sheet beneath her damp.

'Where were you?' she said, waking. But her voice was strained, and when he touched her face he found her teeth were chattering.

'Why didn't you answer me, Pazel?'

'Answer you? When?'

'I saw you, but you wouldn't speak. I heard Marila crying, but that was – I don't know when. And the birds. Thousands and thousands, all flying east.'

He was terrified. He made her sit up. Her skin like something fresh from an oven. He groped for her water flask and wrenched it open.

'Drink!'

She stared at him in the moonlight. 'Are you really here?'

She was looking right at him, but she wasn't sure. He stood and opened the door and shouted for Neeps and Marila. When he looked at her again she had dropped on her side.

'If that's you, Pazel, give me a blanket. I'm freezing to death.'

She had saved them; she was leaving them. She loathed this world that had made her part of its destiny. *Idiotic choice. Look what it's earned you. Now I'm dying and taking your saviour Erithusmé along for the ride.*

The pain grew. A cold pain from deep in her gut, moving outward. As a child Thasha had once been struck by a galloping illness: sweats and vomiting that felled her in an hour and made her imagine death. What she felt now was quite different. It was more like *blanë*, though the ixchel's poison was merciful compared to this. *Blanë* had hurt for a heartbeat or two. This pain went on and on.

Pazel was kissing her cheeks, asking questions: yes, he was really here. She tried to sit up a second time, at his urging. She drank a little water but it scalded her tongue. Then a stabbing light: Neeps and Marila in the doorway, staring, one of them bearing a lamp. Pazel shouted and waved his hands.

'Get Ramachni! Get Hercól!'

Neeps sprinted away. Felthrup was on the bed, flying in circles, sniffing. 'There is no infection about her. No bile, no blood. What is it, Thasha? Who did this, my dearest darling girl?'

'I can't feel you,' she said. 'Felthrup, why can't I feel you with my hands?'

Marila brought a moist cloth and Pazel drew it over her face. If only he would drop it, caress her with his hands alone. He was talking to the others: '... *just fine when I went topside ... weaker by the minute ... doesn't know where she is.*'

Thasha screamed. Some organ inside her had turned to glass, then shattered, exploded. Or else it was fire, or acid, or teeth.

'*She's too cold!*'

'*Her shirt's blary dripping, mate.*'

'*Get some dry clothes. Get a towel—*'

Time blurred. People spoke and then disappeared. Hercól and Bolutu were on either side of her; Bolutu's webbed fingers probed her stomach, her abdomen.

'*There is no hard mass, and no swelling. Thasha, did you eat something strange?*'

'Not me,' she said. 'It was still breathing. I couldn't just eat it alive.'

'*Delirious,*' said Bolutu.

She could have told them that.

They were fighting panic. Thasha watched them tearing through books, fumbling pills, arguing, turning away when their eyes grew moist. The cold advanced into her chest. She saw Ramachni by her shoulder, felt his paw touch her cheek. Dimly, she was aware that he was shocked.

At a distance, in the shadows, an ixchel woman stood watching her. 'Diadrelu?' she said.

But no, Dri was dead. The woman had to be Ensyl, or Myett.

Pazel was looking at Ramachni with a rage she'd never known was in him. 'I didn't hear you say that. You *didn't* just say that. Erithusmé's own Gods-damned spell?'

A blackness descended, and when it lifted there was daylight through the porthole, but the cold was even worse. Her friends were fighting. Pazel was kneeling by the bed. Thasha tried to reach for him but could barely lift her hand.

'Then she is our enemy, and has betrayed us from the start,' said Hercól.

'No,' said Ramachni.

'Yes,' said Pazel. '*Credek*, Ramachni, if the wine's to blame, and she poisoned it—'

'Then it needed to be poisoned.'

'How do you mucking *know*?' Neeps had joined the shouting match; that was bad. 'You haven't seen Erithusmé in what, seventeen years! Pazel talked with her five weeks ago! People change.'

'She did not change the wine of Agaroth from her hiding place in Thasha's mind,' said Ramachni. 'That was done long ago, and for a good purpose, even if we cannot now guess what it was.'

Pazel was seething. 'Erithusmé *told* me to give Thasha the wine.'

'As a last resort. And she warned you that the consequences would be dire.'

'She *hinted*. Why did she hint? Why couldn't she just say, "Give her the wine if the world's ending. Marvel at my cleverness. Let Thasha save you one last time, and then watch her—"'

'Pazel, be *quiet*!' Marila shouted.

Tears, and more darkness. This time it did not lift when Thasha opened her eyes. Her legs were useless, two frozen logs. She swung her eyes left and right. The porthole still glowed dimly. The opposite wall, behind Hercól and Mr Fiffengurt, was simply gone. Black shapes rose in the distance: barren trees. Above them, the birds, that endless flock racing east. Her friends' voices faded. Neeps had pulled Pazel lower, wrapped his arms about his head. They were waiting, weren't they? They had tried everything they knew.

'Keep fighting, Thasha,' Myett whispered in her ear. 'Don't go, don't let it take you. I almost did. I was wrong.'

Now the bed lay in a forest. A terrible place: the forest she'd seen in *blanë*-sleep. The trees with eyes, oily and cruel. The steam and whispers from holes in the earth, the cold that hurt her lungs. She could see her own breath, but not that of her friends. They were becoming shadows, and she was leaving them, leaving with her work undone.

'The wine,' said Myett. 'Do you hear me, Thasha? The *wine*.'

Thasha wished she would be quiet. She knew it was the wine. But Myett was still there beside her pillow. Dimly, Thasha felt the touch of her hand.

'Look at me.'

She looked. The ixchel woman beside her was not Myett but Diadrelu, their murdered friend. She was clearer than the others. Her face brightened when Thasha turned.

'Mother Sky, I thought you'd never hear me! Thasha, the wine is the poison *and the cure*. You must drink it again, immediately. Where is it, girl? Where is the wine of Agaroth?'

'Too late,' whispered Thasha.

A voice laughed, high with delight. There he was, Arunis. Crouched on the limb of a tree, sharply visible like Diadrelu, and leering.

'Yes,' he said, 'far too late. Never mind the crawly, little whore: your battle is done. Agaroth surrounds you, and Death's border is but a short walk from where you lie. But we must settle our accounts first.'

He sat back on the limb. Grinning, he opened his robe at the collar and showed Thasha his neck. A thin diagonal gash ran all the way across it. No, *all the way through it*. The gash was the one she herself had cut, with Ildraquin, when she beheaded him by the ruined tower.

'I scarred you with a necklace, once,' said Arunis. 'You returned the favour with a sword. But it is my turn again, and three is the charm.'

Thasha tried to move, but only managed to roll her face skyward. They were not birds, those shapes overhead. They were the souls of the fallen, racing above this Border-Kingdom and into death's own country. As every soul flew in time. As she would, at any moment: a little death among the millions, a leaf in a hurricane, a speck.

'No!'

Diadrelu slapped her with the full force of her arm. 'Thasha Isiq! Warrior! Raise yourself, raise yourself and call to your friends before they vanish! The wine, girl, the wine!'

Nothing she had ever attempted was half so difficult. Her lips were all but dead, her voice was a fingernail rasping on a door. No one turned; they were weeping. She tried again. They didn't hear a thing.

But Arunis did, and the fact that she could manage even this much scared him, evidently. He leaped down from the tree and advanced – and Diadrelu whirled like a tiger to face him, drawing her ixchel sword.

'Now we come to it! Can you hurl death-spells in Death's antechamber, mage? Is your soul stronger than mine? Take her from me, then! Come, come and take her!'

With that Diadrelu leaped from the bed, and when her feet touched the forest floor she was suddenly the size of Arunis, raging and deadly. Thasha gasped – and in that other world, the shadow that was Ramachni heard her.

'Silence, everyone!' he roared. 'Thasha, did you speak?'

Arunis began to circle the bed, hunched low, a shadow among the trees. Diadrelu matched him step for step, keeping herself between Thasha and the mage. She taunted him, whirling her sword.

'You could not defeat them in life. You will never do so in death. You will not touch this girl.'

Thasha forced the last of her energy into her voice. She found it, wheezed a single, barely intelligible word. Again and again.

'Wine!' cried the shadow-Felthrup. 'She is asking for the wine! Run, run and fetch it!'

A figure turned and vanished into the dark.

Suddenly Arunis dropped to his knees and plunged his arm into one of the steaming holes. A voice from underground gave a cry. Arunis jerked his arm free. In his hand was a war-axe, double-bladed and cruel, but a skeleton-arm came with it. The arm was moving, fighting him for the weapon. Arunis tore the arm away and flung it into the trees.

Then he charged, and the battle joined. It seemed that Diadrelu was right: Arunis could not attack with spellcraft. Yet he was a terrible opponent, fast and vicious and strong. He swung the axe in two-handed arcs at shoulder height, or flashing down from above. Thasha was appalled by his skill. But Diadrelu was an ixchel battle-dancer: a fighter who would have shamed Turach or *sfvantskor* or Tholjassan war-master, if they had ever faced such a foe of human size. Whirling, spinning, her blade like a solid ring about her, she moved at twice the mage's speed. The trouble was that her spectacular movements were better at evading an enemy than holding ground against him. From childhood, ixchel learned to weave and dodge and slip through human fingers. They did not hold ground. Diadrelu had to fight her very instincts to keep Arunis from reaching Thasha's bed.

Except that there was no bed any longer. Thasha lay on bare earth, head propped on a stone, the roots of the evil trees wriggling beneath her. Alifros was nearly gone: nothing of it was visible save the porthole, a slight discolouration of the darkness. Her friends' shadows lacked definite shape; their voices had dwindled to meaningless sounds.

But Diadrelu was improving. She slipped inside the sorcerer's blows, stabbing at him, forcing him to parry with the axe. When he tried to grapple with her, she twisted under him and whirled and clubbed him down with her sword-hilt.

Arunis rolled, and swung the axe one-handed, expertly. Dri leaped back, sucking in her stomach, and the blade passed within a hair's breadth of her ribs. Arunis swung again, sensing his advantage, driving her back towards Thasha. Dri's balance was lost. She dodged a third blow, reeling now, and Arunis came at her with a gleam in his eye.

His fourth blow was too eager, and hence his last. Dri whirled out of range, then spun back again and kicked the mage hard in the chin. Arunis staggered, and whiplash-quick, Dri wrenched the axe from his hand and clubbed him down. With one foot upon his neck, she swung the mage's own weapon. The axe severed his arm at the wrist.

Arunis howled. But the wound did not bleed: perhaps there was no blood in Agaroth, as there was no true and final death. Diadrelu snatched up the severed hand and flung it with all her might into the dark.

'Go!' she said to Arunis, 'and if you return, I will take your other hand, and both feet, and give them to the corpses in those holes.'

A shadow appeared beside Thasha, hovering over her, speaking without words.

Arunis groped to his feet and plunged into the darkness. When he was nearly gone from sight he turned and shouted: 'You cannot prevail. Night comes for Alifros! The Swarm will devour these maggots you defend. There is no stopping it. I have already won.'

With that he fled, cradling the stump of his arm. Then Thasha felt a gentle hand lifting her head, and cold liquid against her lips.

The wine was delicious, here in the land where it was made. Thasha felt life returning even before she swallowed. A vibrant energy rushed through her from head to toe. The shadow closest to her took shape: it was Pazel. She could hear him, feel the warmth of his hand.

Diadrelu rushed to her side. 'They've done it, haven't they?' said Dri. Evidently she could not see the others in the cabin, or the bottle at Thasha's lips. 'Not too much!' she cried. 'Two swallows, and no more.'

Thasha had just swallowed for a second time. With effort, she turned her head away. 'Dri,' she said, 'is this really death?'

'It is death unfinished,' said the ixchel woman. 'Agaroth is a strange and frightening land, but still more like the world of the living than what comes next, I think. The dead may reach backwards from here. It is that reaching that keeps them from sailing on with the tide of souls.'

'The ghosts that walk the *Chathrand*—'

Dri shook her head. 'Ghosts are different. They are souls who have yet to come even this far. They are trapped in a living world, a world with no use for them. I think they suffer more than those in Agaroth. Captain Rose is among them, now.

'But listen carefully, Thasha, while you can still hear my voice. I have been to the dark vineyards where this wine was made, and spoken with those decrepit spirits who guard its secrets.'

'You did that for us?'

'Listen! Erithusmé's spell on your bottle was a sound precaution, given the wine's evil past. The Fell Princes used it for a century: they sipped the wine slowly, making each bottle last years. This allowed them to wield the Nilstone for years as well – and they did so, to the sorrow of Alifros. They exterminated whole peoples, made pyres of cities, withered entire lands.

'Erithusmé wished to leave a weapon hidden on the *Chathrand*, but she could never risk creating another tyrant. Hence the curse, which forces the drinker to finish the wine in a matter of days. Each sip gives a few minutes of perfect fearlessness, and so the ability to use the Nilstone. But each sip also forces the drinker to sip again within two days. Otherwise the poison is activated.'

'I think Ramachni detected the spell at last, after it was triggered,' said Thasha. 'I heard them fighting about it. But Dri, what happens when I run out of wine?'

'Very simple: you swallow the dregs at the bottom. They contain the final cure. Better yet, pour off the wine and swallow the dregs immediately. Only then will you be out of danger.'

'But I can't do that, Dri. We *need* this weapon!'

'This weapon nearly killed you.'

Suddenly Pazel's voice cut through the fog: '*Thasha! Can you hear me? Come back, please come back—*'

She could dimly make out his features, now – but Agaroth was fading, and with it Diadrelu. Thasha was suddenly, almost unbearably conscious of how much she had missed the ixchel woman. 'Don't go. Not just yet.'

'It is you who are going, Thasha, back to the living world. But I have one last discovery to share with you first. You are bound for Gurishal, to cast away the Nilstone. But Gurishal is immense, and overrun with the Shaggat's worshippers. You will have no time to search it shore to shore. Look for a sea rock called the Arrowhead, Thasha. Can you remember that?'

'The Arrowhead?'

'That is where you must land, if you have any hope of sending the Nilstone back to the land of the dead. Oh, if only you could place it in my hands! For *I* shall soon be crossing over, and would bear it gladly, and rest fulfilled.'

'But Dri, how did you learn about this rock, this Arrowhead?'

'By making a nuisance of myself. Many come to this land by the River of Shadows. They told me of a terrible fall into an abyss, down a stone tunnel, with a last round glimpse of blue sky above them, and endless darkness below. Some had heard whispers of the place before they reached it, and knew it lay near the shores of Gurishal, at the spot marked by the Arrowhead. Remember, Thasha.'

The light was growing. Diadrelu's form grew paler still, and Thasha fought back tears. 'I'll remember. Oh Dri, what they did to you, Taliktrum and the others—'

'Never mind. Show them a better example, as you always have done.'

'You're the best of us all, Dri, and the strongest.'

The ixchel woman smiled. 'From childhood I thought my reason for living was to fight for my people. I was right about that. But it took a great deal longer to find out who my people were.'

'Hercól still loves you.'

Dri paused, then looked up at the sky, where the ceaseless flow of souls went on. 'I must leave soon. I do not know what awaits me in the land of the dead. But make certain he knows that I died undefeated, with a heart made whole by him. And say that I will look for him when his turn comes to make the final journey. But Thasha – tell him not to wait for that day, and a reunion that may never come. Do you hear me well?'

'I hear you.'

'Tell him the kiss I send with you is a command. He must go on living. Embrace every joy that still awaits him, every scrap and crumb of life. That is my wish for dearest Ensyl, too. It is my wish for you all.'

She bent down, and pressed her lips to Thasha's own, and Thasha lifted her arms and embraced her. For an instant she felt the hard strength of the woman's shoulders, the warmth of her lips. Then both sensations were gone. Dri's body lifted, escaping Thasha's arms like smoke. The darkness vanished, and with it Agaroth, and Dri herself.

The room was dazzling. Her friends were beyond words. They only embraced her, repeated her name, bathed her in tears of relief. Pazel was kneeling and kissing her hands again and again. She tried to hold him still but it was impossible; he was overcome.

Even Ramachni was shivering with emotion. 'You have aged me today, Thasha Isiq,' he said. 'By the time I guessed the nature of the curse, it was too late for any treatment I could devise. I nearly put you in the healing sleep, which slows poisons to a crawl. But by then you were too weak.'

'How long has it been?' she said. 'I mean, how long since I drank the wine?'

'Perhaps ten minutes, dear one,' said Hercól. 'Why do you ask?'

Thasha closed her eyes, furious with herself. 'I lost a chance to use the Nilstone, that's why. I could have done something. Changed the winds, maybe even parted the Red Storm. There are just a few swallows left. I can't be wasting them.'

'Wasting?' said Neeps. 'Thasha, that mouthful brought you back from the dead.'

Thasha looked at him. *Back from the dead*. It was close enough to the truth. She'd gone much deeper this time than before, during the *blanë*-coma. She looked at their bright, beloved faces. They could never know, never grasp what she had seen. *It will stand between us*, she thought.

'I was … told things.'

'Told?' said Marila. 'By whom?'

'Give her a little time,' said Ramachni.

'And some food, if there is any. I'm famished. Oh Pazel, *stop*.'

He was devouring her hands with kisses. She raised his chin, and understood: he'd been hiding his face, afraid he'd break down once again. Thasha kissed him squarely on the lips.

'Out, everyone, and let me dress. You too, Pazel, go on.'

They obeyed her, limp with exhaustion. But as Hercól made to leave Thasha touched his hand. The warrior turned and looked her in the eye.

'Stay a moment,' she said. 'I have something for you.'

30

Deadly Weapons

15 Fuinar 942
303rd day from Etherhorde

Thasha's brush with death had several immediate consequences. One was an end, for the moment at least, to any sign of division between Neeps and Marila. Pazel could not tell if they were truly reconciled, if the shock of nearly losing Thasha had made Neeps wake up to the danger of losing Marila as well; or if they were both simply making an effort to believe that his heart was not torn. Perhaps Neeps did not know himself. For now Pazel was simply glad to see him trying.

Thasha had also managed to devastate Hercól. This second encounter with Diadrelu had come only through Thasha's lips (in two senses), and yet it proved harder to surmount. In the wilderness he had faced new tasks and dangers by the hour. On the *Chathrand,* others took the lead, and no matter how busy he kept himself with shipboard labours, his mind was free to brood. He was kind and grateful to Thasha, but his mood clearly darkened in her presence.

In a broader sense, of course, Thasha's news had brought hope to them all. They had more than a vast island to aim for, now: they had a landing place, or at least a sign pointing the way.

Neda confirmed at once that the Arrowhead was real. '*Tabruc Derelem Na Nuruth,* we call it,' she told Pazel. 'The great standing stone that ought to fall, but doesn't. Cayer Vispek told us of it once. He said it was a holy place before the rise of the Shaggat.

The elders of the Faith sometimes went there to die.'

'Die how? Is there a great shaft, an abyss, like Thasha's talking about?'

Neda shrugged. 'After the Shaggat's rise we were forbidden to speak of the place. Cayer Vispek was bending the rules even to speak about the Arrowhead. He said there was a legend that the great rock would fall when the Unseen takes its gaze from Alifros, and leaves us alone in the night.'

Pazel asked if she knew where along that massive shoreline they should seek the Arrowhead. Neda shook her head, then laughed. 'Ask the Shaggat,' she said, 'if you can get the marines to stand aside.'

Ott and Haddismal had kept the Shaggat locked in the manger, hidden away from everyone but a few hand-picked Turachs. 'I could, maybe,' said Pazel. 'Haddismal's not spiteful like Ott; he just likes to win. And he might want to question the man himself. He doesn't speak a word of Mzithrini.'

'The Shaggat doesn't speak a word of sane,' said Neda. 'He's the devil.'

'Maybe he's calmed down,' said Pazel. 'And you're a beautiful woman. He might drop his guard.'

She looked at him blankly. Then she turned and showed him her tattooed neck. 'See the hawk? That's a *sfvantskor* emblem. I'm not a woman to the Shaggat Ness. I'm an enemy, a heretic, a spawn of the Whore of the Third Pit. You don't talk to the likes of me. You kill us and mutilate our bodies and put what's left on stakes by the roadside. And I feel the same way about him, do you understand? The only talking I'll ever do is with a blade.'

The ship ran west, and the Red Storm weakened further. Captain Fiffengurt kept double lookouts aloft, and ordered redundant inspections of every element of their fighting arsenal. Still the grey-green seas lay empty.

'Rose built the fire-control teams into a force like you've never seen, after the Behemoth launched those blazing monstrosities at us,' he told Pazel, shortly after Thasha's ordeal, 'but I hope we never

673

put 'em to the test. Wood and tar still burn, and flaxen sails as well.'

As for the wine of Agaroth, Thasha's friends urged her desperately to take Dri's advice and pour it out, swallowing only the dregs. 'In two days you'll collapse again,' said Pazel. 'You can't put yourself through that.'

'Or you,' said Thasha, 'and I won't. I'll take another sip in plenty of time.'

'And delay the poison by two more days? What's the point? What if we drop the bottle and it shatters?'

'Guess I'll lick the deck, won't I?'

No one could change her mind: they would still be prisoners in Stath Bálfyr, she observed, if she had never dared to drink. But that night the choices before her loomed stark and grim, and in the morning she took Ramachni aside.

'You said you thought of putting me to sleep. To slow the poison.'

'I did.'

'Could you still do it? Could I sleep until we need the power of the Stone again. For days, or weeks?'

Ramachni seemed disinclined to answer, but Thasha would not be put off. At last he turned his black eyes on her fully. 'It can be done,' he said, 'but you will get no closer to freeing Erithusmé in your sleep.'

'Why not? I found other answers in my sleep. Felthrup learned *volumes* in his sleep.'

'Felthrup is a dreaming prodigy. And you found your answers on the shores of death, not natural sleep. But we are confusing the matter, Thasha. I want that poison out of you.'

His concern touched her, and then gave her a fright. *Night Gods. He doesn't trust his mistress either.*

Still, she did not dispose of the wine. The hours ticked by, and her debates with her friends became arguments. They begged and cajoled, and even tried to shame her. At one point Neeps and Pazel marched her into her old cabin, demanded the silver key, and opened the safe where the Nilstone lay.

'Erithusmé had this idea that we could never succeed without her magic,' said Pazel. 'You're beginning to sound just like her. Use the mucking Stone, then. Pour off the wine, drink the dregs and use it one last time. Maybe you really *can* part the Red Storm.'

Thasha held the bottle in the crook of her arm. 'I'll drink before the night is out.'

'Another little sip,' said Pazel, accusing.

'The dregs will still be there, damn it all! I'll drink them when I have to. Don't worry about that.'

Neeps shook his head, grinning, furious. 'I love you, nutter girl. But it takes gall to say *don't worry*, straight to Pazel's face.'

Thasha wondered if the tarboys could possibly make things harder. 'Forgive me,' she said, 'I'm not trying to—'

'No,' said Pazel. 'I won't forgive you, if you get sick again.'

He closed the safe and walked out of the cabin. Neeps looked at her a moment, then followed. Thasha sat on her old bed, clutching the ancient bottle, feeling the cold bite her fingers. Dusk was here; the poison had struck at sunrise. She had some twelve hours left.

'SAIL! ABAFT THE PORTSIDE BEAM! SAIL, SAIL!'

It was the alarm they'd all waited for, and dreaded. When it came Pazel was aloft himself, tightening bolts along the main topsail yard in the weird red glow. He had no telescope, and could see no ship. Above him, the lookout howled: 'A five-master, she is! Five masts and thirteen miles!'

Those last words nearly made Pazel fall from the yard. *Just thirteen miles? Was he sleeping? Rose would skin that man alive!*

He raced down the mast. Below, men were pouring onto the deck, and Fegin was striking the ship's bell as though trying to break it. When Fiffengurt emerged from Rose's cabin, however, he did not run, but only climbed with swift decorum to the mizzen yard. He was a new captain, performing the role of the unruffled leader, and everyone knew it and expected no less.

Pazel was running aft when Kirishgán appeared out of the crowd. 'It is the *Death's Head*,' he said softly. 'Macadra has found us at last.'

675

'But thirteen miles? How did the lookouts miss her?'

Kirishgán gestured at the Red Storm. 'Our back is to the bonfire, Pazel. She came out of the dark. We were dazzled, though we did not know it.'

Pazel looked at him, stunned. It was such a simple thing, but who aboard had ever sailed alongside a bonfire? 'And now, *credek*, they have the wind advantage too – it's turned in our faces again. Is that Macadra's doing?'

'Very likely,' said Kirishgán. 'She did as much when she first tried to take the *Promise*.'

'But this time she's flanking us. She'll close that gap in no time.'

'Unless we find *our* gap first,' said Kirishgán.

They hurried to the quarterdeck, through the multitude of rushing, frightened sailors. Fiffengurt's orders had gone out: skysails, studding sails, a third jib strung from the spankermast. Pazel knew it could not add much to their speed. Nothing could, save a change of wind or an about-face, or some massive jettison of supplies.

Mr Coote was bent over the tonnage hatch. 'Gunnery! Fire brigades! Come on, lads! Move like you mean to save this ship!' Coote looked too old to bear the duties of a bosun. *And we've no quartermaster, no doctor, no second mate. Fiffengurt's running this ship with half a team.*

Pazel's friends began to congregate around the Silver Stair. Marila was holding Felthrup; Neeps was holding Marila. Ramachni and Thasha stood a little apart, the mage perched atop a 48-pounder cannon that had just been run out through a gunnery door in the portside rail. The others were handing around Isiq's fine telescope, examining the *Death's Head* and quietly cursing.

Because his mind-fit had struck before the first attack, Pazel had never glimpsed Macadra's vessel. What he saw when his turn came chilled his blood. The *Death's Head* truly was a second *Chathrand*, but a *Chathrand* in terrifying disguise. From the water line to her fighting-tops she was armoured: crude, thick skins of cast iron enveloping the hull, which showed through only here and there. Even her figurehead (a great black bird) was made of metal.

Huge and mysterious devices cluttered her deck, some throwing off long cattails of orange sparks that scattered on the wind.

'Are those ... *weapons?*'

'They are,' said Hercól. 'We saw them in action from the deck of Nólcindar's vessel. We had good luck then: I doubt her weapons were precise enough to wound the little *Promise* without dropping her to the sea floor, along with the prize. Today Macadra's reckoning may be different.'

'But take heart,' said Felthrup. 'However vile, however truly *sanguinary* those weapons prove, they are nothing compared to the Behemoth. That was like being attacked by a whole city. And yet we survived.'

'The Behemoth was slow, Felthrup,' said Marila.

'And this time we are,' said Hercól. 'Fiffengurt will blame himself for our predicament, but what else could he have done? We had nowhere to hide, except in the bay of Stath Bálfyr. We could not sail north, and didn't dare head south again.'

'So all Macadra had to do was guess whether we'd turn east or west?' said Marila.

'Right, and that was simple,' said Neeps. 'She can tell that the Storm's paler to the west, and she must know we mean to pass through. This is an ugly business, mates.'

Pazel crossed the deck to the 48-pounder cannon, where Thasha stood with Ramachni. The mage was still perched atop the gun, looking southwards, and holding exceptionally still. Thasha put a finger to her lips. Ramachni was up to something. They waited, leaning slightly together, as gun crews stormed around them and topmen scrambled in the rigging like nimble cats and battle-netting was stretched overhead.

At last Ramachni turned from his vigil. He looked at them sombrely. 'We must prepare,' he said.

'For a firefight?' said Pazel. 'But that's exactly what we're doing.'

'Not just for a firefight. We must prepare for slaughter. Macadra has no plans to capture us. If she offers clemency, it will be a ruse to secure our surrender. She wants us dead.' He paused. 'She also thinks the *Chathrand* will burn much longer than the *Promise*.'

'You read her mind?'

'The surface, Pazel. The outer thoughts and feelings, as Arunis did with many of you before his death. It could be a façade, or some other subtle ploy, but I doubt that. She is not in a subtle mood.'

'Why does she care how long the *Chathrand* will burn?' asked Thasha.

'Because she is prepared to torch us entirely and then pluck the Nilstone from the flames.'

Pazel had a sense that the world was about to implode. As though they were all trapped in a crate and hearing the approach of some gigantic wheel. Thasha gave him a searching look. He dropped his eyes in shame.

'Don't say it. I was wrong. I'm glad you still have some wine.'

'Can you stop her, Ramachni?' Thasha asked.

'Stop her? I would stand some chance, if it came to a duel. But that hardly matters now. I cannot protect us from the *Death's Head*, and its terrible weapons. Still, we have gained one advantage: this close to the Storm, Macadra will not likely be able to harness the winds, for the Storm itself is one great weather-spell, and mightier than any she could cast.'

A sudden cry from above made Pazel flinch with apprehension. This time, however, the news was better than he or anyone had dared to hope. The gap had been sighted, some twenty miles dead ahead.

The men cheered, though the terror of the enemy was great in them. Pazel took Thasha's hand and drew it quickly to his lips. He caught Neeps' eye from across the deck, and saw a new light there, an almost unbearable hope.

Fiffengurt descended from the mast and made straight for the quarterdeck, shouting as he went: 'To the braces with your teams, gentlemen! We shall come about, full to starboard! Mr Elkstem, lean on that wheel!'

There was a new explosion of activity; five hundred men attacked the ropes. Thasha looked at Pazel, bewildered. 'What's he doing?'

'Tacking closer to the Storm, but damned if I know why.'

'We'll go faster downwind.'

'Of course, but how far? We have to break east or west eventually.'

Fiffengurt climbed the ladder and helped Elkstem at the wheel. For many hours they had been obliged to follow a zigzag stitch across the seas. Exhausting tacks, endless reversals: but no ship could sail straight into a headwind. There was always, moreover, the danger of drifting into the Storm. Now Fiffengurt had them running straight for it.

'*Death's Head* trimming sails to match, Captain,' boomed Fegin. 'She's got keen eyes, that witch.'

'Right you are, first mate. Mr Coote, take thirty men to the cable tiers. I want extra stays on all five masts, coiled and ready to deploy. But keep 'em on the deck below, hard by the hatches but out of sight.'

'The Turachs won't like it, Captain – all that rope in their space.'

'Perhaps they'd prefer six hundred enemy boarders in their space, bosun. You may enquire.'

The *Chathrand* sliced a clean, sharp path towards the Storm. Pazel and Thasha went below with Coote's thirty and helped wrestle the vast, awkward ropes up to the main deck. Pazel had the uncomfortable feeling that the effort was pointless, that Fiffengurt was merely trying to appear as though he had a plan. The winds were steady, but hardly strong enough to call for doubling the mast supports.

'About six miles to the Storm front, Captain,' shouted Fegin. 'And still sixteen or more to the gap, if it's really there. Enemy holding steady behind.'

When they returned to the topdeck Ramachni was speaking with Kirishgán.

'Your captain and his ship are as one,' said the selk. 'See how the men at each station look to their watch-captain, and the latter to the quarterdeck? They are speaking without words. Even Nólcindar would be impressed.'

'Fiffengurt's spent most of his life on this ship, the same as Captain Rose,' said Pazel.

'Which of them persuaded augrongs to join the crew?' asked Kirishgán.

He nodded in the direction of the No. 4 hatch. Pazel smiled. Refeg and Rer, the enormous anchor lifters, were slouching to points on either side of the mainmast. The sailors smiled at them too, from a distance.

'Rose found them, and they're worth their weight in gold,' said Pazel, 'but I can't imagine what they're doing up here. They've never helped out with the rigging before.'

'We've never been so short-handed before,' said Thasha.

'Quite so,' said Ramachni. 'We may need every advantage left to us. I too must beg your pardon, Thasha: you were right to keep the wine. For once I am glad of your stubborn—'

He broke off, his fur standing on end. His eyes snapped to the quarterdeck.

A figure stood there, facing Elkstem and Fiffengurt, who recoiled in horror. A tall woman, chalk-white of skin, so gaunt and narrow-boned that she appeared almost stretched. Her eyes were fixed on the captain, and a long, bony finger was pointing at his heart. Pazel knew at once that he was looking at Macadra.

Ramachni leaped from the cannon and raced towards the quarterdeck. Pazel and Thasha chased after him, though Pazel had no idea what they might be preparing to do. Up the ladder they rushed. The hideous woman turned her head and studied them – with recognition, Pazel thought, at least in Thasha's case. *But she's never seen Thasha before. What does she sense?*

Ramachni stood between the sorceress and the wheel, teeth chattering with rage.

'Macadra Hyndrascorm,' he said, 'we have slain your Plazic servants, your devil-dogs, your Thrandal ogress and the demon for whose services you mortified your flesh. We have slain your foul brother Arunis. Do you think you will be spared, if you impede us?'

Her brother! thought Pazel.

Macadra threw her head back violently, as though her neck had snapped. High laughter rang across the deck.

'Impede us! Do you mark his words, Arunis? I had best break off the attack and run for Bali Adro, and leave the Nilstone in the keeping of Erithusmé's mascot, and this ship of the diseased, the murderous, the mad.' She lowered her head and pointed at Fiffengurt. 'Turn the ship away from the Storm, Captain Fiffengurt! There need be no killing today. Strike your sails and await my vessel, and we will spare all your lives.'

Pazel had a great urge to shout at her: *No you won't!* But Thasha squeezed his arm, and almost imperceptibly shook her head. Pazel shuddered at the recklessness of what he'd nearly done. For what if Macadra didn't know that Ramachni could hear her thoughts? Why give away an advantage like that?

'Yes,' said Ramachni, 'you must break off the attack, and run. There is power here to destroy you. Very soon it will reveal itself, and strike.'

Macadra sneered. 'With the Nilstone? I think not. Across the Ruling Sea you carried it. Through the wilds of Efaroc, the hell of the Infernal Forest, the snows of Urakán. And never in all that time did the Nilstone serve you. Even Arunis failed to wield it, save in his last suicidal hour. Why keep it, Captain? What a danger and a horror it has been! Give it to me, and I will heal your people and send you benevolent currents to waft you home.'

'Aye, madam,' said Fiffengurt, 'and when killers creep in at my window, I'll put knives in their hands.'

'A killer *has* crept in at your window, old fool. Turn your vessel, or watch me destroy it.'

Pazel risked a glance ahead. What was Fiffengurt doing? They were flying fast towards the Red Storm: could he possibly mean to sail straight in?

Ramachni looked back over his shoulder. 'I love an albatross, don't you, Captain?'

'An albatross?' Fiffengurt was startled only for a moment. 'Yes, *sir*, I do adore 'em. But where's a rat when you need one?'

'Here I am!' Felthrup squirmed in a frenzy. Hercól took him from Marila's arms and raised him to the quarterdeck, where he scrambled to the captain's feet.

'Felthrup here is my negotiator,' said Fiffengurt. 'If you want the Nilstone, talk with him.'

'If you want to live, turn your ship around, and clear the deck of these rodents.'

'Rodent,' said Felthrup. 'Singular. My lord Ramachni is a *mustelid*, and specifically a mink. Now pay attention, sorceress! Without my consent the Stone will remain for ever beyond your reach.'

Without a glance at Felthrup, Macadra said, 'No place is beyond my reach.'

'But what an immodest trickster you are! Why, the Storm itself threatens to snatch away your prize. And the seabed? Perhaps you hope you can recover it from such depths, but surely you have some doubt? Otherwise, why didn't you burn the *Promise* to ashes, when the Stone was aboard?'

'I saw no reason to kill,' said Macadra.

'You lie, but what of it? However great your reach, some doors are still closed to you. The door of the Orfuin Club, for example.'

Macadra froze. Slowly, for the first time, she turned her gaze on Felthrup.

'Yes, unpleasant person!' he said. 'I was there, and watching you. I do not fear the River of Shadows. And within this ship are doors to lands you do not know, and will never find. Erithusmé built some; others were made by the Bali Adro shipwrights, and still others were accidents, fissures opened by too much powerful spellcraft in a single place. Burn the *Chathrand* and you destroy the doors. Will you gamble that you can steal the Nilstone away from us before we hide it in another world? If so, you have less sense than many a rodent I could name.'

Pazel was shocked. *Felthrup! When did you become so fierce?*

But Macadra only laughed again. 'Rat! You have surprised me. There may be a place for you at court in Bali Adro, if you are wise enough to rethink your allegiances. Quick wit is not something to be wasted—'

'Oh no, no indeed! Consider the parable of the nine golden—'

'—but we both know your bluff is empty. You cannot take the Nilstone through one of those doors. Living flesh is one thing, but death takes its leave from Alifros by one path only, and that is through the River of Shadows. Of course, that is why you are making for Gurishal. That was Erithusmé's plan from the start.'

Felthrup pinched his eyes shut, rubbed his paws against his face. He was gasping a little; Pazel feared he had been beaten. Then the rat's eyes opened wide and he shrilled, louder than ever:

'How gravely, grossly, wantonly you wade in error, sorceress! Have you forgotten your great-uncle, Ikassam the Firelord? *He* knew a thing or two about journeys by night!'

'He taught me the art, vermin. But how did you learn of him?'

'In a book, in a book, a special book you may not borrow. Ikassam the Firelord, the tamer of beasts. His brother was your grandfather, and said that you should be hanged, and instead you hanged him. His father crossed the Ruling Sea and married the queen of Opalt, and *their* grandson had the tail of a pig.'

'Turn your ship, Captain,' said Macadra.

'You may ask what this has to do with giving you the Nilstone,' Felthrup went on, nearing her and gesticulating with his paws. 'Everything, everything! For who are you but the product of your history? And who are we but the servants of our own? And this transaction, this epochal surrender you seek – someone must understand it, record it, write it down for the sake of history. And what of Sathek?'

'Sathek?' shrieked Macadra, staring down at him again.

'Yes, yes – no. Sathek himself is not the point. But his Sceptre! Who can forget? Your Raven Society tried to steal it, just as you did the Nilstone, three times in six centuries, and Arunis makes four, last year on the Isle of Simja. He had a demonic servant too, and sent it to make off with the Sceptre, but instead our wonderful

Neda used it to bludgeon the little demon to death – I was under the chair, the chair!'

Felthrup was squealing and hopping and running circles around her boots. Macadra seemed appalled and transfixed.

'Orfuin's chair, I was beneath it I say! Not a rat, not a rodent, I was the little wriggly thing called an *yddek*, Arunis called me a masterpiece of ugliness, Orfuin invited you to gingerbread and you ignored him, you went on scheming, but you schemed in bad faith, bad faith, bringing two servants with you instead of coming alone, now again you make promises, how can we ignore such evidence, Macadra, some of us have a sense of history and this, this is a HISTORY OF DUPLICITOUS INTRIGUE—'

Macadra wrenched her eyes away from Felthrup. Pazel did the same, and only then did he realise that five hundred sailors had quietly set their hands to the ropes. *Pitfire*, thought Pazel, *the wind—*

'HEAVE BOYS IT'S NOW OR NEVER!' screamed Fiffengurt.

The wind was turning, swinging round to blow from the east, and gaining strength by the second. Roaring in unison, the men hurled themselves at the bracelines, scrabbling for purchase on the heaving deck. The augrongs heaved alongside the humans, bellowing like bulls. The masts groaned; the huge squaresails turned; Fiffengurt and Elkstem all but leaped upon the wheel.

The Great Ship came violently about, rolling deep on her starboard quarter. '*That's* what I like!' cried Fiffengurt with a cockeyed grin. Men aloft swung like marionettes; those on deck seized the nearest fixed objects and held fast. Pazel snatched up Felthrup while Ramachni sheltered between Thasha's feet. Only Macadra did not sway: her feet touched the boards so lightly she almost seemed to float like a tethered balloon.

The ship made her turn, levelled out, and began to fly downwind. 'Shore up those stays, Fegin!' roared the captain. 'We're in a ripper and we mean to ride 'er like one!'

Suddenly Macadra charged at Fiffengurt, hands raised before

her like talons. But Ramachni was faster. He leaped from the deck straight at her. Just before his claws reached her, however, she vanished without a trace. Ramachni twisted in mid-air and landed on his feet.

'Ha! I expected that. Macadra was never truly here: we were addressing a phantom. But her mind certainly was here – and what a fine job you did of keeping it occupied, Felthrup my lad. You need no weapon but words.'

'Another minute and I should have been forced to improvise,' said Felthrup.

'But where did this mad wind come from?' cried Pazel.

'Ah, Pathkendle, you were distracted too!' said Fiffengurt, laughing aloud. 'We saw, didn't we Ramachni? Two albatrosses. Two lovely birds moving like avenging angels, but hardly flapping their wings. *Coasting*, that is, due west along the edge of the storm. If we're lucky, and I think we are, then we'll find this wind's gushing right through the gap ahead, like a breeze through a window.'

The ship was now racing west, and when the log was tossed the midshipman cried out their speed: eighteen knots.

'Eighteen's grand, but we'll see twenty-eight when Fegin's done, boys. There's still two reefs to let out.'

'The *Death's Head* will catch the wind too, soon enough,' said Kirishgán.

'But she won't catch us. Not before we reach that gap.'

A shout went, up; a hand pointed forward. There! Pazel saw it, twelve or thirteen miles out: a ragged, roiling edge to the scarlet light.

'What if she follows us *through* the gap?' asked Elkstem.

After a moment's pause, Thasha said, 'She won't.'

She descended the quarterdeck ladder, and Pazel followed. Most of their friends were still gathered below. 'Warn the crew,' Thasha told them. 'Tell everyone to brace for a shock. I'm going to put an end to this.'

'Stay with her, Pathkendle,' said Hercól.

The next moment a shock did come, although Thasha had nothing to do with it.

'FIRE! FIRE! ENEMY ORDNANCE!'

Everyone groped for cover. Pazel glanced at the *Death's Head* and found it wreathed in smoke. Then the sound reached them: clustered explosions, ten or twelve strong.

'Hold fast to your stations!' roared Fiffengurt, swinging his telescope skyward. 'You can't run, lads, you can only keep the blessed *ship* running! Think what Captain Rose would say if—'

He choked on the words. A look of disbelief washed over him. 'Aloft there, lookout! Those are no fireballs! What in the Pits are they throwing?'

'SWEET TEARS OF RIN, CAPTAIN! I CAN'T TELL YOU, BUT THEY'RE ALMOST—'

'TAKE COVER! TAKE COVER!'

Something slammed into Pazel, lifting him right off his feet. It was Hercól. He had tackled Pazel and Thasha both, knocking them flat upon the deck. From above came a scream like cannon-fire – but not *quite* like cannon-fire. Pazel twisted his head around and looked up. Through the netting he saw a dozen black, undulating shapes fly over the *Chathrand*, scattershot. Then a roar went up from the topmen. A shadow fell. Close at hand something began to sizzle, and then Hercól gave an enormous lurch and rolled with Pazel and Thasha clutched tight in his arms.

They came to rest in a dogpile with Neeps and Neda and half a dozen sailors. Pazel looked back where they had lain. A huge, viscous black glob hung suspended in the battle-nets, eight feet above the deck. It smoked and stank of burning tar. Large droplets oozed and separated and fell bubbling upon the deck.

More cries from aloft. Pazel looked and saw that one of the projectiles had struck the main topsail and splattered like an enormous black egg.

Night Gods, what sort of weapon—?

Then he understood. The tar was running down the sail – and devouring it, like acid. It took just seconds: where the white flax had been there was a lengthening hole.

Fiffengurt stood waving his arms, howling: 'Cut the mainsail free! Get it *out* of there!'

Too late: the sticky mass had reached the foot of the topsail. The cloth split. Black tar poured down upon the mainsail, the largest canvas on the ship.

Further forward, there were howls of pain. Another of the bombs had landed near the forecastle, coating some twenty men in scalding tar. Pazel shut his eyes. No hope. Their screams were like knives to his brain. A few men, near the edges, escaped by shedding their clothes or shoes. Others fell, upon their knees, or their faces.

'Where are the Gods-damned fire-teams?' bellowed Coote.

'Thasha, Pathkendle: go!' shouted Hercól. 'We will do what we can here, but I fear it will not be enough. We have just lost half our speed.'

'She's going to lose more than speed,' said Thasha. With that she was gone, racing down the Silver Stair, and Pazel was rising, stumbling after her, shouting her name.

'Be careful, damn it!'

She was well ahead of him. Pazel wasn't sure what he was afraid of – would she forget to drink the wine before she touched the Stone, would she hold it too long in her fury? – but he knew that if he wasn't beside her in the crucial moment he would never forgive himself. Down the Silver Stair he plunged, through mobs of rushing sailors, through the Money Gate, along the passage of abandoned luxury chambers, through the invisible wall.

Thasha's dogs were barking. She was already in the stateroom; she had left the door ajar.

'Thasha, Thasha! Wait!'

She screamed. A wordless agony. Pazel thought his heart would stop. He flew into the chamber and thrashed towards her cabin, only to collide with her in the doorway as she tried to exit again, still screaming.

'What's wrong?'

'I'm a mucking fool, that's what's wrong! The key, the silver key! I can't get to the Nilstone without it. Do you have it?'

'*Me?*'

'When I was poisoned, did you—'

'No! I've never touched it!'

Thasha tore at her hair. 'Marila. Oh Pitfire. I gave it to Marila – didn't I?'

Back to the topdeck, faster than they had descended. The bombardment had stopped. Were they reloading? Heating more tar? Whatever had caused the delay, the *Chathrand* was still moving, however erratically, towards the gap. But now the *Death's Head* had caught the ripping wind along the Storm's edge, and was coming up behind them with terrible haste.

'What do you mean you don't have it? Marila!'

Thasha's cry was soon echoed by Neeps, who seized his wife by the shoulders.

'You can't have mucking lost it!'

'Lost it! I never *had* it!'

'On the table! I saw it on the table by the biscuit tin!'

'That was *days* ago, fool!'

What could they do? All four charged back to the stateroom, with Neda and Bolutu and Felthrup in tow. Pazel heard the first cannon-shots as he entered the chambers: the *Death's Head* was close enough to try conventional fire, now. The dogs howled, frightened less by the explosions than the onslaught of people (shouting, frustrated, furious) who set about tearing the stateroom apart. Pazel himself did not know where they had all come from: Mr Druffle was here, bug-eyed, reeking of rum; Myett and Ensyl were searching every inch of the floor.

'It *has* to be in Thasha's cabin!'

'Or the master bedroom. We were all there, she was dying—'

'Someone fetched towels, where did *they* come from?'

'The washroom—'

'Chadfallow's medical bag—'

'If you say *biscuit tin* one more time—'

Thasha was already holding the bottle of the Agaroth wine. 'Just calm down and think,' she shouted. 'Who does remember holding it, that night?'

CRASH. Horror. A direct hit on the wardroom, just below. Glass, chairs, timbers atomised; Pazel felt the shot burst through the compartment wall and carry on into the lower gun deck, heard the screams of the men on the chaser guns. They had yet to fire a single volley.

Another hit: the rigging, this time. The *Chathrand* pitched; the room heaved skyward. Thasha stumbled, cradling the bottle to her chest.

'Gods damn it, people! Where's that key? You can't *all* have never touched it!'

BOOM. A third hit, horribly close, maybe just above the master bedroom. From the latter, Bolutu and Neda cried out. Through the open doorway, Pazel saw part of the ceiling collapse.

'Neda! Bolutu!' They staggered from the bedroom, choking but unhurt. Dust and smoke billowed from the doorway. It was the chart room that had been hit, and its ruined contents had just collapsed into the master bedchamber.

'Thank the Gods the chart room was deserted,' said Ensyl.

'Oh no,' said Neeps. 'Oh no, no, no.'

'What is it?' said Pazel. 'Did you remember something?'

'Maybe I had the key.'

'Maybe?'

Neeps looked at them in panic. 'Yes. I definitely had it.' He gestured at the smoking doorway. 'I put it down on the bed, when Thasha was waking up. I didn't think about it. I was so glad she was alive.'

Marila's glare could have melted an anchor-plate. 'Just be glad *you* are, because when this is done I'm going to kill you.'

She charged into the bedroom. The others followed on her heels.

On the topdeck all was mayhem. Eight sails had been destroyed, and the bow was digging deep after each wave: they were in danger of foundering. The *Death's Head* had come within three miles, and dlömic soldiers were already mustering on her deck. Somehow the *Chathrand* was still weaving towards the gap in the Storm.

Three hits at three miles, thought Captain Fiffengurt. *Tree of Heaven, they've got fine gunners aboard. But so have we. Drop us a mast, Mr Byrd.*

They were firing back at last. The mad pitch of the *Chathrand* – bow dropping, stern lifting like a pump-handle – had forced the men at the stern chasers to Rin knew what sort of alterations to the gun carriages, and the strange angle would do nothing for their aim. Still, there was hope, and every shot fired was a taste of it. And the gap was drawing near.

If only their mage ... No, it wasn't right to ask more of Ramachni. He stood abaft the wheelhouse, gazing fixedly at the *Death's Head*, with the selk man attending him silently. Not a safe place for either of them, as Fiffengurt had already pointed out. He glanced at the Silver Stair. *Where are you, Thasha? Now would be a dandy time.*

'Why haven't they thrown more tar?' demanded Lady Oggosk. She had hobbled out in the midst of the carnage and demanded to be helped onto the quarterdeck. She never did like to miss out on a massacre.

'Who knows?' he said. 'Maybe they threw all they carried. But there's a monster gun on that forecastle, and it ain't fired a shot. I hate the sight of it, I must say.'

'What does it do?'

'For the love of Rin, Duchess, do you think I'm keeping it a secret?'

Elkstem actually laughed. Fiffengurt wished he hadn't; the man's eyes were a bit unhinged. Then Kirishgán stepped into the wheelhouse. 'The gun throws fire, Captain,' he said, almost in a whisper. 'Liquid fire. I have seen such devices slaughter a whole ship's company in minutes, from a distance of five or six hundred yards.'

Fiffengurt swallowed. 'There's ten or twelve bastards working it right now.'

The selk nodded. 'They are preparing.'

But meanwhile the *Death's Head* kept blasting away with her bow chasers. Fiffengurt watched a ball shatter the crests of two waves, and in the same instant felt the *thump* as it struck near the keel: heart-sickening, but no death-blow. The waves had slowed the ball, and the cloudcore oak shrugged it off.

What if it had missed those mucking waves?

He gazed at his ship, saw five hundred sailors at a glance. He was fairly certain he knew all their names. *Don't think of them burning. Don't see it.* Of course he saw it with terrible vividness, the scorched and writhing bodies of these boys who had never given up, whom nothing had broken, these lads who trusted him with their lives.

'Your weapons cannot pierce their armour,' said Kirishgán.

'Our carronades might.'

But the big carronades were not stern-mounted, and could not be moved in time. Another error. Fiffengurt bit the knuckle of his thumb. What, then? Smoke shots, to foul their aim? Useless in such a wind. Dump the fresh water, gain some speed? No, it would not be enough.

Turn into the Storm?

He could still do it. One more tack, hard to starboard, straight into that scarlet light. Even if the *Death's Head* followed they would be unable to attack. The light was blinding, though it inflicted no damage or pain. And based on what they'd met with on the southward journey, there was no reason to expect rough weather. Only a falling forward, a plunge through time.

Cross that line, and lose everything. Give the order, and never again see Anni, never know your child.

Another *boom*, and Fiffengurt saw a man plucked from the rigging and carried by the iron ball out over the sea. He fell at least three hundred yards off the bow. Something Fiffengurt had never seen in all his years of sailing.

Then Kirishgán pointed back at the *Death's Head*. 'There! Look there! Arpathwin has done it!'

Fiffengurt raised his telescope. The enemy ship's forecastle was burning. Tall flames surrounded the giant gun and trickled back along both rails. Men scattered and fell, their bodies like torches. Several hurled themselves into the sea.

'That is your mage's work,' said Kirishgán. 'He was searching for the minds of those gunners, and he found them. He knew he could not affect them greatly, or for long. But one does not need long: only a brief confusion, with matches and that horrible fuel.'

The flame trickled down the vessel's armoured sides. The cannon stopped firing. The jibsail burst into flames, and then the flying jib above it. But the flames spread no further. Already a large team was dousing the blaze.

Ramachni came back to the wheelhouse. 'Bless your soul, you've delivered us,' shouted Fiffengurt.

'Not for long,' said the mage. 'After this attack, Macadra will not even pretend to offer quarter. Nor will she permit any further mind-assaults. How soon will we reach the gap?'

'If we're not slowed further, thirty minutes.'

'Thirty minutes!' cried Oggosk. 'In thirty minutes that sorceress will be standing here in our place, or this boat will be in splinters.'

She was right. Fiffengurt saw it, the next fifteen or twenty minutes, the several forms that ruin could take.

New explosions; new shots screaming by like furies. They had recovered already.

He walked out to the quarterdeck rail, fighting his body, and the urge to cling to the wheel, to pretend. When he was certain his voice would not betray him, he shouted the order to his crew. Hard to starboard. Into the Storm.

They dragged nearly the whole contents of the bedroom out into the central chamber. They ran with armfuls of books and charts, dumping them, sifting them, running back for more. They combed through the remains of the limewood desk from the chart room, the shards of floorboards, the shattered cups and inkwells, magnifying glasses and drafting instruments, Rose's tactical chalk-board, Elkstem's brass spittoon.

'Did you *feel* that?' cried Pazel. 'That was a direct hit to the hull.'

'Glancing, not direct,' snapped Mr Druffle. 'Drop that rubbish, Undrabust! I told you I checked it!'

'And you watch those blary boots,' Neeps shot back. 'That's Myett you nearly trod on.'

They fetched lamps, got in each other's light. They shook out the bedclothes in which Thasha had lain. They found Pazel's mother's ivory whale, last seen before the ship reached Bramian; and a diamond earring that could only have belonged to Syrarys, which Thasha hurled at the wall.

'We're changing tack again,' said Thasha, stumbling to the porthole. 'Oh Gods, he's heading into the Storm!'

They flung aside the horsehair mattress, the remains of the brass bed. They kicked and scrabbled through the ruins, checking everything again, waving at dust clouds, cutting their hands.

Suddenly, from the topdeck a great collective scream. Midnight blackness drowned the glow of the Storm.

Felthrup wailed as though his heart would break – 'No! No! Not yet!' – and then Ensyl found the key, caught beneath the broken foot of the dressing mirror, still bolted to the floor.

It came out of the east like a sentient cloud. It had swollen, larger than the bay of Stath Bálfyr, larger perhaps than the island itself, and it flew arrow-straight and arrow-swift for the gap in the Red Storm. Kirishgán gave a keening cry and turned his face away. Ramachni faced it, but his tiny body shook.

The Swarm of Night. Hercól looked at the thing that had leaped skyward months ago, when Arunis held the Nilstone. Leaped from the River of Shadows, no larger than a little fish. It was obscene, solid, writhing like a clot of black worms. It reached the *Death's Head* first, and only then did Hercól realise that it was lower than the mast-heads. The Swarm flowed around the high timbers, and those sailors who did not dive into the sea were swallowed by it, and when the Swarm moved on the ship's rigging was devoid of life.

'Abandon masts!' Hercól screamed, waving his arms. 'Down, down for your lives!' A few men heard; a few were quick enough to live. Then the thing was above them, swallowing the masts as low as the topsails, and not even screams escaped.

There above the *Chathrand* the Swarm of Night stopped dead, like a cat with a mouse beneath its foot. The ship heaved; the masts were immobilised, and the waves wrenched and tore as though the ship had run aground. Hercól braced himself for the snapping that would mean death to them all. But it did not come. The masts held; the Swarm flowed on, anxious for the gap. The red light of the Storm washed over them again. But of the sixty men who had been working the upper masts, not one was left alive.

The Swarm entered the gap, racing towards the North and its bloodshed, its feast of death. It had almost vanished when a new light appeared on the *Chathrand*. A strange, white-hot light, pouring out through her gunports, and then up from the Silver Stair.

'Thasha!'

She looked like a woman possessed. The light came from the Nilstone in her naked hand. Hercól shouted again but there was no reaching her; she knew what she meant to do. With the Stone thrust high she reached out with her free hand, as if to seize the vanishing Swarm. And indeed her fingers seemed to close on something. Thasha screamed, in fury or agony or both, and every muscle in her body tightened with effort. She threw her head back; she clawed at the air. Miles away, the Swarm of Night faltered, swerved.

Thasha gave a violent wrench of her arm. The Swarm leaped sideways, right out of the gap and into the Red Storm's light. There was a brief flash and it was gone.

Not a voice could be heard. Thasha straightened, flexing her shoulders and her neck. A wild fury still glowed in her eyes. The ship was spinning, bobbing like a derelict. She staggered to the rail and Hercól followed. The light of the Nilstone was dimming.

When he drew near her he caught the smell of burning skin.

'Put it down, Thasha! Put it down before it kills you!'

She nodded. She made to drop the Stone at his feet. Then her eye caught something beyond the rail, and she froze.

The *Death's Head* had spun into view, no more than half a mile away. Replacement crew were scaling her masts, and even as they watched, cannon were sliding out through the gunports, sixty or eighty strong.

Thasha stared at the vessel. She looked as though vomit or blood might be rising in her throat. But what she unleashed from her chest was a howl of rage and madness, and a force that leaped the water and slammed like a hurricane into Macadra's ship. The *Death's Head* rolled onto her beam-ends, the dlömu who had raced up the masts were swept away. Hercól fell on his knees, covering his ears, feeling the noise shake the *Chathrand* to her frame.

Thasha gave a strange, feline twist of her head and dropped the Nilstone. Hercól's foot shot out and held it still, even as Thasha collapsed in his arms. Pathkendle appeared, and the others close behind. Hercól looked at the *Death's Head*. It was not sunk, but its rigging was destroyed, and two of its five masts had been flung like straws across the sea.

Fiffengurt began to shout: 'Strike the jibs! Get that mess off the jiggermast, we can't steer a blary wreck! *Fast* boys, we're drifting!'

Thasha raved: 'Pazel, help me. Oh Gods. Oh Gods.'

Pazel turned over her hand, and stifled a cry: Thasha's palm was a mass of blisters, white and oozing. 'Get some bandages, Neeps! She's scalded!'

Thasha spoke through her gasps. 'Doesn't matter ... I have to kill them, Pazel ... bring the wine.'

No one moved to obey her; no one was even tempted. Hercól raised his eyes. 'Look, girl! We're going to make it, thanks to you.'

They were in the mouth of the gap. It was undulating, and rafts of red light drifted across it like icebergs, but it was wide enough, and the wind they had ridden was pouring through it into the North. For a moment Hercól saw the world beyond: their own world, their own time. Then he felt Thasha's fingers tighten on his arm. Her fury had rekindled. 'Bring the wine, Pazel,' she said.

'No,' said Pazel. 'No more, not for a while, anyway. You held the Stone much too long, Thasha. You can't just pick it up again.'

'Can't I?'

Thasha straightened, pushing away from Hercól, and began to stalk across the quarterdeck. His foot was still upon the Nilstone; he could not follow her. When Pazel did she turned him a glare so vicious that Hercól could scarcely blame the lad for hesitating.

But Fiffengurt did not see the look. Passing the wheel to Elkstem, he ran to intercept her.

'Miss Thasha, enough! You don't need to strike them again; they're barely afloat! And that foul wine's gone to your head—'

Thasha threw her shoulder against him, brutally. Fiffengurt was knocked off his feet, and Thasha crossed to the ladder, shouting: 'Damn you all! Hercól, don't you *dare* move the Nilstone!'

She threw herself down the ladder, onto the main level of the topdeck, and began to march towards the Silver Stair. But after just a few steps, something changed. Her feet slowed; her shoulders drooped. She cursed and stumbled. By the time she reached the Silver Stair the fight was over. She knelt, leaning heavily against the hatch coaming. She raised her eyes with effort, scanned the frightened faces. Then she toppled gently on her side.

Ramachni gazed down at her from the edge of the quarterdeck. 'Sleep and heal,' he said.

Pain flared suddenly in Hercól's foot: the Nilstone was burning him, straight through his boot. He switched feet, staring into the impossible darkness. 'Pathkendle,' he said, 'fetch me those gauntlets, before I kick this thrice-damned thing into the sea.'

The tarboy did not move. 'Pathkendle! For Rin's sake—'

Pazel had gone rigid, his face full of wonder and fear. All around them, pale, nearly invisible particles of light were swirling, drifting like a fine scarlet snow. A silence engulfed them, like the closing of a vault. Hercól raised his hand and saw the particles adhering to his skin. Unlike snow they did not melt.

The gap was imperfect. The substance of the Storm was thin here, but not gone. Only the world was gone. Behind them, ahead of them, North and South, Hercól could see nothing but a featureless glow. The veil of Erithusmé's spell had fallen. And when it rose again, how much of their world, their time, would it have stolen away?

The light began to coat the topdeck, the surviving rigging, the dead men sheathed in tar. Pazel was on his knees, beating the deck with both fists, unable to make a sound. Hercól longed for an enemy, for a reason to pull Ildraquin from its scabbard and whirl into battle with all his strength and skill. He closed his eyes but it made no difference; the light was inside.

31

The Editor's Companions

I see them sometimes, in the lanes and gardens of this academical village, this haven untouched by war. Among the lecture halls in red brick and green marble, the rose beds and Buriav lilacs, there suddenly will shamble Fiffengurt, scowling, kindly, pushing a pram with a burbling daughter, studying the path before him with his one true eye. A little further, and there is Big Skip Sunderling carving meat in the butcher's shop, up to his elbows in the job as always, happily a mess. Neda Pathkendle I have seen at the archery range, a strong, straight-backed woman of forty, teaching students to use a killing tool as a kind of diversion, a means of disciplining hand and eye, a game. I have seen Teggatz in a doctor's coat, Bolutu pushing a broom, Lady Oggosk in the tavern where the fire is never lit, cloudy eyes on the window, eating alone.

They do not know me, of course; or if they do they know the professor whose reputation is so odd and dubious that all familiarity is feigned, A very good day to you, sir, and how are you enjoying this fine summer morn? I don't like it when they speak to me. Not their fault, of course, but whoever could have guessed that in telling their story I should also be afflicted with their faces, that a girl in her first student year would glance up from her book and pierce me with Thasha's beauty, those questing eyes, that hunger for experience, for change?

Nilus Rose teaches physics in the Advanced Science Building; Marila storms by in a barrister's robes; Ignus Chadfallow haunts the faculty club in the guise of the eldest waiter, who will tell you softly that food is not an entertainment but a sacrament, that the rice dishes are superior to the soups. Pazel has made but one appearance, at twilight on the wooded path behind the graveyard, hand in hand with an ethereal beauty whose face was not familiar at all.

They are here until they speak, or until I look a second time, until I summon the memories that sweep phantoms away. Sometimes I will look for them, when I am grumpy and tired of solitude, when living for the past seems less noble than cowardly, a betrayal of the warm blood still in me, a waste. The old spook at the faculty club, who is almost a friend, asked once if I didn't also see myself about the school? Oh yes, frequently, I answered, and let it go at that. He is a gentleman; he assumes that I am sane. What would become of that charity, if he knew where my own doppelgängers appeared? The flash in the alley, the desperate little life, always hungry, always hunted, with senses too sharp for his own happiness, addicted to dreams that call him, nearer, ever nearer, dreams that terrify when they seem most true.

32

Men in the Waves

—⁓—

The world lurched, and Thasha woke in the sling they had fashioned to keep her from being tossed from her bed, and for a time
she could not be made to understand.

It was Neda's turn at her bedside, and their lack of a strong
common language made things harder. Bright spots danced before
Thasha's eyes, and her fingertips were numb.

'We're out of the Storm, then?'

Neda mumbled something. Thasha repeated her question,
louder.

'No, no, Thasha. You are not feeling it?'

What she felt was the *Chathrand* heaving violently beneath her
– climbing mountainous waves, clawing over the crests, rushing like
a landslide into the troughs – and the soreness of muscles flung
too many times against the canvas sling. What she saw was her old
cabin, swept clean of any objects that could fall or fly; and Neda,
balancing with *sfvantskor* grace, barely touching the bolted bed-
frame; and the sea foaming grey and furious over the porthole glass.

The bright spots were shrinking. Thasha breathed in warm, wet
air.

'I mean that we're out of the *Red* Storm,' said Thasha.

'Of course.'

'And smack in the middle of a blary gale. A killer.'

'Not middle. Ending, maybe. I wish you sleep through it, sister.'

Thasha reached for Neda's hand. *Sister*. To wake and find one
watching over you. A sister, something new under the sun. The
voyage had brought her far more than loss.

'How long has it been?' she said.

The ship rolled and heaved. The noise of the storm was strangely distant. Neda looked at her and said nothing.

'Well?'

'You're awake. I am calling Pazel; he is exciting for you.'

Thasha didn't release her hand. 'Just tell me, Neda.'

'Five years.'

'FIVE YEARS! RAMACHNI PUT ME TO SLEEP FOR *FIVE GODS-DAMNED YEARS*?'

'No, no.'

Thasha freed herself from the sling and was thrown at once upon the floor. Her balance gone, her limbs sleep-clumsy. Neda helped her to her feet. 'You sleeping fifty-three days,' she said.

'Then what's this rubbish about – Oh. The Red Storm.'

'Yes,' said Neda.

'It threw us forward in time after all. But how in Pitfire do you know? Have we made landfall?'

'Not yet,' said Neda. 'We knowing by stars. Some stars turning like wheel, over and over the same. But the special stars – they are drifting, *tachai*? Little bit each year. Old sailors know. Captain Fiffengurt checking Rose's book, also Ramachni knows, also Lady Oggosk. Is the truth, Thasha. We lose five years for ever. Or six, if counting travel.'

'But the war—'

'Maybe over. Or very big, or huge.'

Thasha was shaking. 'The Swarm, Neda. I … pushed it out of the gap, into a deeper part of the Red Storm.'

'More in future. You saving us, giving us time. These fifty-days we not seeing the Swarm.'

'Neda, what about your dreams, yours and Pazel's? The ones where your mother speaks to you?'

Neda turned a little away, looking angry or confused. 'Nothing. Silence. Maybe she is getting dead. Or thinking us dead, giving up.'

And her father: he'd surely have given up. 'Oh Gods,' said Thasha.

'Where's the Nilstone? What have they done with the wine? I've got to do something about all this—'

'Foolish talk.'

'I think I'm going to be sick.'

Neda's hand seized her chin. Thasha looked up into the fierce warrior eyes.

'Kill that fear,' said Neda. 'You taking Swarm in your hands and throwing sideways. Then striking Macadra's ship like toy. Now no whimper. Be quiet. Put the raincoat. We are going up into this storm.'

It might have been noon. Or sunset, or dawn. The wind was monstrous, the light dull nickel; the globular thunderheads seemed low enough to touch. Thasha clung to the Silver Stair hatch coaming, appalled. The rain like fistfuls of tiny nails flung endlessly at her face. The *Chathrand* was the toy; and what did that make her crew? A towering wave seemed frozen above the portside bow, then the illusion shattered and the great wave pounced, and somehow, impossibly, they slithered up its flank and toppled over the crest. Then the sick plunge, the weightlessness, the vanishing horizon and the next wave looming like death.

The gale had blown for seven days already, Neda shouted. 'And you sleeping through first one.' The crew was thin, frantic, exhausted, grinning welcome-back smiles at Thasha like gap-toothed ghouls. The next wave pounced. They had been pouncing for seven days.

Thasha frowned: something was definitely wrong with her hearing. The whole battle with the storm was occuring in cottony undertones. Even the mad wolf-howls of the wind through the rigging were subdued.

Neda told her that Pazel and Neeps were aloft, somewhere, but in the maelstrom Thasha could hardly recognize a soul. She wanted to lend a hand on the ropes, but she was weak: she'd had no food in fifty-three days. Nor could she imagine swallowing a morsel in weather like this.

She found a job passing flasks of fresh water to the men on the ropes. The officers had to scream at the men to drink: they were sweating away their life's water despite the soaking and the chill. Hours passed. She met her friends, haphazardly. Bolutu sang out with joy and kissed her on both cheeks; Marila dropped the buckets she was hauling and hugged her, tight barrel-belly pressing Thasha's own. Thasha touched it: three months to go. 'Chew this!' Marila told her, taking a somewhat dusty, leaf-wrapped ball of *mül* from her pocket. 'Trust me, they don't make you sick. Some days it's the only thing I can eat.'

'I still wish I knew what's in those blary things.'

'Eat it, Thasha. You're paler than a cod.'

They met Ramachni near the galley (he could venture nowhere near the topdeck). 'What? Your ears?' he said. 'I save you from destroying yourself with the Nilstone, and you complain about your ears? I ask you, girl: has there ever been a better time to be deaf?'

'I'm not laughing, Ramachni.'

'No, you're not. Well, Thasha, you will not be deaf for long. The healing sleep dulled all your senses; they return at different speeds. But you are still in mortal danger. The sleep cooled your hunger for the Stone, but it could do no more than slow the poison in your blood. The latter has been slowed a great deal: it may be weeks before the poison strikes you again.

'But it will strike, Thasha, and when it does you must be ready. Hercól carries the silver key, and is never parted from it. The wine remains in your cabin. At the first sign of illness you must drink it *all*: down to the dregs, and the cure. Swear that you will obey me in this.'

'Then I'll never use the Stone again.'

'You were never meant to, Thasha. Erithusmé was. And use it she will, when you release her.'

How can you still believe that? she wanted to ask. But she gave Ramachni her word.

The storm raged on. Thasha kept working, biting off chunks of the rubbery *mül*, gnawing at them until they dissolved. A little of her strength returned. She began to carry heavier loads, and to broom water from the gun decks into the drains. After two hours she rested, gasping, flat on her back in the stateroom on the bearskin rug. Jorl and Suzyt curled up against her. Felthrup chattered about the days she had missed.

It seemed that every last soul had gone blind and senseless in the Red Storm, which poured its strange light even into their minds. When their senses returned, they found the ship adrift and heaving on great Nelluroq swells, and barely saved her from foundering. Nólcindar's navigational advice was rendered useless, for there was no land in sight, and no telling just where the Red Storm had released them. 'We've made fine speed north since the Red Storm,' said Felthrup, 'but north from *where*? That we cannot determine. We could be three months from landfall, Thasha. Or three days.'

'Landfall where?'

Felthrup just shook his head. How far east or west they had drifted was beyond all reckoning.

When she ventured out again she met Hercól, who embraced her warmly, but somehow would not meet her eye. Thasha studied him, alarmed. Could he still be hurting from that kiss?

The storm finally ebbed. The waves shrank to mere fifty-footers, and a pulsing behind the clouds suggested the existence of a sun. Down from the masts came Pazel and Neeps and fifty others: rope-whipped, spray-blinded, near-naked monkeys, all muscle and bone. The two tarboys waved and grinned from across the tonnage hatch. Beside her, Marila looked from Thasha to Pazel and back again. 'Why aren't you married yet?' she asked.

The sun peeked out. Captain Fiffengurt poured blessings on the crew. 'You're beautiful, my lads: you're magnificence itself! You've got the blood of blary titans in your veins!' But it was on Thasha that the most praise was heaped. Every man aboard knew how she'd saved them from the *Death's Head*, and every man aboard wanted to kiss her or touch her fingers or kneel down and offer his service, or his life. Even Sergeant Haddismal snapped his heels together sharply and offered a salute – a gesture mimicked at once by every Turach in sight.

'You've done it at last,' said a voice in her ear, as Ensyl leaped nimbly to her shoulder.

'Done what?'

'Made the ship safe for crawlies, Thasha. Or at least for Myett and myself. Not that we've dared come near the topdeck since the storm began. *Héridom*, this ship is a mess.'

'Ensyl,' said Thasha with feeling, 'we haven't talked. You don't know—'

'That you saw Diadrelu, on the night you almost died?'

'Hercól told you?'

'No,' said Ensyl, 'he didn't have to say a word. I saw your face, Thasha: I knew you were going to kiss him before we stepped out of your cabin. And I heard what you said: *I have something for you. Something you were passing along from another.*'

Thasha bit her lips. Dri had sent the same words of hope to Ensyl and Hercól – but the kiss, that had been meant for just one. She wished she could lie, could spare this woman's feelings. 'Dri loved you deeply,' she said.

Ensyl had the grace to smile. 'I knew the fates would punish me, for unchaste dreams of my mistress.'

'Oh, Ensyl – rubbish!'

'Maybe. But the dreams were not.'

Thasha caught up with Pazel and Neeps on the berthdeck, where they had collapsed against a wall among a dozen others fresh from the rigging, every one of them asleep. Pazel's hand was closed around a half-empty cup of rum. Neeps lay with his head on Pazel's shoulder, opened-mouthed and drooling.

Thasha took the cup from Pazel's hand, and he woke and reached for her. Neeps opened his eyes and sat up. 'Hello, Thasha,' he said. Then he rolled away and retched. Seconds later he was asleep against the man on his right.

'He took a beating up there,' said Pazel.

'And you didn't?'

She dabbed at his cuts with her soggy sleeve, and felt quite married, and then recalled that that would never do. She might have to die; this boy had to live, unhitched, unentangled, free. He'd do the living for both of them.

'Did you dream of me?' asked Pazel.

'Endlessly. Dragonflies and buttercups and little songbirds and you. For fifty-three days and nights.'

'Come back to the stateroom with me, Thasha.'

'Oh you fool.'

'I want children. With your eyes. Don't you want that at all?' She kissed him. 'No.'

Pazel went on smiling. He didn't believe her, the egotist. She didn't know if she believed herself.

Then Pazel's eyes darkened. 'You don't know, do you? About them.'

'Who? Neeps and Marila? What are you talking about?'

Pazel reached over and tugged up Neeps' shirt. On the smaller boy's chest, roughly over his heart, was a tattoo of a black and sinuous animal. 'Mr Druffle did that for him. He's a box of hidden talents, the old drunk.'

'Is that supposed to be Ramachni?'

Pazel looked at her. 'It's not a mink, Thasha. It's an otter.'

Thasha sat back. 'Lunja. They called her the Otter, didn't they?'

Pazel nodded. 'She's all he thinks about.'

'Wake him up,' said Thasha, 'so I can slap him back to sleep.'

Instead they just left him there and headed for the stateroom. Thasha was feeling weak again, and her thoughts were awhirl. One sip of wine left. One last, brief use of the Nilstone. She could quell this storm, maybe, and bring fair winds. But could she ask the Stone where in Alifros they were?

What else, in three minutes of magic? Could she find the Swarm, and push it back through the Red Storm a second time? Could she fix Hercól's broken heart, make Neeps forget Lunja, tell Pazel's mother that her children were alive?

They had barely reached the ladderway when the shouting began: Failed rigging! Emergency! All hands above to save the mainmast!

'*Credek*,' Pazel swore, and he was gone, running. Thasha trailed behind him, exhausted. On the topdeck she found disaster averted, the mainmast straightening, the men's hands torn and bleeding on the backstays. Thasha stood and watched. She loved these men, these worker ants. Nothing could kill them. They bore everything and went on serving the ship.

Then the wind rose and the waves climbed higher and they fought the storm all night, and all the next day and night, and when the sun rose at last on a clear calm morning they found two men still out on the bowsprit, dangling where they'd lashed themselves, drowned by rain and spray.

Neeps was among those sent to retrieve the corpses. He had napped for forty minutes in the last twenty hours, and had dreamed of Uláramyth, the bamboo grove, long dark limbs entangled with his own. The woman loved him; she was saving his life. He threaded his fingers through hers and told himself he would never let go. Then he woke. The hand he held was all wrong. Not webbed, not black. Marila asked about his dream, but *Uláramyth* was a word that she could never hear.

'I dreamed of home,' he said. 'Nonsense stuff. Can't remember a thing.'

Marila looked at him, then laid her round cheek on his arm. 'I am home,' she said.

He ought to say something to that. Something grand and gentle. About how he'd felt the child kick, as he had, when Marila's tight spherical belly pressed his own in the night, trying to nudge him off the bed. He stroked her hair, kissed her forehead, saw Lunja in the galley of the *Promise,* back against the door, eyes in *nuhzat,* angry. *Give me something, give me something back, boy. Quickly, quietly. Now.'*

Marila raised her head. 'Are you crying?'

'Don't be daft. Let's get out of this bed.'

Lunja had arms like a wrestler's. She had whispered the whole time, but the words melted into sounds, just sounds, urgent and then more urgent, and Neeps thought her voice had become like the sea's voice for an old mariner, inescapable, behind and under everything for the rest of his life. But not that day. Three minutes and it was over, for the last time, and later she did not speak to him at all.

'Nothing blary fits any more,' said Marila, struggling into her pants.

They went out. The sun rose; the dead men were discovered. Coote's crooked finger directed Neeps to the team scrambling out along the bowsprit. Marila stood and watched, making him clumsy, making him nick himself with the knife. The dead men were so cold and tangled. Their eyes wide open, astonished. Neeps couldn't help himself: he followed the dead man's gaze.

So it was that he, Neeps Undrabust, saw the light that flashed on the horizon. *Blink ... blink-blink...blink.* A lantern, not a mirror-signal. In another minute it would have vanished in the brightening day.

For all the changes in his life and heart, Neeps was still a tarboy, and knew his Sailing Code. The light was a distress signal – from an Arquali ship. Neeps stood and shouted, and marked the light's position relative to the sun, and by midday they were fishing survivors from the sea.

Their commander said his name was Captain Vancz, his boat an Urnsfich grain-hauler, its doom a sudden gale that carried her south into the Ruling Sea. 'We were halfway to Pulduraj, Captain Fiffengurt. Sixth year in a row I've been hired as a barley-boat. Never saw a storm like that one, by all the Gods.'

He was a young captain with a sleek brown moustache and wary eyes, one of twenty men they'd found bobbing like corks on the waves. Now Vancz and a handful of his men had been brought to Rose's cabin. They sat in a circle, wearing the last, precious dry clothes on the *Chathrand*, drinking hot grog. Except for one bewildered, grey-bearded senior they were all young and fit: the sort you would expect to find still fighting for life twenty hours after a shipwreck.

'You're an Urnsfich man yourself, sir?' asked Pazel.

'Born and raised, worse luck,' said Vancz.

'Your boat's prow was still above the waves this morning, when you signalled us,' said Fiffengurt. 'How'd you manage to lose her *slowly*, way out here? You can't have struck something?'

Vancz shook his head. 'Not in these depths. She was just smack-battered by the storm and sprang a fatal leak. We never did find it. The end was slow, but not that slow.'

'You look a mite familiar,' said Fiffengurt. 'Have we met?'

Vancz glanced quickly at his men before he answered. 'I'd be surprised if we hadn't,' he said. 'Perhaps it was in Ballytween, a few years back? At that public house, what's it called now – the Merchant Prince?'

'No doubt,' said Fiffengurt.

No doubt at all, thought Pazel, *because everything he's saying is a lie.*

The man did not speak a word of the Urnsfich tongue: Pazel had called him a dung-eating sow, and got a vague grin in return. Pazel glanced at his shipmates. Lady Oggosk was chewing her lips, furiously impatient: she knew. So did Neeps and Hercól and Felthrup. Sergeant Haddismal was less certain, but more threatening: he stood behind Vancz, sighing like a hippopotamus, his massive hands on the rescued man's chair. Each time Vancz leaned back he met the Turach's knuckles.

Pazel glanced at Thasha. For some reason she looked ready to laugh.

'This truly is the Great Ship,' said Vancz for the third time, 'but how can it be? You struck a reef off Talturi. You went down with all hands. I saw the story in the *Mariner*. I'll never forget it. That awful summer of Nine-Forty-One. Just before the start of the war.'

His listeners moved uneasily. *The start of the war*, thought Pazel. *He's already forgetting it. Rin's eyes, but this is going to be hard.*

'Tell me, Vancz,' said Fiffengurt, 'do you have much trouble with our lads in uniform, out Urnsfich way? I mean the Imperial navy?'

'What, Arqual's navy? Why should we have any feud with them, Captain?'

No one answered. Vancz looked at his men again. 'Why are you all staring at me?' he blurted at last. 'What kind of rescue is this? And what in Rin's name was that creature on your topdeck – you called it a *Bolutu* – that black thing with fishy eyes?'

'Smack him!' said Lady Oggosk. 'The man answers questions with questions! You should have left him squirming in the sea!'

'Now Duchess, have a heart,' said Fiffengurt. 'Captain Vancz, when a man does you a good turn, you ought to be generous awhile. If he asks something small of you, for instance, you hand it over with a smile. Call it plain gratitude, if you like.'

'The principle of reciprocity!' squeaked Felthrup.

'The principle of intelligence,' said Haddismal.

Vancz looked at his hands. 'Right you are, Captain Fiffengurt. And I do hope I can show you a little *intelligence*. The kind any skipper from Arqual has a right to expect.'

Pazel started: something in the man's voice had thrown open a door. *Arqual. He gets more nervous every time he speaks the word.*

Fiffengurt pressed on. 'Those bits of hull we found floating all around you – they weren't from cannon-fire?'

Vancz looked shocked. 'But of course not! *We've* seen no combat, sir. We're neutral in the whole affair.'

'What affair?'

Vancz started, closed his mouth.

'Would you indulge us,' said Hercól, 'by naming the date?'

'The date?'

'Today's date, you prevaricating worm!' shrieked Oggosk. She exploded to her feet and hobbled towards him. Vancz looked rather more afraid of her than of Haddismal.

'Modoli the twenty-sixth!' he said. 'Or the twenty-seventh; I can't swear I didn't lose a day in the storm! Rin's blessings, lady, there's no need to – *Ouch!*'

Lady Oggosk had poked him in the eye. 'No need! If Captain Rose were still alive you'd be dangling from the main yard by your thumbs! We are on a mission of death, you bit of flotsam, and you're spreading lies thick as kulberry jam! Fiffengurt, if you won't get the truth out of this man let the tinshirts get it for you. *Glaya Lorgus!* I never thought I'd miss Sandor Ott!'

At the mention of the spymaster the man visibly paled. Then Thasha put a hand on Oggosk's arm. She *was* laughing, now. 'Duchess, stop,' she said. 'There's no need for any of this. Commander, you're a navy officer yourself. Don't bother to deny it.'

'But my dear lady—'

'Not you,' said Thasha. She pointed at the older, grey-bearded survivor of the wreck. 'He's the man you should be talking to, Captain Fiffengurt.'

The old fellow gaped at her, eyes wide with amazement.

'The beard almost threw me,' said Thasha, 'but I know you now. My father used to point you out in parades.'

'P-parades?' gasped the bearded man.

'What's going on here?' barked Haddismal. 'You're saying *he's* Vancz?'

'There isn't any Vancz,' said Thasha. 'This man's name is Darabik, Purston Darabik. Why have you been lying to us, Commodore?'

'Darabik?' said Captain Fiffengurt.

'Darabik?' Haddismal straightened his back.

Another stunned pause. Then Lady Oggosk shrieked the name a third time, hobbled over to the old man and starting beating him about the face.

'Stop, stop!' cried the old man.

'Darabik!' cried Oggosk. 'You chased Captain Rose across the seas for thirteen years! You made our lives a living hell!'

'Of course I did!' The man's voice and bearing had utterly changed. 'Rose was a common criminal! He swindled everyone from the *Chathrand*'s owners to the Boy Prince of Fulne!'

'He saved our lives, over and over,' said Pazel. 'I guess he was a criminal, but there was nothing common about him.'

The one they had called Vancz looked fearful. 'Sir, I told 'em just what you said – they muddled me—'

'Drink your grog and be quiet, you – *Ouch!* Gods damn it, Fiffengurt, can't you get this pet vulture of yours under control?'

'Is that an order, *Commodore?*'

'It blary well is! Flaming devils, where did this mad ship *come* from?'

Then, for the first time, Ramachni spoke. 'She came from across the Ruling Sea. Your Emperor Magad launched her, and Magad's operatives held sway aboard her for many thousands of miles. But all is changed today. From Captain Rose to the youngest tarboy, from Brother Bolutu to the ixchel, we have all forged new alliances. Our loyalties evolved. That is one reason we are still alive.'

'Sandor Ott's loyalties evolved?'

Ramachni shook his head sadly. 'No, not his.'

Darabik's mouth twisted. 'You see now why I did not announce myself. Lady Thasha, from you alone will I beg forgiveness for this act. We thought you dead. And even when the witch's dreams told us otherwise, we still thought you a prisoner of these people.'

Thasha stepped towards him, barely breathing. 'We?' she said.

Darabik nodded. 'I speak of the leadership of our rebellion, Lady Thasha. Including its military commander, Prince Eberzam Isiq.'

Thasha cried out, laughing and sobbing at once. Her friends embraced her, and Felthrup gave a piercing squeal. Pazel had no idea what minor queen or princess Admiral Isiq had married, but who cared? Thasha's father was alive.

'Rebellion, is it?' Haddismal moved to the cabin door and flung it open. 'You there, marines! Draw and enter! All of you, *move!*'

Move the Turachs did. In seconds there were twenty or more shoving into Rose's cabin with swords in hand.

'Our loyalties haven't evolved either,' growled Haddismal. 'We serve the Ametrine Throne, and will do so 'til our hands drop the swords. Be careful, mage.'

'I have never been otherwise in your presence, Sergeant. But I think you will find the commodore's visit an act of providence. At least, I hope you will.'

'What's that supposed to mean?'

Darabik stood abruptly. His eyes were hawklike in their ferocity: all pretence had dropped away. 'It means,' he said, 'that for years I have placed myself before men like you, and called on them to *keep* their oaths, not break them. To prove their courage and the hard steel of their loyalty—'

'Well, then—'

'—by daring to fight for the only one who, by law and Rin's favour, deserves to sit in the Chamber of Ametrine. I mean Her Majesty the Empress, Maisa daughter of Magad the Third. She lives, and many thousands of true Arqualis are fighting, bleeding, dying for her cause. We were not wrecked in a storm, Turach. We were fired upon by the warships of the Usurper, Magad the Fifth.'

Haddismal started forward, snarling. '*Usurper!* You're speaking of His Supremacy, you traitorous son of a whore!'

'His Supremacy's own grandfather named Maisa to the throne,' said Hercól quietly. 'And *your* grandfathers, dare I remind you, swore an oath to that man.'

The Turach hesitated. He looked hard at Darabik again. 'You weren't making for Pulduraj,' he said. 'Where were you headed, and why?'

Darabik paused, studying the face of the huge marine before him. 'We were bound for the island called Serpent's Head, and a gathering of all Maisa's forces.'

'And Maisa?' asked Haddismal. 'Will she be there, rallying her turncoat troops?'

Darabik shook his head. 'That I cannot say.'

The Turach's eyes narrowed. 'Beg to differ, *Commodore*: you can.'

Never taking his eyes from Haddismal, the old commodore unbuttoned his shirt. Pazel recoiled: the man's chest was like a window cracked by a stone, but the cracks were raised red scars. They had very clearly been made with a knife.

'The Secret Fist thought so too,' he said. 'I chose not to betray our country to the Secret Fist. Do you think I will betray them to you?'

Sergeant Haddismal was leaning forward, hands in fists. But he made no move against the commodore.

'It has been a savage fight, but a proud one,' said Darabik. 'Generals and governors, princes and counts have joined our rebellion. Whole legions have broken with Etherhorde. And Magad faces other enemies, too: the Mzithrinis still bleed him to the west; Noonfirth has cut supplies from the east. The Crownless Lands support us with shelter and armaments and food.'

'The Crownless Lands,' scoffed Haddismal. 'So you're begging from waifs. Doesn't sound like a winning hand to me.'

'We are not winning, but we have not lost. This time last year our forces numbered ninety thousand.'

'*Ninety thousand!*' cried Hercól, his eyes flashing.

'Ninety thousand my bleedin' arse,' growled a Turach. 'Commander, this is all rot and betrayal.'

'Aye, lad, it *is* betrayal,' said Darabik sharply. 'You marines were the first betrayed, when you were told all manner of lies about your Empress. You have given your lives and blood for a false king, a warped image of the Arqual you deserve. Oh, to the Pits with you all—'

Darabik spread his hands wide. 'Kill me and be done with it. Or be as brave and true as you have sworn to be, and choose the harder fight.'

A terrible stillness followed. The Turachs stood like wolves before the pounce. But it was Hercól who moved. With a speed Pazel had only ever glimpsed in Sandor Ott, he struck the sword from the hand of the Turach nearest him, then twisted around Haddismal's sudden thrust so that he stood behind the man. Hercól's left arm slid over Haddismal's shoulder; his elbow caught the marine under the chin.

Hercól gave a brutal backward heave. Both men crashed to the floor and were suddenly still: Haddismal flat on his back, Hercól beneath him, with Ildraquin across the sergeant's throat.

'Stay!' wheezed Hercól. 'Sergeant Haddismal, hear me: I did not wish to assault you. Indeed I fear what I have done.'

'You should,' said Haddismal.

'We cannot go on divided,' said Hercól. 'If shipmate kills shipmate again, we shall all be lost. I feel this in my heart's core, Sergeant Haddismal. I am not an Arquali, nor wish to be. Yet I have served the true Empress of Arqual in secret these many years. I trust this Darabik. And I shall trust you, now: with my life, and the life of Alifros itself.'

'Hercól – no!' cried Thasha. She tried to shove a path towards him, but the Turachs seized her arms.

'Be *still*, Thasha!' cried Hercól. 'All of you, be still! Turachs, I disarmed your leader so that you might know that it was hope, not fear, that led me on. Now I say the same as Darabik: stand with us, or kill us. We will not kill you.'

He opened his hand, and Ildraquin fell to the floor. Instantly a Turach lowered the tip of his sword to Hercól's neck. Haddismal rolled to his feet and took the weapon. His gaze was murderous.

'You were a mucking fool to disarm,' he said. After several gasping breaths, he added, 'Or a saint. I don't know. Corporal Mandric's risked his *own* life since he returned, swearing you're all in the right, that the Nilstone's the enemy, that your quest is the only one that counts. He called Magad a fraud. I had to throw him in the brig or throw him to the fishes.' Haddismal swallowed. 'He ain't with the fishes, yet.

'As for *you*—' the sergeant shot a glance at Darabik '—you sound like the kind of officer my old man was. The kind who could hold his head up, before the world and Rin's judgement. Get up, Stanapeth, and take your weapon back. I'll stand with you lot. I'm mucking tired of lies.'

33

Nightfall

28 Modoli 942
*360th sailing day from Etherhorde**

Burned, battered, weary, leaking, lost. And for all this, a ship united. The other Turachs followed Sergeant Haddismal's lead, and few appeared to regret it. Many even looked relieved to be siding with Pazel and his allies, and nodded to them when they passed, as though they'd been conferred some honorary rank. Corporal Mandric was let out of the brig.

Marila said that the ground had been shifting since Ott's murder of Captain Rose. 'For a while everyone pretended not to know. If you said out loud that Ott had killed him, the Turachs might kill *you*.' Now even the Turachs began to speak of Ott with contempt. Something in Pazel felt healed. The *Chathrand* was one ship, and this time no one had died for her.

Thanks to Darabik, moreover, they were not lost for long. The commodore knew with some accuracy where his ship had gone down: just fifty or sixty miles south of the Baerrid Archipelago, and some eight days west of Bramian. Fiffengurt kept the *Chathrand* on her northern course, and by six bells land was in sight: two tiny

―――――

*One year to the day (subjective ship time) from the *Chathrand*'s launch from Etherhorde. The anniversary passed unnoticed by all aboard. When we did take note, some days later, we struggled to believe that only twelve months had passed in our lives. Over time this became even harder to remember, as the five lost years became real for us. - EDITOR

islands, little nuggets of tree-crowned stone, the serpent's verte-brae. Yes, these were the Baerrids. Fiffengurt had seen the island chain several times over the years – from the north side, of course.

'You haven't lied about our position, anyway,' he told Darabik.

'I rarely lie,' said the commodore, 'but perfect honesty – well, that is a luxury reserved for those who suffer neither want nor pain. I have suffered both. After Maisa launched her rebellion, we divided our naval forces into thirds. I said goodbye to Thasha's father in Ormael, and sailed east across the Nelu Peren. On the third day, a huge force of warships from Etherhorde surprised us, and decimated my squadron. My own quarterdeck was blown out from under my feet. I fell into smoke and darkness, and when I awoke I was in the hands of the Secret Fist.

'For months they tortured me, body and soul. I prayed for death. I told them lies, then truth. At last I confused the two myself, and said whatever I thought would make them stop. Nothing made them stop. I tried to starve myself; they injected me with a poison that left me limp, and forced gruel down my throat.

'But a day came when I was delivered from agony. Only then did I learn that I had been taken to Etherhorde, and tortured in the bowels of Castle Maag itself, somewhere beneath those pretty walks and gardens. Word of me had reached the admiralty, and Emperor Magad surrendered me to my brothers-in-arms. Above all he feared a soldiers' revolt. He got it anyway, of course.'

'It's gone that far, has it?'

'Much further, in fact. Burn the Lord Admiral and his son to death in their kitchen and you'll pay, even if you do wear the crown.'

'Night Gods, Commodore!'

Darabik shook his head. 'A shameful tale, and a long one. The point is, there was a revolt: nearly a third of the Home Forces abandoned the Usurper, fled west, and joined Maisa's campaign. I went with them, and have been fighting ever since. In that time I have won more battles than I have lost. But things have changed recently, and not for the better. Captain, you must make for Serpent's Head.'

The gathering of Maisa's forces was to occur on the fifth day of Teala, barely one week away. They could still make it, said Darabik. Fiffengurt reminded him that their task was to rid Arqual of the Nilstone, not the Emperor of Arqual.

'Yes, the Nilstone,' said Darabik uncertainly. 'Prince Eberzam spoke of it with dread. I still don't know what exactly it is.'

'And you don't want to,' said Fiffengurt. 'You've got the Gods' own luck anyway. We'll take you to Serpent's Head, by way of the archipelago. There's no safer course to Gurishal from here.'

Darabik had gone suddenly rigid. 'To ... *Gurishal*?'

Fiffengurt grinned the grin of a suicide.

'But that is madness, man. You cannot hope to slip past the Mzithrinis.'

'Hope? What's that? But you're right, Commodore. That's why Ott sent us off into the Ruling Sea to begin with, you know: to get around the White Fleet, and come up on Gurishal from behind.'

'Madness,' said the commodore again. 'Perhaps before the war, the western flank of Gurishal was left unguarded. But not today. The Sizzies know Ott wanted to give the Nessarim back their Shaggat – we told them, we announced it to the world! Every harbour is watched, and every approach. The whole island is under quarantine.'

Fiffengurt's grin was melting away. 'You can't quarantine an island that enormous,' he said.

'Can't you? If it's bursting with fanatics awaiting the return of the greatest mass-murderer in history?'

'Trouble is, Commodore, we *have* to go to Gurishal.'

'You can't.'

Darabik said no more, and Fiffengurt was left blinking at the sunset, and trying to calm his nerves. But when darkness fell, Pazel and his allies gathered in the wheelhouse and spoke to the commodore again. Darabik's mood had also darkened. He asked that they light no lamp. On that moonless night they could barely see his face.

'I told you we numbered ninety thousand a year ago,' he said.

'That is true, and I might have said more: we took Opalt, for a time, and held the mainland all the way to the banks of the River Ipurva. But this year the fight has gone poorly. Magad has turned the east into a war-making machine. We sink a ship, and two more launch from the Etherhorde shipyards.'

'North and South begin to mirror each other,' said Kirishgán sadly.

Darabik took no notice. 'The Mzithrinis are willing to sell us ships, but our coffers are empty,' he said. 'Without gold we are nothing to the Black Rags. Lately they have seen fit to drive us from their waters, into the teeth of our enemies. And ... there is another rumour, though I do not know whether to believe it.'

A deep note of worry had entered his voice. 'Tell us,' said Ramachni.

Darabik hesitated, then his dark shoulders gave a shrug. 'A cloud that kills. They say it is as large as Bramian, and that in movement it is less like a cloud than a living thing. Nonsense, probably. Tall tales sprout like weeds in wartime.'

The allies sat in rigid silence, barely breathing, until Darabik asked them what was wrong.

All through the night the *Chathrand* sped west. With the first glimmer of dawn Fiffengurt sent men aloft to spread more canvas, indeed all the canvas she could bear. More rain fell, lashing and cold. More jagged islands appeared off the starboard bow. The ship followed these Baerrid Isles, tacking along one side of the snake. No one who had heard Darabik's words repeated them – the crew was close enough to despair as it was – but they could not stop themselves from glancing at the sky. The Swarm was here already, and it had grown huge.

The days passed, grey gloomy light. Between the wave-tortured islands the lookouts spotted ships, plying the calmer waters of the Nelu Rekere, but they were too distant to be identified. Darabik was confident that they were Maisa's forces, but Fiffengurt took no chances, and lit no flares. The nights were cool, but Pazel could not sleep. When he closed his eyes he felt the darkness crushing him, drowning him, a black wax pouring down from the sky.

In the outer stateroom Neeps and Marila shouted at each other, and some of the last dinner plates were smashed. The dogs howled and Felthrup wept. But late at night Pazel would creep out and find Neeps and Marila sleeping under the gallery windows, curled up together like children, arm in arm.

They are children. They were. All of us were, so recently.

Lying awake one night, Pazel saw a flicker of red in the window glass. He reached out a hand: the glass was trembling in its frame. Quietly, he left Thasha's cabin. In the outer stateroom he found Felthrup staring out at the *Chathrand*'s wake.

The rat crept to his side. 'You saw it too,' he whispered. 'We are almost there, Pazel. I can smell the reek of the volcano.'

They went above. The rain had stopped and the night was clear. There off the port bow stood Serpent's Head, a tall black mountain-mass, spitting fire in great arcs over the western ocean, like a queen throwing riches to a mob. Pazel could smell it now, too: the rotten-egg smell of sulphur, the world's carbolic breath.

The burning mountain terrified Felthrup. 'Why would anyone choose to hold a gathering *there*?' he asked.

'Because no one lives on Serpent's Head,' said Pazel. 'No villagers, no fishermen.'

'No one to talk about you later, to an enemy?'

'Or be tortured for their silence. That's my guess.'

For the rest of the night they watched the strange island grow nearer. Several times ash fell from the heavens, a black sticky snow. But Serpent's Head was not all smoke and fire: steep hills dominated the eastern half of the island, and at daybreak Pazel saw palm trees silhouetted against the sky.

There was also a ring of jagged islets about Serpent's Head: spires of magma, coughed out by the volcanoes over the centuries. By the growing light, Pazel saw that their course would soon take them between these islets and Serpent's Head.

'I'll be damned,' he said to Felthrup. 'Someone aboard knows this place. Look there, off to starboard. Do you know what that is?'

'A seagull?'

'A beach, Felthrup. Not much of one, but definitely a beach. And these little islets, they're as good as a sea wall.'

'Meaning that we could land a boat there?'

'We could try.'

A moist hand dropped on Pazel's shoulder. 'We *will* be trying, lad.'

It was Mr Druffle: stone sober, grinning. 'Don't look so shocked. The twenty-foot launch can handle these waves. At least that's the captain's expectorant.'

Pazel and Felthrup blinked at him. 'Expectation,' corrected Felthrup.

Druffle shrugged. 'Go roust your mates,' he said. 'Them as want to go ashore should assemble in ten minutes flat.'

'Ten minutes?' cried Pazel. 'But Mr Druffle, they're not even awake!'

'Tough blubber, my Chereste heart. Empress Maisa's officers are already landing on the north shore. It's five Teala: her war-council starts today. And sure, the waves are becalmed here, in the lee of them lava-isles. But there's a ripping strong current too. We can't hold position, unless we anchor, and what fool would anchor here? No, the ship's better off out in the Nelluroq, where she'll have no company. She'll circle round and collect us tomorrow, after we learn what Maisa's rebels can give.'

'But why not just head to the north shore ourselves?'

'Because we're a weird sight, that's why. Think, Pathkendle! This ship was at the heart of Magad's blary conspiracy, and no one's seen her in six years! We can't just pop up like the provisional weasel.'

'Provisional!' shrilled Felthrup. 'Sir, your imprecisions are disastrous. First of all, the word is *proverbial*. Second, there is no proverb; there is only a nonsense rhyme.'

'A school-master rat,' muttered Druffle. still grinning. 'Riddle out this one, then: *Froggy and field mouse walked to the fair. Froggy said to field mouse, 'Tie back your hair—'*

'Impossible!'

The argument was cut short by the peal of the ship's bell. At once boots began to pound, and orders began to fly: mainsails in, capstan teams to their stations! Fegin blew shrill notes on his whistle. Mr Druffle slapped Pazel on the back.

'Get your mates on their feet! Bite 'em, pour soup on 'em, kick 'em 'til they curse! We're going ashore!'

The landing was dismal. The twenty-foot launch flipped in the breakers. Groping at the hull in the icy froth, Pazel watched their food parcels sink like stones. The next wave lifted him, thrashed him down, ground him between the boat's gunnels and the sand. Pazel just waited; the sea shrugged the boat aside. When he stood the wind's bite was colder than the sea's.

They fought the vessel ashore, counting heads. Druffle, Darabik, Thasha, Neda, Neeps, Bolutu, Hercól, Kirishgán: no one was missing; everyone was bruised. Neda spat a mouthful of sand and blood; Neeps kicked the boat, then cursed and grabbed his foot. Darabik cursed with more flair and passion than Pazel had ever heard in an officer. It was his second dunking in a week.

Only Ramachni was dry: he had leaped from the boat in owl-form, glided to the beach, and resumed his normal shape. He watched their struggle from atop a warm-looking stone.

'I did call for the forty-footer,' he said.

'Go to the Pits,' said Thasha.

Hercól laughed aloud. 'No harm in a brisk morning swim. But for the sake of our more delicate comrades we should get out of this wind.'

'And across this mucking island,' said Darabik. 'Her Majesty's council is surely already convened on the north shore. If you truly mean to attempt this lunacy involving Gurishal, you will need all the help we can provide.' He shook his head. 'Of course, it will not be enough.'

'Walk now, and mope later,' said Druffle. 'Follow me, shipmates! Never mind your little bumps!'

His good spirits did not flag as he led them inland. He claimed to know Serpent's Head – it was a famous stop for smugglers – but could that account for his glee? Now that Pazel thought about it, Druffle had been grinning since the rescue of Darabik's men. Now he walked along laughing softly to himself, and making a happy buzzing sound in his throat.

It was an exhausting morning. Though not mountainous, this end of Serpent's Head was mostly desolate, criss-crossed with dry rivers of lava twisting down like mammoth tree-roots from the heights. There were cracks and fissures and bare bulbous hills. Above them, the volcano moaned and hissed.

But the trees Pazel had seen were real too: they stood in clumps like islands in the dead landscape, oases spared by chance. There were young palms and rugged tree-ferns, vines and sprays of scarlet flowers, hummingbirds and ants. Pazel found them all the more lovely for their delicate, doomed courage. As for Mr Druffle, he ran up breathlessly to each oasis, studying the treetops. Each time this happened his smile faded, only to break out again as his eyes moved to the next clump of trees.

Thasha was questioning Darabik for the twentieth time about her father. 'Yes, m'lady, I do expect him,' said the commodore. He allowed himself a grudging smile. 'Needless to say he won't be expecting *you*.'

'Will he be coming ashore?'

'Will he! I'd like to meet the man who could stop him! No, the admiral never waits for us to secure an island. With the deepest respect, Lady Thasha, your father is an impossible man.'

'It runs in the family, Commodore,' said Pazel, dodging Thasha's fist.

For five hours they trudged and scrambled. When they grew thirsty Druffle showed them how to suck dew from the fern-fronds. There were no trails, but now and then they passed small mounds of clam shells. Druffle claimed they were trail markers, and over time he was proved correct: the mounds led them sensibly enough through the lava-maze.

'I can hear the surf on the north shore,' said Kirishgán. 'When we pass over that next hill I think we shall see it.'

The hill in question was large and crowned with a particularly lovely stand of trees. They began to climb, drinking in the birdsong. Pazel turned and looked back to the south. He could see the coast in the distance, but not the *Chathrand*: she was gone until tomorrow at the earliest.

Suddenly Druffle exploded: 'There! There! D'ye see it? Sweet teacups in heaven, my darlings! It's honey!'

He dashed up the rest of the hill, and before anyone could stop him began to scale a palm. In his manic state he had found the agility of a young man, if not a monkey. Pazel shielded his eyes: near the fronds at the treetop, bees were boiling. The others saw them too, and they all shouted warnings. But Druffle paid no heed. Up the tree he went, straight to the hive, and when he reached it he plunged in his hand to the wrist. Drawing it out again, he held up a mass of something sticky and pale. He took a great bite of it and hooted with joy.

'What did I tell you? Island honey! Straight from the fuzzy arses of the gentlest creatures in Rin's green earth. Stingless bees! What do they need stingers for, eh?'

Pazel was laughing in spite of himself; most of the others were as well. 'Blary lunatic,' said Neeps.

'Come and taste, come and taste! They don't need stingers. No bears in the islands to steal *this* gold. Only me, only lucky Druffle, whose dream just came—'

A sharp sound. Druffle's back arched terribly. He fell forward, the honey-hand still raised, and as he dropped Pazel saw the arrow buried deep in his ribs.

'Oh Gods, no!'

Pazel and Neeps raced up the hill, deaf to the shouts of those behind them. It occurred to Pazel that he might be running towards his death. He could not stop. Druffle, the hapless fool, lay writhing on the ground. The arrow had passed through him. It was holding his chest off the ground like a stilt.

As the boys reached the man, a dark-robed figure burst from the underbrush. Pazel saw the flash of the falling sword and tried to dive away. Too slow. This was death.

Steel met steel with a clang.

Hercól. He had stopped the killing blow with Ildraquin, and now he leaped and dealt the man a lashing kick to the chest. The dark-robed attacker was no clumsy fighter, however; he absorbed the blow and spun around to strike again, expertly, his sword making an arc for Hercól's chest.

Once more Hercól was faster. Ildraquin flew up, inside the arc of the other weapon. Hercól's sword barely slowed as it severed the man's arm. Pazel did not see the downward stroke that followed. But he heard it, and saw the man fall headless to the ground.

The hilltop was suddenly swarming with men. Druffle wheezed. Blood was foaming about the wound: a pierced lung, Ignus would have said. Pazel pressed his hands about the wound, and Druffle raised a weak hand as if to help him. The honey-coated hand. A few harmless bees still crawled on his flesh.

Druffle lay still.

Pazel wondered at his own dry eyes. This man who had purchased him from slavers. Who had been a slave himself, to Arunis. Who had played the fiddle like an angel and swilled liquor like a fiend. Who had escaped all his tormentors, tasted sweetness one last time.

He looked up. No one was fighting. Sixty or more dark-robed fighters stood about them in a circle, swords pointing inwards. Men and women, with kohl dabbed on their cheekbones and tattoos on the backs of their necks. The Mzithrinis had been lying in wait.

The landing party was disarmed and made to kneel. Their hands were tied behind them, and their ankles bound fast. Six guards surrounded Neda, who was face down in the dirt, with a female soldier's boot on her neck. The Mzithrinis retrieved the severed arm and head of the man Hercól had killed, washed them with oil and bore the corpse into the trees. Druffle's body they left where it lay.

Pazel glanced around. Ramachni was nowhere to be seen.

Their captors still had not addressed them, but they stared with frank astonishment at Bolutu and Kirishgán. Pazel caught their whispers: 'What in the black Pits of damnation *are* they? Demons in the flesh? Can they work curses with those eyes?'

'Brothers, listen to me—' Neda began in Mzithrini. Their captors barked at her to be silent, and one kicked her in the side.

An hour passed. They were given water and moved into the shade. Despite their shock at encountering a dlömu and a selk, their captors actually paid them little attention: they appeared somewhat preoccupied. About half had vanished into the trees atop the hill.

The sun sank low. The volcano moaned and rumbled. At last Pazel heard footsteps approaching, and a Mzithrini officer in a spotless black-and-red uniform stepped out from among the trees. His face unreadable, his movements precise. The guards snapped to attention: the man was evidently of some rank. An aide approached and handed him a ledger-book. The officer glanced from the book to the captives and back again, several times. Then he nodded and walked up to Pazel's sister. The female soldier took her boot from Neda's neck. The officer pointed at Hercól.

'This man killed our brother in fair combat, and to save his friend. That is no dishonour, and he need fear no special punishment. Inform him.'

Neda looked up at Hercól. 'He says—'

'I understand you, sir,' said Hercól in Mzithrini.

The officer whirled. 'You as well! Do you *all* speak our tongue?'

'No, brother,' said Neda. 'Only he and—'

The officer spat in her face.

'Call *me* brother, will you? A rebel *sfvantskor* gone over to the Arqualis!'

Neda's eyes blazed with fury. She tried to rise, but six sword-tips jabbed at her, and the female soldier pressed down again with her boot. Neda spoke through the mud and grass about her face. 'I serve no Arquali, now or ever—'

'Bitch in heat. You lie.'

'I was sent to kill them,' said Neda. 'I failed. They took us prisoner.'

'Which is why you laughed at the fool in the tree, and gazed at this swordsman with open lust. Keep silent, vow-breaker, or I will cut those ensigns from your flesh.'

He meant her tattoos, Pazel realised with horror. Neda twisted beneath the soldier's boot, glaring up at him fearlessly. But she held her tongue.

Hercól's eyes were no less deadly, though his voice was controlled. 'You call her vow-breaker,' he said, 'and you are right: she is that. But it is a greater crime to raise youths in a windowless cell, and then demand vows pertaining to the world beyond. Those who break such vows may be many things, but they are never weak.'

'Where did you learn Mzithrini?' demanded the officer.

'In my own windowless cell. From my old masters, and your arch-enemies, the Secret Fist. I too broke certain vows. I was expected to use my life to kill your people, to destroy your country from within.'

The officer held his gaze for a long moment. Then he turned and studied their faces one by one. 'What are these creatures?' he said.

'The black man is a dlömu. The other is a selk. They are no more your enemies than—'

'Shut up.' The officer pointed at Druffle's corpse and addressed his men: 'Bury this one. Mark the spot.' Then, speaking once more to Hercól, he indicated Darabik.

'That man is too old to fight. He was not guiding you, like the idiot in the tree. He carries himself like a general. Is he in command?'

'We have no commander ashore,' said Hercól.

'Then you have no commander at all.'

Hercól frowned.

'You doubt me?' said the officer. 'Very well: untie their legs. Hold the swordsman and the traitor-girl like the deadly snakes they are. All of you, get up.'

Legs freed but hands still tightly bound, the captives rose stiffly to their feet. The officer led them into the greenery, along a trail beneath the palms. Within, the evening shadows were already dark, but Pazel caught glimpses of many warriors: resting, eating, sharpening their swords. The captives filed past them in silence, nudged on by the blades of their guards.

When they emerged from the oasis they stood on the hill's far shoulder. The officer stood aside, and the captives gasped. The whole north side of the island spread below them, all the way to the coast of the Narrow Sea, and there—

Aya Rin!

Ships beyond counting, slaughter beyond words. At first Pazel could see no order in any of it. Large vessels, smaller ones, burning, blasting, listing, going down. Flashes of fire, wreaths of smoke.

'Startling, isn't it, how little one hears?' said the officer. 'Blame the west wind for that, and the volcano of course.'

Pazel's eyes began to sift what he saw. There was a huge force of heavy warships pressing south, towards Serpent's Head and the westernmost isles of the archipelago. It was easily the largest flotilla Pazel had ever seen in the Northern world, and it was decimating a force about one-third its size. The latter ships were in disarray. Some were tacking west, into the wind; others had turned to engage their enemies head-on. A few were fleeing south between the islands, towards the Ruling Sea. The fight was not completely one-sided: vessels on both sides were burning, sinking. But Pazel could see no hope for the lesser fleet.

'You are witnessing the end of an insurgency,' said the officer. 'The smaller force is trapped between the Nelluroq and Magad's great flotilla. They have been dying all morning, and will go on dying through the night.'

No one in the landing party could speak. Pazel could hear the cannon-blasts, now, just barely, over the rumbling of the volcano.

He felt dizzy, defeated. On his left, Commodore Darabik's face was ashen, and Hercól too looked appalled.

'They fight bravely,' said the Mzithrini officer. 'They have stung Magad's fleet, and will keep on doing so until the very end. Yes, they certainly have heart. Everything else, of course, is against them. Wind, numbers, ammunition, luck. Some have managed to reach the shore, after their boats were pulverised. They will die tomorrow. Magad has men enough to flush them out like rats, once the sea battle ends. And do you know who they are, those rats? Maisa's rebels. The remains of her naval forces. They were planning to gather here, to regroup and try once more to topple the canni-bal-king. But then you know all this. You're Maisa's agents too.'

No one denied it. Commodore Darabik walked forward, drag-ging his feet. 'We were betrayed,' he said. 'The Usurper knew about the gathering of our forces. He *knew*.'

Hercól looked at the officer. 'Magad's land forces will find you as well, tomorrow,' he said.

'Perhaps,' said the officer calmly. 'We may be forced to surrender to the cannibals. For an hour or two.'

He turned and pointed to the northwest. There was rain and haze in the distance. 'You cannot see it, yet, even with a telescope—'

'I can see it,' said Kirishgán. 'Another fleet, even larger than this one. They are fierce vessels, all painted white, and bristling with cannon, every one. There are many men aloft, but they have spread no canvas. The fleet is standing still.'

Once more the officer was stunned. 'Feather eyebrows and eagle eyes,' he said. 'Yes, our White Fleet is coming. Not to rescue Maisa's rebels – that is no task of ours – but to destroy the Arquali navy, which is a force for evil in this world.'

He gestured at the hill nearest to where they stood. It was barren, but at its peak lay an enormous mound of sticks and palm fronds. 'Soaked in chemicals, special chemicals that burn long and bright. We will watch the battle, and when Maisa's rebels have done us all the good they can do, we will light this beacon and summon our fleet. By then it will be past midnight, and Arqual will be wounded, tired, short of ammunition. Then it will be Arqual's turn to be caught between the hammer of a stronger enemy and the anvil of the Ruling Sea.'

'You did this,' said Pazel. 'You told Arqual where Maisa's forces were gathering.'

'Fool,' said the officer. 'We will not shed our blood for your rebellion, but why should we help Arqual to crush it? No, the Secret Fist learned of this gathering all by itself. After years of blundering along without Sandor Ott, it seems they are once more a functioning spy agency. You can't lay the blame on us. Now then—' he turned and raked them all with his eyes '—tell me how you came to be here, and who exactly you answer to in Maisa's ranks.'

There was a long silence. Darabik broke it at last. 'I serve under Her Majesty's royal husband, Prince Eberzam Isiq. This girl is his daughter, who was the Treaty Bride. They are all crew on the Great Ship, the *Chathrand*, which has just returned from across the Ruling Sea.'

At first the Mzithrinis just stared at them, lost. Then as one they roared with laughter. Even their commander gave in. 'Of course,' he wheezed, drying his eyes. 'Why didn't I guess? And this explains why so many of you speak our language. And why a lapsed *sfvantskor* travels with you. And why the idiot was hooting and signalling from the tree.' He waved at his men. 'Go on, search the island. Maybe Empress Maisa herself is down there somewhere, wandering among the rocks.'

'I'm Thasha Isiq!' shouted Thasha, enraged.

This nearly finished them. 'She got the name right, Captain!' said one of the soldiers. 'It *was* Thasha, the girl who died in Simja—

'No, you ass, that was Paca, Paqui, something—'

'Syrarys! Syrarys Lapadolma!'

'How can you be so *ignorant*?' bellowed Thasha. 'Syrarys was my father's consort, and she tried to kill us. Pacu Lapadolma was my maid-in-waiting, who took my place when I was nearly strangled. Have a look at my Gods-damned neck; you can still see the scars!'

Silence.

'Well, come on! It's not that mucking complicated!'

She had shouted in Arquali, of course. None of the Mzithrinis had understood her, but they had sobered nonetheless. 'She sounds just like him,' muttered one of the soldiers.

The officer rubbed his chin. He ordered Thasha gagged, and then walked away into the trees. Pazel could not see what was happening within the oasis, but a few minutes later he heard a number of people approaching, and the officer's voice.

'Turn him. The old fool's looking the wrong way.'

Then a deeper voice boomed from the trees: 'Oh Tree of Heaven! Oh sweet and merciful Rin!'

Crashing, stomping, and then out he came: a bald, barrel-chested man, trailing leg irons, trying to run in them, holding out his arms to Thasha. His tattered uniform trailed leaves and vines. He didn't notice. With a flick of his hand he tore Thasha's gag away, then knelt and embraced her. Thasha, hands still bound, laid her cheek atop his head and wept.

'Prahba.'

'My darling girl, my beauty—'

Eberzam Isiq. Pazel had thought of him many times since the Red Storm. The admiral had looked old and unsteady since Pazel's first glimpse of him on the quay in Etherhorde. But now if anything he looked six years *younger*, not older. His flesh had colour; his limbs looked strong and hale.

He's free of the deathsmoke, Pazel realised. *No one's poisoning him any more.*

'Thasha, Thasha,' said Isiq. 'I let them hurt you, take you from me, I'll never ask you to forgive—'

Thasha *shh'd* him through her tears. Pazel wished he could blow everyone away from the spot, give them this moment, let them be alone together for a time. Isiq rose to his feet and pressed her cheek against his breast. Only then did he take in the rest of them.

'Stanapeth! Undrabust! Pazel Pathkendle! Bless you, Darabik, you found them!'

'They found me, Your Highness,' said the commodore.

The Mzithrinis were wonder-struck. 'You really are Thasha Isiq,' said the officer. 'Is the rest of your mad story true?'

Isiq was looking straight at Pazel. Uncertainly, he extended a hand. Pazel stepped forward and gripped it, not a handshake but a tight, fierce clasp.

'You gave me your promise,' said the admiral. 'In Simja, on the road from the shrine. I asked you to protect her—'

'I remember,' said Pazel.

'I meant her body. I thought it was a dead girl you were carrying away.'

'Yes, sir.'

'You've stayed with her. You all have. You've kept my angel safe.'

'Oh, *Prahba*,' said Thasha, laughing through her tears.

'We've helped each other, sir,' said Pazel, 'and Thasha's done more than anyone.'

'We feared for *your* life as well, Admiral,' said Hercól. 'For a time, Neda and Pazel's dreams brought us glimpses of you, or at least of their mother's thoughts of you.'

'Many thoughts,' said Neda, in her broken Arquali. 'Always good thoughts, loving.'

Isiq looked at her, and seemed astonished both by her words and by the fact of her existence. 'If Rin takes me today, I will die a happy man,' he said.

Then the distant explosions reached his ears. For the first time he raised his eyes to the battle, and Pazel watched horror change the admiral's face. His lips trembled. He shook his head, imperious, helpless: this thing must not be.

'Now he knows why I kept him away in the palms,' said the officer, not without sympathy.

Isiq looked at the officer, then at Pazel. 'He must stop this. Tell him, Pathkendle. If Maisa's navy is destroyed she will never recover, never take the throne of Arqual. Emperor Magad will be stronger than ever, and so will his will to destroy the Mzithrin. Tell him I'm begging, begging him to signal his fleet.'

Pazel took a deep breath, and repeated the admiral's words in

Mzithrini. The officer shook his head. 'I have lived to see things beyond the visions of the seers,' he said. 'Admiral Isiq himself, begging the White Fleet to destroy the Arquali navy. Tell him not to worry: destroy it we will. But as for his rebellion: too late, too late. Even if I lit that beacon now, there would be little left of Maisa's forces by the time they arrived.'

'You wouldn't have to arrive,' said Pazel. 'Just bring your fleet close enough for Magad's forces to notice. They'll have to break off fighting the rebels and sail north to face you. Or turn and run.'

The officer smiled. 'Ah, but we don't want that, do we? You are forgetting the hammer and the anvil. Magad's forces have your rebels where they want them: we will engage Magad in the same place.'

'There is more at stake here than one victory at sea!' said Hercól. 'If Empress Maisa fails, so too does the best chance for peace between the Empires. Maisa has sworn to end the conflict, to make peace once and for all.'

'The famous Arquali hunger for peace,' said the officer. 'Perhaps she will suggest another treaty-signing on Simja. Enough! You will tell the rest of your story to my lieutenant. Your presence here changes very little – although I grant you have made this day … stranger.'

'Things are even stranger than you suppose,' said Ramachni.

The soldiers whirled; blades whistled from sheaths. The mage was seated on a rock some ten feet away. The red rays of sunset glowed in his eyes. 'Hold your fire,' he said. 'I make a much better friend than foe.'

'A woken animal,' said the officer, 'what next? Come down from there, little circus-freak, before we put a shaft through your heart.'

Ramachni stood up slowly, eyes locked on the commander. 'If you think that you will slaughter *me* as you did our harmless companion, you are mistaken,' he said.

Nothing obvious had changed, but somehow Ramachni seemed larger, and in his stillness there was something of a threat. The

Mzithrinis glanced nervously at their commander. He too looked shaken, but he stood his ground.

'If you're not a woken animal, what in the Black Pits are you?'

'An ally, if you will permit it,' said Ramachni. 'Our tale is true, Commander, and the *Chathrand* has returned. You must have heard of the conspiracy that sent her forth. But you cannot possibly grasp the doom that calls her back. The Swarm of Night has been unleashed on Alifros. To defeat it we must make a landing on Gurishal, at a place marked by a sea-rock called the Arrowhead.'

The officer shook his head in disbelief. 'That is a declaration of lunacy.'

'I am quite the sanest person you are likely to meet,' said Ramachni.

'You're not a person at all,' said the officer, 'and Gurishal is sovereign territory of the Pentarchy, despite its occupation by the Shaggat heretics. We do not let enemies parade through our waters.'

'You could help us,' said Pazel.

'Certainly,' said the officer, 'if I were a traitor, and in want of a swift execution.'

'They *could* help us, you know,' said Pazel, glancing at Ramachni. 'They must have a vessel hidden somewhere. They could escort the *Chathrand*.'

The soldiers laughed again, and even the officer smiled as he turned away. 'No more,' he said. 'I have a battle to observe.'

'The carnage below means nothing,' said Ramachni.

The officer glanced at him again. 'Nothing, eh? You jabbering freak. By dawn tomorrow, the balance of power in this world will have shifted for ever.'

'Yes, I fear so,' said Ramachni.

His unblinking eyes remained fixed on the Mzithrini commander. On the next hill, a spark leaped to sudden life, and with a *whoosh* the oil-soaked mound of brush went up in flames.

*

The officer's response was commendable, Pazel had to admit. He did not kill anyone. Indeed he ordered no reprisals, although it was clear that his prisoners were somehow to blame. His only command was to attack the beacon-fire, to smother it, drown it, snuff it out. The task proved impossible, however. The 'special chemicals' were everything the man had claimed. The fire roared like a blast furnace; the soldiers could do nothing but watch. From out at sea it might have appeared that a new and tiny volcano had erupted in this quiet end of Serpent's Head.

Kirishgán looked into the distance. 'The White Fleet is setting sail,' he said. 'Already the vanguard is heading this way.'

'They were prepared,' muttered the officer, snapping open his telescope. As he studied the horizon, he ordered his men to break camp. 'The Arqualis will see the fire too, and mark the spot. No sense waiting for them to come ashore and investigate. We'll sleep tonight at Yellow Cliff.' He turned to Ramachni. 'Well, mage, you've proved you can light a match at fifty paces. Any other tricks at your disposal?'

Ramachni just showed his teeth.

'Do you intend to fight eighty soldiers of the Pentarchy? For that is the only way we will give your prisoners up.'

'I will not hold you to that boast,' said Ramachni, 'but I will not fight you either – yet.'

The officer shrugged, then gestured at the prisoners. 'Get some food in their mouths, unless you want to carry these lunatics.'

Once more Pazel was amazed by his calm. The soldiers brought them meat and bread, and then marched them, at the centre of the battalion, down the hill and back into the maze of rocks and lava-flows and gullies. The soldiers walked in single file. Ramachni scrambled alongside the column, always safely out of reach.

Darkness came quickly. Hands still tied, the prisoners stumbled often on the rugged ground. They were marching generally uphill, but avoided peaks or vantage points of any kind, and Pazel soon lost all sense of where they were. He slogged on, footsore and anxious. He thought the commander had probably ordered Druffle's killing in the same casual way with which he had called for his telescope. The only passion the man had shown was his contempt for Neda, whom he had looked ready to kill.

Hours passed. Pazel's wrists and shoulders went from painful to numb. The moon rose but vanished at once into dense clouds. Occasionally, by the light of particularly powerful lava-bursts, Pazel saw that they had indeed climbed much higher into the volcanic foothills. He never once glimpsed the sea, but at some point late in the night Ramachni called out to them softly in the tongue of Arqual:

'Do not give up! Magad's forces spotted the White Fleet before darkness fell, as I hoped. They have ended their attack on Maisa's ships, and are regrouping to face the new threat. Alas, most of their work was done. Many lives have been saved, but the Empress has lost her navy, or the bulk of it.'

'What about the *Chathrand*?' Pazel whispered. But the soldiers hissed for silence, and Ramachni said no more.

One more weary hour, and they reached a stand of tall pines, and pitched camp. It could not have been more than an hour before dawn, but the darkness was nearly absolute, and the Mzithrinis did not so much as strike a match. The prisoners were chained together by the ankles, and the ankle-chains secured to the trees. Only then were their wrists untied. Pazel collapsed among his friends, and thought the pine needles beneath him the most perfect bed he had ever known. He heard the soldiers murmuring, something about the war's approaching end, but before he could consider just what they meant he was asleep.

Drowning. Sinking. Buried alive.

Pazel woke with a gasp. A dream, horrible and vague, a sense of being crushed beneath some monstrous weight. He sat up. There was daylight, but it was dim and strangely sidelong. In the trees, birds sang uncertainly. Was it morning or not?

The air was distinctly cold. His friends were waking, moving slowly in their chains. All the soldiers were on their feet. Something was very wrong. They were peering up at the sky, and even by the faint light Pazel could see that they were afraid. He stood, felt a cold claw in his stomach. The weight of the air. The pressure, the chill.

Neeps rose beside him, steadying himself on a tree. He gave Pazel a look of knowing dread. Beside them, Thasha's father was fumbling on hands and knees. 'What is it, boys, tell me!' Not a prince or an admiral in this moment, just an old man in chains.

'The Swarm is here,' whispered Pazel. 'I think it's just above our heads.'

'The what?'

Ramachni crept from the shadows. 'Death has come between us and the mountain,' he said, looking up. And Pazel realised it was true: he could no longer hear the volcano. Only birdsong – that, and the pines, which were bending and creaking, although there was no wind.

The others were all awake now and struggling to rise. Murmurs of terror were spreading among the troops. Pazel could see their breath, white and ragged in the unnatural cold.

Suddenly all the birds fell silent. The Mzithrinis were whispering prayers. Then came a curious sound: a soft thumping, as if small purses were raining down on them by the score. It lasted just seconds. Pazel stretched out a foot, felt the tiny body, and knew: the birds had fallen dead from the trees.

A soldier bolted. Seconds later dozens of others followed his example, their comrades cursing and shouting *Come back, come back, you whimpering dogs!* Then the ones who had been shouting began to run.

For a terrible moment the prisoners were left alone, still shackled to the bending trees. Then a pair of soldiers came crashing out of the gloom, and one of them began to unlock their leg-irons. 'You must go to the commander,' he shouted. 'This way, near the overlook. Run!'

Soldiers and captives blundered through the pines. Ahead the light was a little stronger – and the hideous underbelly of the

737

Swarm more plain to see. It was combing the treetops, flowing north like a suspended tide. A black tide, pulsing, animate, a tide of worms and flesh.

'Don't look, Admiral!' shouted Hercól, as he and Thasha supported Isiq by the arms.

The trees ended, and they stumbled out into a barren stretch of earth scarred with ashes and yellow, sulphurous stones. Pazel saw that they were on much higher ground than yesterday's hill. Just ahead, the commander and some twenty of his men were crouching near the top of a cliff.

In their eyes, naked horror. The hideous mass stretched for miles in every direction, over land and sea. It had flowed around the volcanoes to the west of them. South and east Pazel could see no clear border, just a pale glow near the horizon to prove it did end, somewhere. Only the Swarm's northern edge was plain to see, and this too was growing swiftly away from them.

'Now do you believe us, Commander?' asked Pazel.

The officer just stared up into the Swarm. He appeared to have lost the power of speech.

'Gods above, it's as big as the whole Rekere!' said Darabik.

'It has feasted on death since last we saw it,' said Ramachni, 'and it will soon do so again.'

They reached the cliff where the soldiers stood. Pazel looked north, in the direction the Swarm was growing: dark island, dark coast. The limping remains of Maisa's forces. Ten or fifteen miles of empty sea—

And there it was: the Swarm's prey.

Under vast clouds of cannon-smoke, the two greatest navies in the Northern world were blasting, pummelling, burning, and hurling every manner of deadly ordnance at each other. The Arquali loyalists had no intention of being pinned against the anvil of Serpent's Head. They had sailed out into the Nelu Rekere, engaged the Mzithrinis head-on. *The scale of it.* There was so much fire, so much flung iron and splintered wood, that Pazel wondered that the clash did not end instantly, each side torn to pieces by the other's onslaught. But in truth neither was prevailing. The Mzithrinis were more numerous, and the wind was still at their backs. The Arqualis had heavier armour, longer guns. Their attack formations had crossed, splintering. Masts had toppled; rigging burned in sheets.

'Commander, the mage is here!' said the soldier with the keys. Still the Mzithrini officer only stared into the Swarm.

'Mage,' said the soldier, 'did you summon this cloud? Banish it; banish it and name your price!'

Ramachni looked sorrowfully at the man. 'I did not bring it here,' he said, 'and nothing I can do will prevent what is to occur.'

The Swarm passed over Maisa's forces. It was accelerating as it neared the battle-front. Pazel felt its cold in his bones. He wondered how many of the sailors had noticed it, through that pall of cannon-smoke.

'Turn away, soldiers,' said Ramachni. 'Do not force yourselves to see this thing.'

Pazel reached out instinctively, pulling Neeps and Thasha close. He would not shut his eyes. How could they fight something they could not bear even to see?

The soldiers had forgotten them. They stood in a line along the cliff's edge, staring. The edge of the Swarm reached the first of the warships.

'No,' said the commander, suddenly coming to life. He gave a sharp gesture, then shouted: 'No! Men, men! This isn't going to happen, what you think is going to happen cannot possibly—'

The Swarm dropped.

It was a river pouring over a cataract, a curtain of gore, a great formless limb of the floating mass above. It fell to sea level, swallowing forty or fifty miles in an instant – and the battle was gone. No light or sound escaped. From the edge of the mass, dark tentacles groped across the waters, snatching at the few boats that had fallen outside the initial onslaught, dragging them within. Pazel couldn't move. He'd thought he was hardened to horror but this, but this. Someone was laughing, a sick sound like the whinny of a goat. Their commander buckled at the knees. A man was violently sick. The blackness throbbed and quivered; it was a diseased muscle, it was clotted death. Pazel heard his friends swearing, weeping, almost choking him with their arms, and he was doing the same, bleeding inside; was it over, was he allowed to look away? The Swarm twisted, writhed, and fragments of ship began to leak from it like crumbs through teeth. Make it stop. Make it end. From the men around him came sounds of lunacy and damnation; a soldier was eating gravel, a soldier flung himself over the cliff; others were crawling, fighting, shouting blasphemies, their faces twisted like masks.

The Swarm rose again into the sky.

Beneath it sprawled the remains of the warring fleets. Gigantic, mingled, dead. Some vessels were crushed and sinking; others were intact but drifting like corks. Not a gun sounded. The pall of smoke had disappeared. Every fire had been extinguished, and every life.

The commander had curled into a ball. He was pale and utterly still; perhaps he too was dead. Perhaps you, Pazel, are dead. No, no. Your mouth is bleeding, you've bitten your tongue and the blood is warm and trickling. You can taste it. You can kiss your friends and see your blood on their foreheads. You're alive.

The commander turned to look at Ramachni. 'Tell me exactly what you need,' he said.

34

⚊⚊

Monday, 22 Teala 947. Surely this is how men feel on the Redemption Path through the Tsördons, at the end of six months afoot, looking up at the last, steep slope of the Holy Mountain. *I can't climb that. I must climb that. If I climb another foot something in me will shatter. If I don't climb, Rin's light will never again warm my soul.*

We are that close, & that desperate. Sixteen days north from Serpent's Head, most of them in the Swarm's frigid shadow, fighting leaks we cannot locate, fighting scurvy, numb with fear. Who will remember for us? Not me, not good Captain Fiffengurt: I can't remember last night's dinner, though Teggatz has served the same three Gods-damned dishes for a month. A poor memory is one reason I fill these pages. Another is because the very hunt for words helps me stumble on through this fear. Towards what? An end to the Nilstone? A dream of Anni & our child, my seven-year-old boy or girl? Or the cold end of Alifros, the Swarm grown larger than the world it hovers over, the sun extinguished, the *Chathrand* crushed like an eggshell by the frozen sea.

In the year 900 I went ashore in Uturphe & paid eight pennies for a peep show, as tarboys will. When I stepped out again my mate said there were Mzithrinis in the city trying to burn the docks. We were thrilled. We raced each other to the port. I was fast then & left him behind, but I didn't know Uturphe & misjudged the distance. Before I knew it I was at the waterfront & there I saw a Mzithrini soldier gut a man like a mackerel. The victim was flat on his back & holding the killer's forearm as though offering assistance & his face was like a mackerel's too. The Sizzy glanced up at me & saw my abject horror & grinned. I ran & hid in a basement until Arqual retook the port. That was my first death. I thought I'd never recover, & in a sense I was right. The foolish, open-hearted scamp who ran to those docks vanished there; it was a changed, colder boy who got away.

Now look at the sea of blood through which he's passed. Hundreds slain on this voyage. The whole of humankind dead or mindless in the South. Dlömu killing dlömu, armadas burning cities, mages & generals wielding engines of death. In the North, a Third Sea War's raging, the 'Big One' of which we've all lived in fear. Now this. A levitating horror. A shapeless mass that swallows fleets, that has grown so large we have spent the last nine days beneath it, never glimpsing its edge. We are freezing & afraid. Night brings infinite blackness. Dawn brings a feeble twilight that lasts all day.

The *Chathrand* is talking to me: she is full off odd shudders, unsettling creaks. And her stern is riding strangely low. We shift ballast forward; she levels off. But the next day there is a hint of the problem once again. I cannot account for it: we have sprung no leak, & no cargo or armaments have been shifted to the stern. This is no crisis, yet, but it is a mystery, & one more nail in the coffin of my hopes for sleep.

What solace I find is in the new faces. We are part of a flotilla, now: five warships, nine lesser gunboats, twenty ragtag service vessels. That is all that remains of Maisa's great rebellion, or at any rate her navy. After the slaughter at Serpent's Head, of course, her loyalist enemies back home are hardly better off.

Admiral Isiq spent five days with us on the *Chathrand*, days in which he & his dear girl were inseparable, of course. Now Isiq & Commodore Darabik have gone back to *Nighthawk*, the rebel flagship. Still with us, though, are some hundred rebels, the vast majority from Etherhorde. Our homesick lads must be driving them to distraction, begging for stories of home. The rebels for their part listen to our talk of Bali Adro & Floating Fortresses with a weird mix of terror & resignation. They can't really doubt us, for just overhead is something stranger than any part of our tale. Something you could look at for a month & still think *That just can't be.*

A less enjoyable passenger is a certain stiff-necked Mzithrini commander, who was camped on Serpent's Head with a small battalion. I hate him: Bolutu tells me he shot Mr Druffle on a lark & tried to leave the rest of our people chained to trees. All the same, he had wisdom enough to hide his own ship (a sleek little gunboat with lovely lines) well out of the fighting, in a cove on the island's NW quarter. That vessel is our escort, now, & I am glad to have a Mzithrini in the lead as we sail into enemy waters.

Stiff-Neck is blunt with us, all the same: 'You are sailing to your deaths. The bulk of our navy has been destroyed, but what remains could still make a gruel of this little force. Around Gurishal we keep a wide perimeter guard, and a second patrol force near the island's shores. They will destroy you easily – unless the Swarm has devoured them all.'

Rin forgive me, I brightened at the thought, but Ramachni declared it all but impossible. 'That is not how the Swarm does its work. Look at Serpent's Head: men were still dying among Maisa's forces, but the Swarm passed over them, attacked the epicentre of death, and flew on in search of another place where the war was at its height. Always it hunts the largest prey. But that will only protect us while there is large prey left to hunt.'

'And the Nessarim?' added Stiff-Neck. 'Who will protect you from them? We control the seas, but they own the land, and guard it like war-dogs.'

'But this whatsit, this Arrowhead Sound we're making for – Neda says it's blary remote.'

'They will be there, regardless,' said Stiff-Neck.

After Serpent's Head we had a week of cold & blackness. Then a dawn came when even the Turachs wept with joy, for half the sky was free of the Swarm. That ugly malignancy had glided northwards, & its terminal edge was almost directly above us.

Here was a proof that raised our hearts: proof that the thing did not yet fill all the skies of Alifros. Proof that we were not too late. We felt the sun for a good eight hours before it drifted back again & plunged us into the dark. Now it has been nine days, & I begin to wonder if we shall ever see blue sky again.

It was in those eight bright hours that I made a play for Stiff-Neck's trust. Pazel's sister & Hercól urged me to it, & I see now that they were right. What we did was take him down to the manger, to the Shaggat's filthy lair. We let him bring his men-at-arms, but told them nothing before we arrived. Neda insisted on that point.

I unlocked the door & swung it wide. His Nastiness (as Rose called the Shaggat) stood in the middle of the chamber, wearing nothing but a rag about his privates, holding a large & soiled book. A massive chain linked his ankle to the stanchion. Chadfallow had fitted a brass cap over the stump of his left hand. The nails on his right were long & yellow, like the teeth of rats. He was glaring. He seemed somehow to be expecting us.

Neda was first into the room. But before she entered she spat on the threshold, rubbed the spittle with her boot, & spoke some words in Mzithrini in a kind of sing-song, like an incantation or a charm.

'That's him,' I said to Stiff-Neck. 'Your devil incarnate, your hated man.'

Stiff-Neck looked at me, scandalised. 'Liar,' he said. 'The Shaggat drowned forty years ago. Why do you Arqualis insist on peddling this tale?'

We filed inside. Neda's hand was on her knife-hilt. She glared at the Shaggat with a loathing that transformed her pretty face. The Shaggat did not move, but his eyes, like a marionette's, followed our every move. I found his calm almost as disconcerting as his frothing rage had been. Then those eyes turned on me.

'Warden,' he said, 'have you brought me the Stone?'

The Sizzies circled him, muttering, unable to look away. Neda spoke to them in their own tongue, & pointed to the Shaggat's tattooed neck.

'She speaks the truth,' said Hercól. 'Our ship was to convey the Shaggat to Gurishal, that he might lead his throng against you once more. We were a minority on this ship, but we fought their wicked plan from the start.'

'No one fights me,' said the Shaggat. 'Men and Gods, murths and demons: all are my tools. I use them, break them as I please. As I burned alive the army of King Morlach, and starved his masses, saving only the daughters for my legion's delight, so shall it be in this kingdom. And you who dream of opposing me, opposing your Living God, shall suffer first and longest.'

I saw belief dawning in the Sizzies' looks. Belief, & rage, & something else I couldn't yet identify. They kept their distance. When Neda spoke to them, they quickly shook their heads.

'You draw near Gurishal,' said the mad king, 'but I have flown ahead of you. Already I have touched my people, woken their anger, slain the faint-hearted, rewarded the bold. I am there, and in every land. You cannot escape me, Warden. All Alifros is mine.'

I cleared my throat. 'See here, Commander, I figure this man belongs in your hands—'

Stiff-Neck cut me off, his voice strange & thin. 'He calls you *warden* – that is a kind of jailer, yes? You kept this monster in secret. It's all true. Your depravity exceeds our wildest dreams.'

'The cold has come, and the darkness!' boomed the Shaggat suddenly. 'My wrath has brought them, and will devour you.'

'Oh shut up, it ain't your doing,' I said.

The Shaggat's eyes were still locked on my face. 'It is long since I saw you kneel,' he said.

'You've *never* seen it, you old bilge-mop.'

'Warden,' he said, 'I am going to rip open your skull, stake you writhing to the ground, slash your stomach open and pour in scalding—'

Neda gave an eagle's scream. She jumped high, turning in mid-air like a temple dancer, & as she came to earth she buried her knife in his chest.

The Shaggat gave a little cough, shut his eyes deliberately, & fell

745

forward, dead, with a crash that dislocated his jaw.

'*Partha*, it is done,' she said.

Hercól was the first to come to life, jumping between Neda & the Sizzies. I don't know what he expected, but their response floored everyone but Neda. They ran. Even the commander leaped for the door, naked fear in his eyes. Only then, after all this time, did I grasp the power of the Shaggat cult. These men had always loathed him & all he stood for. They'd all have sworn on their grandmothers that he'd died long ago – that was the official story of their faith. But they still feared him. They still thought he might be a God, or a devil. They expected us all to be blasted right out of the manger.

'Stay, stay!' bellowed Hercól. 'By the Unseen you revere, be brave! He was a man, nothing more, and now he is dead!'

The soldiers were out the door already. But Stiff-Neck raised his hands & grabbed the door frame, as though restraining himself by brute force. He struggled there a moment, then turned with a jerk to stare at the corpse.

'Your sister has killed the Shaggat Ness,' said Hercól.

The man was trembling, drenched in sweat. I didn't think he would ever find his voice. But at last he looked at me & spoke.

'Embalm him. Now, very quickly. Can you do it?'

'We can manage,' I said.

'And the knife: do not clean it! His blood, his blood must be left there, to dry.'

'I'll send for a coffin.'

He whirled on Neda, hissing something, & Hercól drew Ildraquin with a *swish*. But the man wasn't threatening her. Bending low, he touched her feet. Neda blinked in amazement & made him rise.

I got no more Arquali out of Stiff-Neck; he was too moved to use our tongue. But hours later over a cup of selk wine (the Shaggat in vinegar, Neda's knife sealed in a box), Hercól explained what had transpired.

'She gave them his death,' he said, 'but also his body. His

unmistakable body, with all its tattoos and birthmarks and legendary scars. The Mzithrinis have tried to stamp out the Shaggat cult for decades, Captain. But how do you prove a man dead without his corpse? Now that they have it, they believe they can at last eradicate belief in this madman, and heal their faith. Of course, none of this will matter, unless we triumph at Gurishal, and lift the curse of the Swarm.'

'What about Neda?'

'They are already calling her the Assassin, and speaking of her like a saint.'

Hercól looked a bit unsteady, & I told him so. He smiled wistfully.

'I am fond of the girl, that's all. I wish no destiny upon her, or her brother for that matter. They have both seen trouble enough.'

Fond of her, is he? Rin bless 'em both, though nothing is likely to come of it. Neda Pathkendle is still too much the Mzithrini, & Hercól likes his women small. As in eight inches.

'There's something else gnawing at you, though, ain't there?' I asked.

After a moment, he nodded. 'I have been to see my old master,' he said.

'What, you mean *Ott?* In the brig behind the Green Door and all?'

'I had to tell him, Fiffengurt. About what Neda did. All his life Sandor Ott has dreamed of destroying the Mzithrin. His plot was brilliant, to stoke the fires of the Shaggat cult to war again. But now it seems that all his effort could have the opposite effect. He has, perhaps, done them the greatest turn of any Arquali in history.'

'You said that to Ott, did you?'

'Not for gloating's sake. I merely needed him to see how things had ended.'

'What did he do?'

Hercól took a thoughtful sip of wine. 'He called me a traitor, as he always does. Then he sat down and wept.'

*

Thursday, 25 Teala. My worst fear is realised: the keel has cracked a second time. I can hear the rasping, the splintering, feel the shudder in the keelson when we crest. I do not know if the repairs in Masalym have failed, or the Nelluroq storms have broken her along some other part of her spine. Perhaps this is why her stern rides low? Who can tell? In these waters there's no hope of an inspection, let alone a patch. We must simply pray that her strength does not give out before the mission's end. Oh dear Grey Lady, what we've asked of you.

Friday, 26 Teala. The lamp oil is running out. We are freezing, groping about in the dark like human moles. Stiff-Neck frowns and paces the forecastle. He's in an odd fix: surrounded by enemies in his Empire's home waters, escorting a ship launched to destroy his people, guarding a corpse that could heal their divisions, racing with his foes against a common doom.

And there's more. At five bells today we passed an islet no larger than a castle & shaped like a broken tooth. The Sizzies took one glance at it & starting muttering afresh. Pazel listened in & reported to me: they knew that barren rock, & did not understand how we could be anywhere near it without encountering patrols.

Even with the damaged keel I have pushed the *Chathrand* to her limits, & we have left the other ships in our flotilla behind – all save Stiff-Neck's own vessel, & the warship *Nighthawk*, with Darabik at the helm. But just where are we? Stiff-Neck responds to my question with a stare, as though perhaps I don't deserve to be told. Then he grits his teeth & says, 'Close to Gurishal. Within days of her, in fact. They must have disbanded the wide-perimeter guard, to add more ships to the battle at Serpent's Head. But the inner guard still awaits us.'

Perhaps, but his men still gaze fearfully into the distance. And tonight there were strange lights to the north: bright flashes, orange & green. To my mind they were obscurely familiar.

Saturday, 27 Teala. Another black dawn, another day on sunless seas.

No land, no stars. Among the men, no talk or smiles or appetite. Felthrup & Marila are tearing through the pages of the *Polylex*, for what aid I cannot fathom. Thasha sits in her room facing the wall, Pathkendle says, with her face clenched in furious concentration. Lady Oggosk is praying on the quarterdeck.

In short, despair, & Captain Fiffengurt has no special immunity. But when I retreated to my cabin this evening I found a gift beneath my pillow, & I record it here as the day's token source of hope – and a peace offering, maybe. I know who brought it, though it came with no card. It is a great blue pearl.

Sunday, 28 Teala. Another glimpse of the sky: miles off to westward, and receding. It was night, but a little moonlight bathed the sea. How many has the Swarm killed, now? How many shiver beneath it, waiting for the end? And the animals: pity the creatures, mad with fear, running from the writhing mass above and never escaping. Off with this lamp now; my oil ration too is spent.

Monday, 29 Teala. I stood on the (slightly aft-tilted) quarterdeck & made a speech about the ixchel. How many are left alive (besides Ensyl and Myett) we do not know, I told them, but we must show forbearance if they appear again. The world is dying, I said, and I've reason to think they know it too. Let us be practical, I said. We may find they're a help to us in the final hour.

It was not a brilliant speech: I lack Rose's gift for rousing a crew. Mutterings & murmurs swept the topdeck. 'They have a talent for ship-sinking, Captain,' someone growled.

'Who do you think you're educating, damn you?' I fairly shouted, on the point of telling them about the *Adelyne*, my drowned uncle & his babe of three. Instead I just dismissed them, with a warning that the man who harmed an ixchel would answer to me.

An utter fiasco. If Talag was offering peace or help with that gift of a pearl, his spies will warn him now to keep his distance. I am a weak captain and a fool.

*

Wednesday, 1 Freala. Horror, horror. Very well, let it come. Annabel, you're the keeper of my heart; I close this journal until I hold you again, in this world or the next. We have reached Gurishal, but we are not the first. Macadra's ship is here, guarding the entrance to the Arrowhead Sound, & a demon crouches on the burning wreck of a Mzithrini patrol. They are waiting. They are daring us to approach.

35

Last Actions

—⚬—

'Just *bring* it, Hercól.'

Thasha plunged down the Silver Stair, not once looking back. From her tone Pazel knew she expected to be obeyed. He and Neeps raced after her, fighting through the press of sailors dashing to their stations. Over the drums and the bellowing of the officers, Neeps said, 'She's right this time. We all wanted her to drink off the wine, save herself from the poison. She said a day might come when we needed her to use the Nilstone again. Well this is the day, mate.'

Just before they entered the ladderway, Pazel felt Neeps grip his arm. The tarboy was gazing off to starboard at the dark shape of Gurishal. Or rather, above it.

'By the Pits, mate: those are *stars!*'

Pazel's heart leaped at the sight: ten, no, twelve stars, exquisitely normal, unbearably lovely, from a patch of naked sky. After a moment Pazel's eyes could make out the edge of the gap, round and ragged, in the fabric of the Swarm.

'That's a big hole,' he said. 'More than a hundred miles, I expect.'

Neeps looked at him soberly. 'It's big … unless it's *all that's left*. Unless the rest of the world is already under the Swarm.'

Pazel snorted, incredulous. Then he looked at the gap again, and shivered. Neeps could be right. But if that hundred-mile hole was all that remained, why would it just happen to be here, so close to them? Could the Swarm be avoiding Gurishal by some sort of instinct? He remembered how it had leaped from the River of Shadows in the heart of the Forest, at the moment Arunis brought it into the world. And there on Gurishal the River surfaced again, before it poured into death's kingdom. Could that portal be exerting some force that actually pushed the Swarm away? And if so, what effect might it have on the Nilstone?

Such questions would have to wait, he knew. They fought their way down the Silver Stair to the upper gun deck. Somewhere in the crowd, the Mzithrini commander was shouting: 'Why this panic? We are three warships, and she cannot manoeuvre with her back to the cliffs! Is the *maukslar* so very deadly?'

Neeps and Pazel stepped through the invisible wall and raced along the aft-leaning corridor to the stateroom. Most of their friends were already here. Thasha had gone straight to her cabin, leaving the door ajar.

'Macadra!' shrilled Felthrup. 'She is every bit as vile as her brother! But is she mindless, too? Can she be blind to the abomination above us?'

'No,' said Ramachni, from the bench by the gallery windows, 'but perhaps she believes that with the Nilstone in hand she can simply banish the Swarm. If so, she is deluded. The Swarm is close to swallowing Alifros, as a snake gulps down an egg. No spell will affect it now.'

'But how did they manage to repair the *Death's Head* so quickly?' asked Marila. 'They needed two masts just for starters.'

'They did not act quickly,' said Kirishgán. 'Don't you see, Marila? The sorceress needed only to choose a better moment than we did to plunge through the gap in the Red Storm. It was weakening, after all. For every day she waited, she could expect to reach this side *earlier*, not later. The *Death's Head* may have spent a month in some sheltered harbour in the Island Wilderness, cutting and fitting those masts, and yet arrived well ahead of us.'

'They made short work of the Mzithrini patrols boat, in any case,' said Bolutu. 'Who knows? Perhaps they have driven the Shaggat's worshippers inland, if there were any nearby.'

'Or enlisted them,' said Neeps.

Pazel moved to the gallery windows. The Arrowhead Sound. It

was a great fjord, wide at its mouth but narrowing as it pierced the towering cliffs of southwest Gurishal. And right in the mouth of the fjord stood the Arrowhead itself: a truly monstrous stone, the size of five hundred *Chathrands*. It had evidently once been part of Gurishal, for it stood as tall as the cliffs. But the rock had eroded from the waves upwards, leaving the base much thinner than the crown. The arrow was balanced on its tip.

He thought of his sister's words. The rock that ought to fall, but doesn't. The place the old masters went to die.

And from atop the Arrowhead, he knew, the *maukslar* was watching them. It had flown there, clutching a half-eaten Mzithrini sailor, when the burning patrol ship finally sank. You could see the demon plainly through a telescope, though not with the naked eye. The *Chathrand* stood four miles out, and Fiffengurt was keeping them here until they chose their next move. Pazel could see the *Death's Head*, however. She stood at anchor beneath that massive stone, as though tempting fate. They could not possibly enter the sound without confronting her.

Hercól arrived and made at once for Thasha's chamber. Pazel and the others followed. Thasha had opened the outer door of the hidden cabinet. The bottle of Agaroth wine stood on her desk beside the *Polylex*. On her bed lay the two halves of Big Skip's steel box and the gauntlets from Uláramyth. Thasha looked straight at Hercól and held out her hand.

Reluctantly, Hercól passed her the silver rod. Neeps was right: they had no choice but to prepare. Thasha had used the Nilstone twice already and survived. Once more and it would all be finished: the wine, the poison, the temptation.

Thasha turned the key in the round hole, then seized the handle and gave a fierce tug. With a shriek of metal the iron slab slid out into the room.

Everyone winced: the Nilstone was throbbing, blazing with an energy so fierce it was like the heat of a bonfire. And yet there was no heat. Pazel shielded his eyes. Was it because they were so near their goal, so near the end of the River of Shadows, so close to death's kingdom? Was the Nilstone reaching out for the land it came from?

Thasha returned the key to Hercól and put on the gauntlets. 'What do you mean to do, Thasha?' asked Felthrup.

'Show Macadra the Stone,' said Thasha. 'If she clears out I'll let her go. But if she so much as aims one cannon our way, I'll hit the *Death's Head* so hard she'll have nothing left to repair.'

'Alas for my brothers aboard,' said Bolutu. 'Some of them serve only out of fear or hunger, I expect.'

'Like soldiers everywhere,' said Kirishgán. 'But Lady Thasha, hear me a moment. Macadra will have mighty telescopes, and things more powerful than telescopes, trained on us. I do not think you should show her the exact location of the Nilstone.'

'Kirishgán's right,' said Pazel. 'Remember the *Promise*. She wants to take the Stone, not sink it to the sea floor. That may be the only reason she hasn't—'

A howl cut him off: a cry of abject terror from the topdeck, on five hundred throats.

'It's started,' said Hercól simply, leaping for the stateroom. The others followed. Through the gallery windows, Pazel saw that a ball of red fire had risen from Macadra's ship. It was hurtling towards them, slower than a cannonball but still very fast, illuminating the black underbelly of the Swarm.

'Away, away from the windows!' howled Felthrup. 'Thasha, call your dogs!'

Neeps was standing on the window bench. 'Get *down* from there, idiot!' screamed Marila, hauling at his arm. Neeps tugged his arm fiercely away.

'Look! That ball's off-target. It's going to miss us by a mile. Unless—'

The fireball screamed by the *Chathrand* to portside. There came a *boom* and a blinding flash. Literally blinding: Pazel groped forward, seeing nothing but white-hot stars. As his vision returned he saw that someone had thrown open the door to the reading room, which had a view to portside. Through the doorway he saw the

Mzithrini ship in flames. The ball, it seemed, had exploded against her stern.

The ship was devastated. Her sternpost split in two. The decks above the waterline were pulverised; the quarterdeck collapsed into the inferno below. Already the sea was gushing in through the shattered hull.

Oh Gods. All those people.

There were two hundred men on the Mzithrini ship.

'Now we know what happened to all those Mzithrini patrols,' said Marila.

Thasha looked Pazel straight in the eye. Her face was set, her look beyond fury. She removed the selk gauntlets, let them fall to the floor.

He almost stopped her, almost said *Wait* – but how could he? The next target would be the *Nighthawk*. What exactly were they waiting for?

They followed her back into the cabin. Thasha lifted the bottle from her desk and stepped in front of the pulsing Nilstone. Then she tore open the stopper, tilted the bottle to her lips and drank it dry.

Her gaze softened. She lowered the bottle and passed it to Marila. In the sudden silence Pazel heard Fiffengurt giving orders for a rescue operation. Thasha placed a hand on her chest.

'I'm … cured,' she said. 'The poison is gone. I can feel it.'

Pazel threw his arms around her, undone with relief.

'And if I touch the Stone again, I will die.'

The feeling of doom that gripped Pazel in the next few minutes was unlike anything he could recall. The dregs of the Agaroth wine had done their work, but had given Thasha no last moment of fear-lessness. She would never use the Nilstone again – not as Thasha, at any rate. And now they were helpless. Macadra had weapons they could never hope to match, and the *maukslar* as well. Pazel glanced at Neeps and saw an echo of his own shame. They had never admitted it, but they had counted on Thasha to save them once more.

755

'Say nothing about this,' urged Hercól. 'Let the men hope: if they cease to, we are finished.'

They sealed the Nilstone in the cabinet and returned to the top-deck. All was mayhem. Eight or ten lifeboats were already in the water, and the rowers were pulling with all their might for the Mzithrini ship, already more than half submerged. 'Hard to port, Elkstem, bring us up behind them,' shouted Fiffengurt. 'Mr Coote, the *Nighthawk* is following in our lee! Where's your blary signal?'

'Already sent, Captain. They ain't listening, is all.'

'Gods damn the old fool!' bellowed Fiffengurt. 'Does he want his people killed as well?' Then, seeing Thasha, he cried, 'Get up here, Missy, and show yourself to your father! He's watching us through a scope this very minute. Wave him off, for Rin's sake, before Macadra fires on the *Nighthawk*. One more boat can't help us now.'

Still in shock, Thasha hauled herself up the ladder. She took the signal-flags from Coote and mimicked his *Desist and withdraw* signal, her movements jerky, her face a blank. But the *Nighthawk* held its position, cannon at the ready, men-at-arms upon her deck.

The rescue effort, meanwhile, was well underway. The first life-boats were already reaching the Mzithrinis. Dlömu had swum ahead of them, seeking out the wounded and the weakening, pulling them towards the boats. And now the *Chathrand* herself was drawing near. Jervik was standing by with a stretcher-team. Accordion-ladders snaked down the hull.

Then the *Death's Head* fired again.

'Cover, cover, fore and aft!' howled Fiffengurt.

The fireball rose from Macadra's ship. But once again they were not the target. 'That one's for the *Nighthawk*!' shouted Coote.

It was all so swift. The fireball closed. Thasha cried out, the sound of a heart breaking if Pazel had ever heard it. And then, explosions – eight, twelve, sixteen cannon, booming from the stern windows of the Arquali warship.

Mere yards from the *Nighthawk*, the fireball disintegrated. Its flame swept on, parting like water around both sides of the hull.

But it had not exploded. It had been torn to bits, and the *Nighthawk* emerged from the short bath of fire apparently unscathed.

'What happened?' cried Ensyl, from Hercól's shoulder.

'I'll tell you what happened,' said Fiffengurt. 'Grapeshot! The admiral filled his stern chasers with grapeshot, and took that blary projectile apart! Rin's gizzard, he's a tough old bird!'

The 'old bird' did not need more urging to withdraw, however. As Thasha wept with relief, the *Nighthawk*'s mainsails rose and billowed, and the warship began to glide away from shore.

Pazel turned to face the Arrowhead, and the small, menacing shape that was the *Death's Head*. One ship had been driven off, another destroyed. And Macadra's vessel hadn't even moved.

Corporal Mandric appeared on the quarterdeck. 'Captain,' he said to Fiffengurt, 'my sergeant's advice is that we fall back too. Approach Gurishal from somewhere else, get the Nilstone ashore that way, carry it overland to this death-portal, wherever it is.'

'No, Mandric, we cannot withdraw,' said Ramachni. 'Have you forgotten how Dastu taunted us at the beginning? How he said that even those who studied Gurishal, and lived here, had never heard of that portal? We have no time to go searching, to fight our way up cliffs and through mountains, to say nothing of battling the Nessarim. It is darker today than yesterday. Tomorrow, the darkness may be complete. And remember that Macadra, too, must act before the Swarm kills us all. I do not think she will permit us to sail away.'

Ramachni looked at Hercól, Fiffengurt, and the youths in turn. Pazel gazed into his black eyes, breathed deep, and nodded.

'Captain—' he said.

'Save your breath, Pathkendle, I understand,' said Fiffengurt. Then, raising his voice to a roar: 'Mr Elkstem, bring us around if you please. Fegin, Coote, to your stations, and lit matches on the gun decks. This is it, gentlemen: we go forward, or we go down.'

They were a ship of lunatics, thought Pazel, and so much the better for it. The men perhaps only dimly grasped what they hoped to do in the Arrowhead Sound. But they knew the goal – to wipe away that hideous cloud – and they knew that death alone would follow, if they failed.

He and Neeps helped set the mizzen topsail. The *Chathrand* turned neatly, despite her wallowing stern, and began to plough straight for the *Death's Head*. From four miles out, it appeared that they could enter Arrowhead Sound on the opposite side of the great rock, avoiding Macadra altogether. But that would only have told the sorceress that she had nothing to fear – and a bluff, Hercól noted grimly, might be their only chance.

'But *is* it even a chance?' Neeps whispered to Pazel, tightening the sword-belt he had just strapped about his waist. 'Last time Thasha was here with the Nilstone in her hand, and Macadra saw her, sure as Rin makes rain.'

'I know,' said Pazel, sliding his own sword half out of its sheath. 'This may not fool anyone, but there's nothing else we can do, unless we bring Thasha up on deck waving a pumpkin.'

The tarboys were on the forecastle, gazing straight ahead. Thasha had agreed to stay below until the charge was over. As it would be, soon: the *Chathrand* was gaining speed. And now at last the *Death's Head* too was spreading canvas. Macadra had no intention of being pinned down against the cliffs. She was sailing out to meet them.

Three miles between the ships, now. Fegin blew his whistle, hustling a crowd of gawking steerage passengers below. Lady Oggosk stood alone by the mainmast, the high wind tearing at her hair and shawl. Refeg and Rer, for once, were already on deck, pacing, breathing like bulls. Someone had had the foresight (and courage) to wake them. Niriviel wheeled in circles overhead.

Pazel glanced around the deck. 'Where's your wife, mate?'

Neeps jumped, looked at him sharply.

'Pitfire, what's the matter with you?' said Pazel. 'Didn't you marry her? Didn't you *want* to?'

'Don't talk rubbish. Of course.' But Neeps' voice was bitter, and his eyes were cross. After a moment, he said, 'If you had to die for someone – no, forget that. If you had to die *next to* someone, are you sure you know who you'd choose?'

'Yes.'

Pazel's certainty did not help his friend at all. 'Well good for you, damn it, but I'm not such a – never mind, you can't – oh, *Gods damn it.*'

Neeps shut his mouth. Two miles. Pazel went to Hercól and borrowed his telescope. There were dlömic soldiers crowding the deck of Macadra's vessel, and standing thick upon her spars.

'They could be an amphibious unit, like the ones we fought at Cape Lasung,' said Hercól. 'That would be one way of taking the *Chathrand* without sinking her.'

'I guess we'll know,' said Pazel, 'if they start diving into the sea. But that's not what I'm worried about. Our stern is riding lower than ever. If they strike us there, who knows how fast we'd flood and sink? And it can't be the crack in the keel that's causing it – we'd *already* have sunk if the keel were that far gone. In fact we don't have a clue why it's happening.'

'I have a clue – or a guess at least.' said Ramachni. Pazel jumped: he had not heard the little mage approach.

'Tell me, then,' he demanded.

'Later, Pazel. Right now, I must ask you to remember the clock. Thasha's clock. If we should have to evacuate this ship, do not leave it behind. Remember that it belonged to my mistress.'

'That's a good reason to leave it behind,' said Pazel.

'Pazel,' said Hercól.

'Many things have failed to go as Erithusmé hoped,' said Ramachni, 'but that does not mean that she acted without reason. She always had a reason.'

Pazel looked away. He could not bear to think of Erithusmé. She was here, even now, a soul within Thasha's soul. And she could save them, slap the *Death's Head* away like a gnat. But it wouldn't happen. A wall no one could see or touch or explain had thwarted her, and now they stood alone.

'We will take it, Ramachni,' said Hercól.

'Good,' said the mage. 'And now I'd best be on my way.'

'*What?*' shouted Pazel. 'You're leaving *now*, by the festering Pits? Leaving us again?'

Ramachni just looked at him, unblinking. Then the cry went up: 'The demon, the *maukslar*! It's taken to the air!'

Pazel whirled. He could see it, a moving speck in the half-light, swooping towards them from the summit of the Arrowhead. When he looked for Ramachni again the little mink was gone, and a black owl was climbing into the sky above the *Chathrand*, making for the distant enemy.

'I'm a blary idiot,' he said aloud.

'But we tolerate you somehow,' said Hercól.

The *maukslar* was closing with frightful speed. Pazel could see the broad, leathery wings, the searchlight eyes, the sputtering glow of its fire-spittle. The owl that was Ramachni looked smaller and smaller as the two forms converged.

'Motion on the *Death's Head*,' said Hercól, his eye to the telescope again. Then his voice rose to a warning howl. 'Dlömu in the water! They're diving, diving by the score! Ah, *Dénethrok, take cover! They're aiming those Plazic guns!*'

The warning swept the ship. There were curses and terror, but no panic: the men had left that emotion behind. Pazel and Hercól stood their ground. Above them, the *maukslar* spat a huge glob of liquid fire, straight at Ramachni, but some unseen power summoned by the mage parted the fire in a wedge to either side of him, and the owl flew on.

The *maukslar* gave a sinuous twist. Ramachni swerved in answer, but he was too late: the creature was past him, hurtling for the *Chathrand*. Behind him, Neeps was shouting: 'Clear the deck, clear the mucking deck! It's going to burn us to a crisp!'

Sudden flashes from the *Death's Head*. Pazel and Hercól threw themselves flat as the thunder of cannon smacked the ship. But no fire or cannonball followed, no burning tar. Pazel rolled over to face the sky.

Oh, Gods.

Ramachni was diving, closing the gap. Even as Pazel watched he reached the *maukslar*, fanned his black wings – and exploded into *eguar*-form.

The *maukslar* screamed. The huge black reptile seized it with jaws and talons, and the two spun flailing in the air. No fire, demonic or otherwise, could harm Ramachni now. He tore at his foe, merciless and deadly. But he had not counted on the force of the *maukslar*'s own dive. They carried forward as they fell. Men screamed and dived for any cover they could find. The two creatures struck the deck just astern of the forecastle, like a bomb.

Fire and ruins were everywhere. Shrouds and bracelines snapped; the longboat was crushed like an eggshell; the jigger-mast collapsed into the sea. The two foes roared, rolled, twisted, an impossible writhing mass of flame and fangs and talons and blood. Sailors ran for their lives, hurling themselves down the hatches, even leaping over the sides. Pazel, Neeps and Hercól stood pinned against the bowsprit. Suddenly Pazel recalled the mage's words at Stath Bálfyr, after the killing of the sharks: *You must not depend on me if it comes to fighting again.*

That was exactly what they were doing. But how could they help? The eguar's fumes alone were so strong that men were dropping senseless at thirty feet.

The warring creatures rolled to the portside rail, splintering it to pieces, nearly toppling into the waves. Then the *maukslar* tore itself away from Ramachni and leaped upon the forecastle. Its tail crushed a sailor against the foremast, then wrapped around another and began to squeeze.

Hercól looked at Pazel, a strange twinkle in his eye. 'You're not a bad diver, Pathkendle,' he said.

'What?'

'Prove it again. Hold your breath.'

He took a great gulp of air and leaped to the attack. Terrified, Pazel knew he must find a way to do the same. He circled left. The *maukslar* was spitting fire at Ramachni, still below on the main deck, but its tail seemed to have a mind and malevolence all its own – that long, lethal tail which had plucked Big Skip from the bridge over the Parsua Gorge. The sailor tried to stab at the coils, but they tightened, crushing his chest. The tail let him drop and groped for another victim.

What it found was Ildraquin. Hercól brought the dark sword down in a flashing arc, biting deep into the flesh.

With an infernal scream the maukslar turned its fell eyes on Hercól. Bleeding but still serpent-quick, the tail circled his waist, raised him high and dashed him down against the deck. Hercól fought on even then, hacking with his one free hand.

Ramachni, seizing the moment, began to haul his elephantine body onto the forecastle. The *maukslar* tossed Hercól away and closed on him, hissing. Pazel saw his chance. He leaped once, twice, over the whiplash tail. Just as the *maukslar* crouched down to leap upon the *eguar*, Pazel stabbed downwards with his sword, two-handed, and pinned the demon's tail to the deck.

The *maukslar*'s lunge fell short. Recoiling with a scream, it tore Pazel's sword from the deck plank, struck him aside like a trifle, and spread its wings.

A roar. The *eguar* pounced. Its crocodilian jaws snapped shut on the demon's snake-like neck. Its talons shredded the wings, then gripped the creature's torso. It ripped. With a gush of black blood the *maukslar*'s neck parted from its body. It fought on, biting and snapping, as Ramachni thrashed it against the forecastle. At last the red eyes went dark, and the thing lay still.

Pazel fell on all fours, gagging. Everyone left alive on the forecastle was struggling to breathe. The eguar looked at the devastated ship, the burned and dying men. Its eyes turned last of all to Pazel. Then it leaped at him.

Pazel was knocked off his feet. The creature landed almost atop him, its toxic vapours like a blow to the stomach. Pazel's vision dimmed. *Ramachni*, he thought. *You're killing me. Why?*

A monstrous *crack* rent the air, followed by the pop and zing of snapped cables. The foremast fell and shattered across the *eguar*'s back.

The creature's legs buckled. With a groan of agony, it shrugged off the mast to one side of Pazel. It was bleeding, black blood that sizzled where it fell. One white-hot eye passed over Pazel, Hercól, Neeps, the whole of the ruined ship. Then the eguar leaped over the starboard rail.

Pazel tried to stand up, and failed. He crawled, and burned his hands and knees. Then Hercól loomed over him, wheezing, bloody from scalp to shoulders. Pazel felt the warrior lift him and begin to stagger away. The two most terrible languages his Gift had forced on him – those of the *eguar* and the demon itself – were roiling and seething in his brain:

I will never (ITHAPRIGAL codex of hatred heartsblood burning blistered eater of life) speak another (IMGRUTHRIGORHIDISH realms of damnation codex of pain) word (CURMASINDUNIK nine Pits nine lairs nine soul-shattered Gods Arunis among them eater of worlds kill the fair kill the gentle the morning mountains minerals rivers forests insects oceans angels newborns hope) for as long as I (codex of misery) live.

Hercól slapped him. 'Breathe, lad! Get that poison out of your lungs!'

Pazel gasped and bolted upright. The battle raged on. From the *Death's Head*, bursts of fire were still leaping, and now the *Chathrand* had opened up with her own forward guns. Along the rails, Turachs and ordinary seamen – and Mzithrinis, by Rin – stood with pikes in hand, ready to repel boarders, gazing down into the waves. They looked hurt and tired. How many had just been killed?

He became aware that his whole body was one agonizing itch. He turned and saw Neeps beside him, recking, vomit-covered. Simply disgusting.

'Hold still.'

Someone began to douse him repeatedly with seawater. Feeling stronger, he looked up to see Swift and Saroo, his old antagonists, gazing down at him with concern.

'I'm all right,' he said.

The brothers looked at him, a bit shamefaced. 'Yeah, *Muketch*, I reckon you are,' said Swift. They leaned down and helped Pazel to his feet.

The *Chathrand*'s guns were deafening: Fiffengurt was throwing everything they had into the forward batteries. Still the *Death's Head* came on: Pazel could see her white sails looming beyond the wreckage of the forecastle. 'How many dlömu are attacking?' Neeps bellowed in Swift's ear.

'Lots of 'em. Hundreds.'

Hundreds? Pazel looked at the ship's defenders, strung out along the rail. Where was his own sword? No time for it: he found a cutlass in a tangle of rigging, the hilt still smeared with the blood of the man who'd dropped it. Then he pushed his way to the rail.

The sea was full of dlömu, swimming as only dlömu could. The fastest were already close to the *Chathrand*'s pitching hull. The *Death's Head*, barely a mile off, was firing its regular guns, firing with a will. But something strange was happening: all the shots were falling hopelessly short. And some of the *Chathrand*'s defenders were putting down their pikes, and casting about the deck for other tools.

'What's going on?' he shouted.

A face glanced up at him: Mandric. 'Don't ye blary see, they—'

BOOM.

A great fireball rose from Macadra's ship. 'Oh hang me from Heaven's Tree!' snarled Mandric, as they dropped below the rail. The fireball screamed, then detonated – twenty yards from the *Chathrand*. The flame licked her hull, but there was nothing left in easy reach to burn.

Except the dlömu in the water.

Pazel looked at Mandric and the others near him: they were holding ropes and life preservers. *The dlömu were deserting Macadra's ship.*

They stood up. The sea looked empty. Then a black leg surfaced. Then a body without a head.

'That hag,' said Mandric. 'She don't want to sink us and lose the prize, but she's fine with killin' her own. She just slaughtered a third of her mucking crew.'

Beside the Turach, Bolutu's eyes were bright. 'They almost made it. We could have pulled them aboard.' He looked at Pazel in sudden wonder. 'There was a selk among them.'

'A selk?' said Pazel. 'A selk aboard the *Death's Head*?'

Cries from the opposite rail. Confusion, then wild urgency, pointing fingers, laughs. The dlömu were surfacing on the far side of the *Chathrand*. The protected side. Nearly all had dived in time to escape the fireball, crossed under the *Chathrand*'s belly, risen unscathed.

Pazel sprinted for the far rail. Neeps was there ahead of him, beckoning. 'Pazel, *look!*'

He leaned out over the rail. Among the two hundred or so black-skinned, silver-haired dlömu, one pale olive face stood out. It was Nólcindar.

Nólcindar!

'Macadra didn't kill everyone on the *Promise*,' said Neeps. 'She took prisoners. And that means—'

'Olik!' cried Bolutu. 'Prince Olik!'

There he was, stern and serene as ever, helping a wounded dlömu seize the accordion ladder someone had just sent clattering down the hull.

Pazel could scarcely believe what he was seeing: Arqualis and Mzithrinis, helping dlömu (and one selk warrior) out of the waves.

A second ladder appeared. Once on deck, the dlömu knelt in surrender, unbidden. Some kissed the humans' feet. Prince Olik, among the last from the water, knelt as well.

Sergeant Haddismal pushed forward. 'Your Highness,' he said, 'Captain Fiffengurt's just spoken. You have the freedom of the ship, but these sailors crewed a boat that's attacked us twice. We're to bind them, at least until the fighting's done. We've been double-crossed too many times.'

'Then bind me also,' said the prince.

'And me,' said Nólcindar. 'None of these men are officers. They served like slaves on the *Death's Head*, and risked their lives to free us from the brig where we were held and tortured. Some leaped overboard and swam to the beach inside the Arrowhead Sound. Those Macadra did not slay fled into the mountains, chased by savage-looking men with tattooed necks.'

The Nessarim, thought Pazel.

The dlömu were holding out their wrists. 'Bind us!' they said. 'Tie us, lock us up. Only do not send us back to her, back to the White Raven. Better to die than to return!'

Something, a surge of anguish, made Pazel turn. The main top-sail was gone: the *Death's Head* had struck it dead-centre with one of the burning tar projectiles it had used during the chase along the Red Storm.

'Tree of Heaven, what does it matter if they're on our side or not?' said Saroo. 'There's enough of 'em still manning those blary weapons. Just look at this ship.'

'He's right, Your Highness,' said Mandric. 'You should have taken your chances ashore. We're beaten, and she's still comin' on.'

'We are *not* beaten,' said a sharp, high voice.

It was Felthrup. Pazel turned and saw him standing on Captain Fiffengurt's shoulder. And beside them, between her dogs—

'Thasha Isiq,' said Hercól sternly, 'you promised to stay below.'

'For as long as it made any difference,' said Thasha. 'But it doesn't, not now. Macadra's not a fool. She knows I'd have used the Stone to save the *Chathrand* if I could. And if it comes to a fight – well, I killed her brother. I can kill her too.'

'Macadra does not have the Nilstone,' said Felthrup, 'and while she lacks it, we still have a card to play.'

'Rin's truth,' said Fiffengurt. 'She's hurt our rigging, not our hull. We may be dead in the water, but we're blary far from sunk. Change of orders, Sergeant.' He waved a hand at the dlömu. 'These men don't need shackles, they need swords in their hands. Get busy!'

The crew raced back to their stations. The dlömu who were able leaped up and cried out their readiness to fight.

Pazel put his arm over Thasha's shoulders. He looked across the dwindling space between the vessels. The deck of Macadra's ship was a confusion of fires, gears, struggling men, clouds of smoke.

'Nólcindar!' Kirishgán raised his kinswoman and embraced her warmly. But Nólcindar's eyes were grave.

'The humans are valiant,' she said in the selk tongue, 'but if the White Raven closes, all is lost. That ship is full of killers and madmen. They will burn the crew off the topdeck, and kill them below with canisters of gas. Any survivors will be torn apart by *athymars*, or simply left to drown once she takes the Nilstone and staves in the hull.'

'We can barely move,' said Kirishgán. 'How are we to prevent her from closing?'

Nólcindar had no chance to respond, for at that moment a bird of prey cried just overhead. It was Niriviel, of course. They looked up: the falcon crouched on the main yard, leaning forward, gazing intently at the *Death's Head*. Then he shrieked: 'By the Throne of Arqual! *That* one!'

He shot away towards Macadra's ship. 'What was that about?' asked Thasha. 'What in Pitfire did he see?'

Kirishgán narrowed his eyes. 'There is something ... a small bird, I think. But it flies as if wounded. Yes, that is what Niriviel is aiming for.'

Then both selk winced. 'Too late,' said Nólcindar. 'The bird has fallen into the sea. Unless – well! Your falcon dives better than a fish-eagle. He has snatched the little bird up in his claws.'

Dimly, Pazel saw the falcon returning. Then his eyes were dazzled by several concurrent flashes from the *Death's Head*. Three fireballs streaked skyward. But what sort of attack was this? One shot climbed so high that it entered the Swarm, where it vanished without a trace. The other two, wildly off-target, exploded over the empty sea. Cannon-fire followed, but it too was erratic.

Then Pazel saw why.

The *Death's Head* was sinking.

Roars of war-engines, howls of fear and rage. Some of those

manning the ship's terrible arms were still trying to bring them to bear on the *Chathrand*. There were more wild cannon-shots, even as the *Death's Head* wallowed deeper.

Pitfire, what's happening to her?

Gradually the frenzy on the *Chathrand* subsided; her crew stood transfixed. The vessel's stern was sinking fastest. On the top-deck, men were fighting, shoving forward and backwards at once. Suddenly, by dint of greater numbers or greater panic, the for-ward-pushing mob prevailed, and the whole throng moved in a rush. But the shift in weight was catastrophic. On the next wave, the bow came thundering down, and the sea flooded in through the chaser gunports.

The deck was awash. Some dlömu were making for Gurishal; many simply vanished into the swirling sea.

'They were getting ready to board us,' said Thasha. 'They're in armour. Gods of death.'

Not one figure was swimming for the *Chathrand*.

Pazel had never seen anything like it. Their deadly enemy had foundered. A ship the size of the *Chathrand*, lost in ten minutes flat.

Hercól approached, with Ensyl on his shoulder. 'How did it happen?' Thasha asked her mentor. 'We never managed to scratch her, did we?'

'Not through that armour-plating,' said Ensyl. 'I cannot guess what breached her, but that iron hastened her sinking, beyond any doubt.'

'Along with the weapons heaped on her like scrap,' said Hercól. 'Still, she *must* have been seaworthy. She did not fly over the Nelluroq, and—'

His voice trailed off. He gazed at the vanishing wreck, suddenly quite still. Then he exploded, leaping up and catching the main-mast shrouds, and bellowing over the heads of the crew:

'On guard! On guard! She is coming, the sorceress is coming! It can only be her!'

Pazel never saw it coming. It was simply, suddenly there: a

coagulating black smoke that moved like a flock of blackbirds, all around them, touching them with a horrible chill, then pulling together into a low column between the mainmast and the forecastle. The apparition shimmered, formed a torso, limbs, a face.

Macadra stood upon the deck.

Instantly Hercól lashed out with Ildraquin. But just as the blade reached her head, the figure became smoke once again, tunnelled through the air, and reformed closer to the quarterdeck.

She loomed over them: tall and bone-white and deathly. 'Where is it?' she shrieked. 'Bring it to me. Act quickly, and I will let you land this carcass of a ship.'

Nólcindar lunged, faster even than Hercól. This time Macadra did not vanish, but merely shouted a spell-word so powerful it crackled in the air. Nólcindar's knife shattered like a thing of glass. The selk warrior fell upon the deck, rigid, unable to move a muscle.

Then something rather astonishing happened. The entire crew attacked the sorceress. No one called for it, no one shouted *Charge!* But charge they did, from every side, and not a soul held back.

Macadra threw up her arms. A pale white light swept away from her. Pazel felt it strike him in the face, and then he felt himself fall, along with scores of others. He was conscious, but his strength had suddenly vanished, and so had that of everyone within ten yards of Macadra. The sorceress stood alone in a wide ring of bodies. She laughed.

'Come, see reason,' she said. 'I could kill you as easily as I have lain you flat. But what if I could not? Suppose you drove me from the *Chathrand*, what then? Do you know how close you are to death? Thirty hours: that is how long you have before the Swarm seals this world beneath its pall. Shall I tell you what will happen then? It will drop from the skies, and become the death-skin of Alifros. And still it will grow, deeper, thicker, until it is nine miles thick, and the last cold bacterium has perished at the bottom of the Ruling Sea. Then the Night Gods will declare my brother one of their circle, and free him from the kingdom of twilight. But for you it will be too late.

'I alone can prevent this. Frail creatures like yourselves die at the Stone's touch, but I will use it to put an end to death. I can do it. I can banish the black horror that even now is destroying your minds. You can feel it, can you not? The madness claiming you, the madness born of too much fear? Come, I am your only saviour. Give me the Nilstone, and live.'

'Never,' said Captain Fiffengurt from the quarterdeck. 'You'll not divide us, and we'll not give the Nilstone up. We've not sailed round this blary world for nothing. We mean to remove the Stone from Alifros.'

'By floating it away down the River of Shadows, into death's Kingdom?' said Macadra. 'Has Ramachni truly made you believe it can be done? Simpletons! If only I had time to watch you try!'

Pazel felt a tingling in his toes. His strength was trickling back. Around him, the spell's other victims were also stirring. *That spell cost her. She's not as strong as she wants us to believe.*

'You fear to land on Gurishal, is that it?' said Macadra. 'You fear the Shaggat's lunatics will come upon you in the night and slit your throats? Well, I will not pretend there is no such danger. But the one who speaks up, and tells me where the Stone is secreted – him I will bear away on wings of sorcery, to a land of his choosing, or to my fair court in Bali Adro, if he prefers, where he will know ease and pleasure and the thanks of Macadra. Only speak. Even your shipmates will thank you, when the Swarm departs the skies.'

She turned in a circle. Only now did she appear to realise that the whole ship had fallen silent, and that hundreds of eyes were upon her.

'Well?' she demanded. 'Who will tell me where they keep it? Who among you wants to live?'

No one moved, no one spoke. Pazel was breathless with pride and gratitude. Every soul on the deck was standing firm.

Then a voice said, 'I will show you.'

Pazel looked up, and wished he could die. The voice was Myett's. The ixchel woman stood on the main yard, thirty feet above their heads. And she was not alone: at least one other ixchel was crouching near her, all but hidden by the spar. Further out along the timber crouched Niriviel, eyeing the sorceress with hate.

From the tangle of bodies, Ensyl cried out, heartbroken: 'Myett! No, sister! You can't!'

'It's the only way,' said Myett.

'Be silent, you up there!' snapped Fiffengurt. 'That's an order!'

Macadra was staring up at Myett, perplexed and doubtful. 'I'll show you!' Myett repeated, with a note of desperation. 'Only don't let them punish me, and don't leave me here! I don't want to die!'

The paralysis ended; Macadra's victims began to struggle to their feet. 'Mucking crawlies,' said Haddismal. 'Every Gods-damned time.'

'Myett, who's up there with you?' shouted Thasha.

'Another back-stabbing, ship-sinking louse with legs, that's who,' shrieked Oggosk. 'Kill them!'

Someone hurled a broken timber. Myett dodged, but a hail of objects followed: boots, bottles, hammers, knives. The falcon shrieked: 'Stop, fools, stop!' but no one heeded it. Myett leaped for the mast and began to climb. Then a well-aimed chisel struck her in the legs, and she fell.

She never reached the deck. A whirl of black smoke passed under her, lifted her, and bore her away at great speed along the deck. Roaring, the sailors who were still on their feet gave chase. But Macadra was too fast. Pazel saw Myett lift a hand to indicate the tonnage shaft. The black whirlwind flowed over the rail and down into the ship's dark depths, and Myett went with it.

All was still. The crew stood trapped between confusion and despair. Pazel looked at Thasha. Thasha looked at Hercól. Neeps looked down at Felthrup, and the rat, for once in his life, held stock-still, too mystified even to squirm.

Then, of all people, old Dr Rain spoke up. 'It isn't *that* way, silly crawly. Everyone knows the Nilstone's in Thasha's cabin. You should have used the Silver Stair.'

Hercól was looking up at the main yard.

'You there! Show yourself at once!'

To Pazel's surprise his command was obeyed: two ixchel men rose and stepped to the edge of the massive beam. One of them was Saturyk, Lord Talag's enforcer. And the other—

'You,' said Hercól.

It was Ludunte: Diadrelu's former disciple, and the one who had lured her into the trap that took her life.

Ensyl leaped for the mast and began to climb.

'Sister,' said, Ludunte, a pleading note in his voice, 'just give us a moment, please—'

'I have something else to give you,' said Ensyl. In all their trials and danger together, Pazel had never heard her like this, enraged to the point of madness, longing to kill. 'Hercól!' she shouted, almost snarling, 'did you love her or not? Is her memory sacred to one of us alone?'

Hercól set a hand on the mainmast. Pazel saw the struggle on his face. He too wanted to kill, and was making a terrible effort to restrain himself.

'Something is not right, Ensyl,' he said.

'Nothing is right! She died, they live!'

Ludunte! thought Pazel. *Of all the ixchel to show his face, after so long. And what in Pitfire did you say to Myett?*

A third ixchel, on hands and knees, appeared at the spar's edge and looked down. He was clearly wounded and quite feeble. As he struggled to rise Saturyk noticed him and cried out: 'My lord!'

Too late. The man's strength gave way, and he toppled from the spar. Hercól lunged, but the distance was too great. The tiny figure struck the deck and lay still.

Pazel and his friends rushed to the spot. Hercól was already kneeling. He lifted the figure, cradling him in both palms. His eyes filled with wonder, and new pain.

It was Lord Taliktrum.

He was struggling to breathe. He wore the remains of his old robe of office, the swallow-suit. But the plumes were scorched, almost melted, and so caked with blood that Pazel doubted the suit could ever again be removed.

'Fiffengurt,' he rasped, bloodshot eyes blinking.

The captain appeared moments later, pushing through the crowd. He had already removed his hat.

'You told me,' murmured Taliktrum. 'Not to leave the clan for ever. Not to swear I'd not come back. You were right, in your way. Ah, Olik: well done. The dogs never caught up with you. I am glad.'

'Warrior and friend,' said Prince Olik, 'what last thing would you ask of one who owes you his life?'

Taliktrum only shook his head feebly. Then, with a startling *whoosh*, another ixchel dived into their midst: Lord Talag. He wore the other swallow-suit, but he bore no weapon, nor even a shirt beneath the robe. His face, nearly always stoic and severe, was like an open wound.

He alighted, and fell to his knees beside his son. They spoke in their own language, and none save Pazel could hear them.

'Father—'

'Hush, my child. I wronged you, wronged the clan from the start. Don't say you forgive me: there are sins too deep for pardon. Only know I love you, and will work no more evil in this world.'

'I set four charges in their hold, Father, and all four exploded. It was easy. Under all that metal the ship was a twin of the *Chathrand*. And such an arsenal. They never missed the black powder.' He managed a ruined smile. 'And they'd never had an ixchel problem before.'

Talag closed his eyes. His voice when he found it was low and strained. 'Four charges. Well, I suppose you're proud of yourself.'

'The last one caught me. I was burning as I flew. If the falcon hadn't seen me I'd have drowned along with the giants. You would have done better, sir.'

'No!' Talag's eyes snapped open. Then, more gently, he said, 'That isn't true, my son.'

Taliktrum paused, and the smile played again upon his lips. 'It was glorious,' he said. 'It was a work of art.' His eyes passed over the crowd of humans, and once more he bent his voice for their ears. 'You say so much that's vile and ignorant about my people. But one thing you say is true enough. We know how to sink ships.'

He rolled on his side and coughed a little blood.

'Lord Taliktrum!' cried Felthrup, in sudden desperation. 'Do you have no word for Myett?'

Taliktrum raised his head, and his eyes lit briefly at the name. Then they closed, and the young lord lay still. From above, Saturyk called out, his gruff voice full of sorrow:

'For whatever it's worth, rat, he told her. For all the good it can do her now.'

The black force that was Macadra swept through the mass of fallen rigging that clogged the tonnage shaft. Myett, suspended within the whirlwind, could hear the mage's voice in her mind.

What are you? Are you magically cursed, to be so small?

'I am an ixchel,' said Myett, 'and no, I'm not cursed.'

And at last she believed it.

You will be worse than that if you dare lie to me. Which way?

'To the orlop deck, then forward. The Nilstone is in the brig.'

Locked away from fools who would try to master it, and kill themselves in the bargain!

'I wouldn't know,' said Myett. 'Take the starboard passage. Will you spare me, Mistress?'

Which way, you louse?

Myett pointed. She had never been more frightened, or more certain of her choices.

'There's the door ahead. The small green one.'

It stood slightly ajar, exactly where Saturyk had promised she would find it. Her clan still existed, still studied the *Chathrand*, still knew where to find a door that came and went like a mirage. But Macadra was instantly suspicious.

Just there, unguarded? Behind that crumbling door?

'I'm not lying, Mistress.'

The whirlwind surged down the passage. Around Myett there was a sudden crackle of excitement.

I feel it! The Nilstone! You spoke the truth!

The Green Door flew wide. Myett felt herself carried down the black, cluttered hallway, towards the antique lamp whose glow increased as they approached. Now came the greatest terror. Now she would win life or everlasting torment. It didn't matter, so long as she won.

The black whirlwind paused in the centre of the chamber. Two of the four cells stood empty. The third held an ancient corpse. And in the last, seated on a chest, was the human being Myett hated most in the world. Sandor Ott.

'Crawly, is that you?' he said, squinting at the sudden light.

Myett felt cold fingers take shape around her: Macadra had resumed her natural form.

At the sight of the ghastly figure, Ott shrank back with a squeal of fear. 'Mercy, mercy!' he cried. 'Where did you come from? Don't punish me, I've done nothing to anyone! Don't hurt a poor old man!'

'It's there, there in his chest,' said Myett. 'Will you protect me, Mistress? Let me serve you in the life to come? I may be small, but—'

The mage flung her viciously to the ground. She advanced to the cell in two strides and flung open the door. 'Back away, old man!' she shrieked.

Ott was only too happy to oblige. As he leaped away, Macadra threw herself on Captain Rose's sea chest. When she raised the lid, a black light bathed her face.

She made a fist of her bone-white hand. She closed her eyes and mumbled a spell – or could it have been a prayer? Then her hand plunged into the chest, and emerged holding an orb that burned darker than the soul of midnight.

Cackling, triumphant, Macadra lifted her prize. 'It does not kill me! Can you see me, Arunis? I am its mistress – not you, brother, never you! It will be Macadra Hyndrascorm, not Arunis, who takes her place in the court of the eternal ones, who disposes of worlds as she sees fit, who—'

A harsh clang, metal on metal. Sandor Ott had stepped out of the cell and closed it behind him.

Macadra took in his changed expression: the terror and the simpering were gone. The little louse-woman's face had changed as well. Then she knew. An enchanted brig, of course the *Chathrand* would have one, why hadn't she *guessed*? But what of it? No magic in the world could stand against her now. She lowered her hand, grinning despite herself, and summoned the power of the Stone.

Nothing happened.

Macadra stared at the throbbing black orb. Sandor Ott turned to Myett, spread his hands and smiled with what looked almost like beneficence. Myett scowled at him.

'It wasn't for you,' she said.

'You do not love me, then?' said Sandor Ott. 'Not even a little, after all this time?'

His smile widened into something unpleasant. But Myett stared him down. 'Love,' she said at last. 'You shouldn't be allowed to speak the word.'

She ran from the chamber. Ott started to follow, then paused and turned to face the cell with the corpse.

'Thank you for the intelligence, Captain Kurlstaff. And my compliments to Rose, if you should see him. It seems his trinket was good luck after all. Madam—'

He bowed mockingly to the sorceress, then raced down the passage and through the Green Door, a free man and a patriot, without a moment to lose.

Macadra stood staring. The Nilstone felt heavy in her hand. She closed her fist about it, tightly, commanded it to obey her, to reveal all its secrets.

And it did. The black light went out. In her hand lay a small glass eyeball, a panther's maybe, or a leopard's. A folly. A trinket. Macadra hurled it away, flew at the door that had no lock, that did not open, that would never open again. The lamp grew dim. And as the darkness deepened, Macadra heard, very faintly, the laughter of invisible men.

36

The Wave

The disc of stars was shrinking.

Pazel gazed up at the twinkling lights and wanted to speak to them, to offer thanks, or perhaps farewell. The Swarm's mouth was closing, converging on all sides towards a point somewhat inland from the Arrowhead Sound. It might, he reflected, be the last starlight his world would ever see.

The sound was only slightly wider than the gigantic rock that marked its entrance. At first the dry, eroding cliffs ran parallel; then they drew much closer together, and the sound become a flooded canyon, crooked and deep. Into this strange fjord they tacked, on two masts and tattered sails. Great black birds swept over them: vultures, probably, although it was too dark to be sure. Their flapping echoed morosely between the silent cliffs.

There was no wind to speak of. Pazel looked up at the limp canvas: it seemed almost a miracle that they could move at all. But they were moving, and rather smartly. Elkstem and Fegin manned the wheel together, sweating and scrambling. The lookouts strained their eyes for rocks.

After two miles, a long, grey beach appeared under the western cliffs. Pazel squinted, then felt nausea strike him like a blow to the face. The beach was strewn with bodies: dlömic bodies, and human. Nothing moved but the carrion-birds, hundreds strong and feasting. All over the *Chathrand* sailors made the sign of the Tree.

Prince Olik raised his hand and pointed: a stone staircase, also strewn with bodies, wound its way up the cliff and vanished into the hills.

'The *Death's Head* came this far, searching for you,' he said, 'and here some of my people tried to flee. A few escaped into Gurishal, but most were driven back to this shore by the Nessarim. Macadra did not discriminate between them: she launched a terrible glass cube over the beach. It exploded, filling the sky with needles, and everyone ashore fell dead. After this Macadra dared sail no farther, but turned her vessel back to the sea.'

'Of course she did,' said Fiffengurt, 'and let me say this perfectly clearly: we *won't* be able to turn back, if this canyon narrows any further. There's depth here, I'll grant you. But a ship needs seaway too. It's blary suicidal to be squeezing her into this sort of crack.'

'The only act of suicide would be to hesitate, Captain,' said Hercól, 'though it gives me no joy to say so. Could the tides offer us no hope of escape?'

'The tides!' Fiffengurt gave an appalled little laugh. 'A tidal race would carry us out to sea again, to be sure. In bits and pieces, after the rocks and cliffs had finished with us. As for the keel – well now, the keel . . .'

Fiffengurt let his voice trail off. Pazel knew he must be struggling to keep his mind on higher things, despite all his instincts as a mariner, and as a man who'd served the *Chathrand* most of his life. Suddenly Pazel wished he could put an arm around the man's weary shoulders. What was it doing to him, to know that his ship's long tale was ending?

Another mile, another silent beach. There were no bodies here, but as they glided past, Kirishgán's sharp eyes caught sight of a small black animal. It was running alongside them in the surf, trying to keep up. 'Arpathwin!' he cried. 'Hurry, change! Take owl-form and fly to us!'

The black mink did not change, and was soon falling behind. Fiffengurt called for shorter sails. But as the men furled canvas, his face grew puzzled. The *Chathrand* did not appear to be slowing.

Thasha looked at the others in alarm. 'I don't think he can change at all,' she said. 'I think his powers are gone.'

'Then we will bring him ourselves!' said Bolutu. 'Come, Prince—'

Before they could dive, however, Niriviel leaped from the rail. 'Stay, the bird is swifter,' said Hercól, 'and he has carried heavier loads than one exhausted mink.'

'Undrabust, heave the blary log,' said Fiffengurt. 'I could swear we're *gaining* speed.'

Neeps gathered the knotted rope and threw the weighted end into the sound. Moments later he had a reading: 'Six knots, Captain.'

Fiffengurt tugged at his beard. 'You there, aloft!' he cried at last. 'Strike the mains, and the topsails also. No, by the Tree, strike *all* the canvas. You heard me, lads: go to.'

There was not much canvas left to strike. In short order the two surviving masts stood naked. But the *Chathrand* plowed on, unchanged. Like a man in a dream, Fiffengurt walked to the rail, snatched off a midshipman's hat and flung it overboard.

'It's just bobbing there on the surface,' he declared. 'There's no current at all. Blue devils, what's making *us* move?'

'The cargo,' said Marila.

Everyone started. 'How do you figure?' asked Neeps.

Marila looked at him. 'The way most people do. You should try it.' To the others, she said, 'Look at Elkstem and Fegin.'

The two sailors were barely managing to control the wheel. They looked, Pazel had to admit, rather clumsy and inept.

'They know how to sail,' said Marila, 'but we're not sailing. I'll bet you all the gold on this ship that if they dropped the wheel we'd spin around and float backward.'

'The Nilstone,' said Thasha, wonder in her voice. 'It's in my cabin, near the stern. Marila – you think it's *pulling* us?'

'Or pushing,' said Marila, 'as long those two can keep us from spinning around.'

The notion was, to say the least, disconcerting. Pazel could not dismiss it, however. Just hours ago, he and Neeps had wondered what might happen to the Nilstone as they neared their goal. If Marila was right they had their answer.

Niriviel returned bearing Ramachni, and Thasha ran to him and took him in her arms. Ramachni looked gaunt and haggard, and his fur was singed, but his black eyes gleamed even here in the darkness.

'Gently!' he said. 'I am spent as you have never seen me, dearest.' He looked over the ship. 'You have roped off the forecastle: just as well. The poison there will linger a long time.'

'Longer than this ship has to live,' said Niriviel. 'I will scout ahead.'

'I would feel better if his master were still in a cage,' said Bolutu, as the falcon climbed into the night.

'The clan will find him,' said Ensyl. 'Isn't that right, Lord Talag?'

The old lord glanced at her and nodded briefly. His face was careworn; he had barely spoken since the death of his son. Beside him, Myett's expression was even more distant. Her eyes were glassy; her hands hung limp at her sides. Pazel's heart went out to her. She had expected her lover to survive his burns. It made no sense, except in the language of the heart.

Neda touched Hercól on the elbow. In the Mzithrini tongue, she said, 'We can test Marila's theory, *Asprodel*. Just put on the gauntlets and move the Nilstone to another part of the ship.'

Hercól blinked at her. 'You're a genius, Neda Pathkendle.'

A small crowd descended to Thasha's cabin; Bolutu carried one of the last lamps with oil left to burn. Thasha donned the gauntlets from Uláramyth as Pazel opened the cabinet. But he could not budge the iron slab. Hercól stepped up beside him Together, muscles straining, they just managed to move it.

The Nilstone slid into the chamber. Everyone flinched and moved back a step. It had not grown, and Pazel could feel no heat or other force that he could have given a name. But he could feel its power, and its utter wrongness. Looking at it was like gazing down into a bottomless pit.

'The slab wasn't stuck like before,' said Pazel. 'The Nilstone's gotten heavier, somehow. Much heavier.'

Thasha put her gauntleted hand on the Nilstone. '*Credek*,' she swore, 'I can't move it an inch.'

'Give me those things,' said Hercól.

When both gauntlets covered his hands he squeezed the Nilstone between them, bent low at the knees, and lifted. He groaned with effort. Veins stood out on his neck and forearms. At last he stopped and shook his head.

'Now we know why Erithusmé made that slab as strong as a ship's anchor.'

'And why the stern's riding so low,' said Marila.

'Can't you make up your mind?' said Neeps. 'A few minutes ago you told us the Stone was pulling us deeper into the canyon. Now you say it's pulling down.'

Again, Marila directed her reply to the others, never glancing at Neeps. 'It's pulling towards this "door to death's kingdom." Which is somewhere ahead of us *and* down. That's what I think, anyway.'

'So do I,' said Hercól, 'for if the Stone is truly so heavy that it can alter the balance of the *Chathrand*, we should not have been able to move that slab with any effort. So why could we? Because the Stone's own forwards pull was helping us.'

Neeps was blushing. 'Marila,' he said, 'you're one smart woman.'

Marila pinned him with a glance. 'I'm not sure about that,' she said, and walked out of the room.

An awkward silence. Neeps, defiant and ashamed at once, could not meet anyone's eye. 'Let's just get out of here,' said Thasha at last. She left the cabin, and the others, relieved, filed after her. But at the stateroom door Pazel seized his friend by the elbow.

'I want a word with you.'

Thasha stayed as well. Neeps looked from one to the other. 'Save your breath,' he said. 'You're not going to take my side, I can tell that already.'

'Gods damn it, I don't know what your side *is*,' said Pazel.

'You wouldn't, would you?'

'What's that crack mean, then?'

'It means you're a one-note whistle,' said Neeps. 'You have Thasha. You don't need anything else. You've got it all worked out. But then nothing's ever mucked with *your* head, has it?'

'Oh no, mate, never,' said Pazel acidly.

'You know what I mean!'

'There's no time for this,' said Thasha. 'Listen, Neeps, *everything* mucks with our heads. Living, dying, magic, hunger, falling in love, falling out of it—'

'Who says I have? Who in the Pits do you two think you are?'

Crash.

The deck lurched, and they crashed to the floor. Howls erupted from above and below. The ship had struck, and struck badly. She was rolling, twisting on whatever rock was grinding beneath her keel. The noise! Cracking, splintering, groaning of the ancient wood. Pazel could almost feel it, like a mutilation with a dull instrument of torture.

Another lurch. The *Chathrand* had twisted free of the rock and righted herself. But Pazel knew what he had heard. Not damage, but a death-blow. From the lower decks men were screaming already:

'She's breached! She's staved! Abandon ship, abandon ship!'

'Marila!' shouted Neeps. He flew from the stateroom and into the dark passageway. 'Be *careful*, damn it!' Pazel shouted, following as fast as he could.

On the Silver Stair it was pitch-black. Men were streaming upward, groping, shoving from behind. Pazel heard Mr. Teggatz sob in the darkness: 'Lost, lost, my home is—'

Crash.

A second strike. The ladderway became a chute of bodies. Pazel was hurled backwards onto the landing, and five or six men fell atop him. Somewhere above Neeps was still shouting Marila's name.

'Out, out or drown!' men were screaming. The sweaty mass of men groped upward, towards the weak starlight, the slanting deck. Many helped one another. Others trampled and fought. Pazel at last found Neeps, pushing against the tide, and shouting for Marila with rising fear.

'Oh Gods, sweetheart—'

Pazel joined the blind search. Thasha was here as well, but all they found were more sailors, dazed and bleeding, trying to drag themselves up the ladderway. Then Hercól's voice reached them faintly over the din.

'It's all right, Undrabust. She's up here, on the topdeck. She's unharmed.'

Pazel was glad of the darkness, for his friend's sake. Neeps had burst into tears.

The youths crawled out through the hatch. It was very dark: the Swarm's mouth had closed even tighter; the disc of starlight above them had shrunk. They were careening between the cliff walls, thumping over one submerged rock after another, still with remarkable speed. Most of the crew had already reached the topdeck, and were clinging for dear life to the rails, davits, hatch coaming, anything fixed and solid. The captain and Mr Elkstem remained on the quarterdeck, but no one was at the wheel. The last vestige of control was gone.

The ship rolled, and Pazel found himself sliding back and forth like a shuffle-puck from port to starboard. He saw Lady Oggosk clinging to Thasha, wailing; Hercól with one arm hooked over a cleat and the other around Neda, who clung to him, arms about his waist. He clawed his way to where Felthrup was holding on by his teeth to the remains of a halyard, and seized him by the scruff of the neck.

'Hold still! I've got you.'

Felthrup did not hold still, but he let Pazel lift him up against his chest. 'Thank you! But you're utterly filthy, you know, and you are bleeding from the chin. Did I ever tell you of my fondness for soda bread?'

'Oh Felthrup, please shut up.' Pazel flung himself over heaps of wreckage that shifted beneath his feet. The rat squirmed up to his shoulder.

'For you I will, Pazel Pathkendle. Yes, soda bread, and the pumpkin fritters they make in Sorrophran. And higher education. I think I shall try to become a professor of history.'

'Do that.'

'Ah, but now you are flippant, when I am only motivated by a wish to share some last intimacies with you, before the voyage ends. And it has almost ended, Pazel. As you would know if you looked over your shoulder. In fact it is ending *n*—'

CRASH.

Pazel fell, and managed to curl into a ball with Felthrup at the centre. He rolled wildly across the deck, alongside countless others. This third collision was not like the first two. It was soft, but massive, affecting the whole ship at once. Pazel came to rest on the stomach of one of the augrongs, who was in turn sprawled atop his brother, who was flat against the wall of Rose's cabin. A few feet away Neeps lay holding Marila, like a man who would never let go.

For an instant no one moved on the *Chathrand*. Then out of the pile of bodies, Sandor Ott rose and dusted himself off 'Well, traitors,' he said cheerfully, 'welcome to Gurishal.'

It was a narrow beach, filling the canyon wall to wall, as the sea had done up to this point. The ship lay wrecked with massive dignity, leaning only slightly to starboard, not fifty feet from shore.

Pazel stood in the shallows with his hand on the hull, watching the evacuation. Four accordion-ladders snaked down to the water's edge, and the midship portal, sealed since Bramian, had been thrown open. Sailors were leaping into the water, splashing and sputtering; the frail and the wounded crossed the fifty feet on makeshift rafts. When they touched ground, the Arqualis knelt and kissed it, intoning the ritual words:

'Hail Cora, Proud and Beautiful. Hail Cora, Earth-Goddess, embracing us at journey's end. Hail, hail . . .'

Sergeant Haddismal had taken it upon himself to save at least part of the Imperial treasure. The Turachs laboured by candlelight, prying open boards in the inner hull, wrenching out thin iron cabinets, hauling them jingling ashore. Sandor Ott, leaning against the mainmast, watched him through narrowed eyes.

There was moonlight, now: a pale search-beam through that

last, closing aperture of the Swarm. By its glow they could see that the beach climbed into dunes, and the dunes in turn gave way to small, rugged trees. But the selk could see farther.

'The cliff walls draw very close together, about a mile from where we stand,' said Kirishgán, 'and between them, a vast wall rises, sealing off the canyon. It is sheer and mighty, like a cliff unto itself. But there is a staircase carved into the cliff on one side. Or rather, many staircases, one above another.'

'Twenty, by my count,' said NN. 'They climb all the way to the top of the wall. And above the wall one may scramble up the bare mountain to a high table-land. There are meadows in that place, and a gentleness to the earth.'

'Twenty staircases?' said Pazel. It was not much, beside all that they had come through to reach this place. But just now it felt like a death-sentence.

'And long, each one of them,' said Nólcindar. 'I think this wall is the work of the First People.'

'First at what?' asked Fiffengurt.

'She means the Auru, Captain,' said Ramachni, 'who built the tower at whose foot we killed Arunis, and who stood guard for centuries wherever the River of Shadows surfaced in this world. That wall is no surprise. Indeed it would be strange if they had *not* built some edifice on Gurishal.'

'And if Dri had it right, death's kingdom is entered by an abyss, somewhere beyond that wall,' said Hercól.

Nólcindar raised her sapphire eyes. 'The falcon returns,' she said.

At her words, Sandor Ott started to his feet. He had been sitting apart from everyone, refusing to help with the evacuation, or to take part in any discussion of their next move. They had killed the Shaggat, and with it his savage dream. Their cause be damned, he'd said. He would not end his life aiding traitors to the Crown.

Ott raised his eyes. He'd wrapped one arm in sailcloth, and Pazel had thought him wounded there. Now he knew better: the thick cloth was to serve as his falcon-glove. Niriviel was his last, loyal servant, and he had yet to see the bird since his escape from the brig. From the darkness, the bird gave a shrill, fierce cry.

Ott lifted his arm and cried out, 'Niriviel, my champion!'

The bird swooped past him, alighting on the sand near Hercól. Ott turned and gaped. He looked like a man whose child had just left him to die.

'We are in the right place,' Niriviel said to the others. 'Our goal lies straight ahead.'

'*Our* goal?' cried Sandor Ott.

The falcon trained one eye on the spymaster. 'Yes,' he said, 'ours. All my life I let you guide me, Master. But your teachings were selfish, and your conspiracies have brought us only death. I would face death clothed in something better than your lies.'

'I created you.'

'You caged me,' said Niriviel, 'first in body, then in mind.'

Ott was shaking with fury. 'Service to one's rightful lord is no cage. And I *am* your lord, Nirviel. I speak for Arqual. I act by writ of His Supremacy.'

The bird gazed at him in silence. 'That is nothing to me any longer,' he said at last. 'I renounce you, old man.'

He turned back to the others. 'I saw it,' he said. 'A black funnel sloping down into the earth, with a pit of darkness at its heart no light will ever pierce, and a river vanishing into it, like a trickle of rain down the side of a well.'

'Thank all the Gods,' said Prince Olik.

'Do not thank them,' said the bird. 'You will never reach that abyss. It lies beyond the wall at the top of those long stairs. Fifty miles beyond, at the minimum.'

A horrified silence fell: once more the specter of defeat stood among them. 'The canyon runs on beyond the wall,' said Niriviel, 'but there is no path, nor even level ground. There are only endless rocks, crevasses, slides and scrambles. You will not reach it in one day, or three.'

'Well, let's blary try,' said Neeps. 'There'll be daylight soon enough. Maybe we have longer than we think '

Hercól shook his head. 'Look at the Swarm, Undrabust. In the last six hours, the gap above us has shrunk by half. We might have another six hours, perhaps even eight. But we do not have days.'

'And to judge by the way our stern was wallowing,' added Fiffengurt, 'that blary Stone weighs more than all the cannon on the ship put together. How are we to carry it up those stairs, let alone over fifty pathless miles?'

Despite himself Pazel glanced at Ramachni. 'No, Pazel,' said the mage, 'I have tapped the wellspring of my power until the water turned to salt, and then I tapped again, and yet again. There is not even salt water now. It may well be a year or two before I can so much as change the colour of my eyes.'

This is why Erithusmé believed we'd fail without her, Pazel thought. *This is why Thasha's got to come through.*

Bolutu started at a sudden thought. 'Pazel, *your* power is not all gone. You still have a Master-Word.'

'Right, and some of us have wolf-shaped scars,' said Pazel, 'but what does that matter now, Bolutu? Dri and Rose are dead. There was a moment when those scars could have given us the answer, but the moment's come and gone. It's the same with my Master-Word: I missed the chance, somehow. If the chance ever came.'

'You don't know that,' said Neeps.

'Fine, mate,' said Pazel. 'The last word is one that *blinds to give new sight*. Go on, tell me who I'm supposed to blind, and what mucking good it will do.'

'What about that magic clock of yours, then?' said Fiffengurt. 'Ain't there nobody on the other side you could call on, Ramachni?'

'If I could summon such help, would I not have done so already?' said Ramachni. 'There is no one left, Captain Fiffengurt. We are alone.'

'Then we've had it,' said the tarboy Saroo, from the edge of the circle. 'Face facts, why don't you? This is where we make peace with our Gods, and commend ourselves to their care.'

'You sound like a fool,' snapped his brother Swift. 'And anyway, just yesterday you said that the Gods don't exist.'

'They exist, all right,' said Marila. 'At least the Night Gods do. Arunis made a deal with them, remember?'

Thasha looked up at the black lips of the Swarm, so close above them now, closing in from all sides. 'The Night Gods,' she said. 'They're coming, aren't they?'

'Lower your gaze, Thasha Isiq,' said Ramachni. 'And hear me, all of you: however else we spend the time that remains to us, we will *not* spend it fighting one another. We have six hours. Let us plumb our minds and hearts for an answer. We are not defeated yet.'

Her spine was cracked, her hull giving way, her seaworthiness ended after six hundred years, but the *Chathrand* still had a duty officer committed to ringing the hour. Whoever it was gave the old bell two strikes. One hour had slipped away already.

It was very cold, now: frost was spreading lacework fingers over porthole glass. The moon had set, but dawn had not yet come. Most of the crew had gone ashore. Pazel had heard more than one man say he preferred to die *anywhere but on that ship*. Thasha, however, had boarded her again, and Pazel had followed. If he was to die he would do it beside her – even if, as it seemed now, she was barely aware of his presence.

For her old distance had suddenly returned. He had watched it come over her, there on the beach, when Ramachni said with finality that there was no help he could give. Pazel knew he should feel for her: she thought the world was perishing on her account, through some moral cavity in her heart, some perverse defeat it meant to deliver to Erithusmé. But that absent look made him furious. He wanted to strike her, cause her pain until she noticed him, until her eyes moved to his with recognition. He couldn't bear the thought that when the end came she might glance at him for the last time with the indifference of a stranger.

They were crossing the lower gun deck, rounding the cold galley (where Teggatz still worked by candlelight, banging pots and blubbering), tripping over wreckage, over bodies, smelling deathsmoke in corners where addicts had gathered, waiting for the end.

'Where are we going?' he demanded.

He had to repeat the question twice before she deigned to answer. 'I don't know about you,' she said. 'I'm going to sickbay.'

'What for?'

'Chadfallow's papers. That table he made, to help him find the Green Door.'

'Thasha!'

'I'm going to let Macadra out. She thinks she can use the Stone: who are we to say she's wrong?'

'Don't be a mucking fool. She's a lunatic. She won't use its power just to toss it away. And she *can't* use it to fight off the Swarm. Ramachni said so. Pitfire, Erithusmé told me that herself. Anyway, Chadfallow's papers aren't in sickbay anymore. Felthrup wanted them. I brought them back to the stateroom.'

Thasha turned so suddenly that they collided. She shoved past him. He turned to follow.

'Let's go back to the others,' he pleaded, 'maybe Hercól has thought of something.'

'We'd know. There'd be shouting.' Thasha stalked on, not looking back.

They passed out of the compartment, around the entrance to the Silver Stair and down the long corridor. Dust and soot coated the magic wall, rendering it visible. Thasha stepped through it and turned to him. The dirt had come off on her face and clothes, leaving a vaguely Thasha-shaped window through which they faced each other.

'Macadra's our last hope,' said Thasha. 'Sometimes lunatics come to their senses, when things get dark enough. Look at Rose, for instance.'

'Sometimes the darkness just makes them crazier. Look at Ott.'

'Do you have a better idea? Do you have *any ideas at all*?'

His cold breath fogged the wall between them. 'No,' he admitted, 'not yet.'

'Then you can't come in.'

'What?'

She turned away, marching for the stateroom door. He moved to follow – and for the first time in almost a year, the wall stopped him dead. It answered to her even now. She had withdrawn her permission; she was shutting him out.

'Don't do it,' he heard himself say. 'Don't leave me before we die. Neeps is right, Thasha, I am a one-note whistle. Nothing matters to me anymore but being with you.'

She stopped with her hand on the doorknob. She turned and struck the passage wall with her fist. She was weeping. He called to her, begging, and the third time he did so her shoulder slumped, and the wall let him through. He ran to her and dried her tears away.

'Stop it,' she said.

'Why?'

Thasha shook her head. When he touched her hair again she started, then took his hand and dragged him brutally into the stateroom and kicked the door shut. She put her hands beneath his clothes, kissed him wildly, avoiding his eyes. She pressed her body against his own.

'What are you doing?' he said, appalled.

'Make love to me.'

'Thasha, stop. What in the Pits is wrong with you?'

She tripped him, threw him down upon the floor. In Pazel's mind instinct took over, and he pulled her down with him as he fell. They grappled, smashing against the admiral's reading chair, the samovar, the tea-table from which he'd snatched a piece of cake on his first visit to the stateroom. The time he'd nearly walked out of her life. He did not know if this was a real fight or something else altogether, if she was angry or aroused. Whatever it was, he didn't want it: not this way. He stopped resisting, letting her win. Glaring, she pinned his back to the floor.

'You still don't trust me,' he said. 'After everything, you're still not sure I'm on your side.'

'What mucking rubbish.'

'If you trusted me, you'd just tell me what was wrong.'

Thasha's slapped the floor beside his head. 'Would I? Would that help? Will anything help us now?'

'You're giving up?'

'I'm going to pick up the Stone myself. Erithusmé created me. She made my mother conceive. It won't kill me as fast as it kills other people. I might have a minute or two.'

'Oh, Thasha—'

'But you have to stay away. If you're there I won't be able to make myself do it.'

'It took you five minutes to get the ship out of the bay at Stath Bàlfyr, with that wine in your stomach. And you only had to move the ship a mile.'

'I know that, bastard. I was there.'

Then the words began to spill from her, a wild, almost delirious plan for moving the Nilstone down that canyon, an idea so ludicrous it made him ache to hear the desperate hope she placed in it; a fantasy, a dream.

'In two minutes?' he said.

'Maybe I'll have longer. I could fight the Stone. Fight back.'

'Do you think you can do it, Thasha? Just tell me the simple truth.'

Her eyes were furious. She was going to hit him, bite him, burn him with her hate. She laid her head down on his shoulder. One hand found his cheek and rested there, gently. It grew quiet. He could hear the waves breaking softly against the stern.

'No,' she said.

He put his arms around her, and they both lay still. Through the tilted windows he could see the Swarm boiling out towards the horizon, growing before his eyes.

'In the mountains,' she said, 'when you lifted Bolutu's pack by the cliff, I didn't think you were going to throw it over the edge. I thought you were going to jump.'

'I considered it,' he said. 'That bastard with the Plazic Knife might have had a harder time lifting me and the Stone together.'

Thasha began to cry – not hysterically, this time, but with a deep, despairing release. 'I wanted to stop you,' she said. 'I reached deep into my mind and called to her, begged her to break down the wall and stop you. I gave her my blessing, my permission. And nothing happened. Even to save your life I couldn't bring Erithusmé back. That's when I knew I never would.'

'You will,' he said, 'somehow.'

'The wall's too strong, Pazel. I take a hammer to it in my dreams. There's a crack, but it closes before I can lift the hammer again. It heals stronger than before.'

'What's it made of?'

'Stone. Steel. Diamond.'

He shook his head. 'Thasha, what is it made of?'

She fell silent, her hand still resting on his face. At last she said, 'Greed. My greed, for a life of my own. No matter what Erithusmé told you there's a part of me that thinks I'll die when she returns. The woken part of me is brave enough to face that. But there's another part I can't control, and it takes over. Every time. Once in a while I just throw myself at the wall like a madwoman, and Erithusmé feels it, and does the same on the other side, raging and smashing, and I start to think we might just do it, might just tear the wall to pieces. That's when the other part of me begins crying out, and it doesn't stop until every crack is sealed.'

'Crying out to whom?'

Thasha froze, as if deeply shocked by the question. 'Who do you mucking think?' she said.

Her tears grew stronger, racking her body. The loyal officer struck three bells. Pazel held her tighter, heartbroken and deeply afraid. Was he supposed to save her, sacrifice her? Was there any reason to keep trying, to torture her with hope in these final, blessed moments before the end?

As he lay there facing the ceiling, blinking his own tears from his eyes, Pazel felt something small tickle the back of his neck. He shifted his gaze and saw a hint of blue and gold. Thasha's Blessing-Band. The embroidered ribbon from the Lorg School, meant for the wedding ceremony on Simja. He lifted it:

the silk was partly torn, but he could still read the ambiguous words:

YE DEPART FOR A WORLD UNKNOWN, AND LOVE ALONE
SHALL KEEP THEE

Within him, something changed. Thasha felt it. Still weeping uncontrollably, she moved her hand to his face, probing.

'What happened?' she said. 'Have you started hating me?'

'Oh, Thasha—'

'You don't have to hide it. I wouldn't. I'd tell you the truth.'

Then he told her to stop crying, kissed her hand, her hair, and promised her he wasn't crazy, that he loved her now and had done so since the day she first pinned him to the floor in the adjoining cabin, that they must get up and call the others together, that they must hurry, because at long last he knew.

The wall was indeed enormous, the stairs many and steep. In the pale light of early morning Pazel and Thasha watched the long procession. Men, dlömu, ixchel, augrongs, selk. Not that you could really tell them apart. He smiled. From this distance they were simply his crew.

And they were making good time, he thought, even though some were bearing stretchers, and others splints. But then they had to be quick. Dry land would soon be scarce, if things went as planned.

Their friends looked back often, and waved: Bolutu, Olik, Nólcindar, Hercól and Neda linking hands. Above them, already blurred with distance, climbed Neeps and Marila. They had started early, in case Marila had to set a slower pace. Pazel smiled. No chance of that.

Only the Mzithrinis were slow, for they carried the heaviest and strangest burden: the Shaggat's corpse, embalmed in the mariner's fashion, in a coffin sealed in wax. They still had a task to perform with it, a cult of murder to destroy.

Murder. It made Pazel think of the one figure who was missing from the crowd. Sometime in the last few hours, Sandor Ott had simply disappeared. No one had seen him depart, but their last sweep of the ship had turned up nothing. Had he raced ahead of them? Was he hiding out among the trees? Or could he have escaped into a vanishing compartment? Was he sitting, even now, on that speck of an island just vacated by the ixchel, beside that other *Chathrand*, and a graveyard sinking into the sand?

They might never find out. Pazel merely hoped that Ott was finished with his bloody intrigues. That he would stop hurting others, perhaps even himself.

'Well, Felthrup,' said Thasha, 'it's time you were on your way.'

'But I do not wish to leave you, Thasha,' he said.

'The dogs will not climb without you,' said Ramachni, 'and neither, for that matter, will I. Come, rat-friend; you know this is the only way.'

'It is cruel.'

'Perhaps, but not only cruel. And the alternative does not bear thinking about. Go, Jorl; bear him off. Suzyt and I will catch you by the second switchback.'

At a gesture from Thasha, the great mastiff bent down, and Felthrup, sniffling, crawled onto his back. 'Do not forget me, Thasha!' he said. 'If we do not meet again, remember that I loved you with all the heart I had.'

Thasha bent down and kissed his muzzle on both sides. 'That's more heart than anyone I know,' she said. 'But this isn't the end. I'll find you. Just be strong until that day comes. And remember for us, will you?'

'It would appear I have no choice. I will wait for you above, Pazel Pathkendle.'

'Don't wait,' said Pazel. 'Get to the ridgetop, and for Rin's sake, be sure there's no one left behind you. Except me, of course.'

Thasha kissed her brave Jorl too, and stroked him and whispered loving words into his ear. Then she pointed to the mountain stair and said, 'Go on.' Reluctantly, Jorl obeyed, with Felthrup crouched low upon his back.

Now only Ramachni and Suzyt were left beside them. The mage looked at each youth in turn. 'I knew,' he said. 'When I first saw you together, I knew I beheld a power to redeem this world.'

'That makes one of us,' said Thasha, holding Pazel tight.

'Do what you must do, Pazel,' said the mage, 'and then take the stairs at a run. If you drown I shall never forgive you. As for you, Thasha my champion—'

He gazed at her a long time. 'What words can be enough?' he said at last. 'Know this: that long ages ago, there was one for whom I felt so deeply that I dreamed of renouncing magic, living a natural life, knowing human love. I made the right choice: this mission proves it, and there have been other proofs across the centuries. But the pain of that choice was so great that I had to flee not only my friends and family, but my body, and my world. Casting everything aside let me forget that pain, and no one ever evoked such feelings in me again. Until your birth. In you, I saw the daughter that might have been mine, the life I had chosen to forsake. That is why I asked my mistress to name me your guardian. Never was anyone so grateful for his charge.'

They walked with him into the trees, and along the path to the foot of the first staircase. Thasha lifted him a last time and squeezed him tight against her neck. 'I'm all out of tears,' she said.

'Then smile for me, and for your triumph,' said the mage, 'and know that I, too, plan to see you again – in this world or the next. Come, Suzyt.'

The great dog bounded after Jorl, with Ramachni clinging tight to her back. Thasha and Pazel watched them until they reached the top of the first flight and vanished around a rock. Then they walked back towards the water until the trees began to thin. They could see the huge, empty ship canted over on her side. The Swarm was closing. The starry window above them like a porthole, now, but all the more beautiful as it shrank.

Thasha glanced to their left. A soft light was flickering among the trees. 'What's that?' she said.

'A gift from Neeps and Marila,' said Pazel.

'What is it, a campfire?'

Pazel nodded, and led her to the clearing, the sweet smell of crackling pine, the heat on his legs. There was a folded blanket. He turned to Thasha and brushed the hair from her eyes.

'Now I'll make love to you,' he said.

He knew it was what he wanted, and knew also that it would increase the pain to come, and it did. To do in haste what they would rather have done gently, slowly; to kiss her and taste her and try to know every inch of her; to risk now what they hadn't risked before, because now was what they had and all they might ever have: yes, it would hurt for the rest of his life. And maybe sustain him, gladden him in whatever future he found.

'It might not last,' she said. 'The effect, I mean. It might fade in month or two, or even less.'

They hadn't moved yet. He said nothing, kept his chin on her shoulder, his mind on what he'd felt, could still feel, would never feel with any other. He wouldn't say *Yes, you're right you know, we might be back here by nightfall*. He didn't want to start lying, to Thasha or to himself.

'It will last, though, won't it?'

'It will,' said Pazel. 'Long enough. Maybe forever.'

'You could just *tell* me about yourself. If you kept at it I'd believe you.'

He raised his head a few inches. She made a small sound of grief and clutched his hips, not letting him leave. Pazel moved his hand to her breast and cupped it, and doubted anything Ramachni had learned in twenty centuries could be worth losing this.

A memory came. Another fire, beside a cold lakeshore in the mountains, far away in the South. Thasha drying his hair with a towel, then plucking from it an exquisite shard of crystal. A shard that melted in her hand. We can possess a thing but not its loveliness: that always escapes. Kirishgán had warned him, but no warning could be enough. Thasha met his eyes, and slowly loosened her grip. Pazel rolled away, trying not to let go of her, and then they groped for their clothes.

Thasha stood. 'I think I'd best face away from you.'

'Towards the *Chathrand*?'

'That'll do.'

She tightened a bootlace, looked up at him with a grin. 'I'm glad we weren't careful this time. A child would fix her.'

'It can't be what she has in mind.'

They smiled for each other. He was grateful when she didn't force herself to laugh.

'I'll be looking for you, you know,' she said. 'When I can. If I can.'

'Don't promise me that, Thasha.'

She nodded, wiped her eyes, kissed him swiftly once more. Then she turned away from him, and without looking back handed him the Blessing-Band.

'Trust feels good,' she said.

'Nothing better,' he agreed, and spoke the word that blinds to give new sight.

This time there was no concussion, no bending of reality, no darkening of the sun. A little pulse went through his temples, dizzying him, but it passed in a heartbeat, and he felt unchanged. Thasha tilted her head as though at a curious thought. Her back was to him, but he could have touched her. A moment ago it was so easy. He wasn't even dry from their lovemaking.

He watched her walk away onto the open sand.

When she had gone twenty paces she looked up at the Swarm. Then into the distance. Slowly she raised her arms and wrapped them around her head. Pazel waited, barely breathing. Thasha lowered her arms, looked at her left palm, and cursed— 'Bugger all, she did it! The wretched girl did as she was told!'

Thasha's voice, but not Thasha. She moved her hands

experimentally, felt the contours of her body. His lover's body. Then she whirled and looked at him, affronted.

'What the devil?' she cried. 'Is this *Gurishal*? Am I standing by the Arrowhead Sound?'

He said yes, that was where she was. Then he told her the rest of what she needed to know.

'I do recognise the vessel,' she said sharply. 'It's mine, after all. And I'm well aware that the Nilstone is aboard. I could feel it, even from – a great distance away. Never mind. Why are you skulking around behind me? What is it you want?'

Pazel stared at her.

'Speak up, boy!' she shouted. 'Have we met?'

'Gods,' he said, 'I never thought it would work on *you*.'

He had directed the Master-Word to blind Thasha to his existence, to make her forget she'd ever known someone named Pazel Pathkendle. But Master-Words could be brutal, or least brutally imprecise. This one had swept right through Thasha's mind, and erased Erithusmé's memory of him as well.

Now her look contained the hint of a threat. 'Work on me?' she said.

He did his best to explain. 'Your disciple Ramachni gave me the words. This was the last of them. And yes, we've met before.'

'Where and when, pray?'

'A few months ago, in—'

His voice froze. The magic of Uláramyth still sealed his tongue.

She waved at him irritably. 'I think you are touched in the head. If you're not, or not too badly, start running for your life. I may have to do some terrible things in the next few minutes.'

'Oh, you do,' he said. 'Look in your shirt pocket.'

She jumped, looked at him with even more vexation. She raised her hand to her pocket and removed a bit of folded parchment. 'Whose writing is this?' she demanded.

'Yours. I mean hers, Thasha's. The idea was hers, too.'

'She thought of this plan? The *girl*?'

'Why do you find that so strange?'

'I believe I shall do it,' said Erithusmé, amazed at her own words. 'The force should suffice. It could be the *only* force that will suffice.' She glanced at him again. 'Did I not say that you should run?'

'I mean to,' said Pazel. 'But Erithusmé: remember your promise. When the Nilstone is gone, you'll give that body back to her, you swore—'

'*Never in two thousand years have I broken an oath!*' she shrieked. 'Get on, you needling brat! This is the last deed of my life, and you are making it unbearable!'

'It's because I love her,' he said.

She laughed, indifferent. Then she blinked, turned to gaze at him with deeper understanding. 'And she you.'

He nodded.

'Desperately,' she said. 'That was it, that was what made her keep fighting me. That was the power that kept rebuilding the wall. She could want to give way to me, let me return and deal with the Nilstone. But she couldn't ever truly want to lose you. She mated with you, with doom hanging over you both like a pall.'

'Something you can't understand.'

The mage considered. 'Quite right. I cannot. But I know power when I feel it. And I will return Thasha her body when this job is done – and only then. Now for the last time, run.'

He ran. The dunes fought him, swallowing his feet. He doubled back to grab the blanket but could not find it, and then, in the thicket of trees, he could not find the stairs. When at last he did he took them two at a time, ambushed by the fear of having waited too long.

If he drowned today she'd be searching for a dead man.

At the top of the fourth staircase he saw her climbing an accordion-ladder. By the time he topped the seventh, the gunports were sealing themselves, one by one. He was already winded. Thirteen to go.

Far above, the last of the climbers were spreading out along the ridgetop, hundreds of feet above the saddle where the canyon began. There were Jorl and Suzyt; there was Marila's round belly, and Neeps holding her close.

Twelve staircases behind him. Now he could look back over the sound, all the way to the Arrowhead, the stone that ought to fall. Thirteen staircases. On the beach, the *Chathrand* suddenly righted herself, slid into deeper water, turned her prow to face the wall.

Fourteen staircases. A tremor shook the earth.

Pitfire. Pitfire. I'm too late.

He could barely feel his legs, but they still served him, he still climbed. *Not high enough. You can't stop. Keep going.* He was dizzy, falling and bouncing to his feet again, scraping his hands. Was this the fifteenth staircase? The sixteenth? He was no longer sure.

The wall still loomed above him. He was crawling. And that wouldn't do.

Then the Arrowhead fell.

'Oh *credek*, no!'

It toppled straight inland, like a tree. Millions of cubic feet of rock struck the water in an instant. And then the wave came, like a second mountain. Like an act of vengeance by the Gods.

He was seeing stars. The wave was big enough. That was all he could think of, all that mattered. It would lift the ship and everything else on that mile-long beach, and would not stop for anything, anyone, between here and death.

A monstrous roaring filled the canyon. As the canyon narrowed the wave grew taller and taller still. He crawled a few more steps. A wind rose that nearly knocked him flat.

Yes, it was big enough, and Erithusmé was there with her hand on the Nilstone, holding her broken ship together by will and sorcery. That was enough. It would have to be enough. He had earned his rest.

'Get up you damned fool!'

Neda. Neeps. They had come out of nowhere and seized his arms, one on each side, and all but carrying him they flew up the stairs, swearing in Sollochi and Ormali and Mzithrini, dashing and stumbling beside drops of five or six hundred feet, looking back with horror in their eyes. They were above the wall, now, and Pazel saw the long, dismal canyon, and a black funnel in the distance, a place even the Swarm could make no darker than it was.

The wave crested thirty feet above the wall, and twenty below the spot where Neeps and Neda ran out of strength and dropped beside him in the dirt. Then the wall collapsed, and stones the size of mansions blasted into the canyon beyond. Then the *Chathrand* came, pitching and rolling but beautifully afloat, and the Goose-Girl swept them with her wooden eyes.

The water swept like lightning down the canyon. The three of them lay there, spent, the wind still tearing at them, and watched the unfathomable torrent's progression. By the time the wave reached the abyss they had lost sight of the *Chathrand*. But the abyss swallowed the wave, and surely everything it carried. And everyone.

Pazel waited. The Swarm felt almost close enough to touch. He was not going to flee it down the mountain again, into that flooded devastation. He was finished.

Nor did he have to flee. Before his eyes the great mass began to shrink, to implode. Faster and faster it shrunk, the sky brightening by the minute, and the withering shadow it had cast over land and sea contracting too. He stood up. The Swarm contracted to the size of the Arrowhead, then the size of the beach. At last it too began to race towards the abyss, as though it were tied by an invisible cord to the Nilstone, and the cord had at last run out. Pazel shielded his eyes and saw it falling, a black star, leaving Alifros for the land where its evil was no evil but the order of things. He watched it vanish. He felt the warmth of the sun.

For a time no one spoke. Pazel could hear Jorl and Suzyt barking hysterically in the meadows above.

'Thank you,' he said at last.

Neeps turned around and looked at him. 'You're a nutter,' he said. 'What in Pitfire were you doing down there?'

'Woolgathering.'

'Sense of humour, too. What are you, a tarboy?'

Pazel grinned at him. Neeps did not grin back. Slowly Pazel's smile began to fade. Neda said, 'You are on *Chathrand*, since Serpent's Head?'

'Neda!'

His sister jumped. So did Neeps. 'Listen, mate: who are you? How do you know her name? We know you're one of Darabik's boys, but why'd you bother to come aboard, if you were just going to hide out below?'

'I am seeing him before,' said Neda. 'I think so. Maybe.'

Pazel tried to speak again, and failed. At last Neeps shook his head.

'Maybe he's afraid of *sfvantskor* tattoos, Neda. After all we've just been through! Well, come up and join us, mystery boy, when you're done quaking in your boots. We're all on the same side, you know.'

They trudged wearily up the ridge, leaving him sitting there. Pazel put his head in his hands. The Master-Word had done its job, all right. But it had not stopped with erasing him from Thasha's mind. It had reached up the mountain and touched his best friend, and his sister. And who knew how many more.

He climbed up to the meadows, among the hundreds of men and women with whom he'd crossed the world. Some were laughing with relief; others were crying, or just lying flat and spread-eagled, making love to the earth. A few looked at him with curiosity, or pity when they saw his distress. But not with recognition, none of them. Even Neda merely frowned at him, puzzled. Fiffengurt sat beside the travel case into which Thasha had packed her clock. Hercól offered him water. Marila stood up and brought him something wrapped in her kerchief.

'It's called *mül*,' she said. 'It doesn't look like food, but it is.'

He held the tiny package, dumbstruck, lost. 'Thanks,' he whispered at last.

Disconcerted, Marila went back and sat beside Neeps. They were talking about Thasha, speculating on her fate. Pazel moved past Bolutu and Prince Olik, who nodded at him distantly. When he crouched in front of Felthrup, the mastiffs growled.

'Hush, you boisterous brutes!' said Felthrup. 'Never mind them, sir. They're a bit uneasy around strangers, but they will do you no harm.'

'Look what I found in my pocket,' said Hercól. On his palm lay the ivory whale Pazel's mother had given him so long ago. 'Rin knows where it came from,' said Hercól, 'or why it especially caught my eye. You want it, Neda Phoenix-Flame?'

Pazel climbed a little higher and sat on a rock. They had their arms around each other. They were tending the wounded, wiping away tears, wondering aloud how soon the *Nighthawk* would come for them, and what would happen next. Even laughing, just a little. They were starting to allow themselves to imagine their lives going on. It was a conversation in which he played no part.

An hour passed, and the survivors of the voyage began a careful descent. 'You there, lad!' Hercól called to him. 'I don't know your story, or how you came to be aboard. But never mind that. You're alive, and the world is new. Get up, come along with us. This is still a dangerous island. You don't want to stay here alone.'

'I'll be right behind you,' Pazel heard himself say.

It was a lie, of course. He wasn't going to move. As for being alone, that was something he'd be getting used to.

A slight sound: he turned and saw Ramachni seated beside him, gazing as he was at the canyon, the water still draining backwards into the sea.

'Not all forms of blindness endure, my lad,' he said.

'You know me?'

'I know you, curiously enough. Perhaps because I was the one who gave you the Master-Words to begin with, or perhaps because I am a mage. But there is a certain flavour to permanent transformation, and another to the temporary sort. This is the latter. They will remember you, in time.'

'How long? Days?'

'Longer, I think.'

'Months? *Years?*'

Ramachni gazed at him quietly. 'I don't know, Pazel. But I can tell you this: Erithusmé, and Thasha within her, left the world aboard the *Chathrand*. My mistress called out to me in the mind-speech as she passed. And her last words were these: *Tell him my promise stands.*'

Pazel caught his breath. 'What does that mean? Her promise to return Thasha's body, to let her live?'

'Unless she made you some other.'

'But how can she keep that promise *now*?'

Ramachni turned and looked towards the abyss. 'By passing through death's kingdom, and out the other side. Erithusmé has the strength to attempt such a journey, but it will not be an easy one, or short. Thasha's soul will be protected, in that back chamber of the mind where Erithusmé dwelt so long. She will not age, or suffer any harm.'

Deep in Pazel's chest a spark flared up. It had almost been extinguished, but he thought he might just keep it burning now.

'You must temper your hopes,' said Ramachni. 'Like other portals you have passed through—the River of Shadows, the Red Storm – any return from the land of the dead runs the risk of metamorphosis. If you find her again, she may have taken a different shape, a different name. She may be older than you, or have stayed frozen in time while you yourself have aged.'

'I don't care. I don't care at all.'

Ramachni leaped up into his lap, and rested his chin on Pazel's knee. 'But you do care, Pazel Pathkendle, and that has made all the difference, in the end.'

37

The Editor Pauses For a Drink

My time has come; my inkwell runs dry. This hand is a paw once more. When I gnaw through the string that holds the quill in place, I will not be able to tie it again. The voyage of the *Chathrand* ends, and with it my voyage in human form.

I have shrunk, too: no longer can I reach the tower window. But the sounds from the courtyard reach me better than ever: the roar of the students (they have rallied to the Fulbreech Society), the shouts of the Academy Police, the clatter of hooves on the cobblestones, the murmur of the swelling mob. The Academy's donors are here for their conference, and are witnessing the scene. I have caused a scandal. I have spent their money on something other than the greater glory of the Academy.

Here at last is the final sound: a battle on the staircase, harsh cries from the flikkermen, steel against steel. There are eight stone floors between us, yet. I cannot tell who is storming the tower: my allies, or the chancellor's thugs? Are they coming to carry off my manuscript or consign it to the fire? Will history be rescued or erased this day?

Allies or enemies, they will find no mad professor here. Only his clothes, and his gold spectacles, and a black rat named Felthrup Stargraven. I see him now, his face reflected in the dish of water from which I drink. He has been swimming a long time. He has spent their gold on truth, to which no glory attaches, now or ever. He has tried to rescue the past as a gift to the future, and he only hopes the gift will suffice. Take it, Alifros. Call it my parting prayer.

Ah, but the battle is still raging, and the words still come. Let us play a game, shall we? Let us see how far I can get.

Epilogue

The *Nighthawk* could not enter the sound, now that the Arrowhead lay barely submerged across its mouth. But the following morning the rest of Maisa's ragtag fleet caught up with her, and the smaller boats shuttled the survivors offshore. Admiral Isiq divided them according to his boats' capacities, but he kept all those who had been closest to Thasha at his side. Thus what remained of the circle of friends stayed together, for a time.

Ramachni put two requests to the admiral. The first was that he extend his personal protection to the whole of Ixphir House, until their new leader, Lady Ensyl, decided where the most travelled clan in history might start anew. This Isiq granted gladly. 'If they wish it, they may dwell in the vessels I command until we take back the Throne of Arqual, and beyond,' he said.

The mage's second request was that the mystery boy, who called himself Pazel Chadfallow, be kept aboard the *Nighthawk* as well.

'Done,' said Isiq. 'What else?' He would have given Ramachni the moon, in a saucer with caramel and cream. The mage had sworn to him that his daughter, though missing, was still very much alive.

'But I am curious about your tarboy,' he added. 'Is he quite sane? He makes no serious claim to kinship with the late doctor, I hope?'

'Not in my hearing,' said Ramachni, with a voice that made it plain the matter was closed.

After a crossing of twenty days they touched ground on tiny Jitril. There they learned that the Defender of the Crownless Lands, King Oshiram of Simja, now commanded the largest surviving fleet in Northwest Alifros, for the simple reason that no large part of it had engaged in battle after the Swarm spread its cloak. They learned too that the black cloud had swept some twelve battlefields clean, though none half so great as the ocean of slaughter at Serpent's Head. It had also frozen much of the Northern harvest in the ground, and a hungry winter was expected. Above all, the people of Alifros had been frightened out of their minds.

The pious declared it heaven's final warning. Practical men knew it was a chance to change the world. In twenty days, peace had replaced war as the fascination of princes, merchants, even generals, even priests. For some, this new passion was to become a sturdy faith. But others felt war's charms returning even before the spring.

Maisa's forces were made to wait at Jitril for a fortnight, until Oshiram himself gave leave for their passage through the Crownless Lands. Then the first separations occurred, with part of the little fleet heading east to Opalt, where rumours of a great new insurrection against Etherhorde had arisen, and others making south to Urnsfich, where the Mzithrinis were to be collected by their countrymen. The *Nighthawk*, however, headed north to Simja. There Oshiram heard their story and professed to believe it. He called them the saviours of Alifros, and promised that every refugee from the *Chathrand* would be granted sanctuary in Simja for as long as they needed it, and citizenship if they desired to stay.

But the king was a busy man, and his ministers took him at his word. Only recognised members of the *Chathrand*'s crew were extended this welcome. Others would have to apply like any normal refugee, and inhabit the barges set aside for them in the Bay of Simja until their appeals could be heard. Pazel took one look at those floating houses of misery and asked Ramachni to help him get across the Straits of Simja to Ormael.

'I will do it, Pazel,' said the mage, 'but have you not heard what they are saying? Ormael may be free, but it is poor and ravaged; it changed hands five times during the war. And there is still fighting in all the lands surrounding the city. It could be a hard place, even for a native son. But how much simpler if you would tell your friends the truth! I would gladly help you explain.'

But Pazel could not bear the thought. He had spoken the truth to one of their number already: to Corporal Mandric, as it happened, just before the Turach left to join the Opalt campaign. Mandric had laughed at first, then grown cross, trying to find a flaw in Pazel's story. At last he had become strangely meek and quiet, nodding at Pazel's every word.

'Do you believe me, then?' Pazel asked.

'Oh I do, lad, sure enough! You were with us, right? On that whole Rinforsaken expedition, 'course you were. I remember.'

'You *remember?*'

'Yes. No, I mean – no. I believe you, that's it. Well, er, shipmate, goodbye.'

They shook hands awkwardly, and Mandric hurried off to take his leave of the others. Pazel saw then that he would never know if his friends believed or merely pitied him, if they were speaking from affection or fear.

So he refused. Ramachni sighed, and spoke again to the admiral, and in four days his passage was arranged. It was Neeps who brought the news, late one night as Pazel was stringing up his hammock on the *Nighthawk*.

'Mystery boy. Roll up your things in that hammock and step lively. There's a boat waiting for you.'

'A boat? Whose boat?'

'Just hurry, if you want to catch it. These louts are kind of impatient.'

It had never crossed his mind that he would leave this way, another mad scramble in the darkness, with his friends asleep in scattered beds across the city, and no chance to say goodbye. Not to his sister and Hercól, who were inseparable now. Not to Felthrup. Not to Fiffengurt. Not to Olik or Nólcindar or Bolutu, or the old admiral, father of the woman he loved. Not even to Ramachni, who would have known who stood before him, saying goodbye.

Neeps led him up the ladderway, with that half-awake stumble Pazel knew so well.

'Hey, stop.'

Startled, Neeps looked back over his shoulder.

'I need to ask you a question. About Marila. How did you . . . come to be sure?'

'Sure of what? That I loved her? That's kind of a personal question, mate.'

'Right,' said Pazel, furious with himself. 'Just forget it. I'm sorry.'

Neeps came back down the ladderway. 'No, I'm sorry. You're not much of a talker, and I reckon you wouldn't ask unless it mattered a lot. You have a woman, then?'

Pazel just looked at him. 'I'm not sure,' he said at last.

'Well that's common enough.' Neeps took a deep breath. 'I was forced to dive once, into a shipwreck. We got into some trouble with sea-murths. The girls touch you, and suddenly you can breathe water. But the same spell makes you fall in love with the one you touched. And that one lures you away from the others and kills you. They got half a dozen of us that way.' He looked at Pazel for a moment, then plunged on. 'It happened to me again, you see, with another sort of woman. Just one touch. Only she didn't want to kill me. She was saving my life. And the love was real. I mean, Pitfire, I don't know that there's any other sort of love.'

'What about the murth-girl? Do you still think about her?'

'Oh, not at all. That was just a charm, just a little confusion. Magic can't change the heart, Pazel. They told me that in – well, in a place where they know about such things. And I found it out myself, the hard way. Trust me: if it lasts more than an hour, it's real.'

He looked over his shoulder, then leaned close to Pazel and said, 'You remember Thasha, don't you? Thasha Isiq? The one who stayed on the ship?'

Pazel spoke very carefully. 'I remember her just fine.'

'They say she'll come back one day. From the land of the dead.' Neeps' eyes were moist. 'Lunja, my woman Lunja, won't be coming back. But if she did—'

He broke off. Pazel wanted to embrace him. They looked away

from each other, suddenly abashed. 'I have no idea why I'm talking to you,' said Neeps.

'Because you're a good bloke, that's why.'

'Lunja made me a better one. She made me larger, you see. She made room in my heart. And that's better for everyone, I guess.'

Marila stood wrapped in a blanket under the starlight, bedraggled and enormously pregnant. 'Hello, tarboys,' she said sleepily, as Neeps pulled her close. 'What took you so long? They got tired of waiting. They're running a loop out there somewhere, and coming back for you, Pazel.' She yawned. 'I don't know why they're crossing in the middle of the night.'

'You didn't have to get up,' Pazel said.

'I wanted to,' she said simply. 'Oh, and Ramachni sent you a package; it's already aboard.' She looked at him, thoughtful. 'He cares a lot about you. Why is that, if you don't mind me asking?'

'We have friends in common.'

It was too vague an answer for Marila, but this time she merely shrugged. 'Be careful out there, will you? The world is stranger than you think.'

'That's hardly possible,' he said. 'All right, then. Good luck with that school.'

They smiled. Long ago Marila had admitted that she wanted to start a school for the deaf. The dream was still with her, and Neeps, it appeared, had begun to see the possibilities as well.

Pazel looked at Marila's round belly. 'What about a name?' he asked. 'Have you chosen one yet?'

They hesitated, glancing sidelong at each other. 'It's strange, really,' said Neeps. 'We're agreed that if it's a girl we'll call her Diadrelu, after a friend who died. But if it's a boy – well, that's the odd part. We chose one. We both remember making a decision, and being very sure. But we can't for the life of us remember what it was.'

'It was such a *good* name,' said Marila, looking at him earnestly.

'So good we don't want to talk about any others, just yet. We're still hoping we remember.'

Pazel looked at her with wonder. 'I hope so too,' he said at last.

'Well, here's your boat,' said Neeps, a bit relieved, as a sleek little clipper drew alongside. 'Goodbye, Pazel. If you ever make it out Sollochstol way, you've got friends.'

'I'll remember,' he said. Then he took their hands and held them a long while, until he knew he had made them uncomfortable. On the clipper, a man was shouting. *All aboard who's coming aboard.*

'Thank you for everything,' said Pazel, and let them go.

He spoke as little as possible to the men on the clipper. He did not look back to see if Neeps and Marila were still standing by the rail. They were bound for the Outer Isles, and it seemed likely that he would never see them again. At the moment the thought was more than he could bear.

The package was heavy. Inside, he found a purse of gold: fine gold cockles from the wreck of the *Chathrand*, a bit of the fortune that Sergeant Haddismal had saved. The purse did not a fortune make, but it was enough to live on, frugally, for a few years at least. There was also a sharp knife, and some clothing. At the bottom of the crate, wrapped carefully in oilskin, lay Thasha's copy of the thirteenth *Merchant's Polylex*.

When he did begin to speak to the men, he learned at once why they were crossing by night. They were freebooters, smugglers, dodging the new tariff collectors of the Crownless Lands. 'These upstarts have got nothin' on the old Arquali Inspectorate,' said one of the men, cheerfully. 'We'll have some good years here, before they learn our tricks.'

'And there must be scarcity, too?' said Pazel.

'Oh, aye, lad, scarcity!'

'So higher prices, higher profits for you.'

'Right on the kisser!' laughed the man. 'You talk like you know the trade. Do you drink as well?'

He took a drink. They were the happiest people he had seen

since Uláramyth. Pazel was almost beginning to enjoy himself when his mind-fit struck.

The freebooters scratched their chins. They set him up on the fife-rail, where everyone could watch him babble and moan. Pazel could not tell whether they thought him possessed, but if so, they worried less about having a devil aboard than the attention it might bring in Ormaelport. They conferred awhile, then gave him a wineskin and locked him in the hold. Pazel wished he could thank them. When he drank, his legs gave out, and he knew he had been drugged.

Days later, when he came to his senses, he was far from the city of his birth. The clipper was running north along a foggy coast-line. New freebooters were aboard, and one of them evidently out-ranked the captain, for he had taken over the man's cabin, and could be heard inside, with a woman. Each time the man laughed Pazel found himself staring at the door.

Later that morning, the man sent for him. Pazel was shown right into the bedchamber. There in blue pajamas, beside a rosy-cheeked woman Pazel had never seen, was Gregory Pathkendle.

He was older – so much older! All the hair that remained to him was grey. Still his eyes were bright with mischief as he beck-oned Pazel to take a seat.

'Pazel Chadfallow, is it?' he said, making a face, as though the name tickled the back of his throat. 'Afflicted with some permanent magic, they tell me? Well never mind, my daughter's just the same.'

'Which daughter's that, love?' said the woman.

'I don't mind a man with problems he owns up to,' said Captain Gregory, 'but there's one thing I can't abide. Can you guess what it is?'

'Domesticity?' said Pazel.

'Beg your pardon?'

'No sir, I can't guess.'

'Boasting, that's what,' said Gregory. 'So I have in mind to find out if you were boasting when you told my boys you knew your way around a ship.'

He drilled Pazel for some ten minutes concerning sails and rigging and the standard etiquette of the sea. Then he asked Pazel about his surname.

'I knew a Chadfallow. He was a doctor, and a great man, although he was too close to the Usurper in Etherhorde. He was one of the most powerful men in Alifros, in his time. Do you know the man I'm speaking of?'

'Ignus Chadfallow,' said Pazel uneasily. 'I knew him. I'm his son.'

The woman burst out laughing. But Captain Gregory just looked him up and down. Pazel found himself remembering certain mornings when the woman beside Gregory had been his mother, and the window behind the bed had looked out on plum orchards. There had been mornings when this man made griddle-cakes, or took Pazel out to edge of the Highlands to spot foxes and deer. A small, sweet life. A life he'd never thought would end.

'Hush your cackling,' Gregory told the woman. 'The lad didn't lie about his sailing smarts; why should he lie about his father? And even the noblest among us may sew a few wild seeds.'

'You're proof of that.'

Gregory kissed her. 'Even dry old Chadfallow had a passionate side. I happen to know that for a fact.' He winked at Pazel. 'There's a past behind every man, ain't there, my boy?'

Pazel signed on with Gregory's freebooters that very day, and in the two years that followed he saw more of the Northern world than he had on all his years on merchant vessels. With his new shipmates he camped in bogs and salt marshes, danced with Noonfirth courtesans, smuggled arms, liquor and living men across the battle-lines. He was aware that he had realised his oldest dream: to sail with the man he'd always believed to be his father. But that had been a childish dream. Gregory's passion for ribald jokes, for helping orphans, for bedding women whose languages he didn't speak and whose very names he confused: all that had been carefully hidden. Pazel only now began to know the man.

Gregory's friendship with the Empress was something more

than strategic: he had despised Arqual even before it invaded his homeland. He took countless risks for Maisa's rebels, whether by sharing intelligence in secret letters or hiding swords in sacks of meal. 'I'm no idealist, Pazel,' he confided once, 'I just know how to pick the winning team.'

Pazel hoped Gregory was right, but doubted anyone could be sure. Maisa's rebels had yet to launch a single raid on Etherhorde. Still, defectors continued to join her ranks, and the noose about the capital was tightening. After one bloody week in springtime, Ulsprit fell. Pazel was there in the city when Maisa rode through as a liberator, waving from an open carriage beside Prince Eberzam Isiq. Pazel was surprised to see a little bird swoop down and land on Isiq's shoulder. Prince Eberzam turned it a blazing smile.

But if Gregory had aged, Thasha's father was actually venerable, and Maisa was almost ancient. Her iron will was apparent in every glance, but her frame was skin and bone, and her hands shook as she waved. And for the first time Pazel wondered who, if anyone, these two were grooming as an heir.

That night Gregory did not come back to the ship, and the next day they sailed for Dremland without him. As Ulsprit dwindled on the horizon, the bosun let it slip that Gregory had stayed behind for a woman.

'Of course he did,' said Pazel. It had happened before: Gregory leaving his ship in other hands, arranging passage with friends or fellow schemers, rejoining them in some distant port. But the bosun said that this woman was a special case. 'They were married once, you see. She was his wife.'

'His wife? His wife *Suthinia*?'

'Aye, the witch. So he's told you about her, has he?'

Pazel looked back at Ulsprit. It was hard to find the words. 'I know about her,' he said at last.

In Dremland, late at night, he wrote a letter to Gregory and slipped it under his door. Then he bundled his things into his hammock and slipped onto the dock. He had forged papers and fine seamanship, and thirty languages to his name. He'd spent less money than he'd earned in Gregory's service. He knew how to get along. *How* was never likely to be a problem, he decided. The harder questions were *where*, and *why*.

He went on wandering. Now and then he took a drink. There were times when his loneliness rose up and seemed to smother him, and other times when he recalled Ramachni's words on Gurishal, and felt glad, and was determined to hold on.

He bribed his own way across the battle-lines and walked the streets of Etherhorde, and stood in front of the old Isiq mansion on Maj Hill. That upper window, her bedroom. That garden, where Hercól taught her to fight. Then he found his way to Reka Street, and was admitted to the Physicians' Temple, and lit a candle for Dr. Ignus Chadfallow, and stayed there in silence for a time.

By evening he was anxious to be gone: too many women in Etherhorde looked like Thasha Isiq. He fled to Uturphe, and grew drunk on Uturphan brandy, and stumbled into the flikkermen's quarter in a daze. The flikkermen chased him, cracking their whips, until they realised he was cursing them in their own language, flawlessly. At once they grew affectionate, and fed him raw river eel, and never wanted him to leave.

The next month he stopped in Simja, and visited the taverns there, and listened to the sailors' gossip. To his amazement, he heard them speaking of the Shaggat Ness.

'What's that?' he said, breaking in. 'You have that wrong, surely? The Shaggat's dead.'

'Oh, the father, aye, on Gurishal. But this is his son, lad. On Bramian. Ain't you heard? The Usurper raised him like a pet snake, with thousands of his crazies, up a big river in the jungle. He even built them a fleet. And the Shaggat's boy sailed off just like they wanted, to make war on the Mzithrinis. It was all according to plan.'

'Somebody's *ugly* plan,' his friend added, with a belch.

'Until one day the son wakes up and says, "It's over. My father the Shaggat is dead. I am going home to set the white monkeys free." And he turns his fleet around and sails back to Bramian, and sets up a kingdom on that riverbank, and starts to bring the tribals into his fold. The island's full of savages, you know. And the poor old Secret Fist! They can't take Bramian back from him. They don't have the manpower these days.'

Seaside taverns were better than the *Polylex*, Pazel decided. A day later he heard an even stranger rumour, concerning Gurishal. As planned, the Mzithrinis had paraded the body of the Shaggat Ness before his worshippers, and that had crushed their spirits, all but destroying the faith. But on Gurishal too a new cult had arisen: the Shaggat Malabron. A scepter-wielding madman with the powers of a sorcerer, who was quickly taking control of the great island. At his side he was said to keep a strange, foreign counsellor, an old man with scars and a wolfish grin.

Pazel sighed, and drank up. They had killed one Shaggat, but two had taken his place.

At long last he made his way home to Ormael. The city was rank, crowded, penniless, beautiful. He saw his own home, with kindly-looking strangers behind the windows and mewling cats in the yard. He walked up into the plum orchards and helped himself to a plum. He sat in the late afternoon sun and closed his eyes and knew an hour's peace. He thought that love had nearly killed them all but love had also saved them, more times than he could count.

Later that year he bought a passage to Opalt. He had no clear purpose in going there, except to lose himself in bustling Ballytween, one of the greatest cities of the North. In the flood of strangers' voices, he thought he might not hear the one voice that followed him everywhere. And that would bring relief, of a kind.

Things did not go as planned. On his first walk through the port district, he saw a public house called Annabel's. The place was large and crowded, and he walked right by. But at the corner he paused, looking back at the bright doorway. Then he walked back and stepped inside and bought himself some ale and fritters at the bar. He was finishing his second pint when he saw Fiffengurt at a corner table, playing chess with Felthrup.

He took the table beside them, and started chatting when the opportunity arose. Captain Fiffengurt was the brother of the bar's owner; he was also very drunk. Felthrup drank only water; he was intent on winning the game. But they seemed to like talking to him. They stayed, even as the crowd grew thinner, and Pazel bought them ale and food and asked them to tell their stories, and they obliged. By midnight they had forgotten the chess match, and were telling Pazel of the great waterworks of Masalym. By closing time they had brought him to the wreck on Gurishal.

'I ran her clean aground,' put in Fiffengurt. 'But that wasn't the end, was it, Ratty? Oh no. We watched her from the meadows on the clifftops. Watched her swept away to perdition, and Lady Thasha still aboard. I still, still dream—'

He staggered away from the table, looking sick. 'Why does he drink so much?' Pazel asked.

'You might too, Pazel, if you had lost five years of your life, and come back to find everything changed.'

Pazel looked down into his tankard: nearly empty. The rat had a point.

'And Captain Fiffengurt has his sorrows,' Felthrup continued. 'Oh, he calls himself lucky, very lucky, to be here again with his beloved Annabel, and to know his dear daughter. They fled here from Etherhorde, during the worst part of the fighting. And it has been good for everyone: there are no beer-wars on Opalt, no breweries torched by rivals.'

'What's his worry, then?' asked Pazel.

'Anni married his brother, Pazel. Years before our return. She is quite fond of him; the man is a good husband and father. But the child is Fiffengurt's. You must keep that last fact to yourself.'

Pazel rested his chin on his hand, and sighed. 'I won't tell a soul.'

'Good,' said Felthrup. 'I have a feeling I can trust you. In fact I will now share a secret of my own. I mean to become a historian.'

'Do that!' Pazel slapped the table and laughed.

'Ah, you are flippant, but I spend every day in the archives, here in Ballytween; it has become a second home. But there is something more. Where that voyage is concerned I have a special advantage. Do you know what I did, when the Great Ship lay smashed on the beach?'

Pazel thought about it. 'No, I don't.'

'I drank the blood of the keel. They brought me to shore on a raft, and while the others were boarding I caught a strange, warm, resinous smell, and then I saw it dripping, dripping from a crack in the good ship's spine, where it arched overhead. I licked the spot. It tasted like nothing I have ever experienced. And the next day the memories began.'

'Memories?'

'Of everything, my lad. I can summon the memories of everyone who made that voyage with us. The cook. The tarboys. The anchor-lifters. The ixchel. Erithusmé's ship had a soul, Pazel Pathkendle, but the difference is this: it was a composite soul. All of us together made up that soul, and now it speaks to me. And I must listen and remember. That is the least I can do.'

'Felthrup?'

'Yes, lad?'

'You just used my last name. But I never told it to you. Did I?'

Felthrup nibbled his fritter, thinking. 'No, it was Diadrelu who told me. Before you and I ever met.'

'Felthrup!'

'Yes, lad!'

'You remember me! I mean, you *just started* to remember me. When I walked in here you didn't know who I was!'

The rat looked at him blankly. Then he squealed so loudly that he stopped all conversation, and even the piano player. He leaped over the table into Pazel's lap. He began to hop up and down.

'I forgot you! I forgot you! And then I remembered, and forgot that I had forgotten!

Oh, Pazel Pazel *Pazel*—'

The lamentable truth is that he wet himself, and Pazel in the process. Pazel could not have cared less. He held the lame rat against his cheek and tried not to cry. Nearly four years had passed since anyone had looked at him with recognition.

Of course Felthrup at once shared all he knew of their friends. Bolutu had remained in Simja, and with the King's blessing – and the help of one particularly talented dog – opened the Royal Inter-Species Institute. 'He sent a letter not two months ago. They've purchased a villa with extensive grounds. The humans who come there will learn from woken animals, and vice versa, and both will take their understanding out into the world. I dare say the work is needed. Many a dog, horse, hare and raven still lives in fear of opening their mouths.'

'But you're not afraid. You're right here in the middle of the pub, playing chess.'

'That's because he's Felthrup Stargraven,' boomed Fiffengurt suddenly. 'Where've you been the last few years, lad? This rat's a hero of Alifros. He's battled sorcerers and pudgy devils, and an ugly, nasty daddy-rat, *GRAAAA—*'

He dropped to all fours and did an impression of Master Mugstur, to the other patrons' delight.

'Never mind him,' said Felthrup. 'I have news of your sister.'

'Neda! Tell me, for Rin's sake!'

'She and Hercól are together, and deeply in love. They are Empress Maisa's special envoys to the Mzithrin, and have done a great deal to ensure that the peace will never again be broken, so long as Maisa is a power in this world.'

'They're married, are they?'

'Alas, no,' said Felthrup. 'In his last letter, Hercól said he dared not ask your sister for her hand, "while so many enemies remain to contend with, and so much evil flourishes in the dark." I fear for them, Pazel. I am very much afraid they will undertake a mission into the heart of Gurishal, to confront the Shaggat Malabron, and Sandor Ott. Both of them feel bound to the task.

'But enough! It is late. You must stay with us tonight, my boy. And change those smelly breeches, for shame!'

Felthrup and Fiffengurt shared rooms above the tavern. Pazel set the rat on his shoulder, passed through the kitchen and up a darkened stair. The rooms, when they entered, surprised him pleasantly. They were spacious and fine.

'We do not go hungry,' admitted Felthrup. 'Sergeant Haddismal divided up the *Chathrand* treasure among all the survivors, and Admiral Isiq gave us more ere we separated. Fiffengurt handed his share over to Miss Annabel, saying that he had gone to sea for the sake of her family's debts, and wouldn't neglect them now. Anni used it to purchase this house, and from that day she has considered Fiffengurt a business partner. Now change. You'll find clean things in that dresser, beneath the clock.'

Pazel smiled as he stepped into Fiffengurt's pants: the wiry sailor had grown rather stout. Then he froze. The clock on the dresser was unmistakable. It was Thasha's, the beautiful mariner's clock, with its face shaped like a gibbous, mother-of-pearl moon.

'Ah yes,' said Felthrup. 'Ramachni left that in our keeping. He has long since departed for his own world. And he says that I must join him there, one day.'

'What? You? Why you, Felthrup?'

'Pazel, the Waking Spell has been the cruelest sort of blessing. I am a rat, in a rat's frail form. I have plans and hopes that far exceed my body's limitations, and its life span. When I depart down the tunnel in that clock, Ramachni tells me that I will find myself in another body, human or dlömic or some other long-lived race, on the other side. And he will present me to a certain learned academy, and even vouch for my studious nature.'

'Felthrup! That's wonderful! But ... how long do you have?'

'Before I leave? This body's aches will tell me that. A few years, I hope. But there is something more astonishing, my boy. That other world, Ramachni's? It is our future. Or rather, a future that *might* be ours.'

'Might be.' Pazel rested a hand on the clock, feeling sudden loneliness. 'You mean the way the *Chathrand* might have ended up on that empty island, where Lord Talag hid his clan?'

'Correct,' said Felthrup. 'Ramachni's Alifros is linked to our own by a thin footpath, winding through endless mountain-chains of years. But in the actual walking we find that the path divides almost endlessly. Some paths lead down into fertile valleys, others to ice and fear. There is no telling, deep in the mountains, whether you have strayed or not.'

Pazel stayed on in Ballytween, and thanked the Gods for Felthrup Stargraven. He took a room in the port district with a view of the sea. He tutored children in many languages, and became a celebrity at Annabel's. On free days he went with Felthrup to the city archives, and learned many things about the world they had saved.

Fiffengurt still did not know him, and when Coote and Fegin paid their old captain a visit they did not know him either. Nor did the half dozen other survivors of the *Chathrand* who passed through Ballytween that year. If the Master-Word's effects were waning, they were taking their time.

He was twenty-one and considered handsome. The serving-girls fought bitterly over the right to bring him beer. Some of them were beautiful, many of them were kind. Now and then he found he could kiss them, or even go through the motions of love. But he could not court them seriously. The kindest and the loveliest he avoided: they stirred a pain in him he could not bear.

His drinking grew worse. A morning came when he woke up knowing that he had spent the whole night at Annabel's, buying rounds for the house, switching languages as often as he switched tables, slapping the backs of strangers, avoiding Felthrup's worried eye. He had an idea that several tarboys from the *Chathrand* had shown up that night, some of them with sweethearts, and it frightened him to realise that he might just as easily have imagined them in his stupor. He threw up into a basin. He lay back thinking of death.

Then his hand went to his collarbone. There was a warmth there that had nothing to do with alcohol. He had almost forgotten the sensation, golden sunlight in his veins, a thing so beautiful that no one who felt it should ever speak of sorrow again.

Land-boy, land-boy, can you still hear me? Do you think I have forgotten you?

It was dawn. He pulled on his shoes and stumbled out through the dirty city and along the coast road until he came to the beach. A sign warned of rip tides, and declared swimming forbidden. He undressed. He felt it was Thasha undressing him, her loving hands, her knowing smile.

He swam offshore with easy strokes. The current bore him swiftly out, and soon the land looked small and notional above the swells. When he tired, he let himself sink, and stayed there until he saw Klyst coming for him, her murth-beauty breathtaking, her teeth like a shark's.

He would have to tell her of Thasha, that his heart had many chambers, that he dreamed of another's return.

Serpentine arms went around him. He was still holding his breath. *It's not forever*, he would have to say. But as he tried to form the words in her language, he found that 'forever' did not exist in the murthic tongue. There were words for now and later, for tomorrow, for tonight. But not forever. The effort tied him in knots.

'Land-boy, do you love me?' she asked. 'Will you come with me today?'

Today. *Iriritha*. That was a lovely word, he thought.

He closed his eyes. Last chance. But then her lips brushed the shell beneath his collarbone, and there was no more waiting, no more doubt. He put his arms around her, buried his face in the kelp-forest of her hair. Klyst was laughing as he kissed her. 'You can breathe again,' she said.

Here ends
The Night of the Swarm
and
The Chathrand Voyage
Quartet

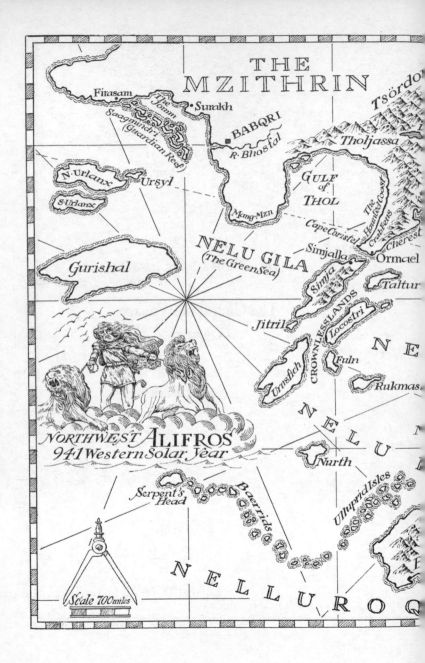

THE
MZITHRIN

Firasam
The Jomm
Surakh
Ssaag'munch'i
(Guardian Reef)
BABQRI
R. Bhosfal
Tholjassa
Tsördo

N. Urlanx
Ursyl
GULF
of
THOL

S. Urlanx
Mang-Mzn
Cape Coristel
The Haunted Coast
Crab Fens
Cherest

Gurishal
NELU GILA
(The Green Sea)
Simjalla
Ormael

Simja
Taltur

Jitril
Locostri
CROWNLESS ISLANDS
N E

Urnsfich
Fuln
Rukmas

NORTHWEST ALIFROS
941 Western Solar Year
N E L L U

Nurth

Serpent's
Head
Baerrids
Ullupri Isles

N E L L U R O Q

Scale 700 miles

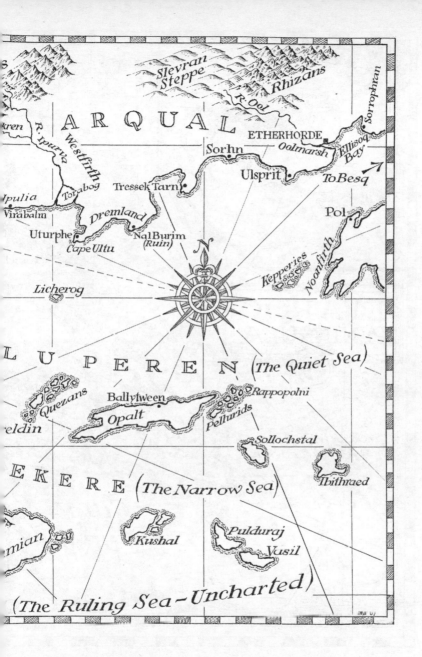

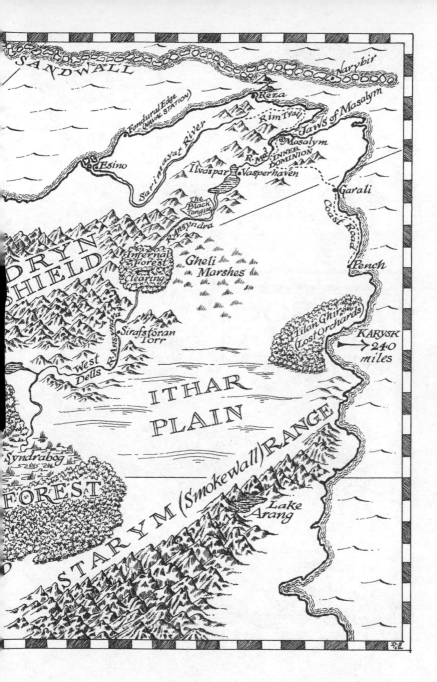

Acknowledgements

Kiran Asher's love, good humour, patience and faith soared with me in the good times and saw me through the bad. For nearly a decade *The Chathrand Voyage* was the third resident in our household: part beloved child, part tone-deaf dinner guest who never said goodnight. Thank you, amor de mi vida, for not banishing the child or poisoning the guest, and for restraining me when I was tempted to do the same.

Holly Hanson, Stephen Klink, Jan Redick, Edmund Zavada, Kiran Asher, Mary Link and William Spademan all shared their wise and generous thoughts on the book as I wrote it. Mary and William were especially generous during the last, frantic days. My debt to them all is profound, and my thanks heartfelt.

I would also like to thank Simon Spanton, John Jarrold, Tricia Narwani, Brendan Plapp, Bruce Hemmer, Betsy Mitchell, Kaitlin Heller, Charlie Panayiotou, Jon Weir, Marcus Gipps, David Moench, Linda Moore, Mira Bartók, Gillian Redfearn, Nat Herold, Robert Silverberg, Stephen Deas, Michaela Deas, Bénédicte Lombardo and all my writer friends in the Cushman/ Mosaic nexus.

Since Book One hit the shelves, countless readers have contacted me, sharing their affection for the story and the characters. You know who you are, but you'll never know how much you've helped me, in times when I felt in danger of shipwreck, or too exhausted to sail on. Thank you with all my heart.

Dramatis Personae, Books I – IV

———

ALYASH: Bosun on the *Chathrand*. Recruited in Simja after the death of Mr Swellows.

ARIM, LORD: Elder selk of Uláramyth.

ARUNIS [Arunis Wytterscorm, 'the Blood Mage']: A mighty sorcerer; founder of the Raven Society; corruptor of the Empire of Bali Adro; arch-enemy of both Erithusmé and Ramachni.

BABQRI FATHER: A high priest and elder of the *sfvantskor* order. Neda Pathkendle's teacher.

BOLUTU, DR BELESAR: A veterinarian and monk of the Rinfaith, assigned to I.M.S. *Chathrand* to care for its shipment of animals.

BURNSCOVE, KRUNO: Founder and leader of the Burnscove Boys gang from Etherhorde. Arch-enemies of the Plapps.

CHADFALLOW, DR IGNUS: Imperial Surgeon of Arqual; a favourite of Emperor Magad V; erstwhile Imperial Envoy to Ormael; former lover of Suthinia Pathkendle and protector of her children.

DARABIK, PURSTON [Purcy]: Commodore in the Arquali navy.

DASTU: Arquali tarboy. Secret protégé of Sandor Ott.

DIADRELU [Lady Diadrelu Tammariken ap Ixhxchr, also 'Dri']: An ixchel noblewoman and former commander of Ixphir House. Sister of Lord Talag.

DOLDUR, PAZEL: A mage and historian. Editor-in-Chief of the in-famous 13th Edition of the *Merchant's Polylex*. Suthinia Pathkendle gave Doldur's first name to her son.

ENSYL: An ixchel warrior and student of Lady Diadrelu.

ERITHUSMÉ [Erithusmé the Great]: Mightiest of latter-day mages; first successful wielder of the Nilstone since ancient times; creator of the Waking Spell and the Red Storm; teacher of Ramachni. Born in Nohirin in the Mzithrin lands, she crossed the Ruling Sea repeatedly with the Nilstone's aid. Erithusmé gave up the Nilstone in 925, and was immediately set upon by the Ravens, and particularly Arunis.

FELTHRUP [Felthrup Stargraven]: A woken black rat from Noonfirth.

FIFFENGURT, GRAFF STARLING: Long-serving quartermaster on the *Chathrand*. Passed over more than once as captain.

FULBREECH, GRAYSAN: Errand-boy from Simja.

GARAPAT, PROFESSOR J.L.: An historian who comes to Felthrup Stargraven's aid in the Orfuin Club.

IBJEN: A young dlömic boy from Masalym.

ISIQ, ADMIRAL EBERZAM: Highest field-serving admiral in the Arquali navy; the appointed Imperial ambassador to Simja; father of Thasha Isiq.

ISIQ, CLORISUELA: Deceased wife of Admiral Eberzam and mother of Thasha.

JALANTRI: A *sfvantskor*, trained alongside Neda Pathkendle.

KET, LIRIPUS: A merchant from Opalt, specialising in soaps and solvents.

KIRISHGÁN: Selk who befriended Pazel Pathkendle in the Temple of Vasparhaven (Book III) and later travelled with his company.

KLYST: A young sea-murth from the Gulf of Thól. Klyst and her sisters killed a number of the divers seeking the Red Wolf off the Haunted Coast.

KUMINZAT, ADMIRAL: Famous Mzithrini officer. Commander of the *White Reaper*, pride of the White Fleet, lost in battle south of Bramian.

KURLSTAF, CAPTAIN. Former captain of the *Chathrand*. Many considered him the only captain in 600 years to approach Nilus Rose in cunning and resourcefulness.

LAPADOLMA, PACU: Niece of Lady Lapadolma Yelig, owner of the

Chathrand. Thasha Isiq's maid-in-waiting. Later her replacement as Treaty Bride.

LATZLO, ERNOM: Ormali merchant. A dealer in live animals and suitor of Pacu Lapadolma.

LUDUNTE: An ixchel. Sophister (student) of Lady Diadrelu.

LUNJA, SERGEANT ['The Otter']: Dlömic soldier from Masalym, loyal to Prince Olik.

MACADRA [Macadra Hyndrascorm, The White Raven]: Bali Adro sorceress who controlled the mind and decrees of the senile Emperor Nahundra.

MAGAD V [His Supremacy; also 'The Usurper']: Ruler of the Empire of Arqual. Son, heir and possible murderer of the previous Emperor. Magad V approved and funded the plot to destabilise the Mzithrin Empire through the return of the Shaggat Ness to his followers on Gurishal.

MAISA: Rightful Empress of Arqual, daughter of Magad III. Deposed by her brother Magad IV in 899 and driven into exile.

MALABRON: Trainee *sfvantskor* in Neda Pathkendle's band.

MARILA: Sponge diver from Tholjassa.

MUGSTUR [Master Mugstur]: A woken rat and messianic psychopath.

MYETT: An ixchel woman. Consort to Lord Taliktrum.

NAHUNDRA: Emperor of Bali Adro, under the sway of Macadra and the Ravens.

NESS, ERTHALON: Deranged son of the Shaggat Ness, held with his father, brother and Arunis for decades on the prison-island of Licherog.

NÓLCINDAR: a selk warrior, sailor and shipwright.

OGGOSK, LADY: [Lady Gosmel Pothrena Oggosk, Duchess of Tiroshi]: A witch and special advisor to Captain Rose.

OLIK, PRINCE [HRH Prince Olik Ipandracon Tastandru Bali Adro]: Lesser prince in the ruling dynasty of the Empire of Bali Adro; second cousin to the Emperor.

ORFUIN: A philosopher; owner of the Club that bears his name in the River of Shadows.

OSHIRAM II, KING: Monarch of Simja and host of the Great Peace.

OTT, SANDOR: Imperial Spymaster and chief assassin of Arqual.

PATHKENDLE, GREGORY: Ship's captain from Ormael and husband of Suthinia Pathkendle. Named a traitor, questionably, for his role in the sinking of an Ormali warship. Later a famous freebooter (smuggler) operating in and around the Crab Fens and the Haunted Coast.

PATHKENDLE, PAZEL: A tarboy from Ormael, pressed into service in the Arquali navy after the invasion of his home country in 936.

PATHKENDLE, SUTHINIA: An amateur mage and student of Pazel Doldur. Mother of Pazel and Neda Pathkendle. Suthinia came to Ormael in 924, married Captain Gregory the same year, and largely renounced magic.

PLAPP, DARIUS: Leader and founder of the Plapp's Pier gang from Etherhorde. Arch-enemies of the Burnscove Boys.

RAIN, DR CLAUDIUS: Doctor (?) assigned to the I.M.S. *Chathrand*.

RAMACHNI [Ramachni Fremken, Arpathwin]: Powerful mage with a gift for shape-shifting; his usual form is that of a black mink. Ramachni is a visitor to Alifros from an unidentified land, and Thasha Isiq's lifelong friend.

REFEG AND RER: Anchor lifters. Augrongs (enormous, scaly, ogre-like creature native to the Arquali interior. Close to extinction.). Refeg and Rer dwell in an Etherhorde slum when not at sea.

ROSE, CAPTAIN NILUS ROTHEBY: Commander of the I.M.S. *Chathrand*; notorious thief, smuggler and sadist.

ROSE, CAPTAIN THEIMAT: Father of Nilus Rose. Great trader and strongman in the Quezan Islands. Widely famous for his cruelty.

SATHEK: [the Demon-Mage, the Soulless One]: Long-dead wizard and warlord whose rule first united the Five Kingdoms of the Mzithrin; creator of the Sceptre that bears his name. Sathek gave posthumous aid to Arunis in his hunt for the Nilstone.

SATURYK: An ixchel of Ixphir house. Lord Talag's chief of security.

SHAGGAT [The Shaggat Ness]: A mad king and founder of a religious cult that fractured the Mzithrin Empire. Believed dead but held secretly by Arqual for 40 years. The core of Arqual's plot against the Mzithrin was to return the Shaggat to his worshippers on Gurishal, thus reviving the fanatic cult and weakening the Mzithrini state enough for a swift Arquali invasion.

STANAPETH, HERCÓL: Tholjassan warrior and former assassin with the Secret Fist of Arqual; protégé of Sandor Ott. Thasha Isiq's combat instructor and lifelong ally.

STELDAK: An ixchel man. Captain Rose's prisoner and poison taster.

SURIDIN: An apprentice *sfvantskor* trained by the Babqri Father in the same cohort as Neda Pathkendle. Daughter of Admiral Kuminzat.

SWELLOWS: Bosun on the *Chathrand*. Long-time crony of Captain Rose.

SYRARYS [Syrarys Isiq]: A former slave given as consort to Eberzam Isiq.

TALAG, LORD: An ixchel nobleman. Co-founder and leader of Ixphir House; architect of the ixchels' campaign aboard the *Chathrand*. Father of Lord Taliktrum and brother of Lady Diadrelu.

TALIKTRUM, LORD: Son of Lord Talag; eventual commander of the ixchel aboard the *Chathrand*.

THAULININ: A selk warrior and leader.

UNDRABUST, NEEPARVASI: Tarboy from Sollochstol.

USKINS, PIDETOR: First mate of the I.M.S. *Chathrand*.

VADU, COUNSELLOR: Commander of the Bali Adro armed forces in the city of Masalym. Bearer of a Plazic blade.

VISPEK: A *Cayer* (master or teacher) of the Mzithrini *sfvantskor* guild of warrior-priests. Cayer Vispek was one of the teachers and instructors of Neda Pathkendle.